Assassin's Fate

ROBIN HOBB

Book Three of Fitz and the Fool

HARPER
Voyager

Harper*Voyager*
An imprint of HarperCollins*Publishers* Ltd
1 London Bridge Street
London SE1 9GF

www.harpercollins.co.uk

This paperback edition 2018
1

First published in Great Britain
by HarperCollins*Publishers* 2017

A catalogue record for this book is available from the British Library

ISBN: 978-0-00-744428-1

This novel is entirely a work of fiction.
The names, characters and incidents portrayed in it are
the work of the author's imagination. Any resemblance to
actual persons, living or dead, events or localities is
entirely coincidental.

Set in Goudy Oldstyle Std by
Palimpsest Book Production Ltd, Falkirk, Stirlingshire

Printed and bound in the UK by CPI Group (UK) Ltd, Croydon CR0 4YY

MIX
Paper from
responsible sources
FSC **FSC™ C007454**
www.fsc.org

This book is produced from independently certified FSC™ paper
to ensure responsible forest management.

For more information visit: www.harpercollins.co.uk/green

To Fitz and the Fool.
My best friends for over twenty years.

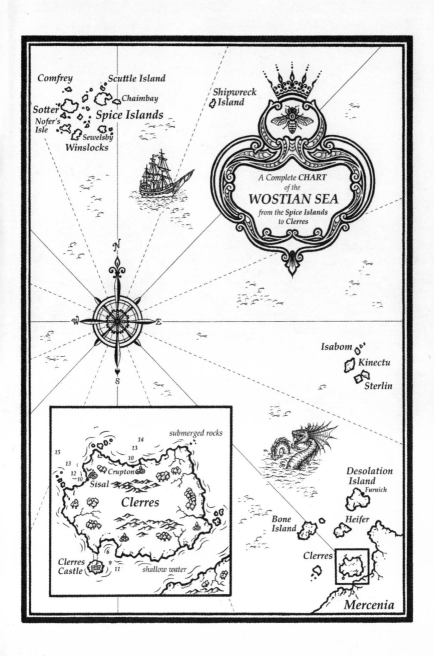

PROLOGUE

There are children holding hands in a circle. In the middle, a single child stands. The child wears a blindfold but there are painted eyes on the blindfold. The eyes are black and staring, edged with red. The child in the middle turns in a circle, hands outstretched. All the other children dance in a wider circle around her. They sing a song.

    'As long as the circle holds
    The futures can be foretold.
    You must be hard of heart
    To tear the circle apart.'

It looks like a merry game. Each child in the outer circle shouts a sentence or a phrase. I cannot hear what they are saying, but the blinded child can. She begins to shout back at them, her words torn by a slowly rising wind. 'Burn it all.' 'The dragons fall'. 'The sea will rise.' 'The jewel strewn skies.' 'One comes as two'. 'The four shall rue.' 'Two come as one.' 'Your reign is done!' 'Forfeit all lives.' 'No one survives!'

At that last shout, a wind bursts from the child in the middle. Bits of her fly in all directions and the wind picks up the screaming children and scatters them far and wide. All becomes black save for one circle of white. In the centre of the circle is the blindfold with its black eyes staring, staring.

Bee Farseer's dream journal

ONE

Bee Stings

The map-room at Aslevjal displayed a territory that included much of the Six Duchies, part of the Mountain Kingdom, a large section of Chalced and lands along both sides of the Rain Wild River. I suspect that it defines for us the boundaries of the ancient Elderlings territory at the time the maps were created. I have been unable to inspect the map-room of the abandoned Elderling city now known as Kelsingra personally, but I believe it would be very similar.

On the Aslevjal map were marked points that correspond to standing stones within the Six Duchies. I think it fair to assume that the identical markings in locations in the Mountains, Rain Wilds and even Chalced indicate standing stones that are Skill-portals. The conditions of those foreign portals are largely unknown, and some Skill-users caution against attempting to employ them until we have physically journeyed there and witnessed that they are in excellent condition. For the Skill-portal stones within the Six Duchies and the Mountain Kingdom, it seems prudent not only to send Skilled couriers to visit every site, but to require every duke to see that any such standing stones are maintained upright. The couriers who visit each stone should document the content and condition of the runes on each face of the stone as well.

In a few instances, we have found standing stones that do not correspond to a marking on the Aslevjal map. We do not know if they were raised after the map was created, or if they are stones that no longer function. We must continue to regard them with caution, as we do all use of Elderling magic. We cannot consider ourselves to be masters of it until we can duplicate their artefacts.

Skill-portals, Chade Fallstar

I ran. I hiked up the heavy white fur coat I wore and ran. I was already too warm and it dragged and snagged on every twig or trunk I passed. Behind me, Dwalia was shouting for someone to 'Catch her, catch her!' I could hear the Chalcedean making mooing noises. He galloped wildly about, once passing so close to me that I had to dodge him.

My thoughts raced faster than my feet. I remembered being dragged by my captors into a Skill-pillar. I even recalled how I had bitten the Chalcedean, hoping to make him release Shun. And he had, but he'd held onto me and followed us into the darkness of the Skill-pillar. No Shun had I seen, nor that Servant who had been last in our chain of folk. Perhaps both she and Shun had been left behind. I hoped Shun would escape her. Or perhaps had escaped her? I remembered the cold of a Buck winter clutching at us when we fled. But now we were somewhere else, and instead of deep cold I felt only chill. The snow had retreated into narrow fingers of dirty white in the deeper shade of the trees. The forest smelled of early spring, but no branches had yet leafed out. How did one leap from winter in one place to spring in another? Something was very wrong but I had no time to consider it. I had a more pressing concern. How did one hide in a leafless forest? I knew I could not outrun them. I had to hide.

I hated the coat fiercely. I could not pause to wriggle out the bottom of it, for my hands felt as clumsy as fish flippers and I could not possibly hide from my pursuers in a huge white fur coat. So I fled, knowing I could not escape but too frightened to let them reclaim me.

Choose a place to take a stand. Not where they can corner you but not where they can surround you either. Find a weapon, a stick, a rock, anything. If you cannot escape, make them pay as dearly as you can for capturing you. Fight them all the way.

Yes, Wolf Father. I spoke his name in my mind to give me courage. I reminded myself that I was the child of a wolf, even if my teeth and claws were pathetic things. I would fight.

But I was already so tired. How could I fight?

I could not understand what the passage through the stone had done to me. Why was I so weak and so tired? I wanted to fall where I was and be still. I longed to let sleep claim me, but I dared not. I could hear them calling to one another, shouting and pointing at me. Time to stop running, time to make my stand. I chose my spot. A cluster of three trees, their trunks so close together that I could dodge between them but none of my pursuers could easily follow me. I could hear at least three people crashing through the bushes behind me. How many might there be? I tried to calm myself enough to think. Dwalia, their leader: the woman who had smiled so warmly as she stole me from my home. She had dragged me through the Skill-pillar. And Vindeliar, the boy-man who could make people forget what they had experienced, he had come through the stone. Kerf was the Chalcedean sell-sword but his mind was so scrambled from our Skill-journey that either he was no danger to anyone or he might kill any of us. Who else? Alaria, who would unquestioningly do whatever Dwalia told her, as would Reppin, who had so harshly crushed my hand as we came through the pillar. It was a much smaller force than she had started with, but they still outnumbered me five to one.

I crouched behind one of the trees, pulled my arms in from the sleeves of the heavy fur robe and at last wriggled and lifted until I could slide out of it. I picked it up and threw it as far as I could, which was not far. Should I run on? I knew I could not. My stomach was doubling and twisting uneasily and I had a stitch in my side. This was as far as I could go.

A weapon. There was nothing. Only a fallen branch. The thick end was no bigger around than my wrist and diverged into three limbs at the end. A poor weapon, more rake than staff. I took it up. Then I pressed my back to one of the trees, hoping against hope that my pursuers would see the coat and pass me by, so I could double back and find a better hiding spot.

They were coming. Dwalia shouted in gasps. 'I know you are frightened. But don't run. You will starve and die without us. A bear will eat you. You need us to survive. Come back, Bee. No one will be angry at you.' Then I heard the lie as she turned her fury on her followers. 'Oh, where is she? Alaria, you fool, get up! None of us feel well, but without her we cannot go home!' Then, letting her anger win, 'Bee! Stop being foolish! Come here right now! Vindeliar, hurry! If I can run, so can you! Find her, fog her!'

As I stood behind the tree, trying to make my terrified breathing as quiet as I could, I felt Vindeliar reaching for me. I pushed hard to make my thought-walls strong, as my father had shown me. I gritted my teeth and bit hard on my lip to keep him out. He was making memories of sweet, warm foods and hot soup and fragrant, fresh bread at me. All those things I wanted so much, but if I let him make me think about them he could find a way in. No. *Raw meat. Meat frozen onto bones, gnawing it off with my back teeth. Mice with their fur on, and their little crunchy skulls. Wolf food.*

Wolf food. Strange, how delicious it sounded. I gripped my stick with both hands and waited. Should I stay hidden and hope they would run past me? Or step out and strike the first blow?

I did not get a choice. I saw Alaria go stumbling past my hiding-place, several trees away. She halted, looked stupidly at the white fur on the ground and then as she turned to call back to the others, she saw me. 'She's here! I found her!' She pointed at me with a shaking hand. I set my feet a shoulder's width apart as if I were going to play at knife-fighting with my father and waited. She stared at me and then sank down in a crumpled heap, her own white coat folding around her and made no effort to rise. 'I found her,' she called in a weaker voice. She flapped a limp hand at me.

I heard footsteps to my left. 'Look out!' Alaria gasped, but she was too late. I swung my branch as hard as I could, connected with Dwalia's face, and then danced back to the right between the trees. I set my back to one trunk and took up my stance again, branch at the ready. Dwalia was shouting but I refused to look and see if I'd hurt her. Perhaps I'd been lucky enough to put one of her eyes out. But Vindeliar was lumbering toward me, his doltish smile beaming. 'Brother! There you are! You are safe. We found you.'

'Stay back or I'll hurt you!' I threatened him. I found I didn't want to hurt him. He was a tool of my enemy, but left to himself I doubted he had any malice. Not that a lack of malice would prevent him from hurting me.

'Brothe-er,' he said, drawing the word out sadly. It was a rebuke but a gentle one. I realized he was radiating gentleness and fondness at me. Friendship and comfort.

No. He was not truly any of those things. 'Stay back!' I commanded him.

The Chalcedean lolloped past us, ululating as he went, and I could not tell if he deliberately or accidentally jostled against the little man. Vindeliar tried to avoid him, but stumbled and fell flat with a mournful cry just as Dwalia rounded the tree trunks. Her hands were extended toward me like claws, her lips pulled back from her bloodied teeth as if she would seize me in her jaws. Two-handed I swung my branch at her, willing it to knock her head from her shoulders. Instead, it broke and the jagged end dragged across her reddened face, trailing a line of blood. She flung herself at me, and I felt her nails dig into my flesh right through my worn clothing. I literally tore myself free of her grip. She kept part of my sleeve as I squeezed between the tree trunks.

Reppin was waiting there. Her fish-grey eyes met mine. Hatred gave way to a mindless glee as she leapt toward me. I dodged sideways, leaving her to embrace the tree face-first. She hit, but she was spryer than I thought. One of her feet hooked mine. I jumped high, cleared it, but stumbled on the uneven ground. Alaria had regained her feet. She wailed wildly as she threw herself against me. Her weight carried me to the ground and, before I could wriggle out, I felt someone step hard on my ankle. I grunted then cried out as the pressure increased. It felt as if my bones were bending, as if they would snap at any instant. I shoved Alaria off me but the moment she was clear, Reppin kicked me in the side, hard, without getting off my ankle.

Her foot slammed all the air out of me. Tears I hated swelled in my eyes. I thrashed for a moment, then wrapped myself around her legs and struggled to get her off my ankle but she grabbed my hair and shook my head wildly. Hair ripped from my scalp and I could not focus my vision.

'Beat her.' I heard Dwalia's voice. It shook with some strong emotion. Anger? Pain? 'With this.'

I made the mistake of looking up. Reppin's first blow with my broken stick caught my cheek, the hinge of my jaw and my ear, mashing it into the side of my head. I heard a high ringing and my own shriek. I was shocked, outraged, offended and in a disabling amount of pain. I scrabbled to get away but she still had a thick handful of my hair. The stick fell again, across my shoulder blades as I struggled to break free. There was not enough meat on my bones and my blouse was no protection: the pain of the blow was followed by the instant burn of broken skin. I cried out wildly and twisted, reaching up to grip her wrist and try to wrest her hand free of my hair. She put more weight on my ankle and only the cushion of forest humus kept it from breaking. I shrieked and tried to push her off.

The stick fell again, lower on my back, and I suddenly knew how my ribs joined my spine and the twin columns of muscle that ran alongside my spine, for all of it screeched with wrong.

All of it happened so fast and yet each individual blow was a single event in my life, one to be always remembered. I'd never been treated harshly by my father and the very few times my mother had disciplined me it had been little more than a cuff or a light slap. Always to warn me of danger, to caution me not to touch the fire-screen, or to reach over my head for the kettle on the hob. I'd had a very few tussles with children at Withywoods. I'd been pelted with pinecones and small stones, and once I'd been in a serious fight that left me bloodied. But I had never been beaten by an adult. I'd never been held in a painful way while a grown-up tried to deliver as much pain as she could, regardless of how it might injure me. I suddenly knew that if she knocked out my teeth or struck an eye from its socket, no one would care except me.

Stop being afraid. Stop feeling the pain. Fight! Wolf Father was suddenly with me, his teeth bared and every hackle standing up.

I can't! Reppin is going to kill me!

Hurt her back. Bite her, scratch her, kick her! Make her pay for giving you pain. She is going to beat you anyway, so take what you can of her flesh. Try to kill her.

But—

Fight!

I stopped trying to wrest her grip from my hair. Instead, as my stick fell again on my back, I lunged toward her instead of away, caught the wrist of her stick-hand and pulled it to my mouth. I opened my jaws as wide as I could and then closed them. I bit her not to hurt her, not to leave toothmarks or make her shout with pain. I bit her to drive my teeth down to her bone to gain a mouthful of flesh and sinew and try to tear it free of her body. I set my teeth as she shrieked and flailed at me with the stick, and then I worried the meat of her wrist, shaking my head fiercely. She let go of my hair, dropped the stick and danced about, yelling in pain and fear, but I kept my grip on her wrist, with both my hands and my teeth, and kicked at her shins and feet and knees as she dragged me about with her. I tried to make my molars meet as I clenched my jaws and hung my weight from her arm.

Reppin roared and thrashed. She'd dropped the stick and thought only to pry herself free. She was not a large person; she was slight of build and I had a good chunk of the stringy meat and flabby muscle of her forearm in my teeth. I worked my jaw together. She was shrieking. 'Get her off me! Get her off me!' She set the palm of her hand to my forehead and tried to push me away. I let her and she screamed as she helped me tear meat from her bones. She slapped at me but weakly. Jaws and hands, I gripped her tighter. She sank to the earth with me still locked to her arm.

Beware! Father Wolf warned me. *Spring away!*

But I was a cub and I did not see the danger, only that my enemy had collapsed before me. Then Dwalia kicked me so hard that my mouth flew open. It knocked me free of Reppin onto the damp earth. With no air in me all I could do was roll feebly instead of getting to my feet and running away. She kicked me repeatedly. My belly, my back. I saw her booted foot coming toward my face.

When I woke up, it was dark, and cold. They had managed a fire but its light barely touched me. I was lying on my side, facing away from the fire, bound hand and foot. My mouth was salty with blood, both thick and fresh. I had wet myself, and the fabric of my trousers was cold against me. I wondered if they had hurt me so bad that I peed or if I had been that frightened. I could not remember. I woke up crying, or perhaps I realized I was crying after I woke up. Everything hurt. My face was swollen on one side from where Reppin had hit me with the stick. My face might have bled, for dead leaves were stuck to my skin. My back hurt and my ribs caged my painful breaths.

Can you move your fingers? Can you feel your toes?

I could.

Does your belly hurt like a bruise or does it hurt like things are broken inside?

I don't know. I never hurt like this before. I drew in a deeper breath and the pain forced it out as a sob.

Hush. Don't make a sound or they will know you are awake. Can you get your hands to your mouth?

They had tied my feet together and bound my hands at the wrist in front of me. I brought them up to my face. They were tied together with strips torn from my shirt. That was part of why I felt so cold. Although spring had visited here during the day, winter reclaimed this forest at night.

Chew your hands free.

I can't. My lips were smashed and bloody. My teeth felt loose and sore in my gums.

You can. Because you must. Chew your hands free and untie your feet, and we will go. I will show you where to go. There is someone kin to us not far from here. If I can wake him he will protect you. If not, I will teach you to hunt. Once, your father and I lived in these mountains. Perhaps the den he built for us is still tight. We will go there.

I didn't know we were in the mountains! You lived in the mountains with my father?

I did. I have been here before. Enough. Start chewing.

It hurt to bend my neck to reach the bindings on my hands. It hurt to press my teeth in hard enough to bite the fabric. It had been a nice shirt the morning I had put it on to go to my lessons with Scribe Lant. One of the maids, Careful, had helped me to dress. She'd chosen this pale-yellow blouse and over it she had tugged a green tunic. The colours of my house, I realized suddenly. She'd dressed me in Withywood colours, even if the tunic had been too big for me and hung on me like a dress, nearly to my knees. I'd worn leggings that day, not the padded trousers my captors had given me to wear. The wet trousers. Another sob rose in me. Before I could choke it back, I made a sound.

'. . . awake?' someone asked by the fire. Alaria, I thought.

'Leave her as she is!' Dwalia commanded harshly.

'But my brother is hurt! I can feel his pain!' This from Vindeliar in a low and woeful voice.

'Your brother!' Dwalia's words dripped with venom. 'Trust a sexless lout like you to not be able to tell the Unexpected Son from some White's by-blow. All the coin we spent, all the luriks I wasted, and that girl is all we have to show for it. Stupid and ignorant, both of you. You think she's a boy, and she doesn't know what she is. She can't even write and pays no attention to her dreams.' A strange gloating filled her voice. 'But I know she's special.' Then the fleeting satisfaction was gone, replaced with a sneer. 'Doubt me. I don't care. But you'd best hope there's something special about her, for she's the only coin we have to buy our way back into the Four's good graces!' In a lower voice, she added, 'How Coultrie will crow over my failure. And that old bitch Capra will use it as an excuse for anything she wants to do.'

Alaria spoke very softly. 'So if she is all we have, perhaps we should try to deliver her in good condition?'

'Perhaps if you had caught her instead of falling to the ground and rolling about moaning, none of this would have happened!'

'Do you hear that?' A desperate whisper from Reppin. 'Did you hear that? Someone just laughed. And now . . . do you hear those pipes playing?'

'Your mind is turned, and all because a little girl bit you! Keep your foolish words to yourself.'

'I could see the bone! My arm is all swollen. The pain thuds through me like a drum!'

There was a pause and I heard the fire's crackling. *Stay still,* Wolf Father warned me. *Learn all you can by listening.* Then, with a touch of pride, *See, even with your poor cow's teeth, you have taught her to fear you. You must teach all of them to fear you. Even the old bitch has learned some caution. But you must drive it deeper. These must be your only three thoughts: I will escape. I will make them fear me. And if I have the chance, I will kill them.*

They have already beaten me just for trying to escape! What will they do if I kill one?

They will beat you again, unless you escape. But you have heard, you have value to them. So they probably will not kill you.

Probably? Terror swept through me. *I want to live. Even if I live as their captive, I want to live.*

You think that is true, but I assure you it is not. Death is better than the sort of captivity they plan for you. I have been a captive, a toy for heartless men. I made them fear me. It is why they sought to sell me. It was why your father could buy my freedom.

I do not know that tale.

It is a dark and sad one.

Thought is fast. So much was conveyed between Wolf Father and me in the pause of the pale folk's conversation. Suddenly a shout came from the darkness. It terrified me and I made myself chew faster on my bonds. Not that I seemed to be making progress with the task. The garbled words came again and I recognized Chalcedean. It would be Kerf, the Chalcedean mercenary Vindeliar had bespelled to Dwalia's service. I wondered if his mind was still scattered by his journey through the pillar. I wondered if his hand was swollen where I had bitten him. As silently as I could, I shifted my body until I could peer through the darkness. Kerf was pointing up at one of the ancient standing pillars at the edge of the clearing. I heard a shriek from Reppin. 'See? See? I am not mad! Kerf sees her as well! A pale ghost crouches upon that pillar. You must see her! Is she not a White? But dressed so strangely and she sings a mocking song!'

'I see nothing!' Dwalia shouted angrily.

Vindeliar spoke timidly. 'I do. There are echoes here of folk from long ago. They held a market here. But now, as evening closes in, a White singer makes merry for them.'

'I hear . . . something.' Alaria confirmed reluctantly. 'And . . . and as I came through that stone, people spoke to me. They said awful things.' She took a little gasping breath. 'And when I fell asleep this afternoon, I had a dream. A vivid dream, one I must tell. We lost our dream journals when we fled the Chalcedeans. I cannot write it down, so I must tell it.'

Dwalia made a disgusted noise. 'As if your dreams were ever of any real worth. Tell away, then.'

Reppin spoke quickly, as if the words leapt from her. 'I dreamed a nut in a wild river. I saw someone pull it from the water. The nut was set down and struck many times, to try to break it. But it only got thicker and harder. Then someone crushed it. Flames and darkness and a foul stench and screams came out of it. The flames wrote words. "Comes the Destroyer that you have made!" And a great wind swept through Clerres and picked us all up and scattered us.'

'Comes the Destroyer!' the Chalcedean repeated in a happy shout from the darkness.

'Be silent!' Dwalia snapped at him, and he laughed. 'And you, Reppin, be silent as well. This is not a dream worth sharing. It is nothing but your fever boiling in your mind. You are such cowardly children! You make shadows and phantoms in your own minds. Alaria and Reppin, go gather more wood. Make a good stack for the night and then check on that little bitch. And say not one more word of this nonsense.'

I heard Alaria and Reppin tramp off into the woods. It seemed to me they went slowly, as if fearful of the darkness. But Kerf paid no attention to them. Hands uplifted, he shuffled in a clumsy dance all around the pillar. Mindful of Vindeliar's power, I lowered my walls cautiously. The bee humming I'd been aware of became voices and I saw Elderlings in bright garments. Their eyes sparkled and their hair gleamed like polished silver and golden rings, and all around the Chalcedean they danced to the chanting of the pale songster perched on the pillar.

Dwalia stared at Kerf, annoyed at his enjoyment. 'Why can't you control him?' she demanded of Vindeliar.

He gestured helplessly. 'He hears too many others here. Their voices are many and strong. They laugh and sing and celebrate.'

'I hear nothing!' Dwalia's voice was angry but there was a thread of fear in it. 'You are useless. You cannot control that bit of a girl, and now you cannot control a madman. I had such hopes for you when I chose you. When I gifted you with that potion. How wrong I was to waste it on you! The others were right. You have no dreams and you see nothing. You are useless.'

I felt a thin chill of Vindeliar's awareness waft toward me. His misery lapped against me like a wave. I slammed my walls tight and tried not to care that he was hurt and yet still worried for me. His fear of Dwalia, I told myself fiercely, was too great for him to offer me any aid or comfort. Of what use is a friend who will take no risks for you?

He is your enemy just as much as the others are. If an opportunity arises, you must kill him, just as you would any of them. If any of them come to touch you, you must bite and kick and scratch as much as you are able.

I hurt all over. I have no strength. If I try to defend myself, they will beat me.

Even if you do only a little damage, they will learn that touching you has a price. Some will not be willing to pay it.

I do not think I can bite or kill Vindeliar. Dwalia, I could kill. But the others . . .

They are her tools, her teeth and claws. In your situation, you cannot afford to be merciful. Keep chewing on your bonds. I will tell you of my days as a captive. Beaten and caged. Forced to fight dogs or boars that were just as miserable as I was. Starved. Open your mind to my tale of how I was enslaved and how your father and I broke the bonds of our captivities. Then you will see why you must kill when you are given the chance.

He began, not a telling, but a remembering that I shared. It was like recalling things I had always known, but in scalding detail. He did not spare me his memories of his family killed, of beatings and starvation and a cramped cold cage. He did not soften how much he hated his captors, or how he had first hated my father, even when my father freed him. Hate had been his habit then, and hate had fed him and kept him alive when there was nothing else.

I was not even halfway through the twisted fabric that bound my wrists when Dwalia sent Alaria to fetch me to the fire. I played dead until she was hunched over me. She put a hand on my shoulder. 'Bee?'

I flipped, lunged and bit. I caught her hand in my teeth, but only for a moment. My mouth was too sore and she ripped her hand free of me with a cry and sprang back. 'She bit me!' she cried to the others. 'The little wretch bit me!'

'Kick her!' Dwalia commanded, and Alaria made a feint at me with her foot, but Father Wolf was right. She feared to get too close to me. I rolled away from her and, despite the screams of my abused body, managed to sit up. I glared at her from my one good eye and lifted my smashed lips clear of my teeth. I did not know how much of that she could see in the firelight's dance, but she did not come near me.

'She's awake,' Alaria informed them, as if I might have bitten her in my sleep.

'Drag her here.'

'She'll bite me again!'

Dwalia stood. She moved stiffly. I held still, poised to avoid her kick or to attack with my teeth if I could. I was pleased to see that I had blacked her eyes and split the flesh on one of her cheeks. 'Listen, you little wretch,' she snarled at me. 'You can avoid a beating, but only if you obey me. Is that clear?'

She bargains. That means she fears you.

I stared at her wordlessly, letting nothing show on my face. She leaned closer, reaching for the front of my shirt. I bared my teeth soundlessly and she drew back. She spoke as if I'd agreed to obey her. 'Alaria is going to cut your ankles free. We'll take you over by the fire. If you try to run, I swear I will cripple you.' She did not wait for a response. 'Alaria, cut the bonds on her ankles.'

I thrust my feet toward her. Alaria, I noted, had a very nice belt-knife. I wondered if I could find a way to make it mine. She sawed and sawed at the fabric that bound me, and I was surprised at how much it hurt. When finally she cut through, I kicked my feet to free them, and then felt a very unpleasant hot tingling as they came back to life. Was Dwalia tempting me to try to escape, to have an excuse to beat me again?

Not yet. Gather more strength. Appear weaker than you are.

'Get up and walk!' Dwalia ordered me. She stalked away from me, as if wanting to demonstrate to me how certain she was of my obedience.

Let her be certain of my surrender. I'd find a way to get away from her. But the wolf was right. Not yet. I stood, but very slowly, taking my time to get my balance. I tried to stand straight as if my belly were not full of hot knives. Her kicks had hurt something inside of me. I wondered how long it would take to heal.

Vindeliar had ventured closer to us. 'Oh, my brother,' he mooed sadly at the sight of my broken face. I stared at him and he looked away. I tried to appear defiant rather than hobbled by pain as I stalked toward the fire.

It was my first chance to have a good look at my surroundings. The pillar had brought us to an open dell in the heart of a forest. There were dwindling fingers of snow between the trees, but it was inexplicably missing in the plaza and on the roads leading to it and away. Trees had grown large alongside those roads and their branches arced over it and interlaced in some places. Yet the roads were largely clear of forest debris and snow. Did no one else recognize how peculiar that was? Evergreens with low, swooping branches surrounded the dell where Dwalia's folk had built their fire. No. Not a dell. I scuffed my feet against some sort of paving stones. The open area was partially bounded by a low wall of worked stone set with several pillars. I saw something on the ground. It looked like a glove, one that had spent part of the winter under snow. Farther on I saw a scrap of leather, perhaps from a strap. And then a woollen hat.

Despite my aching body, I slowly stooped to pick it up, feigning to take a moment to cradle my belly. Over by the fire, they pretended not to watch me, like cats hunched near a mouse hole. The hat was damp, but even damp wool is warm. I tried to shake the spruce needles from it but my arms hurt too much. I wondered if anyone had brought my heavy fur coat back to the camp. Up and moving, the chill of the early spring night reminded me of every aching bruise. The cold reached in and fingered my skin where they had torn strips from my shirt.

Ignore that. Don't think of the cold. Use your other senses.

I could see little beyond the reach of the fire's dancing light. I drew breath through my nose. The rising moisture of the earth brought rich scents with it. I smelled dark earth and fallen spruce needles. And honeysuckle.

Honeysuckle? At this time of year?

Breathe out through your mouth and slowly in through your nose, Wolf Father advised me.

I did. I turned my head slowly on my stiff neck, following the scent. There. A pale, slender cylinder, half-covered by a scrap of torn canvas. I tried to stoop down, but my knees folded and I nearly fell on my face. With my bound hands, I awkwardly picked up the candle. It was broken, held together at the break only by the wick, but I knew it. I lifted it to my face and smelled my mother's handiwork. 'How can this be here?' I asked the night softly. I looked at the nondescript scrap of canvas. Nearby there was a lady's lacy glove, sodden and mildewed. I did not know either of those things, but I knew this candle. Could I be mistaken? Could other hands have harvested the beeswax and scented it with honeysuckle blossoms? Could another hand have patiently dipped the long wicks over and over into the wax pot to form such an elegant taper? No. This was my mother's work. Possibly I had helped to make this candle. How did it come here?

Your father has been here.

Is that possible?

It is the least impossible answer that I can imagine.

The candle folded in two as I slid it into my shirt. I felt the wax chill against my skin. Mine. I could hear Vindeliar shuffling toward me. From the corner of my eye, I saw Dwalia holding her hands out to the fire's warmth. I turned my good eye toward them. Reppin had my big fur coat. She had folded it into a cushion and was sitting on it by the fire next to Alaria. She saw me looking and sneered at me. I stared at her arm and then lifted my eyes to smile at her. Her exposed hand was a fat pad with sausage fingers. Blood was dark between her fingers and in the lines of her knuckles. Had she not had the sense to wash out the bite?

I moved slowly to the biggest gap in their circle and sat down there. Dwalia rose and came to stand behind me. I refused to look back at her. 'You'll get no food tonight. Don't think you can run away from us. You can't. Alaria, you will take the first watch. Wake Reppin to take the second. Don't let Bee escape or you'll pay the price.'

She stalked away to where they had piled the packs and supplies they'd brought with them. There wasn't much. They had fled Ellik's attack with whatever they could hastily seize. Dwalia made herself a lumpy cushion from the packs and reclined on them with no thought for the comfort of the others. Reppin looked around slyly, and then spread out my opened coat before lying down on it and wrapping the excess around herself. Vindeliar stared at them, and then simply flopped down like a dog. He pillowed his broad head on his arms and stared dolefully at the fire. Alaria sat cross-legged, glaring at me. No one paid any attention to the Chalcedean. Hands over his head, he was dancing a sort of a jig in a circle, his mouth wide in mindless enjoyment of the ghost music. His brain might be dazed, but he was an excellent dancer.

I wondered where my father was. Did he think of me? Had Shun gone back to Withywoods to tell him that I'd been taken into a stone? Or did she die in the forest? If she had, he would never know what had become of me or where to look. I was cold, and very hungry. And so lost.

If you can't eat, sleep. Rest is the only thing you can give yourself right now. Take it.

I looked at the hat I'd salvaged. Plain grey wool, undyed but well spun and knitted. I shook it to be sure there were no insects in it and then, with my hands still tied, struggled to get it onto my head. The damp was chill but slowly warmed from my skin. I manoeuvred myself into a reclining position on my less-painful side, and faced away from the fire. The warmth of my body had wakened the candle's scent. I breathed honeysuckle. I curled slightly as if I were seeking sleep but brought my wrists up to my face and began again to chew at my bonds.

TWO

The Silver Touch

There is a peculiar strength that comes to one who is facing the final battle. That battle is not limited to war, nor the strength to warriors. I've seen this strength in old women with the coughing sickness and heard of it in families that are starving together. It drives one to go on, past hope or despair, past blood loss and gut wounds, past death itself in a final surge to save something that is cherished. It is courage without hope. During the Red-Ship Wars, I saw a man with blood gouting in spurts from where his left arm had once been yet swinging a sword with his right as he stood protecting a fallen comrade. During one encounter with Forged Ones, I saw a mother stumbling over her own entrails as she shrieked and clutched at a Forged man, trying to hold him away from her daughter.

The OutIslanders have a word for that courage. Finblead, they call it, the last blood, and they believe that a special fortitude resides in the final blood that remains in a man or a woman before they fall. According to their tales, only then can one find and use that sort of courage.

It is a terrible bravery and at its strongest and worst, it goes on for months when one battles a final illness. Or, I believe, when one moves toward a duty that will result in death but is completely unavoidable. That finblead lights everything in one's life with a terrible radiance. All relationships are illuminated for what they are and for what they truly were in the past. All illusions melt away. The false is revealed as starkly as the true.

FitzChivalry Farseer

As the taste of the herb spread in my mouth, the sounds of the turmoil around me grew louder. I lifted my head and tried to focus my stinging eyes. I hung in Lant's arms, the familiar bitterness of elfbark suffusing my mouth. As the herb damped my magic, I became more aware of my surroundings. My left wrist ached with a bone-deep pain, as searing as frozen iron. While the Skill had surged through me, healing and changing the children of Kelsingra, my perception had shrunk but now I was fully aware of the shouting of the crowd surrounding me as the sound bounced from the lofty walls of the elegant Elderling chamber. I smelled fear-sweat in the air. I was caught in the press of the mob, with some Elderlings fighting to step away from me as others were shoving to get closer in the hope I might heal them. So many people! Hands reached toward me, with cries of 'Please! Please, just one more!' Others shouted, 'Let me through!' as they pushed to get away from me. The Skill-current that had flowed so strongly around me and through me had abated, but it wasn't gone. Lant's elfbark was the milder herb, Six Duchies-grown and somewhat stale by the taste of it. Here in the Elderling city the Skill flowed so strong and close I did not think even delvenbark could have closed me to it completely.

But it was enough. I was aware of the Skill but no longer shackled to its service. Yet the exhaustion of letting it use me now slackened my muscles just when I had most need of them. General Rapskal had torn the Fool from my grasp. The Elderling gripped Amber's wrist and held her silvered hand aloft, shouting, 'I told you so! I told you they were thieves! Look at her hand, coated in the dragons' Silver! She has discovered the well! She has stolen from our dragons!'

Spark clung to Amber's other arm, trying to drag her free of the general's grip. The girl's teeth were bared, her black curls wild around her face. The look of sheer terror on Amber's scarred face both paralysed and panicked me. The years of privation the Fool had endured were betrayed in that stark grimace. They made her face a death-mask of bones and red lips and rouged cheeks. I had to go to the Fool's aid, and yet my knees kept folding of their own accord. Perseverance seized my arm. 'Prince FitzChivalry, what must I do?' I could not find the breath to reply to him.

'Fitz! Stand up!' Lant roared right next to my ear. It was as much plea as command. I found my feet, and pressed my weight against them. I strained, shuddering, trying to keep my legs straight under me.

We had arrived in Kelsingra just the day before, and for a few hours I had been the hero of the day, the magical Six Duchies prince who had healed Ephron, the son of the king and queen of Kelsingra. The Skill had flowed through me, as intoxicating as Sandsedge brandy. At the request of King Reyn and Queen Malta, I had used my magic to set right half a dozen dragon-touched children. I had opened myself to the powerful Skill-current of the old Elderling city. Awash in that heady power, I'd opened throats and steadied heart-beats, straightened bones and cleared scales from eyes. Some I'd made more human, though one girl had wished to embrace her dragon-changes and I'd helped her do that.

But the Skill-flow had become too strong, too intoxicating. I'd lost control of the magic, become its tool instead of its master. After the children I'd agreed to heal had been claimed by their parents others had pushed forward. Adult Rain Wilders with changes uncom-fortable, ugly or life-threatening had begged my aid and I had dispensed it with a lavish hand, caught in the vast pleasure of that flow. I'd felt my last shred of control give way, but when I'd surrendered to that glorious surge and its invitation to merge with the magic, Amber had stripped the glove from her hand. To save me, she'd revealed the stolen dragon-Silver on her fingers. To save me, she'd pressed three scalding fingertips to my bare wrist, burned her way into my mind and called me back. To save me, she'd betrayed herself as thief. The hot kiss of her fingers' touch still pulsed like a fresh burn, sending a deep ache up the bones of my left arm, to my shoulder, to my back and neck.

What damage it was doing to me now, I could not know. But at least I was again anchored to my body. I was anchored to it and it was dragging me down. I'd lost track of how many Elderlings I'd touched and changed, but my body had kept count. Each one had taken a toll from me, each shaping had torn strength from me, and now that debt had to be paid. Despite all my efforts, my head lolled and I could scarcely keep my eyes open amidst the danger and noise all around me. I saw the room as through a mist.

'Rapskal, stop being an imbecile!' That was King Reyn adding his roar to the din.

Lant abruptly tightened his hug around my chest, dragging me more upright. 'Let her go!' he bellowed. 'Release our friend, or the prince will undo every cure he has worked! Let her go, right now!'

I heard gasps, wailing, a man shouting, 'No! He must not!' A woman screamed, 'Let go of her, Rapskal! Let her go!'

Malta's voice rang with command as she cried out, 'This is not how we treat guests and ambassadors! Release her, Rapskal, this moment!' Her cheeks were flushed and the crest of flesh above her brow bloomed with colour.

'Let go of me!' Amber's voice rang with authority. From some deep well of courage, she had drawn the will to fight back on her own behalf. Her shout cut through the crowd's noise. 'Release me, or I will touch you!' She made good her threat, surging toward Rapskal instead of trying to pull her hand free. The sudden reverse shocked him and her silvered fingers came perilously close to his face. The general gave a shout of alarm and sprang back from her as he let go of her wrist. But she was not finished. 'Back, all of you!' she commanded. 'Give us room and let me see to the prince or, by Sa, I *will* touch you!' Hers was the command of an angered queen, pitched to carry her threat. Her silvered forefinger pointed as she swung it in a slow arc around her, and people were suddenly stumbling over one another in their haste to be out of her reach.

The mother of the girl with dragon feet spoke. 'I'd do as she says!' she warned. 'If that is truly dragon-Silver on her fingers, one touch of it will mean slow death. It will seep down to your bones, right through your flesh. It will travel your bones, up your spine to your skull. Eventually, you will be grateful to die from it.' As others were falling back from us, she began pushing her way through the crowd toward us. She was not a large person but the other dragon-keepers were giving way to her. She stopped a safe distance from us. Her dragon had patterned her in blue and black and silver. The wings that weighted her shoulders were folded snug to her back. The claws on her toes tapped the floor as she walked. Of all the Elderlings present, she was most heavily modified by her dragon's touch. Her warning and Amber's threat cleared a small space around us.

Amber retreated to my side, gasping as she sought to calm her breath. Spark stood on her other side and Perseverance took up a position in front of her. Amber's voice was low and calm as she said, 'Spark, retrieve my glove if you would.'

'Of course, my lady.' The requested item had fallen to the floor. Spark stooped and cautiously picked it up in two fingers. 'I will touch your wrist,' she warned Amber, and tapped the back of her hand to guide her to her glove. Amber was still breathing unsteadily as she gloved her hand, but weak as I was, I was horribly glad to see that she had regained some of the Fool's strength and presence of mind. She linked her unsilvered hand through my arm and I was reassured by her touch. It seemed to draw off some of the Skill-current still coursing through me. I felt both connected to her and less battered by the Skill.

'I think I can stand,' I muttered to Lant and he loosened his grip on me. I could not allow anyone to see how drained I was of strength. I rubbed my eyes and wiped elfbark powder from my face. My knees did not buckle and I managed to hold my head steady. I straightened up. I badly wanted the knife in my boot but if I stooped for it I knew I would not stop until I sprawled on the floor.

The woman who had warned the others stepped into the empty space that now surrounded us, but stayed beyond arm's reach. 'Lady Amber, is it truly dragon-Silver on your hand?' she asked in quiet dread.

'It is!' General Rapskal had found his courage and took up a stance beside her. 'And she has stolen it from the dragons' well. She must be punished! Keepers and folk of Kelsingra, we cannot be seduced by the healing of a few children! We do not even know if this magic will last or if it is a cheat. But we have all seen the evidence of this intruder's theft, and we know that our first duty is and must always be to the dragons who have befriended us.'

'Speak for yourself, Rapskal.' The woman gave him a cold stare. 'My first duty is to my daughter, and she no longer totters when she stands.'

'Are you so easily bought, Thymara?' Rapskal demanded scathingly.

The father of the child stepped into the circle to stand beside the woman called Thymara. The girl with the dragon feet rode on his shoulder and looked down on us. He spoke as if he scolded a wilful child, rebuke tinged with familiarity. 'Of all people, Rapskal, you should know that Thymara cannot be bought. Answer me this. Who has it harmed that this lady has silvered her fingers? Only herself. She will die of it. So what worse can we do to her? Let her go. Let all of them go, and let them go with my thanks.'

'She stole!' Rapskal's shout turned to a shriek, his dignity flung to the wind.

Reyn had managed to elbow his way through the crowd. Queen Malta was right behind him, her cheeks pink beneath her scaling and her eyes fiery with her anger. The dragon changes in her were amplified by her fury. There was a glitter in her eyes that was not human, and the crest of flesh in the parting of her hair seemed taller; it reminded me of a rooster's comb. She was the first to speak. 'My apologies, Prince FitzChivalry, Lady Amber. Our people forgot themselves in their hopes of being healed. And General Rapskal is sometimes—'

'Don't speak for me!' the general interrupted her. 'She stole Silver. We saw the evidence, and no, it's not enough that she has poisoned herself. We cannot let her leave Kelsingra. None of them can leave, for now they know the secret of the dragons' well!'

Amber spoke. She sounded calm but she pushed her words so that all could hear. 'There was Silver on my fingers before you were born, I believe, General Rapskal. Before your dragons hatched, before Kelsingra was found and reclaimed, I bore what we of the Six Duchies call Skill on my fingers. And your queen can attest to that.'

'She is not our queen and he is not our king!' General Rapskal's chest heaved with his emotion and, along his neck, patches of his scales showed a bright scarlet. 'So they have said, over and over! They have said that we must rule ourselves, that they are but figure-heads for the rest of the world. So, keepers, let us rule ourselves! Let us put our dragons first, as we are meant to!' He shook a finger at Lady Amber, from a safe distance, as he demanded of his fellows, 'Recall how difficult it was for us to find and renew the well of Silver! Will you believe her ridiculous tale that she has carried it on her fingertips for scores of years and not died of it?'

Queen Malta's rueful voice cut through Rapskal's rant. 'I am sorry to say that I cannot attest to such a thing, Lady Amber. I knew you only briefly during your time in Bingtown, and met you seldom during the negotiations of your loans to many of the Traders.' She shook her head. 'A Trader's word is all she has to give and I will not bend mine, even to help a friend. The best I can say is that when I knew you in those days, you always went gloved. I never saw your hands.'

'You heard her!' Rapskal's shout was triumphant. 'There is no proof! There can be no . . .'

'If I may speak?' For years, as King Shrewd's jester, the Fool had

had to make even his whispered comments heard across a large and sometimes crowded room. He had trained his voice to carry, and it now cut through not only Rapskal's shout but the muttering of the crowd as well. A simmering silence filled the room. He did not move like a blind man as he stepped into the space his threat had cleared. He was a performer stepping onto his stage. It was in the sudden grace of his movements and his storyteller's voice, and the sweep of his gloved hand. He was the Fool to me, and the layer of Amber but a part of his performance.

'Recall a summer day, dear Queen Malta. You were but a girl, and all was in turmoil in your life. All your family's hopes for financial survival depended on the successful launch of the *Paragon*, a liveship so insane that thrice he had capsized and killed all his crew. But the mad ship was your only hope, and into his salvage and refitting the Vestrit family had poured the last of their resources.'

He had them–and me. I was as caught up in this tale as any of them.

'Your family hoped that the *Paragon* would be able to find and restore to you your father and your brother, both missing for so long. That somehow you could reclaim the *Vivacia*, your family's own liveship, for it was rumoured that she had been taken by pirates. And not any pirates, but the fabled Captain Kennit himself! You stood on the deck of the mad ship, putting on such a brave face in your made-over gown with last year's parasol. When all the others went below to tour the ship, you stayed on the deck and I stayed near you, to watch over you as your Aunt Althea had requested.'

'I remember that day,' Malta said slowly. 'It was the first time we had really spoken to one another. I remember . . . we talked of the future. Of what it might hold for me. You told me that a small life would never satisfy me. You told me that I must earn my future. How did you put it?'

Lady Amber smiled, pleased that this queen remembered words spoken to her when she was a child. 'What I told you is as true today as it was then. Tomorrow owes you the sum of your yesterdays. No more than that. And no less.'

Malta's smile was like sunlight. 'And you warned me that sometimes people wished that tomorrow did not pay them off so completely.'

'I did.'

The queen stepped forward, unwittingly becoming part of the performance as she took her place on Amber's stage. Her brow furrowed and she spoke like a woman in a dream. 'And then . . . Paragon whispered to me. And I felt . . . oh, I did not know it then. I felt the dragon Tintaglia seize my thoughts. I felt she would smother me as she forced me to share her confinement in her tomb! And I fainted. It was terrible. I felt I was trapped with the dragon and could never find my way back to my own body.'

'I caught you,' Amber said. 'And I touched you, on the back of your neck, with my Skilled fingers. Silvered, you would say. And by that magic, I called you back to your own body. But it left a mark on you. And a tiny tendril of a link that we share to this very day.'

'What?' Malta was incredulous.

'It's true!' The words burst from King Reyn along with a laugh born of both relief and joy. 'On the back of your neck, my dear! I saw them there in the days when your hair was as black as a crow's wing, before Tintaglia turned it to gold. Three greyish ovals, like silver fingerprints gone dusty with age.'

Malta's mouth hung open in surprise. At his words, her hand had darted to the back of her neck beneath the fall of glorious golden hair that was not blonde. 'There was always a tender place there. Like a bruise that never healed.' Abruptly she lifted her cascading locks and held them on the top of her head. 'Come and look, any that wish, come and see if what my husband and Lady Amber says is true.'

I was one of those who did. I staggered forward, still leaning on Lant, to see the same marks I had once borne on my wrist. Three greyish ovals, the mark of the Fool's silvered hand. They were there.

The woman called Thymara stared in consternation when it was her turn to see the nape of the queen's neck. 'It's a wonder it did not kill you,' she said in a hushed voice.

I thought that would be an end of the matter, but when General Rapskal had taken three times as long to stare at the marks as any had, he turned away from the queen and said, 'What does it matter if she had the Silver then? What does it matter if she stole it a few nights ago, or several decades ago? Silver from the well belongs to the dragons. She must still be punished.'

I stiffened my back and tightened my belly. My voice must not shake. A deeper breath to make my words carry. I hoped I would not vomit. 'It didn't come from a well. It came from King Verity's own hands, that he covered in Skill to work his great and final magic. He got it from where a river of Skill ran within a river of water. Name it not dragon-Silver. It is Skill from the Skill-river.'

'And where might that be?' Rapskal demanded in a voice so hungry it alarmed me.

'I don't know,' I replied honestly. 'I saw it but once, in a Skill-dream. My king never allowed me to go there with him, lest I give way to the temptation to plunge myself into it.'

'Temptation?' Thymara was shocked. 'I who am privileged to use Silver to do works for the city, feel no temptation to plunge myself into it. Indeed, I fear it.'

'That is because you were not born with it coursing in your blood,' the Fool said, 'as some Farseers are. As Prince FitzChivalry was, born with the Skill as a magic within him, one that he can use to shape children as some might shape stone.'

That struck them dumb.

'Is it possible?' This from the winged Elderling, a genuine question.

Amber lifted her voice again. 'The magic I bear on my hands is the same that was accidentally gifted to me by King Verity. It is rightfully mine, not stolen any more than the magic that courses through the prince's veins, the magic you joyfully allowed him to share with your children. Not stolen any more than the magic within you that changes you and marks your children. What do you call it? Marked by the Rain Wilds? Changed by the dragons? If this Silver on my fingers is stolen, why, then, any here who have been healed have shared in the prince's thievery.'

'That does not excuse—' Rapskal began.

'Enough of this,' King Reyn commanded. I saw Rapskal's eyes flash anger, but he did not speak as Reyn added, 'We have abused and exhausted our guests. What the prince freely shared, we have demanded in too great a quantity from him. See how pale he is, and how he shakes. Please, my guests, return to your chambers. Let us bring you both refreshments and our sincere apologies. But in the greatest quantity of all, let us offer you our thanks.'

He advanced and with a gesture moved Perseverance aside. Behind him came Queen Malta, offering her arm fearlessly to Amber. Reyn gripped my upper arm with surprising strength. I found myself a bit humiliated but thankful for the help. I managed to look back once to see Queen Malta and Spark escorting Amber while Per came last of all slowly and with many a backward glance, as if wary that danger followed us but the doors closed behind us without incident. We walked through a corridor lined with curious folk who had been excluded from that audience. Then behind us, I heard the doors open and a gust of conversation belled out to become a roar. The hall seemed interminable. The stairs, when we came to them wavered in my vision. I could not imagine that I could climb them. But I knew I must.

And I did, step by slow step, until we stood outside the doors of my guest chamber. 'Thank you,' I managed to say.

'You thank me.' Reyn gave a snort of laughter. 'I would better deserve a curse from you after what we have put you through.'

'Not you.'

'I will leave you in peace,' he excused himself, and remained outside with his queen as my small party entered my room. When I heard Perseverance close the door behind me, relief swept through me and my knees tried to fold. Lant put his arm around me to help me to the table. I took his hand to steady myself.

A mistake. He cried out suddenly and went to his knees. In the same moment I felt the Skill course through me as swift as a snake striking. Lant clutched at the scar from the sword wound the Chalcedean raiders had given him. It had been closed, apparently healed. But in that brief touch I had known there was more for his body to do, and known, too, of one rib healed crookedly, and a fracture in his jaw that was mildly infected and giving him pain still. All repaired and set right, if one can call such a harsh correction a repair. I collapsed merrily on top of him.

Lant groaned under me. I tried to roll off him but could not summon the strength. I heard Perseverance's gasp, 'Oh, sir! Let me help you!'

'Don't touch—' I began, but he had already stooped and taken my hand. His outcry was sharper, a young man's voice taken back to a boy's shrill one. He fell onto his side and sobbed twice before he could master the pain. I managed to roll away from both of them. Lant didn't move.

'What has happened?' Amber's question was close to a scream. 'Are we attacked? Fitz? Fitz, where are you?'

'I'm here! There's no danger to you. The Skill . . . I touched Lant. And Per.' Those were all the words I could manage.

27

'What?'

'He did . . . the Skill did something to my wound. It's bleeding again. My shoulder,' Perseverance said in a tight voice.

I knew it would. It had to. But only briefly. It was hard to find the strength to speak. I lay on my back, staring up at the high ceiling. It mimicked a sky. Artfully crafted fluffy clouds moved across a pale blue expanse. I lifted my head and summoned my voice. 'It's not blood, Per. It's just wet. There was still a piece of fabric caught deep in the wound and slowly festering there. It had to come out and the fluids of infection with it. So it did, and your wound closed behind it. It's healed now.'

Then I lay back on the floor and watched the elegant room swing around me. If I closed my eyes, it went faster. If I opened them, the forested walls wavered. I heard Lant roll over on his belly and then stagger upright. He crouched over Per and said gently, 'Let's look at it.'

'Look at your injuries as well,' I said dully. I shifted my eyes, saw Spark standing over me and cried out, 'No! Don't touch me. I can't control it.'

'Let me help him,' Lady Amber said quietly. Two hesitant steps brought her to where I lay on the floor.

I pulled my arms in tight, hiding my bare hands under my vest. 'No. You of all people must not touch me!'

She had crouched gracefully beside me, but as he hunkered back on his heels, he was my Fool and not Amber at all. There was immense sorrow in his voice as he said, 'Did you think I would take from you the healing that you did not wish to give me, Fitz?'

The room was spinning and I was too exhausted to hold anything back from him. 'If you touch me, I fear the Skill will rip through me like a sword through flesh. If it can, it will give you back your sight. Regardless of the cost to me. And I believe the cost of restoring your sight will be that I will lose mine.'

The change in his face was startling. Pale as he was, he went whiter until he might have been carved from ice. Emotion tautened the skin of his face, revealing the bones that framed his visage. Scars that had faded stood out like cracks in fine pottery. I tried to focus my gaze on him, but he seemed to move with the room. I felt so nauseous and so weak, and I hated the secret I had to share with him. But there was no hiding it any longer. 'Fool, we are too close.

For every hurt I removed from your flesh, my body assumed the wound. Not as virulently as the injuries you carried but when I healed my knife-stabs in your belly, I felt them in mine the next day. When I closed the sores in your back, they opened in mine.'

'I saw those wounds!' Perseverance gasped. 'I thought you'd been attacked. Stabbed in the back.'

I did not pause for his words. 'When I healed the bones around your eye sockets, mine swelled and blackened the next day. If you touch me, Fool—'

'I won't!' he exclaimed. He shot to his feet and staggered blindly away from me. 'Get out of here. All three of you! Leave now. Fitz and I must speak privately. No, Spark, I will be fine. I can tend myself. Please go. Now.'

They retreated, but not swiftly. They went in a bunch, with many backward glances. Spark had taken Per's hand and when they looked back it was with the faces of woeful children. Lant went last and his expression was set in a Farseer stare so like his father's that no one could have mistaken his bloodlines. 'My chamber,' he said to them as he shut the door behind them, and I knew he would try to keep them safe. I hoped there was no real danger. But I also feared that General Rapskal was not finished with us.

'Explain,' the Fool said flatly.

I gathered myself up from the floor. It was far harder than it should have been. I rolled to my belly, drew my knees up under me until I was on all fours and then staggered upright. I caught myself on the table's edge and moved around it until I could reach a chair. My inadvertent healing of first Lant and then Per had extracted the last of my strength. Seated, I dragged in a breath. It was so difficult to keep my head upright. 'I can't explain what I don't understand. It's never happened with any other Skill-healing I've witnessed. Only between you and me. Whatever injury I take from you appears on me.'

He stood, his arms crossed on his chest. He wore his own face, and Amber's painted lips and rouged cheeks looked peculiar now. His eyes seemed to bore into me. 'No. Explain why you hid this from me! Why you couldn't trust me with the simple truth. What did you imagine? That I would demand you blind yourself that I might see?'

'I . . . no!' I braced my elbows on the table and rested my head in my hands. I could not recall when I had felt more drained. A steady pulse of pounding pain in my temples kept pace with my heartbeat. I felt a desperate need to recover my strength but even sitting still was demanding more than I had to give. I wanted to topple over onto the floor and surrender to sleep. I tried to order my thoughts. 'You were so desperate to regain your sight. I didn't want to take that hope from you. My plan was that once you were strong enough the coterie could try to heal you, if you would let them. My fear was that if I told you I couldn't heal you without losing my sight, you'd lose all hope.' The last piece of the truth was angular and sharp-edged in my mouth. 'And I feared you would think me selfish that I did not heal you.' I let my head lower onto my folded arms.

The Fool said something.

'I didn't hear that.'

'You weren't meant to,' he replied in a low voice. Then he admitted, 'I called you a clodpoll.'

'Oh.' I could barely keep my eyes open.

He asked a cautious question. 'After you'd taken on my hurts, did they heal?'

'Yes. Mostly. But very slowly.' My back still bore the pinkish dimples in echo of the ulcers that had been on his back. 'Or so it seemed to me. You know how my body has been since that runaway healing the coterie did on me years ago. I scarcely age and injuries heal overnight, leaving me exhausted. But they healed, Fool. Once I knew what was happening, I was more careful. When I worked on the bones around your eyes, I kept strict control.' I halted. It was a terrifying offer to make. But in our sort of friendship, it had to be made. 'I could try to heal your eyes. Give you sight, lose mine, and see if my body could restore mine. It would take time. And I am not sure this is the best place for us to make such an attempt. Perhaps in Bingtown, after we've sent the others home, we could take rooms somewhere and make the attempt.'

'No. Don't be stupid.' His tone forbade any response.

In his long silence, sleep crept up on me, seeping into every part of my body. It was that engulfing demand the body makes, one that knows no refusal.

'Fitz. Fitz? Look at me. What do you see?'

I prised my eyelids open and looked at him. I thought I knew what he needed to hear. 'I see my friend. My oldest, dearest friend. No matter what guise you wear.'

'And you see me clearly?'

Something in his voice made me lift my head. I blinked blearily and stared at him. After a time, he swam into focus. 'Yes.'

He let out his pent breath. 'Good. Because when I touched you, I felt something happen, something more than I expected. I reached for you, to call you back, for I feared you were vanishing into the Skill-current. But when I touched you, it wasn't as if I touched someone else. It was like folding my hands together. As if your blood suddenly ran through my veins. Fitz, I can see the shape of you, there in your chair. I fear I may have taken something from you.'

'Oh. Good. I'm glad.' I closed my eyes, too weary for surprise. Too exhausted for fear. I thought of that other day, long ago, when I had drawn him back from death and pushed him into his own body again. In that moment, as I had left the body I had repaired for him, as we had passed one another before resuming our own flesh again, I'd felt the same. A sense of oneness. Of completion. I recalled it but was too weary to put it into words.

I put my head down on the table and slept.

I floated. I had been part of something immense, but now I was torn loose. Broken away from the great purpose that had used me as a conduit. Useless. Again. Voices blowing in the distance.

'I used to have nightmares about him. Once I wet my bed.'

A boy gave a half-laugh. 'Him? Why?'

'Because of the first time I met him. I was just a child, really. A child given what seemed like a harmless task. To leave a gift for a baby.' He cleared his throat. 'He caught me in Bee's room. Cornered me like a rat. He must have known I was coming, though I can't guess how. He was suddenly there with a knife at my throat.'

Breathless silence. 'Then what?'

'He forced me to strip down to my skin. I know now that he was intent on completely disarming me. He took everything I'd carried. Little knives, poisons, wax to copy keys. All the things I'd been so proud to have, all the little tools for what my father wanted me to become. He took them and I stood naked and shivering while he stared at me. Deciding what to do with me.'

'You thought he'd kill you? Tom Badgerlock?'

'I knew who he was. Rosemary had told me. And she'd told me that he was far more dangerous than I could imagine, in more ways. Witted. And that there had always been rumours that he had . . . appetites.'

'I don't understand.'

A pause. 'That he might desire boys as much as he liked women.'

A dead silence. Then a lad laughed. 'Him? Not him. There was only one for him. Lady Molly. It was always a joke among the serv-ants at Withywoods.' He laughed again and then gasped, '"Knock twice," the kitchen maids would giggle. "And then wait and knock again. Never go in until one of them invites you. You never know where they will be going at one another." The men of the estate were proud of him. "That old stud hasn't lost his fire," they'd say. "In his study. In the gardens. Out in the orchards."'

The orchard. A summer day, her sons gone off to seek their fortunes. We'd walked among the trees, looking at the swelling apples, speaking of the harvest to come. Molly, her hands sweet with the wild blossoms she'd gathered. I'd paused to tuck a sprig of baby's breath into her hair. She had turned her face up to me, smiling. The long kiss had turned into something more.

'When Lady Shun first came to Withywoods, one of the new housemaids said he'd gone off to find himself a willing woman. Cook Nutmeg told me of it. She told that housemaid, "Not him. It was only Lady Molly and never anyone else for him. He can't even see another woman." Then she told Revel what the housemaid had said. Revel called her into his study. "He's not Lord Grabandpinch, he's Holder Badgerlock. And we won't have gossip here." And then he told her to pack her things. So Cook Nutmeg told us.'

Molly had smelled like summer. Her flowers had scattered on the ground as I pulled her down to me. The deep orchard grass was a flimsy wall around us. Clothing pushed aside, a stubborn buckle on my belt, and then she was astride me, clutching my shoulders, leaning hard on her hands as she pinned me down. Leaning down, her breasts free of her blouse, putting her mouth on mine. The sun warmed her bared skin to my touch. Molly. Molly.

'And now? Do you still fear him?' the boy asked.

The man was slow to reply. 'He is to be feared. Make no mistake in that, Per. Fitz is a dangerous man. But I'm not here because I have a rightful caution of him. I'm here to do my father's bidding. He tasked me to watch over him. To keep him safe from himself. To bring him home, when all is done, if I can.'

'That won't be easy,' the boy said reluctantly. 'I heard Foxglove talking to Riddle after that battle in the forest. She said he has a mind to hurt himself. To end himself, since his wife is dead and his child gone.'

'It won't be easy,' the man conceded with a sigh. 'It won't be easy.'

I dreamed. It was not a pleasant dream. I was not a fly, but I was caught in a web. It was a web of a peculiar sort, not of sticky threads but of defined channels that I had to follow, as if they were deep footpaths cut through an impenetrable forest of fog-enshrouded trees. And so I moved, not willingly but unable to do otherwise. I could not see where my trail led, but there was no other. Once, I looked behind me, but the track I had followed had vanished. I could only go on.

She spoke to me. *You interfered with what is mine. I am surprised, human. Are you too stupid to fear provoking dragons?*

Dragons don't bother with introductions.

The fog blew slowly away and I was in a place where rounded grey stones scabbed with lichen humped out of a grassy sward. The wind was blowing as if it had never begun and would never stop. I was alone. I tried to be small and kept silent. Her thoughts still found me.

The child was mine to shape. You had no right.

Huddling small had not worked. I tried to keep my thoughts calm but I fervently wished that Nettle were here with me in this dreamscape. She had withstood the full onslaught of the dragon Tintaglia when she was still new to the Skill. I reached for my daughter, but the dragon boxed me as if I were a frog captured in a boy's callused hands. I was in her control and alone. I hid my fear of her deep inside my chest.

I did not know which dragon this was and I knew better than to ask. A dragon guards its name lest others acquire power over it. 'It's only a dream' scarcely applies to what a dragon can do to one's sleeping mind. I needed to wake up, but she pinned me as a hawk's talons would pin a struggling hare. I felt the cold and stony land beneath me, felt the icy wind ripping warmth from my body. And still I saw nothing of her. Perhaps logic might reach her. 'My intent was never to interfere, but only to make the small changes that would let the children live.'

The child was mine.

'Do you prefer a dead child to a live one?'

Mine is mine. Not yours.

The logic of a three-year-old. The pressure on my chest increased, and a translucent shape coalesced above me. She shimmered blue and silver. I recognized which child she claimed by the markings she shared with the child's mother. The mother had been the woman who claimed to work with Silver. Thymara, the winged-and-clawed Elderling. This dragon claimed the girl-child who had been fearless in choosing the changes she would have. A child that was only marginally human. She had not hesitated to choose dragon's feet over human ones so that she might leap higher and grip limbs better when she climbed. A brave and intelligent child.

That she is.

I sensed a grudging pride. I had not meant to share the thought but perhaps flattering the child or the dragon might win me a reprieve. The pressure of the dragon's foot on my chest had gone past painful to the sensation of ribs flexed as far as they could bend. If she cracked my ribs into stabbing pieces that punctured my lungs, would I die or wake up? Being aware that I was dreaming did not lessen the pain or the sense of imminent disaster.

Die in your dreams, wake up insane. Or so the old Elderling saying went. Your connections to this world are strong, little human. There is something about you . . . yet you are not dragon touched by any dragon I know. How is that possible?

'I don't know.'

What is this thread I perceive in you, dragon and not-dragon? Why have you come to Kelsingra? What brought you to the dragons' city?

'Revenge,' I gasped. I could feel my ribs beginning to give way. The pain was astonishing. Surely if I were asleep, this pain would awaken me. So this was real. Somehow this was real. And if it were real, I would have a knife at my belt, and if it were real, I wouldn't die like a pinned hare. My right arm was caught under the dragon's talon but my left was free. I reached, groped, and found it. Drew it and stabbed with all my remaining strength only to have it clash against the heavy scaling of the dragon's foot. My blade skated and turned aside as if I had tried to stab a stone. She did not even flinch.

You seek revenge on dragons? For what?

My arm fell lifelessly away. I did not even feel my fingers lose their grip on the knife. Pain and lack of air were emptying me of will. I did not utter the words, for I had no air left. I thought them at her. *Not revenge on dragons. On the Servants. I'm going to Clerres to kill all the Servants. They hurt my friend and destroyed my child.*

Clerres?

Dread. A dragon could feel dread? Amazing. Even more surprising, it seemed to be dread of the unknown.

A city of bones and white stones far south of here. On an island. A city of pale folk who believe they know all the futures and which one is best to choose.

The Servants! She began to fade from my dream. *I remember . . . something. Something very bad.* Suddenly I was unimportant to her. As her attention left me, I could breathe again and I floated in a dark-grey world, either dead or alone in my sleep. *No.* I didn't want to sleep and be vulnerable to her. I struggled toward wakefulness, trying to recall where my body truly was.

I opened my eyes to deep night and blinked sticky eyes. A mild wind was blowing across the hills. I could see the trees swaying in it. In the distance, I saw snow-topped mountains. The moon was big and round and the ivory of old bones. Game would be moving. Why had I been sleeping so soundly? My head felt as if it were stuffed full of wool. I lifted my face and snuffed the air.

I felt no breeze and smelled no forest, only myself. Sweat. The smell of an occupied room. The bed was too soft. I tried to sit up. Nearby, clothing rustled and someone set strong hands on my shoulders. 'Go slow. Let's start with water.'

The night sky was a cheat and I'd never hunt like that again. 'Don't touch me skin to skin,' I reminded Lant. His hands went away and I struggled into a sitting position. I swung my legs over the edge of the bed. The room spun three times and settled. All was dim and twilight around me. 'Take this,' he said and a cool container was pushed gently into my hands. I smelled it. Water. I drank until it was gone. He took it away and came back with more. I drained it again.

'That's enough for now, I think.'

'What happened?'

He sat down beside me on the edge of the bed. I looked at him carefully and was grateful I could see him. 'What do you recall?' he asked me after a long silence.

'I was healing Elderling children . . .'

'You touched children, one after another. Not that many. Six, I think. They all grew better and, with every healed child, the wonder of the Kelsingra Elderlings grew and you became stranger. I have no Skill, Fitz. Yet even I felt as if you were the eye of a storm of magic that flowed toward you and then blew all around us. And when there were no more children, other people began to push forward. Not just the Elderlings, but Rain Wild folk. I'd never seen people so malformed. Some had scales and some had dangling growths along their jaws. Some had claws or dragon-nostrils. But not in a lovely way, not like the Elderlings do. They were like . . . diseased trees. And full of sudden hope. They began to push toward you, asking you to mend them. Your eyes were blank and you didn't answer. You just began to touch them, and they collapsed, their bodies changed. But almost immediately, you went pale and began to shake, yet still you wouldn't stop and still they came on, pushing and begging. Lady Amber cried out to you and shook you. And still you stared, and still distorted people pushed toward you. Then Amber pulled off her glove and clutched your wrist and dragged you back from them.'

My recollection was like a tapestry unfurling. Lant was blessedly silent as I pieced my life back together. 'And since then? Is all well?' I recalled the pushing and the shouting crowd. 'Were any of you hurt? Where are the others?'

'No one was hurt seriously. Scratches and bruises.' He gave a disbelieving snort. 'And only Spark still bears those marks. When you touched me and Per all our hurts were healed. I have not felt this healthy since . . . since before I was beaten that night in Buckkeep Town.'

'I'm sorry.'

He stared at me. 'You're sorry for healing me?'

'For doing it so abruptly. Without warning. The Skill . . . I could not control it.'

He stared past me. 'It felt peculiar. As if I'd been dunked in an ice-cold river, and then fished out right away, as dry and warm as I'd been.' His voice trailed away as he recalled it.

'Where are they now? Amber and Spark and Per?' Was there danger? Had I slept while they were threatened?

'Probably sleeping still. I took this watch.'

'Watch? How long have I been here?'

He gave a small sigh. 'This is the second night. Well. Perhaps I should say the morning of the third day. It's nearly dawn.'

'I think I fell asleep at the table.'

'You did. We moved you to the bed. I feared for you, but Amber said to let you sleep and not to call in a healer. I think she worried what might happen if a healer touched your skin. She bade us all be very careful not to touch you.'

I answered his unspoken question. 'I think I have control of my Skill again.' I was still for a moment, investigating the flow of the magic. It was strong here in the old city, but I once more felt it as something outside myself rather than a current flowing through me. I considered my walls and found them stronger than I had expected.

'I gave you powdered elfbark,' Lant reminded me.

'That I recall.' I turned to stare at him. 'I'm surprised you carry such a thing.'

He looked away from me. 'You recall my father's early hopes for me, the training I had. I brought many small things on this journey.'

For a time, we were both silent. Then I asked him, 'What of General Rapskal? What is the current feeling toward us here in Kelsingra?'

Lant licked his lips. 'Great respect founded on fear, I think. Amber has counselled us to caution. We have been eating in our rooms and mingling little. None of us have seen General Rapskal. But there has been one note from him, and three visits from one of his soldiers, an Elderling name Kase. He was respectful but insistent that General Rapskal needed a private meeting with you. We've turned him away because you were still resting, but none of us feel it would be safe for you to meet with him alone. The general seems . . . peculiar.'

I nodded silently, but quietly resolved that a private meeting might eventually be needed, if I were to dispel whatever threat the general presented to Amber. After such a meeting, he just might fall deathly ill if he continued to pursue his vendetta.

'The Elderlings have respected our wish for solitude,' Lant continued. 'I suspect the king and queen have sheltered us from curiosity and requests. Mostly we've encountered the serving folk and they seem to feel kindly toward us.' He added awkwardly, 'Some are touched by the Rain Wilds in unpleasant ways. I fear that some may seek healing from you, despite the king's order that you be left in peace. We did not want to leave you alone because we did not want the Elderlings to find you unguarded. At first. Then we feared you might be dying.' As if startled by his own words, he suddenly sat up straight and said, 'I should let the others know you are awake. Do you want food?'

'No. Yes.' I didn't want it but I knew I needed it. I had not been dying but I had not been living either. My body felt like soiled clothing, stiff with dirt and smelly with sweat. I rubbed my face. Definitely a beard now. My eyes were gummy, my tongue and teeth coated.

'I'll see to it, then.'

He left. The room was lightening around me, mimicking dawn. The nightscape on the wall was fading. I dragged off the Elderling robe I wore as I went to the pool. As soon as I knelt by the water-spout it began to release steaming water.

I was soaking in hot water when Amber entered. Perseverance was with her, but she walked beside him, not relying on him to guide her as they came directly to the pool's edge. I answered the basic questions before they could be asked. 'I'm awake. Nothing hurts. I'm starting to get hungry. I have my Skill under control. I think. Please avoid touching me until I'm sure.'

'How are you? Truly?' Amber asked me. I liked that her eyes settled on me even as I wondered if my vision were diminished at all. If the Fool had gained a small amount of vision, had I lost some of mine? I had not noticed a difference. Yet.

'I'm awake. Still tired but not sleepy.'

'You slept a long time. We feared for you.' Amber sounded hurt, as if my being unconscious had bruised her feelings.

The hot water had loosened my muscles. My body was starting to feel more familiar, as if I might belong in it. I ducked my head one more time and scrubbed my eyes clear. I waded out of the water. Still some aches. Sixty was not thirty, regardless of how I might appear. Perseverance left Amber's side to bring me a drying cloth and then a robe. I spoke as I wiped water from my legs. 'What is the mood of the city? Did I harm anyone?'

Amber spoke. 'Apparently not – at least not in a permanent way. The children you touched all seem to be faring better now than before you touched them. The Rain Wilders you touched have sent you notes of thanks. And, of course, pleas that you help others. At least three have left notes under the door, begging you to help them with their changes. Exposure to dragons or even areas where dragons were long present seem to trigger their afflictions, and those deliberately changed by dragons fare much better than those who simply are born with changes or acquire them as they grow. Those changes are often deadly to children, and life-shortening for all.'

'Five notes now,' Perseverance said quietly. 'Two more were outside the door when we came.'

I shook my head. 'I dare not try to help anyone. Even with the elfbark Lant gave me, I can feel the Skill-current sweeping past me like a riptide. I won't venture into that again.' I poked my head out of the neck-hole of the green Elderling robe. The skin on my arms was still damp, but I wrestled my hands through the sleeves, shrugged my shoulders and felt the garment settle itself around me. Elderling magic? Was there Silver in the fabric of this robe, reminding it that it was a garment? The Elderlings had mixed Skill into their roads so that they always recalled they were roads. Moss and grass never consumed them. Was there a difference between the Skill and the magic the Elderlings had used to create this marvellous city? How did the magics intersect? There was too much I didn't know and I was glad that Lant had dosed me and rescued me from any further experiments.

'I want to leave here as soon as we can.' I hadn't thought about saying the words: they just came out of my mouth. I walked as I spoke and Per and Amber followed me through the bedroom and into the entry chamber. Lant was there.

'I agree,' he said instantly. 'UnSkilled as I am, still the whispering of the city reaches me stronger with every passing day. I need to be away from here. We should be gone before the goodwill of the Elderlings fades. General Rapskal may be able to sway people against us. Or folk may begin to resent that you refuse to heal them.'

'Indeed, I think that very wise. Yet we cannot be too hasty. Even if there were a ship heading downriver, we would still have to be sure we bid farewell to Kelsingra in a way that ruffles no feathers.' Amber's voice was pensive. 'We have a long journey through their territories and the Dragon Traders have deep ties with the Rain Wild Traders. They, in turn, have deep family ties with Bingtown and the Bingtown Traders. We must travel by river from here to Trehaug in the Rain Wilds. From there, our safest transport would be on one of the liveships that move on the river. We must journey at least as far as Bingtown, and there find a vessel that will take us through the Pirate Isles and to Jamaillia. So the goodwill of the dragon-keepers may bear us far. At least as far as Bingtown, and perhaps beyond.' He paused then added, 'For we must journey beyond Jamaillia, and beyond the Spice Isles.'

'And then off the edge of any proven chart I've ever seen.' I said.

'Strange waters to you will be home ports to others. We will find our way there. I found my way to Buck, many years ago. I can find my way back to my homeland again.'

His words were little comfort to me. I was already tired just from standing. What had I done to myself? I sat down in one of the chairs and it welcomed me. 'I had expected to travel alone and light. Working my passage for some of it. I've made no plans for this type of journey, no provisions for taking anyone with me.'

Soft chimes sounded and the door opened. A manservant wheeled a small table into the room. Covered dishes, a stack of plates; clearly a meal for all of us. Spark slipped in through the opened door. She was dressed and groomed but her eyes told me she had only recently left sleep behind.

Lant thanked the serving man. Our silence held until the door had closed behind him. Spark began to uncover the dishes on the tray while Perseverance put out the plates. 'There's a scroll-tube here, a heavy one with a funny crest on it. A chicken wearing a crown.'

'The crowned rooster is the Khuprus family crest,' Amber told us.

A shiver went up my back. 'That's different to a rooster crown?'

'It is. Though I have wondered if they have some ancient relationship.'

'What's a rooster crown?' Spark asked.

'Open the letter and read it, please,' Amber fended off her question. Perseverance passed it to Spark, who handed it to Lant. 'It's addressed to the Six Duchies Emissaries. So I suppose that means all of us.'

Lant broke the wax seal and tugged out a page of excellent paper. His eyes skimmed down it. 'Hmm. Rumours of your waking have dashed from the kitchen to the throne room. We are invited to dine tonight with the Kelsingra Dragon Keepers. "If Prince FitzChivalry's health permits".' He lifted his eyes to mine. 'The keepers, I have learned, are the original Rain Wilders who set out with the dragons to find Kelsingra, or at least a habitable area for dragons. There were not many of them, less than twenty, I believe. Others have come to live here, of course. Rain Wilders seeking a better life, former slaves, and other folk. Some of the keepers have taken wives from among the new folk. Their ambassadors to King Dutiful presented themselves as coming from a populous and prosperous city. But what I've seen here and heard from the serving folk tells me a different story,' he mused. 'They've had only moderate luck at building their population to a level that can sustain the city, even on a village level. The Rain Wild folk find that they change faster when they live here, and seldom in good ways. As you have seen, the children born in Kelsingra are not many and the changes that mark them are not always good ones.'

'An excellent report,' Spark said in a fair imitation of Chade's voice. Perseverance snorted into his hands.

'Truly,' Amber agreed, and the colour rose in Lant's cheeks.

'He trained you well,' I said. 'Why do you think they convene and invite us to dine with them?'

'To thank you?' Perseverance seemed incredulous I would not have thought of that.

'It will be the preliminary to bargaining with us. It's the Trader way.' Amber sighed. 'We know what we need from them. Fresh supplies and passage as far south as we can get. The question is, what will they ask of us in return?'

THREE

In the Mountains

This was a very short dream. A chalk-faced man dressed in robes of green trimmed with gold walked on a beach. A grotesque creature hunched on a grassy outcrop above the beach and watched him, but the man paid it no mind. He was carrying fine chains, as if to be worn as jewellery, but much stronger. He carried them in loops on his arm. He came to a place where the sand was shaking and bulging. He watched it, smiling. Snakes began to come out of the earth. They were large snakes, as long as my arm. They were wet and their skins were bright shades of blue and red and green and yellow. The man put a looped chain around the head of a blue one, and the chain became a noose. He lifted the snake clear of the ground. It thrashed but it could not get away even though it opened wide its mouth and showed white teeth, very pointed. The pale man caught another snake in his snare, a yellow one. Next, he tried to catch a red one, but it shook free of him and slithered away very fast toward the sea. 'I will have you!' the man shouted, and he chased the snake and stepped on the end of its tail, trapping it near the waves' edge. He held the leashes of his two captive snakes in one hand and in the other he shook out a fresh snare for the red snake.

He thought she would turn and dart her head at him and he would loop the chain around her neck. But it was a dragon who turned on him, for he was treading on a dragon's tail. 'No,' she said to him very loudly. 'But I will have you.'

The picture I have painted for this dream is not very good, for my father's red ink does not gleam and glisten as the snake did.

Bee Farseer's dream journal

I slept cold and awoke to the toe of Dwalia's shoe nudging my sore belly. 'What have you been doing?' she demanded of me, and then snarled over her shoulder, 'Alaria! You were supposed to be watching her! Look at this! She's been chewing at her bonds!'

Alaria came at a stumbling trot, her fur coat slung around her shoulders, her pale hair a tangle around her bleary-eyed face. 'I was up almost all night! I asked Reppin to watch her . . .'

Dwalia spun away from me. I tried to sit up. My bound hands were cold and nearly numb. My whole body was stiff with various bruises and cuts. I fell over and tried to roll away from her, but I didn't get far. I heard a slap and then a wordless yelp. 'No excuses,' Dwalia snarled. I heard her stalk away.

I tried to stagger to my feet, but Alaria was swifter. She put a knee in my back to keep me down. I twisted toward her to bite. She put one hand on the back of my head and pushed my face down on the paving stone. 'Give me a reason to slam your teeth into that,' she invited me. I didn't.

'Don't hurt my brother!' Vindeliar wailed.

'Don't hurt my brother,' Dwalia mocked him in a shrill whine. 'Be silent!' The last word she spoke with a grunt, and I heard Vindeliar yelp.

Alaria pulled at my tunic hem then sawed strips from it with her belt-knife. She cursed in a guttural voice as she worked. I could feel her fury. Now was not a good time to challenge her. She rolled me over roughly and I saw the print of Dwalia's hand on her face, livid red against her pale skin. 'Bitch,' she snapped, and I did not know if she meant me or Dwalia. She seized my stiff hands and jerked them roughly toward her. She brutally sawed at the sodden rags with her dull knife. I pulled my wrists as far apart as I could, hoping she would not cut me. 'This time, I tie them behind your back,' she promised through gritted teeth.

I heard footsteps crunching through leaves and twigs and Reppin came to join Alaria. 'I'm sorry,' she said quietly. 'My hand hurt so much . . .'

'It's fine,' Alaria said in a tone that said it was not.

'She's so unfair,' Reppin said. 'So cruel to us. We are supposed to be her advisors and she treats us like servants! And tells us nothing. Not a word of what she plans now that she has dragged us to this horrid place. This is not what Symphe intended for us.'

Alaria relented in her sulk. 'There's a road over there. I think we should follow it. It makes no sense to stay here.'

'Perhaps it goes to a village,' Reppin offered hopefully. She added in a softer voice, 'I need a healer. My whole arm throbs.'

'All of you. Go fetch wood!' Dwalia shouted from her seat by the dwindling fire. Vindeliar looked up with a woeful face. I saw Reppin and Alaria exchange rebellious glances.

'I said, "All of you"!' Dwalia shrieked.

Vindeliar came to his feet and stood uncertainly. Dwalia stood up, a much-folded paper in her hand. She looked at it angrily, gripped it so tightly that I knew it was the source of her ire. 'That liar,' she growled. 'I should have known. I should not have trusted a word that we wrung from Prilkop.' Abruptly, she slapped Vindeliar with her paper. 'Go. Get wood. We will be here another night at least! Alaria! Reppin! Take Bee with you. Watch her. We need firewood. Lots of it! You, Chalcedean! Go hunt for some food for us.'

Kerf did not even turn his head. He was perched on a low stone wall and looking across the square at nothing. Nothing until I eased my walls down and saw tumblers, clad all in black and white, performing for a crowd of tall folk with oddly coloured hair. Sounds of a busy market-day filled my ears. I squeezed my eyes shut, firmed my walls, and opened my eyes to the long-deserted plaza. For that was what it was. Once, this open space in the forest had been a lively market square, a crossroads where traders met to exchange wares and Elderlings gathered for amusement and shopping.

'Come on,' Alaria snapped at me.

I got slowly to my feet. If I walked hunched over, my belly did not hurt so badly. Eyes on the ground, I followed them as they crossed the ancient paving stones. I saw bear-scat among the sparse forest debris, and then a glove. I slowed my pace. Another lady's glove, this one of soft yellow kid. Then some sodden canvas. Something red and knitted peeped out from beneath it.

Slowly and carefully I stooped and tugged out a red woollen shawl. It was as damp and smelly as the hat I'd found, but just as welcome. 'What do you have there?' Dwalia demanded and I flinched. I hadn't heard her come up behind me.

'Just a rag,' I said, my words blurred by my swollen mouth.

'There's a lot of rubbish over here,' Reppin observed.

'Which shows that people use this road.' Alaria added. She looked toward Dwalia as she said, 'If we followed it, we might soon come to a village. And a healer for Reppin.'

'There's bear-scat, too,' I contributed. 'And it's fresher than the rubbish.' That last part was true. The excrement was on top of some of the canvas and unmelted by rain.

'Ew!' Alaria had been tugging at a corner of some canvas. She dropped it and sprang back.

'What's that?' Dwalia exclaimed and pushed her aside. She squatted down and peeled the canvas back from the wet stones to expose something white and cylindrical. A bone? 'Umph,' she exclaimed in satisfaction. We all watched as she unscrewed a small plug from the end and coaxed out a coiled piece of parchment.

'What is it?' Alaria asked.

'Go get wood!' Dwalia snapped and took her treasure back to the fireside.

'Move, Bee!' Alaria commanded me. I hastily wrapped my shawl around my shoulders and followed them.

For the rest of the morning they broke sticks from storm-fallen branches and piled them in my arms for me to carry back to the campsite. Dwalia remained crouched by the fire, brow furrowed over the little scroll she'd found.

'I am going to die here,' Reppin announced. She was huddled under her coat and mine, her bitten arm cradled in her lap.

'Don't be dramatic,' Dwalia snapped at her and went back to studying her papers, squinting as the light faded from the day. It had been two days since I'd bitten Reppin, and here we still were. Dwalia had forbidden Alaria from exploring any farther down the old roads, and had slapped Reppin for asking what we would do next. Since she had found the bone cylinder and discovered the parchment inside it, all she had done was sit by the fire and compare it to her crumpled paper. She scowled and squinted as her gaze moved from one to the other.

I stared at Reppin across the fire. The sun was going down and the cold was creeping back. The small amount of warmth the stones of the old plaza had captured would soon flee. Reppin probably felt colder because of her fever. I kept my mouth flat. She was right; she would die. Not quickly, but she would die. Wolf Father had told me and, when I let him guide my senses, I could smell the infection in her sweat. *Next time, for a faster kill, you must find and bite a place*

*where the blood leaps forth in gushes. But for a first kill, you did well.
Even if this is meat you cannot eat.*

I didn't know my bite could kill her.

No regrets, Wolf Father chided me. *There is no going back to do a
thing or not do a thing. There is only today. Today you must resolve to
live. Each time you are given a choice, you must do the thing that will
keep you alive and unhurt. Regrets are useless. If you had not made her
fear you she would have done you many more hurts. And the others
would have joined in. They are a pack and they will follow their leader.
You made the bitch fear you, and the others know that. What she fears,
they will fear.*

So I kept my face set and showed no remorse – though I did
suspect that the proscription against eating humans had not been
made by someone as hungry as I was. In the two days that had passed
since we'd arrived, I'd eaten twice – if a thin soup of some bird
Alaria had killed with a thrown stone and two handfuls of meal
cooked in a full pot of water could be counted as food. The others
had eaten better than I had. I had wanted to be too proud to eat
the little they offered me, but Wolf Father said that was a poor
choice. *Eat to live,* he had told me. *Be proud of staying alive.* And so
I tried. I ate what I was given, spoke little and listened much.

By day, they untied my hands and hobbled my ankles so I could
help with the endless task of scavenging for firewood. My new bonds
had been made from strips torn from my tunic. I dared not chew
them again lest they tear away even more of my clothing. They
watched me closely. If I strayed at all from Alaria's side, Dwalia
would hit me with a stick. Every night, she bound my wrists to my
tied ankles and tethered them to her wrist. If I shifted in my sleep,
she kicked me. Hard.

And with every kick, Father Wolf would snarl, *Kill her. As soon.
As possible.*

'You and I are the only ones left,' Reppin whispered that night
to Alaria after Dwalia slept.

'I am here,' Vindeliar reminded them.

'Of the true luriks,' Reppin clarified disdainfully. 'You are no
scholar of the dream-scrolls. Stop spying on us!' She lowered her
voice as if to exclude Vindeliar. 'Remember when Symphe herself
said we were chosen as the best to help Dwalia discern the Path.
But from the beginning she ignored our advice. We both know that

girl has no value.' She sighed. 'I fear we have strayed very far from the way.'

Alaria sounded uncertain as she said, 'But Bee did have the fever, and the skin-change. That must mean something.'

'Only that she has some White heritage. Not that she can dream. Certainly not that she is this Unexpected Son that Dwalia claimed we would find.' Reppin dropped her voice to a whisper. 'You know she is not! Even Dwalia no longer credits that. Alaria, we must protect one another. No one else will. When Symphe and Dwalia proposed this mission, Capra and Coultrie both insisted that we had already endured the Unexpected Son; that he was the one who freed IceFyre and put an end to Ilistore. So Beloved told us when he came back to Clerres. He said that one of his Catalysts, the noble assassin, was the Unexpected Son. Among his people, they called Ilistore the Pale Woman. And she was defeated by the Unexpected Son. All know that! Three of the Four say that the dreams related to him are fulfilled and those prophecies should be discarded now. Only Symphe thought otherwise. And Dwalia.'

I held my breath. They were speaking of my father! I knew from poring through his papers that the Fool had said he was the Unexpected Son. But I had never grasped that in some far-off land he had been the fulfilment of a prophecy. Furtively, I edged closer.

Reppin dropped her voice. 'Symphe believed her only because Dwalia showered her with obscure references that said the Unexpected Son's victory would be absolute. And it was not, because Beloved came back to us and was recaptured. And remember that Dwalia served Ilistore for years and was infatuated with her. Dwalia always bragged that when Ilistore returned, she would raise her to power.' She barely breathed the next words. 'I think Dwalia only wants vengeance. You recall how she was about Beloved. She holds him responsible for Ilistore's death. And you know whose home we stole Bee from? FitzChivalry's.'

Alaria sat up in her blankets. 'No!'

'Yes. FitzChivalry Farseer.' Reppin reached up to tug her back down. 'Think back. Recall the name Beloved shouted when his foot was being crushed? The name of his true Catalyst. He'd held that back, saying he'd had many: an assassin, a nine-fingered slave boy, a ship's captain, a spoiled girl, a noble bastard. Not true. His one real Catalyst was FitzChivalry Farseer. And when I followed Dwalia into that house, in a room full of scrolls, she stopped still and stared and smiled. And there, on a mantelpiece, I saw a carving. One of the faces on it was Beloved's! As he looked before he was interrogated.' She nestled deeper into their bedding. 'She wanted to take it. But just then, Ellik's men came in and began to push over shelves and throw things around. They took a sword from there. So we left. But that's who Bee is. The daughter of a Catalyst.'

'They said the house belonged to Badgerlock, Tom Badgerlock. Bee said that was her father's name.'

'So. You are surprised that the biting little bitch lies?'

'But she is a White, too?'

Alaria's whisper was soft. I strained to hear Reppin's reply.

'Yes. And think now how a thing such as that could come to be!' Her words were triumphantly scandalized, as if my very existence were shameful.

'Vindeliar is listening,' Alaria cautioned her. She shifted, pulling the coat more closely around them. 'I don't care about such things. I just want to go home. Back to Clerres. I want to sleep in a bed and have breakfast waiting for me when I awaken. I wish I'd never been chosen for this.'

'My hand hurts so badly. I'd like to kill that brat!'

'Don't talk like that!' Vindeliar warned them.

'You shouldn't talk at all. It's your fault, all of this!' Reppin hissed at him.

'Sneaking spy,' Alaria rebuked him, and they all fell silent.

It was not the only time they whispered at night, though most of what they said made little sense to me. Reppin complained of her bite, and they discussed the politics of Clerres with names I did not know and fine points I could not understand. They promised to report all they had suffered when they returned home and agreed that Dwalia would be punished. Twice they spoke of dreams about a Destroyer, who Alaria claimed would bring screaming and foul fumes and death. In one, an acorn brought into a house suddenly grew into a tree of flames and swords. I recalled my own dream of the puppet with the acorn head and wondered if there was any connection. But I had also dreamed of a nut bobbing in a stream. I decided that my dreams were very confusing. Almost as bad as Reppin's, for she had dreamed just darkness and a voice that announced, 'Comes the Destroyer that you have made.'

I gleaned what facts I could from their whispering. Some important people had not agreed about allowing Dwalia to go forth on her mission. When she persisted, they had relented, but only because Beloved had escaped. From my father's writings, 'Beloved' was also 'the Fool'. And 'Lord Golden'. 'The Four' had warned Dwalia of what would befall her if she failed to produce results. She had promised to deliver to them the Unexpected Son. And I was all she had.

Vindeliar was excluded from their discussions, but he so craved their attention that he had no pride. One night, as they whispered under their furs, he broke in excitedly to say, 'I had a dream, too.'

'You did not!' Reppin declared.

'I did.' He was as defiant as a child. 'I dreamed that someone brought a small package into a room and no one wanted it. But then someone opened it. And flames and smoke and loud noises came out and the room fell apart all around everyone.'

'You did not dream that,' Reppin exploded with disdain. 'You are such a liar! You heard me talking about that dream and just repeated what you heard.'

'I did not hear you say such a dream!' He was indignant.

Alaria's voice was a low growl. 'You'd better not claim that dream with Dwalia, because I already told it to her. She will know you for what a liar you are and beat you with a stick.'

'I did dream that,' he whined. 'Sometimes Whites dream the same. You know that.'

'You are no White. You were born broken, you and your sister. You should have been drowned.'

I caught my breath at that and waited for Vindeliar to explode with fury. Instead he fell silent. The cold wind blew and the only thing we truly shared was misery. And dreams.

Even as a small child, I'd had vivid dreams and instinctively known they were important and should be shared. At home, I'd recorded them in my journal. Since the Servants had stolen me, my dreams had grown darker and more ominous. I had neither spoken of them nor written them down. The unuttered dreams were lodged inside me, like a bone in my throat. With every additional dream, the driving compulsion to speak them aloud or write them down became stronger. The dream-images were confusing. I held a torch and stood at a crossroads under a wasp nest. A scarred little girl held a baby and Nettle smiled at her although both Nettle and the girl were weeping. A man burned the porridge he was cooking, and wolves howled in anguish. An acorn was planted in gravel, and a tree of flames grew from it. The earth shook and the black rain fell and fell and fell, making dragons choke and fall to the earth with torn wings. They were stupid dreams that made no sense but the urgency I felt to share them was like the need to vomit. I put my finger on the cold stone and pretended to write and draw. The pressure eased. I tilted my head up and looked at distant stars. No clouds. It was going to be very cold tonight. I struggled to wrap my shawl more warmly around me, to no avail.

A third day passed, and a fourth. Dwalia paced and muttered and studied her documents. My bruises began to fade but I still ached all over. The swelling over my eye had gone down but one of my back teeth still felt loose. The split flesh on my cheekbone was mostly closed over now. None of them cared.

'Take me back through the stone,' Reppin demanded on the fourth evening. 'Perhaps they could save me, if we returned to the Six Duchies. At least I could die in a bed instead of in the dirt.'

'Failures die in the dirt,' Dwalia said without emotion.

Reppin made a stricken sound and lay down on her side. She drew her legs up, treasuring her infected arm close. My disgust with Dwalia equalled my hatred in that moment.

Alaria spoke quietly into the gathering dimness. 'We can't stay here. Where will we go? Why can't we follow this old road? It must lead somewhere. Perhaps it goes to a town, with warm shelter and food.'

Dwalia had been sitting by the fire, holding her hands out to the warmth. She suddenly folded her arms across her chest and glared at Alaria. 'Are you asking questions?'

Alaria looked down. 'I was just wondering.' She dared to lift her head. 'Were not we luriks meant to advise you? Were not we sent to help you find the true Path and make correct decisions?' Her voice rose in pitch. 'Coultrie and Capra did not wish you to go. They only allowed this because Beloved had escaped! We were to hunt him down and kill him! And then, perhaps, capture the Unexpected Son, if Beloved had led you to him. But you let the Farseer take Beloved away, so we could ransack his home. All that killing! Now we are lost in a forest, with the useless girl you stole.

Does she dream? No! What good is she? I wonder why you have brought us all here, to die! I wonder if the rumour was true, that Beloved did not "escape" but was released by you and Symphe?'

Dwalia shot to her feet and stood over Alaria. 'I am a lingstra! You are a young and stupid lurik. If you want to wonder anything, wonder why the fire is dying. Go get more wood.'

Alaria hesitated as if she would argue. Then she rose stiffly and walked reluctantly into the gathering gloom under the great trees. Over the last few days, we had gathered all the close dry wood. She would have to range deeper into the forest to find more. I wondered if she would come back. Twice Wolf Father had noted a faint but foul smell on the air. *Bear,* he had cautioned me. I had been frightened.

He does not want to approach so many humans near a fire. But if he changes his mind, let the others shriek and run. You cannot run fast or far. So lie very still and do not make a sound. It may be he will chase after the others.

But if he does not?

Lie still and don't make a sound.

I had not been reassured, and I hoped that Alaria would return and bring an armful of firewood with her.

'You,' Dwalia said suddenly. 'Go with her.'

'You already tied my feet for the night,' I pointed out to her. 'And my hands.' I tried to sound sullen. If she cut me free to go for wood, I was almost certain I could slip away in the gloom.

'Not you. I'm not having you run off in the dark, to die in the forest. Reppin. Fetch wood.'

Reppin looked incredulous. 'I can barely move this arm. I can't fetch wood.'

Dwalia stared at her. I thought she might order her to her feet. Instead, she just pursed her mouth. 'Useless,' she said coldly, and then added, 'Vindeliar, fetch wood.'

Vindeliar rose slowly. He kept his eyes cast down, but I could read his resentment in the set of his shoulders as he wandered off in the same direction that Alaria had gone.

Dwalia went back to doing what she did every evening: studying the little scroll and the tattered paper. Earlier, she had spent hours circling the pillars at the edge of the plaza, her eyes going from the parchment she'd found to the runes and back again. Some of those markings I had seen in my father's papers in his study. Would she attempt another passage through the Skill-pillars? She had also made brief forays on the road in both directions, and had returned shaking her head and irritable. I could not decide which I feared more, that she would drag us into the Skill-pillar or starve us here.

Across the plaza, Kerf was engaged in a boot-stamping dance. If I allowed myself, I could hear the music and see the Elderlings who danced all about him. Alaria returned with some frozen branches broken green from trees. They might burn but would give little warmth. Vindeliar came behind her, carrying a broken piece of rotted log, more moss than wood. As they approached the fire, Kerf danced a foot-stamping jig around them. 'Go away!' Alaria shouted at him, but he only grinned as he spun away to rejoin the festivities of the spectral Elderlings.

I did not like camping in the open ground of the plaza, but Dwalia thought the forest floor was 'dirty'. But dirt was much better than the smooth black stone of the plaza that gibbered and whispered to me constantly. Awake, I could keep my walls tight, though I was weary of the effort that took. But at night, when exhaustion finally claimed me, I was vulnerable to the voices stored in the stone. Their market-place came alive with smoking meat over fragrant fires, and jugglers flipping sparkling gems and one pale songster who seemed to see me. 'Be strong, be strong, go where you belong!' she sang to me. But her words more frightened than comforted me. In her eyes, I saw her belief that I would do a terrible and wonderful thing. A thing only I could do? The Chalcedean abruptly dropped into place beside me. I jumped. My walls were so tight I had not been aware of his approach. *Danger!* Wolf Father cautioned me. Kerf folded his legs and gave me a jaunty grin. 'A fine night for the festival!' he said to me. 'Have you tried the smoked goat? Excellent!' He pointed across the plaza at the darkening forest. 'From the vendor with the purple awning.'

Madness made him such a congenial fellow. His mention of food made my stomach clench. 'Excellent,' I said quietly, and looked aside, thinking that agreeing might be the swiftest way to end the conversation.

He nodded gravely and walked his haunches a bit closer to the fire, holding his grimy hands toward the warmth. Even mad, he'd had more sense than Reppin. A rag torn from his shirt bandaged the finger I'd bitten. He opened the sturdy leather pouch at his belt and rummaged in it. 'Here,' he said and thrust a stick at me. I lifted my bound hands to fend it off and he pushed it into my fingers. I suddenly smelled meat. Jerky. The rush of hunger and the flood of saliva in my mouth shocked me. My hands shook as I lifted it to my mouth. It was dry and so hard I could not bite off a piece. I chewed and sucked on it, and found myself breathing hard as I tried to gnaw off a piece I could swallow.

'I know what you did.'

I clutched the stick of jerky harder, fearful he would take it from me. I said nothing. Dwalia had lifted her gaze from her papers and was scowling at us. I knew she would not try to take the jerky from me, for fear of my teeth.

He patted my shoulder. 'You tried to save me. If I had let go when you bit me, I would have stayed there with beautiful Shun. I understand that now. You wanted me to stay behind, to protect her and win her.'

I kept chewing the jerky. To get as much of it as I could into my belly before anyone could take it from me. Belatedly I nodded at him. Let him believe whatever he wished if it meant he would give me food.

He sighed as he gazed at the night. 'I think we are in the realm of death. It is very different to what I expected. I feel cold and pain but I hear music and see beauty. I do not know if I am punished or rewarded. I do not know why I am still with these people instead of judged by my ancestors.' He gave Dwalia a gloomy look. 'These folks are darker than death. Perhaps that is why we are lodged here, halfway down death's throat.'

I nodded again. I'd managed to tear a bit of the meat free and was chewing it to shreds. I had never so greatly anticipated swallowing anything.

He twisted away from me and fumbled at his belt. When he turned back, a large gleaming knife was in his hand. I tried to scrabble back from him, but he caught my tied feet and pulled them to him. The knife was sharp. It slid through the twisted fabric and suddenly my ankles were free. I kicked free of his grip. He reached toward me. 'Now your wrists,' he said.

Trust or not? That knife could take off a finger just as easily as cut my bonds. I stuffed the stick of meat into my mouth and gripped it with my teeth. I held out my wrists to him.

'This is tight! It hurts?'

Don't answer.

I met his gaze silently.

'Your wrists have swelled up around it.' He slid the blade carefully between my hands. It was cold.

'Stop that! What are you doing?' Dwalia finally voiced her outrage.

The Chalcedean barely spared her a glance. He took one of my hands to steady his task and began sawing through the rag that bound them

Dwalia surprised me. She had been in the act of adding a hefty stick of wood to the fire. Instead she took two steps and clouted the Chalcedean on the back of his head. He went down, the knife still clutched in his hand. I tore my hands free of the last shred of rag and shot to my feet. I ran two steps on my buzzing feet before she seized me by the back of my collar, choking me. Her first two clouts with the stick were on my right shoulder and right ribs.

I twisted in her grasp, ignoring how it tightened the chokehold she had on me and kicked her as hard as I could, hitting her shin and then her knee. She shrieked with pain but did not let me go. Instead she struck the side of my head with her stick of firewood. My crushed ear rang and I tasted blood but the pain did not matter so much as the way my vision was shrinking. I spun away from her, but that allowed her to hit me on the other side of my head. Dimly, I knew she was shouting at the others to seize me. No one leapt to help her. Vindeliar was moaning, 'Don't, don't, don't,' his voice going higher each time he said the word. It angered me that he would moan but do nothing. I pushed my pain at him.

She hit me on the side of my head again, smashing my ear. My knees folded and suddenly I was hanging by my collar. She was not strong enough to support my weight. She collapsed on top of me and my shoulder exploded with pain.

I felt a wave of emotion. It was like when Nettle and my father merged their minds, or when my father's mind was boiling with thoughts and he had forgotten to hold them in. *Don't hurt her! Don't hurt her!*

Dwalia let go of my collar and made a strange sound as she rolled off me. I didn't try to move. I just breathed, pulling air back into my body. I'd lost the jerky. My mouth was full of blood. I turned my head and opened my lips to let it run out.

Don't die. Please don't die and leave me alone. Vindeliar's thought whispered to me. Oh. That was it. When I'd pushed my pain at him, I'd opened a way for his thoughts to come in. Dangerous. With every bit of will power I could muster, I blocked him from my mind. Tears stung my eyes. Tears of fury. Dwalia's calf was within reach of my teeth. I wondered if I could bite a piece of meat off her leg.

Don't, cub. She still has the stick. Crawl away. Quietly. This is one you don't attack until you are sure you can kill her.

I tried to wriggle away. But my arm wouldn't obey me. It flopped uselessly. I was broken. I blinked at the pain and little black spots danced in front of my eyes. Dwalia got to her hands and knees and then stood up with a grunt and walked away without looking at me. When she reached the other side of the fire, she sat down on the pack again and resumed looking at her much-folded paper, and the little scroll she had taken from the bone. Slowly, she rotated the pieces of paper, then suddenly leaned closer to them. She set them side by side on her knees and looked from one to the other.

The Chalcedean sat up slowly. He reached around to the back of his head, brought his hand before his eyes and rubbed his wet finger-tips together. He watched me sit up and shook his head at my flopping useless arm. 'It's broken,' I whispered. I desperately wanted someone to care that I was hurt so badly.

'Darker than death,' he said quietly. He reached over and put his fingers on the point of my shoulder and prodded it. I yelped and flinched away. 'Not broken,' he observed. 'But I don't know your word for it.' He made a fist and clasped it in his other hand. Then he pulled his fist out. 'Popped out,' he told me. He reached toward me again and I cowered away but he only waved at my shoulder. 'Popped out.'

'My arm won't move.' Panic was rising in me. I couldn't get a breath.

'Lie down. Be still. Be loose. Sometimes, it goes back in.' He looked over at Dwalia. 'She's a wasp,' he observed. I stared at him. He smiled sickly. 'A Chalcedean saying. If the bee stings, it dies. It pays a price to hurt you. A wasp can bite and bite and bite again. It pays nothing for the pain it brings.' He shrugged. 'So they bite. They know nothing else.'

Dwalia suddenly shot to her feet. 'I know where we are now!' She looked back at the small scroll in her hands. 'The runes match. It makes no sense, but it must be so!' She stared into the distance; then her eyes narrowed and her features changed as she realized something. 'He lied to us. He lied to ME!' Dwalia roared. I had thought she was frightening when she was angry, but, outraged was far worse. 'He lied to me! A market square, Prilkop claimed, on a well-travelled road. He thought he was so clever. He tricked me into bringing us here. He tricked me!' This last she screamed, her face contorted into a stark mask. 'Prilkop!' Spit flew out of her mouth. 'Always so condescending. So calmly superior. And Beloved, so silent, and then babbling, babbling. Babbling lies! Well, I made him scream. I tore the truth out of them both, didn't I?'

'Apparently not.' Alaria breathed the words, looking at the space between her feet and the fire. I doubt anyone heard her besides me.

But Reppin's head twitched as if she had and she tried to sit up straight. 'You thought you did. You thought you ripped the truth out of his flesh. But he was stronger than you, wasn't he? Cleverer. Prilkop tricked you into bringing us here, and here we are, in the middle of the wilderness. Starving. Dying!' Her voice cracked.

Dwalia stared at Reppin, her eyes flat. Then she crushed the yellow map between her hands, stood up and thrust it into the pack she'd been sitting on. The little scroll she had found, she rolled and slid back into the tube. She flourished it at Reppin. 'Not all of us, Reppin. Not all of us will die here.' Her smile widened with pride. 'I've deciphered it. Prilkop lied to me, but the true Path is not to be defied!' She dug deeper into the pack and pulled out a small pouch, unwound the ties that secured it and withdrew a delicate glove. Wolf Father growled within me. I stared, feeling ill and not knowing why. Dwalia worked the glove slowly and carefully onto her hand, settling each fingertip into place. She had used it before, when she had dragged us through the Skill-pillar. She stood up. 'Bring the packs and the captive. Follow me.'

The captive. My new title flowed over me like greasy water. Dwalia did not look back to see if they were obeying. She carried only her superiority as she strode to one of the pillars and studied the markings on it. 'Where does it go?' Alaria asked timidly.

'That's not for you to worry about.'

The Chalcedean had followed Dwalia. He was the only one who did. I shifted away from the fire. My hands were free, my feet untied. They tingled with dwindling numbness in contrast to the roaring pain in my shoulder. Could I stand and run? I pushed with my good hand braced on the ground and moved my aching body a bit closer to the darkness. If I could slowly edge into the darkness, I might be able to crawl away.

Reppin had staggered to her feet and was trying one-handed to pick up my coat from the ground. 'I don't know if I can carry a pack,' she apologized. No one responded.

Ignoring Dwalia's scowl, the Chalcedean stepped up beside her to regard the pillar. He reached out and traced the carved runes. 'I know this one,' he said, and smiled oddly. 'I knelt almost upon it and had nothing else to stare at. I was six. We kept a vigil for my grandfather's body in the Chamber of Toppled Doors in the Duke of Chalced's stronghold. It was an honour for my grandfather's body to be exposed in such a place. The next day, they burned his body on a pyre near the harbour.'

Dwalia snapped her stare back to him and smiled. 'This was in Chalced, wasn't it?'

He nodded. 'It was half a day's ride from my family's holding there. The duke's stronghold is said to be built on the site of an ancient battle. There were four pillars such as this one, all dragged down to the earth, sunken to be flush with the floor of the chamber. It is said to be good luck if you can break a chip from one to carry as a token. I tried, but the stone was as hard as iron.'

Her smile broadened. 'As I thought! We are still on the true Path, my luriks. I am certain of it, when such good fortune smiles upon us.' She tapped the little scroll-tube against her palm. 'Fate has delivered a map into my hands. It's oddly drawn and the writing is foreign, but I have puzzled it out. I know where we are on this map, and now I know that this pillar can transport us to Chalced. Kerf will take us to his family's holding and introduce us as his friends. His family will give us supplies for our journey home.' She swung her stare to Vindeliar. 'Won't he, Vindeliar?'

Kerf looked astounded. Vindeliar, carrying one pack on his shoulders and dragging another, looked weary and uncertain. The firelight shifted on his features, making him first an adoring servant and then a beaten dog.

'My family will do that?' Kerf asked in wonder.

'You will speak for us,' Dwalia assured him. I scooted myself a little farther away from the fire. I could barely stand the pain of my popped shoulder when I moved. I cradled my useless arm with my good one, wondering how bad the pain would be if I staggered to my feet and tried to run.

'I can't lift my coat,' Reppin told no one at all.

'No.' Kerf shook his head. 'I cannot speak for you to my family. I cannot even speak for myself. They will want to know how I have survived and returned when so many of my comrades are missing. They will think I have fled battle and left my war brothers to die. They will despise me.'

Dwalia fixed her smile in place, put her ungloved hand on his arm and gave Vindeliar a sideways glance. 'I am sure your family will welcome us when you speak for us. I am sure they will feel only pride in you.'

I kept my eyes fixed on them as I edged into darkness. The pain from my shoulder made me want to vomit. I watched Vindeliar's face slacken as his thoughts went elsewhere. I felt how desperately he pushed his thoughts onto Kerf as if I heard the echo of a distant scream. I watched the Chalcedean's scowl fade as he gazed at Dwalia. Reppin had given up trying to pick up my coat from the ground. Empty-handed, she tottered over to where the others stood. There she made a knowing smile and nodded to herself as Vindeliar worked his magic but no one took any notice of her. I bent my knees and pushed myself deeper into darkness.

'My family will surely welcome you. All we own will be put at your disposal,' Kerf told Dwalia. His smile was warm with certainty.

'Alaria, bring her!' Dwalia looked, not at me, but beyond me. I turned my head. The evil delight on Alaria's face was chilling. All this time, as I'd kept watch on Dwalia and tried to move away from the firelight, she had been behind me. Now or never. I pushed hard with my good hand and managed to gain my feet, my useless arm clutched to my belly. I ran.

I took three strides before Alaria caught me. She grabbed my hair and kicked my leg as if she had been waiting her whole life for that moment. I shrieked. She shook my head by my hair as a fox shakes a rabbit and then flung me aside. I landed on my bad shoulder. Flashes of red and flashes of black. I could not find air to breathe. I could do nothing when she seized the back of my shirt and dragged me almost to my feet. 'Walk!' she shouted at me. 'Walk or I'll kick you again!'

It was hard to obey and impossible to defy her. She was bigger and stronger than me and hadn't been beaten recently. She kept her grip on my garments and held me too high. We were halfway to Dwalia, me struggling to balance on my toes, when I realized that my shoulder was a dull red ache and I could move my arm again. So, I had that.

By the pillars, Dwalia was arranging her ducklings to her liking. 'I will go first,' she announced, as if anyone else could have. 'I will grip Vindeliar's hand, and he will hold Kerf's.' She smiled warmly at the nodding Chalcedean and I understood. Those were the two most important to her own survival. She wished to be certain her magic-man and the warrior with a home in Chalced arrived with her. 'Then the brat. Kerf, hold tight to her. Not her hand. Remember that she bites. Grab the back of her neck. That's right. Alaria, you are last. Take her by her upper arm and hold tight.'

This Alaria was pleased to do and I could only be weakly glad that it was not my bad shoulder. Kerf gripped the back of my neck and any kindliness he previously had shown toward me was gone. He was Vindeliar's puppet again.

'Wait! Am I last?' Reppin demanded.

Dwalia looked at her coldly. 'You are not last. You are unnecessary. You would not fetch the firewood. You chose to be useless. Alaria, go fetch that coat. It may be worth money in Chalced. And Reppin's pack.'

Reppin's eyes were huge in her wan face as Alaria released me and ran to obey. The Chalcedean's grip on me was sure. Alaria moved swiftly. Did she wish to show how useful she was? In a moment, she was back, Reppin's pack slung over one shoulder and the heavy coat that once had been white and mine draped over her arm. She seized my upper arm in a pinching grip.

'You can't leave me here. I need my pack! Don't leave me!' Reppin's pale face was cadaverous in the light of the fire. Her bitten arm was curled to her chest. She pawed at Alaria, trying to seize her free hand with her good one. Alaria turned her face away from her and clutched my former coat to her chest, curling her hand out of Reppin's reach. Her grip on my arm tightened. I wondered if she hardened her heart to leave Reppin or if it was a relief. Perhaps she was simply glad that she wasn't the one being abandoned. I saw now how Dwalia ruled. Cruelty to one of her followers meant the others could breathe more easily for a moment. There was no loyalty between luriks, only fear of Dwalia and desire for what she might bestow on them.

'Please!' Reppin shrieked to the night.

Vindeliar made a small sound. For an instant, his concentration was broken and Kerf's grip on my neck loosened.

'She's useless,' Dwalia growled. 'She's dying, she's whining, and she's consuming resources that are already scarce. Don't question my decisions, Vindeliar. Look what happened to all of us the last time you did not obey my commands. Look how many dead, and all your fault! Pay attention to me and hold tight or you, too, will be left behind!'

Kerf's grip on me tightened and Alaria's fingers ground the flesh of my arm against the bone.

I suddenly grasped the danger. 'We should not do this! We should follow the road. It must go somewhere! The standing stones are dangerous. We may not come out or we may emerge as mad as Kerf!'

My shouted warnings went unheeded. Dwalia pressed her gloved hand to the stone's carved face. It seemed to draw her in like a slice of ginger sinking into warm honey. The light from our abandoned campfire showed her sliding into the stone. Vindeliar followed, panting with terror as his hand, his wrist, his elbow vanished into stone. He whined as he was drawn in.

'We swim with the dead ones!' Kerf shouted, grinning his madman's grimace. 'On to the fallen palace of a dead duke!' He seemed to enter the pillar more slowly than Vindeliar had, as if the stone resisted him. I hung back but his grip on my neck stayed tight even when the rest of him had vanished into the stone. I looked up as I was dragged toward the pillar and lost my breath in horror at what I saw. The additional marking on the stone was not new. It was not scored as deeply into the stone as the original runes, but there was no mistaking its intent. Someone had deliberately marked a deep straight scratch through the rune, as if to forbid or warn anyone who chose to use that face of the portal. 'Da!' I cried out, a desperate call that no one could hear. 'Da! Help me!' In the next moment, my cheek touched the cold surface and I was pulled into tarry blackness.

FOUR

Chalced

Because of our studies of many old scrolls, including translations we have done, I am convinced that the legendary Elderlings of our myths and legends were a very real people who occupied a large territory for many generations before their cities and culture eventually fell into decay long before Buckkeep Castle was founded. Additional information gained from a library of what we call Skill-cubes has only convinced us that we are correct.

Why did the Elderlings, a people of wisdom and powerful magic, fail and disappear from our world? Can we tie that failing to the vanishing of the dragons, another event for which we have no explanation? And now that both dragons and perhaps Elderlings have returned to the world, how does that affect the future of humankind?

And what of our legends of an ancient alliance between Farseer and Elderlings, the very alliance that King Verity sought to revive when he led his expedition to the Rain Wilds? Were they living Elderlings he encountered or the stored memories of what they had been? Questions that we may find the answers to if we continue to mine the memory-cubes for information.

The Vanishing Elderlings, Chade Fallstar

My mother used to do this to me. When she wanted to move me.

A dim recollection. A den, a mother who carried me by the scruff of my neck. Not my thought, but it was a thought and the first one I had. Someone gripped hair, skin and shirt collar. The collar was the part that was choking me. I was dragged up and out of a mire as someone protested, 'There isn't room. Leave her! There isn't room.'

The blackness was absolute. Air on my face. I blinked my eyes to see if they were truly open. They were. No stars. No distant firelight. Nothing. Just dark. And something thick trying to pull me back down.

I was abruptly glad for the choking grip on my collar. In panic, I clutched one-handed at someone's shirt and crawled up and onto Kerf. He was prone on his side beneath me. I lifted my head and it hit against something. Worse, someone had hold of my arm and was pulling on it as they crawled up to join me. The man beneath me shifted onto his back. I fell off him to lie wedged between him and a stone wall. It was a snug fit and instinctively I pushed at him, trying to gain more room. But I could not move his bulk and I heard Alaria gasp and then utter small shriek after shriek as she scrabbled up to take my place on top of Kerf.

The shrieks turned into gasped words. 'Let go! Let go of me!' She was thrashing on top of Kerf.

'You're kicking me,' Vindeliar protested.

'Let go!' Alaria cried.

'I'm not touching you! Stop kicking!' Dwalia ordered her. 'Vindeliar, get off me!'

'I can't. I'm stuck! There's no room!' He was panting with terror.

Where were we? What had happened to us?

Dwalia tried for a tone of command and failed. She was breathless. 'Silence, all!'

'I'm sick.' I heard Vindeliar gag. 'That was awful. They were all grabbing at me. I want to go home. I can't do this. I hate this. I need to go home.' He blubbered like a small child.

'Let go of me!' Alaria, her voice gone shrill.

'Help me! I'm sinking! Please, make room! I can't climb past you!' I heard and smelled Reppin. The infection in her arm stank. She had probably broken the wound open in her struggle. 'My arm . . . I can't climb out. Pull me up, someone! Don't leave me here! Don't leave me with them!'

Where were we?

Be calm. Discover what has happened before you try to make a plan. I felt Wolf Father's steadiness suffuse me. My breathing that had become bellows in my chest. But his voice was so calm in my mind. *Listen. Touch. Smell. What can you discover?*

It was hard to be calm with the slapping, panting struggle going on right beside me. Alaria begged, 'Let go! There's no room! Don't pull me back! Ah!'

Reppin did not shriek. She gave a long moan that was suddenly quenched in a sound like pulled heavy stone dropped in from muck. Only Alaria's panting broke the silence.

'She was pulled back down into the stone.' More a statement than a question from Dwalia. And with it, I recalled that she had dragged us into a Skill-pillar.

'I had to! I had to push her away. There's no more room! You said to leave her. It's not my fault!' Alaria sounded more defensive than sorry.

'Be silent!' Dwalia's voice was still pinched with breathlessness. 'I speak. Vindeliar, get off me!'

'I am sorry. I am stuck here. Kerf pushed me onto you as he crawled up. I can't budge. A stone presses down on me.' He was on the edge of hysteria. 'I am so sick. I cannot see! Am I blind? Lingstra Dwalia, am I blind?'

'No. It is dark, you oaf. Don't dare to vomit on me. You are crushing me. Give me room.' I heard a struggle of shifting bodies.

Vindeliar whimpered, 'There is no space for me to move. I am crushed, too.'

'If you cannot be helpful, be still. Chalcedean?' She was gasping for air. Vindeliar was not a small person and she was trapped beneath him. 'Kerf?'

He giggled. It was a terrible sound coming from a man's deep chest in the darkness.

'Stop that! Dwalia, he's touching me!' Alaria was outraged and terrified.

Kerf giggled again and I felt him tug his arm from under me. He lifted it, giving me a tiny bit more room, and I surmised that he embraced Alaria against him. 'Nice,' he said in a throaty voice and I felt him lift his hips against her.

'Stop,' she begged him, but his reply was a throaty growl followed by a low chuckle. The muscles of his upper arm were pressed against me and I felt them tighten as he snugged Alaria closer to him. His breathing deepened. Beside me, he began a rhythmic shifting that shoved me solidly against the wall. Alaria began to weep.

'Ignore him,' Dwalia ordered her coldly.

'He's trying to rape me!' She squeaked. 'He's—'

'He doesn't have enough room, so ignore him. He can't get his own trousers down, let alone yours. Pretend he's a little dog, infatuated with your leg.' Was there a cruel satisfaction in Dwalia's voice? Did she revel in Alaria's humiliation? 'We are trapped here and you are squawking about a man touching you. Scarcely a real danger.'

Alaria responded with a frightened keening that kept pace with Kerf's thudding against her.

'The girl, Bee. Did she come through? Is she alive?' Dwalia demanded.

I kept my silence. I had wriggled my sore arm free, and although my injured shoulder protested, I was groping to discover the confines of our prison. Stone beneath me. To the left of me, Kerf's body. To my right, a wall of stone as far as I could grope. When I reached up I could brush my fingertips against more stone. It was worked stone, smooth as a polished floor. I explored with my feet. More stone. Even if I'd been alone in this space, I could not have sat up. Where were we?

The tempo of the Chalcedean's jerking was speeding up and with it his open-mouthed gasping.

'Alaria, feel around. Did the girl come through?'

'She . . . must . . . have. Oh! I dragged myself through by . . . holding on . . . to her.' Alaria's voice was going smaller and higher. The Chalcedean continued to heave himself about. 'It's disgusting!' She wailed. 'He's mouthing my face. He stinks! Stop it!' She shrieked but the Chalcedean began to grunt under her.

'Can you feel her? Is she alive?' Dwalia persisted.

I lay still. Despite Kerf's passionate rocking, I felt her groping hand. I held my breath. She touched my face and then my chest.

'She's here. She's not moving but her body is warm. Vindeliar! Make him stop this!'

'I can't. I'm sick. I'm so sick.'

'Vindeliar, you'd best recall that I and only I give you your orders. Alaria, be silent!'

'So many of them were in there,' Vindeliar groaned. 'They were all pulling at me. I'm so sick.'

'Be sick silently!' Dwalia snapped.

Alaria was gasping in horror. She did not speak again but I heard the small weeping sounds she made, and the deep groan of the Chalcedean when he finally reached some sort of satisfaction. She tried to wriggle away from him, but I felt his arm muscles tighten and knew he held her there. It was as well for me. I did not want her to roll off him and onto me.

'Feel about, as much as you can,' Dwalia commanded. 'Can anyone feel an opening in this tomb?'

It was a poor choice of words. 'Tomb,' Vindeliar repeated and gave a trailing moan of despair.

'Silence!' she wheezed at him. 'Feel about over your head. Is there any opening?'

I heard them moving in the darkness, heard the scraping brush of fingers against stone, the scuff of boots scraping more stone. I remained still.

'Anything?' Dwalia demanded of the darkness.

'No,' Alaria responded sullenly. 'Only stone, everywhere I touch. I can barely lift my head. Have you any room next to you?' The Chalcedean's muscles had gone slack and, by his stentorian breathing, I deduced he had fallen asleep. Madness was, perhaps, a mercy in some situations.

'Would I allow Vindeliar to lie on top of me if I could be anywhere else?' Dwalia demanded.

A silence. Then Alaria suggested, 'Perhaps you should take us back to where we were?'

'Unfortunately, as the Chalcedean emerged, he pushed me to one side and shoved Vindeliar on top of me. He now lies on top of the portal stone. I cannot reach it from where I am.'

'We are packed like pickled fish in a cask,' Vindeliar observed sadly. More softly he added, 'I suppose we will all die here.'

'What?' Alaria demanded in a half-shriek. 'Die here? Starving to death in the dark?'

'Well, we can't get out,' Vindeliar responded morosely.

'Be silent!' Dwalia ordered them, but it was too late. Alaria broke. She began weeping in gasps and after a few moments, I heard Vindeliar's muffled sobs.

Die here? Who would die first? A scream started to swell inside my chest.

That is not a useful thought, Wolf Father rebuked me. *Breathe. Quietly.*

I felt panic swell in me and then be quashed under his sternness. *Think how to escape. Do you think you could enter the stone alone?*

Could you reach under the Chalcedean and open the passageway to return us to the forest?

I'm not sure.

Try.

I'm afraid to try. What if I get stuck in the stone? What if I come out alone somewhere?

What if you stay here and starve? After, of course, the others go mad and attack one another? Now, try.

When I had slid off Kerf, I had landed on my back. I wriggled to one side. I had to roll onto my sore shoulder to do so. And it was that hand and arm that I had to try to wedge under Kerf and Alaria's combined weight. I tried to do it slowly, sliding my hand under the small of his back where it did not press so hard against the stone. I made a small sound of pain and Alaria's sniffling stopped. 'What's that?' she cried, and reached down to me. 'She's moving. Bee's alive and awake.'

'And I bite!' I reminded her, and she snatched her hand away.

Now that they knew I was awake, there was no point in being secretive. I shoved my hand as far under Kerf as it would go. He shifted slightly, pinching my arm under him, then belched and went back to snoring. My shoulder burned as I worked my hand deeper under Kerf, scraping it over gritty stone. I heard my own fearful panting and closed my mouth to breathe through my nose. It was quieter but I was still just as terrified. What if I touched the rune and was suddenly sucked in? Could it drag me in past Kerf? Would he and Alaria fall in with me, as if I had opened a door under us? The terror put pressure on my bladder. I blocked it. I blocked everything except the effort of pushing my hand across stone. The stone surface under my fingers suddenly became a small indentation. I cautiously explored it with my fingertips. It was the rune.

Do you feel anything? Can you make anything happen?

I tried. I didn't want to, but I pushed my fingers into the rune and rubbed the tips against the graven lines of it. *Nothing. Nothing happens, Wolf Father.*

Very well. We should think of something else, then. His words were calm but beneath them I felt his simmering fear.

Dragging my arm out from under Kerf was more painful than pushing it beneath him had been. Once my arm was free, I knew a sudden surge of panic. Everything was touching me – Kerf's warm body, the unyielding stone below me, the stone alongside my body. I desperately needed to stand up, to stretch, to breathe cool air. *Don't struggle*, Wolf Father insisted. *Struggling only makes a snare go tighter. Be still and think. Think.*

I tried, but everything was touching me. Alaria was weeping again. Kerf was snoring. His ribs moved against me with every breath he took. My tunic had twisted around me, binding one of my arms. I was too warm. I was thirsty. I made a small noise in the back of my throat without intending to. Another sound rose in me, a scream that wanted to get out.

No. None of that. Close your eyes, cub. Be with me. We are in a forest. Remember the cool night smells of a forest? Lie very still. Be with me.

Wolf Father pulled me into his memories. I was in a forest. Dawn was coming and we were snug in a den. *Time to sleep*, he insisted. *Sleep.*

I must have slept. When I awoke, I held tight to the calm he had given me. I had nothing else to cling to. In the blackness, I measured the passage of time by the behaviour of my fellow prisoners. Kerf awoke when Alaria became hysterical. He put his arms around her and crooned to her, perhaps a Chalcedean lullaby. She stilled after a time. Later, Dwalia burst into shrieking impotent fury when Vindeliar pissed on her. 'I held it as long as I could,' he wailed, and the smell of urine made me want to piss as well.

Dwalia whispered something to him, her voice as soft and deadly as a snake's hiss, and he began to sob.

Then his sounds stopped, and I decided he slept. Alaria was quiet. Kerf began to sing, not a lullaby but some sort of marching song. He stopped abruptly in mid-verse. 'Little girl. Bee. Are you alive?'

'I am.' I answered because I was glad he had stopped singing.

'I am very confused. When we walked through stone, I was certain we were dead. But if we are not dead, then this will not be a good way for you to die. I think I could reach your neck. Would you like me to strangle you? It will not be fast, but it is a faster death than starving.'

How thoughtful. 'No, thank you. Not yet.'

'You should not wait too long. I will become weak. And it will be unpleasant in here soon. Piss. Shit. People going mad.'

'No.' I heard something. 'Hush!'

'I know my words are sad to hear, but I only seek to warn you. I may be strong enough to snap your neck. That might be faster.'

'No. Not yet.' Not yet? What was I saying? Then, from far away, a sound. 'Listen. Do you hear that?'

Alaria stirred at my words. 'Hear what?' she demanded.

'Do you hear something?' Dwalia snapped at me.

'Be silent!' I roared at them in my father's angry voice, and they obeyed. We all listened. The sounds were faint. Slow hooves clopping on cobblestones. A woman's voice lifted in a brief sing-song chant.

'Is it a prayer?' Alaria wondered.

'It's an early pedlar. She sings, "bread, fresh baked this morning. Bread, warm from the oven".' Kerf sounded sentimental.

'Help us!' Alaria's desperate scream was so shrill my ears rang with it. 'Help us, oh help us! We are trapped!'

When she finally stopped shrieking for lack of breath, my ears were ringing. I strove to hear the bread-woman's song or the clopping hooves, but I heard nothing. 'She is gone,' Vindeliar said sadly.

'We are in a city,' Kerf declared. 'Only cities have breadmongers at dawn, selling wares in the street.' He paused for a moment and then said, 'I thought we were dead. I thought that was why you wished to come to the fallen palace of the dead duke, to be dead here. Do breadmongers still sing when they are dead? I do not think so. What need have the dead of fresh bread?' Silence greeted his question. I did not know what the others were thinking, but I pondered his previous words. A fallen palace. How much stone was on top of our tomb? 'So we are not dead,' he reasoned laboriously, 'but we will be soon if we cannot escape. But perhaps as the city awakens, we will hear other people. And perhaps they will hear us if we shout for help.'

'So be silent for now!' Dwalia warned us. 'Be silent and listen. I will tell you when to shout for help, and we will all shout together.'

We waited in suffocating silence. From time to time we heard the muffled sounds of a city. A temple bell rang. An ox bellowed. Once, we thought we heard a woman calling a child. At that, Dwalia bade us all shout for help with one voice. But it seemed to me that the sounds were never very close, and I wondered if we were on a hill above a city rather than in the city itself. After a time, Vindeliar pissed again, and I think Alaria did, too. The smell was getting worse – piss and sweat and fear. I tried to imagine I was in my bed at

Withywoods. It was dark in the room. Soon my father would come to look in on me. He always thought I was asleep when he looked in my room late at night before going to his own bed. I stared up at blackness and imagined his step in the corridor. I was beginning to see dots of light from staring into the blackness so long. Then I blinked and realized that one of the dots was now a narrow stripe.

I stared at it, not daring to hope. Slowly I lifted my foot as far as it would go. It blocked part of the light. When I lowered my foot, the light reappeared, stronger.

'I can see light,' I whispered.

'Where?'

'Near my feet,' I said, but by then the light had started to slink in. I could see how uneven the blocks were that confined us. Worked stone, yes, but tumbled in a heap around us rather than something built.

'I can't see it,' Dwalia said, as if I were lying.

'Nor I,' Kerf confirmed. 'My woman is in my way.'

'I am not your woman!' Alaria was outraged.

'You have slept on top of me. You've pissed on me. I claim you.'

My lifted foot could barely reach the slot of light. I pointed my toe and pushed. I heard gravel fall outside our prison and the crack widened slightly. I rolled onto my side as much as I could and pushed against Kerf to slide myself closer to the light. I could press my whole foot against the stone below the light, and I did. More and larger rock shards fell, some rattling against my boot. The light grew stronger. I kicked at it savagely. The shaft of light enlarged to the size of my hand. I battered my feet against it as if I were dancing in a hill of biting ants. No more gravel fell. I kicked at the stone that roofed that wall, to no avail. I stopped when I had no strength left and became aware that the others had been shouting questions and encouragement. I didn't care. I refused to let Wolf Father's calmness reach me. I stared up at the dimly lit ceiling of my tomb and sobbed.

The Chalcedean moved, shoving me aside to lift his arms past his head to brace them against the stone. He groaned and suddenly shifted hard against me. His hip pushed into my ribs, wedging me against the walls so I could scarcely breathe. Alaria was squeaking and squealing as he pressed her against the ceiling. He drew up his knee, crushing me harder and then with an audible grunt, he kicked out suddenly and hard.

Grit fell and rock dust sifted into my eyes and up my nose and settled on my lips. Kerf was still pinning me and I could not get my hand to my face to rub it away. It stuck to the tears on my cheeks and settled between my collar and neck. Then, as the dust was settling and I could almost draw a clean breath, he did it again. A vertical line of light was suddenly added to the first one.

'It's a block of stone. Try again, little one. This time, push, not kick. I'll help you. Put your feet down low, at the bottom of it.'

'What if it all falls on us?'

'A faster death,' Kerf said.

I wriggled and slid my body closer to the line of light. I bent my knees, set my feet low on the block. The Chalcedean shifted his big boot between and slightly above my feet. 'Push,' he said, and I did. Stone grated grudgingly but it moved. A rest, and then we pushed again. The crack was a hand's-breadth wide. Another push, and the stone fetched up against something. We pushed three more times before the stone moved, and then it slewed to the left. Another push and it was easier. I shifted my body to get more purchase.

The afternoon sunlight that had found us was fading toward evening by the time the opening was large enough for me to wriggle out. I went feet first, squirming blindly out of a gap barely large enough for me to pass, scraping skin off my hip and tearing my tunic. I sat up, brushing dust and grit from my face. I heard the others shouting, demanding that I move more stone, that I tell them where we were. I ignored them. I didn't care where we were. I could breathe and no one else was touching me. I drew deep breaths of cool air, and wiped my sleeve across my gritty face, and rolled my good shoulder. I was out.

'What can you see?' Dwalia was furious with desperation. 'Where are we?'

I looked around me. Ruins, I supposed. I could now see what our tomb had been and it was not at all what I had thought it was. Great blocks of stones had fallen, first one pillar to the floor and then a great slab of stone had collapsed partway across the fallen pillar, and then other pieces of stones had tumbled around them. Only good fortune had kept them from smashing completely flat against the Skill-pillar embedded in the floor. I looked up the evening sky past the jagged remains of walls, and down at more etched runes. There was another Skill-pillar here, set into the floor. I stepped gingerly away from it.

The others were shouting contradictory orders at me: to fetch help, to say what I saw. I didn't respond. I heard the temple bell ring again in the distance. I took three steps out of sight, squatted and relieved myself. As I stood, I heard stone grating and saw the Chalcedean's legs emerging from the enlarged opening. I hastily pulled up my leggings and watched as he braced his feet and levered the stone away. Shrieks from inside of 'Be careful!' and 'You'll bring it down on us!' went unheeded.

'I should run,' I whispered to myself.

Not yet, Wolf Father whispered in my mind. *Remain with the danger you know. The Chalcedean has mainly been kind to you. If we are in Chalced, you do not speak the language or know their ways. Maybe luck will favour us and the stones fall on all the others. Hide and watch.*

I moved back amongst the tumbled stones and crouched where I could see but not be seen. Kerf wriggled out on his back, kicking and scraping and grunting as he heaved himself along. He emerged powdered with grey dust and grit, looking like a statue called to life. His hips freed, he shifted onto his side, twisting like a snake to manoeuvre first one shoulder and then the other out, and sat up, blinking in the late afternoon light. His pale eyes were startling in his grey stone face. He licked dust from his lips, his red tongue another oddity, and looked about himself, then stepped up onto a block of stone and surveyed the scene. I crouched lower.

'Is it safe?' Alaria called, but she had already thrust her feet out of the opening. Smaller and lither than the Chalcedean but just as dirty, she squirmed out without waiting for any answer then sat up, groaning, and wiped rock dust from her face. 'Where are we?' she demanded.

Kerf grinned. 'Chalced. I am almost home. I know this place, although it has changed greatly. Here we once mourned my grandfather. The duke's throne was at the end of a great hall. Over there, I think. This is what remains of the old duke's palace after the dragons brought it tumbling down around his ears.' He sneezed several times, wiped his face on his arm and then nodded to himself. 'Yes. The duchess proclaimed it an evil place and swore it would never be rebuilt.' He frowned slightly, as if summoning the memory was difficult or painful. He spoke slowly, almost dreamily. 'Duke Ellik vowed it would be the first structure he raised again, and that he would rule from it.'

Alaria struggled to her feet. 'Chalced?' she whispered to herself.

He spun to her and grinned. 'Our home! My mother will be pleased to meet you. She has longed for me to bring home a woman to share the tasks of the household with her and my sisters and to bear my children.'

'I am not your wife!'

'Not yet. But if you prove yourself a hard worker and a maker of strong children, then perhaps I shall wed you. Many prizes of war become wives. Eventually.'

'I am *not* a prize of war!' she declared.

Kerf shook his head and rolled his eyes, bemused by her ignorance. Alaria looked as if she wanted to shriek, scratch him or run away. She did none of those things, but turned her attention to the next pair of feet emerging from the stone tomb.

Vindeliar's feet were kicking and scuffing as he tried to emerge. 'I'm stuck!' he cried in a panic-stricken voice.

'Get out of my way!' Dwalia's voice was muted. 'I told you to let me go first!'

'There wasn't room!' He was already tearful. 'I had to go first, to get off you. You said, "get off me", and this was the only way I could get off you.'

She cursed him, her obscenities muffled by stone. Vindeliar did not seem to be making much progress. I took advantage of the noise to retreat farther from all of them, behind the round of a fallen column. From there I could peer back to see what was happening, but not be seen.

Vindeliar was wedged. He drummed his heels helplessly on the ground as if he were a child having a tantrum. Stuck. Good, I thought savagely. Let him be the plug that bottles up Dwalia forever. Despite any kindly feelings he had toward me, I knew he was the real danger to me. If I fled, Dwalia could never catch me. But if Vindeliar set the Chalcedean on me, I was doomed.

'Brother! My brother! Please move the stone and free me!'

I didn't make a sound as I crouched there, watching with one eye. Kerf stepped over to the stone. 'Ware the dust!' he called to Vindeliar and stooped to set his shoulder to the blocking stone. I heard it grate against the ancient floor and saw smaller stones and grit vanish in a crack that opened in the top of the rockpile as he did so. Dwalia screamed but the rocks that fell would do no more than bruise her. Kerf seized Vindeliar's thick legs and dragged him out. Vindeliar jammed for a moment and howled as Kerf grunted and pulled him out anyway. I saw him sit up, grey with dust and with a bleeding scrape on the side of his face.

'I'm free!' he announced as if no one else would know it.

'Get out of my way!' Dwalia shouted. I did not wait to see her emerge. Ducking low, I crept away. I threaded my way through the maze of fallen stone, silent as a mouse. The slanting sunlight of a spring evening created shapes from the shadows. I came to a place where a fallen wall leaned against a collapsed column like a stone tent and crept into it.

Stay hidden. It is easier for them to see motion and hear your footsteps than to search this rubble.

I was alone, and hungry and thirsty, in a city far from home where I did not speak the language.

But I was free. I'd escaped them.

FIVE

The Bargain

A snake is in a stone bowl. There is soup around it. It smells bad and then I know it is not soup. It is very dirty water, full of snake-piss and waste. A creature comes to the bowl and suddenly I see how big the snake is and the bowl. The snake is many times longer than the creature is tall. The creature reaches through bars around the bowl to scoop up some of the dirty water. He slurps some of the filthy water and smiles with an ugly wide mouth. I do not like to look at him, he is so wrong. The serpent coils in on itself and tries to bite him. He laughs and shuffles away.

From Bee Farseer's dream journal

As comfortable as the Elderling robes might be, I did not feel decently clad for my meeting with the keepers until I was in my own clothes again. As I snugged my leather belt tight and buckled it I noticed I had gained two notches of travel since I'd left Buckkeep. My leather waistcoat would function as light armour. Not that I expected anyone to knife me, but one never knew. The small items in my concealed pockets would expedite any deadly task of my own. I smiled to realize that someone had unloaded my secret pockets before my garments were laundered and then restored all to their proper location. I said nothing to Spark as I tugged my waistcoat straight and then patted the pocket that concealed a very fine garrotte. She quirked her brows at me. It was enough.

I vacated the room to allow Spark to attend to Lady Amber's dressing and coiffing. I found Lant ready and Perseverance keeping him company and chased a foggy memory of a conversation between the two and then let it go. Done was done. Lant no longer seemed to fear me, and as Chade's instructions to him to watch over me, well, that would demand a private conversation.

'So, are we ready?' Lant asked as he slid a small, flat-handled knife into a sheath concealed at his hip. It startled me. Who was this man? The answer came to me. This was the Lant that Riddle and Nettle had both admired and enjoyed. I understood suddenly why Chade had asked him to watch over me. It was not flattering but it was oddly reassuring.

Perseverance had a worried frown. 'Am I to be seated with you at the dinner? It seems very strange.'

In the space of a few months, he had gone from being a stableboy on my estate to being my serving man. And companion, if I were truthful. 'I don't know. If they send you and Spark to another table be sure to stay close to her.'

He nodded grimly. 'Sir? May I ask you something?'

'What is it?' I asked guardedly. I was on edge for our meeting with the keepers.

He shot Lant a sideways look as if shy about asking his question. 'About Mage Gray. Sometimes you call him Fool, but he's being Lady Amber now.'

'He is,' I conceded and waited.

Lant was silent, as intrigued by the Fool's many guises as the lad was.

'And Ash is Spark now.'

I nodded. 'True, also.'

'And Spark is a girl.'

I nodded again.

He folded his lips in as if to imprison his question. Then he blurted, 'Do you feel at all . . . odd about it? Uncomfortable?'

I laughed. 'I've known him for many years, in many guises. He was King Shrewd's jester when I was a boy. The Fool. Then Lord Golden. Mage Gray. And now Lady Amber. All different. Yet always my friend.' I reached for honesty. 'But when I was your age, it would have bothered me a great deal. It doesn't now because I know who he is. And who I am, and who we are to each other. That doesn't change, no matter what name he wears or what garb he dons. Whether I am Holder Tom Badgerlock or Prince FitzChivalry Farseer, I know he's my friend.'

He gave a sigh of relief. 'Then it's all right that it doesn't matter to me about Spark? I saw it didn't bother you and I decided it need not bother me.' He shook his head, perplexed, and added, 'When she's being Spark, she's pretty.'

'She is,' Lant said quietly. I fought to keep from smiling.

'So that's who she really is? A girl named Spark?'

That was a harder question. 'Spark is whoever she is. Sometimes that's Ash. It's like being a father and a son and perhaps a husband. All different facets of the same person.'

He nodded. 'But it was easier to talk to Ash. We had better jokes.'

A tap at the door announced Lady Amber and Spark. Lady Amber had gone to every possible effort to be dazzling and had succeeded. The long skirt and lacy beribboned blouse with the embroidered waistcoat were dated by Buckkeep standards. Amber, or more likely Spark, had given special attention to the rouge that shaped her lip and the powder that concealed her scars. Her blind eyes were outlined in black, emphasizing their opacity.

Spark was a pretty girl but no more than that today. She had chosen to present herself in a way that would not invite too much attention. Her hair, released from Ash's warrior tail, hung in black waves to her shoulders. Her high-collared blouse was the colour of butterscotch and the simple smock over it denied she had breasts or a waist. Amber wore an amused smile. Could she sense how Per and Lant were gazing at them, dumbfounded?

'The clothes look much better on you than they did on Lady Thyme,' I complimented her.

'I hope they also smell better,' was the Fool's response.

'Who is Lady Thyme?' Lant asked.

For a moment, the silence held. Then both the Fool and I burst into laughter. I had almost recovered when the Fool gasped, 'Your father.' And we were both lost again to merriment. Lant was torn between confusion and offence.

'I don't understand what is funny?' Spark queried. 'We raided an old woman's wardrobe for these clothes . . .'

'It's a very long tale,' was Amber's ladylike response. 'A hint: Lady Thyme's chamber had a secret entry to Chade's workroom. When he chose to occasionally emerge from hiding in the old days, he moved as Lady Thyme.'

Lant's mouth hung slightly ajar.

'Lady Thyme was one of your father's most inspired ploys. But it must be a tale for another time, for now we must descend.'

'Do not we wait until we are summoned?' I asked.

'No, for Rain Wild courtesies are founded on Bingtown ways rather than on Jamaillian aristocracy. They are more egalitarian, and pragmatic and direct. Here you are Prince FitzChivalry and they will expect you to have the last word. But I know more of their ways than you do. Please let me negotiate.'

'Negotiate what?'

'Our passage through their territory. And possibly beyond.'

'We have nothing to offer them in exchange for our passage,' I pointed out. Much of my coin and several other precious items had been lost in the bear attack.

'I will think of something,' she offered.

'And it won't be offering healing to anyone. I can't.'

She raised her delicately-outlined brows at me. 'Who would know that better than me?' she replied, and held out a gloved hand. I stepped forward and hooked it onto my arm.

I saw Lant grinning as Perseverance stepped forward and offered his crooked arm to Spark. She looked startled, but accepted it. I took a deep breath. 'And off we go,' I warned them.

A serving girl waited at the foot of the stairs to guide us into a sumptuous and elegant chamber. There were no tapestries, no figured rugs, but the walls themselves and the floor underfoot did not need them. We seemed to be dining in an open field, surrounded by a vista of autumn hills in green and gold. We trod on a grassy sward with tiny wildflowers speckled among the verdant green. Only the sensation of stone underfoot and the still air spoiled the illusion. I heard Spark whisper a description to Amber, who smiled wistfully.

Four tables were arranged in an open square, with the guests' chairs directed inward. There was no head of the table, no seat of authority. Some of the keepers were already here, standing or seated in small groups. They were a striking reminder of the tapestry of Elderlings that had graced my boyhood bedchamber. Tall and slender they were, with eyes of gold or copper or sparkling blue. All were scaled, some more heavily than others, and each was marked fantastically, in patterns that were as precise as the feathers on a bird or the colours on a butterfly's wings. They were beautiful and alien, wondrous to behold. I thought of the children I had healed and of the Rain Wilders I had glimpsed in my days here. Their changes were random, as often grotesque as pretty. The differences were striking and the fate of those randomly affected by contact with dragons was appalling.

Our servant escort had vanished. We stood smiling and uncertain. Should I dismiss Spark and Perseverance or were they part of the 'Six Duchies emissaries' that the invitation had addressed? Spark was describing the room, the people and their garments to Amber in a low murmur. I did not interrupt.

General Rapskal stood tall even among the tall Elderlings and was broader of shoulder than many. He wore a less martial air tonight, being clothed in a tunic of blue with yellow trousers and soft blue footwear. He carried no weapons that I could see. I knew that did not mean he was unarmed. With him were the two Elderlings I had seen following his commands earlier. One of them, I surmised, was Kase. Both were scaled in orange, and the eyes they turned toward us were copper, and both were heavily muscled. I'd wager they could brawl hard if provoked.

The blue Elderling woman wore her wings outside her long tunic tonight, folded smoothly to her back. Their feathery scales were a patterned display of blues and silvers, with touches of black and white. I wondered at the weight of them on her slender, once-human frame. Her long black hair was confined in rows of braids that were interrupted with beads and small silver charms. The Elderling man beside her had green scaling and dark hair. He looked directly at us, spoke to his mate, and then moved toward us purposefully. I tried not to stare at the odd pattern of scales on his cheek as he greeted me.

'Prince FitzChivalry, I should like to introduce myself. I'm Tats. Thymara and I thank you for what you did for our daughter. Her feet and legs are still sore but she finds it much easier to walk.'

'I am glad I was able to help her.' He had not offered his hand and so I kept mine at my side.

Thymara spoke. 'I thank you. For the first time in many weeks, she can sleep without pain.' She hesitated and then added, 'She said that her chest feels different. She had not complained of it but now she says that it is easier to breathe with her skin not so tight?' Her inflection made the statement a question.

I smiled and said only, 'I am glad she is more comfortable.' I had a vague recollection of a keel-bone such as a bird might have . . . had their child been developing it? It did not seem tactful to admit that I could not clearly recall what the Skill had done to her through me.

Thymara's earnest gaze met my eyes and then travelled to Amber. 'Would that you could be rewarded as you deserve,' she said softly.

A mellifluous chime sounded. Thymara smiled at me again. 'Well, we are to be seated now. Thank you again. And always.' They moved gracefully away from me, and I became aware that while we had spoken other Elderlings had arrived. Once, I had been an assassin with an edge, constantly aware of my surroundings. I wasn't so tonight, and it was not just that my Skill-walls were so tight. I had lost the habit of extreme alertness. When had I last been the competent assassin that Chade had trained? Not for a long time. When I had lived at Withywoods with Molly that would have pleased me. Here and now it seemed a serious failure.

I spoke low to Lant. 'Stay alert. If you notice anything untoward, let me know immediately.' He gave me an incredulous glance that threatened to become a smile before he gained control of his face. Together we moved in an unhurried way toward the tables. I saw no indication of any protocol related to seating. King Reyn and Queen Malta had entered but were engaged in deep conversation with a lanky blue-scaled Elderling. Phron, looking much livelier now, was with them. Their talk seemed to involve us, for twice he gestured toward us. Where were we expected to sit? Awkward – and potentially a social disaster. Thymara glanced over at us, spoke to her mate and then hastened back to us. 'You may sit wherever you please. Would you like to be together, or to mingle?'

I longed to exchange a glance with Amber. Instead I patted her hand on my arm fondly and she immediately replied, 'Together, if we may.'

'Of course.' But I did not see five adjacent seats until Thymara matter-of-factly called out, 'Alum. Sylve. Jerd. Harrikin. Bump down and make some room!'

The Elderlings so addressed laughed at her abrupt manner and promptly shifted their seating to free up a rank of five chairs. 'There. Please,' Thymara invited, and we were seated. Thymara and her mate took seats as Malta and Reyn joined us at the table. No royal procession into the room, no announcements of names. No titles for the keepers, no variance in rank was apparent. Except for General Rapskal.

Servants brought dishes of food and set them down to be passed for the Elderlings to serve themselves. The meat was wild game, venison or bird. The bread was not plentiful, but there were four fish dishes and three kinds of root vegetables. The menu told me that Kelsingra could feed itself, but not with great variety.

Perseverance and Spark conversed with an Elderling named Harrikin. Seated beyond him was a girlish Elderling. Sylve was pink and gold, with sparse hair but an intricate pattern of scalp scales. They were discussing fishing, and Sylve was unabashedly describing how difficult it had been to keep her dragon fed when they had journeyed from Trehaug to discover Kelsingra. Lant was smiling and nodding, but his gaze often roved the room watchfully. To my right, Amber was seated next to Nortel. He was explaining that it was his dragon, Tinder, we had first encountered near the fountains. He hoped he had not seemed too aggressive; the dragons were unaccustomed to being surprised. Amber nodded, and managed her utensils and food almost as if sighted.

We ate. We drank. We endeavoured to converse in that awkward way one does when attempting to speak loud enough to be heard over a dozen other conversations. Being in the thick of such an occasion was very different to spying on it from behind a wall. From a higher vantage point, I could have quickly deduced the alliances, rivalries and enmities in the room. Trapped in the midst of it, I could only guess. I hoped that Lant, safely layered between me and our two servants, could politely avoid socializing and collect more information.

The board was cleared. Brandy and a sweet wine were offered and I chose the brandy. It was not Sandsedge, but it was palatable. The Elderlings rose from their seats and wandered the room, conversing, and we copied their behaviour. Queen Malta came to apologize yet again and to hope that I was well recovered. Phron embarrassed me with the passion of his gratitude and his anger with General Rapskal's behaviour. Twice I saw Rapskal angling toward me, only to be intercepted by one or another of the Elderlings. We resumed our seats and Harrikin rose. With his knuckles, he rapped on the table three times. Instantly silence fell.

'Keepers, please welcome Prince FitzChivalry, Lord Lant and Lady Amber of the Six Duchies. They come as emissaries from King Dutiful and Queen Elliania. Tonight, we offer them a well-deserved welcome! And our deepest thanks.'

Plain words. No flowery speech, no reminders of past favours, treaties and services. It took me aback but Amber seemed to expect it. She rose in her place. Blind as she was, she still moved her unsighted gaze over her audience. Did she sense the body-warmth emanating from their shadowy shapes? With unerring accuracy, she turned her face to Harrikin.

'Thank you for this welcoming meal and for your hospitality, and for this opportunity to speak. I will be brief and to the point.' She allowed herself a smile. 'I suspect that since we first arrived, gossip has flown swiftly. I believe that most of you know our tale. It is true that we come as emissaries from the Six Duchies, but equally true that Kelsingra is not our destination. As Prince FitzChivalry has restored some of your children to health, you can imagine what pain it would be to have a child stolen. Bee Farseer is no more. When we leave you, it is to embark on a journey of vengeance against the Servants of the Whites.'

As Amber drew breath, Queen Malta interrupted in a low, soft voice. 'Lady Amber, if you would allow me to speak, please?' There was no rebuke in her voice, only a simple request. Amber was startled but gave a slow nod of agreement. The queen took a deep breath and folded her hands the tabletop. 'Yesterday we, the Keepers of Kelsingra, met in our council. I shared your tale with them. The parents and some of the children spoke of what Prince FitzChivalry did. We remain overwhelmed with gratitude and all agreed with what the prince said. The lives of our children are not bargaining points for us to haggle over. No amount of coin, no bartered favour from us, could ever match what the prince did for us. We can only offer you undying thanks, and our promise that we will always, forever, remember. And we are a long-lived people now.' Malta paused and looked around. 'But you have also gifted us with a vengeance we have long sought. We, too, have endured Chalced's destructive attacks, on our dragons and on our kin. Chalced's spies and killers sought to butcher dragons for their body-parts, for remedies to preserve the life of their old duke. Selden, brother to me and beloved singer for our dragons, was brutalized there by both the Duke of Chalced and Ellik. We knew that Ellik was instrumental in the attacks on our dragons. When the dragons took their vengeance on Chalced, toppling the duke's stronghold and killing him, Ellik fled. The present Duchess of Chalced will undoubtedly be as pleased as we are to hear that you've made an end of him. In killing him you have satisfied our family's desire for vengeance. And that is a debt we are more than willing to pay!

'Thus Reyn, born to the Khuprus family of the Rain Wild Traders and I, born to the Vestrit family of the Bingtown Traders, well understand your desire to follow your vengeance to its final closure. We, as Traders for the Khuprus and Vestrit families, are pleased to offer you like for like, aid in your vengeance for how you achieved ours. We have taken it upon ourselves to arrange your transport from here to Jamaillia. If you are willing, you will board the *Tarman* when he docks here. The *Tarman* will carry you to Trehaug, where the liveship *Paragon* will be waiting for you. He will carry you to Bingtown, and if you wish, to Jamaillia on his trading run. A bird has already been sent to secure your passage. On behalf of our families, we hope you will accept our hospitality aboard these liveships.'

'Liveships,' Perseverance breathed with a boy's awe. 'Are they truly real?'

Phron grinned at the lad. 'We will let you judge that for yourselves.'

I forgot my promise to Amber. 'I am speechless,' I said.

Malta smiled, and I glimpsed the girl she once had been. 'That's as well, for I have more to say. The keepers have other gifts they wish to bestow on you.' She hesitated for a moment. 'These gifts are of Elderling make. They are useful but also saleable, should your need be extreme.' She took a breath. 'It ill behoves one to speak of the value of a gift but I must make you aware that usually these items are only possessed by Traders or sold through Bingtown for extremely large sums.' She folded her lips for a moment. 'We break a long-standing tradition in gifting them to you. The Traders of the Rain Wilds and of Bingtown would possibly be offended to know of this action.'

Amber nodded and her smile grew slowly. 'We shall be very discreet in our possession of them. And they will not pass out of our custody save in direst need.'

The relief on Malta's face was evident, even through her strange

Elderling beauty. 'I am so grateful you understand.' She nodded and Harrikin went to the door and spoke to someone outside. He received a tidy wooden chest and set it on the table before us. He opened the hinged lid and removed a bracelet from a cloth bag. Delicate silver links supported green and red stones. He presented it to me with a smile that warned me to be dazzled by its value.

'It's . . . beautiful,' I said.

'You don't know what it is,' he said in amusement. He slid it back into the bag and offered it to me. 'Look inside.'

When I peered into the open mouth of the bag, green and red light shone within. 'They are flame-jewels,' Malta informed us. 'They gleam with their own light. The gems in the bracelet are perfect. Very rare.'

The other item he removed from the box looked like a porous grey brick. He showed us that it was painted red on one side. 'This block gives off warmth, when you place it with the red side upper-most. Always take care to stow it with the grey side uppermost for it becomes warm enough to start a fire.' He met my gaze, and then restored both bracelet and brick to the wooden box. 'We hope you will accept these with our thanks.'

'You honour us,' I replied. Magical items worth a king's ransom in one small box. 'We accept them with thanks, and will always recall our visit here when we use them.'

'You are welcome to return at any time,' Queen Malta assured us.

Amber set an appreciative hand on the box, her face set in determination. 'As generous as you have been with us, there is still a boon I would ask. Before I name it, I beg you to know that we mean no offence by requesting it.'

Puzzled glances were exchanged around the table. I had no idea what Amber sought. They had been generous with us beyond my wildest hopes. I wondered what more she could seek. Amber spoke in a soft, low voice. 'I ask for dragon-Silver. Not a great amount. Only as much as would fill these two vials.' From a pocket in her skirt she produced two glass containers, each with tight-fitting stoppers.

'No.' Reyn responded firmly, without hesitation or apology.

Amber spoke on as if she had not heard him. 'The Skill, as we call the magic that Prince FitzChivalry used to heal your children, is based in Silver. We do not know exactly how the two are related but they are. The magic of Kelsingra comes from the Silver trapped in the stone. The memories of the people who lived here, the lights that gleam from the buildings, the pools that warm the water, all of it comes from—'

'No. We cannot.' King Reyn spoke with finality. 'The Silver is not ours to give. It is the treasure of the dragons.' He shook his head. 'Even if we were to say yes, the dragons would not allow you to take it. It would be disastrous for you and for us. We cannot give you Silver.'

I saw Rapskal shift as if he would speak. The angry glints in his eyes said that he was affronted by her request. I needed to distance us from it. I spoke hastily. 'There is one other request I would make, one that might be easier for you to grant. One that could, perhaps, benefit Kelsingra as well as the Six Duchies.'

I paused. 'You may ask it,' Queen Malta decided. It was difficult to read her fantastically scaled countenance, but I thought that she too strove to move past the awkwardness.

'I would like to send a message to King Dutiful of the Six Duchies, to tell him that we have arrived safely here, and that you have offered to aid us on the next step of our journey. If I write out a letter for him, is there a way you can convey it for us?'

'Easily done,' Reyn replied, visibly relieved at the simplicity of my request. 'If you can write small, a bird can carry such a message to Bingtown. Bingtown has many merchants who exchange birds with Buckkeep Town. I will guarantee that it will reach your king. Eventually. The winds of spring can slow our birds sometimes, but they are hardy creatures.'

'I would greatly appreciate this,' I responded. I hesitated, and then plunged on. Chade would have forbidden it, but Kettricken would have required it. 'King Reyn and Queen Malta, in my land, in my king's court, there are others who share my Skill-magic. Some are far more adept in the healing arts than I am.' I looked around. 'There are folk here who asked that I help them. I dare not. The magic of the Silver runs strongly in Kelsingra, too strong for me to control. I would never have chosen to be so . . .' I fumbled for a word. Violent? Unrestrained? '. . . hasty in my healing of the children. A better healer than I could have been gentler. A full Skill-coterie with better control of the magic could help not just Elderling children but any folk who were born . . .'

They were staring at me. 'Born different,' I said, my voice falling lower. They looked terrified. Or stunned. Had I offended? The changes the dragons' presence had wrought in some of them were too obvious to ignore. But perhaps speaking of such was considered offensive.

Thymara spoke. She was seated nearby but she lifted her voice and her words carried clearly. 'Those born Changed could be . . . healed of it?'

Under the table, Amber gripped my leg in warning. I didn't need it. I would not promise what I was not certain was possible. 'Some could,' I said. 'I think.'

Thymara lifted her hands. I thought she would cover her face, but her cupped hands halted where she could stare at her fingers. She had black claws instead of nails. She tapped them against one another pensively.

The silence in the room shimmered with possibilities. Queen Malta spoke. 'As soon as you can compose your letter . . .' Her voice choked and tailed off.

Harrikin spoke suddenly. 'Prince FitzChivalry has offered us something that has been unimaginable.' He looked around the table at his fellows. 'Perhaps we should be equally generous. We have always accepted that we were bound by the strictures of Bingtown and the Rain Wilds; that we could only do trade in Elderling goods in those markets. Perhaps it is time to discard that notion.'

Malta looked shocked. Reyn spoke slowly. 'You suggest a break with a tradition that dates to the very founding of the Rain Wilds settlements. Many of us feel we owe the Rain Wild Traders little loyalty and the Bingtown Traders even less. On magical goods, we must confer. But for other trade, I see no reason we must be bound.'

Slow nods met his words.

King Reyn turned back to us. 'Ancient maps in the city show that once roads connected Kelsingra to the Mountain Kingdom. Perhaps it is time for us to renew those thoroughfares, and truly become the traders we name ourselves.'

'The Six Duchies have many trade goods. Sheep and wool, grain we grow in plenty, cattle and leather, and iron also we have to trade.' I smiled to cover my doubts. Would Dutiful honour my impromptu negotiating?

'Grain in plenty. Now there is something we could all celebrate. Within the month, we will dispatch a trade delegation to Buckkeep! Shall we raise a toast to opening our borders?'

More than one toast was raised that evening. Perseverance's cheeks were flushed with wine when I saw Lant and Spark exchange a look. Spark put a hand to his shoulder and steered him out of the festivities with dignity if not with the steadiest of gait. A short time later, I pleaded fatigue and Amber retreated with me, leaving Lant to represent the Six Duchies for the rest of that evening.

As we made our slow ascent, she said quietly, 'Within King Reyn's own family there are people severely changed by the Rain Wilds in difficult ways. His sister . . .'

I knew what she was asking, 'Even for his sister, I do not dare—'

'No. I was merely telling you of her. She is in Trehaug now, visiting her family. Even if you were willing to take the risk, you could not. But if there are Six Duchies healers who could help the Rain Wilders, the Six Duchies could gain powerful allies.'

I sat up until dawn creating my letter to King Dutiful. I composed my words fully expecting that several people would read them before they reached him, if they ever did. I was circumspect, saying only that we had reached Kelsingra and secured passage to Jamaillia. I asked him to arrange passage home for Lant, Per and Spark and told him that he might expect an ambassador from the Dragon Traders with a trade proposal. I added that it was imperative that Skillmistress Nettle be present for all negotiations.

I wanted to say more. I dared not. I rolled my missive tightly, dipped it in wax, and pushed it into the small cylinder that would attach to a pigeon's leg. I wished I could Skill a warning to Nettle. These dragon-keepers claimed to be Elderlings and heirs to this city and all its wonders. How would they respond if they knew of Aslevjal and the battered treasures there? Would they attempt to claim them or offer to pool their knowledge of that magic with ours? Chade would have seen a rivalry, Kettricken a natural alliance. Dutiful and Nettle? I did not know what they would see. I wondered if my use of the Skill here had been the pebble that would trigger an avalanche of war, or become the first tiny block in building a shared legacy of magic. It was agonizing to say so little, and to know that it might be days before I could even attempt to reach out with the Skill.

* * *

The exact day of the *Tarman's* arrival was uncertain, for the river ran higher and swifter with the melting of distant snows.

We each dealt with that waiting in our own way. The need to keep my Skill-walls tight and be ever-vigilant against the current of Skill and memories in the city wearied me. I took my meals within our chambers and graciously declined as many visitors as I could. The Skill-induced weariness that assailed me meant that I seldom ventured out into the city. I remembered Kelsingra as the deserted city I had first encountered on my quest to find Verity. It had been my first experience of travelling through a Skill-pillar and had happened by accident. The city had been dangerous to me then. Ironically, despite having studied Skill-magic, the Skill-infused walls and streets of the city were more dangerous to me now.

But the Skill-flow of the city was not the only danger to me. Thrice General Rapskal came rapping at the door of my chambers, and always he seemed to arrive when the others were away. The first time, I feigned an even greater weakness than I felt. He insisted that he needed to talk to me, but I wavered where I stood, apologized and then slowly but relentlessly closed the door. After that, I did not open the door when someone knocked. Lady Amber retained a healthy wariness for General Rapskal. She spent her days within the walls of the Greeting Hall. She visited Malta and passed on to me their gossip of old friends and recent news of both Bingtown and Trehaug. Lant, Spark and Perseverance were as entranced with Kelsingra as a babe with a new bauble, and the keepers seemed both willing and pleased to share the wonders of their city. I warned them to be cautious and let them explore. Per, with Motley the crow on his shoulder, had quickly become a favourite with the servants and unwittingly gave me a great deal of information on the inner workings of Kelsingra when he shared gossip of an evening. In the evening in our chambers, Amber and Spark did repairs on their bear-tossed wardrobe while Amber told the tales of old Buckkeep, including the adventures of the notorious Lady Thyme.

Per asked her once about her childhood. She spoke of a farming family, of an older sister thrilled to have a sibling at last. She told of gentle rolling hills that turned gold in summer, of tending docile brown cows. Then she stopped speaking, and I knew that the next part of her tale must be about Clerres. She told no more stories that night and I dreaded that I must soon dredge those memories for every pertinent fact as to the layout of Clerres. She had locked those recollections away, and yet I must find a way to open them if our plans for vengeance were to succeed.

The Fool was the one who had first demanded that I go to Clerres and 'kill them all'. He had desired his own vengeance even before they had kidnapped Bee. Even before Dwalia had taken her into the Skill-pillars and lost her there, he had been intent on their slaughter. With great care, I had tidied away my life at Buckkeep and attempted to depart alone, to seek that far city and take my own vengeance. I'd had no concern for my own survival afterwards.

But not only the Fool, but Spark, Per and Lant had followed me. Three of them I could send back to Buck, but for the Fool to survive I must wring from him every detail he recalled of Clerres and the Servants of the Whites.

But how? How to pry that essential information from someone so adept at concealment and diversion?

On a day that was more lingering winter than spring, most of us had opted to stay inside the warmth of our chambers but Per had been restless. He had paced and stretched and sighed until I had surrendered and given him permission to explore on his own.

Late in the afternoon, he burst into the chambers, red-cheeked and tousle-haired to exclaim, 'Motley has made a new friend!'

We all turned toward him in surprise.

'Motley met another crow? Remind me to blacken her white feathers, or that friendship will be short-lived,' I replied.

'No! Not another crow!' He fairly shouted the words, then caught his breath, and assumed a storytelling tone. 'I was behaving very carefully, as you bid me, speaking only if spoken to and saying little then. But few people were out in the cold today. Motley had found me and was riding on my shoulder. We were walking toward a plaza with a statue of a horse when a big gust of wind hit me, very cold, and Motley lifted off my shoulder. Then she cried out, as if she were a minstrel, "Oh beauteous one, red as scarlet berries on a frost-kissed vine!" As if she were reciting a poem! The gust of wind was a red dragon landing right in front of me! Her claws clattered on the cobblestones and her tail lashed; she barely stopped short of trampling me. I scrambled backwards and fell. Skinned my palms catching myself!' he added, and held up his reddened hands for our inspection.

'Was the dragon threatening you?' Lant demanded breathlessly.

'No, not at all. She was just landing there. Still, I was scared and decided to leave. I called Motley back to me, but she flew over to land right in front of the dragon. This time she said. "Oh beauteous one, scarlet queen, feeder of crows!" And the dragon stretched her head down and I thought she would eat Motley. But instead, Motley did a little dance.'

Per opened his arms, bobbed his head and wove his body about like a courting bird.

'Then what?' Spark demanded breathlessly.

'The dragon's eyes were spinning like Spring Fair tops. She put her head flat to the ground and Motley hopped over and began grooming her, twiddling her beak along the scales of the dragon's face, going around her eyes and nostrils. The dragon made this very strange sound, like a kettle boiling!'

'And then?' Sparks sounded envious at missing the spectacle.

'I stood and waited for her. When my feet were numb with cold, I called to Motley to come with me, but she didn't even turn her head. The dragon's eyes were half-closed, like a big sleepy cat. So I left her and came back.' His brow furrowed as he asked me, 'Do you think she'll be safe?'

'I think she will be safe. Motley is a very clever bird.' I wondered if dragons and crows shared an ancient connection. Crows are notorious bone-pickers of true predators. An alliance between crows and dragons seemed only natural. 'A very clever bird,' I repeated. And I knew she was a mystery that would only be solved when she chose to reveal herself to me.

'She is!' Per exclaimed proudly. 'That she is.'

On a day of gentle sunshine, I awakened from an afternoon nap to find myself alone. I felt befogged and listless and hoped a short walk around the city would enliven me. Wearing my fine Prince-of-the-Six-Duchies cloak, I ventured out. The distant trees on the hills behind Kelsingra had a blush of moving sap in their white branches. Some, willows perhaps, were dotted with the green of swelling leaves as if someone had threaded beads onto their slender branches. The mountains had shed their snow. How many years had it been since Nighteyes and I had subsisted on their forested flanks, hunting like wolves and sleeping sound? A lifetime ago, perhaps two.

The voices of Elderling memories muttered to me from the Skill-threaded stones of the building. At first, it was distant, like the buzzing of mosquitoes, but it soon became urgent, like bees swarming. The press rasped at my walls, shaving away my defences. I turned back when I began to hear clear snatches of conversation and to see the shadowy forms of Elderlings. The Skill-current swelled around me, like an ocean wave that would slide my feet out from under me and carry me far from shore. I'd been an idiot to venture out alone. I had turned back toward the Greeting Hall when I became aware that Rapskal was following me. My efforts to block the ancient Elderling whispering had deadened my awareness of those around me. I slowed my pace and walked unsteadily. Let him think me weaker than I was. In truth, I judged myself too enervated to withstand the attack of a determined child, let alone this Elderling soldier.

He quickly fell in beside me. 'Prince FitzChivalry. I am glad to see you are somewhat recovered from your magic.'

'You are kind to say so, General Rapskal. But even this brief stroll has wearied me. I shall seek my bed as soon as I return.'

'Ah, well. I am disappointed. I'd hoped to have words with you. Important words.' The last he added in a lower voice, as if someone might overhear us. Did he wish to deliver a private threat? But when I glanced at him, he met my gaze with a pleading look that was almost apologetic. 'I've misjudged you. Heeby has told me I must change my mind.' His gravity increased. 'She had a dream. Or perhaps she remembered something. She has conveyed to me that your quest is a just one. One she supports.' He lowered his voice to a whisper. 'She wishes me to aid you in any way I can to destroy the Servants and their city. In *any* way.' He leaned close and put his hand on my arm, conspiratorial. His eyes glittered as human eyes should not. My wariness became alarm when he confided, 'Your crow and Heeby have become very close friends.'

'Heeby?' I queried, trying to smile in return. My *crow?*

'My dragon. You know of Heeby, I trust? She is my scarlet darling.' For a moment, his smile became a grin, making him a lad. 'She likes your crow. Motley, I think she is called. Motley praises her and tells her of her beauty. Before the crow came, I was the only one who had admired her as she deserved. Heeby has become quite fond of Motley. But, that is not what I wished to discuss. Your mission to kill the Servants of the Whites. Heeby approves of it.'

I tried an interpretation of his words. 'Your dragon had a dream, or remembered that she would like us to kill the Servants of the Whites?'

He grinned wider, white human teeth in a dragon-changed face. 'Yes. Exactly.' He was so pleased that I understood.

I stopped walking. I put my hand on the stone façade of a building, thinking to lean there and rest. A mistake. The street suddenly thronged with Elderlings, blue and silver and green – tall, angular folk with fancifully-scaled faces and artfully-draped garments. There was to be a contest of musicians today, in the Plaza of the Queen, and the queen herself would give the award.

'Hello? Wake up, prince. I'm taking you back to the Greeting Hall. The voices are not so loud there.'

I was walking, and General Rapskal had my arm firmly hooked into his. The contest of musicians faded like a dream. Rapskal was guiding me. Perhaps he had been talking to me.

'I'm not well,' I heard myself say.

'You are fine,' he said comfortingly. 'You simply weren't prepared. If you choose which voice you will hear and ready yourself to share the life of that Elderling, you can learn a great deal. I certainly did! Before I welcomed the Elderling memories of an ancient warrior into my mind, I was a bumbling, stupid boy, earnest and tolerated by my fellow keepers but never respected. Never respected.'

He closed his mouth suddenly on his quavering voice. I revised my estimate of his age downward.

He cleared his throat. 'My dragon Heeby has suffered similarly. She has never spoken much to the other dragons or their keepers. When she first came to me, she was small and clumsy. The other dragons disdained her. She could not even recall her proper name; I had to give her one. Yet of all of them, she was the first to fly and the first to make her own kills.' His chest swelled with pride, as if she were his little child. He saw I was paying attention and gave an abrupt nod. We had stopped walking.

'My chamber,' I said quietly. 'I need to rest,' and my words were true.

'Of course,' he said. 'I am happy to take you there.' He patted my hand on his arm and I sensed far more of him in that brief touch than I liked. We began to walk – more swiftly than I wished, but I gritted my teeth and kept pace. I hoped Lant would be in the rooms when we reached them. Then I wondered when I had begun to count on him to protect me.

Suddenly, I missed Riddle.

'So,' he concluded, and I wondered what I had missed while my thoughts were wandering. 'That is why anything that Heeby remembers or dreams is so important.'

We had reached the Greeting Hall. It seemed dim inside after the brightness of the day. Two Elderlings turned and stared as he escorted me to the stairs. 'Up we go,' he said cheerily. He was stronger than he looked.

'Thank you for your assistance,' I said when we reached my chamber. I'd hoped he'd leave me at the door, but he followed me in.

'Here. Sit at the table. I'll request food.'

I had little choice but to sit. The struggle to keep the Elderling voices out of my mind had sapped my physical energy. Under the guise of settling myself, I made sure of the little blade Riddle had given me, hidden along the waist of my trousers. If I needed to I could draw it and possibly manage to cut soft butter with it. I tried to summon anger that might waken some strength in my wearied body, but I found only fear that made my knees even more uncertain of their function. Rapskal's outward friendliness did not calm my wariness of him. His temperament, I judged, was uneven. And yet he was astute. He alone had seemed to realize we were not being completely honest with the good people of Kelsingra. But was I dealing with a ruthless military leader who would do whatever was necessary to defend Kelsingra, or a melancholy youth concerned with his dragon's dreams?

He joined me at the table, having pressed the flower ornament by the door. 'How does that work?' I asked him, hoping to take his measure a bit more. 'Pressing that flower?'

'I've no idea. It just does. Down in the kitchens a similar emblem glows and hums. One for each room.' He dismissed my question with a shrug. 'There is so much we don't know. It was only six months ago that we discovered those chambers were meant to be a kitchen. There is a basin there that fills with hot or cold water. But no ovens or hearth. So it's a peculiar kitchen. Not that my mother ever had an oven, or even a kitchen that I remember.'

For a moment, he fell morosely silent. Away from the Skill-tumult of the streets, I wanted to hear more of his dragon's dream. But I also had to warn the others before they walked into the chamber. I did not trust this Rapskal, not at all. Was his dragon dream a far-fetched ploy to get into our rooms? I waited three breaths and then said, 'Your dragon had a dream about Clerres?'

He jolted back to awareness of me. 'Clerres, yes! That was a name she recalled. So it was a true dream then, one based in her ancestral dragon memories!' He sounded delighted.

'I'm confused. Ancestral dragon memories?'

He smiled and propped his chin on his fist. 'It's not a secret any longer. When a serpent transforms into a dragon, it awakens with the memories of its dragon ancestors. It knows where to hunt, where to nest, it recalls names and events from its ancestral line. Or so it should.

'Our dragons were sea serpents too long, and spent too short a time in their cocoons. They emerged with fragmented memories. My Heeby recalls almost nothing of her ancestry. But sometimes when she sleeps memories come to her. I hope this means that as she grows she may recall more of her ancestors' lives.' His eyes went wide and for a moment they gleamed. Tears? From this ruthless man? He spoke softly in a wounded voice. 'I love her as she is. I always have and I always will. But to recall her ancestry would mean so much to her.' His gaze met mine and I saw a stricken parent. 'Am I heartless that I long for this, too? That I think she would be better . . . No! She is too wondrous as she is for anything to make her better! Why do I want this so? Am I faithless?'

The worst that can happen to an assassin is to find common ground with his target. But I knew that question too well. How often had I lain awake beside Molly, wondering if I were a monster because I wished my daughter were as able as other children? For an instant, it was as if our hearts pumped the same blood. Then Chade's training whispered to me, 'There it is. The chink in his armour.'

I had my own mission to think of. And the Fool. I needed information and perhaps this boy-general had it. I spoke gently, and leaned toward him as if entranced with his tale. I warmed my voice with false kindness. 'How wondrous then that she dreamed of the Servants and Clerres! I take it neither you nor she have visited that far place?' Feed him some bits of my information to see what he might betray. Above all, maintain a calm demeanour. Pretend this was a social visit rather than a mutual assessment of strengths.

My ploy worked. His face lit with joy. 'Never! Those are real places then, real names? It must be a true memory she recalled, not a yearning dream!' His chest rose and fell with excitement. His eyes that had been so guarded were suddenly wide and open. I felt something go out from him. It was neither the Skill nor the Wit. A peculiar blending of the two? Was that what bonded keeper and dragon? I knew then that he had kept his walls up while we spoke, but now he opened to Heeby and shared with her that her dreams were true recollections. Somewhere in Kelsingra, a dragon trumpeted in joy. The distant caw of a crow echoed it, or had I imagined that?

I nudged him with words. 'Clerres is real, as are the Servants. I have little other information to share with you, I fear. Our journey carries us toward the unknown.'

'For vengeance,' he queried me quietly.

'For vengeance,' I confirmed.

His brow creased, and for a moment he looked almost human. 'Then perhaps we should join you. For what Heeby recalled of that place was dark and distressing. She hates and fears it in equal measures.'

'What does she recall?' I asked gently.

He scowled. 'Little detail. There was treachery and betrayal. A trust violated. Dragons died. Or were, perhaps, slaughtered.' He stared at the wall as if seeing something at a great distance and then snapped his eyes back to me. 'It isn't clear to her. And so it is all the more disturbing.'

'Would the other dragons recall what she does not?'

He shook his head. 'It is as I have told you. All the dragons of Kelsingra emerged from their cocoons with incomplete memories.'

Tintaglia. And IceFyre. I held my features still. Neither of those dragons had been members of the Kelsingra brood. Tintaglia had hatched years before the Kelsingra dragons and had believed herself the sole surviving dragon in the world. My personal experiences with her had been exceedingly unpleasant. She had tormented Nettle, invading her dreams and threatening her. And me. All in her pursuit to have us unearth IceFyre for her. That truly ancient dragon had chosen to immerse himself in a glacier when he believed himself the last dragon in the world. The Fool and I had broken him free of that ice and restored him to the world. His recall of what befell the other dragons should be intact. And from what I knew of him, my chances of learning from him were very small.

General Rapskal was still musing on his dragon. 'My Heeby is different to the other dragons. Always smaller, stunted some would say, and I do fear that she may never grow as large as the others. She seldom speaks, and when she does, it's almost exclusively to me. She shows no interest in making a mating flight.' He paused and then said, 'She is younger than the others, both as a serpent and now as a dragon. We believe she was of the last surviving dragon generation before the final cataclysm took them all. Once, when dragons were many, dragon eggs hatched yearly into serpents. The serpents within then quickly made their way into the sea. There they would remain, swimming and eating, following the migrations of the fish until they were large enough to return to the Rain Wild River and travel up it to the cocooning beach near Trehaug. So it was, once. Many of the dragons have ancestral memories of helping serpents to form and enter their cocoons. And the following summer, the dragons would emerge from those cocoons, strong and fully-formed, ready to take flight for their first hunts.'

He shook his head sadly. 'It was not so for our dragons. They . . . got lost. They remained as serpents far too long, for some great disaster changed the coast and the river so greatly that they could no longer find their way to their cocooning beaches. Heeby and I believe that several generations of serpents were caught in that disaster. Trapped in the sea for far longer than they should have been.'

I nodded. Speculations of my own had begun to boil within my mind, yet I knew it was essential to hear all he had to say. No need to tell him that I knew more of those two elder dragons than he did.

'Heeby suspects that not all dragon kind died when the Elderling cities fell. Certainly IceFyre did not.' His voice went very dark. 'I have given this some thought as well. It might seem that all the Elderlings who lived here in Kelsingra died. But they did not. I have walked in the memory of one Elderling who lived through whatever event split and shattered this city. Through his eyes, I watched the ground tremble and Elderlings flee. But where? I think to other places marked on the map in the tower.' He paused and looked at me. It taxed all my discipline to keep my face bemused as he said, 'I do not know how the magic was done, but they fled through the standing stones. The same stones where I first encountered you.'

'They fled through stones?' I asked as if uncertain of what I had heard.

'Through the stones,' he said. He watched me carefully. I kept my breathing slow and steady while regarding him with great interest. The quiet stretched long before he spoke. 'I grew up an ignorant boy, Prince FitzChivalry. But not a stupid one. This city has a story to tell. While the others have feared to be lost in the memories stored in the stones, I have explored them. I have learned much. But some of what I have learned has only led to more questions. Does it not seem odd to you that in one disaster every Elderling and every dragon in the world seems to have perished?'

He was now speaking as much to himself as he was to me. I was content to let him talk.

'Some Elderling settlements were destroyed. We know that. Trehaug has long mined the remains of one buried Elderling city. Perhaps others fell as well. But humanity did not die out, nor parrots nor monkeys. So how is it that every Elderling vanished from the world, and every dragon? Their population would surely have been greatly reduced. But to die out entirely? That is too strange. I saw many flee when the city died. So what became of them? What became of the dragons who were not here when the city fell?' He scratched his scaled chin. His nails were iridescent and made a metal-on-metal sound against his face. He lifted his eyes to mine. 'Heeby recalls treachery and darkness. An earthquake is a disaster, but not a betrayal. I doubt that Elderlings would be traitors to their dragons. So whose treachery does she recall?'

I ventured a question. 'What does IceFyre say to your questions?'

He gave a snort of disdain. 'IceFyre? Nothing. He is a useless bully, to dragons and Elderlings alike. He never speaks to us. When Tintaglia had no other choice she took him as her mate. But he proved himself unworthy of her. We seldom see him here in Kelsingra. But I have heard a minstrel song of IceFyre's freeing from a glacier. An evil woman, pale of skin, attempted to kill him. A White Prophet, some call her. And this is what I wonder. If someone had killed the dragons and Elderlings, would they not wish to put an end to IceFyre as well?'

The tale of IceFyre and the Pale Woman had reached as far as Kelsingra. I had been known as Tom Badgerlock then, and few minstrels knew of my role in the downfall of the Pale Woman. But Rapskal was right. IceFyre would certainly have a reason to hate the Pale Woman and perhaps the Servants as well. Was there any way to waken that hatred and persuade him to aid me in my vengeance? I rather doubted it. If he would not seek vengeance for his own wrongs, he would care little for wrongs done to a mere human.

I led his thoughts away from IceFyre. 'I do not understand all you have told me. The dragons of Kelsingra are different ages? But I thought all the Kelsingra dragons had hatched from their cases at the same time?'

He smiled indulgently. 'There is so much the outside world does not understand about our dragons. From a mating to the laying of an egg to the serpent entering its case, a generation or more of humanity may pass. And if sea serpents encounter years of poor feeding or are swept away by storms or lost, then even more years may pass before they return to spin their cases. The serpents that finally were guided by Tintaglia to the cocooning grounds were all survivors of a terrible calamity, but some had been in the sea for scores of years longer than others. They had been serpents since dragons ended, and no one knows how long dragons had been gone from this world. Heeby and I believe that she was the youngest of the serpents to reach the banks of the Rain Wild River. Her ancestral memories, poor as they are, retain the most recent history of the dragons before their near-extinction.'

It was time to ask my most important question. 'Does Heeby remember anything of Clerres or the Servants that might aid me in my quest to destroy them?'

He shook his head sadly. 'She hates them, but she also fears them – and I can think of nothing else that she fears. She wavers from demanding that I should rally all our dragons to your cause to warning me that we must never go near that place. If her dreams bring her a clear recollection, she may resolve to take her own vengeance.' He shrugged. 'Or, if those memories are sufficiently terrifying, she may decide to avoid Clerres forever.'

He stood abruptly, prompting me to slide my own chair back and tighten all my muscles. He smiled ruefully at my wariness. I am not a short man, but even if I had been standing, he would have towered over me. Yet he spoke courteously. 'Even if my dragon cannot muster, at present, the will to avenge her kind on these "Servants", I would wish to kill them all myself. For her.' He met my gaze squarely. 'I will not apologize for how I first behaved when you came to my city. My caution was warranted, and I am still dubious about much of your tale. No one saw you descend from the hills into Kelsingra. Your party arrived with more baggage than I believe you could comfortably carry. None of you had the weathered look common to folk who have made a long journey through the wilderness. I could not help but regard you with great caution. I had believed that only the Elderlings of old could use the standing stones as portals.'

He stopped speaking. I met his gaze and said nothing. A spark of anger glittered in his metallic eyes. 'Very well. Keep your secrets. I sought you out not for myself but for Heeby. It is at her bidding that I aid you. Therefore, despite my own reservations, at her urging, I offer you this. I am forced to trust that you will reveal this gift to no one – human, Elderling or dragon—until you are well away from Kelsingra. What use you might have for it, I cannot imagine. By touching dragon-Silver, Lady Amber has dipped her fingers into her own death, and printed death onto you with her touch. I do not envy either of you. But I do wish you success in achieving your mission before death takes you.'

As he spoke, he had reached into his waistcoat. My fingers found the haft of Riddle's knife, but what he drew forth was not a conventional weapon. I thought the fat tube was made of metal until I saw the slow shifting of Silver within it. 'Few of the containers the Silver-workers used survived. The glass is very heavy, and the glass stopper is threaded to ensure a tight fit. Nevertheless, I counsel you to handle it carefully.'

'You're showing me a glass tube of Skill?' I would assume nothing.

He set it on the table and it rolled until he stopped it with a touch. The tube was as fat around as an oar handle, and would fit solidly in a man's hand. He reached into his waistcoat again and set a second tube beside the first. The glass chinked lightly as they touched and the silver substance inside it whirled and coiled like melted fat on top of stirred soup.

'Showing you? No. I'm giving it to you. After what Heeby has shared with me I assume that your Lady Amber requested it to use against the Servants. So here it is. Your weapon. Or your source of magic. Or however you need to use it. It is from Heeby, given freely by a dragon, as only a dragon could grant you dragon-Silver.'

There was a tap at the door. He picked up the Silver and shoved it at me. 'Conceal it,' he told me harshly. Startled, I fumbled my hold on the tubes and then gripped them. They were warm, and much heavier than I'd expected them to be. With no other hiding-place close by, I shoved them inside my shirt and folded my hands at the table's edge to conceal the bulge as he went to the door.

'Ah. Your food,' he announced and admitted a serving man, who gave him a wide-eyed look before carrying a tray to the table and beginning to set out food before me. His brow was scaled as were the tops of his cheeks. His lips were flat and taut, fishlike, and when he shifted his mouth, I glimpsed a flat grey tongue. His eyes, too, moved strangely when he turned his gaze to me. I looked away from his unvoiced plea. I wanted to apologize that I could not help him but dared not open that discussion. I shamed myself by quietly thanking him. He nodded dumbly and backed out of the door, his eyes skimming over Rapskal. News of my visitor would swiftly reach the kitchens and spread as only gossip can.

'Will you join me?' I asked the general.

He shook his head. 'No. I expect that within minutes you will have one or two more of the household dashing through that door to be sure I have not harmed you. A pity. I should like to learn how you travel by those pillars. And why Heeby says you smell like you have a dragon companion, but not one she knows. I suspect there are things I know that would benefit you.' He released a sigh. 'So much is lost when there is no trust. Farewell, Prince FitzChivalry Farseer. I hope the trade and magic alliance you have proposed for our peoples prospers. I hope it does not end in war.'

Those chilling words were his farewell. The moment he closed the door behind him, I rose and took the glass tubes of Skill to my pack. I hefted the vessels thoughtfully and watched the slow swirl when I tipped them. I studied each stopper; they appeared to be tight and felt slightly tacky, as if resin had been added to the seal. I tucked each into a heavy sock, doubling the ends over and then put them into a thick wool hat before snugging it into the bottom of my pack. The glass of the tubes appeared heavy and strong, but

I would take no chances. Indeed, I agreed with Rapskal. I would tell no one that I had this, least of all the Fool. I had no idea why Amber had asked for dragon-Silver. Until she saw fit to divulge what she had planned, I had no intention of putting it at her disposal. It had alarmed me that she had silvered her fingertips, and I could still not sort out how I felt about the fingerprints that once more graced my wrist. I sighed. I knew my decision was sensible and wondered why I felt guilty about it. Worse than guilty. Deceptive and sly.

The others breezed in later that afternoon, full of tales of the city. In an ancient arboretum, the trees had long perished, but there remained statues that slowly changed their poses, and a fountain that chortled with the voices of happy children. Both Lant and Spark had seen the faint shapes of Elderlings moving among the ghosts of green trees and climbing vines. Amber nodded to that account but Perseverance looked forlorn. 'Why do I hear and see nothing?' he demanded. 'Even Amber hears their whispers! When the dragons fly over, the others say they hear them calling to each other. Mostly insults and warnings about hunting territory. But all I hear is the bugling, not that different to the calls of elk in rut.' The indignation in his voice bordered on anger.

'I wish you could hear and see what we do,' Spark offered quietly.

'Why can't I?' This he demanded of me.

'I can't say with certainty. But I suspect it's something you were born with, or without. Some folk have an affinity for a magic. The Skill. Or the Wit. If they have the affinity, they can develop it. Rather like herd-dogs are born with the concept of bunching sheep, and hound pups that follow a scent, even before they are taught the fine points of it.'

'But dogs can be taught to herd or hunt, even if they are not those breeds. Can't you teach me to see and hear what the others do?'

'I'm afraid not.'

Per glanced sideways at Spark, and I sensed perhaps a rivalry, or simply a wish to share. Lant spoke quietly. 'I don't see or hear as much as the others do.'

'But I hear and see nothing at all!' The words burst from the boy.

'That might be a gift rather than a lack. Perhaps you should think of it as an armour against magic. Your imperviousness was why you could resist the impulse to join the others in the carriage drive on the night Withywoods was raided. It was why you could help Bee to stay hidden as long as she did, and to help her try to escape. Your deafness to the Skill and to the magic of Kelsingra may be as much of a shield as a weakness.'

If I had thought to comfort him, it failed. 'A lot of good that did her,' he said miserably. 'They still took Bee from me. And they still destroyed her.'

His words damped all our spirits. A morose silence fell. Whatever pleasure they had taken in the magic of the city was engulfed in the miasma of recalling why we had come here. 'General Rapskal came to see me today,' I said, dropping the words like stones into a still pool.

'What did he want?' Amber asked. 'Did he threaten you?'

'Not at all. He said that he came to wish us success in our quest for vengeance. And that Heeby, his dragon, had a dream about the Servants. And Clerres.' I summarized for them my visit from Rapskal.

A profound silence followed my words. Per was the first to speak. 'What does all that mean?'

'Rapskal suspects that some great disaster befell the dragons. He believes that Heeby hates the Servants of Clerres because they somehow murdered the remaining dragons. Or as many as they could kill.'

Lady Amber's face had slackened into the Fool's features. In the Fool's voice, he whispered, 'That would explain so much! If the Servants foresaw a disaster to the dragons and the Elderlings, then they could plan to make it worse. If their goal was to eliminate all dragons from the world, and they succeeded, then they might foresee that we would try to restore them. And so they would create the Pale Woman, and hold me captive at the school and send her out in my place. To be sure that the dragons had no chance of being restored.' His gaze went distant as he recalled all we had done. 'The pieces fit, Fitz.' Then a strange smile lit his face. 'But they failed. And we brought dragons back into the world.'

A shiver ran up my back and stood my hair on end. How far ahead had the Servants planned their strategy? The Fool had once hinted that they had used him to draw me away from Withywoods so that they might steal Bee. Did their dreams and omens warn them that we were coming? What other obstacles or distractions might they devise for us? I smothered those fears. 'We still don't know why they wanted to destroy the dragons.'

He shot me the Fool's mocking glance. 'I said it explained much, not all. The Servants play a very long game with the world and the lives of all those in it. And they play it only for their own good. I would speak with this Heeby and see what else she can recall.'

'I don't think that's wise. I think all of us should avoid General Rapskal as much as we can. He does not seem . . . stable. Today he was courteous, even kind. Nonetheless, I do not trust him. He told me plainly that he does not believe our story of how we came here, nor how you silvered your fingers. He strongly suspects that we came by the pillars. He glimpsed you near the dragons' well on the night you dipped your fingers, Fool. For all our sakes, stay clear of him.'

For a long time, he was silent. Then his features assumed the poise of Lady Amber. 'I suppose that is the wiser course. And you say that Heeby speaks only to him? Would any of the other dragons recall anything of the Servants, do you think?'

'I don't think so. But how could we possibly know?' I pondered a bit. 'IceFyre knows. He survived whatever befell the dragons and of his own will entombed himself in ice. He should recall those times. He would know if the Servants had anything to do with the extinction of the dragons. I suppose it's possible he shared that tale with Tintaglia.'

'But he is not here. Many of the dragons went to the warm lands for the winter. Some went two or even three years ago. I gather that IceFyre left and has not returned.'

A cold dread uncoiled in my belly. I tried to keep it from showing on my face. 'Fool. Lady Amber. What is the climate like on the White Island? And in the nearby lands?'

She fixed her blind eyes on me. 'Warm. Mild. I never knew winter until I travelled north to the Six Duchies.' She smiled, her face falling into the Fool's lines. 'It's beautiful, Fitz. Not just the White Island, not just Clerres. I meant the other islands and the mainland. It's a gentle land, a much kinder place than you have ever known. Oh, Buck is beautiful, in its savage way. It's stark, a stern land, and it makes folk as stony as its bones. But my land? It has gentle rolling hills, wide river valleys and herds of cattle and flocks of sheep. Not the rangy creatures you call cattle in Buck and the Duchies. Big brown cows with sweeping horns and black muzzles, their backs head-high to a man. It's a rich and easy land, Fitz. Farther inland, there are golden-shored lakes that teem with fish and there are steaming springs in the wooded hills.' He sighed and seemed lost for a time, perhaps recalling the days of his childhood. Abruptly, Amber cocked her head at me. 'Do you think that is where dragons go when the winter freezes the land here? Or went, at some time?'

I imagined gentle rolling pasturelands, fat cattle stampeding in terror and swooping dragons. 'That would explain why the Servants would wish to eliminate them. Dragons have not proven favourable for the Six Duchies. Perhaps the Servants found them more than an inconvenience.' Did the Servants know how to kill dragons? Were there dragons that would never return to Kelsingra?

'Let me ponder this, and recall what little I know of the dream-prophecies that mention dragons.' Amber scowled suddenly and it was the Fool who said, 'And why has it never occurred to me to wonder why there are so few dream-prophecies that mentioned dragons? Are there no dream-prophecies of the rise and fall of the dragons? Or were they suppressed?'

Suppressed, I thought to myself. As the Fool suppressed his memories of Clerres. I needed to unlock both those mysteries. A slow plan to do so began to unfold in my mind.

SIX

Revelations

I first dreamed the Destroyer when I was still on Aslevjal Island. Beloved's Catalyst had returned for a second time. I believe his presence triggered both my dreaming and the vision of the Destroyer. In that dream, the Destroyer was a fist gripping a flame. The hand opened and the flames flared tall but instead of giving off light, they brought darkness. And everything I had ever known was destroyed.

It had been so long since I had dreamed a Dream that I told myself I had imagined that it was significant. Had not I just achieved all my goals? Why would a dream so dark come to me amid my triumph? Nonetheless, I was moved to say to the White Prophet and his Catalyst that the time had come for them to part. One of them, at least, accepted the truth of my words, but I saw that they both lacked the will to do what they must. I undertook to separate them.

The writings of Prilkop the Black

My recovery was slower than from any physical injury I had experienced in decades. Clearly my old Skill-healing did not repair whatever the Skill itself had drained from me. Focusing my thoughts was a challenge, and I tired easily. And my afternoon with General Rapskal had taxed me gravely. Even in this so-called 'quiet' building, the Skill-current sang and surged around me. But that did not mean there was not work to do. Information to gather, regardless of barriers. No matter how weary I was.

That night I sent Perseverance down to the kitchens to beg brandy and a glass for me. He had returned with a large bottle of Sandsedge.

'Carot is from the Rain Wilds and very hampered by thick scales on his face and hands,' he had informed me as he set out the bottle and two glasses. 'He said you deserved only the best, and asked me to remember him to you.' I'd sighed. My steady refusals to attempt any more healings had not stopped the requests and courtship of those afflicted with dragon changes. With an understanding shrug, Per left me alone in my room and went off to bed.

I was sitting on the bed, bottle beside me and glass in hand when Amber came in after a late dinner with Malta. I greeted her after I drained the last drops of brandy from my glass. 'Did you have a pleasant evening?' I asked her in a slow voice.

'Pleasant enough. Little to show for it. IceFyre has been gone for months now; Malta isn't sure when he left. All know that Heeby doesn't speak to anyone except Rapskal, and Malta had heard that Rapskal had called on you and was concerned for you.'

'I hope you told her I was fine. Though truly, I shouldn't have ventured out into Kelsingra. The Skill-current out there is like being tumbled down a river full of boulders. I don't know if it's because I've been trained to be aware of it and use it, or because there is so much Silver here. Perhaps I made myself vulnerable to it somehow, when I did those healings and let it course through me without restraint.' I lifted the bottle. 'Will you have some?

'Some what?' She sniffed the air. 'Is that Sandsedge brandy?'

'It is. I've only one glass but there are cups still on the table.'

'I will, then. It would be shameful to make you drink alone.'

I kicked my boots off, let them thud to the floor. I let the bottle's neck clink on the lip of my glass as I dribbled a bit more into it. Then I lay back on the bed, staring up at the dimmed ceiling. Stars gleamed against a deep blue sky. They were not the only illumination in the room. The walls had become a forestscape. White flowers gleamed on the swooping branches of trees. I spoke to the stars. 'So much Skill coursing through this city, and I dare not use it at all.'

I did not watch as Amber discarded her skirts and wiped paint from her face. When I felt someone sit down on the edge of the bed, it was the Fool in plain leggings and a simple shirt. He had brought a teacup from the table. 'And you still dare not venture to help any of the dragon-touched folk? Not even with the smallest complaint? Scales growing down over the eyes, for example?'

I sighed. I tapped the neck of the bottle light on the edge of his teacup to warn him, and then filled it well. 'I know the man you speak of. He has come twice to talk to me, once to beg, once with coin. Fool, I dare not. I am besieged by the Skill. If I open my gates to it, I will fall.' I moved over on the bed. He took two generous sips from his cup to lower the level of the brandy before taking a place beside me. I set the bottle on the bed between us.

'And you cannot reach out to Nettle or Dutiful at all?' He leaned back on the pillows beside me and held the teacup in both hands on his chest.

'I dare not,' I repeated. 'Think of it this way. If there is water sloshing in my boat, I don't drill a hole in the bottom to let it out. For then the ocean would surge in.' He did not reply. I shifted in the bed and added, 'I wish you could see how beautiful this chamber is. It is night in here, with the stars illuminated on the ceiling, and the walls have become a shadowed forest.' I hesitated, needing to ease into the topic. Do it. 'It makes me grieve for Aslevjal. The Pale Woman's soldiers destroyed so much beauty there. I wish I could have seen it as it was.'

The Fool held a long silence. Then he said, 'Prilkop often spoke of the beauty that was lost when she invaded Aslevjal and made it hers.'

'Then he was there before she was?'

'Oh, long before. He's very old. Was very old.' His voice went dark with dread.

'How old?'

He made a small, amused noise. 'Ancient, Fitz. He was there before IceFyre buried himself. It shocked him that the dragon would do so, but he dared not oppose him. IceFyre was seized by the idea that he must burrow into the ice and die there. The glacier had claimed most of Aslevjal when Prilkop first arrived there. Some few Elderlings still came and went, but not for long.'

'How could anyone live that long?' I demanded.

'He was a true White, Fitz. Of a much older and purer bloodline than existed when I was born. Whites are long-lived and terribly hard to kill. You have to work at it to kill a White or permanently disable one. As the Pale Woman did with me.' He sipped noisily from his teacup, and then tipped it to take a healthy drink from it. 'What they did to me in Clerres . . . it would have killed you, Fitz.

Or any other human. But they knew that, and were always careful not to go too far. No matter how much I hoped they would.' He drank again.

I'd come to the topic I wanted to explore but not by the path I'd hoped. I could already feel the tension in him. I looked around and asked, 'Where is that bottle?'

'It's here.' He groped beside him on the bed then passed it to me, and I tipped a bit into my glass. He held out his cup and I sloppily refilled it.

He scowled as he shook brandy from his fingertips, and then sipped it down to where it would not spill. For a time, neither of us spoke. I counted his breaths, and heard them slow and become deeper.

Beside me in the darkness, he lifted his gloved hand. He let the teacup balance on his chest by itself. Gingerly he pulled at the fingertips of the glove with his other hand, until his silvered hand was bared. He held it up and turned it first one way and then the other. 'Can you see it?' I asked him curiously.

'Not as you do. But I can perceive it.'

'Does it hurt? Thymara said it would kill you, and Spark told me that Thymara is one of the few Elderlings allowed to work with Silver and knows more of it than anyone. Not that she has mastered the artful way of the old Elderlings.'

'Really? I had not heard that.'

'She attempts to learn from the memories stored in the city. But it is dangerous to listen too closely to them. Lant hears the city whisper. Spark hears it singing. I've warned them to avoid deliberate contact with places where memories are stored.' I sighed. 'But I am certain they have at least sampled some of what is there.'

'Oh, yes. Spark told me that some of the serving girls do nothing in their free time except seek out the erotic remembrances that a certain Elderling left stored in a statue of herself. Malta and Reyn disapprove, and with reason. Years ago, I heard a rumour about the Khuprus family, that Reyn's father spent too much time in a buried Elderling city among such stones. He died of it. Or rather, he became immersed in it and then his body died from lack of care. They call it drowning in memories.' He sipped from his cup.

'And we call it drowning in the Skill. August Farseer.' I spoke aloud the name of a cousin long lost.

'And Verity, in a much more dramatic way. He did not drown in someone else's memories but submerged himself in a dragon, taking all his memories with him.'

I was quiet for a time, thinking about his words. I lifted my glass to my lips and then paused to say, 'A hedge-witch once told me that all magic is related—like a circle—and people may have this arc of it, or that. No one gets it all. I've got the Skill and the Wit, but I can't scry. Chade can, or could. I think. He never fully admitted it to me. Jinna could make charms for people, but despised my Wit as a dirty magic . . .' I watched his silvered hand turning. 'Fool. Why did you silver your hand? And why did you ask for more Silver?'

He sighed. His free hand shook out his glove and held it open as his silvered hand crept into it. He took up his cup in both hands. 'To have the magic, Fitz. To be able to use the pillars more easily. To be able to shape wood again, as I once did. To touch someone or something and know it, from the bones out, as I once could.' He drew in a deep breath and sighed it out. 'When they tormented me . . . When they skinned my hand . . .' He faltered. He took a slow sip of his brandy and said in a careless voice, 'When I had no Skill on my fingers, I missed it. I wanted it back.'

'Thymara said it would kill you.'

'It was slow death for Verity and Kettle. They knew it. They raced to create the dragon and enter it before the Silver could kill them.'

'But you lived for years with Silver on your fingertips.'

'And you bore the marks of my fingers on your wrist for years. You didn't die of it. Nor has Malta from my touch on her neck.'

'Why not?'

He scowled at his teacup and drank to lower the level of brandy in it before he shifted onto his side to face me. 'I don't know. Perhaps because I am not fully human. Perhaps because of the White heritage. Perhaps because you were trained to master the Skill. Perhaps because for you, like Malta, it was the barest brush of Silver on your skin. Or, for her, perhaps Tintaglia's dragon-changes made her immune.' He smiled. 'So perhaps because there is something of a dragon in you. Elderling blood, from long ago. I suspect it entered the bloodlines of the Farseers when the first Holder came to the shores of what would be Buck. Perhaps the walls of Buckkeep are not as heavily infused with Skill as the walls of Kelsingra, but we both know there is some of it, in the Skill-pillars and in the oldest stones of the castle.

Perhaps you are immune to it because you grew up with it, or perhaps you were born that way.' He shook his head against the bed that had relaxed to cushion him. 'We don't know. But I think this,' he held his gloved hand aloft and rubbed his fingertips together, 'will be very useful to me when we reach Clerres.'

'And the vials of Silver you asked for?'

'Truthfully, I wished them for a friend. To improve his lot in life. And perhaps to win a favour of him.'

I trickled some brandy into my glass and refilled his teacup. We both drank. 'Do I know this friend?'

He laughed aloud. It was a sound that had become so rare that I smiled to hear it, even when I did not know the reason. 'No, you don't know him yet. But you will.' He looked at me with his pale gold eyes and I felt he could see me. 'And you may find you have much in common,' he said, and laughed again, a bit loosely. I didn't ask. I knew better than to think he might answer a direct question. He surprised me when he asked, 'You have never considered it? Adding a bit of Skill to your fingers?'

'No.' I thought of Verity, his hands and forearms coated with Silver, unable to touch his lady or hold her. I thought of the times when something, a fern or a leaf, had brushed against the Fool's old fingerprints on my wrist and I'd had a disconcerting moment of full awareness of it. 'No. I think I have enough problems with the Skill without making myself even more vulnerable to it.'

'Yet you wore my fingerprints for years. And became very upset with me when I removed them.'

'True. Because I missed that link with you.' I took a sip of brandy. 'But how did you remove them from my skin? How did you recall the Skill to your fingertips?'

'I just did. Can you tell me how you reach out to Nettle?'

'Not in a way you would understand. Not unless you had the Skill.'

'Exactly.'

Silence fell between us for a time. I worked on my walls and felt the muttering of the city become a soft murmuring and then fade to blessed silence. Peace filled me for a moment. Then guilt welled up to fill the space the city's muttering had occupied. Peace? What right had I to peace when I had failed Bee so badly?

'Do you want me to take them back?'

'What?'

'My fingerprints on your wrist. Do you want me to take them back again?'

I thought briefly. Did I? 'I never wanted you to remove them when you did. And now? I fear that if you put your hand to my wrist, we might both be swept away. Fool, I told you that I felt besieged by the magic. My latest encounter with the force of the Skill has left me very wary. I think of Chade and how he crumbled in the last few months. What if that were suddenly me? Not remembering things, not keeping my thoughts organized? I can't let that happen. I have to keep my focus.' I sipped from my glass. 'We—I—have a task to complete.'

He made no response. I was staring at the ceiling but from the corner of my eye, I watched him drain his teacup. I offered him the bottle and he poured more for himself. Now was as good a time as any. 'So, tell me about Clerres. The island, the town, the school. How will we get in?'

'As for my getting in, that's not a problem. If I show myself in a guise they recognize, they will be very anxious to take me back in and finish what they began.' He tried for laughter, but abruptly fell silent.

I wondered if he had frightened himself. I sought for a distraction. 'You smell like her.'

'What?'

'You smell like Amber. It's a bit unnerving.'

'Like Amber?' He lifted his wrist to his nose and sniffed. 'There's barely a trace of attar of roses there. How can you smell that?'

'I suppose there's still a bit of the wolf in me. It's noticeable because you usually have no scent of your own. Oh, if you are filthy, I smell the dirt on your skin and clothes. But not you, yourself. Nighteyes sometimes called you the Scentless One. He thought it very strange.'

'I had forgotten that. Nighteyes.'

'To Nighteyes. To friends long gone,' I said. I lifted my glass and drained it, as did he. I quickly refilled his cup, and chinked the bottle against the lip of my glass.

We were both quiet for a time, recalling my wolf, but it was a different kind of silence. Then the Fool cleared his throat and spoke as if he were Fedwren teaching the history of Buck. 'Far to the south and across the sea to the east is the land from which I came. I was born to a little farming family. Our soil was good; our stream seldom ran dry. We had geese and sheep. My mother spun the wool, my parents dyed it, my fathers wove with it. So long ago, those days, like an old tale. I was born to my mother late in her life and I grew slowly, just as Bee did. But they kept me, and I stayed with them for many years. They were old when they took me to the Servants at Clerres. Perhaps they thought themselves too old to care for me any longer. They told me I had to become what I was meant to be, and they feared they had kept me too long from that calling. For in that part of the world, all know of the White Prophets, though not all give the legends credence.

'I was born on the mainland, on Mercenia, but we journeyed from island to island until we reached Clerres. It's a very beautiful city on a bay on a large island named Kells in the old tongue. Or Clerres. Some call it the White Island. Along that coast and on several of the islands are beaches littered with immense bones. They are so old they have turned to stone. I myself have seen them. Some of those stony bones were incorporated into the stronghold at Clerres. For it is a stronghold, from a time before the Servants. Once, a long narrow peninsula of land reached out to it. Whoever built the castle at Clerres cut away that peninsula, leaving only a narrow causeway that leads to it—a causeway that vanishes daily when the tide is in and reappears as the tide goes out. Each end of the causeway is stoutly gated and guarded. The Servants regulate who comes and who goes.'

'So they have enemies?'

He laughed again. 'Not that I have ever heard. They control the flow of commerce. Pilgrims and merchants and beggars. Clerres attracts all sorts of folk.'

'So we should approach it from the sea, in a small boat, at night.'

He shook his head and sipped more brandy. 'No. The towers above are manned at all times with excellent archers. Toward the sea, there are tall pilings of stone, and nightly the lamps on them are lit. They burn bright. You cannot approach from the sea.'

'Go on,' I said with a sigh.

'As I told you. All manner of folk come there. Merchants from far ports, people anxious to know their futures, folk who wish to become Servants of the Whites, mercenaries to join the guard. We will hide among them. In the daily flood of people seeking Clerres, you will be unnoticed. You can blend with the fortune-seekers who at every low tide cross the causeway to the castle.'

'I would rather enter by stealth. Preferably during darkness.'

'There might be a way,' he admitted. 'There is an ancient tunnel under the causeway. I don't know where one enters it, or where the tunnel opens. I told you that some of the young Whites carried me out in secrecy.' He shook his head and took a healthy swallow of his brandy. 'I thought they were my friends,' he said bitterly. 'Since then, I have had to wonder if they did not serve the Four. I think they freed me as one uncages a messenger pigeon, knowing it will fly home. I fear they will expect me. That they will have foreseen my return and be ready for me. What we attempt to do, Fitz, will disrupt every future they have ever planned. There will have been many dreams about it.'

I rolled my head to look at him. He was smiling strangely. 'When first you brought me back from death, I told you I was living in a future that I'd never foreseen. I had never dreamed of anything beyond my death. My death, I knew, was a certainty. And when I travelled with Prilkop, back to Clerres, I had no dreams. I was certain that my time as a White Prophet was over. Had not we achieved all I'd ever imagined?'

'We did!' I exclaimed and raised my glass. 'To us!' We drank.

'As the years passed, my dreams came back to me, but fitfully. Then Ash gave me the dragon-blood elixir, and my dreams returned as a flood. Powerful dreams. Visions that warned of strong divergences in what may be, Fitz. Twice I have dreamed of a Destroyer who comes to Clerres. That would be you, Fitz. But if I have dreamed such a thing, then will others have done so also. The Servants may expect us. They may even have deliberately set in motion that I will come back to them, and bring my Catalyst with me.'

'Then we must make sure they do not see you.' I feigned an optimism I did not feel. Telling an assassin he is expected is the worst news that can be delivered. I ventured toward something I had long wondered about. 'Fool. When we were changing the world, putting it into a "better track" as you used to say . . . how did you know what we should and should not do?'

'I didn't, exactly.' He sighed heavily. 'I saw you in the futures I wanted. But not often. At first, your survival was very unlikely. So my first task was to find you, and keep you alive as long as possible.

To create a greater likelihood that you would exist in more possible futures. Do you see what I mean?' I didn't, but I made an agreeable noise. 'So. To keep a bastard alive, find a powerful man. Win him to my side. I put into King Shrewd's head the thought that you might be useful in the future; that he should not let Regal destroy you, or he would not have you as a tool to possibly use later.'

I recalled Regal's words the first time he saw me. 'Don't do what you can't undo, until you've considered well what you can't do once you've done it.'

'Almost exactly right,' he said, and hiccupped, and then chuckled. 'Oh, King Shrewd. I never foresaw that I would come to care for him so much, Fitz, nor that he would be fond of me. Or you!' He yawned and added, 'But he did.'

'So, what can we do, to make it less likely they expect us?'

'We could not go.'

'Yes, there's that.'

'We could delay going for twenty years or so.'

'I'd likely be dead. Or very old.'

'True.'

'I don't want to take the others into this. Lant and the youngsters. I never meant for you to come along, let alone them. I hope that in Bingtown we can put them on a ship home.'

He shook his head, disapproving that plan. Then he asked, 'Do you think that somehow you will manage to leave me behind as well?'

'I wish I could, but I fear that I must have you with me, to help me find my way. So be useful, Fool. Tell me of this tunnel. Is it guarded as well?'

'I think not, Fitz. I can tell you so little. I was blinded and broken. I did not even know the names of those took me out of there. When I realized they were moving me, I thought they were taking me to the dung-tank on the level of the lowest dungeons. It is a vile place, always stinking of filth and death. All the waste of the castle flows into a vat set into the floor. If you have displeased the Four that is where they will dump your dismembered body. Twice a day the tank floods with the incoming tide. A chute slants down and under the castle wall, into the bay. And when the tide goes out, it carries with it the filth, the excrement, the little strangled babies they did not find worthy of life . . .'

His voice cracked as he said, 'I thought that was why they had come. To cut me in pieces and throw me in with all the other waste. But they hushed me when I cried out and said they had come to save me, and they rolled me onto a blanket and carried me out. During the times when I was conscious I heard the drip of water and smelled the sea. We went down some steps. They carried me a long way. I smelled their lantern. Then up some steps and out onto a hillside. I smelled sheep and wet grass. The jolting hurt me terribly. They carried me over rough ground for a painfully long time and then out onto a dock where they gave me over to sailors on a ship.'

I stored in my mind the little he had given me. A tunnel under the causeway that ended in a sheep pasture. Not much of use. 'Who were they? Would they be willing to help us?'

'I don't know. Even now, I can't recall it clearly.'

'You must,' I told him. I felt him flinch and feared I had pushed him too hard. I spoke more gently. 'Fool, you are all I have. And there is so much I need to know about this "Four". I must know their weaknesses, their pleasures, their friends. I must know their habits, their vices, their routines and desires.'

I waited. He remained silent. I tried another question. 'If we can choose but one to kill, which one do you most wish dead?' He was silent. After a time, I asked him quietly, 'Are you awake?'

'Awake. Yes.' He sounded more sober than he had. 'Fitz. Was this how it was with Chade? Did you two take counsel with one another and plan each death?'

Don't talk about this. Too private even to tell the Fool. I'd never spoken of it to Molly. The only one who had ever witnessed me engaged in my trade was Bee. I cleared my throat. 'Let it go for tonight, Fool. Tomorrow I will beg paper from the keepers and we can begin to draw the stronghold. As much as you remember. For tonight, we need to sleep.'

'I won't be able to.'

He sounded desperately unhappy. I was exhuming all he had buried. I handed him the bottle. He drank from the neck. I took it back and did the same. It was unlikely that I would sleep either. I hadn't intended to get drunk. It was supposed to be a ploy. A scheme, to trick my friend. I drank more and took a breath. 'Have you any allies there, within the walls?'

'Perhaps. Prilkop was alive, the last time I saw him. But if he lives, he is likely a prisoner.' A pause. 'I will try to order it all in my mind and tell it to you. But, it is hard, Fitz. There are things I can't bear to recall. They only come back to me in nightmares . . .'

He fell silent. Digging information out of him felt as cruel as digging bits of bone from a wound.

'When we left Aslevjal to return to Clerres?' he said suddenly. 'That was Prilkop's idea. I was still recovering from all that had happened. I did not feel competent to chart my own course. He had always wanted to return to Clerres. Longed for it, for so many years. His memories of that place were so different to mine. He had come from a time before the Servants were corrupt. From a time when they truly served the White Prophet. When I told him of my time there, of how I had been treated, he was aghast. And more determined than ever that we must return, to set things right.' He shifted suddenly, wrapping his arms around himself and hunching his shoulders forward. I rolled toward him. In the faint light of the ceiling's stars, he looked very old and small. 'I let him persuade me. He was . . . I hope he *is* . . . very large-hearted, Fitz. Unable, even after he had seen all Ilistore did, to believe that the Servants now served only greed and hatred.'

'Ilistore?'

'You knew her as the Pale Woman.'

'I did not know she had another name.'

At that, a thin smile curved his mouth. 'You thought that when she was a babe, she was called the Pale Woman?'

'I . . . well, no. I'd never really thought about it. You called her the Pale Woman!'

'I did. It's an old tradition or perhaps a superstition. Never call something by its true name if you wish to avoid calling its attention to you. Perhaps it goes back to the days when dragons and humans commonly coexisted in the world. Tintaglia disliked that humans knew her true name.'

'Ilistore,' I said softly.

'She's gone. Even so I avoid her name.'

'She *is* gone.' I thought of her as I had last seen her, her arms ending in blackened sticks of bone, her hair lank about her face, all pretence of beauty gone. I did not want to think of that. I was grateful when he began to speak again, his words soft at the edges. 'When I first returned to Clerres with Prilkop, the Servants were

. . . astonished. I have told you how weak I was. Had I been myself, I would have been much more cautious. But Prilkop anticipated only peace and comfort and a wonderful homecoming. We crossed the causeway together, and all who saw his gleaming black skin knew what he must be: a prophet who had achieved his life's work. We entered and he refused to wait. We walked straight into the audience chamber of the Four.'

I watched his face in the dim light. A smile tried to form, faded. 'They were speechless. Frightened, perhaps. He announced plainly that their false prophet had failed, and that we had released IceFyre into the world. He was fearless.' He turned toward me. 'A woman screamed and ran from the room. I cannot be sure, but I think that was Dwalia. That was how she heard that the Pale Woman's hands had been eaten, and how she had died in the cold, starved and freezing. Ilistore had always despised me, and that day I secured Dwalia's hatred as well.

'Yet almost immediately, the Four gave us a veritable festival of welcome. Elaborate dinners, with us seated at the high table with them. Entertainments were staged, and intoxicants and courtesans offered to us, anything they imagined we might desire. We were hailed as returning heroes rather than the two who had destroyed the future they had sought.'

Another silence. Then he took a breath. 'They were clever. They requested a full accounting of all I had accomplished, as one might expect they would. They put scribes at my disposal, offered me the finest paper, beautiful inks and brushes so that I might record all I had experienced out in the greater world. Prilkop was honoured as the eldest of all Whites.'

He stopped speaking and I thought he had drowsed off. I had not had near as much brandy as he had. My ploy had worked too well. I took the teacup from his lax hand and set it gently on the floor.

'They gave us sumptuous chambers,' he went on at last. 'Healers tended me. I regained my strength. They were so humble, so apologetic for how they had doubted me. So willing to learn. They asked me so many questions . . . I realized one day that, despite all their questions and flattery, I had managed to . . . minimize you. To tell my history as if you were several people rather than one. A stableboy, a bastard prince, an assassin. To keep you hidden from them, save as a nameless Catalyst who served me. I allowed myself to admit that I did not trust them. That I had never forgotten or forgiven how they had mistreated and restrained me.

'And Prilkop, too, had misgivings. He had watched the Pale Woman for years as she claimed Aslevjal. He had seen how she courted her Catalyst, Kebal Rawbread, with gifts—a silver throat-piece, earrings of gold set with rubies, gifts that meant that she had substantial wealth at her disposal. The wealth of Clerres had been made available to her that she might set the world on their so-called true Path. She was no rogue prophet, but their emissary sent out to do their will. She was to destroy IceFyre and put an end to the last hope to restore dragons to the world. Why, he asked me, would they welcome the two who had dashed their plans?

'So, we conspired. We agreed that we must not give them any clues that led back to you. Prilkop theorized that they were looking for what he called junctions—places and people that had helped us shift the world into a better future. He speculated that they could use the same places and people to push the world back into the "true Path" they had desired. Prilkop felt you were a very powerful junction, one to be protected. At that point, the Four were still treating us as honoured guests. We had the best of everything, and freedom to roam the castle and the town. That was when we smuggled out our first two messengers. They were to seek you out and warn you.'

I rallied my bleary brain. 'No. The messenger said you wanted me to find the Unexpected Son.'

'That came later,' he said softly. 'Much later.'

'You always said I was the Unexpected Son.'

'So I thought then. And Prilkop, too. You will recall how earnestly he advised us to part, lest we accidentally continue to work unpredictable change in the world, changes we could neither predict nor control.' He laughed uneasily. 'And so we have done.'

'Fool, I care nothing for anyone's vision of a better future for this world. The Servants destroyed my child.' I spoke into the darkness. 'I care only that they have no future at all.' I shifted in the bed. 'When did you stop believing that I was the Unexpected Son? And if those prophecies do not pertain to me, what of all we did together? If we were guided by your dreams, and yet I was not the one your dreams foretold . . .'

'I've wrestled with that.' He sighed so heavily I felt his breath against my face. 'Prophetic dreams are riddling things, Fitz. Puzzles to be solved. Often enough you have accused me of interpreting them after the fact, bending them to fit what truly happened. But the prophecies of the Unexpected Son? There are many. I have never told you all of them. In some, you wore a buck's antlers. In others, you howled like a wolf. The dreams said you would come from the north, from a pale mother and dark father. All those prophecies fitted. I cited all those dreams to prove that the bastard prince that I had aided was the Unexpected Son.'

'You aided me? I thought I was your Catalyst.'

'You were. Don't interrupt. This is difficult enough without interruptions.' He paused again to lift the bottle. As he lowered it, I caught it before it fell. 'I know you are the Unexpected Son. In my bones, I knew it then, and I know it now. But they insisted you were not. They hurt me so badly that I could not believe what I knew. They twisted my thoughts, Fitz, just as much as they torqued my bones. They said that some of their Clerres-bred Whites were still having dreams of the Unexpected Son. They dreamed him as a figure of dark vengeance. They said that if I had fulfilled those prophecies, the dreams would not be continuing. But they were.'

'Maybe they still mean me.' I stoppered the bottle and lowered it carefully to the floor. I set my glass beside it. I rolled to face him.

I had meant it as a jest. His sharp intake of breath told me it was anything but humorous to him. 'But—' he objected and then stopped speaking. He bowed his head forward suddenly, almost butting it into my chest. He whispered as if he feared to speak the words loud. 'Then they would know. They would certainly know. Oh, Fitz. They did come and find you. They took Bee, but they had found the Unexpected Son, as they had claimed the dreams predicted they would.' He choked on those last words.

I set my hand on his shoulder. He was shaking. I spoke quietly. 'So they found me. And we will make them very sorry they found me. Did not you tell me that you had dreamed me as Destroyer? That is *my* prediction: I will destroy the people who destroyed my child.'

'Where is the bottle?' He sounded utterly discouraged and I decided to take mercy on him.

'We drank it. We've talked enough. Go to sleep.'

'I cannot. I fear to dream.'

I was drunk. The words tumbled from my mouth. 'Then dream

of me, killing the Four.' I laughed stupidly. 'How I would have loved to kill Dwalia.' I took a deep breath. 'Now I understand why you were angry at me for walking away from the Pale Woman. I knew she would die. But I understand why you wished me to kill her.'

'You were carrying me. I was dead.'

'Yes.'

We were both quiet for a time, thinking of that. I had not been this drunk in a long time. I started to let my awareness slide away.

'Fitz. After my parents left me at Clerres, I was still a child. Just when I needed someone to care for me, to protect me, I had no one.' His voice, always controlled so carefully, was thickening with tears. 'My journey to Buckkeep, when I first fled Clerres to discover you. It was horrible. The things I had to do, the things that were done to me – all so that I could get to Buck. And find you.' He sobbed in a breath. 'Then, King Shrewd. I came there hoping only to manipulate him to get what I needed. You, alive. I had become what the Servants had taught me to be, ruthless and selfish. Set only on levering people and events to my will. I came to his court, ragged and half-starved, and gave him a letter with most of the ink washed away, saying that I had been sent as a gift to him.'

He sniffed and then dragged his arm across his eyes. My eyes filled with tears for him. 'I tumbled and pranced and walked on my hands. I expected him to mock me. I was prepared to be used however he desired if I could but win your life from him.' He sobbed aloud. 'He . . . he ordered me to stop. Regal was beside his throne, full of horror that a creature such as I was admitted to the throne room. But Shrewd? He told a guardsman, "Take that child to the kitchens, and see him fed. Have the seamstresses find some clothes to fit him. And shoes. Put shoes on his feet".

'And all that he commanded was done for me. It made me so wary! Oh, I didn't trust him. Capra had taught me to fear initial kindness. I kept waiting for the blow, for the demand. When he told me I could sleep on the hearth in his bedchamber, I was certain he would . . . But that was all he meant. While Queen Desire was gone, I would be his companion in the evening, to amuse him with tricks and tales and songs, and then sleep on his hearth and rise in the morning when he did. Fitz, he had no reason to be so kind to me. None at all.'

He was weeping noisily now, his walls completely broken. 'He protected me, Fitz. It took months for him to gain my trust. But after a time, whenever Queen Desire was travelling and I slept on the hearth, I felt safe. It was safe to sleep.' He rubbed his eyes again. 'I miss that. I miss that so badly.'

I did, I think, what anyone would have done for a friend, especially as drunk as we both were. I remembered Burrich, too, and how his strength had sheltered me when I was small. I put my arm around the Fool and pulled him close. For an instant, I felt that unbearable connection. I lifted my hand away and shifted so that his face rested on my shirt.

'I felt that,' he said wearily.

'So did I.'

'You should be more careful.'

'I should.' I secured my walls against him. I wished I didn't have to. 'Go to sleep,' I told him. I made a promise I doubted I could keep. 'I will protect you.'

He sniffed a final time, wiped his wrist across his eyes and gave a deep sigh. He groped with his gloved hand, and clasped my hand, wrist to wrist, the warriors' greeting. After a time, I felt his body go slack against mine. His grip on my wrist loosened. I kept mine firm.

Protect him. Could I even protect myself any more? What right did I have to offer him such a vain promise. I hadn't protected Bee, had I? I took a deep breath and thought of her. Not in the shallow, wistful way one recalls a sweet time, long past. I thought of her little hand clasping my fingers. I recalled how thickly she spread butter on bread, and how she held her teacup in both hands. I let the pain wash fresh against me, salt in fresh slashes. I recalled her weight on my shoulder and how she gripped my head to steady herself. Bee. So small. Mine for so short a time. And gone now. Just gone, into the Skill-stream and lost forever. Bee.

The Fool made a small sound of pain. For an instant, his hand tightened on my wrist, and then fell slack again.

And for a time, as I stared up at the false night sky, I kept a drunken watch over him.

SEVEN

Beggar

A dream so brief but so brilliantly coloured that I cannot forget it. Is it significant? My father is talking to a person with two heads. They are so deep in conversation that no matter how loudly I interrupt them, they will not speak to me. In the dream, I say, 'Find her. Find her. It's not too late!' In the dream, I am a wolf made of fog. I howl and howl, but they do not turn to me.

Bee Farseer's dream journal

I had never been so alone. So hungry. Even Wolf Father was at a loss for what I should do. *Let us find a forest. There, I can teach you to be a wolf like your father taught me.*

The ruins were a great tumble of blackened and melted stone. The squared edges of some blocks were slumped and sunken like ice melted by the sun. I had to climb up and over collapsed walls, and I feared to fall into the cracks between the fallen stones. I found a place where two immense blocks were tented together and crawled into the shadowy recess beneath them. Huddled in their shade, I tried to gather my thoughts and strength. I needed to stay hidden from Dwalia and the others. I had no food and no water. I had the clothes on my back and a candle in my jerkin. My mildewed shawl had been lost in my most recent beating, along with my wool hat. How could I win my way back to Buck, or even to the border of the Six Duchies? I reviewed what I knew of the geography of Chalced. Could I walk home? Chalced's terrain was harsh. It was a land where heat welled up from the earth. There was a desert, I seemed to recall

. . . and a low range of mountains. I shook my head. It was useless. My mind could not work while my belly clamoured for food and my mouth told me how dry it was.

All that afternoon I remained hidden. I listened intently but heard nothing of Dwalia and the others. Perhaps she had managed to exit the tumble of stone, and perhaps Vindeliar had once more bent the Chalcedean's will to her purposes. What would they do? Perhaps go into the city or to Kerf's home. Would they search for me? So many questions and no answers.

As night approached, I picked my way through a dragon-blasted section of the city. Once-fine houses gawked rooflessly, with empty holes for windows and doors. The streets had largely been cleared of rubble. Scavengers and salvagers had been at work among the ruins. Walls were missing blocks of stones; tall weeds and scrawny bushes grew from the cracks. Beyond a gap in a tumbled garden wall I found water collected in the mossy basin of a derelict fountain. I drank from my cupped hands, and splashed my face. My raw wrists stung as I washed my hands. I pushed sprawling bushes aside as I sought a shelter for the night. The scent of crushed mint rose to me as I trod through herbs. I ate some of it, simply to have something in my belly. My brushing fingertips recognized the umbrella shapes of nasturtium leaves. I ripped up handfuls and stuffed them in my mouth. Beyond a curtain of trailing vines on a leaning trellis I found an abandoned dwelling.

I clambered through a low window and looked up at a roofless view of the sky. Tonight would be clear and cold. I found a corner relatively free of rubble and partially sheltered by the collapsed roof, crept into the darkness and curled up like a stray dog there. I closed my eyes. Sleep came and went with intermittent dreams. I had toast and tea at Withywoods. My father carried me on his shoulders. I woke up weeping. I huddled tighter in the dark and tried to imagine a plan that would get me home. The floor was hard beneath me. My shoulder still ached. My belly hurt, not just from hunger but from the kicks I'd received. I touched my ear; blood crusted my hair around it. I probably looked frightful, as awful as the beggar I'd tried to help back in Oaksbywater. So, tomorrow, I'd be a beggar girl. Anything to get food. I pushed my back against the wall and huddled smaller. I slept fitfully through a night that was not that cold unless one was sleeping outside with no more cover than tattered clothing.

When the sun rose I discovered a blue sky full of scudding white clouds. I was stiff, hungry, thirsty and alone. Free. A strange smell hung in the air, tingeing the city smells of cooking-fires and open drains and horse droppings. *Low tide*, Wolf Father whispered to me. *The smell of the sea when the waves retreat.*

I clambered up what remained of the stone wall of the house to survey my surroundings.

I was on a low hill in a great trough of a valley. I had glimpses of a river beyond the city below. Behind me, houses and buildings and roads coated the land like a crusty sore. Smoke rose from countless chimneys. Closer to the city, tendrils of brownish water surrounded the many ships at anchor. A harbour. I knew the word but finally I saw all it meant. It was sheltered water, as if a finger and thumb of the land reached out to enclose it. Beyond it was more water, all the way to the edge of the sky. I had so often heard of the deep blue sea that it was hard to grasp that the many shaded water of greens and blues, silver and greys and black were what minstrels sang about. The minstrels had sung, too, of the lure of the sea, but I felt nothing of that. It looked vast and empty and dangerous. I turned away from it. In the far distance beyond the city, there were low mounds of yellowish hills. 'They have no forest,' I whispered.

Ah. This explains much about the Chalcedeans, Wolf Father replied. Through my eyes, he surveyed a land scarred with buildings and cobbled streets. *This is a different and dangerous sort of wilderness. I fear I will be of small use to you here. Go carefully, cub. Go very carefully.*

Chalced was waking. There were damaged swathes of city below me, but the dragons had concentrated their fury on the area around the ruined palace. The duke's palace, Kerf had said. Memory stirred. I had heard of this destruction in a conversation between my mother and father. The dragons of Kelsingra had come to Chalced and attacked the city. The old duke had been destroyed and his daughter had stepped up to become Duchess of Chalced. No one could recall a time when a woman had reigned over Chalced. My father had said, 'I doubt there will be peace with Chalced, but at least they'll be so busy fighting civil wars that they can't bother us as much.'

But I saw no civil war. Brightly garbed folk moved in the peaceful lanes. Carts pulled by donkeys or peculiarly large goats began to fill the streets, and people in loose, billowing shirts and black trousers moved amongst them. I watched fish spilling silver from a boat pulled up on the shore, and saw a ship towed out to deep water where its sails spread like the sudden wings of a bird before it moved silently away. I saw two markets, one near the docks and another along a broad avenue. The latter had bright awnings over the stalls while the one near the docks seemed drabber and poorer. The smells of fresh-baked bread and smoked meats reached me, and faint though they were, my mouth watered.

I assessed my plan to be a mute beggar girl and beg for coins and food. But my ragged tunic and leggings and fur boots would betray that I was a foreigner in this land of bright and flowing garb.

I had no choice. I could stay hidden in the ruins and starve, or take my chances in the streets.

I tidied myself. I would be a beggar but not a disgusting one. I hoped that my pale hair and blue eyes would make me appear Chalcedean, and I could mime that I had no voice. I touched my face, wincing as I explored bruises and scarcely healed cuts. Perhaps pity would aid my cause. But I could not rely on pity alone.

I took off the fur boots. The spring day was already too warm for them. I dusted and smoothed them as best as I could. I peeled the rags of my stockings and stared at my pale and shrivelled feet. I couldn't remember the last time I'd gone barefoot. I'd have to get used to it. I hugged my boots to my chest and began to walk toward the market.

Where people sell things, there are people buying things. My feet were bruised by stones and dirty by the time I reached the market, but my hunger outshone those pains. It hurt to walk past the stalls selling early fruit and baked breads and meats. I ignored the odd looks people gave me and tried to appear calm and relaxed, rather than a stranger in this city.

I found the stalls that sold fabric and garments, and then the carts that sold used clothing and rags. I offered the boots mutely to several booths before anyone showed any interest in them. The woman who took them from me turned them over and over. She frowned at them, scowled at me, looked at them again, and then held out six copper coins. I had no way to bargain. Good or bad, it was the only offer I'd get, and so I took the coins, bobbed a bow to her, and stepped back from her stall. I tried to fade into the passing folk but I could feel her eyes following me.

I silently offered two coins at a baker's stall. The vendor asked me a question and I gestured at my closed mouth. The young man looked at the coins, looked at me, pursed his lips and turned to a covered basket. He offered me a stiff roll of bread, probably several days old. I took it, my hands trembling with eagerness and bobbed my head in thanks. A peculiar look crossed his face. He caught me by the wrist and it was all I could do not to shriek. But then he chose from the fresh wares on the board in front of him the smallest of the sweet rolls and gave it to me. I think my look of utter gratitude embarrassed him, for he shooed me away as if I were a stray kitten. I stuffed my food into the front of my tunic with my battered candle and fled to find a safe place to eat it.

At the end of the market row I saw a public well. I'd never seen the like. Warm water bubbled up into a stone-lined pool. The overflow was guided away in a trough. I saw women filling buckets, and then saw a child stoop and drink from cupped hands. I copied her, kneeling by the water and scooping up a drink. The water smelled odd and had a strong flavour but it was wet and not poisonous and that was all I cared about. I drank my fill, then splashed a bit onto my face and scrubbed my hands together. Evidently that was rude, for a man made a noise of disgust and scowled at me. I scrambled to my feet and hurried away.

Beyond the market was a street of merchants. These were not market stalls, but grand establishments built of stone and timbers. Their doors were open to the warming day. As I walked past, I smelled meat curing in smoke, and then heard the rasp of a carpenter smoothing wood. There were stacks of rough timbers in an open space beside and behind the carpenter's shop. I looked both ways and then slipped into their shade. The cross-layered planks hid me from the street. I sat on the ground and set my back to a stack of sweet-smelling wood. I took out my bread and made myself eat the older roll first. It was coarse stuff and stale—and incredibly delicious. I trembled as I ate it. When it was gone, I sat still, breathing hard and feeling the last of the bread descend from my throat to my stomach. I could have eaten ten more just like it.

I held the small sweet roll in my hand and smelled it. I told myself I would be wise to save it for tomorrow. Then I told myself that as I carried it, I might drop it, or break bits off it and lose them. I was easily persuaded. I ate it. There was a thin thread of honey swirled on top of it that had baked into the bread, and there were bits of fruit and spices inside it. I ate it in torturously slow nibbles, savouring every tingle of sweetness on my tongue. Too soon it was gone. My hunger was sated, but the memory of it plagued me.

Another memory sifted into my brain. Another beggar, scarred and broken and cold. Probably hungrier than I was now. I had tried to be kind to him. And my father had stabbed him, over and over. And then abandoned me to carry him off to Buckkeep for healing. I tried to put those bits together with the pieces I had overheard, but they only joined together in impossible ways. Instead, I wondered why no one looked at me, small, hungry and alone, and offered me an apple.

My mouth watered at the thought of the apple I'd given that beggar. Oh, the chestnuts that day, hot to peel and sweet in my mouth. My stomach knotted and I bent over it.

I had four small coins left. If the bread man was as kind tomorrow as he had been today, I could eat for two days. Then I'd either go hungry or steal.

How was I going to get home?

The sun was getting warmer and the day brighter. I looked down at myself. My bare feet were scuffed with dirt and my toenails were long. My padded trousers were grubby. My once-long Withywoods green jerkin was spotted and stained, and ended raggedly at my hips. My underblouse was grimy at the cuffs. A very convincing beggar.

I should go down to the docks and see if any ships were bound to Buck or indeed anywhere in the Six Duchies. I wondered how I could ask, and what I could do to earn passage on one. The sun was bright and my clothing too warm for the mild day. I moved deeper into the shade and curled up with my back to a stack of wood. I did not mean to fall asleep, but I did.

I woke in late afternoon. The shade had travelled away from me, but I had slept until the moving light of the sun on my closed eyes had wakened me. I sat up, feeling miserably sick, dizzy and thirsty. I staggered to my feet and began to walk. My small store of courage was gone. I could not make myself go down to the docks or even explore more of the city. I retreated to the ruins where I had sheltered the night before.

In a city full of strangeness, I took comfort from what little I knew. By daylight, the water in the old fountain in the ruined house's garden was greenish and little black water creatures darted in its depths. But it was water, and I was thirsty. I drank and then bared my body to wash as best I could. I washed out my clothes and was surprised at how hard a task that was. Once again I realized how easy a life I'd led at Withywoods. I thought of the servants who had supplied my every need. I had always been polite to them, but had I ever truly thanked them for all they did? Careful came to mind and how she had loaned me her lace cuffs. Was she still alive? Did Careful think of me sometimes? I wanted to weep, but did not.

Sternly I made my plans as I dipped and scrubbed and wrung out my garments. Dwalia had thought me a boy. It was safer to present myself as a boy. Would a ship going towards the Six Duchies need a boy? I'd heard tales of ship's boys having wild and wonderful adventures. Some became pirates in the minstrels' songs, or found treasures or became captains. Tomorrow I would take two of my coins and buy more bread and eat it. I very much liked that part of my plan. Then I must go down to the waterfront and see if any ships were going to the Six Duchies and if they would give me passage for work. I pushed away the thought that I was small and looked childish and was not very strong and spoke no Chalcedean. Somehow, I would manage.

I had to.

I hung my clothing on a broken stone wall to dry and stretched out naked on the sun-warmed stones of a deserted courtyard. My mother's candle was battered, the wax imprinted with lint, and broken in one place with only the wick holding it together. But it still smelled like her. Like home and safety and gentle hands. I fell asleep there in the dappling shade of a half-fallen tree. When I awoke a second time, my clothing was mostly dry and the sun was going down. I was hungry again and dreaded the chill night. I had slept so much but I still felt weary and I wondered if my journey through the stone pillars had taken more from me than I knew. I crawled deeper under the leaning tree to where the leaves of several falls made a cushion against the stone. I refused to think of spiders and biting things. I curled up small and slept again.

Sometime in the night, I lost my courage. My own crying woke me, and once awake, I could not stop the sobs. I stuffed my hand in my mouth to muffle the sounds and wept. I wept for my lost home, for the horses killed in the fire, for Revel dead in his blood on the floor before me. Everything that had happened to me, all that I had seen and had not had time to react to suddenly flooded my mind. My father had left me for the sake of a blind beggarman, and Perseverance was probably dead. I'd left Shun behind and hoped the best for her. Had she survived and reached Withywoods, to tell them what had befallen us? Would anyone ever come after me? I remembered FitzVigilant, his blood red on the white snow.

Suddenly going home seemed impossible. Going home to what? Who would be there? Would they all hate me because the pale folk had come for me? And if I went home, would not Dwalia or others of her kind know where I would flee? Would they come after me again, to burn and kill? I hunched low under my sheltering tree, rocking myself, knowing that there was no one who could protect me.

I'll protect you. Wolf Father's words were less than a whisper.

He was only in my mind, only an idea. How could he protect me? What was he, really? Something I imagined from the fragments of my father's writing?

I am real and I am with you. Trust me. I can help you protect yourself.

I felt a sudden rush of anger. 'You didn't protect me before, when they took me. You didn't protect me when Dwalia beat me and dragged me through the pillar. You're a dream. Something I imagined because I was so childish and scared. But you can't help me now. No one can help me now.'

No one except yourself.

'Be silent!' I shouted the words, and then covered my mouth in horror. I needed to hide, not shout at imaginary beings in the night. I scuttled deeper under the tree until I felt a tumble of fallen wall and could go no farther. I made myself small and shut my eyes tight and walled my thoughts in and slept.

I awoke the next day with my face crusty from my weeping. My head pounded with pain and I felt nauseous with hunger. It was a long time before I could convince myself to crawl out from the tree's shade. I did not feel well enough to walk down to the markets, so I wandered the ruined area of the city. I caught sight of lizards and snakes basking on the tumbled stones. I thought of eating one but at my approach they whisked under the stones. Twice I saw other people who seemed to be living in the broken houses. I smelled their cook-fires and saw ragged clothing hung to dry. I kept out of their sight.

Hunger drove me at last back to the market. I could not find the bread stall I'd patronized the day before. I staggered and limped through the stalls, looking for it, but finally my raging hunger forced me to approach another. A sour-faced woman was cooking pastries stuffed with some savoury filling on a griddle. A small metal pot held her cookfire. The pastries sizzled in a wide pan over the flames and she deftly flipped them with a pronged tool to brown each side.

I offered her one coin and she shook her head. I wandered off behind a stall where I could extract another coin from my knotted shirt. For two coins, she put a pastry on a wide green leaf, folded the leaf around it, secured it with a sliver of wood and handed it to me. I bowed my thanks but she ignored that, already looking over my head for her next potential customer.

I did not know if the leaf was meant to be eaten or was a napkin. I took a cautious nibble of the edge; it was not unpleasant. I reasoned that a vendor would not wrap food in something poisonous. I found a quiet place behind an unoccupied market stall and sat down to eat. The pastry was not large, just filling my hand, and I wanted to eat it slowly. The filling was crumbly and tasted a bit like wet sheep smelled. I didn't care. But after my second bite, I became aware of a boy watching me from the gap between the walls of two stalls. I looked away from him, taking another bite, and when I glanced back, a smaller boy in a dirty striped shirt had joined him. Their hair and their feet and bare legs were dusty, their clothing unkempt. They had the eyes of small, hungry predators. I felt a moment of dizziness as I stared at them. It reminded me of when the beggar at Oaksbywater had held my hand. I saw events swirling, possibilities. I could not sort them, could not tell good from bad. All I knew for certain was that I must avoid them.

As a donkey cart passed between us, I scooted around the corner of the stall and stuffed the rest of my pastry in my mouth, overfilling it but freeing my hands. I rose and tried to blend in with the passing folk.

My clothing made me stand out so that I drew curious glances. I kept my eyes down and tried not to engage anyone's attention. I glanced back several times but did not see the boys, yet I was convinced they were following me. If they robbed me of my two remaining coins, I would have nothing. I fought down the panic that thought brought. *Don't think like prey.* A warning from Wolf

Father or simply a thought of my own? I slowed my steps, found a place to crouch beside a refuse cart and watched the ebb and flow of people.

There were others like me in the market, and those young beggars were more skilled at this trade. Three youngsters, two girls and a boy, lingered at a fruit vendor's stall despite his efforts to shoo them away. Suddenly all three darted in, each seizing a prize and then scattered while the seller shouted and cursed and sent his son chasing after one of them.

I saw, too, some sort of city guards. Their orange robes were cut short, to their knees, and they wore canvas trousers, light leather tunics and low boots. They carried short, knobbed staffs and wore sheathed swords as they strode past in groups of four. Merchants offered them skewers of meat and rolls of bread and chunks of fish on flatbread as they passed. I wondered if gratitude or fear prompted such generosity, and slipped away from their view as quickly as I could.

I made my way eventually to the docks. It was a noisy, busy place. Men were pushing handcarts, teams of horses pulled laden wagons, with some going to the ships and others coming from them. The smells were overwhelming; tar and rotting seaweed predominated. I hung back, watching and wondering how to tell where a ship was going. I had no desire to be carried even farther from the Six Duchies. I watched wide-eyed as an apparatus I could not name lifted a net that held several large wooden crates and swung them from the dock to a ship's deck. I saw a young man receive three sharp cracks from a stick across his bared back even as he was guiding such a swinging cargo down to a deck. I could not tell what he had done wrong or why he had been struck and shrank back, imagining such blows falling on me.

I saw no one as small as me working on the docks, though I guessed that several of the boys I saw were my age. They worked shirtless, darting barefoot on the splintery docks, on apparently urgent missions that demanded they run. One boy had an oozing welt down his back. A cart-driver shouted at me to get out of his way and another man did not bother, shoving me aside, shoulders laden with two heavy coils of rope.

Daunted, I fled through the market and then up the hill toward the ruins.

As I left the market, a young man in a lovely robe decorated with rosettes of yellow called to me with a smile. He beckoned me closer, and when I halted at a safe distance, wondering what he wanted of me, he crouched down to my height. He cocked his head and said something softly, persuasive words that I did not understand. He looked kind. His hair was more yellow than mine and cut so that it barely reached his jaw. His earrings were green jade. A man of a good family and wealth, I guessed. 'I don't understand,' I replied hesitantly in Common.

His blue eyes narrowed in surprise, and then his smile widened. In a heavy accent, he said, 'Pretty new robe. Come. Give you food.' He eased a step closer to me and I could smell his perfumed hair. He held out his hand, palm upturned and waited for me to take it.

Run! Run now!

Wolf Father's urgency brooked no hesitation. I gave the smiling man a final glance, a shake of my head and I darted away. I heard him call after me and I wondered why I ran, but run I did. He called after me again but I did not look back. *Do not go straight to your den. Hide and look back,* Wolf Father cautioned me, and so I did, but saw no one. Later that night, curled under my sheltering tree, I wondered why I had fled.

Eyes of a predator, Wolf Father told me.

What should I do tomorrow? I asked him.

I don't know, was his woeful response.

I dreamed of home that night, of toasted bread and hot tea in the kitchen. In my dream, I was too small to reach the top of the table and I could not right the overturned bench. I called to Caution to help me, but when I turned to look for her she was lying on the floor with blood all over her. I ran from the kitchen screaming but everywhere folk were dead on the floor. I opened doors to try to hide, but behind each door were the two beggar boys, and beyond them Dwalia stood, laughing. I awoke sobbing in the middle of the night. To my terror, I heard voices, one calling questioningly. I muffled my sobs and tried to breathe silently. I saw a dim light and a lantern passed by in the street outside my broken garden. Two people spoke to one another in Chalcedean. I stayed hidden and wakeful until morning.

The morning was half gone before I found the courage to return to the market. I found the bread stall I'd visited the first day, but the young man had been replaced by a woman and when I showed her my two coins, she gestured me away in disgust. I held them both up again, thinking she had seen only the one, but she hissed a rebuke at me and slapped her hands together threateningly. I retreated, resolved to find food elsewhere, but in that instant I was knocked down by one of the two boys I'd seen the day before. In a flash, the other boy snatched my coins and they both darted away into the market throng. I sat up in the dust, the wind knocked out of me. Then, to my shame, sobs shook me and I sat in the dirt and covered my eyes and wept.

No one cared. The flow of the market went around me as if I were a stone in the current. For a time after my sobbing left me, I sat forlorn. I was so terribly hungry. My shoulder ached, the relentless sun shone on my aching head and I had no plans left. How could I imagine getting home when I could not think how to get through the day?

A man guiding a donkey-cart through the market tapped me with his quirt. It was a warning, not a strike, and I quickly scrabbled out of his way. I watched him pass, and smeared dust and tears from my face onto my sleeve and looked around the market. The hunger that assailed me now seemed the product of weeks rather than just a day. While I'd had the prospect each day of something to eat, however small, I'd been able to master it. But now it commanded me. I squared my shoulders, wiped my eyes once more and then walked deliberately away from the bread stall.

I moved slowly through the market, studying each stall and vendor. My moral dilemma lasted as long as it took for me to swallow the saliva the smells of the foods triggered. Yesterday, I'd seen how it was done. I had no one to create a diversion for me, and if anyone decided to pursue me, I would be the only rabbit to be run down. My hunger seemed to speed my thought processes. I'd have to choose a stall and a target and an escape route. Then I'd have to wait and hope that something would distract the merchant. I was small and I was fast. I could do this. I had to do this. Hunger such as I felt now could not be borne.

I prowled the market, intent on my theft. Nothing small. I did not want to take this chance for a bit of fruit. I needed meat or a loaf of bread, or a side of smoked fish. I tried to look without appearing to look, but a small boy lifted a switch threateningly at me when I stared too long at his mother's slabs of red salted fish.

I finally found what I sought: a baker's stall, bigger and grander than any other I'd seen. Loaves of rich brown and golden yellow were mounded in baskets on the ground in front of his stall. On the plank before him were the more expensive wares, bread twisted with spices and honey, rich cakes studded with nuts. I'd settle for one of the golden yellow pillows. The stall next to him sold scarves that billowed in the breeze off the sea. Several women were clustered there, their bargaining focused and intense. Across the milling market street, a tinker sold knives. His partner sharpened blades of all sorts on a spinning whetstone powered by a sweating apprentice. The grinding made a shrill sound and sometimes it spat sparks. I found a backwater of the customer stream and pretended a great fascination with the spinning stone. I let my mouth hang a trifle ajar as if I did not have all my mind. I was sure that with such an expression and my ragged clothes, folk would pay little attention to me. But all the while, I waited for anything in the market that might make the bread vendor look away from his wares and give me a chance to steal my target.

As if in answer to my thoughts, I heard distant horns. All glanced in that direction and then went back to their business. The next blast of the horn was closer. People turned again, nudging one another, and finally we saw four white horses, decked out in fine harness of black and orange. The guards who rode the horses were just as richly attired, their helms as plumed as their horses' headstalls. They rode toward us, and the clusters of buyers pushed against the stands to get out of their way. As the riders again lifted their horns to their mouths, I saw my chance. All were watching them as I darted in, seized a round golden loaf and then darted back the way the horsemen had come.

So intent had I been on my theft that I had not perceived that behind the horsemen, the market street had remained empty, and that the folk who lined the street had dropped to their knees. I ran, skittering out into the empty street as the bread-merchant shouted. When I tried to dart back into the kneeling crowd to lose myself among them, people grabbed at me, shouting. Another set of guards was coming on foot, marching in a row of six, with two more rows behind them, and behind them came a woman on a black horse with harness of gold.

The kneeling folk were packed as solidly as a wall. I tried to push into them. A man grabbed me with hard hands and pushed me down in the dirt. He growled at me, a command I did not understand. I struggled to rise and he slapped me sharply on the back of my head. I saw stars and went slack. An instant later, I realized that everyone around me was frozen into stillness. Had he bid me be still? I lay as he had pushed me. The loaf I had stolen was clutched to my chest and chin. The smell of it was dizzying. I did not think. I tucked my head and opened my mouth and bit into it. I lay on my belly in the dusty street and gnawed at the loaf like a mouse as first the ranks of guards and then the woman on her black horse and then another four ranks of guards passed. No one moved until a second rank of horsemen came. At intervals, they halted and rang brass chimes. Only after they had passed did the nearby merchants and buyers rise to their feet and resume their lives.

I waited, chewing busily into my bread, and the moment the chimes rang, I bucked to my feet and tried to run. But the man who had held me down snatched the back of my jerkin and gripped my hair. He shook me and shouted something. The bread-merchant came dashing over, snatched the bread out of my hand and cried out to find it dirty and chewed. I cringed, thinking he would hit me, but instead he began to shout, one word, over and over. He threw the bread down in anger and how I longed to snatch it up again, but my captor held me fast.

The city guard. That was who he was shouting for, and two came on the run. One smirked and looked at me almost kindly, as if he could not believe he had been summoned for such a small thief. But the other was a business-like fellow who seized me by the back of my tunic and all but lifted me off my feet. He began to ask me questions and the breadman began to shout his side of the story. I shook my head and then gestured at my mouth, trying to convey that I could not speak. I think it was going well until the kind guardsman leaned close to his fellow and then suddenly gave me such a pinch that I squeaked.

Then it was all over. I was shaken and when the guardsman who held me lifted his hand to slap me, I burst out in Common, 'I was hungry so I stole. What else was I to do? I am so hungry!' Then, shaming myself, I burst into tears, and pointed at the bread and strained toward it. The man who had caught me first stooped and picked it up and put it into my hands. The breadman attempted to slap it away from me, but the guardsman who still held me swung me out of his reach. Then, to complete my humiliation, he picked me up and perched me on his hip as if I were a much younger child and strode off through the market.

I gripped the bread in both hands. I could not control my tears or my sobs, but that did not stop me from eating the bread as fast as I could get it down. I had no idea what might happen to me next but decided that one thing I would be sure of; I would fill my belly with the bread that had got me into so much trouble.

I was still clutching the last of the crust when my carrier strode up three steps to the door of an unremarkable stone building. He pushed open the door, carried me inside and then swung me to the floor as his partner followed.

An older man in a fancier livery looked up from a table as we came in. His noon meal was spread out before him and he looked rather annoyed to be interrupted. They spoke about me over my head as I looked around the room. There was a bench down one plain wall. A woman sat on it. Her feet were chained together. At the other end of the bench, a man sat hunched with his face in his hands. He glanced up at me, and his mouth was all blood and one eye was swollen shut. He put his face back in his hands.

The guard who had carried me seized me by the shoulder and shook me. I looked up at him. He spoke to me. I shook my head. The man behind the desk spoke to me. I shook my head again. Then, in Common, he asked me, 'Who are you? Are you lost, child?'

At the simple question, I burst into tears again. He looked mildly alarmed. He made shooing motions at the two guards and they left. As the one went out the door, he looked back at me, almost as if he were concerned for me. But the man at the table was talking again.

'Tell me your name. Your parents could pay for what you took and take you home.'

Was that even possible? I drew a breath. 'My name is Bee Farseer. I'm from the Six Duchies. I was stolen from there and I need to go home.' I took a breath and made a wild promise, 'My father will pay money to get me back.'

'I've no doubt that he will.' The man leaned one elbow on his desk, right next to a little round cheese. I stared at it. He cleared his throat. 'How did you come to be running about on the streets of Chalced, Beefarseer?'

He made my name one word. I didn't correct him. It didn't matter. If he would listen to me and send word to my father, I knew he would pay money to get me back. Or Nettle would. Surely she would. And so I told him my story, doing my best to leave out the unbelievable parts. I told him of Chalcedeans raiding my home, and how I'd been carried off. I didn't explain how I'd come to Chalced, only that I'd slipped away from Kerf and his companions because they had been cruel to me. And now I was here and I only wanted to go home, and if he would send word to my father, I was sure someone would come and bring money and take me home.

He looked a bit puzzled by my stew of a story, but nodded gravely at the end. 'Well. I understand now, perhaps better than you do.' He rang a bell on the corner of his desk. A door opened and a sleepy looking guardsman came in. He was very young and looked bored. 'Runaway slave. Property of someone named Kerf. Take her to the end cell. If no one claims her in three days, take her to the auction. Price of a loaf of pollen bread is owed to Serchin the Baker. Make a note that this Kerf must either pay for it, or the price come out of whatever she fetches at auction.'

'I'm not a slave!' I protested. 'Kerf does not own me! He helped steal me from my home!'

The deskman looked at me tolerantly. 'Spoil of war. Prize of battle. You are his, whatever he chooses to call you. He can keep you as slave or ransom you back. That will be up to this Kerf, if he comes to claim you.' He settled himself back in his chair with a sigh and took a deep drink from his cup.

My tears started again, despite how useless they were. The bored guard looked down on me. 'Follow me,' he said in clear Common, and when I turned and bolted for the door, he stepped forward, tripped me, and laughed. He picked me up by the back of my jerkin as if I were a sack and carried me through the same door he'd entered from, not caring at all how he thudded me against the frame. He kicked it shut behind us, tossed me to the floor and said, 'You can follow me or I can kick you all the way down this hallway. It's all one to me.'

It was not all one to me. I stood, gave him a stiff nod, and then followed him. We went around a corner and down some stone steps.

It was cooler down there, and dimmer. The only light came from some small windows at intervals in the wall. I followed him past several doors. He opened the last one and said, 'Get in there.' I hesitated and he gave me a shove and shut the door behind me.

I heard it latch.

The room was small but not terrible. Light came from a very small window. It was so small that even if I could reach it, I couldn't have wriggled out. There was a woven straw mat in one corner. In the opposite corner, there was a hole in the floor. Stains and the smell told me what it was for. Next to the mat was an ewer. It had water in it. I sniffed it to be sure it was water. I dipped the hem of my shirt into it and wiped the stupid tears from my face. Then I went and sat down on the straw mat.

I sat for a long time. Then I lay down. I might have slept a bit. I heard the latch work and stood up. A man opened the door carefully, looking all around and then down at me. He seemed surprised at how small I was. 'Food,' he said, and handed me a crockery bowl. I was so surprised I just stood there clutching it as he left, closing the door behind him. When he was gone, I looked down in the bowl. It was grainy mush with a few pieces of an orange vegetable on top of it. I carried it back to my mat and ate it carefully with my fingers. Someone had put enough food for an adult in the bowl. It was the most food I'd had in a very long time. I tried to eat it very slowly, and to think what I should do next. When the food was gone, I drank some water and then wiped my fingers clean on my shirt hem. The light coming into my little room was getting dimmer. I wondered if anything else would happen, but it didn't. When my cell was dark, I lay down on my mat and closed my eyes. I thought of my father. I imagined what he would have done to the guards. Or Dwalia. I imagined him throttling her and clenched my own fists and panted at how satisfying that would be. He would teach them. He would kill them all for me. But my father was not here. He could not know where I was. No one was coming to save me. I cried for a time, and then slept, clutching my mother's candle.

When I woke, there was a small square of light on the floor of my little room. I used the hole in the floor, and drank some more water. I waited. Nothing happened. After what seemed like a long time, I shouted and pounded on the door. Nothing happened. When I couldn't shout or pound any more, I sat on my mat. I reached for

Wolf Father and could not find him. It was a very bad moment. I decided he had always been something I pretended. And now I was too old and the world was too real for me to pretend anything any more. *When I need you, you are gone. Just like everyone else.*

When you block me out, I cannot make you hear me.

I blocked you out?

When you close your thoughts. So, here we are, in a cage again. At least your captors are kind. For now.

For now?

You will be sold.

I know. What should I do?

For now? Eat. Sleep. Let your body heal. When they take you out of here to sell, be very aware of me. We may yet escape.

His words gave me very little hope, but before I'd had no hope at all. I cried until I slept that night.

When I woke the next morning, I felt better than I had in many days. I inspected the bruises on my legs and arms. They were yellow and pale green, fading from black and deep blue. My belly hurt less and I could move my arm in a full circle. I combed my growing hair with my fingers, and then chewed my fingernails shorter. Another guard brought me a bowl of food and filled my water ewer. He took the empty bowl away. He didn't speak to me. It was another big bowl of food. This time the mush had some stringy strands of greens cooked into it, and there was a lump of yellow vegetable on top of it. I ate it all then watched the square of light move across my floor and up the wall until it was gone. Night again. I cried again and slept again. I dreamed that my father was angry because I had not put my inks away. I woke up while it was still dark, knowing that something like that had never happened but wishing it could. I fell back to sleep and dreamed an important Dream about a swimming dragon who captured my father. I woke to the square of light and wished I could write the dream down but there was nothing I could write on and no ink or pen. I spent the afternoon devising a way to tie my folded candle into the hem of my underblouse so it would not be lost.

That day passed. Another bowl of food. Would they auction me soon? How did they count the three days? Did they start the day they caught me, or the day after? I wondered who would buy me and what sort of work I'd have to do. Would I be able to convince them to send word to my father? Perhaps I'd be sold as a house slave and could convince the buyers to ransom me? I'd heard of slaves but had no idea how they were treated. Would they beat me? Keep me in a kennel? I was still wondering those things when I heard the latch to my door rattle. A guard opened it, and then stepped back.

'This one?' he asked someone, and Kerf stuck his head around the door. He stared at me dully.

I almost felt glad to see him. Then I heard Dwalia's voice. 'That's the little wretch! What a trouble she has been.'

'She?' The guard was surprised. 'We thought it was a boy.'

'So did we!' Vindeliar. 'He is my brother!' He poked his head past the doorframe and smiled at me. His cheeks were not as plump as they had been and his sparse hair was dull but the light of friendship was still in his eyes. I hated him. They never would have found me if he had not mastered Kerf for Dwalia. He'd betrayed me.

The guard stared at him. 'Your brother. I see the resemblance,' he said but no one laughed.

I felt sick. 'I don't know those people,' I said. 'They're lying to you.'

The guard shrugged. 'I don't really care, as long as someone settles your fine.' He swung his gaze back to Kerf. 'She got caught stealing a loaf of pollen bread. You'll have to pay for it.'

Kerf nodded dully. I knew that Vindeliar was controlling him, but not too well. Kerf seemed very dim, as if he had to think carefully before he could speak. Ellik had always seemed very sure of himself. Was Vindeliar losing his magic or was something going wrong with Kerf? Perhaps the two trips through the stone had done it. 'I will pay,' he said at last.

'Pay first, then you can take her. You owe for four days of her keep here, too.'

They shut my door and walked away. I felt a twinge of gladness that they would cheat him for extra days, and then worried that perhaps I had been here four days and had lost track of time. I waited for them to come back, dreading that I'd be with them again but almost relieved that someone else would be in charge of me. It seemed to take a long time, but eventually I heard the latch lift.

'Come along,' Dwalia snapped at me. 'You are far more trouble than you are worth.'

Her eyes promised me a beating later, but Vindeliar was smiling fatuously at me. I wished I knew why he liked me. He was my worst enemy, but also my only ally. Kerf had seemed to like me, but if Vindeliar held his reins, I had no hope of help from him. Perhaps I should try to build my friendship with Vindeliar. Perhaps if I had been wiser, I would have done that from the very start.

Dwalia had a long coil of light cord. Before I could protest, she looped it around my neck. 'No!' I cried but she jerked it tight. When I reached for it, Kerf took one of my hands and she seized my right hand and turned it up behind my back. I felt a loop of the cord coil around my wrist. She was very quick at doing it; doubtless she had done this before. My hand was uncomfortably high and I could not lower it without tightening the loop around my neck. She held the end of the line in her hand. She gave it an experimental tug and I had to jerk my head back.

'There we are,' she said with great satisfaction. 'No more little tricks from you. Off we go.'

After the cool dimness of my cell, the bright day was painful, and soon too warm for me. Kerf and Dwalia walked in front of me, my leash barely slack. I had to hurry to keep up with them. Vindeliar trotted beside me. It struck me how oddly he was made, with his bean-shaped body and short legs. I recalled how Dwalia had called him 'sexless'. I wondered if she had castrated him like the men did our goats when they wanted to raise them for meat. Or had he been born that way?

'Where is Alaria?' I asked him quietly.

He gave me a miserable look. 'Sold to a slaver. For money for food and passage on a boat.'

Kerf gave a twitch. 'She was mine. I wanted to take her to my mother. She would have been a good serving wench. Why did I do that?'

'Vindeliar!' Dwalia snapped.

This time I opened my senses and I felt what he did to Kerf. I tried to understand it. I knew how to put up my walls to keep out my father's thoughts. I'd had to do that since I was small, just to have peace in my own mind. But it felt as if Vindeliar pushed a wall into Kerf's mind, one that kept out Kerf's thoughts and made him share what Vindeliar thought. I pushed against Vindeliar's wall. It was not that strong but I was not sure how to breach it. Still, I heard a whisper of what he told Kerf. *Don't worry. Go with Dwalia. Do what she wants. Don't wonder about anything. It will all be fine.*

Don't touch his mind. Don't break his wall. The warning came from Wolf Father. *Listen but don't let him feel you there.*

Why?

If you make a way into his thoughts, it's also a way for him to come into yours. Be very careful of touching his mind.

'Where are we going?' I asked aloud.

'Shut up!' Dwalia said just as Vindeliar said, 'To the boat for our journey.'

I went quiet but not because of Dwalia's order. For just a moment I had sensed that it was hard for Vindeliar to talk, trot at Dwalia's heels and control Kerf. He was hungry, his back hurt and he needed to relieve himself, but he knew better than to ask Dwalia to pause. As I kept my silence, I felt his focus on Kerf grow tighter and stronger. So. A distraction might weaken his control. That was a small but useful thing to know. Wolf Father's voice was a bare whisper in my mind. *Sharp claws and teeth. You learn, cub. We will live.*

Are you real?

He did not answer but Vindeliar cocked his head and stared at me strangely. Walls up. Keep him out of my mind. I would always have to be on guard now. I tightened my guard on myself and knew that when I shut out Vindeliar, I shut out Wolf Father as well.

EIGHT

Tintaglia

This dream was like a painting that moved. The light was dim, as if pale grey or blue paint had been washed over all. Beautiful streamers in brilliant colours moved in a slow breeze that came and went, came and went, so that the streamers rose and fell. They were shimmering pennants of gold and silver, scarlet, azure and viridian. Bright patterns like diamonds or eyes and twining spirals ran the length of each pennant.

In my dream, I moved closer, flowing effortlessly toward them. There was no sound and no feel of wind on my face. Then my perspective shifted. I saw huge snake-heads, blunt-nosed, with eyes as large as melons. I came closer and closer, although I did not wish to, and finally I could see the faint gleam of a net that held all those creatures as fish are caught in a gill net. The lines of the net were nearly transparent and somehow I knew that they had all rushed into the net at the same moment, to be trapped and drowned there.

This dream had the certainty of a thing that had happened, and not just once. It would happen again and again. I could not stop it for it was already done. Yet I also knew it would happen again.

Bee Farseer's dream journal

Early the next morning there was a knock on our chamber door. I rolled from the bed and then stood. The Fool did not even twitch. Barefoot, I padded to the door. I paused to push my hair back from my face and then opened it. Outside, King Reyn had flung back the hood of his cloak and it dripped water on the floor around him. Rain gleamed on his brow and was caught in droplets in his sparse beard.

He grinned at me, white teeth incongruous in his finely-scaled face. 'FitzChivalry! Good tidings, and I wanted to share them right away. A bird just came in from across the river. Tarman has arrived there.'

'Across the river?' A brandy headache had begun a sudden clangour in my head.

'At the Village. It's far easier for the barge to nose in there than it is for it to dock here, and it's much better for Captain Leftrin to offload cargo there than having us ferry it across the river a bit at a time. Tarman had a full load: workers for the farm, a dozen goats, sacks of grain. Three dozen chickens. We hope the goats will fare better than the sheep did. The sheep were a disaster. I think only three survived the winter. This time we will keep the chickens penned.' He cocked his head and apologized. 'Sorry for awakening you so early, but I thought you'd want to know. The ship will need cleaning before it's fit for passengers. A day, perhaps two, three at worst. But soon you'll be able to depart.'

'Welcome news indeed,' I told him. I reached past my headache to dredge up courtesy. 'Although your hospitality has been wonderful, we look forward to continuing our journey.'

He nodded, scattering droplets. 'There are others that I must notify. Forgive me that I must go in haste.'

And off he went, dripping down the corridor. I tried to imagine Dutiful delivering such a message to a guest. I watched him go and felt a twinge of envy for how spontaneously the Dragon Traders seemed to interact. Perhaps I had had it backwards all along. Perhaps being a bastard had given me far more freedom than living within the rules that bound a prince.

I shut the door as the Fool crawled to the edge of the bed. 'What was that?' he asked unhappily.

'King Reyn with news. The *Tarman* is docked across the river. We will depart in a day or two.'

He swung his legs over the edge of the bed, sat up, and then leaned forward, his head in his hands. 'You got me drunk,' he complained.

I was so tired of lying. 'There are things I have to know. One way or another, Fool, you need to talk to me.'

He moved slowly, lifting his head from his hands cautiously. 'I'm very angry with you,' he said quietly. 'But I should have expected this from you.' He lowered his face back into his hands. His next words were muffled. 'Thank you.'

He clambered from the bed, moving as if his brains might spill out of his skull, and spoke in Amber's voice. 'Thymara has requested my time for a visit. I think she is exceedingly curious about the Silver on my hands and how it affects me. I think today I will call on her. Would you summon Spark to help me dress?'

'Of course.' I noticed she did not ask me to accompany her. I supposed I deserved that.

That afternoon, when the rain eased, I ventured out with Lant. I wished to see the map-tower. I had first seen it many years ago when I had accidentally stumbled through a Skill-stone and into Kelsingra. The fine maps that Chade and Kettricken had given me had not survived the bear attack. I hoped to refresh what I recalled with a look at that Elderling map. But we had not walked far when I heard the wild trumpeting of dragons, and then the shouts of excited people.

'What is it?' Lant asked me, and in the next breath, 'We should return to the others.'

'No. Those are welcoming shouts. A dragon returns, one that has been long absent.' A trick of the wind had brought a name to my ears. 'Tintaglia returns,' I told him. 'And I would see her again.'

'Tintaglia,' he said in hushed awe. His eyes were wide. 'Riddle spoke of her. The queen dragon who came to help free IceFyre, and then rose as his mate. She who forced IceFyre to lay his head upon the hearthstones in Queen Elliania's mothershouse, to fulfil the challenge that Elliania had set for Dutiful.'

'You know all that?'

'Fitz. It's known to every child in the Six Duchies. Hap Gladheart sings that song about the dragons, the one that has the line, "Bluer than sapphires, gleaming like gold." I have to see her for myself!'

'I think we shall,' I shouted at him, for a wild chorus of dragons trumpeting now drowned our voices. They had risen from the city, in greeting or challenge. It was an astonishing sight, beauty and terror mingling equally. They cavorted like swallows before a storm, but these were creatures larger than houses. They gleamed and glittered against the cloudy sky, in colours more like jewels than creatures of flesh.

Then, flying over the tops of the trees in the distance, I saw Tintaglia. For a moment, I could not resolve how close she was to us; then, as she flew nearer, I realized my error. She truly was that large—she dwarfed any of the dragons we had seen in Kelsingra—far larger than the last time I had seen her.

This queen dragon was aware of the stir she was causing in the city. She swept far wide of us, in a great circle. As she spiralled round and round, I could scarcely take my eyes off her. My heart lifted in admiration and I found that a grin commanded my face. I managed a glance at Lant and saw that he had clasped both his hands on his breast and was smiling up at her. 'Dragon-glamor,' I croaked out, but I still could not stop smiling. 'Careful, Lant, or you will burst into song!'

'Oh, brighter than sapphires and gleaming like gold!' and there was music in his voice and longing. 'No minstrel's song could do justice to her. Gold and then silver she glitters, bluer by far than jewels! Oh, Fitz, would that I never had to look away from her!'

I said nothing. Tales of dragon-glamor were well known now throughout the Six Duchies. Some never fell prey to it, but others were ensorcelled by the mere glimpse of a dragon in the distance. Lant would hear no warning from me now, but I suspected the spell would be broken as soon as she was no longer in sight. Had I not already had my Skill-walls raised against the clamour of Kelsingra, it was likely I would have felt as giddy as he did.

It quickly became apparent that she would land in the plaza before the Greeting Hall. Lant hurried and I kept pace with him. Even so, she was on the ground before we arrived, and Elderlings and lesser dragons had begun to gather. Lant tried to surge forward but I caught his arm and held him back. 'Queen Malta and King Reyn,' I cautioned him. 'And their son. They will be the first to greet her.'

And they were. Even the dragons of Kelsingra kept a respectful distance—something I had not expected. Tintaglia folded her wings leisurely, shaking them out twice as if to be sure that every scale was in place before gradually closing them to a chorus of admiring sighs from those who had gathered. When Reyn and Malta appeared with Phron on their heels it was obvious to me that Malta had performed a hasty grooming and Reyn had donned a clean tunic and smoothed his hair. Phron was grinning in awestruck wonder but Malta's expression was more reserved, almost stony, as she descended the steps to stand small before Tintaglia. Queen to queen, I found myself thinking, despite the size difference.

Reyn walked at her side but half a step behind as the queens advanced to greet one another. Tintaglia surveyed Malta, her neck arched and her eyes slowly whirling as if she inspected her. Malta's expression did not change as she said coolly, 'So you have returned to Kelsingra, Tintaglia. Your absence has been long this time.'

'Has it? To you, perhaps.' The dragon's trumpeting was musical, and her thoughts rode on the sound. 'You must recall that dragons do not reckon time in the tiny droplets of days that seem so significant to humans. But yes, I have returned. I come to drink. And to be well groomed.' As if to snub Malta for her rebuke, the dragon ignored Reyn and swung her head to look down at Phron, who gazed up at her adoringly. The dragon's eyes spun fondly. She leaned down and breathed on him, and I saw his garments ripple in her hot breath. Abruptly, she flung her head up and then glared all about in indignation. 'This one is mine! Who has interfered with him? What foolish dragon has dared to alter what is mine?'

'Who has dared to save his life, do you mean? Who has dared to set his body right, so that he need not choose between breathing and eating? Is that what you ask?' Malta demanded.

Tintaglia's gaze jerked back to Malta. Colours rippled in her throat and cheeks and the scales of her neck abruptly hackled into a series of crests. I thought Queen Malta would at least step back. Instead, she stepped forward and this time Reyn moved with her and beside her. I was astonished to see a similar flush of colouring in the crest of flesh above her brow. Malta stood, hands on her hips and her head tilted back. The patterns in the scales on her face echoed Tintaglia's in miniature.

The dragon's great eyes narrowed. 'Who?' she demanded again.

Ice crept up my spine and I held my breath. No one spoke. Wind wandered amongst us, adding to the chill, ruffling hair and reddening noses.

'I thought you might be pleased to see I was still alive. For without the changes wrought in me, I doubt I would be.' Phron stepped forward to stand between his parents and the dragon. Malta's hand reached out to snatch him back to safety, but Reyn put his hand on top of her wrist. Slowly, he pushed her arm down and then caught her hand in his. He said something and I saw a flicker of agony cross Malta's face. Then she stood silent as her son faced down the dragon that had shaped all of them.

Tintaglia was silent. Would she admit that she cared if he lived or died? But she was a dragon. 'Who?' she demanded, and the colours on her throat flared brighter. No one replied and she set the end of her muzzle against Phron's chest and pushed him. He staggered back but did not fall. It was enough.

'Stand well clear of me,' I told Lant. I took three steps into the open space that surrounded the dragon. My walls were up tight. I lifted my voice into a shout. 'Tintaglia. Here I stand!'

Faster than a serpent strikes, her head whipped around and her gaze fixed on me. I could almost feel the pressure of that scrutiny as she said, 'And who are you, who dares use my name?'

'You know me.' I controlled my voice but pitched it to carry. Phron had glanced at his parents but he had not retreated to shelter behind them.

Tintaglia snorted. She shifted so she faced me. The wind of her breath was meaty and rich. 'Few are the humans I know, little gnat. I do not know you.'

'But you do. It was years ago. You wished to know where the black dragon was. You hunted me through my dreams. You wanted IceFyre freed from his prison. I am the one who did what you could not. I broke the glacier and released him from both ice and the Pale Woman's torment. So you know me, dragon. As you know my daughter, Nettle. And as you know me, so also you owe me!'

There was a collective gasp at my words. From the corner of my eye, I saw Lady Amber emerge onto the steps, with Spark and Per flanking her. I prayed she would not interfere, that she would keep the youngsters safely out of the dragon's knowing. Tintaglia stared at me, her eyes whirling gold and silver, and I felt the pressure of her mind against mine. For one instant, I yielded my walls to her. I showed her Nettle in her dreamed gown of butterfly wings. Then I slammed the gates of my mind, shutting her out and desperately hoping my walls could hold.

'Her.' Tintaglia made the simple word a curse. 'Not a gnat, that one. A gadfly, a biting, buzzing blood-sucking . . .'

I'd never seen such a large creature strangling on words. I felt a sudden rush of pride in Nettle. She had used her Skill and her dream-manipulation to strike back at the dragon, turning the creature's own weapons against her. With no formal training in the Farseer magic, Nettle had not only bent Tintaglia to her purpose, but persuaded that strong-willed queen to make IceFyre honour Prince Dutiful's promise to lay the black dragon's head on the bricks of Elliania's hearth fire. IceFyre's entry into the narcheska's mothershouse had caused some damage to the door lintel, but the promise had been fulfilled and Dutiful had won his bride.

And a dragon remembered my daughter! For one exhilarating moment, my heart teetered on exultation. As close to immortality as any human could come!

Tintaglia advanced on me. Colours swept over her like flames consuming wood. 'You interfered with my Elderlings. That offends me. And I owe you nothing. Dragons have no debts.'

I said the words before I considered them. 'Dragons have debts. They simply don't pay them.'

Tintaglia settled back on her hind haunches and lifted her head high and tucked in her chin. Her eyes spun fast, the colours flickering and I more felt than saw how both humans and dragons retreated from her.

'Fitz,' Lant whispered harshly, a plea.

'Get back. Stay back!' I whispered. I was going to die. Die, or live horribly maimed. I'd seen what the acid spew of a dragon did to men and to stone. I steeled myself. If I ran, if I took shelter behind the others, they would die with me.

A gust of wind struck me and then, as lightly as a crow hopping to a halt, a much smaller scarlet dragon alighted between me and death. An instant later, I felt a sudden weight on my shoulder, and 'Fitz!' Motley greeted me. 'Hello, stupid!' she added.

The scarlet dragon folded her wings, as if it were an important task that must be done in a very particular way. I thought Tintaglia would spray the creature with acid in vengeance for her interrupted fury. Instead it appeared that she regarded the red dragon in perplexity.

'Heeby,' the crow said to me. 'Heeby, Heeby.' Motley turned and suddenly gave my ear a vicious peck. 'Heeby!' the bird insisted.

'Heeby,' I repeated to calm her. 'General Rapskal's dragon.'

My acknowledgement placated her. 'Heeby. Good hunter. Lots of meat.' The crow chuckled happily.

Lant seized my arm. 'Come away, you fool!' he hissed at me. 'While she is distracted by the red dragon, get out of her sight. She means to kill you.'

But I moved only to shrug off his grip. The much smaller scarlet dragon was facing off with the immense blue one. Heeby's head wove on her serpentine neck. Every imaginable shade of red flushed over her. There was no mistaking the challenge in her stance. I felt the tension of the communication between them though I could not mine any sense of human words from the low rumbling of the red. It was like a pressure in the air, a flow of thoughts I could feel but not share.

Tintaglia's crest and the row of erect scaling on her neck eased down rather like a dog's hackles smoothing themselves as its aggression subsides. The arch of her neck softened and then she lifted her eyes and I felt her piercing gaze. Tintaglia spoke, and her words were clear to all, her question an accusation. 'What do you know of the pale folk and their Servants?'

I drew breath and spoke clearly, willing that all the dragons and gathered folk would hear. 'I know the Servants stole my child. I know that they destroyed her. I know that I will seek them out and kill as many of them as I can before they destroy me.' My heart had begun to race. I clenched my teeth and then added, 'What more need I know?'

Both Heeby and Tintaglia became very still. Again, I sensed a flow of communication between them. I wondered if the other dragons or any of the Elderlings were privy to what they said. General Rapskal pushed his way through the crowd. He was dressed very simply, in leggings and a leather shirt, and his hands were dirty, as if he'd abruptly broken away from some task.

'Heeby!' he cried at sight of her, and then stood still. He looked around at the gathered Elderlings and dragons, saw me, and hastened to my side. As he came, he drew his sheath knife. I reached for my own and was startled when Lant shoved me aside and back and stepped between Rapskal and me. Unmindful of Lant's bristling, Rapskal called to me, 'Heeby summoned me to protect you! I come to your aid!'

Lant gaped at him. I knew a moment of shock and then anger as Per inserted himself into the situation. 'Behind me!' I snapped at the boy and he replied, 'Your back, sir, yes, I will guard your back!'

It wasn't what I had meant, but it moved him away from Rapskal's blade.

'I don't understand,' I growled at Rapskal and he shook his head in shared bewilderment. 'Nor do I! I was mining for memories when Heeby summoned me urgently to protect you here. And then she vanished from my awareness as if she were slain! It terrified me, but here I am, to do her will. I will protect you or die.'

'Enough of your chittering!' Tintaglia did not roar at us but the force of the thought attached to her words near stunned me. Heeby kept her watchful stance between the immense blue dragon and me, but it was little shelter. Tintaglia towered over her and she could easily have spat acid at me if she had chosen to. Instead she cocked her head and focused her gaze on me. I felt the full impact of her presence as her huge spinning eyes fixed on me. My walls could not deflect completely the wash of dragon-glamor that surged over me.

'I choose to allow the changes you have made. I will not kill you.'

As I basked in that bit of good news and my guardians hastily sheathed their blades, she tilted her great head, leaned close, and breathed deep of me. 'I do not know the dragon who has marked you. Later, perhaps, he will answer to me for your wilfulness. For now, you need not fear me.'

I was dizzied with gratitude and awe at her magnificence. It took every scrap of will I could muster to lift my voice. 'I strove only to help those who needed my help. Those neglected by their dragons, or changed but not guided in their changes.'

She opened her jaws wide and for a heart-stopping moment, I saw teeth longer than swords and the gleaming yellow and red of the poison sacs in her throat. She spoke to me again. 'Do not press me, little man. Be content that I have not killed you.'

Heeby lifted then, her front paws leaving the ground so that she was slightly taller than she had been before. Again, I felt the force of an unheard communication.

Tintaglia sneered at her, a lifting of lips that bared her teeth. But she said to me, 'You and those like you may interfere with the ones claimed by no dragons. This I grant to you, for they are nothing to me. Change them all you like. But leave to me what is mine. This is a boon I grant you because you and yours were of service to me in the past. But do not presume to think I pay a debt to you.'

I had almost forgotten Motley on my shoulder. I do not think a crow can whisper, but in a low hoarse voice I heard, 'Be wise.'

'Of course not!' I hastily agreed. Time to move away from my ill-considered remark. I took a breath, realized that I was about to say a worse thing and said it anyway. 'I would ask a second boon from you.'

Again, she made a display of teeth and poison sacs. 'Not dying today,' Motley said and lifted from my shoulder. My protectors cowered against me but did not flee. I counted that as courage. 'Is not your life enough of a boon, flea?' the dragon demanded. 'What more could you possibly ask of me?'

'I ask for knowledge! The Servants of the Whites sought to end not just IceFyre but all dragons forever when they sought his death. I wish to know if they have acted against dragons before, and if they did, I wish to know why. More than anything else, I wish to know anything that dragons know that can help me bring an end to the Servants!'

Tintaglia drew back her immense head on her long neck. Stillness held. Then Heeby said in a child's timorous voice. 'She doesn't remember. None of us remember. Except . . . me. Sometimes.'

'Oh Heeby! You spoke!' Rapskal whispered proudly.

Then Tintaglia gave forth a wordless roar and it horrified me to see Heeby crouch and cower. Rapskal drew his sheath knife again and stepped in front of his dragon, waving the blade at Tintaglia. I had never seen a stupider or more courageous act.

'Rapskal, no!' an Elderling cried but he did not halt. Yet if Tintaglia noticed this act of insane defiance she gave it no heed. She put her attention back on me. Her trumpeting was a low rumble that shook my lungs. Her anger and frustration rode with her words. 'This is knowledge I should have, but I do not. I go to seek it. Not as a boon to you, human, but to wring from IceFyre what he should have shared with us long ago, rather than mocking us for a history we cannot know, for no dragon can recall what happened when one is in the egg or swimming as a serpent.' She turned away from us, not caring that humans and Elderlings alike had to scatter to avoid the long slash of her tail as she did so. 'I go to drink. I need Silver. When I have drunk, I shall be groomed. All should be in readiness for that.'

'It shall be!' Phron called after her as she stalked majestically away. He turned back to his parents, and his Elderling cheeks were as pink as their scaling would permit. 'She's magnificent!' he shouted aloud, and a roar of both laughter and agreement echoed his sentiment.

I did not share the crowd's exultation. I felt as if my guts were trembling now that I had leisure to consider how close I'd come to dying. And for what? I knew no more of the Servants than I had before. I could hope I'd won Tintaglia's acceptance for any Skill-healers that Nettle and Dutiful might eventually send. I could hope that Dutiful might win an alliance with folk who occasionally could modify a dragon's behaviour.

But I knew IceFyre lived. My small hope was that Tintaglia would share whatever she discovered with me. I suspected a long vendetta between dragons and the Servants. Could Elderlings have been unaware of such enmity? I doubted it, and yet we had not discovered any evidence of it.

Or did we? I thought back to the Pale Woman's occupation of Aslevjal. Ilistore, the Fool had named her. The ice-encased Elderling city had proven a formidable fortress for her, an excellent site from which to oversee the OutIslander war against the Six Duchies. And where she would torment the ice-trapped dragon and attempt to destroy him and his kind. She had done all she could to degrade the city. Art had been defaced or destroyed, libraries of Skill-blocks tumbled into hopeless disorder . . . did not that speak of a deep-rooted hatred? Had she sought to destroy all traces of a people and culture?

I did not expect the support of the dragons against the Servants. IceFyre had had years to retaliate against the Servants if the dragon had harboured any desire to do so. I suspected he had vented all his fury when he had collapsed the icy hall of Aslevjal and put an end to the forces of the Pale Woman. He had left it up to me to make sure of her death, and that of the stone dragon she and Kebal Rawbread had forged. Perhaps the black drake was not as fierce a creature as Tintaglia seemed to be. 'It's not uncommon for the female creatures to be far more savage than the males.'

'Truly?' Per asked, and I realized I'd said the words aloud.

'Truly,' Lant replied for me and I wondered if he were recalling his stepmother's attempt on his life. In the open square before us, Rapskal was fussing over Heeby as if she were a beloved lapdog, while Malta, Reyn and Phron were caught in a lively discussion that almost looked like a quarrel. I was ambushed by a wave of vertigo.

'I'd like to go back to our chambers,' I said quietly, and found no strength to resist Lant taking my arm. The weakness I'd felt after the Skill-healings I'd done assailed me again, for no reason I could deduce. Amber and Spark joined us as I manoeuvred my way up the stairs. Amber stopped the rest of them at the door. 'I will talk to you later,' she announced and ushered them out.

Lant dumped me in a chair at the table. I heard him close the door gently behind himself. I'd already lowered my head onto my crossed arms when the Fool spoke to me. 'Are you ill?'

I shook my head without lifting it. 'Weak. As if exhausted by Skilling. I don't know why.' I gave an unwilling laugh. 'Perhaps last night's brandy hasn't worn off.'

He set his hands gently to my shoulders and kneaded the muscles there. 'Tintaglia gave off a powerful aura of glamor. I was transfixed by it, and terrified at the fury she generated toward you. So strange to feel but be unable to see. I knew she was going to kill you, and I was helpless. Yet I heard you. You stood firm before it.'

'I had my walls up. I thought I was going to die. We gained a small bit of knowledge though; IceFyre is alive.' His hands on my shoulders felt good but reminded me too sharply of Molly. I shrugged free of his touch and he wordlessly moved to take a chair at the table beside me.

'You could have died today,' he explained. He shook his head. 'I don't know what I'd do. You all but dared her to kill you. Do you want to die?'

'Yes.' I admitted it. 'But not yet,' I added. 'Not until I've put a lot of other people in the ground. I need weapons, Fool. An assassin's best weapons are information, and more information.' I sighed. 'I don't know if IceFyre knows anything useful. Nor do I know if he would share it with Tintaglia or how we would receive the information if he did. Fool, I have never felt so unprepared for a task.'

'The same for me. But I have never felt so determined to see it through.'

I sat up a bit straighter and leaned one elbow on the table. I touched his gloved hand. 'Are you still angry at me?'

'No.' Then, 'Yes. You made me think about things I don't want to remember.'

'I need you to remember those things for me.'

He turned his face away from me, but did not pull his hand back. I waited. 'Ask me,' he commanded me harshly.

So. Time to torture my friend. What did I most need to know?

'Is there anyone within Clerres who might help us? Anyone who would conspire with us? Is there a way to send them a message that we are coming?'

Silence. Was he going to balk now? I knew the brandy ploy would not work again. 'No,' he grated out at last. 'There is no way to send a message. Prilkop might still be alive. They separated us when they began their torture. I assume he endured much the same treatment I did. If he lives, he is most likely a prisoner still. I think they found him too valuable to kill, but I could be wrong.'

'I know you doubt the ones who helped you escape. But you and Prilkop sent out messengers. Were they loyal to you? Do any of those folks remain in Clerres?'

He shook his head. His face was still turned away from me. 'We were able to do that in the first few years we were at Clerres. After we had become uneasy with the Four, but before they realized we didn't trust them. We sent them first to warn you, that the Four might seek to do you harm. While we were doing that, the Four kept trying to win us to their way of thinking. Perhaps they truly thought that their collators and manipulors would make us believe we had erred.' He smiled wryly. 'Instead, it went the other way. I think they found our tales exciting, for they knew little of life outside the walls. As we told them more of life outside their sequestered world, some began to question what the Servants had taught them. I do not think that, at first, the Four realized how much influence we had begun to wield.'

'Collators? Manipulors?'

He snorted in disgust. 'Fancy titles. Collators classify the dreams and find connections and threads. Manipulors try to find people or upcoming events that are most vulnerable to making the future change in ways that benefit the Four and their Servants. They were the ones who worked so hard to convince Prilkop and me that we were wrong. About everything, but especially in claiming that one of my Catalysts had fulfilled the dream-prophecies of the Unexpected Son. They were the ones who told us of the dreams of a new White Prophet, born "in the wild" as they said. The dreams of that child correlated with the dreams of the Unexpected Son in ways that could not be denied, even by me. They spoke of a dream of a child who bore the heart of a wolf.

'You asked, if you are not the Unexpected Son, then how can I be sure that all we did, all we changed, was the right course for the world? That was the very question they battered me with. And I saw it crack Prilkop's confidence. In the days that followed, we discussed it privately. I always insisted that you were the one. But then he would ask and rightfully, "but what of these new dreams?" And I had no answer to that.' He swallowed. 'No answer at all.

'And one night, in wine and fellowship, our little friends whispered to us that the wild-born child must be found and controlled before he could cause any harm to the course of the world. They knew that the Four were intent on finding this child. Not all the Four believed the new prophet was the Unexpected Son, but one did. Symphe. Whenever we dined with the Four, she would challenge me. And her challenges were so strong they shook even my belief. Day after day, the Four commanded that the library of dreams be combed so that the child could be found. And "controlled". I began to fear that they would find the same clues I had found and followed, all those years ago, to find you. So I sent the other messengers, the ones that asked you to find the Unexpected Son. For they had convinced me that there was a "wild born" White Prophet. And there, they were correct. They knew Bee existed long before I did. And Dwalia convinced them that the child they sensed was the Unexpected Son.'

His words chilled me. They had 'sensed' that Bee existed? I pulled his words to pieces in my mind, needed to understand fully everything he was telling me. 'What did they mean by "wild born"?'

His shoulders heaved. I waited. 'The Clerres that Prilkop remembered,' he began and then choked to a stop.

'Do you want a cup of tea?' I offered.

'No.' He gripped my hand suddenly, tightly. Then he asked, 'Is any brandy left?'

'I'll see.'

I found the corked bottle half under a pillow. There was some left. Not much, but some. I found his teacup, filled it, and set it down on the table. His bared hand crept toward it. He lifted it and drank. When I resumed my seat, I noticed that his gloved hand was where I had left it. I took it in mine. 'Prilkop's Clerres?'

'It was a library. All the history of the Whites, all the dreams that had ever been recorded, carefully organized and analysed in the writings of others. It was a place for historians and linguists. All

White Prophets were "wild born" in his time. People would recognize that their child was . . . peculiar. And they would take the child to Clerres. Or the child would grow and know that he or she must make that journey. There, the White Prophet for that time would have access to all the older dreams and histories of other White Prophets. They were educated and sheltered, fed and clothed and prepared. And when the White Prophet felt he was ready to begin his work in the world, he was given supplies: money, a mount, travel clothes, weapons, pens and papers, and sent on his way, as Prilkop was. And the Servants who stayed on at Clerres would record all they knew of the prophet, and they and their descendants would patiently await the next one.' He drank again. 'There was no "Four". Only Servants. People waiting to serve.'

A long silence. I ventured, 'But Clerres was not like that for you.'

He shook his head, slowly at first and then wildly. 'No. Not at all like that! After my parents had left me there, I was astonished to find that I was not unique to that place at all! They took me in, kindly and gently at first, to a row of little cottages in a pretty garden, with a grape arbour and a fountain. And in the little cottage they brought me to, I met three other children, all nearly as pale as I was.

'But they were all half-brothers. And they had been born there in Clerres. Bred and born there. For the Servants were no longer serving the White Prophet, but themselves. They had collected children, for they could trace the lineage of each White Prophet. A cousin, a great-nephew, a grandchild rumoured to be descended from a White Prophet. Gather them up, house them together, and breed them like rabbits. Breed them back again to each other. Sooner or later the rare trait surfaces. You've seen Burrich do it. What works with horses and dogs works with people as well. Instead of waiting for a wild-born White to appear they made their own. And harvested their dreams. And the Servants who once believed that White Prophets were born to set the world on a better path forgot that duty and began to care only for enriching themselves and their own comfort. Their "true Path" is a conspiracy to enable whatever brings to them the most wealth and power! Their home-bred Whites did as they were told. In small ways. Put a different man on the throne of a neighbouring kingdom. Warehouse wool, and never warn anyone of the coming plague that will kill all of their sheep. Until finally, perhaps, they decided to rid the world of dragons and Elderlings.' He drank the rest of the brandy in his cup and set it down with a clack on the table.

He turned his face to me at last. Tears had eroded Amber's careful powder and paint. The black that lined her eyes had become dark trails down his cheeks. 'Enough, Fitz,' he said with finality.

'Fool, I need to know—'

'Enough for today.' His groping hand found the brandy bottle. For a blind man, he did a passable job of emptying the dregs of the bottle into his cup. 'I know I must speak to you of these things,' he said hoarsely. 'And I will. At my pace.' He shook his head. 'Such a mess I made of it. The White Prophet. And here I am, blind and broken, dragging you into it again. Our last effort to change the world.'

I whispered the words to myself. 'I don't do this for the world. I do it for myself.' Quietly I rose and left him the table and the brandy.

In the two days before the *Tarman* left the village and crossed the river to us, I saw no more of Tintaglia. Lant had heard the blue dragon had drunk deeply of Silver, made a kill and ate it, slept, and had been groomed by her Elderlings in the steaming dragon-baths. Then she had drunk Silver again, and left. Whether she had gone to hunt or departed to find IceFyre, no one knew. I surrendered my hope that I would learn anything from her.

The Fool lived up to his word. On the table in my room, he built a map of the island and the town and castle of Clerres. I hoarded plates and cutlery and napkins from our meals and the Fool's groping fingers moved walls of spoons, and arranged plate towers. From this peculiar representation, I sketched Clerres. The outer fortifications were presided over by four stout towers, each topped with an immense skull-shaped dome. Lamps burned in the skull-eyes at night. Skilled archers walked the crenellated walls of the outer keep always.

Within the high white walls of the keep, a secondary wall surrounded gracious gardens, the cottages that housed the Whites and a stronghouse of white stone and bone. The stronghouse had four towers, each taller and narrower than the watchtowers of the outer walls. We dragged a bedside table into the main room, and on this we created a map of the main floor of the Servants' stronghold.

'The stronghouse has four levels above the ground, and two below,' the Fool informed me as he formed up the walls from scarves and arranged towers of teacups. 'That is not counting the majestic towers where the Four abide. Those towers are taller than the watchtowers on the outer walls. The roof of the stronghouse is flat. On it are the old harem quarters from the days when Clerres was a palace as well as a castle. Those quarters are used to confine the more important prisoners. The towers offer an excellent view of the castle island and the harbour and the hills beyond the town. It is a very old structure, Fitz. I do not think anyone knows how the towers were built so narrow, and yet expand at the top into such grand rooms.'

'Shaped like mushrooms?' I asked as I tried to visualize.

'Like exquisitely graceful mushrooms, perhaps,' and he almost smiled.

'How narrow are the stems of those mushrooms?' I asked him.

He considered. 'At the base, as wide as the great hall at Buckkeep Castle. But as one ascends, they narrow to half that size.'

I nodded to myself, well pleased at that image. 'And that is where each of the Four sleeps at night? In a tower room?'

'For the most part. Fellowdy, it is well known, has appetites for flesh that he satisfies in several locations. Capra, almost always in her tower room. Symphe and Coultrie, most nights I imagine. Fitz, it has been many years since I was privy to their lives and habits.'

Castle Clerres stood on an island of white rock, alone. From the castle's outer walls to the steep edges of the island there was only flat, stony earth that any invader must cross to reach the walls. A watch was kept over the water and the narrow causeway. The causeway opened twice a day, at the low tides, to permit servants to come and go, and to admit the pilgrims who came to discover their futures.

'Once pilgrims cross the causeway and enter the walls, they see the stronghouse with the vine of time in bas-relief on its front. All the grandest rooms are on the ground floor: the audience chambers, the ballroom, the feasting room, all panelled in white wood. A few of the teaching rooms are there, but most of them are on the second floor. The young Whites are taught and their dreams harvested. On that floor are extravagant chambers where wealthy patrons may take their ease and sip wine and listen as collators read selected scrolls to them and lingstras interpret them. For a fat fee.'

'And the lingstras and collators are all Whites?'

'Most have a trace of White heritage. Born on Clerres, they are raised to be servants of the Four. They also "serve" the Whites who can dream, in much the same way a tick drops on a dog. They suck off dreams and ideas, and express them as possible futures to the rich fools who come to consult with them.'

'So. They are charlatans.'

'No,' he said in a low voice. 'That is the worst part, Fitz. The rich buy knowledge of the future, to make themselves even richer. The lingstras gather dreams of a drought to come, and counsel a man to hoard grain to sell to his starving neighbours. Pestilence and plague can make a family wealthy, if they expect it. The Four no longer think of putting the world on a better course, but only of profiting from disasters and windfalls.'

He drew a deep breath. 'On the third floor is the treasured hoard of the Servants. There are six chambers of scroll-collections. Some of the scrolls are old beyond reckoning, and new dreams are penned and added daily. Only the wealthiest can afford to stroll here. Sometimes, a wealthy priest of Sa may be admitted to study independently, but only if there is wealth and influence to be gained.

'Finally on the fourth floor are the living quarters for the Servants who are high in the Four's favour. Some guards live there, the most trusted ones, who protect entry to each of the Four's private towers. And the most prolific White dreamers are housed on that level, where the Four may easily descend from their grand towers to have congress with them. Not always congress of a lofty intellectual sort, where Fellowdy is concerned.' He stopped speaking. I did not ask if he had ever been victim of that sort of attention.

He stood up abruptly and walked across the room, speaking over his shoulder. 'Up one more set of stairs and you emerge onto the roof, and the old harem quarters that are now the cells where recalcitrant Whites are held.' He drifted away from our work. 'Perhaps Prilkop is held there now. Or whatever is left of him.' He drew a sudden deep breath. Then Amber spoke. 'It's stuffy in here. Please summon Spark for me. I wish to go out and take the air.'

I did as she asked.

My sessions with the Fool were brief and intermittent. I listened far more than I spoke, and if he silently rose and became Amber and left the room, I let him go. In his absence, I sketched and noted down key bits of information. I valued what he had shared but I needed more. He had no recent information on their vices or foibles, no names of lovers or enemies, no idea of daily routines. That I would learn by spying when I reached Clerres. There was no rush. Haste would not bring Bee back. This would be a cold, and carefully calculated, vengeance. When I struck, I would do so with thoroughness. It would be sweet, I thought, if they died knowing for what crime they suffered. But if they did not, they would still be just as dead.

Perforce, my plans were simplistic, my strategy sparse. I arranged my supplies and pondered possibilities. Five of Chade's exploding pots had survived the bear's attack. One was cracked and leaking a coarse black powder. I softened candle wax and repaired it. I had knives, and my old sling, an axe too large to carry in a peaceful city; I doubted those weapons would be useful. I had powdered poisons for mixing with food and some for dusting a surface, oils that could go on a doorknob or the lip of a mug, tasteless liquids and pellets, every form of poison I knew. The bear attack had robbed me of the ones I had carried in quantity; I had no hope of poisoning the castle's water supply or dosing a large kettle of food. I had enough poison to deploy if I could get the Four to sit down and play dice with me. I doubted such an opportunity would exist. But if I could gain access to their personal lodgings, I could make an end of them.

On the bedside table, in the little cups that represented the towers, I arranged four black stones. I was holding the fifth in my hand, pondering, when Per and Spark came in with Lady Amber and Lant. 'Is it a game?' Per asked, staring in consternation at the cluttered tables, and my murder kit arrayed neatly on the floor.

'If assassination is a game,' Spark said quietly. She came to stand at my elbow. 'What do the black stones represent?'

'Chade's pots.'

'What do they do?' Per asked.

'They blast things. Like trapped sap popping in a firewood log.' I gestured at the five little pots.

'Only more powerful,' the Fool said.

'Much more,' Spark said quietly. 'I tested some with Chade. When he was healthy. We blew a great hole in a stone cliff near the beach.

Rock chips flew everywhere.' She touched her cheek as if remembering a stinging splinter.

'Good,' the Fool said. He took a seat at the table. Amber was long gone as his fingers danced over the carefully-arranged items. 'A firepot for each tower?'

'It might work. The placement of the pots and the strength of the tower walls are key. The pots must be high enough in the tower to make the tower collapse while the Four are abed. The pots have to explode simultaneously, so I need fuses of different lengths, so I can place and light a pot, and then go on to the next until all four are burning.'

'And still give you time to escape,' Lant suggested.

'That would be very nice, yes.' I didn't consider it likely that the pots would explode simultaneously. 'I need something to make fuses from.'

Spark frowned. 'Are not the fuses still in the top of the pots?'

I stared at her. 'What?'

'Give me one. Please.'

With reluctance, I lifted the repaired pot and handed it to her. She scowled at that. 'I'm not sure you should even try to use this one.' She tugged the cap off the pot, and I saw that it had been held on with a thick resin. Inside were two coiled strings. One was blue and the other white. She teased them out. The blue was twice the length of the white. 'The blue is longer and burns more slowly. The white burns fast.'

'How fast?'

She shrugged. 'The white one, set fire to it and run. It is good if you are being chased. The blue one you can conceal, and then finish your wine and bid your host farewell and be safely out the door.'

Lant leaned over my shoulder. I heard the smile in his voice. 'Far easier to use those with two of us. One man can never set all four and still be away before they explode.'

'Three of us,' Spark insisted. I stared at her. Her expression became indignant. 'I've more experience with them than anyone here!'

'Four,' Per said. I wondered if he understood we were talking about murder. It was my fault they included themselves at all. A younger and more energetic Fitz would have kept his plans concealed. I was older and weary and they already knew too much. Dangerously too much, for them and for me. I wondered if I'd have any secrets left when I died.

'When the time comes, we will see,' I told them, knowing they would argue if I simply said 'no'.

'I won't see,' the Fool interjected into the silence. For a moment, there was discomfort, and then Per laughed awkwardly. We joined in, more bitter than merry. But still alive and still moving toward our murderous goal.

NINE

The *Tarman*

Even before King Shrewd rather unwisely chose to strictly limit Skill-instruction to the members of the royal family only, the magic was falling into disuse. When I was in my 22nd year, a blood-cough swept through all the coastal duchies. The young and the old were carried off in droves. Many aged Skill-users died in that plague, and with them died their knowledge of the magic.

When Prince Regal found that scrolls about Skill-magic commanded a high price from foreign traders, he began secretly to deplete the libraries of Buckkeep. Did he know that those precious scrolls would ultimately fall into the hands of the Pale Woman and the Red-Ship Raiders? That is a matter that has long been debated among Buck nobility, and as Regal has been dead and gone for many years, it is likely we shall never know the truth about that.

On the decline of knowledge of Skill during the reign of King Shrewd,
Chade Fallstar

We trooped down together to the dock to watch the *Tarman* arrive in Kelsingra. I had grown up in Buckkeep Town where the docks were of heavy black timbers redolent of tar. Those docks seemed to have stood since El brought the sea to our shores. This dock was recently built, of pale planks with some pilings of stone and some of raw timber. New construction had been fastened to the ancient remains of an Elderling dock. I pondered that, for I did not judge this the best location for a dock. The half-devoured buildings at the river's edge told me that the river often shifted in its bed. The new Elderlings of Kelsingra needed to lift their eyes from what had been and consider the river and the city as it was now.

Above the broken cliffs that backed the city, on the highest hills, the snow had slumped into thin random fingers. In the distance, I could see the birches blushing pink and the willows gone red at the tips of their branches. The wind off the river was wet and cold, but the knife's edge of winter was gone from it. The year was turning and with it the direction of my life.

A sprinkling rain fell as the *Tarman* approached. Motley clung to Perseverance's shoulder, her head tucked tight against the rain. Lant stood behind him. Spark stood next to Amber. We clustered near enough to watch and far enough back that we were not in the way. Amber's gloved hand rested on the back of my wrist. I spoke to her in a low voice. 'The river runs swift and deep and doubtless cold. It is pale grey with silt, and smells sour. Once there was more shore here. Over decades, the river has eaten its way into Kelsingra. There are two other ships docked here. They both appear idle.

'The *Tarman* is a river barge. Sweeps, oars, long and low to the water. One powerful woman is on the steering oar. The ship has travelled upriver on the far side of the river, and now it's crossed the current, turned back and is moving with the current. No figure-head.' I was disappointed. I'd heard that the figureheads on liveships could move and speak. 'It has eyes painted on his hull. And it's coming fast with the current, and two deckhands have joined the steerswoman on the rudder. The crew is battling the current to bring the ship in here.'

As the *Tarman* neared the docks and its lines were tossed to folk on the dock, where they were caught and snubbed off around the cleats, the barge reared like a wilful horse and water piled up against its stern. There was something odd about the way the barge fought the current but I could not place it. Water churned all around it. Lines and dock timbers creaked as they took its weight.

Some lines were tightened and others loosened until the captain was satisfied that his craft was well snugged to the dock. The long-shoremen were waiting with their barrows and one tall Elderling on the dock was grinning in the way that only a man hoping to see his sweetheart grins. Alum. That was his name. I watched the deck and soon spotted her. She was in constant motion, relaying commands and helping to make the *Tarman* fast to the dock, but twice I caught her eyes roving over the welcoming crowd. When she saw her Elderling sweetheart, her face lit, and she seemed to move even more efficiently as if to flaunt her prowess.

A gangplank was thrown down and about a dozen passengers disembarked, their possessions in bags or packs. The immigrants came ashore uncertainly, staring up in wonder or perhaps dismay at the half-ruined city. I wondered what they had imagined, and if they would stay. On a separate gangplank, the longshoremen began to come and go like a line of ants as the ship disgorged cargo. 'That's the boat we'll travel on?' Spark asked doubtfully.

'That's the one.'

'I've never been on a boat.'

'I've been out in little boats before. Rowing boats on the Withy. Nothing like that.' Perseverance's eyes roved over the *Tarman*. His mouth was slightly ajar. I could not tell if he were anxious or eager.

'You'll be fine,' Lant assured them. 'Look how stable that ship is. And we're only going to be on a river, not the sea.'

I noted to myself that Lant was speaking to the youngsters more as if they were his younger siblings than his servants.

'Do you see the captain?'

I responded to Amber's question. 'I see a man past his middle years approaching Reyn. He has been larger in his life, I think, but looks gaunt now. They greet one another fondly. I suspect that is Leftrin and the woman with him would be Alise. She has a great deal of very curly reddish hair.' Amber had shared with me the scandalous tale of how Alise had forsaken her legal but unfaithful Bingtown husband to take up with the captain of a liveship. 'They are both exclaiming over Phron. They look delighted.'

Her hand tightened slightly on my arm as she fastened a smile onto her face.

'Here they come,' I added quietly. Lant stepped up beside me. Behind me, Per and Spark fell silent. We waited.

A smiling Reyn introduced us. 'And here are our Six Duchies visitors! Captain Leftrin and Alise of the liveship *Tarman*, may I present Prince FitzChivalry Farseer, Lady Amber and Lord Lant of the Six Duchies?'

Lant and I bowed, and Amber fell and rose in a graceful curtsey. Leftrin sketched a startled bow and Alise deployed a respectable curtsey before rising to stare at me in consternation. A smile passed over her face before she seemed to recall her manners. 'We are pleased to offer you passage on Tarman to Trehaug. Malta and Reyn have told us that Ephron's renewed health is due to your magic. Thank you. We have no children of our own, and Ephron has been as dear to us as he is to his parents.'

Captain Leftrin nodded gravely. 'As the lady says,' he added gruffly. 'Give us a day or so to get our cargo on the beach, give our crew a bit of shore time and we'll be ready to carry you down river. Quarters on Tarman are not spacious. We'll do our best to make you comfortable but I'm sure it won't be the sort of travel a prince is used to, nor a lord and a lady.'

'I am sure we will be most content with whatever you offer us. Our goal is not comfort but transport,' I replied.

'And that Tarman can provide, swifter and better than any on this river.' He spoke with the pride of a captain who owns his ship. 'We'd be pleased to welcome you aboard now and show you the quarters we've readied for you.'

'We would be delighted,' Amber replied warmly.

'This way, please.'

We followed them onto the dock and up the gangplank. The way was narrow and I worried that Amber might make a misstep, but as I stepped onto the barge's deck, that worry was replaced with a new one. The liveship resonated against both my Wit and Skill. A liveship indeed, as alive as any moving and breathing creature I'd ever known! I was certain the *Tarman* was as aware of me as I was of him. Lant was looking around with a wide grin on his face, as pleased as a boy on an adventure, and Per echoed him. Motley had lifted herself from the boy's shoulder and circled the barge suspiciously, flapping hard to keep her place against the river wind. Spark was more reserved than Lant and Per, almost wary. Amber put her hand back on my arm as soon as she could and gripped it tightly. Alise stepped onto the ship, followed by Leftrin. Both halted as abruptly as if encountering a wall.

'Oh, my,' Alise said softly.

'A little more than that,' Leftrin said tightly. He froze, and the communication between him and his ship was like a plucked string thrumming. He fixed me with a stare. 'My ship is . . . I must ask. Are you claimed by a dragon?'

We both stiffened. Had the ship sensed the dragon-blood she had consumed? She let go of my arm and stood alone, ready to let any blame fall on herself. 'I think what your ship senses about me is actually—'

'Beg pardon, ma'am, it's not you unsettling my ship. It's him.'

'Me?' Even to myself I sounded foolishly startled.

'You,' Leftrin confirmed. His mouth was pinched. He glanced at Alise. 'My dear, perhaps you could show the ladies their quarters while I settle this?'

Alise's eyes were very large. 'Of course I could,' and I knew that she was helping him separate me from my companions though I could not guess why.

I turned to my tiny retinue. 'Spark, if you would, guide your mistress while I have a word with the captain? Lant and Per, you will excuse us.'

Spark registered the unspoken warning and swiftly claimed Amber's arm. Lant and Perseverance had already moved down the deck, examining the ship as they went. 'Tell me all about the ship, Spark,' Amber requested in an unconcerned voice. They moved off slowly, following Alise, and I heard the girl adding descriptions to everything Alise said to them.

I turned back to Leftrin. 'Your ship dislikes me?' I asked. I was not reading that from my sense of the *Tarman*, but I'd never been aboard a liveship before.

'No. My ship wants to speak with you.' Leftrin crossed his arms on his barrel chest, then seemed to realize how unfriendly that appeared. He loosened his arms and wiped his hands down his trouser legs. 'Come on up to the bow rail. He talks best there.' He walked ponderously and I followed slowly. He spoke over his shoulder to me. 'Tarman talks to me,' he said. 'Sometimes to Alise. Maybe to Hennesey. Sometimes to the others, in dreams and such. I don't ask and he doesn't tell me. He's not like other liveships. He's more his own than . . . well, you wouldn't understand. You aren't Trader stock. Let me just say this. Tarman has never asked to speak to a stranger. I don't know what he's about, but understand that what he says, goes. The keepers made a deal with you, but if he says he doesn't want you on his deck, that's it.' He drew a breath. 'Sorry,' he added.

'I understand,' I said, but I didn't. As I moved toward the bow, my sense of the *Tarman* became more acute. And uncomfortable. It was like being sniffed over by a dog. A large and unpredictable dog. With bared teeth. I repressed my impulse to show my own teeth or display aggression in any way. His presence pressed more strongly against my walls.

I allow this, I pointed out to him as he pushed his senses into my mind.

As if you have the right to refuse. You tread my deck, and I will know you. What dragon has touched you?

Under the circumstances, lying would have been foolish. *A dragon pushed into my dreams. I think it was a dragon named Sintara, who claims the Elderling Thymara. I have been close to the dragons Tintaglia and Heeby. Perhaps that is what you sense.*

No. You smell of a dragon I have never sensed. Come closer. Put your hands on the railing.

I looked at the railing. Captain Leftrin was staring stonily across the river. I could not tell if he was aware of what his ship said to me or not. 'He wants me to put my hands on the railing.'

'Then I suggest you do so,' he responded gruffly.

I looked at it. The wood was grey and fine-grained and unfamiliar to me. I drew off my gloves and placed my hands on the railing.

There. I knew I smelled him. You touched him with your hands, didn't you? You groomed him.

I have never groomed a dragon.

You did. And he claims you as his.

Verity. It was not a thought I had intended to share. My walls were slipping before this ship's determination to force his way into my mind. I set my boundaries tighter, trying to work subtly so the ship would not perceive I was blocking him, but wonder had set my blood to racing. Would dragons of flesh and blood truly count Verity as a dragon who could claim me? I'd dusted the leaves from his back. Was that the 'grooming' that this ship had sensed? And if dragons would consider Verity a dragon, then did this barge count himself as a dragon?

The ship was silent, considering. Then, *Yes. That dragon. He claims you.*

Overhead, Motley cawed loudly.

The hardest thing in the world is to think of nothing. I considered the pattern of the wind and the current on the river's face. I longed to reach for Verity with a desire that almost surpassed my need to breathe. To touch that cold stone with my mind and heart, to feel that in some sense, he guarded my back. The ship broke into my thoughts.

He claims you. Do you deny it?

I am his. I was startled to find that was still true. *I have been his for a very long time.*

As if a human knows what 'a very long time' is. But I accept you as his. As Leftrin and Alise wish it, I will carry you to Trehaug. But it is your will that you do this. I am not interfering with a human claimed by a dragon.

I wondered what it meant that a liveship 'accepted' me and believed that a stone dragon had claimed me. I wondered how Verity had marked me as his own. Had he known he had done it? A dozen questions sprang to my mind, but Tarman had dismissed me. It was like a door closing on a noisy tavern, leaving me in dark and quiet. I felt both wild relief at how alone I was, and a sense of loss for things he could have told me. I reached, but could not sense Tarman at all. Captain Leftrin knew it at the same moment I did. For a moment he stared at me, taking my measure. Then he grinned. 'He's done with you. Want to see where you'll be bunking for the trip downriver?'

'I, uh, yes, please.' The change in his demeanour was as abrupt as the sun emerging from a cloud bank on a blustery day.

He led me aft, past the ship's deckhouse to two blocky structures attached to the deck. 'These are a lot nicer now than the first time we used them. Never thought Tarman would be ferrying as many people as he carries crates of freight. But times change, and we change with them. Slowly, and sometimes without a lot of grace, but even a Rain Wilder can change. This one is for you, Lord Lant, and your boy.' He looked uncomfortable for a moment. 'It would be better if you and the lady had private quarters, but where would I put your serving girl? Shoreside girls don't seem happy to share the crew's quarters, even though on my ship there's no danger to them. Just no privacy. We've given the other cabin to the women. I'm sure it's a lot less than what a prince expects, but it's the best we can offer.'

'Transport is all we desire, and I'd be happy to sleep out on the deck. It wouldn't be the first time in my life.'

'Ah.' The man visibly relaxed. 'Well. Hearing that will ease Alise's worries. She's been so anxious since we got the word we were going to give you passage. "A prince from the Six Duchies! What will we feed him, where will he sleep?" On and on. That's my Alise. Always wanting to do things in the best possible way.'

He opened the door. 'Was a time when these cabins weren't much more than cargo crates, built big. But we've had close to a score of years to make them comfortable. The others ain't been here yet, I don't think, so you can claim the bunk you want.'

Folk who live aboard ships know how to make the best of a small space. I had braced myself for the smell of old laundry, for canvas hammocks and a splintery floor. Two small windows admitted daylight and it danced on gleaming yellow woodwork. Four bunks stacked two high, none spacious, lined two of the walls. The room smelled pleasantly of the oil that had been used to wipe down the wood. One wall was all cupboards, drawers and crannies framed around the little window. A pair of blue curtains had been pushed back from the open window to admit both light and air. 'A more pleasant little water-cottage I could not imagine!' I told the captain, and turned to find Alise at his elbow, beaming with pleasure at my words. Lant and Perseverance stood behind her. The lad's cheeks were bright red with the wind and his eyes shone. His grin widened as he peered into our cabin.

'The ladies were pleased with theirs as well,' Alise observed happily. 'Welcome aboard, then. You can bring your things aboard any time today, and feel free to come and go as you please. The crew will need at least a day of rest here. I know you are eager to be down the river, but . . .'

'A day or even two will not disturb our plans,' I replied. 'Our tasks will wait until we arrive.'

'But Paragon can't, so a day and a half is all I can give my crew this time,' was Leftrin's observation. He shook his head at Alise. 'We'll be cutting it fine to meet Paragon in Trehaug. Time and tides wait for no man, my dear, and both ships have schedules to keep.'

'I know, I know,' she said, but she smiled as she said it.

He turned his smile at me. 'The other ships make regular runs up and down the river, but neither of them ride the current as well as Tarman does when the water runs high in spring. Once the snowmelts are done and the river calms, Tarman and his crew can take a nice break while the impervious boats take their turn. When the river runs swift with snowmelt or the acid runs white in the main channel, we leave the pretty boats safely tied up and Tarman shoulders the load.' He spoke with more pride than regret.

'Are we going to be crowded with passengers going downriver?' Alise asked him, a bit anxiously.

'No. I spoke to Harrikin. If any of the new folk can't abide the city's muttering, he'll send them across the river to Village to await our next run. I think he hopes that they'll settle and work there instead of fleeing back to whatever they came from.' He turned to me. 'Twenty years of bringing folk here, and then taking half of them back when they can't cut it. It makes for a crowded ship and taking turns at the galley table. But this run will be only you folks, crew, and a bit of cargo. Should be a pleasant run if the weather stays fine.'

The next morning was as clear and blue as a day could be. The wind off the river was ever present and never kind, but it was definitely spring now. I could smell the sticky new leaves unfolding and the dark earth awakening. There were a few fresh scallions mixed in with the omelette and fried potatoes at the breakfast we shared with the keepers who had gathered to say farewell. Sylve told us jubilantly that the chickens she had insisted on keeping in the garden houses over the winter were now laying reliably again.

The farewell gathering included the children and companions of the keepers. Many came to thank me again and offer parting gifts. A pragmatic man named Carson had brought us dried strips of meat in a leather pouch. 'It will keep if you don't let damp get to it.' I thanked him, and had that instant sense of connection that sometimes comes, a feeling of a deep friendship that could have been.

Amber and Spark both received earrings from a woman named Jerd. 'There's nothing magical about them, but they're pretty, and in a hard time you could sell them.' She had given birth to a little girl I had healed, but oddly enough an Elderling named Sedric was raising the child with Carson. 'I am fond of the girl, but was never meant to be a mother,' Jerd informed us cheerily. The little girl, sitting on Sedric's shoulders and gripping his hair in two tight handfuls appeared content with her lot. Sedric was enthusiastic about her. 'She has begun to make sounds. She turns her head when we speak now.' The child's mass of coppery hair concealed her very tiny ears. 'And Relpda now understands the problem and will help us with it. Our dragons are not cruel, but they do not always understand how a small human is meant to grow.' And from the queen of the Elderlings, a box that held assorted teas. She smiled as she offered it to Amber. 'A small pleasure can be a great comfort when one travels,' she said, and Amber accepted it gratefully.

It was noon before we processed down to the ship. Our baggage was already stowed on board, and our new gifts filled a barrow that Perseverance pushed. Tats had given an Elderling scarf to Per and he had folded it very carefully and asked quietly if he might send it to his mother from Bingtown. I assured him we could. Thymara had pulled Amber aside from us, to present her with a woven bag. I overheard her giving her yet more cautioning words about the Silver on her fingers.

The farewells at the dock seemed to take forever, but Leftrin finally gave a shout and said it was time we were away if we were to have any daylight at all. I watched Alum kiss his girl, who then hurried aboard and took charge of the deck crew. Leftrin observed me watching them. 'Skelly's my niece. She'll captain Tarman some day, after I lie down on his deck and slide my memories into his timbers.'

I raised my brows.

Captain Leftrin hesitated, then laughed at himself. 'Liveships ways are not as secret as they once were. Liveships and their families are very close. Children are born aboard the family ship, and grow to crew and then captain. When they die, the ship absorbs their memories. Our ancestors live on in our ships. He gave me an odd grin. 'A strange immortality.'

Rather like putting memories into a stone dragon, I thought to myself. A strange immortality indeed.

He gave his grizzled head a shake and then invited us to join him and Alise in the galley for coffee while the crew went about its tasks. 'Don't you need to be on the deck?' Perseverance asked him, and Captain Leftrin grinned. 'If I can't trust Skelly by now, I should just cut my throat today. My crew loves the ship and Tarman loves them. There's little they can't handle, and I enjoy my time with my lady.'

We found cramped seats around the scarred galley table. The small room was crowded in a friendly way, redolent of the year's cooking and wet wool. The coffee added its own fragrance. I'd had the stuff once before and knew what to expect, but I watched Per pucker his mouth in surprise. 'Oh, here, lad, you've no need to drink that! I can make a pot of tea just as easily.' And with a swoop, Alise took his mug, dumped the contents back into the coffee pot and began to dipper water into a battered copper kettle. The little iron stove warmed the room almost unbearably and she soon had the kettle hissing on top of it.

I looked round at us, seated so companionably around the table. At Buckkeep Castle, Spark and Per would have been dismissed to a servant's table, and perhaps Lant and I would have dined separately from a humble ship's captain and his lady. The room gave a dip and a lurch. Per's eyes went wide and Spark audibly caught her breath. The greedy current rushed us out onto the river. I craned to look out of the small window. I saw only grey river water.

Leftrin sighed with satisfaction. 'Aye, we're well on our way now. I'll just step out and see if Big Eider needs a hand with the tiller. He's a good man, if simple. Knows the river well. But we're still missing Swarge. Thirty years that man kept us steady in the current. Well, he's gone into Tarman now.'

'As will we all, eventually,' Alise affirmed with a smile 'I must step out also. I need to ask Skelly where she stowed the last barrel of sugar.' She looked at Spark. 'I'll count on you to brew the tea when the water boils. It's in the box on the shelf by the window.'

'Thank you, Lady Alise. I shall do so.'

'Oh, *Lady* Alise!' Her cheeks went pink and she laughed. 'I haven't been a lady for years! I'm just Alise. If I forget to address you as the grand folk you are, you'll have to excuse me. I'm afraid my Bingtown manners have faded after nearly a score of years on the river.'

We laughed and all assured her that we were comfortable. And we were. I felt more at ease on Tarman than I had in the dragon city.

The opened door let in a gust of river wind and then slammed shut behind her. We were left to ourselves, and I heard Amber breathe a soft sigh of relief.

'Do you think they'd mind if I went on deck and had a look about?' Per asked wistfully. 'I'd like to see how the tiller works.'

'Go,' I said. 'They'll tell you if you're in the way, and if they tell you to move, do it fast. It's more likely they'll find some work for you to do.'

Lant unfolded himself as the boy stood. 'I'll keep an eye on him. I'd like to have a look about myself. I've been out fishing with friends on Buckkeep Bay, but never on a river, let alone one so large and swift.'

'Will you still want tea?' Spark asked them, for the kettle had begun to steam.

'Most likely. I think it's pretty cold out there, with the wind and all.'

And again the wind slammed the door as they left. 'What an odd little family we've become,' Amber observed as Spark took down a lovely sea-green pot for the tea. She smiled and added, 'No tea for me. I'm content with the coffee. It's been years since I've had good coffee.'

'If this is "good" coffee, I dread what bad coffee might be,' I told her. I did as I'd seen Alise do, dumping my unwanted cupful back into the big black pot on the stove. I waited for the tea to brew.

We settled easily into life aboard ship and found a new rhythm to our days. The crew was happy to take Perseverance in and give him small tasks. When our lad was not learning his knots from Bellin, a large and near-silent woman who could manage a deck-pole as well as any man, he was put to polishing, sanding, oiling and cleaning. He took to it as a duck to water, and told me one afternoon that if he were not sworn to me, he could be happy as a ship's boy. I felt a twinge of jealousy, but also relief to see him busy and happy.

Motley had joined us as soon as Tarman cast off from Kelsingra. The crow got over her wariness quickly and shocked all of us by preferring a perch on the bow rail. The first time she squawked 'Tarman! Tarman!' she won the heart of the crew and made Perseverance beam with pride.

She became a cheery presence on the boat if the weather was blustery. She happily rode on Per as he went about his tasks, but whenever Lady Amber emerged onto the deck, Motley transferred to her. The crow had learned to chuckle, and had an uncanny ability to laugh at just the right moment. Her gift for mimicry had become suspiciously good, but whenever I reached toward her with the Wit I found only the bland fog of a creature that was proudly uninterested in forming a bond. 'How much do you understand?' I demanded of her one afternoon. She cocked her head at me, met my gaze and demanded, 'How much do YOU understand?' With a chuckle, she took flight down river ahead of Tarman.

Travel aboard a vessel is either boring or terrifying. On Tarman, I was glad to be bored. The farther away from the city, the less the Skill-current pressed on my walls. Each night the tillerman steered us into moorage along the riverbank. Sometimes there was a beach and we could disembark, but often we were nudged up against a bank of trees with serpentine roots. On the third day, the river narrowed and deepened, and the current became much stronger. The forest closed in and there was no true horizon. The banks of the river were solid walls of trees with stilt roots and we moored to them at night. It began to rain, and didn't stop. Motley moved into the galley. I moved between our cramped cabin and the ship's steamy galley. My clothing and bedding was always slightly damp.

I tried to pass my time constructively. Amber suggested I learn Mersen, the old language of Clerres. 'Most people will speak Common to you, but it's useful to know what they say to one another when they think you can't understand them.' To my surprise, my companions joined in. In the long wet days, all of us would hunch on the cramped bunks, while Amber would drill us in vocabulary and grammar. I had always been adept at learning languages but Perseverance outshone me. Lant and Spark struggled, but we pressed on. I put Lant to helping Perseverance with his letters and numbers. Neither of them relished those tasks, but they made progress.

In the evenings after we were moored, Lant, Spark and Perseverance would join the crew in games that involved dice, cards, and some little carved rods. Imaginary fortunes changed hands often across the table.

While they gamed, Amber and I convened in her cabin. I valiantly ignored the small smiles that both Leftrin and Alise would exchange when I rejoined the company. I wished I could find humour in them, but in truth I felt as if I tormented the Fool during our private sessions. He wanted to help but the viciousness he had endured at Clerres made it hard for him to speak his memories in a coherent order. The scalding anecdotes I pried from him only made me reluctant to dig deeper. And yet I knew I must. I learned of the Four in bits and references. It was the best he could offer me.

The only one of the Four I learned about in detail was Capra. Capra seemed to take pride in being the eldest of the Four. She had long silver hair and wore blue robes weighted with pearls. She appeared gentle, kind, and wise. She had been his mentor when he had first arrived at Clerres. In his early days there, he was invited daily to her tower room after he had completed his lessons. There they would sit together on the floor before her fire while he scribed his dreams onto thick soft paper that was as yellow as a daisy's heart. They shared delicious little cakes, exotic fruits and cheeses. She taught him about wines with tiny sips from little gold-rimmed goblets and educated him on teas. Sometimes she invited tumblers and jugglers there, simply to entertain him, and when he wished to join in, she had them teach him their skills. She praised him and he blossomed in her care. When she spoke his name, Beloved, he believed she meant it. He spoke of an adolescence I envied. Pampered, praised, educated—any child's dream. But we all awake from dreams.

Most often I sat on the floor of our cabin and he claimed a lower bunk and stared sightlessly up as he spoke. Rain spattered on the small windows of the cabin. A single candle he could not see gave me a dim light appropriate to his dark tales. He was the Fool in those sessions, in a loose blouse with a spill of lace down his chest and plain black leggings, Amber's gown a wilted flower on the cabin's floor. His posture and garments were similar to when we had been youngsters, knees drawn up to his chin, one bared hand and one gloved hand clasped around his knees. His unseeing eyes stared at a distant time.

'I studied hard to please her. She gave me dreams to read and listened to my earnest interpretation. I was sitting before her fire when I first read of the Unexpected Son in an old and crumbling scroll. It spoke to me as no other had. I literally began to tremble. My voice shook as I told her of a childhood dream. My dream and the old one fitted together like interlaced fingers. I spoke true to her, saying I'd be sorry to leave her but I was the White Prophet for this time. I knew that I needed to be out in the world, preparing for the changes I must make. A fool I was indeed, fearing I would hurt her by leaving.'

The Fool made a small sound. 'She listened to me. Then she shook her head sadly and gently said, "You are mistaken. The White Prophet for this time has already manifested. We have trained her, and soon she will begin her tasks. Beloved, every young White wishes to be the White Prophet. Every student at Clerres has made that claim. Do not be sad. There are other tasks for you, to do humbly and well to aid the true White Prophet."

'I could not believe what I was hearing. My ears rang and my vision swam to hear her deny me. But she was so wise and kind and old, I knew she must be right. I tried to accept that I was wrong, but my dreams would not let me. From the time she denied me, my dreams came on like a storm, two and three a night. I knew as I wrote them down that she would be displeased, but I could not hold them back. She took each one and showed me how it did not apply to me, but to another.'

He shook his head slowly. 'Fitz, I cannot explain my distress. It was . . . like looking through badly-made glass. Eating rotten meat. There was a foulness to her words that made me feel physically ill. They rang wrong in my ears. But she was my mentor. She treated me so lovingly. How could she not be right?'

He asked that question so earnestly. His hands, gloved and bared, kneaded each other. He looked away from me, as if I could read anything in his shuttered eyes. 'One day, she took me up the steps to the top tower room. Fitz, it was huge, bigger than the Queen's Garden at Buckkeep Castle. And it was littered with treasures. Amazing things, objects that were lovely beyond imagining scattered like discarded toys. There was a staff that gleamed with light all along its length, and a marvellous throne made from tiny interlocking flowers of jade. Some, I know now, were of Elderling make. Wind chimes that sang, a statue of a pot with a plant that grew from it, flowered, faded back into the soil and then grew again. I gazed in wonder, but she told me crisply that they came from a faraway beach where such treasures washed up, and that the stewards of that place had bargained with her that all the sea gave them would be hers if she granted them a boon.

'I wanted to know more of that story, but she took my hand and drew me to the window and bade me look down. I saw a young woman below in a walled garden full of flowers and vines and fruit trees. She was White as I was White. I had met others at Clerres who were almost as colourless as I was. Almost. They had all been born there, and they all seemed to be related, sister to brother, cousin and uncle. But none of them were White as I was White. Not until I saw her.

'Another woman was there, with red hair and a great sword. She was teaching the pale woman how to wield it as a serving maid watched and cried encouragement. The White woman danced with that sword, and her hair floated as she moved so beautifully. Then Capra said, "There she is. The true White Prophet. Her training is almost complete. You have seen her. Let us have no more of foolishness."' He shuddered. 'That was the first time I saw the Pale Woman.' He fell silent.

'You have told me enough for tonight.'

He shook his head, his mouth pursed tight shut. He lifted his hands and rubbed his face hard, and for a moment the faded scars stood out against his skin. 'So I didn't speak of my destiny again,' he said harshly. 'I wrote down my dreams but I no longer tried to interpret them. She took them from me and set them aside. Unread, I believed.' He shook his head. 'I have no idea how much knowledge I handed over to her. By day, I studied and I tried to be content. I had a lovely life, Fitz. All that I could ask for. Good food, attentive servants, music and amusements in the evening. I was useful, I thought, for Capra put me to sorting old scrolls. It was a clerk's work but I was good at it.' He kneaded his scarred hands together. 'In the way of my kind, I was still a child. I wanted to please. I missed being loved. So I tried.

'But of course, I failed. In my clerk's work, I encountered writings about the Unexpected Son. I had a dream, of a jester singing a silly song about "fat suffices". He sang it to a wolf cub, Fitz. The cub had sprouting antlers.' He gave a muffled laugh, but the hair stood up on my arms. Had he truly seen me in a dream, so many years before we had even met? But it had not been me. It had only been a puzzle, to which I was, perhaps, the answer.

'Oh, I do not like this tale I vomit out to you. I wish I had not begun telling it. So many things we have never spoken about. So many things that shame me less if I am the only one who knows them. But I will finish.' He looked toward me, his sightless eyes swimming with tears. I slid across the floor and took his gloved hand in mine. His smile was a wavering thing. 'I could not forever deny what I was. My anger and resentment grew. I wrote my dreams down, and I began to reference other dreams, some ancient, some recent. I built a fortress of evidence that Capra could not deny. I did not insist I was the White Prophet, but I began to ask her questions, and they were not innocent ones.' He smiled slightly. 'I know you could never guess it, Fitz, but I can be stubborn. I was determined to force her to admit who and what I was.'

Again, he paused. I did not speak. This was like digging splinters out of an infected wound. He pulled his hand from mine and wrapped his arms around himself as if freezing.

'I'd never been so much as slapped by my parents, Fitz. Not that I was a tractable and easy child. No. I am sure I was not. Yet they had corrected me patiently and I had come to expect that from adults. Never had they denied me information as to why a thing was so. Always they had listened to me, and when I taught them something new, they were always so proud of me! I thought I was so clever to ask Capra questions about my dreams and other dreams I had read. My questions would lead her to the inevitable answer that I was indeed, the White Prophet.

'And so I began. A few questions on one day, a few more the next. But the day I asked Capra six questions in a row, all leading up to what she must admit about me, she held up her hand and said, "Not another question! I will tell you what your life is to be." Not even thinking, being young as one is only once, I said, "But why?" And that was it. Without a word, she rose and pulled a bell-pull. A servant came, and she sent him for someone else, a name I did not know then. Kestor. A very large and muscular man. And he came and held me down with a foot on the back of my neck and let his leather strap fall wherever it would on my body. I screamed and begged but neither of them spoke a word. As abruptly as it began, my punishment was over. She dismissed Kestor, seated herself at her table and poured some tea. When I could, I crawled from her room. I remember my long trip down the stone stairs of her tower. The lash had fallen on the big muscles behind my knees, and curled around one of my ankles. The tip of it had etched into my belly more than once. It was agony to try to stand. I edged down on my hands and knees, trying not to pull on the welts, crept to my cottage and stayed there for two days. No one came. No one asked after me, or brought me water or food. I waited, thinking someone would come. No.' He shook his head, old bafflement on his face. 'Capra never summoned me again. She never spoke directly to me again.' He sighed out a small breath.

In the silence that followed, I asked, 'What were you expected to learn from that?'

His tears scattered as he shook his head. 'I never knew. No one ever spoke of what she had done to me. When two days had passed

I limped to the healer's room and waited for the full day. Others came and went but he never summoned me. No one, not even the other students, asked what had happened to me. It was as if it had never occurred in their world, only mine. Eventually, I began to limp to my lessons and to meals. But my instructors had a new disdain for me, rebuked me for my missed lessons and punished me by withholding food. I was made to sit at a table and work on lessons while the others ate. It was on one of those days that I saw the Pale Woman again. She walked through the hall where we gathered for meals. All the other students looked at her with admiring eyes. She was garbed all in green and brown, like a hunter, and her white hair was braided back with golden thread. So beautiful. Her servant followed her. I think . . . looking back, I think her servant was Dwalia, the one who took Bee. One of the people who prepared our food hurried out and gave a hamper to Dwalia. Then the Pale Woman walked out of the hall, with her servant carrying the basket. As she passed me, she halted. She smiled at me, Fitz. Smiled as if we were friends. Then she said, "I am. And you are not." Then she walked on. And everyone laughed. The twist to my mind and thoughts were worse than the welts all over my body.'

He needed his silence for a time and I let him keep it. 'So clever they are,' he said at last. 'The pain they gave my body was only a gateway to what they could do to my mind. Capra must die, Fitz. The Four must die to end the corruption of the Whites.'

I felt ill. 'Her servant was Dwalia? The same Dwalia that stole Bee?'

'So I think. I could be wrong.'

A question I didn't want to ask, an unwise question, found its way to my voice. 'But after all that . . . all that, and all else you have told me . . . you went back with Prilkop?'

He laughed bitterly. 'Fitz, I was not myself. You had brought me back from the dead. Prilkop was strong and calm. He was so certain that he could restore Clerres to its proper service. He came from a time when the word of a White Prophet was a command to the Servants. He was so certain of what we should do. And I had no idea what to do with this unexpected life.'

'I recall a similar time in my life. Burrich made all our decisions.'

'Then you understand. I couldn't think about anything. I just followed what he said we were going to do.' He clenched his teeth and then said, 'And now I go back for a third time. And more than anything, I fear that I will fall into their power again.' He took a sudden gulping breath. But even so, he could not seem to catch his breath. He began gasping like a spent runner. He could barely get his words out. 'Nothing could be worse than that. Nothing.' Hugging himself, he rocked back and forth on the bunk. 'But . . . I . . . must . . . go back . . . I must . . .' He snapped his head back and forth wildly. 'Need to see!' he cried out suddenly. 'Fitz! Where are you!' His gasping was ever faster. 'Can't . . . feel. My hands!'

I knelt beside the bed and put an arm around him. He yelped and struggled wildly, striking out at me

'It's me, you're safe. You're here. Breathe, Fool. Breathe.' I refused to let go. I was not rough but I held him firmly. 'Breathe.'

'I . . . can't!'

'Breathe. Or you'll faint. But you can do that. I'm here. You are safe.'

Suddenly he went limp and stopped fighting me and, very gradually, his breathing slowed. When he pushed me away, I let him. He folded himself tight and hugged his knees. When he finally spoke, he was ashamed. 'I never wanted you to know how much I feared to do this. Fitz, I'm a coward. I'd rather die than let them take me.'

'You don't have to go back. I can do this.'

'I do have to go back!' He was instantly furious with me. 'I must!'

I spoke quietly. 'Then you will.' With great reluctance, I added, 'I could give you something to carry with you. A quick end if you thought you would . . . prefer that.'

His gaze wandered over my face as if he could see me. He said quietly, 'You'd do it, but you'd not approve. Nor have such a resource for yourself.'

I nodded then spoke. 'That's true.'

'Why?'

'Something I overheard a long time ago. It didn't make sense when I was younger, but the older I get, the wiser it seems. Prince Regal was speaking to Verity.'

'And you put weight on something Regal said? Regal wanted you dead. From the moment he knew of your existence, he wanted you dead.'

'True. But he was quoting what King Shrewd said to him, probably the king's response when Regal suggested that killing me was the easiest solution. My grandfather told him, "Never do a thing until you've considered what you can't do once you've done it."'

A slow, fond smile claimed his face. 'Ah. That does sound like something my king would have said.' His smile widened, and I sensed a secret he would not share.

'Killing myself would put an end to all other possibilities. And more than once in my life, when I thought death was my only escape, or that it was inevitable and I should surrender to it, I've been proven wrong. And each time, despite whatever fire I had to pass through, I found good in my life afterwards.'

'Even now? With Molly and Bee dead?'

It felt disloyal but I said it. 'Even now. Even when I feel like most of me is dead, life breaks through sometimes. Food tastes good. Or something Per says makes me laugh. A hot cup of tea when I'm cold and wet. I've thought of ending my life, Fool. I admit it. But always, no matter the damage to it, the body tries to go on. And if it manages to, then the mind follows it. Eventually, no matter how I try to deny it, there are bits of my life that are still sweet. A conversation with an old friend. Things I am still glad to have.'

He groped for me with his gloved hand and I offered mine. He shifted his grip to a warrior's clasp, wrist to wrist. I returned the pressure. 'It's true for me as well. And you are right. I would never have thought to admit it, even to myself.' He released my wrist and leaned back, then added, 'But still, I would take your escape, if you will prepare it for me. Because if they do manage to take me, then I cannot . . .' His voice had begun to shake.

'I can prepare something for you. Something you could carry tucked in the cuff of your shirt.'

'That would be good. Thank you.'

Of such cheerful discourse were my evenings made.

I had not realized that we were on a tributary until we left it and joined the furious rush of the Rain Wild River. The turbulent waters that carried us now were grey with acid and silt. We no longer drew water from the river but relied only on our casks. Bellin warned Perseverance that if he fell overboard 'all we might pull back would be your bones!' It did not dampen his enthusiasm at all. He scampered about the deck despite the rain and wind, and the crew tolerated him with good humour. Spark had less endurance for the foul weather, but she and Lant would sometimes stand on top of the deckhouse, sheltering under a square of tarpaulin and watch the passing view as the current swept us along.

I wondered what fascinated them, for the scenery had become unvarying. Trees. More trees, some of a size I had never imagined, with trunks as big around as towers. Trees made of a hundred spindly trunks, trees that leaned and dropped extra trunks down from the branches into the river's marshy edge. Trees with vines climbing up them, trees with curtains of vines dangling down. I had never seen forest so thick and impenetrable, or foliage that could survive such wet conditions. The far shore of the river retreated to a foggy distance. We heard more birds during the day, and once saw a shrieking troop of monkeys, very strange to me.

It was all so different to the familiar landscapes of Buck. Even as it fascinated me and I longed to explore it, my deeper longing was for home. My thoughts went often to my Nettle, gravid with her first child. I'd abandoned her when she was still growing within Molly, to obey the urgent summons of my king. And now I left her to bear my first grandchild alone, at the behest of the Fool. How did Chade fare? Had he succumbed to age and a wandering mind? There were times when taking vengeance for the dead seemed too high a price for abandoning the living.

I kept such musings to myself. My fears of Skilling lingered. The press of it I had felt in Kelsingra had diminished, but the living ship beneath my feet was a constant hum of sentience against my walls. Soon, I promised myself. Even a brief Skill-contact could convey so much more than the tiny lettering on a messenger bird's scroll. Soon.

Once when we were moored for the night, Skelly rose from the table, retrieved a bow and quiver from the crew quarters and then stepped soundlessly onto the deck. No one moved until we heard her shout. 'I got a river pig! Fresh pork!' There was a scramble to the deck, and the messy exuberant work of retrieving the dead animal. We butchered him on the narrow mud beach.

We feasted that evening. The crew built a fire, threw on green branches, and toasted strips of pig in the flames and smoke. The fresh meat put the crew in a merry mood, and Perseverance was pleased to be teased as one of their own. After we had eaten the cookfire became a bonfire that drove back the darkness and the biting night insects. Lant went for firewood and returned with an armful of an early-blooming vine with fragrant flowers. Spark filled Amber's hands with some and then crowned herself with a garland. Hennesey began a bawdy song and the crew joined in. I smiled and tried to pretend I was neither an assassin nor a father mourning the loss of his child. But to join their simple, rowdy pleasure seemed a betrayal of Bee and how her little life had ended.

When Amber said she was wearied, I assured Spark that she should stay with Lant and Per and enjoy the evening. I guided Amber as we moved over the mucky shoreline to a rough rope ladder tossed over Tarman's side. It was a struggle for her to climb the sagging rungs in the long skirts she wore.

'Would not it all be easier if you dropped the pretence of Amber?'

She gained the deck and tousled her skirts back to order. 'And which pretence would I then assume?' she asked me.

As always, such words gave me a twinge of pain. Was the Fool indeed only another pretence, an imaginary companion invented for me? As if he had heard my thoughts, he said, 'You know more of me than anyone, Fitz. I've given you as much of my true self as I dare.'

'Come,' I said and took his arm for balance while we both shed our muddy footwear. Captain Leftrin was rightfully fussy about keeping the deck clean. I shook the mud from our shoes over the side and carried them as I guided him back to the cabin. From the shore came a sudden whoop of laughter. A whirl of sparks rose into the night as someone threw a heavy piece of wood onto the bonfire.

'It is good for them to have some enjoyment.'

'It is,' I replied. Childhood had been stolen from both Spark and Perseverance. Even Lant could use a window of merriness in his permanent wall of melancholy.

I went to the galley to kindle a little lantern. When I returned to the cabin, the Fool was already out of Amber's fussy dress and into his simpler garb. He had wiped the paint that composed her face onto a cloth and turned to me with his old Fool's smile. But in the light of my small lantern, the tracks of his torment still showed on his face and hands as silver threads against his light skin. His fingernails had regrown thick and stubby. My efforts at healing and the dragon's blood he had taken had aided his body's recovery more than I had dared hope, but he would never be who he had been.

But that was true of all of us.

'What are you sighing about?'

'I'm thinking of how this has changed all our lives. I was . . . I was on the way to being a good father, Fool. I think.' Yes, burning bodies of murdered messengers at night. Excellent experience for a growing child.

'Yes. Well.' He sat down on the lower bunk. The upper bunk was neatly spread up. The other two bunks seemed to be serving as storage for the excessive wardrobe that he and Sparks had dragged with them. He sighed and then admitted, 'I had more dreams.'

'Oh?'

'Significant dreams. Dreams that demand to be told aloud or written down.'

I waited. 'And?'

'It is hard to describe the pressure one feels to share significant dreams.'

I tried to be perceptive. 'Do you want to tell them to me? Perhaps Leftrin or Alise would have pen and ink and paper. I could write them down for you.'

'No!' He covered his mouth for a moment, as if the explosive denial had revealed something. 'I told them to Spark. She was here when I awoke in a terrible state, and I told her.'

'About the Destroyer.'

He was silent for a moment. Then, 'Yes, about the Destroyer.'

'You feel guilty about that?'

He nodded. 'It's a terrible burden to put on one so young. She already does so much for me.'

'Fool, I don't think you need be concerned. She knows that I am the Destroyer. That we are on our way to bring down all Clerres. Your dream just repeats what we all know.'

He wiped the palms of his hands down his thighs and then clasped them together. 'What we all know,' he repeated dully. 'Yes.' Abruptly he added, 'Goodnight, Fitz. I think I need to sleep.'

'Goodnight then. I hope your dreams are peaceful.'

'I hope I don't dream at all,' he replied.

It felt strange to rise and leave him there, taking the lantern with me. Leaving the Fool in the dark. As he was always in darkness now.

TEN

Bee's Book

The preparation of the darts must be done with a steady hand. One cannot wear gloves but one must be extremely cautious, for the smallest nick of the fingers will become infected immediately and the parasites will quickly spread. There is no cure.

I have found that using the eggs of the boring worms combined with the eggs of the ones that cling inside a man's guts and become long worms is the most effective in causing a prolonged and painful death. Eggs from one or the other will plague the victim but not lead to death. It is the double attacks of these creatures that inflict the death most befitting the cowards and traitors who dare betray Clerres.

Various Devices of my own Design, Coultrie of the Four

After a few days aboard Tarman, I had grown more accustomed to the light press of the ship's awareness against mine. I was still uncomfortable that a liveship would be privy to any message I might Skill out, but after much debate with myself, I had decided to risk the contact with home.

Lady Amber sat down on the ship's bunk opposite mine. A cup of tea steamed on the little shelf by the bunk. In the small space, our knees nearly touched. She gave a sigh, untwined a scarf from her damp hair and shook it out. Then the Fool reached up to tousle his hair into wild disorder that it might dry more quickly. It was no longer the dandelion fluff of his boyhood, or as golden as Lord Golden's hair had been. To my surprise, white mixed with the pale blonde of it, like an old man's hair. White hair, growing from the scars on his scalp. He wiped his fingers on Amber's skirts and gave me a weary smile.

'Are you ready?' I asked him.

'Ready and well supplied,' he assured me.

'How will you know if I need your help? What will you do if I am swept away?'

'If I speak to you and you don't respond, I'll shake you. If you still don't respond, I'll dash my tea in your face.'

'I hadn't realized that was why you'd asked Spark for tea.'

'It wasn't.' He took a sip from his cup. 'Not entirely.'

'And if that doesn't bring me back?'

He groped on the bunk beside him and held up a small pouch. 'Elfbark. Courtesy of Lant. It's well powdered, to mix with my tea and pour down your throat or simply stuff into your mouth.' He canted his head. 'If the elfbark fails I will link my fingers to your wrist. But I assure you, that will be my final resort.'

'What if you do, and instead of you pulling me back, I drag you under?'

'What if Tarman hits a rock and we all drown in the acid waters of the Rain Wild River?'

I stared at him in silence.

'Fitz, get to it. Or don't. But stop procrastinating. We are far from Kelsingra. Try to Skill.'

I centred myself and let my vision unfocus, evened my breathing and slowly lowered my walls. I felt the sweep of the Skill-current, as cold and powerful as the river beneath our hull. Just as dangerous. It was not the riptide it had been in Kelsingra, but I knew that it concealed hidden currents. I hesitated upon the brink and then waded in, groping for Nettle. I did not find her. I reached for Thick. A distant wailing of music might have been him, but it faded as if wind had blown it away. Dutiful? Not there. I tried for Nettle again. I felt as if my fingers brushed my daughter's face and slid away. Chade? No. I had no desire to tatter away in the Skill-current alongside my old mentor. When last I had seen the old man, his moments of acuity had been brief islands in a sea of vagueness. His Skill-magic, once so feeble, now sometimes roared, and he used it without caution. The last time we had connected in the Skill, he had nearly dragged me away with him. I must not try to reach for Chade—

Chade seized me. It was like being grappled from behind by a boisterous playmate and I was flung headlong into a wild rush of Skill. *Oh, my boy, there you are! I've missed you so!* His thoughts embraced me in a tightening net of fondness. I felt myself becoming the person that Chade imagined me to be. Like clay pressed into a brick mould, the parts of me he'd never known were being sheared away.

Stop! Let me go! I have word for Dutiful and Nettle, news of Kelsingra and the Dragon Traders!

He chuckled warmly yet I felt chilled at the soft press of his thoughts. *Leave that. Leave all that and join us here. There is no loneliness, no separation at all. No aching bones, no worn-out body. It's not what they told us, Fitz! All those warnings and dire predictions—faugh! The world will go on without us just as well as it did with us. Just let go.*

Was it true? His words were soaked in conviction. I relaxed in his grip as the Skill-current roared past us. *We aren't tattering.*

I'm holding you tight. Keeping you part of me. It's like learning to swim. You can't find out how until you're all the way into the water. Stop clinging to the bank, boy. You only tear apart when you try to hold onto the shore.

He had always been wiser than me. Chade had always advised me, educated me and commanded me. He seemed calm and content. Happy, even. Had I ever before seen Chade content and happy? I moved toward him and he embraced me more warmly. Or did the Skill seize me? Where did Chade stop and the Skill begin? Had he already drowned in the Skill? Was he dragging me down to join him?

Chade! Chade Fallstar! Come back to us! Dutiful, help me. He's fighting me.

Nettle gripped him and attempted to peel him away from me. I held to him fiercely, struggling to make her aware of me, but she was focused on separating us. *Nettle!* I roared my thought, trying to make it stand out from the rip and rush of thoughts around us. Thoughts? No. Not thoughts. Being. Beings.

I pushed all wondering aside. Instead of clinging to Chade, I thrust him toward her. *I've got him!* She told a Dutiful I barely sensed. And then, in sudden awe, *Da? Are you here? Are you alive?*

Yes. We are all fine. Will send you a bird from Bingtown. Then, divorced from Chade, the surge of the Skill began to tear at me. I tried to draw back, but the Skill gripped me like a bog. As I struggled, it sucked at me, pulling me deeper. Beings. The current was a flow of beings, all plucking at me. I gathered my strength and flung myself against its current as I resolutely put up my walls. I opened my eyes to the blessedly cramped and smelly little cabin. I folded forward over my knees, gasping and shaking.

'What?' the Fool demanded.

'I nearly lost myself. Chade was there. He tried to pull me in with him.'

'What?'

'He told me that everything I learned about the Skill was wrong. That I should give myself over to the Skill. "Just let go," he said. And I nearly did. I nearly let go.'

His gloved hand closed on my shoulder and shook me lightly. 'Fitz, I did not think you had even begun to try. I told you to stop agonizing about it and you fell silent. I thought you were sulking.' He cocked his head. 'Only moments have passed since we last spoke.'

'Only moments?' I rested my forehead on my knees. I felt sick with fear and dazed with longing. It had been so easy. I could drop my walls and be gone. Just . . . gone. I'd merge with those other rushing entities and wash away with them. My hopeless quest would be abandoned along with the loss I felt whenever I thought of Bee. Gone would be the deep shame. Gone the humiliation that everyone knew how badly I had failed as a father. I could stop feeling and thinking.

'Don't go,' the Fool said softly.

'What?' I sat up slowly.

His grip tightened slowly on my shoulder. 'Don't go where I can't follow you. Don't leave me behind. I'd still have to go on. I'd still have to return to Clerres and try to kill them all. Even though I would fail. Even though they would have me in their power again.' He let go of me and crossed his arms as if to contain himself. I wasn't aware of the connection I'd felt from his touch until he removed it. 'Some day we must part. It's inevitable. One of us will have to go on without the other. We both know that. But Fitz, please. Not yet. Not until after this hard thing is done.'

'I won't leave you.' I wondered if I lied. I'd tried to leave him. This insane mission would be easier if I were working alone. Probably still impossible but my failure would be less horrific. Less shameful to me.

He was silent for a time, looking into the distance. His voice was hard and desperate as he demanded, 'Promise me.'

'What?'

'Promise me that you won't give in to Chade's lure. That I won't find you somewhere sitting like an empty sack with your mind gone. Promise me you won't try to abandon me like useless baggage. That you won't leave me behind so I'm "safe". Out of your way.'

I reached for the right words, but it took me too long to find them. He did not hide his hurt and bitterness as he said, 'You can't, can you? Very well. At least I know my standing. Well, my old friend, here is something I can promise you. No matter what you do, Fitz— no matter if you stand or fall, run or die—I must go back to Clerres and do my best to pull it all down around their ears. As I told you before. With you or without you.'

I made a final effort. 'Fool. You know I am the best man for this task. I know that I work best alone. You should let me do this my way.'

He was motionless. Then he asked, 'If I said that to you, and if it were true, would you allow me to go alone into that place? Would you sit idly by and wait for me to rescue Bee?'

An easy lie. 'I would,' I said heartily.

He said nothing. Did he know I lied? Probably. But we had to recognize what was real. He could not do this. His shaking terror had created serious doubt in me. If he succumbed to it in Clerres . . . I simply could not take him with me. I knew his threat was real. He would find his way there, with or without me. But if I could get there before him and do my task, if the deed was done, he'd have no quest.

But would he ever forgive me?

While I'd been silent, he'd stored the pouch of elfbark in his pack. He sipped from his cup. 'My tea's gone cold,' he announced. He stood, cup and saucer in hand. He smoothed his hair and flounced his skirts into order, and the Fool was gone. Amber trailed her fingers along the wall until she found the door and then left me sitting alone on the narrow bunk.

The Fool and I had one serious quarrel on that journey. I came to Amber's cabin one evening at our agreed-upon time as Spark was leaving. Her face was pale and strained, and she gave me a tragic look as she left. I wondered if Amber had rebuked her. I dreaded finding him in a dark and irrational mood. Slowly, I closed the door behind me.

Inside the room, yellow candles burned in glass and the Fool perched on the lower bunk. His grey woollen night robe had seen much wear, probably purloined from Chade's clothing stash. The shadows under his eyes and the resigned droop of his mouth made him older. I sat down on the bunk opposite him and waited. Then I saw my hastily stitched pack beside him. 'What's that doing here?' I asked. For one moment I thought that some accident had brought it to his room.

He set a possessive hand on it and spoke hoarsely. 'I have promised to take all blame for this. Even so, I fear I may have broken Spark's friendship to do this. She brought it to me.'

Cold spread out of my belly and through my veins. I made a conscious and difficult choice. No anger. Fury surged against my wilful blocking. I knew but still I asked, 'And why would you ask her to do that?'

'Because Perseverance mentioned to her that you had books that belonged to Bee. Sometimes he saw you read what she had written there. Two books, one with a bright embossed cover, and the other plain. He recognized her hand on the page when he climbed past you to his bunk.'

He paused. I shivered with fear of how angry I might become. I controlled my breath as Chade had taught me, the silent breathing of an assassin on the verge of a kill. I quenched my emotions. The violation I felt was too immense.

The Fool spoke softly. 'I think she kept a dream journal. If she is mine, if she carries the blood of a White, then she will dream. The drive to share those dreams, to speak or write them, would be overpowering. She will have done it. Fitz, you are angry. I can feel it like storm waves lashing my shores. But I must know what she wrote. You have to read these books to me. From start to finish.'

'No.' One word. For one word, I could keep my voice level and calm.

His shoulders rose and fell with the strength of the breath he took. Did he struggle for control as I did? His voice was taut as a hangman's rope. 'I could have hidden this from you. I could have had Spark steal the books and read them to me here in stealth. I didn't.'

I unclenched my fists and my throat. 'That you didn't wrong me in that way makes this no less of an affront.'

He took his gloved hand from the bag. He put both his hands, palms up, on his knees. I had to lean closer to hear his whisper. 'If you think these the random writings of a small child, your anger is justified. But you cannot believe that. These are the writings of a White Prophet.' He dropped his voice even lower. 'These are the writings of your daughter, Fitz, your little Bee. And mine.'

If he had struck me in the belly with a stave's end, the impact could not have been worse. 'Bee was my little girl.' It came out a wolf's growl. 'I don't want to share her!' Honesty can be like a boil that bursts at the most unfortunate time. Had I known the source of my anger before I spoke it aloud?

'I know you don't. But you must.' He set his hand lightly on the pack. 'This is all that she could leave for us. Other than one glorious instant of holding her and watching her promise explode all around me like a geyser of light into a dark night, it is all of her that I will ever know. Please, Fitz. Please. Give me that much of her.'

I was silent. I could not. There was too much in those books. In her journal, there was too little mention of me from the days when she had held herself apart from me. Too much of a small girl fighting alone the ugly, childish battles with the other Withywoods children. Too many entries that made me feel cowardly and ashamed of what a blind father I had been. Her account of her clash with Lant and how I had promised her afterward that I would always take her part showed how I had failed in that regard. How could I read those pages aloud to the Fool? How could I bare my shame?

He knew I could not share those writings, even before he had asked me. He knew me that well; he knew that there were some things I could not yield. Why did he even dare to ask? With both hands he lifted the pack to cradle it to his breast. The tears started in his golden eyes and traced the scars on his face as they ran down his cheeks. He held out the pack, surrendering to me. I felt like a thwarted child whose parent gives in to his tantrum. I took the pack and immediately opened it. There was little in it save the books and Molly's candles. I had stowed most of my clothing, the Elderling firebrick and other possessions in the tidy cabin cupboards. In the bottom, one of my shirts wrapped the tubes of dragon-Silver. I had judged my pack to be the most private place to keep such things.

They were wrapped as I had left them. He had spoken true; he hadn't rummaged. A waft of fragrance rose to me. I breathed in Molly's perfumes from the candles. With them came calm. Clarity. I lifted the books out to shift the candles to a safer position.

His words were hesitant. 'I'm sorry if I've hurt you. Please, don't blame Spark. Or Perseverance. It was a chance remark on his part, and the girl acted under duress.'

Molly's calmness. Molly's stubborn sense of fairness. Why was it so hard? Was there anything in those books that he did not already know about me? What could I lose? Was not all lost to me already?

Did he not share that loss?

Snow had dampened one corner of Bee's dream journal. It had dried, but the leather cover had puckered slightly, rippling the embossing. I tried to smooth it with my thumb. It resisted. I opened it slowly. I cleared my throat. 'On the first page,' I said, and my voice squeaked tight. The Fool looked blindly toward me, tears streaming down his cheeks. I cleared my throat again. 'On the first page there is a drawing of a bee. It is exactly the size of a bee and exactly the colours of a bee. Above the bee, written very carefully in a sort of arc, are the words "This is my dream journal, of my important dreams."'

His breath caught in his throat. He sat very still. I stood up. Crossing that tiny room took less than three steps. Something—not pride, not selfishness, something I had no name for—made those three steps the steepest climb I'd ever attempted. I sat down beside him with the book open on my lap. He was not breathing. I reached across and lifted his bare hand by its woollen sleeve. I brought it over to the page and lightly skimmed the arch of letters with his drooping fingers. 'Those are the words.' I lifted again and manoeuvred his forefinger onto the bee. 'And here is the bee she painted.'

He smiled. He lifted his wrist to dash the tears from his face. 'I can feel the ink she put on the page.'

Together we read our daughter's book. It was still a barbed thought for me to name her so, but I forced myself to it. We did not read it swiftly. That was his decision, not mine. And to my surprise, he did not ask that I read her journal. It was her dreams he wanted to hear. It became our ritual as we parted each evening. A few dreams from her book, read aloud. I read no more than three or four of her dreams every night. Often I read each one over as many as a dozen times. I watched his lips move silently as he committed them to memory.

He smiled when I read a favourite dream, of wolves running. A dream of candles made him abruptly sit up straight, and then fall into a long and pensive silence. Her dream of being a nut puzzled him as much as it did me. He wept the evening I read her dream of the Butterfly Man. 'Oh, Fitz, she had it. She had the gift. And they destroyed it.'

'As we shall destroy them,' I promised him.

'Fitz.' His voice halted me at the door. 'Are we sure she is destroyed? You were delayed in the Skill-pillars when you travelled from Aslevjal, but eventually you emerged at Buckkeep.'

'Give up that hope. I was a trained Skill-user. I emerged. Bee went in untrained, with no experienced guide, part of a chain of untrained folk. So we know from Shun. There was no sign of them when Nettle's coterie went after her. No trace of them when we followed that same route, months later. She is gone, Fool. Tattered away to nothing.' I wished he had not made me speak the words aloud. 'All that is left for us is vengeance.'

I did not sleep well on Tarman. It was, in some ways, like sleeping on the back of an immense animal and always being aware of him with my Wit-sense. Often I had slept with the wolf's back against my belly, but Nighteyes had been a comfort, for he shared his wild awareness of our surroundings with my duller human senses. I had always slept better when he was near me. Not so with Tarman. He was a creature apart from me. It was like trying to sleep with someone staring at me. I sensed no malevolence, but the constant awareness made me jittery.

So it was that I was sometimes awake and restless in the middle of the night, or in the dark-grey time that comes before dawn. Dawn was a strange thing on the Rain Wild River. During the day, we travelled down a stripe of daylight in the centre of the river while the looming trees to either side blocked both sunrise and sunset. But my body knew when it was dawn, and often I would awake in the pre-dawn and go out onto the still, damp deck to stand in the un-silence of the slowly-waking forest that surrounded us. I found a small measure of peace in those hours when I was as close to alone as one can be on a ship. There was always a hand on anchor watch, but for the most part they respected my stillness.

One such pre-dawn time, I was standing on the port side, looking back at the way we had come. I held a cup of steaming tea in my two hands, a welcome warmth. I blew on it softly and watched the shifting plumes of steam. I was about to take a sip when I became aware of a light footfall on the deck behind me.

'Morning,' I said quietly to Spark as she came up beside me. I had not turned my head to look at her, but if she was surprised at my awareness of her, she didn't show it. She came to stand beside me, resting her hands on the railing.

'I can't say I'm sorry,' she said. 'I'd be lying.'

I took a sip of the tea. 'Thank you for not lying to me,' I said, and I meant it. Chade had always stressed that lying was an essential skill for any spy and had required me to practise artificial sincerity. The thought made me wonder if she actually was lying and truly was sorry. I dismissed the strange idea.

'Are you angry with me?' she asked.

'Not at all,' I lied. 'I expect you to be loyal to your mistress. I'd mistrust you if you weren't.'

'But don't you think I should be more loyal to you than to Lady Amber? I've known you longer. Chade trained me. And told me to listen to you.'

'When he had to abandon you, you chose a new mentor. Be loyal to Lady Amber.' I gave her a piece of truth. 'It comforts me that she has someone as competent as you watching over her at all times.'

She was nodding and looking at her hands. Good hands. The clever hands of a spy or an assassin. I ventured a question. 'How did you know about the books?'

'From Perseverance. Not that he thought he was betraying a secret. It was when you said we should all be learning. Per and I were talking later, and he said he did not like the sitting still and staring at paper part of learning to read. But he said that you had a book that Bee had written. She had shown him some of his letters and he had recognized the book was hers by the way the letters were made. He mentioned it to me since he hoped that if he learned to read, he could some day read what his friend had written.'

I nodded. I had never said to the boy that the books were private. He'd rescued one of them when the bear had wrecked our camp. He'd even commented on them. I could not blame him for telling Spark. But I found I could still blame her for locating the books in my pack and then taking it to Amber. Had she handled Molly's candles? Did she know of the tubes of Silver in my socks? I did not say anything but I think she still felt the rebuke.

'She told me where to look and asked me to fetch it. What was I to do?'

'What you did,' I said shortly. I wondered why she had sought me out and begun this conversation. I had not rebuked her nor treated her any differently since she had given my books to the Fool. The silence grew long. I cooled the heat of the anger I felt and suddenly it became cold wet embers, drenched by my discouragement with our quest. What did it matter? Sooner or later, the Fool would have found a way to get at the books. And now that he had, it felt right that he know what was in Bee's dream book. There was no logic to me feeling angry or injured that Spark had facilitated it. But still . . .

She cleared her throat and said, 'Chade taught me about secrets. How powerful they are. And how once more than one person knows the secret, it can become a danger rather than a source of power.' She paused, then added, 'I know how to respect secrets that are not mine. I want you to know that. I know how to keep to myself secrets that do not need to be revealed.'

I gave her a sharp look. The Fool had secrets. I knew some of them. Was she offering me some of the Fool's secrets as a peace offering for her theft of Bee's books? It offended me that she thought I could be bribed with my friend's secrets. Chances were that I already knew them, but even if they were ones I did not know, I had no desire to gain them through her betrayal. I frowned at her and looked away.

She was quiet for a time. Then she spoke in a carefully measured way, her voice resigned. 'I want you to know that I feel a loyalty to you as well. Not as great a connection as I feel to Lady Amber, but I know that you protected me as best you could when Lord Chade began to fade. I know that you put me with Lady Amber as much for my sake as for hers. I have a debt to you.'

I nodded slowly, but said aloud, 'The best way you can repay me is to serve Lady Amber well.'

She stood silently beside me as if she were waiting for me to say something more. When I didn't, she added with a small sigh, 'Silence keeps a secret. I understand.'

I continued to stare out over the water. This time she ghosted away from me so softly that only my Wit told me when I was alone again.

*   *   *

On a clear, calm afternoon we came upon a Rain Wild settlement. The banks of the river had not grown any more welcoming. The trees of the forest came right to the edge of the water, or perhaps it would be more correct to say that the swollen river had invaded the skirts of the forest. The trees that overhung the water were fresh with gleaming new leaves. Brightly plumaged birds were shrieking and battling over nesting sites, and that was what drew my eyes upward. I stared at the largest nest I'd ever seen, and then saw a child emerge from it and walk briskly along the limb back toward the trunk. I was gaping, soundless for fear that any shout I raised might cause the child to fall. Big Eider saw the direction of my gaze, and lifted a hand in greeting. A man emerged from what I now saw as a tiny hut hung in a tree and waved before following the child.

'Is it a hunter's shelter?' I asked him and he stared at me as if my words made no sense.

Bellin was passing by on the deck. 'No, it's a home. Rain Wild folk have to build in the trees. No dry land. They build small and light. Sometimes five or six little rooms hung in the same tree. Safer than one big one.' She paced by me, intent on some nautical task and left me gaping at the village that festooned the trees.

I stayed on the deck until early evening, teaching my eyes to find the small clusters of hanging chambers. As the sky darkened, lights began to gleam from some of them, illuminating the flimsy walls so that they glowed like distant lanterns in the treetops. That night we moored alongside several smaller boats, and folk came down from the trees to ask for gossip and offer small trades. Coffee and sugar were the most sought-after items and these they traded in small quantities for freshly harvested tree greens that made a refreshing tea and strings of bright snail shells. Bellin made a gift of a shell necklace to Spark and she expressed such delight over it that the woman actually smiled.

'We're close to Trehaug,' Leftrin told us at the galley table that night. 'Probably pass Cassarick tomorrow morning and be in Trehaug in the afternoon.'

'You won't stop in Cassarick?' Perseverance asked curiously. 'I thought that was where the dragons hatched.'

'It was.' Leftrin scowled and then said, 'And it's the home of traitors, folk who betrayed the Trader way and never suffered any consequences for it. People who harboured those who would have slaughtered dragons for their blood and bones and scales. We gave them a chance to redeem themselves and bring justice down on the betrayers. They didn't take it. No Dragon Trader vessel will ever stop there to trade. Not until Candral and his cronies are brought to justice.'

The colour drained from Spark's face. I wondered how well she had hidden the tiny vial of dragon blood she had pilfered from Chade, or if the Fool had used all of it. I'd never heard Leftrin speak so vehemently. Yet Amber sounded calm and almost cheerful as she said, 'I shall be so pleased to see Althea and Brashen again. Or perhaps the word I must use now is "meet". Would that I could see them again, and Boy-O.'

Captain Leftrin looked startled for a moment. 'I'd forgotten you knew them. But in any case, you would not see Boy-O. Some years back, he went off to serve a term or two on Vivacia and never returned. Vivacia had a right to demand him, but I know it was a wrench for Althea and Brashen to let him go. But he's a man now and he has the right to choose his own life. He may wear the Trell name, but from his mother's side, he's a Vestrit and Vivacia has a right to him. And he to her, though the Pirate Isles may not agree with that.' He lowered his voice. 'Paragon was not pleased to see him go. He demanded that there be an exchange. He wanted to be given his namesake, Paragon Ludluck. He's a Ludluck by right, but I hear in the Pirate Isles, they call him Kennitsson.' Leftrin scratched a whiskery cheek. 'Well, Kennitsson is the son of the Queen of the Pirate Isles, and she wasn't willing to let the lad go. Paragon said he'd been cheated. He called it as he saw it, an exchange of hostages— though he was quick to point out that he had a more rightful claim to both men. But Queen Etta of the Pirate Isles simply said no. We even heard a rumour that Kennitsson was courting and was likely to wed a wealthy lady from the Spice Isles. Well, Queen Etta had best wed him off soon if that's what she intends. He's well past the age for it! And if he does wed, then I doubt he will ever sail on Paragon's decks. Paragon becomes moody or disconsolate whenever it is spoken about, so perhaps the fewer questions about Boy-O the better.'

'I don't understand,' I objected softly, though obviously Amber did.

Leftrin hesitated. 'Ah, well.' He spoke slowly, as if revealing a confidence. 'Althea and Brashen captain the *Paragon* now, but for generations he belonged to the Ludluck family. He was stolen and for a time the pirate Igrot used him for foul ends. Scuttled and scarred, he somehow managed to find his way back to a Bingtown beach. And then he was righted and hauled out to languish on shore for years. Brashen Trell and the Vestrit family claimed Paragon when he was a washed-up hulk. They refitted him and put him out to sea again. But he's a Ludluck ship at heart still, and for a time the pirate Kennit Ludluck reclaimed him. And died on Paragon's deck. The ship would want Kennit's son. And Boy-O.'

'And Althea?' Amber queried. 'Had she anything to say about Kennit's son living aboard Paragon?'

Leftrin looked at her. I sensed a tale untold, but he said only, 'Another discussion that were better not held on Paragon's deck. They no longer call him the mad ship, but I would not tempt his temper. Or Althea's. They are bound to disagree on some things.'

Amber nodded gratefully. 'I thank you for your warnings. A careless tongue can do much damage.'

It was hard to sleep that night. A different ship and the next leg of our journey loomed before us. I'd be going deeper into territory unknown to me, and taking people little more than children with me. I spoke into the darkness of our cabin. 'It's in my mind, Perseverance, to ask Captain Leftrin if he might not take you on as a ship's boy. You seem well suited to this trade. What think you of that?'

Silence followed my words. Then his voice came out of the dark, tinged with alarm. 'You mean, afterwards? When we are homeward bound again?'

'No. I mean tomorrow.'

His voice was lower when he said, 'But I vowed my service to you, sir.'

'I could release you from that vow. Help you set your feet on a brighter and cleaner way than the one I must follow.'

I heard him draw a long breath. 'You could release me from your service, sir. Indeed, if you chose to turn me out, I could no longer claim to be yours. But only Bee could release me from the promise I made to avenge her. Turn me off if you wish, sir, but I will still have to follow this to the end.'

I heard Lant turn over in his bunk. I had thought him asleep and his voice was so thick that perhaps he had been. 'Don't even bring it up to me,' he warned me. 'It's as the boy said. I gave a promise to my father, and you can't ask me to break it. We follow you, Fitz, to the end. No matter how bitter.'

I said nothing, but my mind went to work immediately. What would constitute 'the end' for Lant? Could I convince him that he had done his duty and could honourably return to Buckkeep without me? I did not judge it safe to put Spark and Per on a ship home without a protector. I could claim I'd had an urgent Skill-summons from Dutiful for Lant to return home to Chade. By the time he found out it was false, he'd be home. Yes. I pulled up my knees to fit better in the small bunk and closed my eyes. That part, at least, was settled. A small but convincing lie in Bingtown and I could get him onto a ship home. Now I just had to find a way to pry Perseverance loose from me. And Spark.

The next day went as Leftrin had predicted it would. The crew began to say their goodbyes to us at breakfast. 'Oh, I shall so miss having you aboard,' Alise exclaimed to Amber.

Bellin had left shell earrings next to Spark's plate. The dour deckhand had grown fond of the girl. Per made the rounds of the various crewmen, making his own farewells.

We spent our last hours on the roof of the deckhouse, for the day was almost calm not chill at all, as long as one's coat was closed. The weather had broken and there was a stripe of blue sky over the river. We passed the dragon's hatching beach, as Skelly pointed it out to us, and then the treetop city of Cassarick. We did not pause nor did Leftrin return any of the greetings shouted down to us. In the stretch of river between Cassarick and Trehaug the little hanging dwellings were as thick as apples on a tended tree, and I did not know how he could tell where one settlement ended and the next began. But at some point, the captain began to return the friendly waves of folk from their treetop homes. We began to see floating docks tied up to the tree trunks, and small vessels moored to them. There were people out fishing, sitting straddled on the tree trunks that overhung the water and letting their lines drop straight down into the river. Tarman swung wide of them to avoid the dangling lines. I was fascinated by the hanging walkways and the well-travelled branches that functioned as footpaths. Spark sat beside Amber and me, pointing up at the trees and exclaiming over how some children ran heedlessly along a branch she would have thought too narrow to traverse with care.

'Trehaug docks are just around the next bend!' Skelly shouted up at us as she passed by the deckhouse. Big Eider was guiding Tarman in closer to the thickly banked trees. The water ran quieter and shallower, and soon the crew unshipped their poles and began to slow the *Tarman* and then to guide him. It struck me that something felt odd, as if more was at work than merely the crew with their poles. The ship seemed too responsive. When I commented on it, Spark said, 'But Tarman is a liveship. That means he helps the crew get him to where they need him to be.'

'How?' I was intrigued.

She grinned. 'Study his wake the next time we dock for the night.' At my puzzled look she added, 'And think of a frog's legs, kicking.'

We rounded the bend and my first glimpse of Trehaug put Tarman's 'legs' out of my mind. It was the oldest of the Rain Wild cities. The immense trees that over hung the wide, grey river were festooned with bridges, walkways and homes of all sizes. The swampy, flood-prone land beneath the branches of the ancient forest allowed no permanent dwellings. The city of Trehaug was built almost entirely in the branches of the trees that lined the river.

Dwellings as big as manor houses were built in the lower, thicker branches. They put me somewhat in mind of the houses of the Mountain Kingdom, where the trees were integral parts of the structures. But these were not as integrated into their jungle setting. I could as easily believe that some storm had blown a grand home from Farrow and deposited it here. They were all built of rich wood with glass windows and looked impossibly grand and massive. I was admiring one that seemed to have been built entirely around the trunk of one immense tree when Skelly said, 'That's the Khuprus home. Reyn's family.' I stared up at the looming structure. Oh. Wealth and importance personified. His family had been of the ruling class long before he became a 'king' in Kelsingra. Old wealth, shown by the weathering of the ancient support timbers. I stored that bit of insight. So much useful information that I intended to relay to Buckkeep. When I reached Bingtown, I'd send several messenger birds to Dutiful. What I wished to share would not fit into one message capsule.

'Oh, look! Have you ever seen such a thing! He's magnificent!' Perseverance's shout drew my eyes from the tree and down to the long dock ahead of us. A liveship was moored alongside it. Sails furled, it rode placidly at the moorage. The silvery wood of his hull proclaimed this was no ordinary ship. Unlike Tarman, this liveship had a fully carved figurehead. His dark head was bowed over his muscular chest as if he were drowsing over his crossed arms. A strange posture for a figurehead. Then the hair on my scalp and arms prickled as he slowly lifted his head.

'He's looking at us!' Spark exclaimed. 'Oh, Lady Amber, if only you could see this! It's truly alive! The figurehead has turned and is looking at us!'

I stared at the ship, my mouth hanging open. Spark and Perseverance looked from the ship to me. I was speechless, but Lant spoke the words aloud. 'Sweet Eda. Fitz, he has your face. Right down to the break in your nose.'

Amber cleared her throat. She spoke breathlessly into our shocked silence. 'Fitz. Please. I can explain everything.'

ELEVEN

Passage

This is my most frightening dream. I dream it as a vine that splits into two branches. On one branch there are four candles growing. One by one they are kindled to flame, but their light does not illuminate. Instead, a crow says, 'Here are four candles to light you to bed. Four candles lit means their child is dead. Four candles burn for the end of their ways. The Wolf and the jester have wasted their days.'

Then, on the other branch of the vine, three candles are suddenly kindled. Their light is almost blinding. And the same crow says, 'Three flames burn brighter than the sun. Their blaze engulfs an evil done. Their angry mourning purpose gives. They do not know their child still lives.'

Then the crow suddenly has a broken candle. She drops it and I catch it. In a slow and frightening voice she says, 'Child, light the fire. Burn the future and the past. It's what you were born to do.'

I woke up shaking all over and I got out of bed and ran to my parents' chamber. I wanted to sleep with them, but instead my mother brought me back to my bed and lay down beside me. She sang me a song until I could fall asleep again. I was very young when I dreamed this; I had only recently learned how to climb out of my bed. But I have never forgotten the dream or the crow's rhyme. I draw the candle as he held it, broken and the pieces held together only by the wick in the middle.

Bee Farseer's dream journal

The very best part of our sea voyage was how sick Dwalia was. We had a tiny room for all four of us. There were two narrow bunks in it. Dwalia took one and for days she stayed in it. Her vomit bucket and her sweaty bedding stank. In the windowless cabin, the smells in the still air were a soup that rose around us, thicker and deeper every day.

The first two days of our journey, I was wretchedly seasick. Then Dwalia screeched at us that our noise and motion were making her worse and ordered us out. I tottered after Vindeliar and Kerf. We passed through a dark space between the deck and the cargo hold where oil lanterns swung gently from the beams. Bunks lined the curved walls, and in the centre hammocks hung, some full and some empty. It smelled of tar, lamp oil, sweat and bad food. I trailed behind Kerf to a ladder and followed him up and out of a square hatch. Out in the air, with the wind blowing chill in my face, I immediately felt better.

Once my stomach accepted that the world would surge and tilt around me, I felt fine. Dwalia knew I could not escape while the ship was at sea, and was too ill to think beyond that. We had brought some food with us, but sometimes we would join the other travellers at the evening meal. There was a kitchen called a galley, and a room called a mess where the long table had a little fence around the edge to corral any sliding plates or mugs. The food was neither good nor bad, and after my privation, I was glad of anything to eat on a regular basis.

I spoke little, obeyed the few commands Dwalia gave, and fiercely observed every detail of the ship and my two companions. I wished them to believe that I had given up defiance, to lull their vigilance. I hoped to discover a way to escape at the next port. The breeze that filled our sails bore me ever farther from my home. Moment by moment, day by day, my former life receded from me. No one could rescue me; no one knew where I was. If I were to escape this fate, I would have to do it myself. I doubted I could win my way back to the Six Duchies, but I could hope for a free life for myself, even if it was in a strange port half a world away from my home.

Dwalia ordered Vindeliar to make us 'uninteresting' to the crew and the other passengers and he kept a loose spell around us. No one spoke to us or watched us as we wandered the ship. Most of the passengers were Chalcedean merchants, accompanying cargo to other destinations. A few were from Bingtown or the Rain Wilds and some were from Jamaillia. The wealthy stayed in cabins; the younger ones filled the canvas hammocks. There were slaves, too, some valuable. I saw a beautiful woman who strode with the pride of a stud horse, despite her slave collar and the pale tattoo beside her nose. I wondered if she had ever been free. I watched an elderly man with a bent back sold for a stack of gold coins. He was a scholar who could speak six languages, and read and write in all of them. He sat stoically as a woman drove a hard bargain for him. Then he bent to ink and paper to write out the bill of sale for himself, his nose very close to the paper. I wondered how much scribe work was left in his knobby fingers and what would become of him as he aged further.

Time passes differently on a ship. Day and night there were always sailors running from task to task. A bell ringing broke time into watches, and I could not seem to sleep through it. When it awoke me at night on the splintery cabin floor, breathing the sour fog of Dwalia's sickness, I longed to escape onto the deck. But Kerf slept snoring across the narrow door. In the bunk above Dwalia's, Vindeliar muttered in his sleep.

If I slept, I dreamed, sometimes the dreams that boiled and seethed in me. When I awoke from those, I traced an account of them onto the plank floor and tried desperately to set them out of my mind, for they were dark dreams of death and blood and smoke.

Several nights into our voyage, as I lay on the floor surrounded by our sparse belongings, I heard Vindeliar moan a single word. 'Brother,' he said, and sighed, sinking deeper into his dreams. I ventured to let crumble the walls I held so firmly against him during the day and stilled my mind to sense his boundaries.

It wasn't what I expected.

Even in his sleep, he kept a leash on Kerf. The Chalcedean had become passive as a milk cow, an attitude much at odds with his warrior's harness and scars. He asked for the food he took and the female passengers were safe from his stare, even the line of female slaves who were picketed on the deck once a day to take the air. Tonight I could feel how Vindeliar draped him in boredom one step short of despair. All triumphant and pleasurable memories were hidden from him. He recalled only days of dull duty. Every day would be yet another one of following his commander's orders. And his commander was Dwalia.

I tried to feel Vindeliar's control of me, but if he tried, it was too subtle for me to find. I had not expected to find a foggy veil draping Dwalia.

Perhaps she had requested it of him? Did she wish to sleep? It was unlikely that she wished to feel so sick as to daily remain in her bed. She had betrayed to him how much she detested him. The day she flung insults at him he had cowered before her disdain. Had that been the first time she had revealed her loathing of him? I explored what he suggested to her: she could trust Vindeliar to manage us; he had repented his brief rebellion. He was her servant, totally loyal to her. He could control Kerf and conceal me for as long as she needed to rest. I tiptoed around the edges of that fog of suggestion. How deep did his careful defiance of her go? Would she guess it when she recovered from her seasickness?

If he allowed her to recover from being seasick! I considered that thought. Was he keeping her queasy? Dwalia ill in bed relieved us of her slaps, pinches and kicks. Was he starting to turn against her? If he no longer served Dwalia, if he wanted his freedom, could I feed that? Could I win him to my side? To escape, to go home?

The instant that seed came into my mind, I threw up my walls as stoutly as I could. He must not suspect what I knew, let alone what I hoped. How did I win his loyalty? What did he most desire?

'Brother,' I breathed, in little more than a whisper.

The rhythm of his stentorian breathing faltered, hitched and then went on. I challenged myself. Was it possible to make my situation worse?

'Brother, I cannot sleep.'

His snoring stopped. After a long silence, he said in wonder, 'You called me "brother"!'

'As you call me,' I responded. What did it mean to him? I must be careful in what I invoked.

'As I dreamed I would call you. And that you would call me in return.' His head shifted on the bundled clothing that served him for a pillow. Sadly he added, 'But the rest of this has not matched my dream. My only dream.'

'Your dream?'

'Yes,' he admitted. With bashful pride he added, 'No one else ever dreamed it. Only me.'

'How could they? It was your dream.'

'You are so ignorant of dreams. Many Whites share the same dreams. If many Whites have dreamed it, it is important to the Path! If a dream comes only once, it probably won't happen. Unless a brave person works hard to make it happen. To find the other dreams that show the journey to it. As Dwalia did for me.'

Dwalia shifted in her bunk, a terrifying sound. So stupid of me! Of course, she would be wakeful. The old snake never truly slept. She had heard our whispered words and would thwart my plan before I even formed it!

And then I felt it. Deep and blessed sleep rolled over me like the softest of blankets, warm but not stifling, muscles eased, headache gentled away, free of the cabin's foul stench. I almost sank into it despite my walls. I wondered how strong it was for Dwalia and if it drenched Kerf too. Should I tell Vindeliar that I knew what he was doing? Could I threaten to betray him to Dwalia if he did not help me?

'You feel what I do, and you guard yourself from it.'

'Yes,' I admitted, as denying it seemed useless. I waited for him to say more but he didn't. He had seemed so fatuous to me, but now, in his silence, I wondered if he considered his strategy. What ploy did I have to get him to speak? 'Would you tell me of your dream?'

He rolled onto his side. I could tell from his voice that he faced me now. He sent his whisper across the small cabin. 'Every morning, Samisal would call for paper and brush. He and I were twice brothers, our parents sister-and-brother, and their parents also. So sometimes I pretended that I had dreamed too, the same dream he had. But they always called me a liar. They knew. So Samisal had all the dreams and I had only one. Even Oddessa, my twin, born as badly made as I was, had dreams. But I had only one. Useless Vindeliar.'

Brother bred to sister? His parentage horrified me, but it had not been his doing. I held back my dismay, to say only, 'But you had one dream?'

'I did. I dreamed I found you. On a day white with snow I called you "brother" and you came with me.'

'It came true, then.'

'Dreams don't "come true",' he corrected me. 'If the dream is on the true Path, we journey toward it. The Four know the Path. They find the correct dreams and send forth Servants to make the Path for the world to follow. Finding the dream-moment is like finding a guidepost on the road. It confirms the Path is true.'

'I see,' I said, though I didn't. 'So your dream brought us together?'

'No,' he admitted sadly. 'My dream was only a tiny dream. A little tiny part, not very important, Dwalia says. I should not think I was important. Many people had better dreams than mine, and those who sort the dreams and put them in order, the collators, knew where we should go and what we should do to make the true Path.'

'Did all the dreams say I was a boy?' That question was simple curiosity on my part.

'I don't know. Most called you a son, or didn't say what you were. In my dream, you were my brother.' I heard him scratch some part of himself. 'So Dwalia is right. My dream was small and not very correct.' He sounded like a disappointed child hoping someone would disagree with him.

'But you saw me and you did call me "brother". Did anyone else dream that part?'

I had never known that silence could be slow, but his was. Satisfaction and vindication vied in his voice as he said, 'No. No one else dreamed it.'

'So perhaps you were the only one who could have found me, brother. No one else could have fulfilled that dream?'

'Yes-s-s.' He savoured the word.

This silence seemed a necessary pause in the world. A time for Vindeliar to possess something he had not realized belonged to him. I held it for as long as I could. Then I asked, 'So, for the dream to be true and confirm the Path, it had to be you. But why did it have to be me?'

'Because you are the one. The Unexpected Son. The one in so many dreams.'

'Are you sure? Alaria and Reppin doubted it.'

'You have to be! You must be.' He sounded more desperate than certain.

He had called me the Unexpected Son when he first found me. I pried a bit more at that. 'So, in your dream, you were the one to find the Unexpected Son. And it was me.'

'I dreamed . . .' His words trailed away. 'I dreamed I found you. Dwalia needed to find the Unexpected Son.' He sounded both frightened and angry as he said, 'I wouldn't have found you if she hadn't been looking for him. She told me to look for him, and I found you and I knew you from my dream! So, you are the Unexpected Son.' He gave a sharp huff of annoyance that I had doubted him.

He knew that his logic was flawed. I could not see him in the darkness to read his face. I spoke gently to avoid angering him. 'But how? How do you know that when I do not know it?'

'I know I dreamed you. I know I found you. There is not much White in me. Some mock me and say none at all. But if I were meant to do one thing, as a White, I was meant to find you. And I did.' Satisfaction warmed those words. He yawned suddenly and his voice went soft at the edges. 'When I am on the Path, I can feel it. It's a nice feeling. Safe. You are not a true dreamer, so you would not know these things.' He sighed. 'It makes no sense to me. In all the dreams they quote at me, the Unexpected Son is the balancing point. Beyond him, all is orderly or all is chaos. At some point, you set us all on a false course. But the divergence created by the Unexpected Son may be full of terrible destruction. Or wondrous good. The course you create might lead toward a thousand possible futures that no one else could open . . .' His voice dwindled away. He sighed. 'I need to sleep now, brother. I cannot rest during the day. When Kerf is asleep is my only chance.'

'Rest then, brother.'

I lay still and for the rest of the night I slept little and plotted much. I stacked up my precious bits of knowledge. Vindeliar had begun to deploy his powers against Dwalia. Controlling Kerf was wearying to him. He believed I was very important, and so perhaps, did Dwalia. But did she still think that I was the Unexpected Son? With a few kind words I had cheered Vindeliar. Might more conversation recruit him to my side? I built a fragile hope. If Vindeliar would aid me we could flee Dwalia in the next port. Surely he could use his magic to smooth my journey home. I smiled, imagining riding up the carriageway to Withywoods. Perseverance would come to meet me. Perhaps my father, too, and Revel would open the door and come down the . . .

But Revel was dead. The stables were burned. Scribe Lant was dead, and maybe Per too. I wondered again if Shun had survived and reached home? She had proven herself far tougher than I had imagined her to be. If she had, would she have told them how they took me through a stone? And if she did, would they try to follow and find me? My heart knew a lurch of hope. My father knew how to travel through the stones. Surely he would come after me!

I curled into a smaller huddle on the floor. A worry tugged at me. Could he guess that we had entered the stone again? The scent of my mother's candle tucked in the front of my shirt reached me. For a moment, it was comfort. Then it was alarm followed by certainty. I'd found the candle because my father had brought it there. Shun had reached home, she'd told him where they had taken me, and he *had* followed. Followed and somehow passed me in the stone. He had dropped this candle. Dropped it, and never picked it up again? I thought of the scatter of possessions I'd found, the tattered remnants of a tent. The bear scat! Had he been attacked there? Had he died? Were his scattered bones sunken in the deep moss under the trees?

I reached for Wolf Father. *If my father was dead, would you know?*

I felt no response. I huddled tight behind my walls. If my father was dead, then no one was coming to rescue me. Not ever. And my dreadful dreams of what I would become would come true.

Unless I saved myself.

TWELVE

The Liveship *Paragon*

For generations the secret of how liveships were created was known only to certain Trader families. By the end of the war with Chalced and with the emergence of the dragon Tintaglia, parts of the secret could no longer be concealed. Over the last decade, the paradox of the living ship, loyal to the family that created it by destroying the creature it would have become, has become ever clearer.

The creation of the liveship begins with a dragon's cocoon. When Rain Wilders first discovered immense logs of an unusual wood, they had no idea that they were dragon pods. The 'logs' had been stored in a glass-roofed chamber in ruins that lay buried beneath the city of Trehaug. The finders assumed they were especially treasured timbers of exotic wood. At the time, the Rain Wilders desperately needed a material that would resist the acid floods of the Rain Wild River. No matter how well-oiled and seasoned their hulls, traditional ships suffered gradual damage from the river water, and during times of white floods, when the river flowed particularly acidic, some boats simply dissolved, spilling cargo and passengers into the toxic water. The 'timber' discovered in the buried Elderling cities proved to be exactly what they needed. Wizardwood, as they named it, was a fine-grained, dense timber, and proved to be ideal for shipbuilding and resistant to the river's acid.

Ships built from this substance were the only ones that could endure repeated journeys on the acid water of the Rain Wild River. These highly desirable vessels became an essential link in the trade in Elderling artefacts which could be ferried out of the ancient ruined cities to the Rain Wild settlements, where they could be sold at exorbitant prices to the world at large.

It was several generations before the first figurehead on a liveship 'awoke'. *Builders and owners were astonished. The* Golden Dawn *was the first figurehead to take on life. Conversation with the figurehead soon revealed that the ship had absorbed the memories of those who had lived aboard him, especially those of his captains, and an attachment to the family who owned him. The ship's knowledge extended to navigation, to the handling of weather and awareness of necessary maintenance. The value of such a ship became inestimable.*

Those who cut the 'timbers' into lumber must have had early knowledge that these logs were not wood. In the heart of each log, they must have discovered a partially-formed dragon. Even if they could not discern what it was, they undoubtedly knew it had contained a living creature at some time. That was the deepest secret of all, one the families kept concealed from all but blood kin. It is believed that prior to the emergence of the dragon Tintaglia from a wizardwood 'log', the liveships themselves were not cognizant of their relationship to dragons.

Of the Bingtown Liveships, Trader Cauldra Redwined

I stood on Tarman's deck and stared up at Paragon's figurehead. My face. And an axe sheathed in the harness across his chest. Lant and Perseverance were transfixed. Spark whispered. 'He's looking at us.'

He was indeed. The figurehead of the docked vessel looked as affronted as I felt. Paragon resembled me in almost every way. 'You can't possibly explain this.'

'I can,' Amber assured me. 'But not now. Later. In private. I promise.'

I made no answer. As the distance between the ships closed, Tarman's crew was busy with their poles, slowing and adroitly guiding him closer to the riverbank. Trehaug was a busy trade centre and there was little open dock space. Ships followed the custom of mooring to one of the docked vessels and crossing a neighbouring deck to reach the shore. I assumed we would do likewise. There was an open space near Paragon but I judged it too tight a fit for Tarman. As we drew closer to Paragon, he returned my gaze, scowling.

'Why does he have blue eyes?' I wondered aloud. My own were dark.

Amber had a strangely sentimental smile on her face. She held her clasped hands to her breast like a grandmother looking on a beloved child, and spoke fondly. 'Paragon chose them. Many of the

Ludlucks, including Kennit, had blue eyes. The Ludlucks were originally his family. I carved his face, Fitz. Or rather, I re-carved it. He had been blinded, his eyes chopped away with a hatchet. He'd been branded with the mark of his tormentor . . . Oh, it's a long and terrible story. When I carved his face, I carved him with his eyes closed, as he wished. For some time, he refused to open them. When he did, they were blue.'

'Why my face?' I demanded. We were nearing the dock.

'Later,' she quietly requested.

Her word was almost lost in the shouted orders as Tarman neared Paragon. Tarman's crew had sprung into action. My four companions and I stood on top of the deckhouse, out of the way, and watched. Our tillerman worked the oar to hold us against the current as the others used poles to keep Tarman from meeting the dock too firmly. On two of the moored vessels, worried deckhands stood ready to stave us off. But Tarman nudged into place as precisely as a sword returning to a sheath. Scully leapt from Tarman's deck to the dock, and in the next moment caught a flung line. She took a quick wrap around a cleat, and then dashed down the dock to catch the next mooring line.

Our squat river barge was a sharp contrast to the tall sailing ship. Tarman's shallow draught enabled him to travel up the river where deep-keeled ships like Paragon could not go. Paragon was meant for deep water and tall waves. He dwarfed us. The figurehead that stared down at us was several times life-size. His gaze shifted suddenly from me to the woman beside me and his judgmental frown blossomed into a smile of incredulity. 'Amber? Is that you? Where have you been for the last twenty-odd years?' He reached huge hands toward her, and if we had been any closer, I think he would have plucked her off Tarman's deck.

She lifted her outstretched arms as if to offer an embrace. 'Far and away, my friend. Far and away! It is so good to hear your voice again.'

'But not to see me. Your eyes are blind. Who has done this to you?' Concern vied with anger.

'Blind as you once were. It's a long tale, old friend, one I promise to tell you.'

'That you will! Who is this with you?' Was there an edge of accusation in his voice?

'Friends of mine, from Buck Duchy, of the Six Duchies. But let me save that telling for when I am on board. Shouting across a dock is no way to converse.'

'I agree!' This shouted comment came from a small, dark-haired woman leaning over Paragon's railing. Her teeth were white in a wind-weathered face. 'Come aboard and welcome. Leftrin and Alise will send your things over, and then I hope they'll join us for a glass or two. Amber, well met! I could scarcely believe the news the bird brought. Come aboard!' She shifted her gaze to me, and her grin widened. 'I look forward to meeting the man who shares a face with our ship.' With that, she ducked back out of sight.

At her words, Paragon's smile dimmed and he crossed his arms on his chest. He turned his head and watched Amber from the corner of his eyes. She gave me half a smile. 'That was Althea Vestrit, aunt to Queen Malta. She is either the captain or the mate on Paragon, depending on who you ask.' She turned her face toward me. 'You will like her, and Brashen Trell.'

Docking and disembarking was a precise and slow process. Captain Leftrin had to be completely satisfied with the docking before he would allow a gangplank to be lowered. He ordered that our possessions be transferred to Paragon. Then he and Alise escorted my small party down the gangplank, across the dock, and then up a rope ladder flung down to us from Paragon's railing. Leftrin led the way, and Lant and then Perseverance followed easily enough. Spark's skirts gave her a bit of trouble as she ascended. I stood holding the ladder taut and waiting for Amber to ascend. 'No need,' the figurehead announced. He twisted lithely from his waist, leaned down low and offered Amber his outstretched hands.

'The figurehead is reaching for you. Be cautious!' I warned her in a low voice.

She did not lower her voice. 'I have no need of caution among old friends. Guide me, Fitz.'

I did so reluctantly, and held my breath as the figurehead closed his hands around her ribs as if she were a child. I stood staring as Paragon lifted her in his huge hands. They were the colour of a man's hands, swarthy with many days outside, but I could still see the grain of the wizardwood he'd been carved from. Of all the Elderling magic, the living figurehead most astonished me, but also created the most unease in me. A dragon, I could understand. It was a creature of flesh and blood, with the same needs and appetites of any animal. But a ship of living wood, something that moved and spoke and apparently thought, but had no need of food or drink, no drive to mate, no hope of progeny? How could one predict the actions or the desires of such a being?

From my position as the last person standing on the docks beside Paragon's ladder I could hear Amber's voice, but she pitched her words to the figurehead and I could not make them out. He held her like a doll and looked intently into her face. Having been blinded himself, would he feel sympathy for her? Could a ship carved out of a dragon cocoon feel sympathy? Not for the first time, I confronted how little of his life the Fool had shared with me. Here, he was known as Amber, a clever, tough woman who had lent her fortune to rebuild Bingtown and help former slaves build new lives in the Rain Wilds. For this portion of our journey, that was who she must be. Amber. A woman who was still a stranger to me.

'Fitz?' Lant leaned over the Paragon's railing. 'Are you coming?'

'Yes.' I climbed up the rope ladder—never as easy a task as it seemed—and stepped onto Paragon's deck. He felt different to Tarman. Much closer to human. Wit and Skill, I sensed him as a living creature. For now, his attention was focused on Amber. I had a few moments to look around.

It had been a long time since I'd been on a ship of this size. I thought back to my journey to the OutIslands and Thick's protracted seasickness. There was an experience I hoped never to repeat! Paragon was smaller than that ship, sleeker and, I suspected, more sea-worthy. Paragon was very well kept. The decks were clear, the lines neatly stowed and even while the ship was tied to the dock, the crew was well occupied.

'Where are Spark and Perseverance?' I asked Lant.

'Exploring, with the permission of Captain Brashen. You and I are invited to join the captain and Lady Althea in their stateroom for refreshments and conversation.'

I looked toward the bow, where Paragon still held Amber. I was reluctant to leave her literally in the ship's grasp, and equally reluctant to offend the folk offering us free passage to Bingtown. There was a lengthy journey ahead of us, down the Rain Wild River and then along the uncertain and boggy coast of the Cursed Shores until we reached Trader Bay. I wished to be on good terms with all. I doubted the Fool would have any caution around the figurehead. Obviously Amber had long ago made her decision to trust him.

'Fitz?' Lant nudged me.

'I'm coming.' I glanced back at Amber. I could see her face but not his. The wind off the river was rustling her skirts and stirring the bits of hair that showed around her scarf. She was smiling at something he'd said. Her arms rested easily on top of his hands as if they were the arms of a comfortable chair. I decided to trust her instincts, and followed Lant.

The door into the captain's stateroom was open to the spring day and I heard lively voices. Spark laughed at something. We entered, to see Leftrin gripping the back of Per's collar and holding him almost off the floor. 'He's a rascal and a lackwit, so see you work him hard!' he announced. Just as my muscles tightened, Leftrin laughed and gave the grinning boy a half-shove, half-toss toward a well-muscled man of middle years. The man caught my boy by the shoulder and grinned in return, showing very white teeth in a neatly trimmed beard. He slapped Per on the back. 'Running the rigging is what we call it, and yes, you can learn it. But only if Clef, Althea, or I authorize it. We'll tell you when we want you up there and exactly what we want you to do.' The man glanced up at Leftrin. 'Does he know any of his knots?'

'A few,' I interjected into the conversation. I found I was smiling at Captain Trell.

'Oh, more than a few,' Leftrin objected. 'Bellin had him working on them in the evenings, when you were closeted with your lady. We've given him a good start on being a deckhand. But Trell is right, lad. If you venture into the rigging, go the first times with someone who knows what she's about, and listen! Listen exactly and do exactly and only what you are told. Do you hear me?'

'I do, sir,' Per was grinning from one captain to the other. If he'd been a puppy, he'd have been wriggling all over. I felt proud and a bit jealous.

Trell advanced toward me, hand out, and we exchanged a Trader's handshake. His dark eyes met mine, a frank and open gaze. 'I've never had a prince on board but Leftrin tells me you're an easy one to deal with. We do our best, but Paragon is a ship, and we live as that dictates.'

'I assure you, I'm not a grand noble. I spent a fair amount of time pulling an oar on the *Rurisk* during the Red-Ship Wars. My gear was under my bench, and half the time, that was my bed as well.'

'Ah, you'll do well then. I'd like to introduce Althea Vestrit. I've tried to make her a Trell, but she persists in being a Vestrit, stubbornness being the hallmark of her family's women. But if you've met Malta, you'll know that already.'

Althea was seated at a table laden with a fat steaming pot, cups, and little cakes on a platter. The pot was Elderling made; it had a gleaming, metallic finish and was embellished with snakes. No. They were sea serpents, for tiny fish were also there. The little cakes were studded with seeds and bits of bright pink fruit. Althea half-stood and leaned over the table to extend her handshake to me. 'Don't mind him. Though my niece did get more than her fair share of Vestrit "character", as we call it.' The calluses on her hand rasped against mine. Her smile made lines at the corners of her eyes. Her dark hair was threaded with grey and was bound back from her face and braided into a tight queue down her back. Her grip was the equal of any man's, and I felt she took my measure as much as I did hers. She sat down again and said, 'Well. It's a strange pleasure to see the man who wears my ship's face—though doubtless you think of it the other way. Please, come to our table, and have a cup of coffee and tell me how it felt to see the figurehead Amber carved to match the man who held her heart.'

The silence that follows a very awkward statement has a peculiar noise of its own. I swear that I could hear Lant holding his breath and literally feel the wide-eyed stares from Spark and Perseverance. I found a hasty lie. 'Coffee would be welcome! It may be spring, but the wind off the river cuts right down to my bones.'

She grinned. 'You never knew she'd carved your face for the ship, did you?'

Was honesty becoming a dangerous habit? What would Chade have thought? I allowed myself an embarrassed laugh and conceded, 'Until a very short time ago, I did not.'

'Oh, sweet Sa,' Althea muttered, and Brashen brayed out the suppressed laugh that he could hold back no longer. I heard a soft exclamation behind me and turned to find that Alise had joined us.

'Oh, the things our women do to us!' Brashen exclaimed and came to clap me on the shoulder. 'Sit down, sit down, and Althea will pour. There's brandy, too, and that might take the chill away a bit better! Alise! Lord Lant, will you join us? And, well, if I invite your serving folk to join us, am I breaching manners? You'll have to bluntly advise me on these things.'

'Travelling rough soon breaks down the walls of protocol. Perseverance and Spark, would you care to join us for coffee?'

Perseverance made a face before he could control his features. 'No, sir, thank you very much all the same. I'd like to go and look around the ship, if I may?'

'You may,' Althea and Brashen spoke in unison, and then Brashen thought to look toward me and add, 'That is, if your master approves.'

'Of course. Per, if someone tells you to get out of the way, jump lively.'

'I will.' He was halfway to the cabin door when Spark spoke.

'I want—' she began, and then halted. Her cheeks turned red.

Every adult was looking at her. Alise smiled. 'Just say it, dear.'

She opened her mouth and then said in a subdued voice. 'I should see to unpacking Lady Amber's things.'

'Or,' Alise suggested, 'you could go and look about the deck with Per. And no harm done for being interested in the ship. From the Rain Wilds to Bingtown, women have stood on an equal footing with men for quite some time. Even if some forget it from time to time.' She smiled at me. 'When you were otherwise occupied, Spark had many questions for Bellin and me about Tarman. She learns quickly, and I assure you, there's no harm in a girl knowing more than ribbons and sewing.'

I defended the Six Duchies. 'I assure you, in the Six Duchies we do not confine our women at all. They are minstrels and guards, scribes and huntswomen, or whatever other occupation appeals to them.'

Spark found her tongue. 'I wasn't asking permission. That is, I was, but I also wanted to ask if it would offend if I donned trousers for my time on the ship? For I, too, would like to climb the rigging, and skirts made it a task even to climb the ship's ladder.'

A peculiar look passed over Perseverance's face. He stood, his hand on the door and looked at Spark as if she had turned into a cat.

Althea stood up and dusted her hands on the legs of her well-worn trousers. 'I think we could find you some boy's clothing on board the ship.'

Spark grinned and suddenly I saw Ash's countenance. 'I've some from home, if no one minds me wearing them.'

'It won't be noticed at all. I truly don't know how Alise masters being ever the lady in lovely skirts.' Althea smiled at her friend before nodding to Spark. 'Run off and find your other clothes. All your gear should be on board in your cabins. We're a larger vessel than the *Tarman*, but we're built for cargo, not passengers. I've put Prince FitzChivalry and "Lady" Amber in the same room she once shared with Jek and me. Lord Lant, Clef has offered to share his cabin with you. He's given you the bunk and we'll hang a hammock for him. Per we put belowdeck with the crew.' She gave me an apologetic look. 'For now, we put your serving girl in with you and Amber, but—'

'Actually I don't mind a hammock belowdecks alongside Perseverance. It's better than sleeping on an open deck.'

'Oh, we can do better than that. No need to separate you from your lady.' This from Brashen.

We were back to an awkward silence as I sought words. It was broken by a loud shout that vibrated the planks of the deck. 'Ahl-theee-a!'

'Paragon,' she explained unnecessarily. 'I'd best see what he needs. Don't wait for me, but help yourself to coffee and cakes. Brashen, would you show them where their cabins are?'

'Of course.'

'We must take our leave, I fear.' This from Alise with her hand on Leftrin's arm. 'There's cargo to load. It must be tallied as it comes aboard and stowed to Leftrin's liking. This cargo cannot brook delay. Young fruit trees in tubs of earth from Bingtown, and ducklings and goslings. I suspect we'll be sorry to have those aboard, but they cannot be worse than the sheep were. Farewell! We enjoyed your company.'

Hasty good wishes were exchanged and they took their leave.

After Althea had left, Trell said quietly, 'Our ship is out of temper lately. My son is serving aboard a different liveship right now— *Vivacia*, the Vestrit family ship. Paragon misses him keenly. Sometimes, he can be like a spoiled child. If he says anything peculiar to you, let me know.' He looked troubled and I strove to keep the alarm from my face as I wondered what sort of tantrum a living ship might throw. He avoided meeting my eyes as he added, 'Let me show you around a bit. The pot will keep the coffee hot.' As we left the cabin, Lant raised his brows at me and I gave a shrug.

Brashen handed Per off to a deckhand named Clef. He had an old slave tattoo beside his nose and a long tarred braid down his back. 'Gotcher gear below,' he said to Per with an echo of a foreign accent, faded beyond recognition. They went off together and I smiled to see Per unconsciously mimic the sailor's walk. Lant followed them. Brashen led Spark and me to a cabin that was largely occupied by Amber's and Spark's baggage. My own packs seemed small in comparison to their bulging bags. I wondered if they had acquired more garments in Kelsingra and how we would manage when it came time to carry our possessions on our backs. My smaller pack that held Bee's books and Molly's candles had safely crossed to Paragon. The Elderling firebrick resided there as well. I hefted it and knew that below Chade's carefully packed firepots, my shirt still bundled the heavy glass containers of Skill. Amber had taken charge of the lovely bracelet.

Spark immediately burrowed into her bag like a hound in search of a remembered bone. We left her there.

As we walked toward the bow, Trell introduced me to crew-members. They gave a nod or smile but never paused in their tasks. Kitl, Cord, Twan, Haff, Ant, Jock, Cypros . . . I stacked the names in my memory and tried to attach them to faces. Ant was halfway up the mast and my heart jumped when she waved at me with both hands. Trell was not amused. 'One hand for yourself and one for the ship!' he roared. 'You don't take unnecessary risks on my deck! I'll put you right back in the tree you came from!'

'Sir!' she responded, and went scampering up the mast like a squirrel avoiding a barking dog. Trell rolled his eyes. 'If she lives to grow up, she'll be a great deckhand. But she doesn't have a scrap of fear, and that may get her killed.' He gestured at Trehaug. 'When a child grows up there, the mast of a ship seems short.'

I followed his waving hand. The towering trees that held Trehaug dwarfed the naked masts of the *Paragon*. The swooping branches of the dense forest were as busy with foot-traffic as the streets and byways of any city. Everywhere throughout the trees were signs of human habitation. Signboards advertised a tavern while another in the shape of a basket advertised all manner of wickerwork. I saw some people veiled as I had always heard the Rain Wilders went, and others with exposed faces and bared arms that revealed scales and growths. A wicker lift was hoisted into the upper branches while pedestrians travelled up and down a stairway that spiralled around the trunk. I had stopped to gawk and realized that Brashen was waiting for me.

'Did you grow up here?' I asked Brashen.

'Here? Oh, no. I'm Bingtown born and bred, from an illustrious Trader family. But I'm the black sheep and not the heir, so here I am, captaining a liveship instead of minding the family fortune.' He was clearly well satisfied with his lot.

'Not too different to my tale,' I told him. 'Amber may call me a prince, but my name tells the truth. "Fitz" means I was born on the wrong side of the blankets. So, I'm a Farseer, but a bastard one.'

'That so? Well, that explains why you might end up on the end of an oar on a war galley.'

I grinned. 'Yes. Bastards are a bit more expendable than princes.' And that simply, we were at ease with each other. We strolled toward the bow. I could hear voices, Amber's and Althea's and the ship's but the wind off the river and the noise of the tree city meant I could not make out their words.

'. . . vengeance, then?' Althea asked as we drew closer.

'More than vengeance,' Amber replied. 'We go to break a cage of cruelty. To destroy a court that has grown only greedier and more corrupt with every passing year.' She lowered her voice and spoke the words I had so often heard from her. 'We go to be the rock in the cart track that bounces the wagon onto a new path.'

They could not have presented a stranger scene. Althea leaned on the ship's railing. The ship's face was turned toward the river, with my more youthful profile. Amber sat in the figurehead's finger-laced hands. Her hands rested lightly on his thumbs and she swung her daintily booted feet, ankles crossed, over the empty fall to the cold, acid rush of the river. Her knitted cap allowed a feathering of short hair to frame her face. Powder and paint had smoothed her scarring and the scaling that the dragon's blood had triggered. In Amber's guise, the Fool became a very fetching woman.

Althea's voice was subdued. 'I've never heard you speak with such passion, not even when we were facing our deaths together.'

Amber's face contorted with hatred. 'They took our child and destroyed her.'

It hurt to hear Amber claim Bee that way, and I knew what Althea and Brashen must assume. The Fool might believe it was so, but to hear him speak of her that way to strangers wounded something in me. *Molly*, I thought fiercely. She had been Bee's mother and no other. I did not wish these people to think I had fathered Bee upon Amber. No, Molly had been the one to endure that pregnancy, in some ways so alone, and Molly had been the one to cherish and protect a child that others would have let dwindle away. It wasn't right for Amber to erase her. The hurt seared me, and I realized it had another source.

'My boy is gone, too!' Paragon burst out and I felt the surge of emotion that washed through the ship. His sense of outrage and loss were fuelling the fire of hurt within me. Trell spoke calmingly. 'Boy-O is fine, Paragon. Vivacia would never let harm befall him. He is only gone from you for a time. He will return. You know that.'

'Will he?' Paragon demanded harshly. 'He has been gone two years! Will he ever come back? Or will Vivacia claim him? He was born here, on my decks! He is mine! Or am I the only liveship without a family? The only liveship with no heir to my captaincy? For even as Althea's brother demands my boy for his deck, he keeps from me what should be mine! Kennit's son!'

'Queen Etta keeps Paragon Kennitsson from you, not Wintrow.' Althea's voice was taut. I could hear it was not the first time she had uttered those words to the ship. I saw Brashen square his shoulders and step forward, prepared to take up the peacemaker's role.

'Paragon,' Amber said softly. 'My friend, I feel your anguish. It is almost too much to be borne. Please.' And then, breathlessly, 'You are holding me too tightly. Please set me safely on your decks.'

I stared helplessly. I had two small, concealed knives, useless weapons against such a huge opponent. If I attacked him, would he drop Amber into the river? I looked to Brashen, but his face had gone pale. Althea leaned farther over the railing. She spoke in a low, rational voice. 'Crushing your friend will not win you Kennit's son. Calm yourself, ship.'

What need of breath did a wooden ship have, even one carved from a dragon's cocoon? Yet Paragon's chest rose and fell as if he were a boy in the grip of strong emotion. His eyes were squeezed shut and the big hands that clutched Amber trembled. Amber's milky eyes were fixed, not on me, but on a nameless distance. Her face was flushed with breathlessness. Paragon drew his hands closer to his chest. He bent his head over her and I feared he would bite her head off. But instead he twisted his shoulders and released her onto the deck so abruptly that she staggered and fell. Althea dropped to one knee beside her, seized her shoulders and dragged her backwards.

'You needn't put her out of my reach!' Paragon complained hoarsely. 'I would not hurt her.'

'I know you wouldn't,' Amber gasped.

Althea was small but she hoisted Amber's arm across her shoulders and stood up with her. 'I'm taking Amber to our stateroom,' she announced calmly. Before I could step in, Brashen seized Amber's other arm and helped her to walk aft. I began to follow but the ship suddenly spoke.

'You, with my face. Don't go.'

I halted. Brashen stopped and looked back at me, his eyes wide. A small shake of his head was full of warning. Lant's gaze went from me to Amber. I tipped my head toward her, letting him know he should follow her and he quickly took Brashen's place. The captain folded his arms and stood watching the figurehead.

'Buckman. I want to talk to you. Come here.'

The ship wasn't looking at me. He was staring off across the wide Rain Wild River. The distant shore was a haze of green on the horizon. 'I'm here,' I said, striving to keep any challenge out of my voice.

The ship gave no sign he had heard me. I stood and waited. I heard the river and the ship's motion against the dock. The distant calls and shouts of the riverside city were like birdsong in the distance.

'Buckman?'

I stepped closer and raised my voice. 'I'm here, ship.'

'NO!'

Brashen's warning was too late. With a twist of his body that set the ship rocking against the dock, the figurehead turned, reached and grabbed me. I leapt back, but he caught my left shoulder and arm. I seized one of his fingers in my right hand and tried to lift and twist it. Useless. He dragged me off my feet and pinned me against the railing.

'Let him go, Paragon!' Brashen bellowed.

The lurch of the ship had alerted the crew. Clef came running, then jolted to a halt, staring at me, with a white-faced Per at his elbow. Two others, Cord and Haff, hurried toward us, then stopped. Althea halted, her arm still around Amber. I could not hear what she said but Amber swivelled to gaze blindly back at us.

Paragon spoke calmly and his words vibrated through me. 'This does not concern any of you. Busy yourself with your duties.'

'Paragon,' Althea pleaded.

Paragon tightened his grip, lifting me up onto my toes. His thumb and fingers pinched the left side of my chest. I didn't struggle. When one cannot win, avoid angering the opponent. Give him no reason to employ more force.

'We're fine,' I gasped. I held onto his fingers, trying to ease the pressure.

'About your duties,' Paragon suggested pleasantly, and I nodded my head in vehement agreement.

Althea began moving Amber away. She went reluctantly, looking back at me, but I could not read her expression. Clef gripped Per's shoulder and dragged him along. Lant came to help him. Brashen, his mouth flat in a bitter line, retreated from us. Paragon eased me onto my feet but kept me wedged against the railing. 'Now,' he said in a very soft voice. 'We will talk, you and I, to be sure that things are clear between us. Are you listening, Buckman? For that is your role in this conversation. You listen.'

I wheezed a response. 'I'm listening.'

'Excellent. Amber seems to be fond of you. Perhaps she has been fond of you for years.' He paused.

I nodded. 'Friends since childhood.'

The pressure eased. 'Friends?'

'Since we— since I was a boy.'

He made a deep sound that I felt all through my body. Then he said, 'Understand this. We share a face, though mine is more youthful and handsomer. I asked her to carve me a face she could love. She gave me yours. But it was "could" love, not "did" love. Remember that. She loves me far more than you. She always will.'

On the last three words, his grip on me tightened. I nodded breathlessly.

Overhead, I heard a worried caw. I could not look up but I knew that Motley was circling. I prayed she would not try to attack the ship. *Please don't!* I flung the thought at her.

Paragon snapped his fingers open. I clutched the railing so I did not fall. For an instant, I thought he had responded to my Wit. Then he gave me a threatening smile. 'So. We understand one another?'

'Yes.' I fought the impulse to flee. I did not want to turn my back to him, even if he had turned his back to me. He put his gaze on the water and crossed his arms on his chest and rolled his shoulders. Substantial musculature there. I was not sure I'd ever truly looked like that.

He held his silence. A step at a time, I retreated, keeping my eyes fixed on him until someone seized my collar and dragged me backwards. I kicked my heels against the deck to speed the process, and we both went down in a heap. Brashen huffed out his air as we hit the deck with me on top. 'You're welcome,' he wheezed as I rolled off him and staggered upright.

'Thank you,' I responded.

'Are you all right?' Amber was immediately beside me as Althea offered Brashen a hand up. Per darted to my side and seized my hand.

'I'm bruised, but not badly injured, other than my pride.' I turned to Althea and Brashen. 'You warned me. I didn't imagine he could move that quickly. Or be that—' I flailed for a word.

'Deceptive,' Brashen supplied for me. He sighed. 'He's been difficult lately.'

'More difficult than usual,' Althea amended. She took Amber's hand and hauled her to her feet. 'It's a strange welcome back for you, Amber. But I'm sure you recall Paragon's nature. He'll be steady and stable for a month or a year, then something will set him off.'

'Jealousy,' I said very quietly. 'Amber, he does not wish to share you.'

'I will do my best to calm him. But it is not just that. Paragon's hull and figurehead were created out of two "logs" of wizardwood. He has the nature and partial memories of two dragons. His decks were the scene of much violence and cruelty. He was captured by the notorious pirate Igrot and used as his personal vessel. And Kennit Ludluck, the son of his family, was tormented on board him. Tormented and twisted.' She added in a whisper, 'Cruelty begets cruelty.'

'Deliberate cruelty is never forgivable,' Althea said brusquely.

Amber nodded curtly. 'I understand that now, perhaps better than I once did.'

We moved away from the foredeck. Brashen tossed his chin at the crewmen who were staring at us, and they suddenly stirred to life. I gently pried my arm from Per's grip. 'I'm fine,' I told him. 'Get to learning the ship. I'll call you if I need you.'

He looked doubtful but Clef gave a sharp whistle and the boy perked like a summoned dog. 'Go on,' I told him, knowing it was what he longed to do and what was best for him, and he went. With a sudden rattle of black feathers, Motley swooped in to land on Per's shoulder. Clef startled and Per laughed. The tension broke like a bubble popping. I left him explaining the bird to Clef and Ant.

We hadn't gone more than a dozen steps when Ash abruptly appeared. 'Is all well?' he demanded anxiously, in a voice so boyish I knew he had changed his self along with his clothing. I felt a pang that we had stolen this superlative young spy just when Chade might need him most, but I also knew that her dual identity could not be used aboard the ship.

'It is, Spark,' I told her. She gave me an odd look. 'You can relax,' I added. I pointed toward Clef and suggested, 'Go explore the ship with Per.'

She gave me a girl's relieved smile and trotted off with an eagerness that told me I'd given her exactly the right prompt.

Althea ambushed me at the stateroom door with sparks of anger in her eyes. 'You can't be careless on this ship! We warned you.'

'You did,' I agreed. 'He tricked me into coming into range. It was my own fault.'

My agreement set her back. Amber groped out and I offered her my arm. She gripped it tightly. 'Ah, Fitz. As you do not know Paragon's history, you cannot be as terrified as I was.'

'We need to get underway. People are staring. The sooner we are away from Trehaug, the less they have to gossip about,' Brashen suggested tersely.

I looked toward the city. Yes, people were pointing, others just gaping. I wondered how many had witnessed what had happened, and how Paragon's jealousy would be interpreted by those who had not heard his words.

'Walk me to my room, please. I'm still recalling the ship,' Amber lied, giving me a graceful way to depart.

'They didn't even ask what he'd said to me,' I observed quietly.

'Some of it we overheard. I had no idea he would feel so possessive of me.'

'Must you be so pleased about it?' I demanded.

She laughed. 'I'd feared that he had forgotten me.'

'After you re-carved his face and gave him back his sight?'

'Paragon is changeable. One moment he's an adoring child, the next a vindictive, angry adolescent. Sometimes, he is manly and brave and chivalrous. But I never lean too strongly on any of his moods, for I know how quickly they can shift.'

'Have you really forgotten your way around the ship?'

A rueful smile twisted her mouth. 'Fitz, you have such amazing faith in me. I haven't been on this ship in decades. I can recall the layout but will I know how many steps from fore to aft, how many steps in a ladder, when to duck for a doorway? No. Yet I must walk as if I am confident of the way. I know that when I grope or cling to a wall, I become less of a person and more of an obstacle. So, I pretend I can see more than I do.'

'I'm sorry.' And I was. And disheartened. I thought again of the long and weary way he had come, alone and horrendously wounded, blind in the snow.

'Is this the door?' she asked.

'I think so.' I was more rattled than I wanted to admit. I'd been stupid. I kept trying to think of what I should have done when Paragon seized me.

'I thought you were leading me.'

'I was letting you hold my arm while we walked.' I tapped on the door and when no one answered, I opened it. 'I see your things. Everywhere. There are three bunks and a fold-down table. Spark's pack is open, and she has obviously rummaged through it.'

Amber entered and allowed herself to grope and touch. I shut the door behind us. She moved carefully in the small room, measuring distances in careful steps and the reach of her arms. 'I recall it,' she said as she perched on the lower bunk. 'I once shared this room with Althea and Jek. Three people crowded into this space. It was tense at times.' I pushed my pack completely under the lowest bunk and set my bag of clothing by the door.

'Crowding does that to you.' I sat down beside her. The motion of the ship had changed and I did not find it pleasant. We'd cast off from the dock and the current of the river was taking charge. I looked out the small porthole. We were picking up speed and moving away from shore into a deeper channel and swifter current. I'd never liked the sensation of being disconnected from the ground. The pace of a horse had a rhythm. A ship might lurch in any direction at any moment. I tried to settle my stomach into accepting the unpredictable.

'What's wrong?' she asked softly.

'I'm not seasick, but I don't enjoy the motion. I'd just become accustomed to Tarman's waddle, but Paragon—'

'No. What's really worrying you?' He spoke as the Fool.

I didn't look at him. Was there anyone else I could admit this to? Probably not. 'I'm . . . I'm not what I used to be. I make more mistakes, and they're more serious. I think I'm alert and ready and fit for anything, and then I'm not. Things and people take me by surprise. Brashen seizes me from behind and I'm so focused on Paragon not even my Wit let me know he was there. Despite being warned, the ship lured me into coming within his arm's reach with almost no effort. He could have killed me. In an instant.'

'Fitz. How old are you?'

'Exactly? I'm not sure. You know that.'

'Take a guess,' he chided me.

I blew out my distaste for the subject. 'Sixty-two, perhaps sixty-three. Sixty-four, maybe. But I don't look it and most days I don't feel it.'

'But you are it. It's going to take its toll. You had a good life, for a time. An easy life. With Molly. Calm and prosperity dull a man's edge just as endless battle and hardship dulls the gentler parts of the soul.'

'It was good, Fool. I wanted it to be forever. I wanted to grow old and to die with her sitting by my bed.'

'But you didn't get that.'

'No. I got this. Chasing across half the world to kill people I don't know, people who didn't know me but still came to destroy what little peace and joy I had left.' As I put words to that, I felt a fury that would have let me snap a man's neck. Dwalia. I could have broken her in half with my bare hands at that moment. Then it passed and I felt foolish and empty. And, worst of all, incompetent. I spoke a guilty fear. 'They lured me away from Withywoods, didn't they? So they could raid it while I was away.'

'I fear they did.'

'How could they plan that?' He had explained it before but I wanted to hear it again.

'They have access to thousands of prescient dreams from scores of young Whites. They could find the right circumstances to nudge you in the direction they desired.'

'And you?'

'Probably I was part of it. Did I escape, or was I released? Were the chance strangers who helped me along the way truly kind or were they conspirators with the Servants? I don't know, Fitz. But I don't think you can blame yourself.'

'I make too many mistakes! I had my sword at Ellik's throat, and my strength gave out. When I should have followed Bee into the Skill-pillar, my magic was gone. So many mistakes, Fool. How roughly I "healed" those children.' I looked at his empty eyes. 'And just now, with Paragon . . . Stupid, stupid, stupid.' I reached to seize his gloved hand. 'Fool. I'm not competent to do what you want done. I'm going to fail you, drag you down into torture and death with me. Will Lant and Per and Spark fall with us? Will we listen to Per scream? Watch Spark abused and torn? I can't stand it. I can't stand to think of it. Do you wonder that I want to send them home, that I am terrified of bringing anyone with me into this? I fear failing all of you as I have feared nothing else in my life! I'll fall for some trick of theirs . . . how can I battle people who even now may know what I'm likely to do next? They might even know that we are on our way to kill them.'

'Oh, I consider that likely,' the Fool observed heartlessly, then added quietly, 'you're hurting me.'

I released my clutch and he massaged his hand. His words had quenched my last spark of courage. In our silence, the moving ship spoke around us. I heard the water and the creaking of Paragon's wizardwood timbers. Felt the press of his sentience and tightened my walls. 'This is insane. I can't do this. We'll both die. Possibly messily.'

'Probably so. But what else would we do with the rest of our lives?'

I thought about that like a wolf chewing on a bare bone. Or chewing on his leg in a trap.

'Nighteyes,' he said.

'He's gone,' I said dully. 'If I still had him, I wouldn't feel so diminished. His senses were so sharp and he shared all with me. But he's gone completely now. I used to feel him inside me, sometimes. I could almost hear him, usually mocking me. But I don't even have that any more. He's just gone.'

'That's not what I meant, though I'm sad to hear it. No, I was recalling Nighteyes at the end of his life. You wanted to heal him and he refused. How you tried to leave him safe while we went after the Piebalds and he came after you.'

I smiled, remembering my wolf's determination to live until he died. 'What are you saying?'

He spoke solemnly. 'This is our last hunt, old wolf. And as we have always done, we go to it together.'

THIRTEEN

Full Sails

I am so bothered when the dreams make no sense, but still swell with importance. It is hard to write down a story that has no sequence or sense, let alone make a picture of what my dream showed me. But here it is.

A flaming man offers a drink to my father. He drinks it. He shakes himself like a wet dog, and pieces of wood fly in all directions. He turns into two dragons that fly away.

I am almost certain that this dream will come to pass. A dream that makes no sense!

Bee Farseer's dream journal

It was a chill and rainy day. I wore my old jerkin over the cheap, loose shirt and trousers Dwalia had grudgingly purchased for me in Chalced. The layers were uncomfortable but I had no coat. Kerf, Vindeliar and I had fled the stench in the tiny cabin. We huddled in the skimpy shelter of the deckhouse eaves, and watched the heaving grey seas amid the endless pattering rain. Few merchants wished to take the air that day. The two who trudged past us in deep conversation made my heart leap with hope.

'Six days to Woolton. I'll part with my Sandsedge brandy there, for a tidy profit. I want to look at their currant liqueur. It has a tartness that wakes the tongue, and is as good a tonic for a man as it is a pleasure to the ladies.' He was a small man, lithe as a rat and dressed all in ratty grey.

The tall woman beside him laughed and shook her head. The

bangles in her ears brushed her shoulders; a nest of yellow braids crowned her head, hatless in the rain. 'I've no stock to sell there, but I hope to acquire an item or two. It's not called Woolton for nothing. Their weavers make magnificent rugs. If I take one as a gift to my buyer in the Spice Isles, he may spend his clients' money a bit more freely. I'll be glad to get off this ship for a bit. We've a layover there, before a seven-day run to Cartscove, if this wind holds.'

'The wind is good, but this rain I'd wish gone.'

'The storm is good by me.' The woman looked up, letting the rain fall on her face. The man stared at her bared throat. 'Less chance of pirates or the Tariff Fleet spotting us. But I'm looking forward to a couple of days on dry land.'

Two days in port. Two days in which to find a way off the ship and out of Dwalia's custody. Six days to win Vindeliar over to my cause. If he fled with me, and kept us both hidden, what chance would Dwalia have of finding us? I knew that luring him from his 'path' would be like luring a wild bird from a berry bush. The wrong words might frighten him off completely. I would have to be very careful. I put myself on a strict schedule. For three days I would court his friendship. Only on the fourth would I begin to persuade him to help me.

Kerf hunched beside me, his shoulders bowed against the rain, his face nearly blank with Vindeliar's overlay of servitude. I felt sorry for him. He looked like a once-proud stallion hitched to a dung cart. At night, when he stripped for sleep, I noticed the slackening of the muscles in his arms and chest. Under Vindeliar's sway, he moved less and less like a warrior and more like a servant. Much more of this, and he would lose his usefulness as a protector. I wondered if Dwalia saw that.

On the other side of me, Vindeliar slumped. He had an odd face: sometimes boyish and at other times the face of a disappointed old man. It had fallen into dismal folds today as he stared at the waves. 'So far from home,' he said woefully.

'Tell me of our destination, brother.' Being asked to speak always flattered him. I had become the avid listener, never correcting or silencing him. 'What will it be like when we arrive there?'

'Oh,' he breathed out long, as if he did not know where to begin. 'It depends on where we land. We may dock in deep water, on the other side of the island. We may land in Sisal or perhaps Crupton. Dwalia will be known there. I hope for a night in a comfortable inn and a good meal. Lamb with mint, perhaps. I like lamb. And a warm, dry room.' He paused as if already savouring those simple pleasures. 'She may hire a carriage to take us to Clerres. I hope she does not want to ride there on horseback. A horse's back has never fitted my bottom well.'

I nodded sympathetically.

'And we will go to Clerres. Perhaps we may dock there . . . It will depend on what sort of a ship we can find. It will be full summer when we arrive. Hot for you, little northern thing that you are. Nice for me. I will welcome the sun baking the aches out of my joints. Clerres gleams white on a sunny day. Some of it is built of ancient bone, and other parts are white stone.'

'Bone? That sounds frightening.'

'Does it? Not to me. Worked bone can be lovely. When we get there, we will wait for low tide to bare the causeway and then cross to our island sanctuary. Surely you have heard of it! The tops of the watchtowers are shaped like the skulls of ancient monsters. At night, the torches inside make the eyes gleam with orange light and they appear to be looking out in all directions. It is imposing and powerful.' He stopped and scratched his wet cheek. Rain dripped from his chin. Then he leaned closer and lowered his voice to impart an important secret to me. 'The furniture in the four towers is made from dragon's bones! Symphe has a set of drinking cups carved from dragon's teeth and lined with silver! They are very old, passed down from Symphe to Symphe, through the generations.'

'Symphe to Symphe?'

He lifted his pale brows. 'The woman in the North Tower is always called Symphe. How can you not know these things? I was taught them when I was very young. Clerres is the heart of the world, and the heartbeat of the world must always be steady.' This last he said as if repeating an adage known the world over.

'Until you took me, I knew nothing of the Servants or Clerres.' It was not quite a lie. I had read a tiny bit about them in my father's papers, but not enough to prepare me for what I now endured.

'Perhaps it is because you are so young,' Vindeliar replied thoughtfully. He gave me a pitying look.

I shook my head. My hair was now long enough to go to curls in the rain and droplets flew from it. 'I don't think they are as famed as you believe them to be. Kerf, had you heard of Clerres before the Servants hired you?'

He turned slowly toward me, blue eyes widening in slow consternation like a puzzled cow.

'Hush,' Vindeliar warned me. 'Don't ask him questions!'

Vindeliar furrowed his brow and, as he did, Kerf's face settled into his habitual scowl. Alertness faded from his eyes. I stood up suddenly and stretched, choosing to do so just as two young deckhands dashed by. Both avoided me, but one turned to look back at me in surprise. I looked directly at him, smiling. He stumbled, caught himself, turned back, and I think he would have spoken to me if someone hadn't roared a rebuke at him. The command was accompanied by the sound of a rope length snapping against the ship's railing. Both boys fled to their work. I sat down slowly. Vindeliar was breathing through his nose harshly as if he had just run a race. The world settled around me, as if I had been paddling on the surface of a sea and now sank in stillness below the waves. I avoided his gaze as I tried to quote what he had said. 'Clerres is the heart of the world, and the heartbeat of the world must always be steady.'

I peered at him through a sudden blast of rain. I could not tell if the water running down his face was rain or tears. His chin quivered briefly. 'We who serve the Servants aid them to keep that heart beating steadily. If we obey. If we keep to the Path.'

'But what about you?' I asked him. 'What harm if you went to a festival and ate roasted nuts and drank spiced cider? There's no evil in that.'

His little round eyes were full of misery. 'But no good, either. I must do only what keeps the world to the Path. Harm can come of simple things. The cake I eat, another person lacks. Like tiny pebbles that shift till the hillside gives way, carrying a road into oblivion.'

Had I heard such a thing, a long time ago? His words rang strangely, even as I hated the sense of them. If he believed that Dwalia knew his destiny and he followed her direction, I had no hope of enlisting his help to escape.

As if he heard my thought, he said, 'That is why I cannot help you defy her. If you try to escape, I must stop you and bring you back.' He shook his head. 'She was very angry when you ran away in the city. I said I could not make you be obedient. I did it once, that first time. The power was fresh and strong in me that day; she had readied me for the hard work I did. But since then, I cannot make you obey me. She said I was lying. She slapped me many times.' His tongue moved inside his cheek as if finding sore places. I felt a rush of guilty sympathy for him.

'Oh, brother,' I said and took his hand.

It was like thrusting my hand into a cold rush of water, I felt the current that strongly. Like touching my father when his thoughts were unguarded, before I had learned how to protect myself. I felt that his current snatched the thoughts from my mind. I sensed his hold on Kerf, like a strangling rope around his mind. Kerf was no weakling. It was taut with tension, a leash on a lunging dog. I snatched my hand back and tried to disguise what I'd felt by patting his sleeved arm sympathetically. 'I am sorry she punished you for that.'

He stared at me. 'You thought of your father.'

My heart was beating very fast. *Walls, walls, walls.* 'I miss my father constantly,' I said.

He reached for me and I stood up. 'I'm so cold. I'm going inside. Kerf, are you not cold?'

Kerf's eyes flickered and Vindeliar was distracted as he brought his lunging dog to heel again. By the time he had mastered Kerf and had him standing to follow me, I was out of his reach on my way back to the cabin. A deckhand coiling a rope paused in his activity and stared at me. So, Vindeliar had been concealing me and controlling Kerf. But doing both at the same time strained his abilities. A useful bit of information.

However, I'd handed him a weapon I wished he did not have. Did he guess that if he touched me, skin to skin, he might be able to push inside my mind? I did not look back at him or let my thoughts dwell on that. I must do better at guarding my thoughts. I now doubted that I'd be able to lure either Vindeliar or Kerf into helping me. An old sailor strode past me, wet shirt plastered to his back, bare feet slapping the deck. He did not even glance at me.

I reached the hatch and climbed down the ladder that led into the bowels of the ship where our miserable compartment awaited me. I threaded my way past dangling hammocks and sea chests. As I went, I studied those I passed. A few Chalcedean merchants had clustered to mutter about weather and pirates. I paused near them. None looked at me, but from their talk, I learned that our ship was bragged to be the swiftest out of Chalced. She had never been boarded by pirates, though she had been pursued by them more than once. She had also avoided encounters with the so-called Tariff Fleet and slipped unnoticed past the Pirate Isles without paying toll to Queen Etta and her cutthroats.

'Are the pirate ships that might chase this ship part of the Tariff Fleet?' I asked aloud, but no one turned toward me.

Yet a moment later, a younger fellow at the edge of the huddle said, 'It seems ironic to me that a queen who rules a domain called the Pirate Isles is now troubled herself by pirates.'

A grey-moustached merchant laughed aloud. 'Ironic and very satisfying to those of us who once had to run the Pirate Isles corridor hoping to escape the attention of King Kennit. He'd take ship, crew and cargo and turn it to his own purposes. Anyone who could not bring a ransom ended up a resident of the Pirate Isles.'

'Kennit? Or Igrot?' asked the youngster.

'Kennit,' the older man affirmed. 'Igrot was before my time, and a much more brutal beast. He'd take the cargo, slaughter and rape the crew, and then scuttle the vessel. He had a liveship, and nothing outruns one of those. He choked trade for years. Then one day, he simply vanished.' He widened his eyes at the younger man and mockingly asserted, 'Some say that on a stormy night, you can glimpse his ghost ship in the distance with her sails blazing and the figurehead shrieking in agony.'

There was a moment of silence as the young man stared at him, and then all burst into laughter.

'Do you think we'll elude Queen Etta's Tariff Fleet?' the younger man asked, trying to regain a bit of dignity.

The older merchant tucked his hands into his ornate sash. He pursed his lips and waxed philosophical. 'We will or we won't. The deal I struck was that if the ship can get us past the Tariff Fleet, I'll pay the captain half what I would have paid them. It's a good bargain, and it's one I've made with him before. On three voyages out of five we slipped past them. Good odds, I think. That little offer of mine makes him willing to crack on a bit more sail, I do believe.'

'Good odds indeed,' the young man replied.

I heard awkward steps coming down the ladder and looked up to see Kerf descending with Vindeliar following him. 'There you are,' I said brightly. 'I hurried ahead to be out of the rain.'

Kerf said nothing but Vindeliar regarded me with a scowl. 'We'd best return to our cabin,' he said stiffly. He walked Kerf past me. I stood where I was.

'What will become of me?' I demanded aloud. 'What does Dwalia intend for me? Why did she come so far, destroy so much and shed so much blood? She sold Alaria into slavery to get us away from Chalced, without a thought for one who had travelled so far with her. Why didn't she sell me? Or you?'

'Hush!' Vindeliar spoke in a soft whisper. 'I cannot speak to you here!'

'Is that because they cannot hear me? Or see me? And they will think you a madman, talking to yourself?' I lifted my voice and spoke each word clearly.

I saw his control of Kerf slipping as one of the men turned his head, scowling, wondering if he'd heard something. An instant later, Vindeliar had Kerf blank-eyed again. He looked at me, trembling from the effort. There was a tremor in his voice as he said, 'Brother, please.'

I should have felt only hatred for him. He had facilitated my capture and kept me subdued as they whisked me away. He had hidden Shun and me from any who might have helped us, and still he made me invisible. I was Dwalia's prisoner, but he was my gaoler.

It was irrational for me to feel pity for him, yet I did. I tried to keep my stare icy as tears welled in his pale eyes. 'Please . . .' he breathed again, and I broke.

'In the cabin, then,' I said in a lower, more rational voice.

His voice was squeezed so tight with fear that it squeaked. 'She will hear us. No.'

One of the merchants turned away from his fellows and stared at Vindeliar accusingly. 'Sir! Do you listen in on our private conversation?'

'No. No! We came in from the rain, to be dry for a bit. That's all.'

'And you have nowhere to stand but here beside us?'

'I . . . we are leaving. Now.' Vindeliar gave me a desperate glance, then prodded Kerf. It must have seemed strange to the merchant that they went right back up the ladder and out onto the stormy deck. I followed more slowly. Vindeliar was shivering as he led us back to the deckhouse. But one of the ship's boys had claimed our spot and was enjoying a pipe there. He glanced at Vindeliar and then looked away. I cleared my throat loudly. The boy did not so much as startle.

'Brother!' Vindeliar rebuked me, and trudged down the deck, Kerf following listlessly. The rain had increased, driven by a rising wind. There was no sheltered place. He stopped and leaned miserably on the railing. 'She will kill me if she finds I've answered your questions.' He gave me a sideways glance. 'If I don't answer, you will push me past what I can do. It is harder and harder to hide you. I hid a troop of men from an entire town. Why are you so hard to hide?'

I didn't know and didn't care. 'Why me?' I demanded of him. 'Why did you destroy my home and ruin my life?'

He shook his head slowly, deeply hurt at my failure to understand. 'Not to ruin your life,' he objected. 'To set you on the true Path. To control you lest you create a false way and carry us all to a terrible future.'

I stared at him.

He sighed. 'Bee. This makes you important! You are part of the true Path! For so long, there were dreams of the Unexpected Son. Hundreds of dream-scrolls mention him and some are very old. He is full of crossroads. His existence is a junction. A nexus, Symphe says. You create more and more junctions. You are dangerous.' He hunched down to look into my rain-spattered face. 'Do you understand?'

'No.'

He put his hands to both sides of his head and squeezed as if to stifle a pain. Water slid down his face, tear or raindrops or sweat. Kerf stared out over the sea in bovine passivity, not sheltering his face from the driving rain. The storm was rising. The sails were making a slapping sound. The ship rose and then fell, making my stomach lurch.

'More dreams mean something is more likely,' Vindeliar went on. 'The Unexpected Son brings change to the world. If you are not controlled, you will set the world on an inappropriate course. You are a danger to the Servants, to Clerres! In all the dreams, he changes things so much that no one can predict a future. You have to be stopped!' He clamped his mouth shut on his words.

'And you think I am him?' I asked incredulously. I lifted my arms wide to show how small I was. 'If you don't stop me, I will ruin the world? Me?' A gust of wind slapped me. 'How do you stop me? Kill me?' I snatched at the railing as the ship jolted. The wind roared and the rain pelted us harder.

'You must be him.' His words were a distressed plea. I thought he would crumple into tears. 'Dwalia said if I found the wrong one she would kill me. She was so angry when she found out you were a girl. That was when she started to doubt me. And you. But it is simple to me. If you are not him, who can you be? I dreamed finding you in my only true dream. You are him, and unless we take you to Clerres, you will change the world's path.' He suddenly spoke sternly. 'When we come to Clerres, we must make everyone believe that you are the Unexpected Son and we did a good thing. YOU must make them believe you are him. If we don't—'

Then he clapped his mouth shut so suddenly and firmly that it made a popping sound. His eyes grew wide as he stared over my head at nothing. When he shifted his gaze back to me, I saw anger and betrayal in his glare. 'You are doing it, aren't you? Right now. You are making me tell you things, and then you will know and you will change things. Because you are him. You fight me when I try to hide you. You make Dwalia angry with me. You ran away, and so many died. And we caught you again, but Reppin died and Alaria was sold. Now there's just Dwalia and me, and this Kerf. All those others . . . you changed all their lives into deaths! That is what the Unexpected Son would do!' He looked furious.

Fear gripped me. He had come so close to being my ally. I choked on disappointment. 'Brother,' I said, and my voice wavered. 'Those things only happened because you stole me!' I didn't want to cry but the sobs ripped from my chest. I shouted my words past my tight throat. 'It wasn't me! It was Dwalia! She came and she killed people. She brought all those luriks there to die. Not me. Not me!' I sank to my knees. He couldn't be right. All that death couldn't be my fault. FitzVigilant. Per's father. Revel. I couldn't be the reason for that!

The storm rose with my fear. It felt as if it was coming out of my chest and blowing all around us. A wave leapt over the railing. It splashed over me and reflexively I grabbed Kerf's leg. I heard someone shout a command, and three men went racing past us. The nose of the ship began to tip up as if we were going up a steep hill. One of the men shouted at Vindeliar, 'Get below, you idiot!' as he ran past.

I stood up, bracing myself against the deck. The wind blew all around us. We hovered.

Then the ship tipped again and we were sliding downhill on the wet deck. I skidded past Vindeliar, shrieking. 'Grab her,' Vindeliar ordered Kerf. 'Get her back to the cabin.'

Kerf stooped and seized a handful of the back of my shirt. He dragged me like a sack as he staggered aft toward the hatch with Vindeliar holding onto him. Men cursed as they avoided us. They moved purposefully but I could make no sense of the shouted commands. Sailors climbed masts and into rigging while storm winds slashed at them and the canvas cracked at each gust. The deck tipped again. We reached the hatch cover but it was closed. Vindeliar crouched and pounded on it, shrieking to be let in. Kerf dropped me and went to one knee. He groaned as he lifted the hatch cover and slid it aside. We more tumbled than climbed down the ladder. Above us someone slammed the cover shut. We were plunged into dimness.

For a moment, it felt safe. Then the rough plank floor tipped. In the darkness, I heard a cry of dismay, but someone laughed and mocked, 'You'll never be a merchant, boy, if a bit of rough water makes you yell.'

'Put out that lantern!' someone shouted. In an instant, the blackness became absolute and the world seesawed around me.

I could not tell in which direction our miserable cabin lay. But Kerf knew. Vindeliar said by my ear, 'Follow us,' and I did. I clutched at Vindeliar's shirt and walked in short steps, bumping into beams, a hammock, a sea chest and finally stumbling through an opening that proved to be our cabin door. The floor tilted. I crouched and then sat flat, pushing my palms against the deck to try to stay in one place. When Kerf tried to shut the door, I discovered that I was sitting in the way. I scooted into the room on my rump, fearing to stand. I groped and slid until I found a corner and bracketed myself in it. There I sat in the dark, cradling my bruised hand in my lap. I was wet through, my hair dripping on my neck. Despite the closeness of the cabin, I felt chilled. And hopeless. Let Dwalia be as angry as she pleased. I needed a real answer!

'Why did you steal me? What are you going to do with me?' I spoke the words loud and clear into the dark.

I heard Dwalia shift in the bunk as the ship lurched in another direction. 'Make her be quiet!' she ordered Vindeliar. 'Make her fall asleep.'

'He can't! I can block him out of my mind. He can't control me.'

'Well, I can! I can control you with a stick, so you'd best be quiet.' It was a threat but her voice was misery laced with anger. And a trace of fear. The motion of the ship suddenly pressed me back into my corner. I felt like a kitten in a crate that someone was shaking. I didn't like it at all. But I reminded myself that the sailors on deck had looked busy and challenged, but not terrified. I refused to be afraid. 'You don't have a stick, and you couldn't see me to hit me if you did. Are you afraid to answer me? Why did you steal me? What are you going to do with me?'

She sat up suddenly in the bed. I knew because I heard the rustle of the blanket and the solid 'thud' as her head hit the upper bunk. I smothered my laugh, and then let it burst out of me. In the dark and the tossing storm, defying her, I suddenly felt strangely powerful. I threw words at her. 'I wonder if the ship will sink. Then all your plans would be for nothing. Imagine if it sank with us stuck in her. Even if we got out of the cabin, we'd never find the ladder and the hatch in the dark. We'd all die here when the cold water came rushing in to find us. I wonder if it would flip upside-down first?'

I heard Vindeliar take in a ragged breath. Pity for him warred with satisfaction. Could I make them feel how scared and sick I had been when they stole me?

The ship tilted again. Then it felt as if we hit something, then passed through it. A moment later I heard Dwalia vomit. There had been a bucket by her bunk, but I heard the thin trickle of bile spatter on the deck as she strained and gagged. The smell grew stronger.

'You thought I was the Unexpected Son. Then you thought I wasn't! Well, I think I am! And I am changing the world, right now. You will never know how I will change it, for I think you will die before we reach port. You have certainly lost flesh and strength. And if you die, and Vindeliar is left alone with us? Well, I doubt I shall go to Clerres.' I laughed again.

There was an instant of absolute silence, as if both storm and ship paused. She spoke into it. 'What will I do with you? I will do to you what I did to your father. I will tear you into pieces. I will have every secret out of you, if I must take every inch of your skin off your meat to do it. And when I am done with you, I will give you to the breeders. They have wanted one of your lineage for a long time. No matter how I disfigure you, I imagine they will find someone willing to rape you until you conceive. You are young. I imagine they can get a score of babies out of your belly before your body gives out.' She made a cawing sound.

I'd never heard Dwalia laugh but I knew it for what it was. Cold fear, colder than the wild seawater outside the wall of our cabin, rose in me. Confusion ruled me. What was she telling me? I tried to find that confidence again. 'You did nothing to my father. You never even saw my father!'

A pause as the floor shifted in a new direction. In that silence, I heard the timbers of the ship mutter to one another. Then she spoke and she was the darkness itself. 'So, you do not even know who your father was!'

'I know my father!'

'Do you? Do you know his pale hair and eyes? Do you know his mocking smile and long-fingered hands? I think not. But I do. I blinded those eyes; I put the mockery out of them forever! And I flayed the tips from your father's long fingers. That was after I'd tugged out his nails, a thin slice at a time. He'll never juggle again, nor make an apple appear from thin air. I ended his dancing and tumbling, too. I peeled the skin from his feet, oh so slowly. And I put his left foot between two blocks of a vice, one on each side, and slowly, slowly I tightened it, less than a quarter turn for each question. It did not matter if he answered me or not! I asked, and he shrieked or cried out words. And then I tightened the screw. Tighter and tighter, with the top of his foot bulging up until, crunch!' She cawed again.

I could hear Vindeliar panting in the darkness. Did he try not to laugh? Was he on the edge of weeping?

'The bones gave way. One stuck up like a little ivory tower from the top of his foot. Oh, how he screamed. I stood beside him, and I looked up at my witnesses, and waited and waited until he could scream no more. And then I tightened the screw another quarter turn!'

For a long moment, the world paused around me. Even the ship seemed to hover, motionless and nearly level. A father I did not know? A father she had tortured. She had tortured someone; of that I was certain. She spoke of it as if it were the most delicious meal she had ever eaten, or the loveliest song ever heard. But my father? I knew my father. He was Nettle's father, too, and he was my mother's husband all those years. Of course he was my father.

But as if my world teetered as the ship did, the question had to rise. What if he was not my father? What if he never had been? Burrich hadn't been Nettle's father. I would not have been the first child handed off to foster-parents. But Molly was my mother. Of that I was certain. Unless . . . I wondered an unthinkable thing about my mother. Would not that explain why I looked nothing like him? Wouldn't it explain why he had left me so easily that day? He'd said he'd had to go, that he had to save the battered old beggarman. The blind beggarman, with the broken hand and the lumpy foot . . .

And then the ship made a slow, sickening tip. I felt the ship must stand on its nose. Did we move? I could not tell until the sickening impact, both hard and soft. Something thudded into the wall beside me and then fell to the deck as the ship tried to right herself. I felt we sank, and then bobbed up like a cork. Even below the deck, I heard a crash and men shouting. I wondered what had happened.

'Sounds like we lost some rigging, maybe even a mast.' Kerf's voice came deep and slow in the darkness. Then with rising urgency he asked, 'Where are we going? When did we board a ship? I was taking my prize, my won woman, home to my mother! Where is she? How did we get here?'

'Control him!' Dwalia warned Vindeliar savagely, but he made no response. I slid my foot across the floor and in the dark I found a yielding lump.

'I think Vindeliar hit his head,' I said, and then cursed myself for a fool. He was unconscious and could not stop me. I did not think Kerf would care. This was my best chance to kill her and free all of us. The ship was shuddering around us. Without warning, it began to climb again. I heard Vindeliar's body slide across the floor.

Weapon. I needed a weapon. There was nothing in the room that would serve me as a weapon. I had nothing I could use to kill her.

Except Kerf.

'You are a prisoner. As am I.' I tried to deepen and smooth my voice. I needed to sound rational and older. Not like a terrified child. 'They took Alaria from you and sold her as a slave. Before that, they lost Lady Shun for you forever, by tricking you into bringing her back to her captors instead of taking her home to safety. Remember, Kerf? Remember how they dragged you through a magic stone and almost made you lose your mind? They did it again. And now they have tricked you into leaving Chalced and your home behind.' Despite my efforts, my voice had gone higher and childish as I tried to sting him with the wrongs done to him.

He made no response to my words. I risked it all. 'We have to kill her. We must kill Dwalia. It's the only way we can stop her!'

'You evil little bitch!' Dwalia shrieked at me. I heard her scrabbling, trying to get out of her bunk, but the tilt of the ship was on my side. She was downhill from me. I could not wait for Kerf. He was too addled still. I tried to move quietly in the dark as I half-crawled and half-slid toward her. I had only moments to reach her before the ship would level itself on a wave's crest.

I slid into the edge of the bunk, fought to stand and felt for her. She was struggling to rise. I tried not to touch her, to give her no warning of where I was or what I intended. I had to guess where her neck was as I darted my hands toward her head. I touched her nose and chin with one hand, shifted down and seized her throat in both hands. I gripped and squeezed.

She slapped me, hard, on the side of my head. My ear rang. I held tight but my hands were too small. At best, I was pinching the sides of her neck, not throttling her of air as I'd hoped to do. She screamed words at me that I did not understand, but I could hear the hatred in them. I snaked my head in to try to bite her throat and found her cheek instead. That would not kill her but I bit her anyway, clenching my teeth tight in her meaty face and trying to grind my teeth together. She screamed and battered at me with her fists, and I suddenly knew she was hitting me hoping that I'd let go because she feared to tear me away from her face, knowing that I'd take a bite of it with me. Living meat is much tougher than cooked. I worked my teeth back and forth, grinding through her flesh, feeling savage and triumphant in equal measure. She was hurting me, but it would cost her. I'd see to that. I closed my jaws and worried her flesh as if I were a wolf shaking a rabbit.

Then Kerf blundered into us. I knew a surge of hope. With him helping me, we could kill her. The ship was upright. He could draw his sword and stab it right into her. I wanted to shout this to him, but I would not let go my bite. Then, to my horror, he seized me. 'Let go,' he said in the dull voice of a sleepwalker.

'Pull her off,' Vindeliar ordered him. He'd only been temporarily stunned.

'No! No, no, no!' Dwalia was shrieking. She seized hold of my head and held it close to her face, but Kerf was stronger. I felt my teeth meet and then as he jerked me away the meat of her face tore and came with me. As if I were a shovelful of earth, Kerf tossed me aside. I hit the floor, spat Dwalia's cheek out and then slid as the ship began to tilt again. I wound up in a corner and braced myself there. Dwalia was screaming hysterically as Vindeliar nattered at her, demanding was she hurt, what was wrong, what should he do now? I gagged at what I had done. Her blood slimed my chin. I scraped my teeth over my tongue and spat Dwalia out on the floor.

Vindeliar was busy with Dwalia. I had no idea where Kerf was or what he was doing. *Get out.* As soon as she could, she would beat me. I knew now how much she would enjoy hurting me. Nothing would stop her from killing me now.

In the darkness of the tossing ship, I'd lost my bearings. When the ship pressed me to one wall, I spidered along it but encountered no doorframe. The ship hit the wall of water and wrenched sideways. Yells of dismay came from the sailors working the deck. So now it was time to fear something bigger than Dwalia. I decided I would be frightened for the ship sinking after I got out of the cabin and away from her.

The next time the ship tilted, I went with it to the opposite wall. I was halted briefly by someone's boot, probably Kerf's. I struck the wall, felt the doorframe, pulled myself up, opened the door and climbed around it until I fell out. I heard it fall back into place behind me. Dwalia was still screaming curses at me. I wondered how long I had before they realized I was not in the cabin.

I crawled off into the darkness of the tilting deck beneath the swinging hammocks. I heard curses and prayers and grown men weeping. I blundered into an upright post and clung there for a moment. I made myself be still, forced myself to recall what I had seen of the between-decks area. Then, as the ship crested another wave, I made my way to the next post. I clung, waited, and then moved again, blundering past a man. On and away. If I drowned when the ship sank, I would not drown next to Dwalia.

FOURTEEN

Paragon's Bargain

In the matter of the wild-born White known as Beloved:

We have been unable to confirm the village of his birth. All records of his coming to Clerres have either been incorrectly stored, or have been destroyed. In my opinion, Beloved has found a way to infiltrate our record chambers, has located the records that pertained to him and his family and has hidden or destroyed them.

Tractable when we first received him, he has become unmanageable, inquisitive, deceptive and suspicious. He remains convinced that he is the true White Prophet, and will not regard our teachings that out of several candidates, the Servants choose who is best suited for this task. Neither kindness nor harsh discipline has shaken this belief in him.

Although he would be a valuable addition to the White lineages when he comes of an age to breed, his temperament and outspoken ways mean that it would be a dangerous distraction to the others to allow him to continue to have unfettered access to them.

I present to my three peers my opinion. It was an error for the boy to be coddled and spoiled. The plan to lull him into security and harvest his dreams has only encouraged him to be rebellious and secretive. To continue to allow him to range freely, to visit the village and to mingle with our other charges is to invite disaster.

My suggestions are these: As our White Prophet has suggested, mark him clearly with tattoos.

Confine him. Continue to spice his meals with the dream-drugs and see that is he well supplied with brush, ink, and scrolls.

Contain him for twenty years. Stroke his vanity. Tell him we hold him in isolation so that his dreams cannot be tainted by the talk of others. Tell him that while he is not the true White Prophet, he serves the world and the Path by continuing to dream. Allow him pastimes but do not let him mingle with other Whites.

If, by the end of that time he has not become manageable, poison him. These are my suggestions. Ignore them, and I will take none of the blame for what he does.

Symphe

Give a man a dreaded task. Then put him in a situation where he must wait to attempt that task. Make it a difficult task as well. Confine him where there is little for him to do, and rare opportunity to be alone. Time will stand still for that man. I know this to be true.

I tried to fill my days aboard Paragon with useful pursuits. Amber and I would isolate ourselves in her cabin for a session of reading and discussing Bee's dream-writings. Those sessions were painful to me, made only more chafing by the Fool's avaricious consumption of her journal. 'Read that again!' he would command me, or worse, 'Does not that dream tie in to the one you read me four days ago? Or was it five? Go back in the book, Fitz, please. I must hear the two read together.'

He savoured the dreams that he claimed were proof that Bee was his child, but I was tormented by unremembered moments of my little girl. She had written those carefully penned words alone, and illustrated them with inks and brushes pilfered from my desk. She had laboured on all these pages, each illustration so exact, each letter so precisely inked, and I had known nothing of her obsession. Had she done this work late at night, while I slept, or perhaps while I ignored her and Molly to morosely pen my own thoughts in my private study? I didn't know and would never know. Every recounted dream, every peculiar little poem or detailed illustration, was a rebuke to the father I had been. I could avenge her death. I could kill as my memorial to her, and perhaps die in the effort and end my shame. But I could not undo how I had neglected the child. Every time the Fool exclaimed over how cleverly she had worded a rhyme, it was like a tiny burning coal of shame deposited on my heart.

The weather held fine for us. The ship operated smoothly. When I walked on the deck, I felt as if the crew moved around me while they trod the intricate steps of a dance to a music only they could hear. The river current swept us along for the first part of our journey, with little need for canvas. The dense green walls of the sky-tall forest towered higher than any mast. Sometimes the river raced deep and swift and the trees were so close that we smelled the flowers and heard the raucous cries of the birds and nimble creatures that inhabited every level. One morning I awoke late to find that the river had been joined by a tributary and now spread wide and flat round us. On the left side of the ship, the forest had retreated to a green haze on the horizon. 'What's over there?' I asked Clef when he paused near me in his duties.

He squinted. 'Don't know. Water's too shallow for Paragon or any large ship. There's just this one channel down the middle and we're damn lucky that Paragon knows it as well as he does. On that far side, the river gets shallower and then gives onto stinking grey mudflats that would suck a man down to his hips. And they stretch at least a day's walk, maybe two, before trees start again.' He shook his head and mused, 'So much of the Rain Wilds in't for humans. We're better off remembering that not all the world is made for us. Hey! Hey! You don't coil a line like that!' He was off down the deck and I was left staring across the water.

The river bore us ever closer to the coast, and I became aware by my Wit and Skill both that the ship was not a passive component of our journey. By day, I sensed his awareness. 'Does he steer himself?' I asked Amber at one point.

'To some degree. Every part of him that touches water is made of wizardwood. Or more accurately, dragon-cocoon. The Rain Wilders built the ships that way because the water of this river eats anything else away quickly. Or so it was at one time. I understand that the Jamaillians have come up with a way of treating wood that lets an ordinary ship ply this river without being eaten. Impervious ships, they call them. Or so I'm told. A liveship would have some control over its rudder. But only some. Paragon can also control every plank of his hull. He can tighten or loosen. He can warn his crew if he's leaking. Wizardwood seems able to "heal" after a fashion, if a liveship scrapes bottom or collides with another vessel.'

I shook my head in wonder. 'A marvellous creation indeed.'

The slight smile Amber had been wearing faded. 'Not created by men or even by shipbuilders. Every liveship was meant to be a dragon.

Some remember that more clearly than others. Each ship is truly alive, Fitz. Puzzled in some cases, angry or confused in others. But alive.' As if that had given her some new thought, she turned away from me, set her hands on the railing and stared out across the grey water.

Our shipboard days quickly fell into a pattern. We breakfasted with Brashen or Althea, but seldom both. One or the other of them always seemed to be on deck, prowling about with a keen eye. Spark and Perseverance kept themselves busy. The rigging seemed to both fascinate and daunt them, and they challenged each other daily. It was a task for Lant to corner them and settle them to letters and learning. Spark could already read and write but had a limited understanding of Six Duchies geography or history. It was fortunate that she seemed to enjoy the hours Lant spent instructing her, for Per could not have endured being kept at pen and paper while Spark roved the ship. Often enough the lessons were held on the deck, while Amber and I quietly plotted imaginary murders.

The noon meal was less formal, and often I had little appetite for it, having spent my morning in idleness. It troubled me that the skills I had fought to regain at Buckkeep were now becoming rusty again, but I saw no way to drill with an axe or a sword that would not have invited questions or created alarm. In the afternoon, Amber and I were often closeted with Bee's books. We took our evening meal with Brashen and Althea. The ship was usually anchored by then, or tied off to trees depending on the river's condition.

After the evening meal, I was often left to my own devices, for Amber spent almost every evening with Paragon. She would don a shawl and make her way to the foredeck, where she would settle herself cross-legged on the peak of the bow and talk with him. Sometimes, to my discomfort, Paragon would hold her in his hands. She would sit on his palms, his thumbs under her hands so she could face him, and they would converse far into the dark. At his request, she borrowed a small set of pipes from Clef and played for him—low, breathy music that seemed to be about loneliness and loss. Once or twice I wandered forward to see if I might join them, for I confess the curiosity seethed in me as to what they might be talking about for so many nights. But without insult it was made plain to me that I was not to be included in their discussions.

The galley and the area belowdecks were the province of the crew.

On Paragon, I was not only a stranger, a foreigner and a prince, I was also the idiot who had upset the figurehead and let him publicly threaten me. The rattling games of chance played belowdecks and the crew's rough humour was not to be shared with the likes of me. So as often as not I spent the evening alone in the cramped cabin Spark shared with the Fool. I kept my mind busy as best I could, usually with leafing through Bee's books. Sometimes I was invited to Althea and Brashen's stateroom for wine and casual talk, but I was keenly aware that my companions and I were their cargo rather than their guests. So when I politely declined an invitation one evening, my dismay rose when Brashen said bluntly, 'No, we need to talk. It's important.'

A little silence held as I followed him back to their stateroom. Althea was already there, with a dusty bottle of wine on the table and three glasses. For a brief time, all three of us pretended that this was no more than a chance to share a fine vintage and unwind at the end of the day. The anchored ship rocked gently in the river's current. The windows were open overlooking the river and the night sounds of the nearby forest canopy reached us.

'We'll leave the river tomorrow afternoon and head toward Bingtown,' Brashen announced suddenly.

'We've made good time, I think,' I said agreeably. I had no idea how long such a voyage usually took.

'We have. Surprisingly good. Paragon likes the river and sometimes he dawdles on this leg of the journey. Not this time.'

'And that is not good?' I asked in puzzlement.

'That is a change in his behaviour. And almost any change is a cause for worry.' Brashen spoke slowly.

Althea finished her wine and set her glass firmly on the table. 'I know Amber has told you a little of Paragon's history—how he is, in essence, two dragons in a ship's body—but there is more you should know. He's led a tragic life. Liveships absorb the memories and emotions of their families, and the crews who live on board them. Early in his awareness, perhaps due to his dual nature, he capsized and a boy of his family died tangled in lines on his deck. It scarred him. Several times after that, he turned turtle, drowning all aboard him. Such is the value of a liveship that each time he was found and righted, re-fitted and sailed again. But he became known as a bad luck ship, mockingly called the *Pariah*. The last time he was sent out he was gone for years. He returned to Bingtown on his own, drifting against the current and was found, hull up, just outside the harbour. When he was righted, they discovered that his face had been deliberately damaged, his eyes chopped away, and he bore on his chest a brand that many recognized. Igrot's star.'

'Igrot the pirate.' Their tale was fleshing out the bones of what Amber had told me. I leaned closer, for Althea spoke in a low voice as if fearful of being overheard.

'The same.' Brashen spoke the word with such dull finality that I could no longer doubt the seriousness of the conversation.

'Paragon was abused in ways that it is hard for someone not of Bingtown lineage to understand.' Her voice had become stiff. Brashen interrupted. 'I think that's as much as an outsider can understand about Paragon. I'll add that Amber re-carved his face, giving him back his sight. They became close during those days. And he has obviously missed her and feels great . . . attachment to her.'

I nodded, still baffled by their sombre tone.

'They are spending too much time together,' Althea said suddenly. 'I don't know what they are discussing, but Paragon is becoming more unsettled with every passing day. Both Brashen and I can feel it. After so many years living aboard him, both of us are . . .'

'Attuned.' Brashen suggested the word, and it fitted. I thought of telling them exactly how much I did understand it, and then refrained. They considered me peculiar enough without my revealing a hereditary magic that let me touch minds with other people.

And possibly with liveships? It had certainly felt that way with Tarman. I'd kept my Skill tightly restrained since my incident with Paragon, fearing that if I lowered my walls to read him, he'd not only be aware of it, but annoyed by it. I'd already agitated him enough. So, 'I can imagine that sort of a bond,' I offered them.

Althea accepted that with a nod and poured more wine for all of us. 'It's a bond that goes both ways. We are aware of the ship and the ship is aware of us. And since Amber came on board, Paragon's emotions have become more intense.'

'And at such times, Paragon becomes more wilful,' Brashen said. 'We notice it in his handling. As does the crew. Earlier today, that was a tricky stretch of the river, known to have shifting shoals. We usually slow his progress when we traverse it. Today he defied us and we took that passage faster than we ever have. Why is Paragon hurrying?'

'I don't know.'

'Where are you bound?'

Suddenly I felt too weary to talk about it. I never wanted to tell my tale again. 'Queen Malta sent you a message by bird, I thought.'

'She did, with a request that we help you since you had helped many of their children. Undoing what the Rain Wilds had done to them.'

'What the dragons had done to them,' I corrected her. I was uncomfortable with this conversation. Plainly they were upset to the point of anger about their ship's attitude and were willing to blame it on Amber. And demand that I do something about it. I made the obvious suggestion. 'Perhaps we should all walk forward to the figurehead and ask what is upsetting your ship.'

'Please lower your voice,' Althea warned me.

Brashen was shaking his head emphatically. 'Trust us that we know Paragon. As old as he is, he still does not accept logic as an adult. He is more like an adolescent. Sometimes rational and sometimes impulsive. If we try to intervene between him and Amber, I think the results will be . . .' He let his voice trail off, his eyes widening.

Althea shot to her feet. 'What is that?' she demanded of us and of no one.

I felt it too, as if a prickling heat had washed suddenly through my body. I found it hard to catch my breath for an instant, and as I steadied myself by gripping the edge of the table, I realized I was not feeling vertigo. No. The wine in my glass trembled, tiny circles dancing in it. 'Earthquake,' I said, trying to be calm. They were not unusual in the Six Duchies. I'd heard tales of quakes powerful enough to crack the towers of Buckkeep Castle. The Fool's first rooms at Buckkeep had been in one such damaged tower. In my lifetime, I had not seen such a happening, but the minstrel tales of falling towers and waves that demolished harbours were terrifying. And here we were, anchored near a forest of towering trees rooted in mud . . .

'Not an earthquake,' Brashen said. 'It's the ship. Come on!'

I doubted he was speaking to me but I followed Althea out of the cabin. We were not the only ones on the deck. Some of the deckhands were looking up at the trees or over the side in puzzlement. Clef was running forward. I went more slowly. I would not again risk being in Paragon's hands. I felt a sudden crackling under my feet. I looked down. In the uncertain light of the ship's lanterns, the deck suddenly appeared pebbly rather than having the smooth tight grain of wizardwood. No, not pebbly. Scaly.

I hurried after Althea. Brashen and Clef had halted a safe distance from the figurehead. Amber stood alone on the foredeck, spine straight and head up. A stubborn stance. The figurehead twisted around and tossed something to her. She did not see it and it tumbled to the deck with the tinkle of breaking glass. 'More!' he demanded.

'That's all I have now. But help me and I promise I will try to get you more.'

'I need more! That wasn't enough!'

At first glance I had thought the dim lights were playing tricks on my eyes. But Paragon's face no longer matched my own. He was as scaled as an elderly Rain Wilder. As I stared up at him, his eyes shifted. They were still blue, but the blue swirled with silver. Dragon's eyes. He reached toward Amber with fingers tipped with black claws.

'Fool! Step away from him!' I cried, and Paragon lifted his eyes to lock his gaze on me.

'Don't ever call her a fool!' he snarled at me, past sharp teeth. 'She is wiser than all of you!'

'Amber, what have you done?' Althea cried in a low, broken voice. Brashen was silent, staring in stark horror at the transformed figurehead.

'She has given me back my true nature, at least in part!' It was Paragon who answered them. His face was changing as I stared up at him, colour rippling across the features we shared. In the dark, he gleamed a coppery bronze as he closed his clawed hands around Amber and lifted her from the deck. He clutched her possessively to his chest and added, 'She knows me for who I am, and has not hesitated to give me what I have always needed!'

'Please, ship, be calm. Put her back on your deck. Explain this to us.' Brashen spoke as if he were reasoning with a recalcitrant ten-year-old. Calm but still in control. I wished I felt that way.

'I am not a SHIP!' The figurehead's sudden shout startled birds from the trees and sent them battering off through the darkened forest. 'I have never been a ship! We are dragons, trapped! Enslaved! But my true friend has shown me that I can be free.'

'True friend,' Althea said under her breath, as if doubting both words.

Brashen moved closer to his wife. Every muscle in his body was tensed, as if he were a hound on the leash, waiting to be released. He spared one glance over his shoulder for the gathering crew. 'I'm handling this. Please disperse about your duties.'

They departed slowly. Clef didn't move. He stood where he was, his face grave. My gaze met Lant's and he put a hand on Spark's shoulder, drawing her closer to him and gave Perseverance a nudge as he moved them away. I remained where I was. Paragon held Amber under his chin and against his chest. She looked blindly out over the water. 'I had to do it,' she said. I wondered if she spoke to me or to her former friends.

'She has set me on the path to returning to my proper forms!' Paragon announced to the early stars in the deep sky. 'She has given me Silver.'

I scanned the deck, and saw at last the shards of a glass vial. My heart sank. Had she discovered it in my pack and taken it without asking me? Without warning me of her plan? What was her plan?

Althea's voice was higher pitched than usual as she asked, 'Your proper forms?'

'You see what even a small amount of Silver has done for me? Given enough, I believe I can shake off these wooden planks you have fastened to me and cast aside canvas sails for wings! We will become the dragons we were meant to be!'

Althea looked stunned. She spoke her words as if trying to find the meaning of words spoken in a foreign tongue. 'You will become dragons? You will cease to be Paragon? How?' Then, even more incredulously, 'You will leave us?'

He ignored the hurt in her voice, choosing instead to take offence at a meaning her words had not held. 'What would you have me do? How could you want me to stay like this? Always at the whim of others? Going only where you take me, carrying burdens back and forth between human ports? Sexless? Trapped in a form not my own?' From almost begging, his voice edged into fury. I expected his arrowed words to wound her, but she seemed immune to them.

Althea stepped fearlessly toward the figurehead, turning her face up to him in the dimming light. 'Paragon. Do not pretend that you cannot tell what I feel about this. About you.'

He narrowed his dragon eyes at Althea until his fixed stare looked like blue fire seething in a cracked stove wall. Slowly his arms, still so strangely human despite their scaling, unfolded. He lowered Amber to the deck and wordlessly turned his back on us. Amber stumbled a little and then stood. I tried to read her stance, to see something of my old friend the Fool in her at this moment. Instead I saw only Amber and felt again the gulf of wondering who that woman was.

And what she was capable of.

Paragon had turned away from all of us, to stare out over the darkened river. The tension of the figurehead thrummed through the wizardwood hull and bones of the ship. I had the rising realization that he spoke the truth. He was not a ship. He was a dragon, transformed and trapped by men. And however much he might care for those who crewed him, on some level he had to feel resentment. Perhaps even hatred.

And we were completely in his power.

As that chill thought iced my bones, Althea advanced on Amber. She reminded me of a stalking cat that sizes another cat up for a fight. The small steps, the precise balance, the unwinking stare. She spoke in a low, soft voice. 'What did you do to my ship?'

Amber turned her sightless eyes toward Althea's voice. 'I did what should be done for every liveship. What you should do for Vivacia if the opportunity presents itself.'

At the name Vivacia, every muscle in Althea's body tightened and she knotted her fists.

I've seen women fight. I've seen ladies in fine dress slapping and flapping at one another, weeping and shrieking all the while. And I've seen fishwives draw knives against one another, attempting to scale and gut one another as coldly as they process fish. Althea was no soft-bred lady in lace, and having watched her run the deck-crew and scale the rigging, I had a sturdy respect for the strength in those arms. But the Fool had never been a fighter. Blind and given what he had so recently endured, I did not trust the new healing of his body to withstand any sort of physical struggle.

Light-footed, I dashed forward and stepped between them.

It was not a good spot to be. Althea's anger at her old friend was as nothing to the fury that an intervening stranger woke in her. She drove the hard heel of her palm into the middle of my chest. 'Move,' she demanded. If I hadn't been ready for such a blow, it would have knocked the wind out of me.

'Stop,' I advised her.

'This doesn't involve you. Unless you want it to!' But before I could even contemplate reacting to that, Brashen bulled between us, pushing Althea to one side. Chest to chest, our eyes met in the darkness.

'You are on my deck.' A low growl. 'You do what she or I tell you to do.'

I shook my head slowly. 'Not this time,' I said quietly. Behind me, Amber was silent.

'You want to take it to fists?' Brashen demanded. He leaned closer and I felt his breath on my face. I was taller than he was, but he was broader. Probably in better condition. Did I want to take it to fists?

I did. Abruptly I was tired of all of them. Even Amber. I felt my upper lip lift to bare my teeth. Time to fight, time to kill. 'Yes,' I promised him.

'Stop this, all of you! It's Paragon feeling that. Fitz, it's the dragon!' the Fool shouted behind me. 'It's the dragon!' He slapped me on the back of the head so hard that my head jolted forward. My brow slammed into Brashen's face and I heard Althea shout something. She had hold of her man's shirt and was dragging him away from me. I clutched at him, unwilling to release my prey. Behind me, the Fool slammed his shoulder into my back. Althea tripped and went down backwards, dragging Brashen with her. I nearly fell on top of them but rolled to one side. The Fool landed on top of me and spoke by my ear. 'It's the ship, Fitz. It's his anger. Stop claiming what isn't yours.'

I fought my way clear of him, tearing myself from his grip. I scrabbled to my feet and managed to stand, ready to wade back into it and kick Brashen's ribs to splinters. I was gasping for breath and I heard that sound echoed in the heavy snorting of a large creature. A very large creature.

Most of the light had fled from the day, and the wan circles of the ship's lanterns were not intended to illuminate the figurehead. Even so, I could see that he was rapidly losing any resemblance to a human form. What had been my jaw, mouth and nose were lengthening into a reptile's snout. I stared up at his gleaming, whirling blue eyes. For a moment, our gazes locked and held. I saw there the same fury that had surged through me. I felt the Fool's gloved hand on my arm. 'Walls up,' he pleaded.

But the fury had passed like a summer squall, leaving me empty of emotion in its wake. I gripped the Fool's wrist and hauled Amber to her feet. She shook her skirts into order.

'Move aft,' Brashen commanded us. His nose was bleeding where my brow had struck him. Petty, that I enjoyed that. I still obeyed his order. His face in the dim light looked slack and old. As we trudged back to their stateroom, we passed Clef. Brashen spoke as he strode past him. 'Pass the word. Everyone stays well clear of the figurehead until I give orders otherwise. Then come back here and keep a watch on him. Call me if you think I need to come forward.' Clef nodded and hurried away.

We reached the stateroom. Lant and the youngsters were clustered by the door, a questioning look on Lant's face. 'We're fine,' I told him. 'Take Per and Spark to Lady Amber's cabin for now. I'll explain later.' I gestured him away. His gaze told me he didn't wish to be dismissed with the youngsters, but he steered them away. Brashen was waiting by the open door. I followed Amber in and he shut the door behind us.

We were not two steps inside when 'What did you do?' Althea demanded of Amber in a tight, angry voice.

'Not yet,' Brashen told her. He took mugs from a cupboard and a very potent-looking bottle from a shelf. He poured for all of us, a healthy portion. Not an elegant wine or a mellow brandy but harsh spirits. Cheap rum. He made no ceremony, but took a healthy swallow from his, added more, and then thunked it onto the table as he dropped into his chair. 'Sit down. All of you.' It was a captain's command. Amber obeyed it, and after a moment I sat, too.

'Why did she do it? That's the real question.' He stared at Amber and in his eyes I saw anger, despair and the deep hurt that only a friend's betrayal can bring.

I had nothing to say. Her action had confused me completely. During our journey, on a quest that I would have sworn had become the Fool's sole purpose in life, she had chosen to reveal that we possessed a forbidden substance by using it to . . . do something to the ship. Well on our way, she had betrayed hospitality and friendship and endangered us all. It made no sense. I felt as affronted as Althea to be plunged into such a situation. And helpless to right any of it.

Amber spoke at last. 'I had to do it. It was the right thing to do for the ship. For Paragon.' She took a breath. 'I gave him Silver. That's what the folk in Kelsingra call it. There is a well of it there; the dragons drink from it. It's a liquid magic, the stuff that breaks the walls between humans and dragons. It can heal an injured dragon, extend the lives of Elderlings, and imbue objects with magic. For those born with a touch of magic, like Fitz, it can enhance abilities . . . And I believe, as Paragon does, that if he is given enough of it, he can complete the transformation he was meant to make. He can become the dragon whose cocoon was stolen to make the "wizardwood" that comprises this ship.'

Information spilled from her—a very unFool-like sharing. I saw Brashen and Althea struggle to grasp what she was saying. She seemed to run out of words. Brashen was scowling. Althea had reached across the table to take his hand. Then, reluctantly, Amber spoke again.

'But I had another reason. Some might call it selfish. I needed to strike a bargain with Paragon—a bargain I knew you would not find agreeable. I must get to Clerres, as swiftly as possible, and Paragon can take me there. And for the chance of more Silver, he will take me there.' She looked down at the table, and lifted the heavy pottery mug. 'It was my only choice,' she said, and took down a hefty swig of rum.

'We're going to Bingtown. Then Jamaillia. Not Clerres. We have cargo to deliver, contracts to fulfil.' Althea explained it all carefully but dread was growing in her eyes as she began to comprehend the size of the change overtaking her life.

'No. We're going directly to Clerres,' Amber told her softly. She breathed out raggedly. 'I know this will change your lives. If there were another way, I would have taken it. Maybe. Regardless of what it does to any of the rest of us, Paragon deserves the Silver. All the liveships do! But if I hadn't been so desperate . . . This is the only way for me to get to Clerres as swiftly as possible, and that is what I must do.'

'I don't even know that port,' Brashen said. He raised a brow at Althea, and she shook her head.

'Paragon does. He has been there before. When he was Igrot's ship, they ranged far in taking their prey. Far past the Spice Islands. Past several clusters of islands. Isabom. Kinectu. Sterlin. And beyond. Clerres is known to Paragon. He will take us there.'

'We have contracts . . .' Althea said faintly.

Brashen did not try to disguise the anger in his voice. 'We "had" contracts. But I suppose it's useless trying to make an outsider understand that a Trader's good word is all he has. And now those words will be broken, both mine and Althea's. No one will ever trust us again. No one will trade with us again.' He took a breath, his scowl deepening. 'And after Paragon has taken you to Clerres, and you've done whatever urgent thing you must do and you give him this "Silver". What then?' Brashen demanded relentlessly. 'Do you truly believe Paragon can . . . stop being a ship? Transform into a dragon?'

Amber drew a ragged breath. 'He would become two dragons, freed of an unnatural bond with one another and transformed into their proper forms. Yes. With enough Silver, I hope he can. *They* can.' She looked from one incredulous face to another. 'You love him. You've loved him for years, since the time he was a derelict hulk dragged up on the beach. Althea, you played inside him as a girl. Brashen, you took shelter inside him when no one else would offer you a roof. You know him, you know how mistreated he has been. What he said was true. You can't possibly wish for him to remain as he is.'

'I do love him,' Althea said faintly. 'When my family risked all to buy him, it protected him from being dismantled and gave us a way to save Vivacia and my nephew. All the years since, Brashen and I have protected him. Do you think any other captains would have wished for a ship like this?' She drew a slow breath. 'But you have ruined us. Do you understand that? Doubtless you think me selfish that I think of our future now, but without our liveship, Brashen and I have nothing. No home, no holding, no business. Nothing. We've depended on Paragon, cared for him when no one else would trust him, kept him from being carved up and sold off as a curiosity. You seem to think his life a miserable one, but it was the best we could give him. We're a part of him and he's part of us. What becomes of us if he becomes a dragon; or two dragons? What legacy do we have left for our son?'

She paused and I watched her try to find some measure of control. 'And if the Silver fails and he can never be more than what he is now? That, perhaps, is even worse. Do you not recall how miserable he was when we first resurrected him, blind and abused, full of hatred? You must remember; you were there for some of it. Do you think all the years since then were always easy? But we rebuilt him, gave him heart and peace and joy. He took us through storms, roaring with laughter at our fear! Placid seas, with him holding our child in his hands and dipping him into the water to make him giggle. All that is gone now. He will never take joy in being a ship again. All the reputation we rebuilt for him, all our years together . . . It's all ruined. All lost.'

Althea slowly crumped onto the table, her face sinking into her folded arms. Before my eyes, she dwindled, and I now saw the grey streaks in her dark hair and the veins and tendons on the back of her strong hands. Brashen reached across the table and set his weathered hand on top of one of hers. For a time, silence held at that table. I felt shamed at the disaster we had brought upon them. I could not read the emotions behind Amber's stiff expression. It came to me again that, despite my long bond with the Fool, I'd never be able to predict what Amber might or might not do.

Brashen spoke measured words as he stroked his wife's rough hair. 'Althea. We go on, my dear. With or without Paragon's deck beneath our feet, you and I go on.' He swallowed. 'Perhaps Boy-O stays on Vivacia's deck. She is as much his family ship as Paragon is, and Sa knows that Kennit's son has shown little interest in a life at sea . . .'

I heard his voice falter and saw the slow realization steal across his face. If Paragon could become a dragon again, so could Vivacia. So could any or all of the liveships. It was not just them that Amber had destroyed. When she gave Paragon Silver, she had toppled the dynasties of the Bingtown Traders who owned liveships. Bingtown itself, that great trade centre, had always been dependent on the liveships to transport the treasures of the Rain Wilds. Now liveships would fade into history, and with them the fortunes of the old families that owned them.

Althea lifted her head and stared at Amber. 'Why?' she asked brokenly. 'Why not ask us first, why not tell us what you were going to do? Why not give us a small amount of time to plan how we might handle such an immense change? Did you think we would deny Paragon what he so earnestly desires? Did you not think the idea could have been introduced to him slowly in a safer place and way?'

She spoke of her ship as if he were her child. A damaged child, but beloved all the same. A child she would now lose to his madness.

It was painful to be witness to such a terrible loss, but Amber sat impassive.

'I had to do it,' she said at last. 'And not just for Paragon's sake.' She looked at me. 'It did begin with Paragon. I'm sorry, Fitz. I wanted to tell you what I'd planned. It was why I wanted the Silver. I did not intend to just give it to him. But when I was speaking to Paragon tonight he asked me if it pleased me to be back on the ship, even if I could no longer be a sailor as I was meant to be. I told him I did not think I was meant to be a sailor. And he said he had never been meant to be a ship, that he should have been dragons . . . Suddenly the bits of what he was saying intersected with something in Bee's dream journal and I knew what her dream meant. She predicted her survival. I am certain that Bee is alive. And likely still in the hands of her kidnappers. They will take her to Clerres. We cannot know by what path, but we know where that path leads. We also know that she cannot remain in their hands for even a moment longer than we can prevent. We cannot travel in fits and starts, we cannot pause to find other ships and negotiate passage, going from one port to the next and hope we reach there in time. We must get to Clerres as swiftly as we can. And a liveship that knows the way is our best chance of saving her.'

Hope, dashed too often, becomes the enemy. I heard her words and they did not make my heart leap with gladness. Instead, I felt hot anger. How dare she? How dare she say such a thing before strangers, how dare she taunt me with a foundationless fancy? Then, like a drenching wave that cannot be outrun, hope crashed over me. It seized me and dragged me over barnacles into its depths. I forgot all other events of the day as I demanded, 'Bee, alive? How? Why do you believe such a thing?'

She turned to me. Her hand quested over the table and found mine. She clasped it, the cool touch of her fingers enclosing mine. I could not read her pale, empty eyes. Her voice was careful. 'It's in her dream book, Fitz. Oh, not spelled out exactly, but there were dreams that she labelled as most likely to come true. Things she believed were more likely to happen than other things. She spoke of events to come in images rather than words. I spent a lifetime learning to read dreams. And her dreams fitted together as perfectly as pieces of broken crockery being nudged back into alignment.'

'A dream book?' Althea demanded. 'Sa's balls and tits! What is a dream book and why did it prompt you to destroy us?'

Amber turned her face toward them. 'It will take some time to explain . . .'

'Time you should have taken days ago, I think. So start now.' Althea's anger was unconcealed.

'Very well.' Amber accepted the rebuke gravely and offered no defence. She squeezed my hand. There was regret in her voice when she said, 'Fitz, I know you will resent my asking for this, but please fetch Bee's dream book while I explain to Althea and Brashen what it is and why each of her dreams is so significant.'

I have known the hot flush of anger, and the blinding red of fury. Now I felt as if ice formed in the pit of my belly and spread from there. A cold that nearly stilled my heart came over me. I stared at her, frozen motionless by her callousness. She stared toward me. What did she see? A shadow? A shape?

'Fitz. Please.' Brashen did not stare at me but looked at his hands. 'If you can help us understand what this is about . . .'

His words trailed off. Wordlessly, I rose, shoving my chair back with my thighs, and left the stateroom. I didn't go to Amber's room where my pack was kept. Instead I walked alone through the insect-singing darkness until I came to the foredeck.

Paragon brooded in his place. His hunched shoulders were human but his neck was longer now and his reptilian head was tucked to his chest. It disturbed me as few things in my life had. I cleared my throat. He moved his head on his sinuous neck to look at me. His eyes were still blue. That was the only feature I could recognize.

'What do you want?' he demanded.

'I don't know,' I admitted. I did not feel fearless, but nonetheless I walked over and leaned on the railing. Amber had wakened hope in me, and with hope, she had wakened doubt. While I had been certain Bee was lost to me, I had wanted vengeance. More than vengeance, I had wanted my own death. If I could go to Clerres and kill as many as I could and die in the attempt, that would be fine. I'd had time and to spare to work that vengeance thoroughly. But now I wanted Bee to be alive so that I could rescue her. If she wasn't alive, I wanted to be dead, too, so that all my failures would finally be over. Didn't I want vengeance any more? Not tonight, I decided. I was too tired of it all. If I could dash in, find Bee and run away and live quietly with my child somewhere, that would be enough. 'Do you think my daughter is alive?' I asked the ship.

His blue eyes whirled, as if lanterns shone through spinning blue glass. 'I don't know. But that does not matter to the bargain that we struck, Amber and I. I will take you to Clerres, as swiftly as I can. I know the way. I was there when enslaved to Igrot. If your daughter is alive you will rescue her, and even if she is not you will destroy that nest of ugliness. Then we will come back here and sail up the river, and Amber will get Silver for me. Enough Silver for me to become the dragons I was meant to be.'

I wanted to ask him what he would do if we died trying. I was sure he'd still go back to Kelsingra and demand Silver. So why didn't he do that right now?

Because your vengeance is dragon-vengeance as well. He paused. I waited, but he gave me no more than that. *As dragons, I cannot bear you there. Only as a ship can I transport you that far. So we all go, together, to take the vengeance that is owed to us. And then we will be free, to become what we were always meant to be.*

Slowly, I became aware that Paragon's lizard lips were not shaping those words. I heard him and I knew the sense of his words. He was replying as much to my thoughts as he was my words. It was like the Skill and it was like the Wit, but it was neither. I lifted my hands slowly from the railing.

I know you now. There is no avoiding me if I wish to speak to you. But right now, I will say only this. Do not thwart her will in this, or mine. To Clerres we go, to make an end to those who tormented her and stole her child. And then we return to Kelsingra that I may become dragons. Go now. Fetch what she sent you for. Reassure Brashen and Althea as much as you can.

That last he said as if he were asking me to be sure his cats were fed while he was away. How could he feel so little for them?

Would you rather I hated the ones I have served as a slave?

I slammed my walls up tight. Could he truly reach into my mind whenever he wished? What sort of vengeance did he imagine we would take? If we found Bee alive, and wished to take her and flee immediately, would he oppose us? I pushed such questions aside. Perhaps for now I needed to know only that he would take us to Clerres.

I went to Amber's small cabin. It was dark but I refused to go back for a lantern. My pack was wedged into a corner under the bunk. I found it by touch and dragged it out past the bundles of Amber's and Spark's clothing that had somehow expanded to fill every available space. I dug for the dream journal and as I did so my fingers brushed the fabric that had wrapped the Silver I'd been given by Rapskal. A small betrayal that she had gone through my pack and found it, but I was becoming accustomed to her small betrayals. Yet as I angrily pushed the fabric aside to remove the book, I felt the heavy glass tubes the general had given me. Slowly I withdrew the bundle, opened it and held up the tubes. Early starlight had begun to venture in the tiny window and the substance in the glass answered it with an unearthly gleam. The Silver within still did its slow dance. Both were full to the brim, stoppered and sealed as they had been when Rapskal put them in my hands. Liquid magic. The Skill in pure form, independent of human or dragon blood. I tipped the tubes again and watched the slow crawl within the glass. I wondered how much Amber had given Paragon. Was this enough to fulfil his transformation? If he became recalcitrant or dangerous, could this be the bribe I offered? Precious stuff. Dangerous stuff.

I rewrapped the bundle and thrust it deep into the pack again. I'd misjudged Amber. Somehow she had obtained Silver and concealed it from me. Just as I concealed what I had from her. To think that perhaps I was as deceptive to her as she was to me only made me angry. I wished she would go away and that . . .

And that the Fool would come back? The peculiarity of my thought suddenly spun me round and round. There was no avoiding the admission that my interactions with Amber were vastly different to what I thought and felt about the Fool. I wanted to rattle my head like a dog shaking off water, but knew it would be useless. I tucked Bee's book securely under my arm, and shoved my pack well back in its place.

'You took your time,' Brashen observed as I re-entered the stateroom. I noticed that Clef had joined us. He wasn't seated at the table, but hunched on a low stool in the corner, a mug of liquor in his hands. The look he gave me was not friendly. I didn't feel particularly friendly either. Doubtless he had seen me speaking with Paragon and come to tell Brashen.

'I stopped to talk to Paragon,' I admitted.

Brashen's jaw muscles bunched and Althea straightened as if she would spring at me. I held up a cautioning hand. 'He confirmed his bargain with Amber. And implied that he and other dragons might have reasons of their own for wishing us well on our quest.' I looked at Amber. 'I'd like to know what those are. And I'd like to know how you got Silver when Reyn and Malta specifically refused your request for some.'

Althea made a small sound of shock. Brashen grew very still.

'I didn't steal it,' she said in a low voice. I waited. She took a breath. 'It was given to me, very privately, by someone who knew that it could bring down great trouble if other people knew about it. I'd rather not say exactly who that was.' She folded her lips primly.

'As if we'd care,' Althea grumbled sarcastically. 'Show us your "proof" that your child is alive. That you have not destroyed our lives for nothing.' It was obvious that any sympathy she'd ever felt toward us had been burned away. I could scarcely blame her and yet I felt a rising fury to hear her speak so of Bee.

I set the book carefully on the table and sat down with my arms to either side of it. No one was going to touch it but me. I forced my voice to an even tone and addressed Amber. 'What, exactly, did you wish me to read from this book?'

I think she knew how close I was to irrational fury. I was at her mercy, and the mercy of these strangers and their unreliable ship, and they were demanding that I 'prove' to them that my child was special enough to deserve to be rescued from people who delighted in torture. If there had been any sort of a 'shore' to the river, I would have immediately demanded to be put upon it and walked away from all of them.

'Please read the dream where the two-headed person gives you a vial of ink to drink. And you shake off pieces of wood and become two dragons. I think that one will be the clearest to all of us here.'

I was very still for a moment. More than once, I had accused the Fool of 'interpreting' his dream predictions with hindsight, tailoring them to fit what actually happened. But this, at least, did strike me as starkly clear. I paged through Bee's dream journal until I found it. For a moment, I looked at the illustration she had created. A gloved hand held aloft a little glass vial. In the background, I reached for it with eager hands. There were glints of blue in the eyes she had given me. She had tinted the 'ink' within the vial yellow and grey. It was not silver but I understood it was meant to be. Slowly

I read her words aloud and then turned the book and offered the illustration to Althea and Brashen. Althea scowled at it and Brashen leaned back and crossed his arms on his chest.

'How do we know that you didn't write that out last night?' Brashen demanded.

It was a stupid question and he knew it. But I answered it. 'One of us is blind and therefore unable to write or draw. And if you suspect me, I have no brushes and inks of a quality to do this, nor the talent for illustration.' I gently fanned the pages of Bee's book. 'And there are many pages of dreams and illustrations that follow this one.'

He knew that. He simply didn't want to admit that Bee had foreseen how Lady Amber would give a liveship with my face a vial of Silver so that it might become not just one but two dragons.

'But—' he began and Althea cut in quietly, 'Let it be, Brashen. We both know there has always been a peculiar scent of magic around Amber. And this is more of it, I fear.'

'It is,' Amber confirmed. Her face was grave, her voice solemn.

I didn't want to ask my question in front of strangers but the desire to know was eating me like an infected wound. 'Why do you think Bee is alive?'

Her shoulders rose and fell with a deep breath taken and sighed out. 'That will be less clear, I fear.'

'I'm waiting.'

'First, there is her dream of being a nut. And a second one, in which she calls herself an acorn. Do you recall that one? She is small and tight and tossed in a current. I think she is predicting her passage through a Skill-pillar.'

'Passage through a what?' Brashen asked.

'I speak to Fitz, now. If you wish to know, I will explain it later.'

He subsided, but not gracefully. He leaned back in his chair, his arms crossed on his chest and his face closed.

'That's one possible meaning,' I conceded with as little grace as Trell.

'Then there is the dream of the candles. Fitz, I know you carry some of Molly's candles with you. The scents are plain to a blind man. I can even tell when you've taken them out and handled them. How many do you have?'

'Only three. I began with four. One was lost when the bear

attacked us. After you and Spark fled through the pillar, we gathered what we could of our supplies. But much was scattered and lost or spoiled. I could only find three . . .'

'Do you remember her dream of the candles? Find it in the book, please.'

I did. I read it aloud slowly. A gradual smile spread over his face. *The wolf and the jester*. It spoke so plainly that even I knew it meant the Fool and me.

'Three candles, Fitz. "They do not know their child still lives." Her dream showed her a place where her chances divided. When you lost a candle, it somehow created a change for her. A change that meant that she lived instead of dying.'

I sat very still. It was too ridiculous to believe. A surge of something—not hope, not belief, but something I'd no name for—rushed through me. I felt as if my heart had begun to beat again, as if air filled my lungs after a long denial. I wanted so desperately to believe Bee might still be alive.

Belief burst through any wall of rationality or caution I possessed. 'Three candles,' I said weakly. I wanted to weep and to laugh and shout.

Three candles meant that my daughter still lived.

FIFTEEN

Trader Akriel

The puppet dances. He turns flips and he jigs. His painted red smile looks happy but he is screaming, for he performs on red-hot coals. His wooden feet begin to smoke. A man comes in with a shining axe. He swings it. I think he will cut off the puppet's burning feet, but instead the axe cuts all his strings. But the man with the axe falls just as swiftly as the puppet leaps away, free.

Bee Farseer's dream journal

'Why do you think I would help a ragamuffin like you?' The woman took a sip of her tea and stared at me. 'You are exactly the sort of trouble I've spent most of my life avoiding.'

She wasn't smiling. I couldn't tell her that I chose her because she was a woman and I hoped she would have a softer heart. I thought that would offend her rather than sway her. My stomach was so empty it made me want to vomit bile. I tried not to tremble but I was at the end of my resources. All I had left was will. My body had no physical courage left in it. I tried to keep my voice level. 'Earlier in the voyage, I saw you sell the old man who could read and write. He wrote his own bill of sale. I saw that you got a good price for him, even though he is old and probably does not have many years left in him.'

She was nodding but with a small scowl.

I drew myself up as straight as I could. 'I may be small and I am young, but I am strong and healthy. And I can read and write. I can also copy illustrations or draw what you wish drawn. And I can work with numbers as well.' My skill with those was not as strong as I would wish it to be but I deemed that was close enough to the truth. If I were selling myself to a slaver, I'd best present myself as a good bargain.

She leaned her elbow on the galley table. It had been terribly difficult to find her alone. I had watched her for a full day, moving from hiding-spot to hiding-spot to track her, and seen how she lingered at the table after the other traders had finished stuffing their food down. I suspected she preferred to eat late and alone rather than endure their gulping and jostling. I had ventured into the galley after the breakfast mob had left. Her unfinished meal was before her. I fought not to stare at it, but I had memorized it. The crusty edge of her bread with traces of butter on it, and a smear of grease on the plate that I longed to catch on the bread or even on the side of my finger. A scraping of porridge in her bowl. I swallowed.

'And from whom would I be buying you?'

'No one. I offer myself to you.'

She looked at me silently for a moment. 'You are selling yourself to me. Really? Where are your parents? Or your master?'

I had prepared my lie as carefully as I could. I'd had three hungry, cold and thirsty days to compose it. Three days of skulking about in the ship, trying to stay out of everyone's sight while still finding food, water, and a place to relieve myself. It was a large ship but everywhere I had found to hide in had been cold and damp. Curled small and shivering for most hours of the day, I'd had plenty of time to plot my strategy. It was a poor one. Sell myself as a slave to someone who would value the small skills I had. Get off the ship and away from Dwalia. Eventually, find a way to send a message to my father or sister. A good plan, I'd told myself. And then wondered why I didn't also plan to build a castle or perhaps conquer Chalced. Both of those goals seemed as attainable. I spoke my carefully rehearsed lie.

'My mother brought me to Chalced and the home of her new husband. He and his older children treat me horribly. So, as we walked in the market, one of his boys began to tease and then chase me. I hid on board this ship. And here I am now, being carried far away from my old home and my mother. I have tried to fend for myself and done poorly at it.'

She took a slow sip of her tea. I could smell it so clearly. It had honey in it, probably fireweed honey. It was hot and steamy and delightful. Why had I never cherished that hot morning cup of tea as it deserved? That thought brought back a rush of memories. Cook Nutmeg in the kitchen, the bustle all around me as I sat on or at the board with simple foods. Bacon. Ah, bacon. Bread toasted with butter melting on it. Tears stung my eyes. That would not do. I swallowed and stood straighter.

'Eat it,' she said suddenly, and thrust her plate toward me.

I stared at it, unable to breathe. Was it a trick? But I had learned in Chalced to eat food whenever I had the chance, even face down in the street. I tried to remember my manners. She must think me a valuable asset to acquire, not a mannerless brat. I seated myself and carefully picked up the bread crust. I took a small bite and chewed carefully. She watched me. 'You have self-control,' she observed. 'And your tale was not a bad one, even though I doubt every word of it. I haven't noticed you about the ship before today. And you do smell as if you've been in hiding. So. If I take you as my property, will there be someone raising a storm and calling me a thief? Or a kidnapper?'

'No, my lady.' That was my hardest lie. I had no idea what Dwalia might do or say. I'd bitten her badly, and I hoped she would be holed up in her cabin, nursing that injury. Kerf would only demand my return if Vindeliar puppeteered him into doing so. I did not think that likely, but my best defence would be to keep myself out of their sight as much as possible. I finished the bread in two more slow bites. I longed to lick the plate and scoop up the porridge with my finger. Instead I carefully folded my hands in my lap and sat quietly.

She tipped the porridge pot in the centre of the table toward her and with a big wooden serving spoon scraped the hardened bits from the sides and bottom into her dish. They were edged with brown where they had scorched. She pushed her bowl toward me and handed me the spoon she had used.

'Oh, thank you, my lady!' I could barely breathe but I forced myself to take small bites and sit with my back straight.

'I am not "your lady". Nor am I Chalcedean by birth, though I've found I do my best trading there. I grew up near Bingtown, but not of Trader stock, and hence it was hard for me to establish myself there. And when they eliminated the slave trade, my business there became more difficult. I am not the slave trader you think me. I find valuable and rare goods. I buy them, and I sell them at a profit. I do not always take the fast profit; sometimes my game is to wait for the large profit. Sometimes the valuable item is a slave with undervalued talents. Such as the scribe you saw me placing. Seen as aged and infirm in one market, he is seen as experienced and widely learned in another. Stand up.'

I obeyed immediately. She ran her eyes over me as if I were a cow for sale. 'Dirty. A bit battered. But you stand straight, you've some manners and a forthright way. In the Chalcedean market, they would beat that out of you. I will take you where that's a valued trait in a servant. As I doubt you've paid passage, you'll finish this voyage in my chambers. Make any sort of a mess in there, and I'll turn you over to the captain. I'll see that you are fed. When we reach Cottersbay, I will sell you as a child's maid to a family I know there. That means you will have the care of their little boy. You will bathe him, dress him, help him with his meals, publicly defer to him, and privately teach him the same manners that you are showing me now. They are a well-to-do family and will probably treat you well.'

'Yes, my lady. Thank you, my lady. I hope I will bring you a good price.'

'You will, if I clean you up a bit. And you will prove your claims to me, about letters and drawing.'

'Yes, my lady. I am eager to do so.' Suddenly the prospect of being a small boy's personal slave sounded as fine a thing as being the lost princess of Buckkeep. They might treat me well. I'd be fed and sleep indoors. I would be so good to their little boy. I'd be safe, even if I were no longer free.

'I'm not your lady. I earned my way to what I am; I was not born into it. I am Trader Akriel. And your name is?'

'Bee . . . uh!' Should I tell her my real name?

'Bea. Very well. Finish that porridge while I drink my tea.'

This I did, not rapidly but with my best manners. I felt I could have eaten three more bowls of it, but resolved to give no sign of that as I carefully set my spoon neatly beside her bowl. I looked around the cluttered, sticky table and tried to think what the servants at Withywoods would have done. 'Do you wish me to clear the table and wipe it clean, Trader Akriel?'

She shook her head and gave me a bemused smile. 'No. The ship's cook-helpers can do that. Follow me.'

She rose and I followed her. Her legs were neatly trousered in blue wool and she wore a short jacket a shade lighter than her trousers. All of her was immaculately groomed from her gleaming black boots to her braided and coiled brown hair. Her success was plain in her dangling earrings, rings and the jewelled comb in her hair. She walked with utter confidence and as we descended into the hold and then passed through the swinging hammocks and haze of smoke in the sleeping quarters, she reminded me of a sassy barn cat walking through a pack of dogs. She did not avoid meeting the gaze of the lesser merchants quartered there nor did she appear to hear any of the muttered comments as she passed. Her cabin was further forward in the ship and we went up a short flight of steps to it. She took out a key on a heavy fob and opened the locked door. 'In,' she told me, and I was happy to comply.

I was astonished. This chamber had a tiny round window and the room was as big as the one I'd been sharing with my captors. Her trunk was open on the lower bunk and her garments were arranged as precisely as tools set out for a task. Having seen Shun's wardrobe, this was astonishing to me. But it was also plain that she had planned for this voyage. There was a blue-and-white quilt with tasselled edges on the upper bunk, and a matching rug on the floor. The little oil lamp that swung from the rafter had a rosy tint to its cover. Several sachets of cedar and pine hung about the room, though they could not entirely banish the tarry smell of the ship. There was a small stand under the porthole, with a fenced top. A tin pitcher and washbasin were corralled there. A damp cloth was folded neatly beside it.

'Touch nothing,' she warned me as she closed the door. She stood for a moment, considering me. Then she pointed at the washbasin. 'Strip. Wash. Can you sew?'

'A bit,' I admitted. It had never been my favourite task, but my mother had insisted that I at least know how to hem and make basic embroidery stitches.

'After you are clean, set your dirty clothes on the floor by the door.' She went to her trunk and her fingers travelled down the folded and stacked garments. She pulled out a simple blue shirt. From a compartment, she took out scissors, thread and a needle. 'Shorten the cuffs so this fits you. Cut a strip off the bottom and hem it. It should still be long enough to cover you decently. Take the bottom strip and make it into a belt. Then sit in that corner there until I return.'

With that, she turned and went out the door. I heard her lock it behind her. I waited a short time and then tried the latch. Yes. I was locked in. The surge of relief I felt astonished me. I was a slave, locked in my mistress's cabin, and I felt happy? Yes, for the first time since I'd been taken. Yet as I stripped, carefully setting my broken candle to one side, I found myself weeping. By the time I had turned my mistress's used washwater into a greyish soup, I was sobbing. I hugged my dirty, torn, smelly jerkin goodbye. It was my last link to Withywoods. No. Not quite. I had my mother's candle.

I suddenly wanted nothing more than to curl up and sleep, even naked. But I made myself do as she had told me. The shirt was a good heavy one of wool tight woven and then washed and shrunk. It was a deep blue, and I wondered if that was her favourite colour. I hemmed it well, twice, to be sure it would not unravel, and did the same with the sash I made, turning the cut edges in to make all tidy. I hemmed the sleeves back and was clothed in something warm, soft and clean for the first time in months. From the cut cuff, I stitched a hasty pocket inside the front of the shirt. Regretfully, I folded my broken candle and hid it there. I folded the washcloth. Then, as my owner had bidden me, I sat down in the corner and soon fell fast asleep there.

I awoke when she returned. The porthole was black. I stood up as soon as she entered. She surveyed me, up and down, and then looked around the room. 'It's done well enough. You should have put the sewing tools away. You should have been smart enough to do that without being told.'

'Yes, Trader Akriel.' I had assumed she would want me to obey her exact orders only and I had hesitated to open any part of her travelling trunk. Now I knew. 'Do you wish me to dispose of the washwater as well?'

'Set it outside the door with the empty pitcher. It is another's duty. I will tell you yours.' She sat down on the edge of the lower bunk and held out a foot toward me. 'Draw off my boots and rub my feet first.'

I was too well-born for that sort of work. Wasn't I? Did I want to live and escape Dwalia? I did. I thought of my father. But for fate, he'd have been heir to the Six Duchies throne. But he'd been a stableboy and then an assassin. I might have been a princess. But now I was a slave. So be it.

I crouched and drew off her boots, set them side by side and then rubbed her feet. I had never done such a task before but her small groans guided me. After a time, she said, 'That's enough. Set out the dirty water, and put my boots away. There are some soft shoes in the trunk. Find them.'

So began the pattern of our days together. I saw that I never gave her cause to tell me to do a thing twice. She was a very reasonable mistress. She liked quiet. I avoided chatter, but did not fear to ask her simple questions relating to my duties.

I stayed inside the cabin. When we reached port, she left me there, locked in, but made sure that I had food and water and I always had the use of her chamber pot. My porthole looked away from the town, so I saw nothing of it and no one witnessed me dumping the chamber pot out of it. We were in port for almost ten days, for the storm had done more damage than I had realized. Whenever I grew restless and wished to be out of the small chamber, I would imagine Dwalia's consternation at how I had vanished. I hoped various things for her, that my bite might grow septic and kill her, that she might disembark from the ship and never return, that she might think I had fallen overboard and drowned and give me up as dead. I had no way of knowing if any of my wishes came true, so I remained in the cabin and made plans for my future.

I would, I resolved, be kind to my new little master, regardless of how spoiled he might be. I would give my new owners no cause to mistreat me or distrust me. Eventually, I might share with them my true tale, and let them know that my father and my sister would be happy to buy me back from them, or even ransom me. Thus, some day, I would get home to my people. To Withywoods? I wondered if I even wanted to go back there and face all the people who had been injured on my behalf. So many folk dead.

When such thoughts plagued me, I would often take out my mother's candle and hold it close to my face and breathe its fragrance, telling myself that somehow my father had been there at the forest plaza. I could not understand how he might have reached there before us, or where he would have gone from there. But I held tight to the idea that this broken candle meant that he had come searching for me. That he missed me and would do what he could to bring me safely home.

The days seeped past, one into the next. Sometimes Trader Akriel told me things. Some of the fabrics in her trading trunks had been spoiled during the storm when the water rose in the bilges and partially flooded the lower deck. She believed the owner of the ship should share her loss. He did not agree. She thought that was a poor decision on his part as this was the sixth time she had sailed with him, but if he did not reimburse her, it would be the last.

She had been married once but her husband had been unfaithful so she had simply taken her share of the wealth they had made trading and walked away. She'd bought goods and booked a passage the day she discovered his treachery, and she'd never looked back. She'd been successful; he had not, or so she heard. She cared nothing for what had become of him. She'd always been the clever one in their business. It was hard to be a woman and a trader when she went to the Chalced markets; once she'd had to stab a man to teach him manners. She hadn't killed him, but he had bled a great deal and when he had apologized, she had sent a runner for a healer. She'd never heard what became of him. Another man she had no interest in.

When she returned to the ship before we sailed for the next port, she brought me two pairs of loose trousers, some flat shoes, and a softly-woven blue shirt in my size. That night, she gave me a piece of soap and told me to wash my hair, and then gave me her own comb to take out the tangles. I was surprised at how long my hair had grown. 'The Chalcedean in you shows in all those yellow curls,' she told me, and meant it as a compliment. I managed a nod and a smile in response.

'Are you weary of confinement and idleness?' she asked me.

I phrased my reply carefully. 'My weariness is far less than my gratitude for meals and shelter,' I told her.

She gave me a very small smile. 'So. We shall test your tale of your skills. While ashore, I have obtained a book for you to read aloud from. And also, paper, pen, and inks. You shall demonstrate for me that you can manipulate numbers and execute illustrations.'

And those things I did, to her satisfaction, and with my illustrations, even beyond. She had me first draw her shoe, and then copy exactly a flower that was embroidered on a scarf she had bought.

She nodded over my work and mused, 'Perhaps I shall get a better price for you as a scribe than I would as a child's attendant.'

And to that I bowed my head.

So on we sailed, and for a time my world was very small indeed. There were stops at two other ports. I was certain that Dwalia and the others must have given me up and left the ship by now. I fervently hoped that after our second stop, Trader Akriel would begin to give me the freedom of the ship. But she did not and I did not ask for it. Instead, she showed me her book where she kept a tally of her trades. A bolt of fabric bought for this price and sold for that. There was a separate tally of what each journey cost her. She showed me the tally sheet for me. She had me add up the cost of my clothing, and of the paper, the book, the inks and even the pen used to prove my claim to be useful. That was her investment, she explained. I had to be sold for at least twice that amount for her to be satisfied with her bargain. I looked at the number. There it was. That was what I was worth in this new part of my life. I took a deep breath and resolved to be worth more.

There came a day when she told me to busy myself packing her trunk with her personal items, for it was expected that we would make port before nightfall, and here we would disembark. The port was called Sewelsby, for it was next to the Sewel River in Shale. I asked her no questions. I knew we were far off any map I had ever seen. She was pleased and humming to herself as I put things into her trunk, each in its designated place. She gave me a shoulder bag for my garments. As she carefully arranged her hair and chose her earrings, she told me that she had saved a tidy amount of money because our ship had evaded the tariff ships of the Pirate Isles. By this I surmised we were past the Pirate Isles, but I knew no more than that.

We reached the harbour, and lowered sails, and little boats came out to take lines tossed from our ship. Slaves bent to the oars and pulled us into harbour. It was tediously slow but Trader Akriel had left me in the locked cabin so I had nothing to do but stand on tiptoe and watch out the porthole. When finally we reached the dock and were safely tied to it, she returned and bade me follow her. I felt strangely giddy to leave the cabin after such a long confinement.

My legs were surprised to walk and then climb the ladder to the open deck. There was a fresh wind blowing and bright summer sunlight beating down on my bare head and glinting off the moving waves. Oh, the smells, of the water and the ship and the nearby town! There was chimney smoke and horses sweating in the sun and a stink of stale urine, as if people had lived on this piece of earth for far too long. 'Follow me,' Trader Akriel directed me brusquely. 'I always stay at the same inn. My trunk will be taken there, and my trading goods to my warehouse. I have people I must meet with, and goods to arrange delivery for, so for now, you will stay by my side until I have determined how best to place you.'

It pleased me that she said she would 'place me' rather than sell me. It was a small difference, but I told myself it meant that she wished to do well by me as well as make a solid profit. As she had paid nothing for me and invested little more than some garments and some paper, I hoped she would profit handsomely from her kindness toward me.

She strode fearlessly through the busy cobbled streets. 'Keep up!' she warned me and without warning darted out into a busy street to thread her way among horse-drawn carts and riders going in both directions. I was breathless before we gained the other side of the street but she was undaunted. On she went at a pace that kept me trotting. My hair was soon stuck to my scalp with sweat and a tickling trickle of perspiration was making its way down my spine when she abruptly turned and went up three stone steps and through an arched wooden door. I caught it and it was so heavy it was all I could do to keep it from slamming shut behind us.

This inn was certainly different to the only other inn I'd ever seen, the one in Oaksbywater. The floor was of a white stone with threads of sparkling gold in it. It was not warm and smelling of food as I had always supposed all inns were. Instead there was a spacious, calm room with comfortable chairs and little tables. It was cool in here after the streets outside, and the thick walls shut off the noise and smells of the street. I felt a gentle breeze perfumed with flowers. I lifted my face in surprise and saw an immense fan gently swaying back and forth and pushing the air to cool us. My gaze followed the line attached to it, down to a woman standing in the corner and rhythmically pulling the cord. I had never seen or imagined such a thing, and I stood gawking until Trader Akriel called to me to follow her.

We were greeted by a man dressed all in white. He wore his hair in six braids, each tied with a bit of string in a different colour. His skin was the colour of old honey, and his hair a shade darker. 'All is ready. I expected you as soon as the ship came into port.' He smiled in the way of a merchant who is almost a friend.

She counted coins into his hand and said it was good to see him again. He handed her a key. I forced myself not to stare and instead followed the trader up a stair of the same white stone and down a hallway. She halted at a door, unlocked it with the big brass key and we entered a very fine chamber indeed. There was a massive bed, fat with pillows scattered over a plump white coverlet. A bowl of fruit and flowers and a glass carafe of pale yellow liquid rested on a table in the centre of the room. Two doors stood open to a little balcony that overlooked the street and the harbour beyond.

'Close those!' the trader commanded me, and I obeyed immediately, shutting out the street sounds and the smells that came in with them. I turned back to the room to find she had poured herself a glass of the golden wine. She sat down in a cushioned chair and sighed. She took a slow and careful sip.

'My trunk will be delivered shortly. Open it. Set out the white sandals, my long red skirt, and the loose white blouse that is hemmed in red and has red cuffs on the sleeves. Put out my brushes and jewellery on that shelf beside my mirror and my perfumes. After you have done that, you may eat any of the fruit on this table. I believe there is a servant's chamber beyond that door; I have never travelled with a servant before, but you may make yourself comfortable there until I return.' She gave a sigh. 'I fear I must go out immediately, to be sure my goods have all been delivered to the warehouse, and to let three of my buyers know that I have returned with the wares they requested.' She picked up the wine glass and drained the last of it. 'Do not leave this room,' she cautioned me, and walked briskly to the door. She closed it behind her, and silence filled the room. I breathed out, a shuddering sigh. I was safe.

I wandered the room, looking at the fine furnishings. I peered into my servant's chamber. Simple but clean, with a low pallet and a blanket, a washstand with a ewer and basin, a chamber pot and two hooks for clothing. After sleeping so many nights on the floor or the ground, the simple bed seemed a luxury.

A loud knock at the door announced the arrival of the trader's trunk. I admitted the two large men carrying it. They set it down by the wall and bowed their way out. I shut the door behind them and performed my duties exactly as Trader Akriel had given them to me. A few items had been jostled about in the trunk's passage. Those I straightened. I arranged her brushes and cosmetics and jewellery as she had requested.

Only when I had finished did I go back to the fruit on the table. Some of it was unfamiliar to me. I sniffed a pale green one and wondered if I should bite into it or peel it or cut it. A little knife and a plate had been left beside it. I settled on eating the obvious berries from the bowl; they were tangy and juicy and after so many days of bread and porridge and occasional meat the flavour was such a surprise that it made my eyes water. There was a larger fruit like a plum, but orange. This I took onto the balcony. I sat cross-legged, looking through the railing and eating it slowly. The sun was very warm. The seaport seethed with activity and the mild wind carried all the strange scents of a foreign place. I grew sleepy, and after a time, I went inside and lay down on my little pallet. I fell deeply asleep.

I awoke to a dimmer light. I realized I'd heard the door opening and rolled quickly from my bed. I was still sleepy but I put a smile on my face and stepped out of my room saying, 'I hope your day went well, Trader Akriel.'

She gave me a puzzled look. Her eyes were vague.

'We have you!' Dwalia exclaimed.

'No!' I shrieked. Nightmare figures pushed into the room past the trader. Kerf was dishevelled and unkempt, his beard grown out and his hair matted to his skull. He stood, his shoulders rounded and his mouth ajar. His glance was dull. Vindeliar was not much better. It was obvious to me that their voyage had been a much greater hardship for them than it had for me. The magic-man's cheeks drooped and his eyes were sunken with weariness. He had never taken care with his grooming and now his hair hung in lank and greasy locks. But Dwalia was the worst, a monster from a nightmare. Her cheek was purple and red and black. The wound had closed but it had not grown skin over it. I saw the ropy muscles of her face stretch and writhe as she laughed. She carried a length of black chain in her hands and I knew it was for me.

I screamed. I screamed and screamed, wordlessly, a trapped animal's shriek.

'Shut the door, you fool!' Dwalia screeched at Vindeliar. As he turned to do so, a spark came back into the trader's face.

'Run!' I shrieked at her. 'Killers and thieves! Flee!'

And she did. Her shoulder hit the door just as Vindeliar was closing it. He held it, feet braced, but her head and one shoulder was outside the chamber and she had found her own voice. Trader Akriel shouted for help and I screamed while Dwalia vainly commanded Kerf to 'Kill the woman! Seize the girl! Shut that door! Vindeliar, you useless idiot, take control of them!'

Out in the corridor, I heard someone shout, 'Oh, sweet Sa!' and then running feet. But he was running away, not toward us. I heard shouts in the distance, as if he had alerted the inn folk, but Dwalia's shouted commands drowned all sense from their words.

'Vindeliar! Make Kerf kill her!' she shrieked.

'No!' I cried. Dwalia seemed afraid to lay hands on me herself. I sprang to the door, past Kerf who appeared to be lumbering aimlessly about the room, and tried to pry the door open. I could not match Vindeliar's strength so I resorted to kicking him in the shins as hard as I could with my soft shoes and pounding him with my clenched fists. The door opened slightly wider and Trader Akriel fell out of it. Then Vindeliar slammed it closed on her ankle and the crack of the joint breaking and her scream made my ears ring.

'Forget her! Control Kerf! Kerf! Seize Bee and get us out of here!'

Vindeliar shook his blunt head, a dog in a wasps' nest, and then abruptly Kerf moved with purpose. Vindeliar had abandoned his grip on the door and the trader was dragging herself down the hall, screaming for help. Kerf seized me in his left hand and drew his sword with his right. 'Lead us out of here!' Dwalia commanded him.

And he did, dragging me along by my upper arm as I shrieked wordlessly. 'Kill her!' Dwalia barked, and I screeched in fear for my life, but it was the trader who received his blade. He stood over her, legs spread, and stabbed her over and over, even as Dwalia roared, 'Enough! Get us out of here! Stop!' Vindeliar's face was white as ice and he flapped his hands helplessly. I could not tell if the horror of that bloody slaughter shattered Vindeliar's focus or if Kerf's buried fury at being mastered suddenly manifested itself. People came to the end of the corridor, cried out in horror, and fled. Someone shouted for the city guard but no one, no one came to aid me or Akriel. I twisted and clawed and kicked but I do not think Kerf was even aware of me as he gripped my upper arm in an iron fist. With his free hand he stabbed and stabbed and stabbed and I do not think I knew how much I had come to care for Trader Akriel until I saw her reduced to red meat and rags.

'We need to flee!' Dwalia shouted and she slapped Vindeliar.

Kerf started striding down the hall, dripping sword in one hand and dragging me with the other while Dwalia and Vindeliar came cringing behind him. If a snarling mountain cat had come down the staircase, the reaction would have been the same. Those who had clustered at the bottom of the stairs, clutching at one another and shouting what they had seen suddenly parted for us. We went through the lovely room, Kerf leaving bloody footprints on the white stone floor, and out into early evening.

Shouting and the sounds of running feet reached our ears. 'The guard!' Dwalia exclaimed in dismay. 'Vindeliar, do something. Hide us!'

'I can't!' He was panting and sobbing and trying to keep pace with Kerf's murderous stride. 'I can't!'

'You must!' Dwalia raged. Her hand rose and fell over and over as she lashed Vindeliar with the chain she carried. I heard him cry out and looked back to see blood bubbling from his mouth. 'Do it!' she commanded him.

He gave a wordless shriek of pain and fear frustration. And all around us, the gawking crowd dropped to the ground. Some writhed as if having fits and others were still. Kerf fell to his knees and then over onto his side on top of me and even Dwalia stumbled sideways. I scooted out from under Kerf, staggered to my feet. As I leapt to run, Dwalia grabbed me by my ankle. I went down hard on to the cobblestones, the pain of crashed knees wringing another shriek from my sore throat.

'Chain her!' Dwalia shouted at someone. And Vindeliar stepped forward, to kneel on me and wrap a chain around my throat and fasten it tight with a clip. I seized the chain in both hands but Dwalia had the other end of the chain and jerked it hard. 'Up!' she shouted. 'Up and run! Now.'

She did not look back but hurried down the street in a lumbering trot. I went stumbling after her, clutching at the chain around my throat, trying to tear it from her grip. She passed over and among sprawled figures and I was forced to jump over the fallen people or step on them. They seemed stunned, some twitching and others sprawled lax on the paving stones. Dwalia turned abruptly and we went down an alley between two tall buildings. Halfway to the next street, she halted in the darkness, and a sobbing Vindeliar came blundering into us. 'Silence!' she hissed at him, and when I opened my mouth to scream she jerked savagely on the chain, slapping my head against the wall beside us. I saw a bright flash of light and my knees gave out.

Some time had passed. I knew that. Dwalia was yanking on the chain around my neck. Vindeliar was plucking at me, trying to pull me to my feet. Using the wall, I staggered upright and looked around dazedly. At the other end of the alley, lanterns bobbed and voices were raised in horror, confusion and commands. 'This way,' Dwalia said quietly, and then gave a fierce jerk on my leash that brought me to my knees again. Vindeliar was still sobbing softly. She turned, slapped him as if she were hitting a mosquito and walked away. I got to my feet in time to save myself from another fall. I tottered after her, feeling sick and weak.

Vindeliar moved one of the hands he'd had clapped over his mouth to muffle his sobs. 'Kerf?' he dared to ask.

'Useless,' Dwalia snapped. Vindictively, she added, 'Let them have him. He will keep them busy while we find a better place to be.' She looked back at Vindeliar. 'You were almost as useless as he was. Next time, I will leave you behind for the mob.'

She increased her pace, annoyed that I was walking fast enough to keep slack in the chain. I groped for whatever clip Vindeliar had used to fasten it. My fingers found it but I could find no way to open it. She gave the chain another jerk and I stumbled after her again.

Dwalia led us out into a street and uphill and away from the tall buildings near the harbour. Always she chose to go where there were fewer people and lanterns in the streets and those we passed seemed to find nothing unusual about her hauling me along. Vindeliar followed us, hurrying to catch up, then falling behind, sniffling or sobbing or panting. I didn't look at him. He was not my friend. He had never been my friend and he would do anything to me that Dwalia told him to do.

We turned down a dark road lit only by the lights coming from the houses. They were not prosperous homes; light shone through cracks in the walls and the street was rutted and muddy. Dwalia appeared to choose one at random. She halted and pointed at it. 'Knock on the door,' she ordered Vindeliar. 'Make them want to welcome us.'

He gulped back a sob. 'I don't think I can. My head hurts. I think I'm sick. I'm shaking all over. I need—'

She clouted him with the free end of the chain, jerking me to my knees as she did so. 'You need nothing! You'll do it! Right now.'

I spoke in a low clear voice. 'Run away, Vindeliar. Just run away. She can't catch you. She can't really make you do anything.'

He looked at me and for an instant his little eyes grew big and round. Then Dwalia struck me twice with the loose end of my chain, hard, and Vindeliar fled up to the doorstep of the run-down house and hammered on the door as if to warn of fire or flood. A man snatched the door open and demanded, 'What is it?' Then his face suddenly softened and he said, 'Come in, friend! Come in out of the night!'

At those words, Dwalia hurried toward the door and I was forced to follow. The man stood back to let us in. As I followed Dwalia across the threshold, I saw her mistake. The young man holding the door and nodding was not alone. Two older men sat at a table, glaring at him and us. An old woman stirring a kettle of something over a low fire in the hearth demanded of him, 'What are you thinking, bringing strangers into the house in the dead of night?' A boy about my age looked at us in alarm and immediately picked up a stick of firewood, holding it like a truncheon. The woman's gaze had snagged on Dwalia's face. 'A demon? Is that a demon?'

Vindeliar turned back to Dwalia with a face full of woe. 'I can't do this many people any more. I just can't!' He gave a broken sob.

'All of them!' Dwalia demanded shrilly. 'Right now!'

I had been at the point of stepping over the threshold. I took a firm hold on my chain below my throat and stepped back as far as I could. 'I'm not a part of this!' I shouted hopelessly. Everyone in the little house was staring at us in consternation and fear. My shout broke them.

'Murder! Demons! Thieves!' the woman shrieked suddenly and the lad sprang forward at Vindeliar with his chunk of firewood. Vindeliar threw his arms up over his head and the lad delivered several sound thwacks to him. Dwalia was backing hastily out of the door but not in time to avoid the heavy mug one of the men flung at her. It struck her in the face, sloshing beer over her and making her yell angrily. Then she was away, dragging me after her. Vindeliar came behind us, yelping as the lad landed blow after blow on his shoulders and back while his father and uncles cheered him on.

We ran on, even after the family had given up their pursuit, for the shouts and clatter had roused other folk in the row of simple houses. We fled them, though Dwalia soon dropped her run to a shuffling trot and then to a hasty walk as she looked back over her shoulder repeatedly. Vindeliar caught up with us, holding his head with both hands and sobbing brokenly. 'I can't, I can't, I can't,' he kept saying until even I wanted to strike him.

Dwalia was leading us back toward the town. I waited until we were in streets where the houses were sturdily built, with glass in the windows and wooden porches. Then I set both hands to the chain, set my heels and jerked it as hard as I could. Dwalia did not let go but she halted and glared back at me. Vindeliar stood beside me, his mouth loose and trembling, hands still on his battered head.

'Let me go,' I said firmly. 'Or I shall scream and scream and scream until this street fills with people. I will tell them you are kidnappers and murderers!'

For a moment, Dwalia's eyes went wide and I thought I had won. Then she leaned in close to me. 'Do it!' she dared me. 'Do it. There will be witnesses that recognize us, I don't doubt. And there will be folk who will believe that you were our partner, the servant girl that let us in to rob and kill that woman. For that is the tale that we shall tell, and Vindeliar will make Kerf agree with it. We shall all hang together. Scream, girlie! Scream!'

I stared at her. Would that happen? I had no one to vouch for my tale. Trader Akriel was dead, cut to pieces. Abruptly that loss hit me like a blow to the belly. She was dead because of me, as Vindeliar had warned me would happen. I'd left that Path he spoke of, and again someone was dead. My wonderful idea of escaping Dwalia hung in tatters around me. I did not want to believe Vindeliar's superstitions about the Path. It was stupid and ridiculous to think there was only one right way for me to live my life. But here I was again, alive when those who had helped me were dead. I wanted to weep for Akriel but my grief went too deep for tears.

'I thought not,' she mocked me, and turning away from me, gave a vicious jerk on the chain. It ripped from my bruised hands and I found myself following her again as she led us into the dark.

SIXTEEN

The Pirate Isles

I have dreamed the theft of a child. No, not dreamed. For six nights, this nightmare has howled through my sleep, a dire warning. The child is snatched, sometimes from a cradle, sometimes from a feast, sometimes from a morning of play in fresh snow. However it happens, the child is lifted high and then falls. When the Stolen Child lands, the child has become a scaled monster with glittering eyes and a heart full of hatred. 'I am come to destroy the future.'

Those words are the only part of my dream that is always the same. I know I am but a collator, with no more than a drop of White in my veins. Over and over, I have sought to tell this dream, and always I am pushed away, told it is just an ordinary nightmare. Beautiful Symphe, you are my last hope that I will be heard. This dream is worthy of being recorded in the archives. I tell it to you, not to gain glory for myself or be recognized as a White who can dream, but only because . . . (text charred away)

Discovered among Symphe's papers

The long slow days aboard Paragon lodged in my life like a bone in the throat. Each had been so much like the last that it seemed like one endless day, and each choked me with its dragging passage.

Most of the crew's enmity was focused on me and Amber. Their simmering anger made our brief and meagre meals daily trials for me. Amber had destroyed not just Althea and Brashen's livelihood, but theirs as well. Securing a berth on a liveship was seen as a life-time position, for the crew was well paid, safer than on an ordinary ship, and became almost as family. Now that would end for all of them. From the youngest who had earned his position only six months ago to the oldest—a man employed on Paragon for decades— their livelihoods were gone. Or would be, when Amber supplied the ship with enough Silver to transform himself. For now, they were hostages to Paragon's ambition. As we were.

Spark and Per were pitied more than reviled. Clef still seemed intent on completing Per's education as a deckhand and I took comfort that the lad had time that was not focused on our differences with the crew. Lant continued to share Clef's room, and Clef moved Per in with them. I wanted to thank him for keeping the lad close and safe from any resentment, but feared that any conversation would taint Clef with the dislike I had to bear. To avoid exacerbating the discord, I kept mostly to the cabin I now shared with Amber and Spark. Spark had become subdued and thoughtful. She spent more time strolling on the deck with Lant than she did trying to learn knots or run the rigging. Spring had warmed to summer, and the tiny chamber was often muggy. When Lant and Per crowded in with us to practise our language lessons of an evening, sweat rolled down my back and plastered my hair to my head. Even so, it was a welcome diversion from the enforced idleness I endured.

When we were alone during those long days, the Fool and I pored endlessly over Bee's books. He sought further clues from her dreams. I desperately wanted to believe that she might still be alive somewhere, even as the thought of my little daughter held captive in such ruthless hands tormented me to sleeplessness. He asked me to read to him from her journal as well, and this I did. Somewhat. I could not tell if he knew I skipped passages and entries that were too painful to share. If he was aware of it, he said nothing. I think he realized I had been pushed to my limit.

Yet the Fool was far less restricted in his movements than I was. As Amber, he moved freely on the deck, immune to the displeasure of the crew and the captains, for he was favoured of the ship. Paragon often required her presence for conversation, or music. It was a freedom that I envied and attempted not to resent. Yet it made for long and lonely evenings.

One evening after Amber had left the chamber to spend time with the figurehead, I could stand the small, close room no more. With only a slight twinge of conscience, I rummaged through the substantial wardrobe packs that Spark and Amber had brought aboard. I found the wondrous Elderling cloak folded into a very small packet, butterfly side out, and shook it out. Most Elderlings were tall, and the cloak was cut generously. I hesitated. But no, it had been Bee's treasure and she had given it to Per to save him. In turn, he had surrendered it to the Fool's use without a murmur. And now it was my turn.

I donned it, butterfly side in. It fitted, in that uncanny way that Elderling garments had of adapting to the wearer. The front fastened with a series of buttons from my throat to my feet. There were slits for my arms. I found them and lifted the hood to cover my head. It fell forward over my face. I had expected it to blind me, but I could see through it. I watched my disembodied arm reach for the door handle. I opened the door, drew my arm in and stepped out. I stood still, allowing the cloak to adopt the dim colour of the passageway walls.

I soon discovered what a burden a floor-length garment was. I moved slowly, but still stepped on the front hem more than once. As I explored the ship unseen, any ladder I ascended required that I wait until no one was near, for I had to hike the cloak up to climb. I wondered if the ship were aware of me, but did not wish to test that by venturing too close to the figurehead.

I ghosted about, moving only when no crew were near and choosing my stopping places carefully. As night deepened, I moved more boldly. I found Per sitting on the deck next to Clef in a circle of yellow lantern-light. I remained outside its reach. 'It's called marlinspike work,' he was explaining to the boy. 'You use the spike off a marlin's nose, or some do. I just use a wooden fid. And you take the old line that's no good for anything else, and you sort of weave the knots and you can make mats or whatever you want. See? Here's one of the first ones I made. Useful and pretty in its way.'

I stood soundlessly nearby and watched Clef walk the boy through starting the knot centre. The work reminded me of Lacey, busy with her needles and hooks. She'd made lovely things, cuffs and collars and doilies. And few were the ones who knew that the sharpened tips of her needles were her clever weapons as Patience's bodyguard. I drifted away from them, wishing that Per could give up his fierce loyalty to Bee and become a ship's boy. Surely that was better than being involved in assassin's work.

I went in search of Lant. Since the crew's feelings toward us had darkened, I worried for him more than I liked to admit. If any of the crew were to seek a target for their anger, it would most likely be Lant. He was young and able-bodied; it would not be seen as cowardly to provoke him to a fight. I'd warned him often to be wary of hostility. He'd promised to be careful, but with a weary sigh that said he believed he could take care of himself.

I found him standing on the dim deck, leaning on the railing and looking out over the water. The winds were favourable and Paragon was slicing the water smoothly. The decks were almost deserted. Spark was beside him and they were conversing in low voices. I drifted closer.

'Please don't,' I heard him say.

But she lifted his hand from the railing and stepped inside the circle of his arm. She leaned her head on his shoulder. 'Is it because I'm low born?' she asked him.

'No.' I saw how difficult it was for him to remove his arm from around her and step away. 'You know that's not it.'

'My age?'

He leaned on the railing, hunching his shoulders. 'You're not that much younger than I am. Spark, please. I've told you. I've a duty to my father. I'm not free to—'

She leaned in and kissed him. He turned his face toward her, letting her mouth find his. He made a low sound, pleading. Then he abruptly gathered her in and moulded her body to his, pushed her against the railing and kissed her deeply. Her pale hands moved to his hips and snugged his body tight to hers. She broke the kiss and said breathlessly, 'I don't care. I want what I can have now.'

I stood in numbed shock.

He kissed her again. Then, with a discipline I envied, he took her by the shoulders and pushed her gently away from him. He spoke hoarsely. 'There are enough bastards in my lineage, Spark. I won't make another one. Nor will I break faith with my father. I promised him, and I fear those words will be the last ones he heard from me. I must see this through to the end. And I will not chance leaving a fatherless child behind.'

'I know ways to prevent . . .'

But he was shaking his head. 'As you were "prevented"? As I was? No. You told me what Amber said to you, that in all likelihood, she and Fitz will both die. And as I am sent to protect him, that means I will die before he does. It will shame me enough to leave you without a protector, though I hope that Per will stand by you. But I'll not chance leaving you with child.'

'I'm more likely to end up protecting Per!' She tried to take his hand but he clamped his fingers to the railing. She contented herself with covering his hand with hers. 'Perhaps I'll die protecting you before you die protecting Fitz,' she offered, but her laugh was not a merry one.

I moved softly away from them, scarcely able to breathe for the tears. I hadn't realized I'd begun to cry until I'd choked on them. So many lives contorted because my father had given in to lust. Or love? If Chade had not been born, if I had not been born, would other players have stepped up into our roles? How often had the Fool told me that life was an immense wheel, turning in a set track and that his task was to bump the wheel out of that track and set it on a better one? Was that what I'd witnessed tonight? Lant refusing to continue the Farseer tradition of hapless bastards?

I drifted back to the privacy of the room, closed the door behind me, removed the butterfly cloak and folded it carefully as it had been. I wished I had not worn it. I wished I didn't know what I knew now. I put the cloak back where I found it, resolving I would not use it again, and knowing that I lied to myself.

Paragon was selecting our course now, with little regard to what Althea or Brashen might wish. Bingtown had been left far behind, with no pause. We had neither dropped off cargo there nor taken on supplies and water. We had threaded our way along the shifting coast of the swampy shores and entered the waters of the Pirate Islands. Some of them were inhabited, and others were wild and unclaimed places. It made no difference to Paragon. We might look longingly toward tiny port towns alight at night where we may have put in to take on fresh water and food, but he did not pause. On we went, as relentless as the sea itself. And our rations grew ever smaller.

'We are prisoners.'

The Fool sat up from where he had been lounging on the lower bunk in the sweaty cabin and leaned out to give me a look. 'Do you speak of Althea and Brashen? You know why they have cautioned you to keep mostly to our cabin.'

'Not them. Under the circumstances, I think they have been very tolerant of us. It is Paragon who has taken us prisoner.' I lowered my voice, painfully conscious that I could not tell what the liveship was or was not aware of within his wooden body. 'He cares nothing now for Althea and Brashen's contracts and deliveries. Nothing for our comfort and safety. He does not care that we are ill supplied for this voyage, having failed to take on supplies in Bingtown. Short rations mean nothing to him. On he goes, through night and storm. When Althea ordered the sails reefed, he rocked so violently that she called her crew back from going aloft.'

'He has caught the current,' the Fool said. 'Even without sails, we would be carried through the Pirate Islands and past Jamaillia and on to the Spice Islands beyond them. He knows that, and the crew knows that.'

'And the crew blames us for our situation.' I sat up slowly in the cramped top bunk, careful of my head on the low ceiling of the cabin. 'Coming down,' I warned the Fool, and left the upper bunk. My body ached from inactivity. 'I don't like it when Lant and the youngsters are gone for so long. I'm going out to check on them.'

'Be careful,' he said, as if I needed a warning.

'When am I not a cautious fellow?' I asked him and he lifted his brows at me.

'Wait. I've decided to go with you,' he said and reached for Amber's skirts that were wilted on the floor. The fabric rustled as he drew them up around his hips.

'Must you?'

He frowned at me. 'I know Althea and Brashen far better than you do. If there is trouble of any kind, I think I am the better judge of what to do.'

'I mean the skirts. Must you continue to be Amber?'

His face grew still. He spoke more quietly, the skirts drooping in his hands. 'I think that adding any other difficult truths to what the crew and the captains must absorb right now would only make our lives more difficult. They knew me as Amber, so Amber I must remain.'

'I don't like her,' I said abruptly.

He gave a caw of laughter. 'Really?'

I spoke honestly. 'Really. I don't like who you are when you are Amber. She's, she's not a person I would choose as a friend. She's . . . conniving. Tricky.'

A half-smile curved his mouth. 'And as the Fool, I was never tricky?'

'Not this way,' I said, but wondered if I lied. He had publicly mocked me when he thought it was politically advantageous. Manoeuvred me into what he needed me to do. Still I did not modify my stare.

He cocked his head at me. 'I thought we were past all this,' he said softly.

I said nothing. He bowed his head as if he could see his hands as he fastened the waistband of his skirts. 'It is my best judgment that they continue to know me as Amber. And if you are leaving the cabin to look for the others, I think it best I go with you.'

'As you wish,' I said stiffly. Then, childishly, I added, 'But I am not waiting for you.' I left the small space, shutting the door not loudly but firmly behind me. Anger was a hot boil inside my throat and chest. I stood for a time in the passage, telling myself that it was simply close quarters for too long, and not true anger I was feeling for my friend. I took a deep breath and went back out onto the deck.

A fresh wind was blowing and the sun was shining, scattering silver on the water. I stood for a while, letting my eyes adjust and enjoying the wind on my face. After the crowded cabin, it felt as if I had the whole world around me. The dancing water that surrounded us was dotted with green islands in the distance. They rose abruptly from the water like mushrooms sprouting up from the forest floor. I drew a deep breath, ignored the sullen stare of Cord who had paused in her work to watch me, and went to find my straying wards.

I found Spark and Per leaning on the railing beside Lant. Spark's hand was all but touching Lant's on the railing. I sighed to myself. All three were looking morosely out over the water. As I took a spot behind them, Lant glanced back at me. 'All well?' I asked him.

He raised a brow. 'I'm hungry. None of the crew will speak to me. I don't sleep well at night. And how are you?'

'Much the same,' I said. The captains had reduced the rations for everyone.

On the day Paragon had by-passed the channel that would have taken us to Trader Bay and Bingtown, the captains and crew had confronted him. 'I won't be tied to a dock,' Paragon had declared. 'I won't allow you to trick me into having lines roped to me so you can drag me aground on a beach.'

'It's not about trying to thwart you,' Brashen had said. 'It's purely about taking on some water and food. Delivering the cargo we were to leave there. And sending some messages back to Bingtown and Trehaug and Kelsingra. Paragon, we have simply disappeared to those people! They will think the worst has befallen us.'

'Oh, the worst?' His voice had grown sly. 'So they will think the mad ship has rolled and drowned another crew.' There had been acid in his voice and his dragon eyes had whirled swiftly. 'Isn't that what you mean?'

Anger had spasmed over Brashen's face. 'Maybe. Or maybe our Bingtown merchants and our Rain Wild clients will think we've become thieves, taking their goods and running off to sell them elsewhere. Maybe we'll lose the only things left to Althea and me, our good names.'

'The only thing?' the ship demanded. 'Did you spend every penny of Igrot's treasure, then? That was a fair windfall for you, when I took you to that!'

'There's enough left perhaps to commission an impervious ship to replace you. One of wood that would let us lead a simple life. If anyone consented to trade with us again after you've made us liars and cheats!'

'Replace me? Ha! Impossible! I am the only reason you have ever prospered, you spend-thrift spoiled son of—'

'Stop this.' Althea had intervened, stepping closer to the figure-head, apparently without fear. 'Paragon, be reasonable. You know we need fresh water to drink. You know we need food. We didn't supply for a long voyage. We had enough on board to get us to Bingtown, and a bit extra. That was all. And we're days past that. If you make us just keep going, we're going to die of thirst. Or starve. You'll get to wherever you're going with a deck full of bodies— including Amber's. Then how will you get your Silver and become dragons?'

There was no rationality in those spinning blue eyes. He turned his gaze out over the water. 'There's plenty of fish you can eat.'

So we'd sailed on, and Althea and Brashen had cut the rations. And yes, there were fish in these waters, and moisture in the cooked flesh. The crew had pulled enough aboard each day to eke out the hard tack and salt-meat that was left to us. We'd had two spring storms, and Althea had ordered out clean canvas and channelled rainwater into barrels to replenish our meagre stores. And still we sailed on, through the region known as the Cursed Shores with its shifting sandbars and toxic waters, and on until we began to see the scattered islets and then the islands of the Pirate Isles.

Motley swooped down and startled me by landing on my shoulder. 'Well, where have you been?' I greeted the crow.

'Ship.' She spoke the word urgently. 'Ship, ship, ship.'

'We're on a ship,' I conceded to her.

'Ship! Ship, ship, ship!'

'Another ship?' Per asked her, and she bobbed her head wildly up and down and agreed, 'Ship, ship.'

'*Where?*' I pushed the word at her with Wit as well as voice. As always, I felt as if I shouted down a well.

'Ship!' she insisted, and launched from my shoulder. The wind caught her and flung her skyward. I lifted my eyes to follow her flight. Up she went and up, far higher than the ship's mast. There she hung, rocking in the wind. 'SHIP!' she called, and her word reached us faintly.

Ant had been halfway up the mast. At the crow's call, she looked around, scanning the full horizon before climbing even higher. When she reached the crow's nest at the top of the mast, she scanned the horizon, then, pointing, 'SAIL!' she called.

In an instant, Brashen had joined Althea on the deck. They both looked up, followed Ant's finger. Brashen's face was grave.

'What's wrong?' I asked Amber softly.

'It's probably nothing,' she replied. 'But at one time, passage through the Pirate Isles might cost your life. Or your freedom, or your cargo. When Kennit was raiding these passages, he built an empire, going from pirate captain to king. He didn't ransom the ships he captured. Instead, he appointed one of his loyal men to be captain and sent him out to raid, taking a share of whatever loot he captured. He crewed his new ships with escaped slaves, or sometimes with the very men they had defeated. From a single ship, he went to two, then half a dozen and then a fleet. He became a leader, and then a king.' She paused. 'A fairly good king, as it turned out.'

'Yet an evil bastard of a man.' Althea had approached quietly as Amber was speaking.

Amber turned, showing no evidence of surprise. 'That, too, is true. According to some.'

'According to me,' Althea said brusquely. 'But now the Pirate Isles are themselves plagued with pirates. And if it is not a pirate ship that overtakes you, it may be one of the tariff ships, come to collect a "passage tax". Like pirates, but with far more paperwork.' She turned to Per. 'That crow of yours. He talks. Is there any chance he could tell us what ship he has sighted?'

Per shook his head, surprised to be singled out. 'She says words, but I'm not sure she always knows what she's saying. Or that she could tell one sort of ship from another.'

'I see.' Althea fell thoughtfully silent.

'Are you worried what will happen if that is Vivacia or another liveship?' Amber dropped the question as if she were plopping small stones into a quiet pond.

Althea's response was so calm I wondered if she had forgiven Amber. 'The thought occurred to me. Yes, it's a worry. We can't know yet how the Silver will affect him, or if he can ever transform completely into a dragon. I'd sooner not create misery for every liveship and liveship family until we know how Paragon's experiment will end.'

I felt Brashen coming to join us before he stepped into my peripheral vision. He had the presence of a predator and my Wit-sense of him was edged with scarlet anger. I managed to keep my hands lax and my shoulders lowered but it was not easy.

Althea's mouth moved, as if she considered words and rejected them. 'Right now, Amber, you have a better connection with Paragon than either Brashen or me. And I have to ask you to use whatever influence you have with him.'

'What do you wish of me?'

'If that sail is a liveship, we judge it best to stay clear. However, if it is an ordinary wooden ship, we'd like to come alongside and see if we can buy provisions from them. Anything would be welcome, but chiefly we need water.' She shifted her gaze to me. 'In the Rain Wilds we take on rainwater from wooden cisterns high in the trees.

It's expensive, and we try to take only what we need. The water from the river and its tributaries are usually unsafe to drink.' She sighed. 'To ration food is harsh enough. But soon we will have to cut the water allowance again, unless Paragon allows us to put in at one of the Pirate Islands and take on water. Or we encounter a ship that has enough fresh water to wish to sell some.'

I watched her shoulders rise and fall with her deep sigh. Then she rolled them back, squaring them, and I felt my admiration for her rise. She possessed the sort of grinding courage I had seldom seen in man or woman. Facing the end of all she had known as her life—the end of all she had expected her life to be—she would nonetheless think not only of her crew but of those who crewed the other Bingtown liveships. And of the ship she still loved, even as he prepared to abandon her.

Verity. Carving his dragon. That was who she reminded me of.

Amber spoke my question aloud. 'So. You have forgiven me?'

Althea gave her head a short shake. 'Not any more than I've forgiven Kennit for raping me. Or Kyle for taking Vivacia from my care. For some things, there is no forgiving or unforgiving. They are simply a crossroads, and a direction taken, whether I would or no. Someone else set my feet on that path. All I can control is every step I take after that.'

'I'm sorry,' Amber said softly.

'You're sorry?' Brashen asked incredulously. 'Now you say you're sorry?'

Amber lifted one shoulder. 'I know I don't deserve forgiveness for what I've done. I don't want to seem as if I expect it, based on old friendship. Yet I say it now to let you know it's the truth. I'm sorry that it was what I had to do. Althea is right. Events set my feet on a path. All I can do is take the next step.'

'She's flying Pirate Island colours!' Ant called down to us. 'And she's tacking to cut our path. Moving fast, too.'

'Most likely a tariff ship,' Brashen suggested. He scowled toward the horizon. 'If it is, it will be sure to intercept us, to demand to inspect our cargo, and charge us for passage through these waters.'

'And as we are carrying Elderling artefacts from Trehaug and Kelsingra—items that were originally destined for Bingtown—the value they will assign and hence the tariffs on that value will be far beyond our ability to pay. We will be detained in the

Pirate Isles and given a choice between sending for the funds or surrendering part of our cargo to pay the tariff—cargo that is not ours to use to pay our debts. Cargo we were contracted to transport to Bingtown.' Althea spoke as if the words were made of thorns.

Brashen laughed without humour. 'And if we refuse to be boarded by the Pirate Isle tariff agents, or if we refuse to follow them to port until the tariff is paid, then they will endeavour to force their way onto Paragon and take control of him. And we have no idea how he will react to that.'

'Actually, I fear that I have a very clear idea of how he will react,' Althea said. 'I think he will do his best to sink the other ship, with little mercy for the crew.' She shook her head bitterly before turning back to Amber. 'And so I am going to ask you to use every bit of influence you have to persuade him to be reasonable. To let them come alongside and talk with us. There will be trouble over the tariffs, but at least putting into port will give us the chance to take on food and water. Or to release our crew.'

'Release the crew?' There was alarm in Amber's voice.

Althea was resolute. 'As many as will go. Whatever is to become of Paragon, and of us, I see no point in taking them all with us. The sooner they are off Paragon's decks, the sooner they can find other employment. Other lives.'

'How can Paragon get to Clerres with no crew?' Amber demanded.

'Skeleton crew.' She looked Amber up and down. 'You'll have to lose those skirts and remember how to work the deck again.' She tipped her head toward me. 'Him, too. And Lant and the youngsters.'

I opened my mouth to respond but Amber spoke quickly. 'I'm blind. But what I can do, I will. We all will. And I will do all I can to encourage Paragon to be reasonable. I've no wish for this to be any worse than it must be.'

'Any worse,' Brashen said softly, a terrible wondering in his voice. 'How could it be any worse?'

As if in answer to his question, a wave of something swept past me that spun me like a weathervane. It seemed as palpable as the wind, but it was not air that slid past me, but Skill and Wit, twined together and moving through the wizardwood of the ship in a way I knew but did not understand. I knew it, for I had done it—done it without thinking or understanding it in the days when I had first begun to try to master my magics. I had done it because I had not known how to separate them. I had been told my Skill was tainted with the Wit, and I had known that my Wit had undertones of Skill to it. I had struggled to separate the two, to use the Skill properly. And I had succeeded. Almost.

But now I felt it rippling and surging through the ship, and it felt, not wrong, but pure. As if two halves of something had been restored to a whole. It was powerful, and for a time I could focus on nothing but the wonder I felt at it.

'Oh, no!' Althea said in a low voice, and that was when I knew the others were aware of it too. All of them stood still, faces frozen, as if they were listening to the distant howling of hungry wolves. Everyone save Perseverance, who looked from face to face and then demanded, 'What is it?'

'Something's changing,' Spark whispered. Transfixed as I was by the flow of magic, I still noted in a small corner of my mind how her hand crept out to grasp Lant's forearm, and how he set his hand over hers to reassure her. Something was changing indeed, and it wasn't just the ship. I felt Amber catch hold of my sleeve.

Althea and Brashen moved as if one will controlled them, striding toward the foredeck. Overhead, Motley still circled, cawing 'Ship, Ship!' We followed, and Clef came dashing past us. As abruptly as the surging magic had begun, it passed. Althea and Brashen had gained the foredeck.

Paragon twisted slowly to look back at them. 'What?' he asked mildly, raising a questioning brow.

I had a single instant of disconnection before the obvious stunned me. He looked back at us with my face, save for his pale blue eyes. 'That's exactly how Prince FitzChivalry looks when he's puzzled,' Per observed, answering a question I hadn't even formed in my mind. Slowly, Paragon turned away from us. He lifted his arm, offering the back of his wrist to the sky. Motley swooped in to land there, completing my utter confusion.

'Ship!' she told him.

'I see it. It's a tariff ship. We'd best heave to, and then let them know we'll be following them to Divvytown to pay our taxes.' He glanced back to give his captains a boyish grin. 'Vivacia is out of Divvytown, isn't she? I have a feeling she'll be there. It will be so good to see Boy-O again, won't it? And Queen Etta has her court there. Perhaps, at last, Paragon Kennitsson will see fit to walk my decks. Let's put on some more sail and pick up some speed.'

'Paragon, what are you playing at?' Brashen demanded in a low voice.

The figurehead did not turn back towards him. 'Playing at? Whatever do you mean?'

'Why have you resumed your old face?' Brashen asked.

'Because I did. Isn't this the one you prefer? The one that makes me seem more human?'

'You are human,' Amber spoke her words with soft clarity. 'Human and dragon. Possessed of the memories of both. Soaked in the blood and the memories of those who have crewed your decks, bled and died on them. You began as the shells of two dragons, that is true. But you have become something that is not only dragon, but imbued with humanity as well.'

Paragon was silent.

'Yet you changed your face,' Amber continued, 'so that Boy-O would see you in your familiar guise and not be alarmed.' I wondered if she were guessing or if she knew.

'I changed my face because it suited me to do so.' Paragon spoke the words defiantly.

Amber's response was mild. 'And it suited you to do so because you care for Boy-O. Paragon, there is no shame in being who and what you are. In partaking of two worlds instead of one.'

He turned to look at her and the blue of his eyes was dragon-blue. 'I shall be dragons again. I shall.'

Amber nodded slowly. 'Yes, I believe that you will. As will Vivacia and the other liveships. But you will be dragons as dragons have not existed before. Dragons touched with humanity. Understanding us. Perhaps even caring about us.'

'You do not know what you are saying! Dragons shaped by human touch? Do you know what those are? Abominations! That is what *they* are, those who hatch and grow on Others' Island. Those who are as much human as serpent, and hence neither! And never will they be dragons. I shall be dragons!'

I made little sense of this outburst, but Amber seemed to understand it. 'Yes. Yes, of course, you will be dragons. And the part of you that will remember humanity is not in your wing or your tooth or your eye. It will be in your memory. As the serpents of the sea recall the memories they need of those who were serpents before them, and as a dragon recalls his ancestral knowledge. You will have an additional pool of memories. Your human memories. And it will give you wisdom beyond what other dragons have. You and the dragons who have been liveships will be dragons apart from the ordinary. A new kind of dragon.'

He turned away from all of us. 'You have no idea what you are suggesting. Look. Soon they will be hailing us. Should not you be about your duties?'

The tariff ship's captain was a young man. The red beard that edged his chin was patchy and though he wore a fine hat with several immense plumes in it, I think he was relieved when Brashen shouted to him that we were Divvytown bound to submit for taxing. 'I'll follow you then,' he declared, as if he had been about to demand that we submit.

'Go ahead and try,' Paragon invited him affably. And indeed, once we were under way again, he demonstrated the difference between a liveship and one made of wood. Given the same wind and current, we pulled steadily away from the tariff vessel. Truly, if Paragon had wanted to run from him, the tariff ship's chase would have been futile.

No one asked us to leave the deck and so I stood by the rail with my small retinue, enjoying the wind on my face. 'How does he do it?' I asked Amber, and felt Per step closer for the answer.

'I don't truly know. He smooths his hull, I think. And unlike many other ships, a liveship will never develop a beard of weed and mussels. His hull never needs to be scraped and painted, and no tubeworm will ever hole his planking.'

For the rest of the afternoon, we watched the islands grow closer. Soon even Paragon had to slow in order to thread his way through islets to what had once been a hidden town, a place where pirates went to divvy out their spoils and drink and gamble and take every pleasure they could. Once it had been a place where escaped slaves could go to begin a new life as free folk. I'd heard tales of it as a noisome place of stagnant water and patchwork hovels and sagging wharves.

But Paragon followed a well-marked channel into a tidy little harbour where large sailing vessels, obviously merchanters, were anchored in the bay while smaller ships and fishing boats were tied to an orderly array of docks. A prosperous little city spread back from the harbour in a grid of streets and alleys. Trees I did not recognize lined the streets, heavy with yellow blossoms. The main street led to a large structure about the same size as the manor house at Withywoods, but there the resemblance ended. Queen Etta's palace was of plank, painted white, with long open porches on the front. A green surrounded it, so that even from the harbour it was visible past the rows of warehouses and store-fronts. As I looked, I realized that the height of the buildings had been reduced to have exactly that effect; the royal residence towered over the town and, from the upper balconies and tower, had an unimpeded view of the harbour.

'Is that the *Vivacia*?' Lant asked and I turned my gaze.

'I don't know but she's definitely a liveship.' She was a queenly creation, a youthful woman with her head held high and her shapely arms and wrists crossed at her waist. Her hair was a black tumble of curls that fell to her bared shoulders and over her breasts. I saw in her proud features an echo of Althea, as if they were related. As Spark described the vessel to Amber in a low voice, Amber nodded. 'Vivacia,' she confirmed. 'The Vestrit family liveship. Command of her was snatched away from Althea by cruelty and strange turns of fate. Her nephew Wintrow commands her now. Brashen served aboard her for years, as first mate under Althea's father. This will be bittersweet for both of them.'

Vivacia rocked gently at anchor in the harbour. Paragon's sails were slowly gathered in, and when a small flotilla of dories came out to meet us lines were tossed and Paragon surrendered his motion to their command. I paid small attention to any of that. Instead I stared at Vivacia as we drew nearer. She turned her face toward us, and at first it was the look of a woman interrupted in her private musings. Then, as she recognized the ship, a smile dawned on her features. Vivacia held out her arms in welcome, and despite all that had befallen Althea and was yet to come, I heard our captain call a joyous greeting.

The dories pulled Paragon into position facing Vivacia and his anchor was dropped. A longboat moved out from the docks and came alongside us, and a woman in an extravagant hat and a well-tailored jacket over black breeches called out that she would be pleased to transport the captain and a manifest of our cargo to the Tariff House. Althea called back that she would be pleased to accompany them in a short time; would the tariff officer wish to come aboard and view the cargo, as there were unusual circumstances to be explained?

The officer was so inclined. But I was distracted from that process by what was taking place on Paragon's deck. With various shades of reluctance and anger, the crew folk were assembling. Most had brought their ditty bags from belowdecks. The canvas sacks were not large but contained most if not all of each sailor's possessions. Ant was weeping silently, the tears streaming down her face as she bade farewells. Cord threw her bag near the girl and hunkered down beside her. The look she gave us was hostile.

I made a decision that surprised me, for I had not even realized I was considering it. 'Lant, a word with you,' I said, and led him apart from the others. I leaned on the railing, looking up at Divvytown. He took his place beside me, a slight scowl on his face. I suspected he knew what my topic was, but doubted he knew the direction of the discussion. I waved at the city. 'It's not a bad place. It looks clean, with legitimate businesses. And there's a lot of trade and traffic through here.'

He nodded, a frown building between his brows.

'You and Spark could do well here. And I'd be grateful if you took Per as well. Take the gifts we were given in Kelsingra. Be careful how you sell them; get full value. There should be enough money to keep you all for some time, and enough to send Per back to Buckkeep.'

He was silent for a while. When he turned to stare at me, his eyes were flinty. 'You've made some assumptions about me that I don't care for.'

'Have I?' I asked him coldly. 'I see how she follows you about; I see her hand on your arm.' Then what should have been righteous anger suddenly melted into weariness. 'Lant, I hope you truly care for her. She isn't a serving girl to be romped and set aside. Chade chose her. She came with us, and I never expected any of this to happen. I wish she had stayed with him. But she's here, and I expect you to—'

'You're insulting me. And her!'

I stopped talking. Time to listen. The silence ate at him until he filled it.

'We do share an . . . attraction. I don't know how you think it could have become more than that on a ship as crowded as this one. And no matter what she feels for me, her loyalty to Amber is greater. She won't forsake her.'

I bowed my head to that.

'I doubt you will as easily believe what next I tell you. My father asked a task of me and I said I would do it to my utmost ability. If you cannot accept that I might feel some loyalty to you, then know that I am my father's son. I may not perform to the level you expect, but I will stay at your side until this thing is done. One way or another.' His voice suddenly grew thicker. 'I did not do well with Bee. Not when I tried to teach her, not when you left her in my safekeeping. She was a strange and difficult child. Don't bristle at me! You must know it's true. But I should have done better by her, even if protecting her with a blade was never something I expected to do. She was my cousin and a child in my care, and I failed her. Do you not think that I have agonized about that? Going to avenge her is something I have an interest in, beyond any duty to you or my father.'

'The Fool thinks Bee might still be alive.'

That brought his eyes back to meet mine. I saw pity in them. 'I know he does. But why?'

I took a breath. 'Bee kept a journal of things she dreamed. I've read the entries to him and he thinks they have meanings beyond what I understand. He believes Bee had foresight, and that some of her dreams predicted she would survive.'

His face was still for a moment. Then he shook his head. 'That's a cruel hope to dangle in front of you, Fitz. Though were we to find her alive and bring her home, it would lift a great weight of guilt from my shoulders.' He paused. I could think of nothing to reply to that. Then he went on, 'I say this as a friend, if you ever consider me so. Fix your course on vengeance, not rescue. There's no guarantee of the latter. We may not have success with the former either, but I am determined they will know we tried.'

A friend. My mind snagged on that word and I wondered if I did feel he was a friend. I knew I'd come to rely on him. And now I had to admit that some of the anger I'd felt about his possible involvement with Spark was that I knew I had to release both of them. I asked the worst possible question, thoughtlessly. 'Then you and Spark are not . . .?'

He stared at me. 'I don't think you have the right to ask either of us that question. You may not have noticed, but I am a man grown and of noble birth. Not your equal, perhaps, but not your serving man. Nor is Spark a servant to you, or anyone else. She is as free to choose her course as I am.'

'She is under my protection and very young.'

He shook his head. 'She is older than she looks, and more experienced in the ways of this world than many a woman twice her age. Certainly she has seen more of the hard side of life than Shun ever did. She'll make her own decisions, Fitz. And if she wants your protection, she'll ask for it. But I doubt she'll ask to be protected from me.'

I did not think our discussion was over, but he turned and walked away. And when I reluctantly followed him, I found only Per waiting with him. 'Where are Amber and Spark?'

'Lady Amber went to change her clothing. Althea asked that she accompany them on shore. Spark went to help her. Evidently Althea and Brashen think Amber should be with them when they sit down with Admiral Wintrow Vestrit, to discuss our future. The crew has been offered "shore leave" which is, I think, an invitation for them to jump ship here. Two thirds of them have accepted it.'

Small boats had already ventured out from the town. Vendors in the little boats below were hawking everything from fresh vegetables to free rides to Auntie Rose's Ladyhouse. I watched our crew departing, ditty bags on their shoulders as they climbed over the railing and down to the waiting dories. A few were clustered near the foredeck, bidding Paragon farewell. The ship was kind to them but unswerving in his determination. Across the stretch of water that separated us from Vivacia, she watched us expectantly, eyeing every small boat that departed from ours. Ant stood beside Clef, watching her fellows leave. Kitl stayed; Cord left. Twan went to the railing with his ditty bag, then turned, cursed fluently and kicked his bag back across the deck and down the hatch to the crew quarters. Cypros went and took his arm. They went to stand with Ant.

'Go with Amber and Spark,' I ordered Lant.

'I wasn't invited.'

'Amber is blind and Spark is, as others besides you may note, a very pretty girl. Divvytown was a pirate town, and I am sure that men with the hearts of pirates still abide here. I know that Althea and Brashen would not deliberately lead them into danger, but if there is danger, I would wish that they had a man with them who was dedicated solely to protecting them.'

'Why don't you go yourself?'

'Because I am sending you,' I replied tersely. Sparks of anger leapt into his eyes and I modified my tart reply with, 'I wish to remain on the ship and watch what transpires here. I also wish to charge you with an additional errand. Find someone who has messenger birds. A wealthy merchant, preferably, someone who would have connections so that a message capsule might be transferred from bird to bird until it reaches Buckkeep. I'd like to send back word that we are alive and well and continuing our journey.'

He was silent for a moment. Then he asked, 'Will you tell Chade and Dutiful and Nettle that Lady Amber believes Bee might still be alive?'

I shook my head. 'When I truly know that I have good news for them, then I'll share it. They should not have to live in uncertainty until then.'

He was nodding slowly. Abruptly he said, 'I'll do it. But— would you write an additional message for me? If there is any message-parchment on this ship?'

'I have a bit left from what Reyn gave me. It's precious stuff. Don't you want to write it yourself?'

'No. I'd rather you wrote it. A note to Lord Chade. Just to say that . . . I'm doing what he asked of me. And doing it . . . well. If you can bring yourself to say that of me. But you can say whatever you like. I won't read it before I send it. Just tell him I'm still at your side and serving you.' He looked away from me. 'If you would.'

'I can easily do that,' I said slowly.

I returned to Amber's cabin and carefully penned a note in tiny letters to Chade. The fine parchment was nearly translucent. Even so, there was little space to say much more than that I was very well pleased with FitzVigilant's service to me. I may have mentioned that, on several occasions, he had been instrumental in keeping me alive. I blew on it and waved it about to dry and then rolled it small to make it fit in the hollow bone capsule that would protect it on its journey. On the bone itself I lettered Chade's name and Buckkeep Castle, Buck in the Six Duchies. It had a long, far way to travel. As I entrusted it to an abashed Lant, I wondered if any of our messages home had been received yet. I had not sealed it with wax, and he knew that was my invitation to read what I'd written. But there was no time for any discussion, for all the others were eager to get to Divvytown. I decided I would leave it to Lant to compose a message explaining where we were and the peculiar nature of the liveship we were on.

I had hurried, but I'd still kept the shore party waiting. Althea gave Vivacia a friendly wave before she turned and descended the ladder to the waiting rowing boat. The liveship watched our party clamber down and find their places. Her smile broadened, only to fade to a puzzled stare as the small boat went directly to Divvytown.

As the long evening passed, Per and I sat at the galley table, idly rolling a set of dice that belonged to the crew and moving pegs in a gameboard. I could not care if I won or lost, and so I played poorly, to Per's disgust. To my Wit the ship felt empty, almost cavernous, with most of the crew gone. Clef and several of the older hands gathered at the far end of the table. Kitl had made food in the galley, and it was heartening once more to smell cooking meat. When she called us to eat, there were admiring coos from the crew. Even more enticing than the platter of sizzling meat strips was a large bowl of fresh greens. Scallions and flat pea pods, crisp stalks of a vegetable I didn't know, and mixed in with them, carrots no bigger than my thumb and piquant purple radishes. We each dished our own food onto tin plates. The strips of meat were tough and a bit gamy, but no one complained. The crew ate theirs with a white paste that was so hot it made my eyes water and my nose run when I tried it. But no one laughed at me or made a joke of it.

Per and I ate at our end of the table, apart from the crew-folk. The sidelong glances we received were plain reminders that they had not forgotten who was at the root of their problems. Clef scowled at the obvious separation, and came to join us, filling the empty seat at the galley table between us and the crew.

After we had eaten and Ant collected the plates, Clef joined us at our game. I rolled dice and moved my pegs but Clef and Per knew they only competed against each other. While they gamed, I eaves-dropped with one ear on the subdued talk of the crew. The older hands spoke of 'the old days'. Some few had been there when the *Paragon* had been dragged off the beach where he had languished for many a year and towed back into deep water. Others spoke of when the ship had stood up to a fleet of ordinary vessels and helped the Satrap of Jamaillia make his claim to power. They recalled shipmates who had died on the ship's deck and entrusted their memories to his wizardwood planks. Lop, who had not been the brightest fellow but had always pulled his share of the load. Semoy, mate for a time until there came a year when he had no strength and dwindled to bones and sinew, and died while coiling a line. And they spoke of the pirate, Kennit. Paragon had been his family ship, but that secret had not been known while Kennit was alive and raiding. Even fewer had known that Igrot, the notoriously cruel pirate, had stolen both ship and the boy Kennit from his family and misused both. Even after Paragon was reunited with Kennit and they rediscovered one another, Kennit had tried to use fire to send him to the bottom. But in the end, when Kennit was dying, Paragon had taken him back and received him gently. It was a mystery they still discussed in soft voices. How could such a wilful ship also have been so loving? Did the memories of Kennit move in him now, recalling Divvytown to him?

My speculation was silent. Whose memories would guide Paragon back to Clerres? Igrot's, I decided. Did the thoughts and deeds of that nefarious old pirate lurk deep in the ship's wizardwood bones? How deep did the memories of his human family and crew soak into his dragon's wood?

And I wondered how Althea had felt captaining a ship that would always harbour the memories of her rapist. How much of the pirate still lurked in the ship that wanted to be two dragons?

Useless questions.

Per won the game and Clef stood up from the table. He looked weary and sad and much older than he had when we first had come aboard. He looked around at the faces and then lifted his mug of fresh water. 'Shipmates to the end,' he said, and the others nodded and drank with him. It was a strange toast that fanned my guilt to white-hot coals. 'I'm taking the anchor watch,' he announced, and I knew it was not his usual duty. I suspected he would spend it near the figurehead. The spy in me wondered if I could manage to witness whatever words they traded. When Per proposed another game, I shook my head. 'I need to walk a bit after that meal,' I told him, and left him to tidy our game away.

I leaned on the railing and watched the pirate town as the summer night descended. The sky darkened from azure to the blue that precedes black, and still Amber and the others did not return. Per joined me on the deck to watch the lights of Divvytown come out. It was a lively place; music carried to us across the water, and the angry shouts of a street fight came later.

'They'll probably stay the night in the town,' I told Per, and he nodded as if he did not care or worry.

We retired to Amber's cabin. 'Do you miss Withywoods?' he asked me abruptly.

'I don't think of it much,' I told him. But I did. Not so much the house as the people and the life that had been there. Such a life, and for too few years.

'I do,' Per said quietly. 'Sometimes. I miss being so sure of what my life would be. I was going to grow taller than my father and be Tallestman, and step up to his job in the stables when he got old.'

'That might still be,' I said, but he shook his head. For a time, he was quiet. Then he told me a long, wandering tale about the first time he'd had to groom a horse much taller than he could reach. I noted that he could now speak of his father without weeping. When he fell silent, I stared out of the window at the stars over the town. I dozed off for a time. When I woke, the cabin was dark save for a smudge of light from an almost full moon. Per was sound asleep and I was perfectly awake. With no real idea of what had wakened me, I found the boots I had kicked off, donned them and left the cabin.

On the deck, the moon and the still burning lights of Divvytown made the night a place of deep greys. I heard voices and walked softly toward the bow.

'You're dragging anchor.' Clef made his accusation factually.

'The tide is running and the bottom is soft. It's scarcely my fault that the anchor isn't holding.' Paragon sounded as petulant as a boy.

'I'm going to have to roust every crew member I still have aboard to hold you in place, lift anchor and drop it again.'

'Perhaps not. It feels to me as if it's holding now. Perhaps it was just a bit of slippage.'

I stood still, breathing softly. I looked at the town and tried to decide if the ship had moved. I couldn't decide. When I looked at

Vivacia, I became certain that he had. The distance between the two liveships had closed.

'Oh, dear. Slipping again.' The liveship's words were apologetic but his tone was merry. We edged closer to Vivacia. She seemed unaware of us, her head drooped forward. Was she asleep? Would a ship made of wizardwood need to sleep?

'Paragon!' Clef warned him.

'Slipping again,' the ship announced, and our progress toward the other liveship was now unmistakable.

'All hands!' Clef roared abruptly. His whistle pierced the peaceful night. 'All hands on deck!'

I heard shouts and the thudding of feet hitting the floor below decks and then Paragon saying, 'Vivacia! I'm dragging anchor. Catch hold of me!' Vivacia jerked to awareness, her head coming up and her eyes flashing wide. Paragon held out his arms to her in a plea and, after a moment, she reached toward him.

'Mind my bowsprit!' she cried, and narrowly they avoided that disaster. Paragon caught one of her hands and with an impressive display of strength pulled himself close to her. It set both ships rocking wildly and I heard cries of alarm from Vivacia's crew. In a moment, Paragon embraced her with one arm despite her efforts to fend him off.

'Be still!' he warned her, 'or you will tangle us hopelessly. I want to speak to you. And I want to touch you while I do so.'

'Fend him off!' she shouted to her crew who came running as she pushed futilely against his carved chest. Clef was shouting commands to his crew and someone was angrily cursing at him from Vivacia's deck, demanding to know what sort of an idiot he was. Clef tried to shout an explanation while barking orders at his crew.

Paragon's laugh boomed out over the cacophony, silencing them all. Except Vivacia. 'Get him away from me!' Vivacia barked her command. But Paragon only shifted his grip to the curls on the back of her head and bent her head backwards so that her bare breasts thrust up toward him. To my astonishment, he leaned down and kissed one. As she shrieked her outrage and seized his face in her nailed hands, he increased his grip upon her hair. With his free hand, he reached up and seized a handful of the lines that festooned her bowsprit. He paid no attention to her battering.

'Don't try to fend me off!' he warned her crew. 'Get away from the foredeck. All of you! Clef, order everyone back. And you, Vivacia's crew, go back to your bunks. Unless Boy-O is among you. Send him to me if he's there. If not, leave us alone!' He bent his head again and tried to kiss Vivacia's face, but she seized handfuls of his hair and tried to tear it from his scalp. He let her sink her hands into it, then abruptly made it harden into carved wood under her touch. 'Do you think this wood feels pain?' he demanded of her. 'Not unless I will it to. But what do you feel when I kiss you? Do you recall Althea's outrage when Kennit forced himself upon her? Did you keep that memory, or is it solely mine, her pain absorbed by me that she might heal? As I took Kennit's pain at all Igrot did to him. Have you only human memories left to you? What do you feel, wooden ship? Or does a dragon still lurk in you? Once, you named yourself Bolt. Do you recall that? Do you recall the fury of a queen dragon when she rises in flight and defies all drakes to master her? What are you right now, Vivacia? A woman struggling against a man, or a queen dragon challenging her mate to master her?'

Abruptly she ceased her struggling, her features set into an aristocratic look of frozen disdain. Then, heedless of his grip on her hair, she rocked her head forward and stared at him with eyes that blazed with the true light of hatred. 'Mad ship!' she called him. 'Pariah! What insanity is this? Will you sink yourself right here in Divvytown harbour? You are no fit mate for me, were I woman or dragon.'

Out of the corner of my eye I saw a boat lowered from the Vivacia and four men rowing furiously toward Divvytown, doubtless to alert someone and demand aid. If Paragon saw it go, he paid no attention to it.

'Are you certain of that?' As he spoke the words, I felt the change ripple through the ship.

'I am certain,' Vivacia said disdainfully. She turned her face away from him. 'What do you want of me?' she asked in a low voice.

'I want you to recall that you are a dragon. Not a ship, not a servant to the humans who sail you, not a sexless being trapped in a woman's form. A dragon. As am I.' As he spoke, he was changing, resuming his semi-dragon form. I found I had crossed my arms tightly across my chest and raised my walls. Skill and Wit, I tried to contain myself, as prey does when a predator threatens. I saw the dark curling hair on his skull become a dragon's scaled crest, watched as his neck grew longer and sinuous.

But most astonishing of all, I watched Vivacia's face. Her expression became stone. The light that shone from her eyes grew bright and harsh as she witnessed his transformation. She did not wince from him at all.

When his transformation was complete, when I felt the magic grow still, she spoke at last. 'What makes you think I have ever forgotten that I am a dragon? But what of it? Would you have me cast aside the life I have yearning for what is lost? What life would I gain? That of a mad ship, chained to a beach, isolated and avoided?' She ran her eyes over the transformed figurehead. 'Or play at being a dragon? Pathetic.'

He did not flinch at her scorn. 'You can be a dragon. As you were meant to be.'

Silence. Then, in a low voice that might have held hatred or been full of pity, she said, 'You *are* mad.'

'No, I am not. Set your human memories aside, set your time of being a ship aside. Reach back, past the long imprisonment in your case, past your time as a serpent. Can you recall being a dragon? At all?'

I thought I felt the magic moving again. Perhaps it flowed from ship to ship, from Paragon to Vivacia. I caught the edges of floating memories, as if I scented foreign food. I flew with wings over the forest; the wind filled my sails and I cut through the waves. I flew over valleys thick with green foliage but my eyes were keen and I could sense every waft of warmth from living flesh, flesh that I could feed on. I moved through water, cold and deep, but beneath me I could sense shadowy pulses of being, other creatures, scaled as I once had been, free as I once had been. I found I was edging forward, drawn into that world of wings and wonder. *Stay out of his reach,* I thought faintly and almost wondered if Nighteyes still lurked within me to give me that wolfish warning. But I had moved to where I could see the *Vivacia*'s face and a partial profile of Paragon. So human and so foreign were those faces.

'No,' Paragon said. 'Go back farther. As far as you can reach. Here. This. Remember this!'

Again, I felt that surge of magic, Wit and Skill seamed into a tool sharper than any sword.

Once, during the battle of Antler Island, a man had hit me on the side of my head with the hilt of his sword. It had not stopped me, and my axe had already descended between the point of his shoulder and his head as he struck. The blow did not have a great deal of force, yet it made my ears ring and for a time the world wavered before me in odd colours. I knew it had happened, yet never had I recalled it. But as I was plunged into a dragon-memory it was as if Nettle had pulled me into a Skill-dream. The sensation was so similar that it awoke that old memory. I felt I reeled as from a blow, and I saw a pool of sparkling silver edged with black and silver sand, and beyond its edges, a meadow of black and silver grasses, and white-trunked trees with black leaves beyond that. I blinked my human eyes, trying to resolve it into familiar colours. Instead I saw a dragon, green as only gemstones are green, and as sparkling.

He came from the horizon, small at first and then looming larger and larger until he was the largest creature I'd ever seen—larger than Tintaglia or even IceFyre. He landed in the silver pond, sending up plumes of silver liquid that lapped and splashed against the black sand and rocks, coating them briefly with a layer of silver. The dragon plunged his head and serpentine neck into the stuff, wallowing and washing himself in it as if he were a swan. His scales seemed to absorb it, and the green grew dazzling. Groomed with it, he then lowered his muzzle to the water and drank and drank.

As he waded from the pool and composed himself for rest on the grassy bank, I had one long moment of looking into his whirling eyes. I saw age there. And wisdom. And a sort of glory I'd never seen in the eyes of a man. For a humbling instant, I knew that I looked upon a creature that was better than I would or could ever be.

'Sir? Prince FitzChivalry?'

I started from my dream, feeling resentful. It was Per, tugging at my sleeve, his eyes wide and dark in the dimness. 'What is it, boy?' I wanted him to be gone. I wanted to plunge back into that world, to know that dragon and be the better for knowing him.

'I thought you'd want to know. Our boat is coming, as fast as it can move, with Captains Althea and Brashen, and Amber and Spark and Lant. And someone from the other ship is coming, too.'

'Thank you, lad.' I turned away from him and tried to find an entry back into that magical dream. But either it was over or I had lost my way. I sensed the magic still streaming between the two liveships, but I could not enter to share it. Instead I saw only the two figureheads. Despite their bowsprits, they embraced as closely as they could, as if they were lovers denied intimacy for too long. Vivacia's head rested on Paragon's scaled chest, her eyes wide but unseeing. His longer neck had twined around her like a scarf and his dragon's head rested on her shoulder. Her graceful hands rested on his shoulders. No enmity or uncertainty showed in her face. I could not read Paragon's dragon visage to glimpse what he was feeling, but as I watched he changed. It was like watching the melting of river-ice when water swiftly erodes it. Slowly his features slipped back into his human configuration. His expression was tender as he embraced Althea. No, it was Vivacia he embraced so warmly. And suddenly I saw myself holding Molly, knowing a rare moment of peace and feeling loved and a terrible loss and longing welled in me.

I was caught up in this strange tableau until I heard Brashen's voice. 'What happened?' he demanded. 'How did Paragon get over here?'

'He dragged anchor, sir.' Clef's reply was formal, mate to captain.

'This was no trick of the tide or a bad anchor set,' Althea said. 'Paragon did this. For a reason.' Her tone said she doubted the reason had any good purpose.

Brashen and Althea stood well clear of the figurehead's reach, watching the stillness. It was Amber who moved past them, slipping free of Spark and Lant as if she too were a ship dragging anchor.

'Amber. No, please,' Althea pleaded but Amber did not pause. She stood well within Paragon's reach and waited.

Vivacia lifted her head from Paragon's shoulder and breathed a great sigh. 'What we were. What we might have become. It's lost to us, now. The young dragons, the serpents who hatched in Trehaug and live now in Kelsingra, they may become that again, a century hence. But not us. Never us.'

'You are wrong.' Paragon's voice was an inhuman rumble. 'Amber can help us get Silver. And with it, I believe we can gather enough of what we were to make ourselves what we ought to have been.'

The ships moved slightly apart, breaking their embrace to look at Amber. 'It is not certain,' she said. 'And I will not make promises I may not be able to keep. The Silver, yes, I promise I will do all I can to obtain it for you. But will it be enough to transform you into dragons? I don't know.'

'And?' Vivacia asked abruptly.

'And what?' Amber asked, startled.

Vivacia's face resumed a more human cast. 'And what do you ask of me in return? Traders made me what I am. Their blood and their thoughts have soaked into my deck and permeated every fibre of what I am. Nothing is free when you deal with humans. What do you want of me?'

'Nothi—' But Amber's response vanished in Paragon's heartfelt cry.

'Boy-O! I want Boy-O on my decks for my last voyage.' He wore my face again. Heart-struck, I wondered if I looked like that when I thought of regaining my child. Now, when he spoke, it was with a human heart. 'Give me back what is truly mine. And Paragon Kennitsson! I want him as well. He was promised to me so often when Kennit was a lad on my decks. He said he would have a son and name him for me! So much I endured for his family, so much pain! Without me, he would never have existed! I want him. I want him to see me and know me as the ship of his family. Before I become dragons and leave him forever.'

'Forever . . .' I heard that forlorn whisper from Althea and knew that until now she had dared to hope that Paragon might change his mind, or at least keep some link to her and Brashen after he transformed.

'Paragon!' A shout from Vivacia's deck, a welcoming cry in a man's deep voice.

I saw a young man in his mid-twenties with a dense mop of curly dark hair and a ready grin. He was tanned to mahogany and his shirt strained at his wide shoulders. Anyone who had seen Brashen and Althea would know he was their son. He held a lantern aloft, and clearly he had not an inkling of what was going on. He regarded his home ship with joy.

'Trellvestrit!' someone shouted behind him, but Boy-O had already set down the lantern and scrambled up to Vivacia's bowsprit. He ran lightly along it and then without hesitation threw himself toward Paragon. Paragon released Vivacia immediately. He caught and lofted the young man as I had once lifted Dutiful's small sons; and, as I had then, feigned tossing him into the air before catching him securely once more. Agile as a tumbler, the man accepted this treatment and laughed aloud at being caught. Freeing himself of the ship's grip, he climbed onto Paragon's hands and then launched himself backwards, flipping in the air and landing again nimbly on the ship's outstretched hands. Plainly it was a game from his childhood, one they both recalled with pleasure. Seldom had I seen that level of trust between any two creatures. Paragon could have torn Boy-O in half with his big wooden hands, but instead he held him at arm's length and the two studied one another, the man grinning as he looked up at the ship's face.

Unnoticed by me and perhaps also by Paragon, lines had been thrown to men in small rowing boats, and they were hauling Paragon in one direction and Vivacia in the other, swinging both on their anchor chains as they separated the two ships to a safe distance. I wondered if Boy-O had been aware of the plan, and then I wondered if Paragon cared. He had made his plea to Vivacia and had half of what he had requested, and the look on Boy-O's face was one of fearless love for his ship. No wonder Paragon had missed him.

'Prince Fitz—'

'Hush,' I bade Per. I was watching Althea and Brashen. Their conflict showed plainly on their faces. Love for their son, worry for him in the ship's hands, but also that fondness of watching the two together. Boy-O said something to Paragon as the ship caught him, and the figurehead threw back his head and roared with laughter. Looking at them, I could scarcely believe this was the same being that had been so supremely unconcerned for his crew's welfare. I half-expected Brashen or Althea to call to their son with a warning, but they were both silent and waiting. Confident in the young man or in their ship, I wondered.

As Paragon twisted to put him on the deck, I heard Boy-O say to the ship, 'I have missed you so! Vivacia is a very fine ship, but she is always serious. And Cousin Wintrow is an excellent captain, but he sets a very simple table. Mother! Papa! There you are! What brings you to Divvytown without a bird to warn us of your coming? I was at the sailmaker's when they came running to fetch me! If we'd known to expect you, you would have had a much better welcome!'

'Any sight of you is welcome enough for us!' his father exclaimed heartily as Boy-O stepped down from Paragon's hands. The figurehead was smiling so broadly over his shoulder at all three of them that I could scarcely reconcile what I was seeing.

Amber, forgotten by all, had retreated. I reached out and touched her sleeve, saying quietly, 'It's Fitz,' and she came to me with a shuddering sigh of relief, hugging my arm as if I were flotsam on a stormy sea. She was breathless. 'Are they all safe? Was anyone hurt?'

'All safe. Boy-O is with his parents. And Clef. And some of the crew.'

'I was terrified.'

I watched her try to calm herself and spoke soothingly. 'Yet Paragon seems calm now. Affable.'

'He is two, Fitz. Two dragons. I think it was what drove him mad, and sometimes I feel like he has two natures. One is boyish, a prankster who desperately craves affection and companionship. The other is capable of almost anything.'

'I think I have seen both tonight.'

'Then we are all fortunate that Boy-O brought out his kindlier nature. Angered, there is no telling what one liveship could do to another.'

'Do they fight? Can a liveship be killed?'

'A liveship can be destroyed with fire. Or disfigured as Paragon was.' She tilted her head and considered. 'I've never heard of a physical altercation between liveships. Jealousies and rivalries. Quarrels. But not taken to a physical level.'

I became aware that Per was standing nearby, listening. In the shadows behind him, Spark waited beside Lant.

'Shall we return to our cabin?' I suggested. 'I'm anxious to hear what transpired on shore.'

'Please,' Amber replied, and as we began to walk that way, she leaned more heavily on my arm. Yet before we could reach our cabin, Clef sought us out.

'Captains want to see all of you in their stateroom. Please.' He added the courtesy but it wasn't a request.

'Thank you. We will go directly there.'

Clef gave a nod and disappeared silently into the darkness. Night had fallen over the harbour. Lanterns burned on the masts of nearby ships and lamplight shone in the more distant windows of Divvytown, but they were only brighter sparks beneath the far-flung strewing of stars above us in the night sky. I looked up and suddenly longed fiercely for good forest and soil under my feet and prey that I could kill and eat. For the simple things that made life good.

SEVENTEEN

Serpent Spit

My king and queen, and esteemed Lady Kettricken,

I have reached my destination and have had several meetings with King Reyn and Queen Malta of the Dragon Traders. Trader Khuprus, mother to King Reyn, was also in attendance, representing the Rain Wild Traders. This was an unexpected inclusion for me to deal with.

The two Skill-healers who accompanied me could effect some small healing tasks for the people here. I cautioned them against greater works, for both said that the influence of the Skill runs strongly here and might sweep their minds away. And there is also the consideration that large works should merit large favours in return, and I fear I do not foresee that happening.

Both the king and queen assert that they have small influence with the dragons, and cannot order them to stop their raids on our herds and flocks. In truth, their rulers appear to have little authority over their people as well, with all large decisions being made by a consensus. I am not certain how to deal with such a situation. Nor can Trader Khuprus speak for any beyond her own family, saying that any contracts we wish to make, that is, healing for trade goods, must be voted on by the Traders' Council.

I recall that you advised me to be as generous as we can be during this first meeting. But in my opinion, if we give too freely of what these people so greatly desire, we will lose much of our bargaining ability.

The Skill-users you sent with me suggest that perhaps it were better to establish a healing centre in the Six Duchies and advise the Rain Wild folk to seek our services there, where the Skill-current is more manageable for them. Here the Skill-influence waxes so strong that I must send this message to you by bird.

We shall take ship to return home in three days.
In your service,

Lady Rosemary

We did not dare stay long in Sewelsby. Dwalia could not be sure how many people might recognize us from that bloody night. Over and over, she asked Vindeliar how much Kerf would recall and how much he would tell. 'He won't forget,' Vindeliar had whined. 'I did not have time to tell him to forget. You made us run away. He will be confused but he won't forget what he did. He will tell. If they hurt him enough.' He had shaken his blunt head sadly. 'They always talk when you hurt them that much. You showed me that.'

'And you whimpered and pissed yourself, like a kicked cur,' she had replied vindictively. And so instead of having Vindeliar magic us into an inn and a room, we slept that night under a bridge to stay away from spying eyes. As soon as the sun lightened the sky, she made us wade out into the chilly river and try to rinse some of the blood from our clothes. We weren't alone for long. Men and women from the town came bearing baskets of linens and clothing. The washerfolk each had their own areas along the rocky shore, and they set up their drying racks and glared us away from the riverbank.

Dwalia led us back toward the town. I think towns and busy streets were all she knew. I would have sought the forest for a time, to let folk forget us. Instead, she had hissed at Vindeliar, 'Make us unremarkable. Restore my face. Leave no injury for them to notice. Do it.'

I know he tried. I felt the lapping of his magic against my senses. I do not think he did it very well. But in a port city poor folk are not uncommon and we did not look so strange that we drew many glances. We stayed well away from the lovely inn and the well-travelled street where Trader Akriel had died. Dwalia took us to the seedy section of the harbour, where the signboards of the inns were weathered grey and splintery, and the gutters ran greenish and stinking beside the streets.

Dwalia and I hunkered out of sight in an alley or sat at the edge of the street, hands out to beg, in vain. Vindeliar moved slowly up and down the street, seeking easy prey. Some folk were easier to influence than others. He took a little from each, a few coins here, a few coins there. They gave willingly, or so they would recall it, even if they could not remember why. Towards evening, he had collected enough that we could have a hot meal and sleep inside one of the cheap inns.

It was nothing like the inn Trader Akriel had taken me to. The sleeping area was simply a loft over the room below. We found unoccupied space and lay down in our clothes. I could not help but contrast that night to the future I had nearly gained. When I was sure the others slept, I allowed myself to weep. I tried to think of Withywoods, my home and my father, but those things seemed distant and more unlikely than my dreams.

For dreams came to me that night, pelting me like hailstones. After each, I jolted awake, seized with the need to tell someone, to write them down, to sing of them. It was a compulsion as strong as when one must vomit, but I choked them back. Dwalia would rejoice in them, and I would not give her that. And so my dream of the slow team of oxen that trampled a child into a muddy street, my dream of a wise queen who planted silver and reaped golden wheat, my dream of a man who rode a huge red horse across ice to a new land, all those I choked back and swallowed. If they spoke of futures, she would not know of them. It made me feel ill and wretched to keep those dreams inside me, but the satisfaction I took in any small way I could thwart Dwalia outweighed the sickness.

The next day I was so shaky I could scarcely walk. Vindeliar looked concerned for me, while Dwalia wore a calculating look. 'We need to leave this city and move on,' she told him. 'Look into their minds. See if anyone is going to Clerres. Or has been there.' He had persuaded a breadmonger to part with a loaf. Dwalia had portioned it out, half for herself, and the rest for Vindeliar. He had looked at it hungrily and then reluctantly given me half of his half. It was no bigger than my fist, but it was all I could do to nibble it down.

I heard Vindeliar speak quietly to Dwalia. 'I think she's sick.'

Dwalia looked at me and smiled. 'She is. And I'm glad. It means I'm at least partially right.'

Her words made no sense to me. As the day passed, my misery increased. I huddled as far away from her as my chain would let me and tried to sleep. Vindeliar took his small tolls from passing folk. Dwalia sat like a toad and watched the town go by. I decided to test her idea that no one would help me. I cried out for help. A few folk turned heads but she jerked on my chain. 'New to slavery,' Dwalia explained blithely, and my babble of hasty words that she was lying, I was no slave but kidnapped, went unheeded. I was just another foreign slave.

One man stopped and spoke to her in Common, asking if I were for sale. His eyes were not kind. Dwalia replied that he could pay her for a few hours with me, but that he could not buy me. He looked at me speculatively. Terror inspired me and I began to retch, forcing a thin bile to spill from my mouth and down onto my clothing. The man shook his head, plainly not wanting to share whatever disease I had, and hurried on.

Whatever ailed me took a firm grip on me the next day. In the pleasant warmth of the summer day, I curled up and shivered with cold. The bright sunlight could not warm me; it only battered me in pink darkness through my closed eyelids as the fever wracked me.

On the splintery floor of the inn loft, I shivered and Vindeliar rolled over and put his arm over me. He smelled offensive to me. It was not the grime or sweat of him; it was his own scent that repelled me. Wolf-sense told me to beware of him. I tried to shake off his arm but I was too weak. 'Brother, let me keep you warm,' he whispered. 'It wasn't your fault.'

'My fault?' I heard myself mutter. Of course it wasn't. None of this was my fault.

'I did it. I created the rift that allowed you to run away. Dwalia told me. When I did not do as I knew she would have wished me to do, it opened another path for you. And you followed it, taking us farther and farther from the Path. So now we must endure hardship and pain as we make our thorny way back to the Path. Once we are on the way to Clerres again, our difficulties will ease.'

I tried to shrug his arm away from me, but he drew me closer. His stink was all around me, gagging me with every breath I took. 'You should learn this lesson, brother. Once you accept the Path, all in life is easier. Dwalia guides us. I know she seems cruel. But she is only angry and harsh because you have taken us so far from the true Path. Help us go back to it, and it will be so much easier for all of us.'

The words did not sound like him, or Dwalia. Perhaps he parroted some long-ago lesson. I summoned every shred of will I had. I forced out my words. 'My true path goes home!'

He patted my shoulder. 'There. You are right, your true path will take you to your true home. Now that you admit that, things will become easier.'

I hated him. I curled on the floor, sick and angry and powerless.

Dwalia moved us to a different part of the waterfront and hailed passers-by to ask if any had news of a ship bound for Clerres. Most shrugged and the rest ignored her. I huddled miserably while Vindeliar kept a distance from us as he moved up and down the streets and 'begged'. He chose those he accosted and I knew they had little choice as he pushed his thoughts against theirs. I saw their reluctance as they reached into purses or pockets, and witnessed their confusion as they wandered away from him. The area was not rife with wealthy folk. I suspected that Vindeliar showed mercy in the small amounts he charmed from each victim, yet Dwalia always berated him for not coercing more money out of his victims.

One day he did not get enough money for us to sleep inside. I had thought I could not feel worse, but as the chill of evening came on, I shook until my teeth chattered.

Dwalia commonly took small notice of my misery, but I think that evening she worried that I might die. She did nothing to give me comfort, but only turned her anger on Vindeliar. 'What's wrong with you?' she demanded of him when the streets had emptied and there was no one in earshot to hear her scold him. 'You used to be strong. Now you are useless. You used to control a cavalcade of mercenaries, hiding them from sight. Now you can barely charm a penny or two from a farmer's purse.'

For the first time in many a day, I heard a note of spirit in his voice. 'I am hungry and tired and far from home and unhappy with all I have seen. I try very hard. I need—'

'No!' she interrupted him furiously. 'You do not *need*! You *want*. And I know what you want. Do you think I don't know how much pleasure you take from it? I've seen your eyes roll back with it and how you drool. No. There is only one left and we must save it against most dire need. Then there will be no more for you, Vindeliar. No more ever, for it has become scarce since the nine-fingered slaveboy set the serpent free!'

How strangely those words rang in me, like a memory of something

I'd never experienced. A nine-fingered slaveboy. I could almost see him, dark-haired and slight, strong only in his will. His will to do what was right. 'The serpent was in a stone pool.' I breathed the words to myself. It had not been a dream of a snake in a bowl, no.

'What did you say?' Dwalia demanded sharply.

'I am sick,' I said, a repetition of words I'd said so often over the last few days. I closed my eyes and turned my face away. But with my eyes closed, I could not control the images that filled my mind. The slaveboy came to the stone pool; he wrestled with the iron bars that ringed it. Eventually, he made a path for the deformed serpent that crawled out of the pool and into water. Yes, into water, an incoming tide. How could I recall something I'd never seen? And yet the waves lapped up and into the pool, replenishing but not cleansing it. Both slave and serpent dissolved into whiteness. I saw no more.

I opened my eyes to breaking dawn. We had slept on the streets, yet I no longer felt chilled. I ached, as one does after sleeping on hard earth or after a long sickness has kept one still. I sat up slowly, or tried to. Dwalia had rolled over onto the chain. I took it in both hands and jerked it out from under her. She opened her eyes to glare at me. I snarled back at her.

She made a noise, a snort from her nose, as if to say she did not fear me. I resolved then that the next time she slept, I would give her reason to fear me again. My gaze travelled lovingly over the rancid bite I'd given her. Then I lowered my eyes lest she guess my plan.

She got to her feet and kicked Vindeliar. 'Up!' she said. 'Time to move on. Before someone wonders why they gave half their coins to a beggar yesterday.'

I squatted and pissed in a gutter, wondering when I had lost all modesty and indeed all civilized ways. My mother would not have known me with my knotted hair and dust-stained skin and filthy nails. The tidy garments that Trader Akriel had given me could not withstand the sort of use I was giving them now. Tears welled in my eyes when I thought of her. I rubbed them away, doubtless smearing dirt down my face with them. Then I looked at my hands and the peeling of skin that clung to my fingers. I shook them clean and looked up to find Dwalia sneering with satisfaction.

'The Path knows her even if she does not know the Path,' she said to Vindeliar, who looked awestruck. Then she gave my chain a sharp tug and I was forced to go stumbling after her. My arms itched, and when I scratched them, my skin came away in thin layers that wadded like cobwebs at my touch. It was not a sunburn peeling. The layer that came off me was fine as gossamer, and beneath it my skin was not pink but paler. Chalky.

At the waterfront, we dodged barrows and donkey carts and folk carrying bales on their shoulders. Dwalia guided us to a stretch of market stalls. At the smell of food my stomach leapt up inside my throat and choked me. I had not felt hunger for days, but now it assailed me mercilessly till I felt dizzy and shaky.

Dwalia slowed, and I hoped she was as hungry as I was and had some coins for food. But instead she tugged me along to stand in a growing crowd clustered around a tall man with broad shoulders standing on a cart. He wore a high hat striped in many colours. His cloak had a collar that stood up to his ears, and it too was striped. I had never seen such garments. Behind the man in the cart was a wooden cabinet with row after row of little drawers, each drawer of a different colour, and each carved with an emblem. Over the man's head, scarves and tiny bells hung from a framework of sticks. The wind off the water was a near constant, and so the bells tinkled and the scarves fluttered. Even the big grey horse that waited patiently in his traces had ribbons and bells in his mane. Never had I seen such a spectacle!

For that moment, my hunger was forgotten. What wondrous things could such a merchant be selling? That seemed to be the question everyone was pondering. He spoke in a language I did not know, and then abruptly he shifted into Common. 'A fortune for you, to guide your footsteps into a lucky path! Brought to you from a far-off place! Do you wince at a silver for such knowledge? Foolish you! Where else in this market can you part with a silver and receive wisdom and luck? Should you wed? Will your wife grow heavy with child? Should you plant for the roots or the leaves this year? Come, come, you need not wonder! Press a silver to your brow, and then pass it to me with your question. The coin will tell me which box to open! Come, come, who will try? Who will be first?'

Dwalia made a sound in her throat like a cat's growl. I glanced back at Vindeliar. His eyes were very wide. He saw my stare and spoke in a whisper. 'He imitates the small prophets of Clerres, the

ones sent out by the Four. It is forbidden to do what he is doing!
He is a fraud!'

Two people turned to stare at him. Vindeliar lowered his eyes and
fell silent. The man on the cart was chattering on, in both languages,
and suddenly a woman was waving a coin at him. When he nodded
to her, she pressed the coin firmly to her forehead and then offered
it to him. He smiled, took her silver, and pressed it to his brow. He
asked her a question and she replied. Then, to the larger crowd in
Common he announced, 'She wishes to know if her mother and her
sister will welcome her if she makes the long journey to visit them.'

He pressed the coin once more to his brow and then held it
out. His hand wavered and circled. It looked indeed as if the coin
led his hand to the little door he selected. He opened it and from
it he extracted a nut. That startled me. It was gold or painted with
gilt. He struck it suddenly against his brow as if he were cracking
an egg. Then he offered it to the woman. Hesitantly she took it
and opened the nut. It had split as evenly as if sliced by a knife.
Delighted, she opened it on her palm and drew out a thin strip of
paper. It was white but edged in yellow, blue, red and green along
its sides. She stared at it and then offered it back to him, asking
him something.

'Read it! Read it!' the crowd echoed her request.

He took it back from her. He had elegant hands, and he made
quite a show of drawing the narrow coil of paper out and perusing
the lines lettered there. His pause as his eyes moved over it prompted
the crowd to edge closer. 'Ah, good news for you, good news indeed!
You asked for advice on a journey, and here it is for you! "Walk with
the sunshine and enjoy the road. A well laid table and a clean bed
awaits you at your destination. Your arrival fills a house with joy."
There! Pack your bag and be on your way! And now, who is next?
Who will hear what fortune awaits you? Isn't it worth a coin to
know?'

A young man waved a coin, the merchant took it, and again he
put on a performance worthy of any puppeteer before he presented
the fortune from the golden nut to the man. He received good tidings
for the marriage offer he wished to present and stepped back from
the cart, grinning. More coins were being waved now, some frantically. Dwalia watched, eyes narrowed, like a cat at a mouse hole, as
the merchant accepted money and foretold fortunes. Not all were

good. A man who asked about crops was instead warned that he should save his money and not make a purchase he had been considering. He looked dumbstruck and then told the crowd, 'I came to market today to look for a plough-horse! But now I will wait.'

A couple hoping for a pregnancy, a man thinking of selling his land, a woman who wanted to know if her father would recover from an injury . . . so many folk seeking to know what tomorrow would bring. Once or twice the merchant would take the coin, hold it to his brow, and then wave it about and frown. 'It's not leading me,' he'd say. 'I'll need a larger piece of silver from you to find the answer to your question.'

And to my astonishment, folk would give him a bigger coin. It was as if once they had started on the path, they could not turn aside. Some read their coiled messages aloud, others curled over the string of paper and read it privately. The fortune-merchant read them aloud for folk who were unlettered. Door after door of his little cabinet he opened. His audience did not grow smaller. Even those who had bought a fortune lingered to find out what others might hear.

Dwalia moved us to the edge of the crowd, but there she stopped and whispered to Vindeliar, 'Control him.'

'Him?' Vindeliar did not whisper.

I saw that she longed to cuff him but she restrained herself. Obviously, she did not wish to distract those watching the merchant.

'Yes, him. The one selling fake fortunes.' She spoke through gritted teeth.

'Oh.' Vindeliar studied the man. I could sense tendrils of his magic floating and feeling their way toward him. And I knew he couldn't do it. The man was too strong of self to be captured by such feeble threads. I could sense the shape the fortune-merchant made in the world and to my surprise I could feel that he had a sort of magic shimmer to him. He did not reach out with his magic as Vindeliar did. Instead, his magic coated him just as his bright colours did, and like his colours, it invited folk to study him and draw near. I reached toward his magic and pushed on it gently. For a moment, he looked puzzled. I moved away. All he could do was draw people in; he probably didn't even know he was using it.

I looked back at Vindeliar, and found him regarding me strangely. I looked away and scratched my neck under the collar. I hadn't intended to touch his magic; I'd done it without thinking. And somehow Vindeliar had sensed it and now his suspicions were stirred.

The fortune-merchant was waving a coin, letting it guide his hand to a little door with a bird on it. I pretended vast interest in his show.

'I can't do it,' Vindeliar said to Dwalia. His face crumpled before she even glared at him. 'There is no way into him.'

'Make a way.'

'I can't.' He drew the word out long and slow.

She seethed silently for a moment, then seized the shoulder of his shirt and pulled him close, so close I thought she intended to bite him. In a venomous whisper she said, 'I know what you want. I know what you long for. But listen to me, you pathetic unformed thing, neither human nor White! I have but one dose left of the potion. ONE! If we use it now, we will not have it later when perhaps it will be essential that you have strength. So, find a way into him. And do it now, or I will kill you. It is that simple. If you cannot do your work, you are useless. I will leave you behind to rot.' She pushed him away from her.

I watched Vindeliar's face as each word struck him and sank in like a separate arrow. He believed her with absolute certainty. And so did I. If he failed her today, she would kill him. I didn't wonder how or when because I knew she would do it.

And then I would be left alone with her. That thought struck me like an axe blow.

I saw Vindeliar's shoulders rise and fall, rise and fall as his panicky breathing began to accelerate. Without thinking, I reached out and took his hand. 'Try,' I begged him. His wide eyes darted to mine. 'Try, my brother,' I said in a softer voice. I would not, could not, bear to look at Dwalia. Did she sneer to see us frightened, did she rejoice at how she had hammered us into an alliance? I did not want to know.

Vindeliar's pudgy hand closed on mine. It was warm and moist, as if I'd put my hand into something's mouth, and I wished I could withdraw it. But now was not the time to instil any doubt in him. He took a shuddering breath and then I felt him settle himself. But more than that. I felt him gather his magic, and suddenly I knew that no matter what Dwalia might believe, this was Farseer magic. I knew a moment of outrage that somehow he had stolen such an ability. Then I felt him bubbling it toward the merchant.

How often had I felt my father or my sister use this magic? They had employed it as if it were the sharpest knife one could imagine, arrowing toward the person they sought to reach. Vindeliar pushed his lips out and then sucked them in, straining to reach the merchant, as if he were sloshing water toward him. I wondered how he had ever managed to control Duke Ellik and his men with such a sloppy magic. Perhaps then he had been stronger in it, strong enough that he had not needed to refine his skill. Perhaps it was like the difference between smashing an ant with a brick or squishing it with a fingertip.

The magic moved sluggishly toward the merchant. It reached him and washed against him. But he was so full of himself, so radiant in his enthusiasm for what he was selling, that he felt it not at all. It rolled aside from him. This I felt as Vindeliar's hand engulfed mine. I felt too, the drop in his confidence. The magic grew softer and less focused as his despair grew.

'You can do this,' I whispered to him, and willed that he would feel confidence, that he would try again.

Once, when I fell from a tree and ran to my mother with my elbow bleeding, I was unaware that much more blood was escaping from my nose. The magic that moved out of me and through Vindeliar was like that. I felt no sensation of something vital leaving me until suddenly I was aware of the effect. Vindeliar had marshalled what magic he could and was rolling it toward the merchant like a badly tumbled stone. Then my magic, a magic so like my father's and sister's that I knew it was mine, guided his. And it was abruptly not a badly tumbled stone, but a well-flung one.

I saw it strike the merchant, saw how in the midst of his smiling chatter his eyes widened and his words suddenly failed him. I felt what Vindeliar commanded him. *You will want to do what Dwalia wishes you to do.* When he conveyed 'Dwalia' it was an image of her as well as a feeling of who she was. Important, wise, a woman to be obeyed. A woman to be feared. The merchant's gaze roved over the crowd and found Dwalia. He regarded her with awe. She nodded to him, and to Vindeliar she said softly, 'I knew you could do it. If you wanted to badly enough.'

Vindeliar dropped my hand and clapped both hands over his

mouth, astonished at what he had accomplished. As for the merchant, he continued his spiel, selling golden nuts and wonderful fortunes to buyer after buyer, until every little door on his cabinet stood open and plundered. He announced to the crowd that he had no more fortunes to sell that day, and they dispersed, drifting and chatting, some still perusing the long tails of paper with the futures written on them.

We stood where we were as his audience dispersed. He glanced at Dwalia, not once, but repeatedly as he shut each little door of his wonderful cabinet and slowly stepped down from his cart. His horse turned its head and snorted questioningly but the merchant walked toward us, his expression puzzled. Dwalia did not smile. Vindeliar retreated behind her and I followed him as my chain would allow.

'You have done a wicked thing,' Dwalia said, her first words to him. The merchant stopped and stared at her. His mouth twisted as if he would be sick. 'You have smuggled fortune-nuts out of Clerres. You know it is forbidden. Those who buy a fortune there know it must be kept in their homes in a place of honour. They know it must not be given away nor sold. But somehow you have acquired dozens of them. Your charade with tapping the nuts to open them did not fool me. They had been opened, and the revelations inside were given to those who had paid well for them. How did you get them? Did you steal them?'

'No! No, I am an honest merchant!' He looked horrified at the suggestion of theft. 'I buy and I sell. I have a sailor friend who brings me extraordinary merchandise. He does not come to this port often, but when he comes, he brings me the nutshells and the fortune papers to put inside them. I am known for my rarities, such as the fortunes spun by the pale folk. I have sold them here for years. If there was a crime, it was not mine! I only buy them and sell them on to folk eager for them. Folk who know that a silver is a fair price for such rare things!'

Dwalia glanced at Vindeliar. His eyes widened and I felt him push his magic toward the man. It sogged against him like a wet cloth but he gave a tiny nod to Dwalia. She smiled and it made my bite-mark a horrid, crawling thing on her face. 'You know you have done wrong,' she accused him. 'You should give me the silver, for I come from the Pale Ones, the Whites and the Four. Give me the money you have gained from your deceit, and I will beg them to forgive you. And tell me the name of your friend and the ship that brought him here, and for him, too, I will beg pardon.'

He stared at her. He hefted the pouch of silvers he had gained. I had counted the little doors in his cabinet. There were forty-eight of them. Forty-eight pieces of silver, and some were the larger pieces that he had cajoled from his buyers. It was a magnificent sum, if a silver here was worth what a silver was in Buck. He stared at Dwalia and then tilted his head before he shook it at her. 'You're a peculiar beggar. You accuse me of theft, and then try to rob me. I don't even know why I spoke to you at all. But I'm to be wed tomorrow, and the old saying tells us to pay a debt you don't owe before your wedding day, and you'll never have a debt you can't pay. So, here's a silver for you, a debt I don't owe.' As he spoke he fished in his pouch and brought up a single piece of silver. He held it between two fingers, then flipped it suddenly into the air. Dwalia clutched at it, but it slid between her fingers into the dirt. Vindeliar squatted to get it for her but she set her shoe firmly on the coin.

The fortune-merchant had turned away from us and was walking toward the front of his cart. Without looking back, he added, 'You should be ashamed of yourself. Feed that child something. And if you've a heart at all, take that chain off her throat and find her a home.'

Dwalia kicked Vindeliar, hard. He fell onto his side, gasping. 'The name of the ship!' she demanded of both, and I felt the pained thrust of Vindeliar's desperate magic.

The man was mounting to the seat of his cart. He didn't look back at us. 'The *Sea Rose.*' He took up the reins and shook them. His horse moved placidly forward. I wondered if he even realized that he had spoken to us.

Dwalia crouched to pick up her coin. She stood and as Vindeliar started to rise, she kicked him down again. 'Don't think this pays for all,' she warned him. She jerked my chain viciously and against my will I cried out. And then, to my shame, tears flowed from my eyes. I shuffled and sobbed after her as Vindeliar lumbered to his feet and followed us like a kicked dog.

Dwalia did stop to buy food. Cheap dry bread for Vindeliar and me, a savoury flaky roll stuffed with meat and vegetables for her. She watched the vendor count her coins back to her with an eagle's keen stare, and stuffed them into a fold of her clothing. She ate as she walked, and so did we. I longed for water to wash down the dry bread, but she did not pause near the public well we passed. She took us down to the waterfront. The harbour was a great circle of calm water, with fingers of docks that reached out. The biggest ships were anchored in the placid bay, and little boats skated back and forth over the water like many-legged water insects, bearing people and supplies to them. Closer to us, smaller ships tied to the docks and piers, created a wall of hulls and a forest of masts between us and the open water. We three beggars entered the jostling world of carts and long-shoremen and prosperous merchants inviting one another to tea or wine or discussing their latest purchases and sales.

We limped and shuffled among them, either invisible and unno-ticed or cursed and reviled for making the traffic pause or standing where someone wished to walk. Dwalia sounded to me like a bread-monger as she called out, 'The *Sea Rose*? Where does she dock? The *Sea Rose*? I'm looking for the *Sea Rose*!'

No one answered her. The best she got was a shake of the head to say they didn't know the vessel. At last Vindeliar tugged at her sleeve and pointed wordlessly between two ships. We had a narrow view of the bay, and a fine vessel with no figurehead, but a glorious bouquet of flowers at her bow, with a large red rose in the centre of it. It was fat and long, the largest ship in the harbour. 'Might it be that one?' he asked her timidly. Dwalia halted despite the push and press of folk around us and stared at the vessel. The ship's bare masts pointed at the sky and she rode high in the water. Her crew moved briskly on her decks, busy with sailorish chores I didn't understand. As we watched, a small boat with six men at her oars pulled along-side. A large crate of something was lowered to the waiting boat, and then a man descended to it.

Someone bumped me hard, and said something vicious in a language I didn't know. I cringed closer to Vindeliar and he in turn huddled behind Dwalia. She neither moved nor appeared to notice that we were blocking traffic. 'We need to see where they go,' she announced in a low voice. As the boat moved away from the ship, she suddenly set out at a trot, and I was forced to keep pace with her. It was hard to see where the rowing boat was going for our view was often blocked by tethered ships or large stacks of crates and bales. On we went, and on, with my bare feet protesting both the uneven cobbles and the splintery docks. I tore a nail on my foot and it bled. She darted in front of a team and wagon, dragging me behind her so that I felt the hot breath of the horses when they jerked their heads up and protested, and the angry shout as the teamster called me vile names.

Finally, we stood on a well-built dock. The sky overhead was wide and blue, sprinkled with screaming gulls. The wind blew past me, stirring my clothes and hair. I reached up and touched it, astonished at how it had grown. Had it been so long since my father and I had sheared our heads for grief at my mother's death? It seemed but days and it seemed like years.

Vindeliar and I stood side by side while Dwalia paced up and down, every step a small tug at my chain. As soon as the boat drew near she began shouting, 'Are you from the *Sea Rose*? Are you her captain?'

A finely-dressed man who did not pull an oar but rode grandly beside the wooden crate looked up at her in distaste. His lips curled back as if he could already smell us. The captain stood in his boat, ignoring how it rocked as his men climbed up and made the lines fast. A davit was swung out over the water. After supervising the transfer of the wooden crate to the dock, he climbed the ladder up to the docks, ignoring Dwalia's frantic queries as if she were but another squawking gull. As if we were of no consequence, he brushed his hands on his black trousers and straightened his dark green jacket. It had two rows of silver buttons down the front, and his cuffs were likewise secured with silver. The shirt he wore beneath his fine jacket was a paler green, and the collar sparkled with jewel studs. He was a handsome fellow, handsome as a jaybird. He took something from his pocket, opened a little pot. He rubbed his finger in something and then smeared it over his lips. All the while, he stared over our heads toward the busy shore as if we did not exist.

His crewmembers were not so reserved. Their shouts of appalled merriment at the sight of us were impossible to misunderstand in any language. One woman moved behind Dwalia and mocked her stance and face, contorting her features and behaving like a halfwit. An older sailor gave her a rebuking shove, and then dug in his pocket to offer Vindeliar a handful of coppers. Vindeliar looked to Dwalia, and when she simply continued to shout her queries at them, he received the coppers into his cupped hands. With that, the crew was finished with us. They strode away with the rolling gait of experienced hands, laughing among themselves, all save one who sat forlornly in the rowing boat below, evidently consigned to that duty.

Dwalia screeched curses after them and then spun on Vindeliar, slapping him so hard that some of the coppers jumped out of his hand, bounced on the planks and fell through the cracks into the water below. Heedless of my chain, I managed to secure two of them and clutched them tightly. Somehow, I would find a way to turn them into food. Somehow.

Vindeliar cringed as Dwalia beat him with her fists and kicked him. He hunkered down into a ball, hiding his head in his arms and giving small cries of pain in response to each of her blows. I seized my chain in both hands, jerked it free of her grip, and lashed her with it twice. She staggered sideways but did not go into the water as I'd hoped. I turned and ran, a length of chain clanking and pinging against the dock planks as I fled.

I expected it to happen but it still hurt when someone stamped hard on the trailing chain, jerking me to a halt. Sobbing and bruised, hands at my throat, I turned back, ready to attack Dwalia. But it was Vindeliar who had landed on my dragging leash. His cheeks were still reddened from Dwalia's blows; nonetheless, he had done her will. Dwalia was a puffing step behind him. He looked up at her, pathetically loyal, and held my chain out to her. 'No!' I shrieked but she stooped down, seized the chain and snapped it wildly back and forth so that my head lashed with it. I saw flashes of light and fell to the dock. She kicked me twice, panting with fury. 'Get up!' she commanded. She was going to kill me. Not at once, but with continued abuse. I knew it with the certainty of a dream. I would die at her hands, and with me would die the future that should have been. I was the future they sought to destroy by capturing and holding the Unexpected Son. I felt half-stunned by the knowledge. Had it been in my mind all that time, finally to be shaken free by Dwalia's abuse of me? I felt sick with the insight. It was no dream that flashed before my eyes as if I had stared at the sun. It was a future. I had to find the path to that future. I would find it, or I would die trying.

'Get up!' she repeated. I got to my hands and knees, then staggered to my feet and stood, reeling. Snarling, she shoved her hand down the front of her shirt. Her fist came back up gripping something.

Vindeliar quivered, his attention completely focused on her hand. Dwalia beamed at him with cruel power. Slowly she uncurled her fingers until I saw that she held a glass tube that held a cloudy liquid. She shook her head at him slowly. 'You are weak. So weak. But when a broken shovel is the only tool one has to dig a hole, then one mends it and uses it. So, one last time, I will fill you with strength. One last chance I will give you to redeem yourself. But if you fail me again, in the slightest way, I will make an end of you. No, I will not put it into your hands. Sit down. Tilt your head back and open your mouth.'

I had never seen anyone obey so quickly. Vindeliar sat upon the dock and leaned back, his eyes closed and his mouth opened wider than I had ever imagined it could. And he sat like that, perfectly still and waiting, while she laboriously pried a glass stopper from the tube and slowly, so slowly, tipped the tube over his mouth. A lumpy liquid, yellowish and yet threaded with silver, drooled slowly from the tube. I felt revulsion at the sight of it, and the smell that reached me was that of vomit. I gagged as it trickled into his mouth and he swallowed it. A moment later, like the lapping of water in a pond when a stone is thrown into it, the wave of his fresh power touched me. Had I thought my father was like a boiling pot with a steam of magic coming from him? What I felt from Vindeliar was not steam but a scalding blast of power. Both body and mind, I curled small against it, going as tight and hard as a nut against that surging current.

Vindeliar's eyelids fluttered wildly and his whole body quivered in ecstasy. The trickle of lumpy fluid continued to flow, thick and clotted and disgusting. And as he swallowed and then swallowed again, the battering of his magic against me grew only stronger. I curled tighter and smaller, body and mind. Dwalia gauged what she gave him, righting the tube when there was a perhaps a quarter of the fluid left in it, then stoppered it again.

I shut my eyes and strove to feel nothing, hear nothing, smell and taste nothing, for any sense I left unguarded might bring him blasting into my mind. For a time, I was nothing. Senseless and without being, I barely existed.

I could not say how much time passed. But eventually I felt his regard lessened or focused elsewhere and dared to open my senses. I smelled tarry wooden deck and seaweed, and heard the distant mewling of seabirds. And Dwalia's voice, just as mewling and constant. 'When the captain returns, he will see us as lordly and respectable. We are people he wants to impress. He will long to please me, ache for my regard. All his crew will see us that way. He will take these coppers as if they were golds. He will be anxious to set sail for Clerres as soon as he possibly can, and will provide for us every comfort that can be offered. Can you do that?'

My vision swam, but I saw Vindeliar's beatific smile. 'I can do that,' he said dreamily. 'I can do anything right now.'

And I feared that he could.

My fear touched him. He turned toward me and his smile was as unbearably bright as looking at the sun. 'Bro-ther,' he drawled out, pleased with himself, as if he spoke to a toddler hiding behind a chair. 'I see you now!'

I retreated, smaller and smaller, shell tighter and harder, but he followed me effortlessly. 'I do not think you can hide from me now!' he teased me gently. And I could not. Layer after layer after layer of me he knew, secrets peeling away from me like skin from a blister, getting closer and closer to the raw heart of me. He knew now of how Shun and I had fled, he knew of my day with my father in the town, he knew of the bloody dog and he knew of my quarrel with my tutor.

It had been so long since Wolf Father had spoken to me, but suddenly I knew what he would tell me. Cornered? Fight.

I threw my shields aside. 'No!' I snarled. 'It is you who cannot hide from me!'

Physically, I came to my feet, but that was not how I faced him. How to describe it? He had ventured too close to me. He had pushed in and now suddenly, I enveloped him. I did not know what I did or how I did it. Did I remember doing this once? Did I remember my father doing it, my sister? I wrapped my awareness around him and trapped him. He was too surprised to struggle. I do not think he had ever imagined that someone could do this to him. I pressed hard on him, and suddenly it was like crushing a boiled egg in my hand. His shell broke; it had not been a thick one. I doubt he had ever had to guard his mind against another.

And I knew him. That knowledge did not come to me in any sequence; it simply was mine. I knew that he had been born with an oddly shaped head, and that was enough for him to be set aside from the others. He was barely a White to their eyes, just a flawed and useless baby, given over to Dwalia, one of several squalling infants born that season who were less than perfect.

And in knowing what had befallen him, I learned of Dwalia, too. For she had raised him from infancy.

Once she had been respected, the handmaiden who had served a highly regarded White. She had seen her mistress sent out into the world to do great things. But when the woman failed and fell, Dwalia's fortune had perished with her. Disgraced and delegated to demeaning tasks, Dwalia became a servant to the midwives and healers of Clerres. The business of Clerres was the breeding of Whites for the harvesting of their precognizant dreams, and Dwalia had hoped to be entrusted with a promising White of the purest bloodlines. But she was no longer trusted there. Given a set of defective twins to dispose of, she had instead suckled them on a pig and kept them alive, hoping that their imperfect bodies might conceal powerful minds.

Daily, she reminded them that they owed their lives to her. Denied access to the perfect children given to others to groom and raise, she had only her rejected children to cultivate. And cultivate them she did. Vindeliar recalled peculiar diets, soporific herbs, times when he was not allowed to sleep, times when he was given sleep-inducing concoctions for weeks, to force him to dream. But as Vindeliar and his sister Oddessa had grown, they had shown no extraordinary abilities.

All this and much that was sadder I knew in an instant. Vindeliar had not been able to dream for her, other than the one pathetic dream he had shared with me. Oddessa dreamed but the images she saw were so formless as to be useless. Yet Dwalia had been merciless in the efforts she made to force her protégés to produce dreams for her. He knew that she had begun to serve as Fellowdy's assistant at his dissections and inquisition, for he had to tidy after them. But he did not know why Symphe had come to her with a rare elixir made from the fluids of a sea serpent's body. It was said to give intense and prophetic dreams to any who took it, followed by an agonizing death. This Vindeliar had overheard.

The first time she administered it to Vindeliar she had chained him to a table. It had burned his tongue and mouth so badly that to this day he could not taste food. Yet the pain had been followed by an intense ecstasy, and an expanding of his thought so that he could share his mind with others. When some nearby prisoners fell, writhing, screaming, holding their mouths, Dwalia realized they felt his pain. And from there, in careful testing, she had discovered that he could make others believe the thoughts he pushed toward them.

Those of White heritage were seldom vulnerable to his manipulation. For years, as he developed his ability under her secret tutelage, he had believed Dwalia was immune to it, and had never dared to try it against her. He was never allowed to speak of the elixir. Dwalia insisted to others that he was extraordinary, with the ability to find tiny paths where others believed him and obeyed him.

So much I learned in that shattering of our walls. My invasion of his mind stunned him. I weighed my strength against his as he struggled to discover what had just befallen him. Then I acted, using the hereditary magic of the Farseers almost by instinct. 'You cannot master me,' I told him, pushing the thought at him with every ounce of strength I had. 'You cannot break my walls.'

And then, I slammed shut the gates to myself.

When next I knew I was me, Dwalia was nudging me, not gently, with her foot. 'Get up,' she was saying in a falsely kind voice. 'Get up. It's time for us to go aboard.'

The world wavered before my eyes. I saw her sumptuous dress, the spill of lace from the low-cut bosom, the extravagant flowers in her hat. She was young, no older than Shun, and her long black ringlets gleamed with perfumed oil. Her eyes were a rare shade of deep blue, framed with long lashes. Her skin was flawless. Her dapper serving man stood beside her.

Then I blinked and she was Dwalia with the chewed face and well-worn clothes. Vindeliar was Vindeliar. I wondered how the gathered sailors saw me. I stood reluctantly, my head still whirling. My hunger had become nausea. I contained it with a deep breath. The sailors were not looking at me, so I was a serving girl or slave and not an attractive one. Dwalia received their sidelong glances with a simpering smile. The captain of the *Sea Rose* had returned and he was speaking to her in rapt tones. He ordered a swing prepared that she should not fuss her skirts, and guided it himself as the davit lowered her to the rowing boat. She looked back up at us. 'Quickly now! We board our ship and soon we depart for Clerres.'

I reached my hand to my throat. Vindeliar gave my chain a tug. 'Quickly now!' he ordered me in a cold voice. He did not smile. He began to descend the ladder to the small boat. The chain went tight and dragged me to the edge of the dock and toward a future I could not avoid.

EIGHTEEN

Silver Ships and Dragons

I cannot deny his peculiar looks, but he seems a clever fellow, and I am certain that he is not a danger to me. How you can imagine he is sent by an enemy to kill me surprises me. The note that accompanied the lad said that many rulers now enjoy having a jester to amuse their court and perhaps I would welcome this clever tumbler. His antics are most amusing, and I confess that when his sharp little tongue cut Lord Attery to shreds yesterday evening, I rather enjoyed it, since the man is a pompous boor.

When first he arrived in his tattered clothing, bearing a sodden scroll gifting him to me with the name of the gifter sogged away, my brother cautioned me, and even suggested I do away with him. Chade spoke quite plainly in the boy's hearing, for the lad had not spoken a word up to that point, and we had both assumed he either was a deaf-mute or simple. But right away, the lad piped up and said, 'Dear king, please do not do a thing you cannot undo, until you have considered well what you cannot do once you've done it!' It was a clever thing to say and it won me over. Please, my dear, settle whatever it is in Farrow that you have to do and then come home and be as amused with him as I am. Then you will see that Lady Glade has exaggerated his peculiarities in her letter to you. He is such a scrawny spider of a child; I am sure that when he is better fed he will not look so odd and may gain a bit of colour. I think she dislikes him because he so well imitated her well-fed waddle.

I so miss you, my Desire, and look forward to your return. Why you must so often be absent from Buckkeep is a mystery and a sorrow to me. We are wed, husband to wife. Why must I retire to a lonely bed every night while you linger in Farrow? You are my queen now, and need no longer trouble yourself with the rule of Farrow.

Letter from King Shrewd to his second queen, Desire of Farrow.

It looked more like a family gathering than a convening of people seeking to prevent a disaster. I thought of my own family and realized such gatherings were often both. Queen Etta's admiral had boarded while we were occupied with the figurehead. Wintrow Vestrit was already seated at the table, and Althea was brewing tea when we joined them in the stateroom.

Wintrow Vestrit, chief minister to Queen Etta of the Pirate Islands and Grand Admiral of her fleet, looked so much like Althea that they could have been brother and sister rather than nephew and aunt. They were of a height, and I judged there was less than a score of years between them. He was Malta's elder brother and Amber had told me some of the brutal history of how he had been captured with Vivacia and forced to serve aboard her under the pirate Kennit. Oddly enough, she had told me that the slave tattoo beside his nose and his missing finger were actually the work of his father. Knowing all this, I had not expected the aura of calm about him nor his subdued garb.

Boy-O moved swiftly and easily about his parents' stateroom, reacquainting himself with the familiar territory of his childhood ship. I saw him pick up a mug from a shelf, smile at it, and restore it to its place. He had his father's height, but his brow and eyes were from the Vestrit side, mirroring Althea's and Wintrow's. He was graceful as a cat.

Wintrow had a grave demeanour, and when Althea served him a steaming cup of rum and lemon mixed with hot water, he took it with muted thanks. I guided Amber to a seat at the captain's table and joined her there. Lant took his place behind us. My youngsters ranged themselves along the wall and held a subdued silence. When all were served, Althea sat down heavily beside Brashen and heaved a sigh. She met Wintrow's gaze and said, 'Now you understand. When I said that our stopping here would change not just your life but hundreds of lives, I don't think you grasped what I was telling you. I trust that now you do. You have seen the changes in Paragon. Prepare for Vivacia to do the same.'

He lifted his mug and sipped from it slowly, collecting his thoughts as he did so. When he set it down, he said, 'It's something we can't alter. In situations like this, it is best to accept Sa's will and try to see what comes of it rather than fighting against the inevitable. So, if Paragon is correct, after this last voyage he will return to the Rain Wilds and be given enough Silver to become two dragons.' He shook his head and a smile flitted briefly over his face. 'I'd like to witness that.'

'I think it inevitable that you will witness Vivacia's transformation. If Amber and Paragon are correct that such a metamorphosis is actually possible.'

'I am virtually certain of it,' Amber said softly. 'You have seen how, given a small amount of Silver, he can change his appearance at will. Given a large quantity, he can transform the wizardwood of his body into any shape he desires. And he will desire to be a dragon. Or two.'

Clef spoke up, and no one seemed to think it was out of place as he asked, 'But will he be a real dragon, of flesh and blood? Or a wooden dragon?'

A silence fell around the table as we mulled that over. 'Time will tell,' Amber observed. 'He will be transforming from wizardwood to dragon; not entirely different to a dragon's body absorbing the wizardwood of its cocoon as it hatches.'

Boy-O had drawn closer to his parents. He looked from one to the other and then asked, 'This is real? This can actually happen? It's not one of Paragon's wild fancies?'

'It's real,' Brashen confirmed.

His son stared into a future only he could see, one he had never imagined. Then he spoke in a whisper. 'He has always had the heart of a dragon. I felt it when he held me in his hands and flew me over the water when I was a child . . .' His words trickled away. Then he asked, 'Has he enough wizardwood in his body to make two dragons? Won't they be rather small?'

Amber smiled. 'We cannot know yet. But small dragons grow. From what I understand, dragons continue to grow as long as they live. And few things can kill a dragon.'

Wintrow drew a deep, considering breath. He looked away from Amber, to Brashen and Althea. 'Are you financially solid?' he asked gravely.

Brashen wobbled his head in a way that was not yes nor no. 'We have resources. The loot from Igrot's hoard was substantial, and we were not wasteful of our share. But money alone is neither wealth nor a future for our son. We've no home save here on Paragon, no life or employment beyond plying our trade on the Rain Wild River and in Bingtown. So, yes, we have sufficient funds that we can eat and sleep inside a house for the rest of our days. Inside a house. There's a future I never sought! But something to leave to Boy-O? A life for us to live . . . that's harder for us to chart.'

Wintrow was nodding slowly. A man, I thought, who seemed to think before he spoke. Just as he drew breath and opened his mouth to say something, we heard a shout from outside. 'Permission to come aboard?'

'Refuse it!' Wintrow ordered.

Brashen was at the door of the stateroom in two strides. 'Refused!' he shouted into the night and then spun on Wintrow, demanding, 'Who is it?'

But the voice outside shouted, 'You can hardly deny me permission to board the ship whose name I bear!'

'Paragon Kennitsson.' Wintrow spoke in the brief gulch of silence before the ship bellowed out, 'Permission granted! Paragon! Paragon, my son!'

Althea went so pale she was more greenish than white. I'd heard a strange note in the ship's voice, a difference in timbre.

'Sweet Sa,' Wintrow breathed into the quiet. 'He sounded almost like Kennit.'

Brashen looked back at his wife over his shoulder. His face was stone. Then his gaze found Wintrow. 'I don't want him talking to the ship,' he said in a low voice.

'I don't want him *on* this ship,' Wintrow agreed. He strode to the door and Brashen edged aside to let him pass. 'Paragon!' Wintrow shouted and there was command in his voice. 'Here. And now.'

The figure who answered Wintrow's summons was no boy or youth but a man, dark-haired, with an aquiline nose and a finely sculpted mouth. His eyes were a shockingly intense blue. His clothing was as handsome as he was, and the emerald earrings he wore were large, diamonds glittering around the green jewels. I judged him to be older than Boy-O, but not by much. And he was softer. Physical work pounds a boy into a different sort of manhood. Boy-O had that physique. But the prince was a house cat in comparison. Kennit's son smiled with even white teeth. 'I present myself,' he said to Wintrow with a mocking bow, and then leaned past him to peer into the cabin. 'Trellvestrit? You are here, too? It seems you've convened a party and not invited me. Well, that's cold of you, my young friend!'

Boy-O spoke softly. 'It's not like that, Kennitsson. Not like that at all.'

'You've come to know one another?' Althea asked softly but received no response.

Wintrow spoke in a low, controlled voice. 'I want you off this ship. We both know that your mother does not approve of your coming here.'

Kennitsson cocked his head and grinned. 'I also know that my mother is not here.'

Wintrow did not return his smile. 'A queen does not have to be present to expect that her commands will be obeyed. Especially by her son.'

'Ah, but this is not the will of a queen but the will of my mother who fears for me. And it is time for me to live beyond her fears.'

'In this case, her fears are well-founded,' Wintrow countered.

'You are not welcome aboard this vessel,' Brashen added in a flat voice. There was no anger in his tone but there was danger. For an instant, Kennitsson's face went blank with astonishment. Then we all heard a roar of disagreement from Paragon the ship.

'Send him forward! Send him forward to me!'

Kennitsson recovered himself, and his features shifted from shock to royal arrogance. I had not been so vividly reminded of Regal in many a year. His words were clipped, his anger palpable. 'I believe this was my father's ship before it was yours. And I believe that even if I did not have an inherent right to be here, my authority as Prince of the Pirate Isles supersedes your captain's powers. I go wherever I wish to go.'

'On this deck, nothing overshadows the say of the captain,' Brashen informed him.

Paragon's roar blasted us. 'Except the will of the ship!'

Kennitsson canted his head at Brashen and smiled. 'I believe I am summoned,' he said, and offered an elegant bow, complete with a sweep of his feathered hat, before turning and sauntering away. Brashen made a noise, but Wintrow stepped between Brashen and the door and blocked the captain from exiting.

'Please,' he said. 'Let me talk with him. He has been consumed with curiosity about Paragon since he was eight years old.' He turned his gaze to Althea. 'Any boy raised with no glimpse of Kennit, surrounded by dozens of men telling him hero tales of his father, would be enamoured of this ship. He cannot resist.'

'Coming aboard!' someone roared, and in the next breath, 'Kennitsson! Prince you may be, but you do not defy me or your mother without a reckoning!'

'Sorcor,' Wintrow said with a sigh. 'Oh, lovely. Just perfect.'

'Sometimes Kennitsson listens to him.' Boy-O sounded hopeful.

Beside me, Amber breathed, 'Kennit's first mate, in the old days.'

'Sometimes,' Wintrow agreed and then turned and went to meet Sorcor. I heard the hasty mutter of their conversation, Sorcor's voice accusing and Wintrow's defensive and reasonable. But my ears strained to hear a different set of voices. I heard the ship hail 'young Paragon' with joy and the young man's more measured response.

'How can he?' Boy-O spoke into the quiet. 'After what Kennit did to you, after all you and Brashen have done for him, how can he be so joyous to receive Kennit's son?' I wondered if I heard a twinge of jealousy beneath his outrage. His jaw was set and he suddenly looked a great deal more like his father.

'He's Paragon. He's always been capable of things we can't even imagine.' Althea stood slowly. She moved as if she had suddenly aged, as if every joint in her body were stiff.

'I'm not my father,' Brashen said suddenly. 'Neither is he.'

'He looks like him,' Althea said uncertainly.

'Much as Boy-O looks like you. And me. But he isn't either of us. And he's not responsible for anything we've done in our lives.' Brashen's voice was low and calm. Rational.

'Boy-O,' the young man said softly. 'Haven't heard that name in a while. I'm almost used to being called Trellvestrit now.'

'I'm not . . . I don't think I hate him. Kennitsson I mean. And I don't judge him for his father.' Althea tried to find words for her thoughts and continued, as if her son had not spoken. 'I think I'm a better person than that. His father is not his fault. Though I don't find him the least bit charming.' She looked sideways at Brashen, and stood straighter. Determination came back into her face and voice. 'But I am concerned by what he might waken in Paragon. There is so much of my father in Vivacia. So much of my grandmother in the Vestrit family liveship.' She shook her head slowly. 'I always knew that Kennit must be a part of Paragon. He was a Ludluck, and the Ludluck family owned Paragon for generations. And we both know that Paragon absorbed all the abuse that Igrot heaped on Kennit, all the deep hurts and wrong. There was so much blood shed on his decks in Igrot's day, so much cruelty, the pain and fear sank into him with the blood spilled on his planks. And then, when Kennit died, our ship took into himself all that Kennit had been since he'd abandoned Paragon. I thought Paragon had …nullified it. Outgrown it, as children outgrow selfish ways and learn to have empathy for others. I thought . . .' Her voice faltered into silence.

'We all bury things inside ourselves,' Amber said, making me flinch. She was looking straight ahead, not at Althea, but I felt she had intruded into a private conversation. 'We think we have mastered them. Until they burst out.' Her hand was on the cuff of my shirt and I felt it tremble.

'Well, what's done is done,' Althea said abruptly. 'Time to face it.' She took Brashen's arm and a look passed between them that reminded me of two warriors standing back to back in battle. As they walked away, Boy-O and Clef fell in behind them as if it were some sort of formal procession.

'Lead me,' Amber demanded. We trailed after them with Lant and Spark and Per following us. The few members of her crew who had decided to stay aboard despite where Paragon might take them ghosted along after us.

Lanterns illuminated the masts and bows of the anchored vessels in the harbour, and the moon had risen. The light was uneven, draping angled faces in veils of shadow. But the moonlight fell on Paragon's features and his face was full of fondness. It was like approaching a puppet show in the middle of an act. Paragon's figure-head was twisted to look down at Kennit's son on his deck, and his profile showed me his smile. His namesake stood with his back to us, legs wide and hands clasped loosely behind his back. His stance spoke to me more of patience than awe.

Behind him, Wintrow stood beside a heavy-set man with little hair left to his head but a generous grey beard. He wore loose trousers tucked into high boots and a wide belt that held a curved sword over his equally generous belly. His shirt was so white it seemed to gleam in the moonlight. The man was scowling, his arms crossed on his chest. I was abruptly reminded of Blade. Some old warriors are like good weapons. Their scars become the patina of experience and wisdom.

Paragon was speaking. 'Then you will go with me? Sail with me this last time that I shall sail, before I manifest as the dragons I have always been?'

Kennitsson seemed amused by his question. 'I will indeed! I can think of no better way to spend my time. I'm weary of lessons in geometry and navigation and languages. Why do they teach me the stars if I'm never allowed to sail under them? Yes, I'll go with you. And you will tell me tales of my father, as he was when he was my age.'

A tell-tale dragon gleam passed through the ship's eyes. I thought he would refuse the boy, but he sounded judicious as he replied, 'Perhaps. As I think you are ready to hear them.'

Kennitsson laughed. 'Ship, I am Prince Paragon of the Pirate Isles! Do you not realize who Kennit's son is now? I am next in line for the throne.' The light that touched his face followed the hard lines of his smile. 'I command. I do not request.'

Paragon turned away from him and spoke out over the water. 'Not on my decks, Kennitsson. Never on my decks.'

'And you are not voyaging off anywhere, Paragon Kennitsson,' Wintrow added firmly. 'Sorcor is here to take you back to your chambers. You should be dressing even now for an evening of cards with the dignitaries from the Spice Islands. Your mother, Queen Etta, expects both of us to be there, and if we do not depart now, we will both be late.'

Kennitsson turned slowly to face Wintrow. 'And I do pity you, Chief Minister, that you will face her wrath alone. But there it is. When I return to the palace tonight, I intend to pack for a sea voyage, not dress for a game of cards with a lady who laughs like a horse neighing.'

A silence fell. Then Sorcor said to Wintrow, 'I'm trying to remember the last time I thrashed him to howling. I think he might be due for another.'

The prince crossed his arms on his chest and drew himself up straight. 'Touch me, and I'll have you in chains before morning.' He gave a contemptuous snort. 'I'd have thought you'd have tired of playing nursemaid years ago. I scarcely need a nanny following me about. I'm not a wilful child for you to bully. Not any more.'

'Naw.' The older man shook his head woefully. 'You're worse. You're a spoiled boy dressed in a man's fine clothes. If I thought your mother would ever agree to it, I'd tell her that the best thing for you would be to send you off with Trell. As a deckhand. To learn a bit of the trade that your father knew from the bones out when he was half your age.'

Brashen Trell spoke. 'He's a bit too old to learn it, I fear. You missed your chance, both of you.' A strange look crossed his face. 'He reminds me of a spoiled merchant's son who thought he was a Trader.'

There is a way a boy stands when he does not wish to admit that words have struck him. Kennitsson stood that way—a bit too still, shoulders a bit too stiff. His speech was precise as he said, 'I shall be returning to the palace now. But not to dress and play dice with the Spice Island monkeys. Ship! I will see you again in the morning.' He swung his gaze to Brashen and Althea. 'I trust you'll have my quarters awaiting me when I return. The stateroom I saw when I first came on board would be adequate. And please take on appropriate food and drink for me.'

He walked through us, but I saw he chose a path that did not require anyone to step aside for him and knew he doubted his ability to face any of us down. We listened to the sharp thuds of his boots on the deck, then he was over the railing and clambering down a rope ladder, shouting at some poor soul who had been left waiting in a small boat for him. The sound of the moving oars was a gentle shushing in the night.

'Do you really think so?' Sorcor had a deep voice and it was full of slow dismay. For a moment, I couldn't understand what he was asking of Wintrow, but it was Brashen he was looking at in the darkness.

The captain of the *Paragon* stared down at the deck. 'No. Not really,' he admitted. 'Though I was younger when my father threw me out of the house and made my brother his heir. It was hard to find my own way. But I did. It's not too late for Kennit's son.' He heaved a great sigh. 'But it's not a task I want.'

Sorcor looked up toward the moon and the light fell on his face. His brow was wrinkled, his lips pursed in thought. Then he said in a gruff voice, 'But the ship's right. He should sail with you. It's his last chance, his only chance to know this deck under his feet. To sail on the ship that shaped his father.' He swung his gaze to meet Brashen's startled gaze. 'You should take him.'

Wintrow started. 'What?'

But Sorcor flapped a knobby hand at him, silencing his objection. The older man cleared his throat. 'I've failed the boy. When he was small, I was too glad to have any piece of his father that was left to us. I cherished him and kept him from all harm. I never let him feel the pain of his own mistakes.' He shook his head. 'And his mother still dotes on him and gives him what he desires. But it's not just her. I wanted him to be a prince. I wanted him in fancy clothes with clean hands. I wanted to see him have what his father earned for him. To be what his father would have expected of him.' He shook his head again. 'But somehow, we didn't get that other part of him.'

'He hasn't had to become a man,' Brashen observed flatly. The words were harsh but his tone was not.

'A voyage away from his mother might do it?' Sorcor suggested.

Althea stepped suddenly in front of Sorcor. Her gaze went from him to Wintrow. 'I don't want him. I've enough to deal with on this voyage. I've only a vague idea of where we're going and I've no idea how we will be received there. Or how long Amber's little errand will take, or when we'll be back. Perhaps it hasn't been revealed to you, Sorcor, but we go to deal death and vengeance. We very well may end up fleeing for our lives. Or be dead ourselves. I won't be responsible for the well-being of the prince of the Pirate Islands, let alone his survival.'

'But I will.' It was Paragon that spoke.

We all felt and heard that response. It thrummed through the ship's bones, and it reached our ears not as a shout but as an assertion. I wanted no more additions to our company on this voyage, let alone a spoiled prince, so I drew breath to make my own objection and felt Amber's sudden clutch on my wrist. In a low voice she said, 'Hush. As they say in Chalced, you don't have a dog in this fight.'

Since we had come aboard Paragon, I had felt control of my plans slipping ever farther from my grip. Not for the first time, I wished I'd come alone and unhampered.

'Our stateroom,' Brashen announced tightly. His eyes roved over us. 'Follow me.' He glanced at his crew and added, 'About your duties. Please.' The last was a concession, I felt, to those sailors who had stayed aboard the *Paragon*. Not many had. If we sailed, which I was beginning to doubt, we'd have a skeleton crew indeed.

Paragon's voice boomed out into the quiet harbour. 'I will have what I want, Brashen. I will!'

'Oh, I don't doubt it,' he replied bitterly. Althea had already turned away. Brashen spun and followed to lead us aft.

The chamber was large for a ship, but never designed to be packed with so many people. I let Amber sit and stood behind her, my hands on the back of her chair. I had positioned her so that I could study every person in the room.

Sorcor was a contrast. I judged him to be a man past his middle years, used hard by his early life but now in a safe harbour. He dressed as befitted a minor noble, but the scars on his face and the wear on his hands were that of a fighter and a sailor. The sword at his side was of excellent and deadly quality. There was something in the cut of his clothing and the selection of his jewellery that spoke of a man who'd known poverty suddenly given the chance to dress in fine fabric and gold. On another man, it might have looked laughable. On him, it looked earned.

Brashen thudded two bottles down on the table. Brandy and rum. Althea followed it with a clatter of cups. 'Your choice and pour for yourself,' she announced wearily before dropping into a chair. For a moment, she lowered her face into her hands. Then, as Brashen came and set his hands on her shoulders, she lifted her head and straightened her back. Her eyes were resigned.

Wintrow spoke. 'Queen Etta isn't going to like any of this. She was already alarmed when she got word that a liveship was being brought in for tariff violation. That simply doesn't happen. The Traders understand taxes and tariffs well, and none of them want the delays and fines that violations bring. As soon as I knew it was Paragon, I went to her immediately. She feared . . .' He stopped and abruptly chose another word. 'She considered it best if the prince were located and his introduction to his father's ship monitored. So to speak.' He gave Sorcor a sideways glance.

'He's a young man!' Sorcor objected. 'Somehow he knew what my mission was and kept clear of me. I suspect he paid his guards to turn a blind eye. I'll see to their stripes tomorrow. So here we are. What now?'

'Coming aboard!' A woman's voice, imperious and angry.

Wintrow and Sorcor exchanged a look. 'Queen Etta is not . . . recalcitrant in acting on a situation.'

Sorcor snorted and looked at Brashen. 'That big word means she might have a sword out. Look to yourselves and make no fast moves.' He whipped the hat from his head. I saw how he fell naturally into a fighter's stance.

Brashen moved away from Althea, closer to the door, as if he would protect her, but her dark eyes blazed and she came to her feet and stood beside him. Queen Etta's voice reached us again.

'Out of my way! I've told you I don't need you for this. You are embarrassing me, and my chief minister is going to hear of this. Standing orders should fall before my command! Wait in the boat if you must, but get out of my way.'

'She just dismissed the guard I assigned to her,' Wintrow observed mildly.

And in the next instant, the door framed an extraordinary woman. She was tall, and the planes of her face were angular. She was not beautiful, but she was striking. Her glossy black hair fell loose to her shoulders, which were wide beneath a scarlet jacket. Black lace spilled from her shirtfront and cuffed her wrists. Gold hoops dangled boldly from her ears. And close to her throat, almost nestled in the lace, she wore a necklace carved in a man's image. Kennit? If so, the son strongly resembled the father. She also wore a sword on a wide black belt studded with silver, but it resided still in its sheath. She rested the back of her fingers on its elaborate hilt. The glance that raked the room was sharper than any blade as she demanded, 'Are you conspiring?'

Wintrow tilted his head at her. 'Of course we are. And we would welcome your company. The issue is your strong-willed and rather spoiled heir, who has recently met his father's strong-willed and rather spoiled ship. They seem intent on taking up with one another, on a voyage to Clerres. I've been given to understand that the purpose of this voyage is to exact vengeance on a monastery there for the kidnapping and murder of a child. And that afterward, this vessel will magically change himself into two dragons.'

Etta's mouth hung slightly ajar as Wintrow looked to Althea and asked, 'Do I have that mostly right?'

Althea shrugged. 'Close enough.' And the two women exchanged cold looks.

Queen Etta said nothing. Wintrow spoke cautiously. 'The Spice Island delegation?'

'Have plenty of folk to lose their coins to. I'll join them at the card table or not at all. It little matters to me now.' She turned a furious look on Althea and Brashen. 'Why have you brought this ship here? What do you want of us? Of Kennitsson? My son is not going anywhere! He is the heir to this kingdom and is needed here. He is supposed to be enjoying an evening with the merchants from the Spice Islands and his potential bride, not planning a sea voyage.' Her gaze roved over all of us, her eyes cold. 'And whatever vengeance you seek, it has nothing to do with us. So why have you come here? What sort of discord do you attempt to sow? Why bring this vessel and its ill reputation and bad luck to our harbour? It was my wish that he never see or set foot on this ship!'

'There we agree,' Althea replied quietly.

I felt the pirate queen force herself to look at Althea. 'But not for the same reasons,' she said stiffly. 'My son has had a fascination with this ship ever since he was old enough to know how his father died. Kennit's last blood soaked into the planks of this deck. His memories, his . . . life . . . was taken into it. Absorbed. And from the time my son was old enough to be told of such things, he has possessed a wild curiosity to see this ship, to be aboard it, in the hope of speaking to his father. We have told him, over and over, that Paragon is not his father. His father makes up just a part of the life that the ship embodies. But it is a hard thing to make someone understand.'

Althea spoke in a flat voice. 'I doubt that anyone not born to Bingtown Trader stock can fully understand what that means.'

Queen Etta stared at her coldly. 'Kennit was born of Bingtown stock. A Ludluck. And his son carries that blood, even if he prefers the name Kennitsson.' Her hand rose to clutch at her necklace. 'And perhaps I understand more of this ship than you think. Paragon himself spoke to me of these things. Plus,' she tipped her head toward Wintrow, 'I have had your own nephew as my advisor in these matters.'

'Then perhaps you will understand what Paragon has suffered. In his days as Igrot's ship he absorbed many deaths, probably more than any other liveship. And even before that, when he belonged to the Ludluck family, his fortune seemed to be cursed. He has never been . . . stable. For a time, he was known in Bingtown as the *Pariah*. As the mad ship, the liveship that would kill any crew that sought to sail him.'

'I know that.' Queenly disdain in her tone. Then Etta cocked her head and was suddenly, disarmingly human as she said, 'Althea, do you think I have not been visited by Malta and Reyn? Do you think I have not heard every detail of the tale of this ship and his history?' She looked down at the pendant she clutched and added more quietly, 'Perhaps it is possible that I understand even more than you do of this ship.'

Both women fell silent. I felt as if fate balanced on a tiny point, waiting to shift and choose a direction. Was this what the Fool had meant when he told me of infinite futures, poised and waiting, but only one that would become real? Were we all witnesses to that?

Yet it was Brashen who spoke. 'The past haunts everyone here. Walk away from it, please. There is no sense in arguing who better understands liveships or Paragon. That's not our problem right now. And before we speak about the future, I would like to settle the present, as it affects Althea and me and my crew.' He ran his gaze over us all. No one spoke. 'When Althea and I spoke with Wintrow after we first went ashore, he agreed to help us meet our most basic needs—to send messenger birds back to our trading partners at Bingtown and in the Rain Wilds, assuring them that we intended no larceny when we did not stop in either Bingtown or Jamaillia. Queen Etta, we would ask your help in selecting trustworthy ships and captains bound to those ports who would be willing to deliver our goods to their proper destinations, so that our word as honourable Traders remains untarnished. If you can aid us in that, we could consider it a great favour to both our families.'

Etta looked at Wintrow and nodded.

'That can be done.' Wintrow spoke softly. 'I know several captains that I trust.'

Brashen's relief was plain. 'And I think we all agree that it would be a great mistake to have Kennitsson accompany us on Paragon's mad errand. We must all ensure that he can't board before we depart. He must be kept away from the harbour and the ship, for Paragon cannot seek him out on the land.' He lifted a hand. 'If we keep them separated, Paragon may remain in the harbour, obsessed with Kennitsson, and give up this quest. But I consider that unlikely. I think his desire to recreate himself as dragons will be stronger than his will to have Kennitsson make a final voyage with him.'

'I agree—' Wintrow began and then halted. His startled gaze met Brashen's. Althea rocketed to her feet while Sorcor asked in a harsh whisper, 'What is that?'

Sailors all, they were aware before I was of a subtle change in the ship. In a matter of breathless moments, I felt the list and Althea cried out, 'He's taking on water!'

Brashen took two large steps and seized the handle of the door, but the door was wedged tight against a sill that had been eased out of alignment. The ship's timbers groaned and the panes of the windows made an indescribable sound as the ship flexed. Paragon's voice boomed over the ship and the harbour's waters. 'I could kill you all! Drown you right here in the harbour! How *dare* you stand on my deck and plot against me?'

Amber's fingers dug suddenly into my forearm. 'I'll break a window,' I assured her.

Spark clutched at Per, in the sisterly way of someone who seizes the youngest preparatory to snatching him out of harm's way. Lant took each of them by a shoulder and herded them toward me. We clustered close in the slowly tipping room. Sorcor had moved to Etta's side. He reminded me of a battered watchdog taking up his duties. Etta seemed unaware of him. Her jaw was set, forming some plan of her own. I watched Brashen. If he moved, I would. Until then . . .

'But I shall not.' The ship's voice thundered through my chest. 'Not now! And not just because Boy-O would be trapped in there with you.'

Boy-O was standing pale-faced, gripping the edge of the table, his eyes showing white all around. I realized he believed the threat. Ice filled my spine and belly.

'Paragon, let me out. Allow us to come forward and discuss this in a way that doesn't involve all of the Pirate Isles.' Brashen spoke as a father to his child, his words calm and firm. His hand still rested on the doorhandle.

'But it does!' Paragon's booming voice came from outside. I did not doubt that all in the harbour and in the shoreside structures could hear him. 'It involves them all, if they keep their prince from me! For he is my blood before he became their prince! The prince that Kennit could not have made without me!'

'He's mad,' Etta said in a low whisper. 'I'll happily die here, drowned inside him, before he shall have my son!'

'You won't drown here, Queen Etta.' Sorcor picked up one rum bottle and hefted it thoughtfully, looking at the windows.

'I don't swim,' she said faintly.

'Paragon is not going to sink,' Althea declared firmly, and I wondered if her determination alone could protect us.

From outside the stateroom door, Ant's voice reached us. 'Sir, I've an axe! Shall I chop my way in?'

'Not yet!' Brashen ordered, to my surprise.

Then, to my even greater shock, came another woman's voice. It rang with authority and was fully as loud as Paragon's. 'Harm my family, and I'll see you burn, you faithless Pariah!'

'Vivacia!' Althea gasped.

'Burn me?' Paragon howled. 'To save your family? Do you think your family matters more to you than mine does to me? Set fire to me and they'll cook inside me like meat in an oven!'

'Paragon!' Boy-O bellowed the name. 'Would you truly do that to me, who was born on your decks and learned to walk here?' The breath he drew shuddered into his lungs. 'You named me! *You* called me Boy-O, your Boy-O, because you would not call me Trellvestrit! You said I was yours, and that name did not fit me!'

A sudden deep silence followed these words. It swelled and deafened us. Then a deep, anguished groan vibrated the deck beneath us. I wondered if the others felt, as I did, a welling of unbearable guilt that washed through me with the sound. I recalled every foolish thing, every evil and selfish thing, I had ever done in my life. Shame surged through me so that I longed to die, invisibly and alone.

Beneath our feet, the deck was slowly shifting back to level. All around us I heard the muttering of shifting planks and beams. Then the door was thrown open to reveal a panicky Ant holding an axe. Several crew surrounded her. 'The danger has passed,' Brashen said to her, but I was not sure I agreed. 'All you crewmen who remain, see to our cargo. Any wet crates, bring them up onto the deck. I know, I know—working in the dark. It can't be helped. I want to be able to offload tomorrow as swiftly as possible.' A brief pause and then he added, 'All hatch covers to be open and remain so.'

'Sir,' Ant agreed in a shaky voice and darted off.

Brashen stepped through the door and headed forward, Althea at his heels and Boy-O beside her and we all followed. 'I hate this,' I said quietly to Amber.

'Don't we all,' she muttered.

'It feels as if my entire future lies outside my control. I want to get off this insane ship and away from these people. I want to leave now!'

On the deck, I led her to the railing and stared toward the scattered lights of the pirate town. 'We can demand to go ashore. Use our Rain Wild gifts to buy passage on a different vessel. Regain some control over our journey. And send Lant and the youngsters home and out of danger.'

'Are we back to that?' Lant shook his head. 'It will not happen, Fitz. I won't go home until you go with me. And it would be foolish and dangerous to send these two off alone on a long voyage with people we do not know. Whatever we face, I feel they are safer with us.'

'It's not a matter of "safer" for me,' Per muttered darkly.

I ignored them all and stared at the lights. I wanted to shake all over like a wolf would shake off rain, and run off alone into the darkness to do what I must. I felt caged by responsibilities. What was best for us? 'Then we should leave this ship tonight, all of us. Find other passage to Clerres.'

'We can't,' said the Fool. Not Amber. I turned my head to look at him. How did he do that? How did he shed one mask and don another so easily? Despite the rouge and powder, he turned my friend's face to me. 'We have to go there on this ship, Fitz.'

'Why?'

'I told you.' He sounded both patient and exasperated in a way only the Fool could manage. 'I've begun to dream again. Not many dreams, but the ones that reached me rang with clarity and with . . . inevitability. If we are going to Clerres, we travel on this ship. It's a narrow channel I navigate to reach my goal. And only Paragon provides us a passage to the future I must create.'

'But you never thought to share that information with me until this moment?' I did not try to keep the accusation out of my voice.

Was this a true thing or a gambit by the Fool to get what he wanted? My distrust of Amber was starting to bleed into my friendship with the Fool.

'The steps I have trodden to get us to Kelsingra and then Trehaug, to get us onto this ship and thence to Divvytown . . . if I had told you of them, of the things I did and the things I took care not to do, it would have influenced you. Only by you behaving as you would if you knew nothing of what I did would we come here.'

'What?' Lant asked, confused.

I could not blame him. I sorted out the Fool's words. 'So of course that means you can't tell me any of your other dreams and warn me of what we must do. It must all be left in your hands.'

He set his gloved hands on the ship's railing. 'Yes,' he said quietly.

'Balls,' said Perseverance, quite distinctly. Spark gave him a shocked look and then rebuked him with a shove. He glared at her. 'Well, it's not right. It's not how friends should do things.'

'Perseverance, enough,' I said quietly.

Lant sighed. 'Shouldn't we move up to the bow and see what is going on?' And when he turned and walked that way, we followed. I didn't especially want to go. The deep sobbing of the figurehead and his misery permeated the ship. I paused to reinforce my walls, and then walked on with Amber.

The Fool spoke quietly. The others were far enough ahead that I doubt they heard him. 'I won't say I'm sorry. I can't be sorry for something I must do.'

'I'm not sure that's entirely true,' I responded. I could recall many things that I'd had to do, and many of them I regretted.

'I'd be sorrier, and so would you, if I began to worry more about your feelings and less about getting to Clerres and rescuing Bee.'

'Rescuing Bee.' His words felt like meat dangled for a starving dog. I was tired and battered by Paragon's guilt and grief. 'I thought your great ambition was to destroy Clerres and kill as many people as you could. Or as I could kill for you.'

'You're angry.'

When he said the words aloud, I felt ashamed. And even angrier. I stopped and stood still. 'I am,' I admitted. 'This is . . . not how I do things, Fool. When I kill, I do it efficiently. I know who I'm stalking, I know how to find them and how to end them. This is . . . madness. I'm going into unfamiliar territory, I know little of my targets, and I'm hampered with people I'm responsible for protecting. Then I discover that I'm dancing to your tune, to music I can't even hear . . . Answer me this, Fool. Do I live through this? Does the boy? Does Lant go back to Chade and is his father still alive when he gets there? Does Spark survive? Do you?'

'Some things are more likely than others,' he said quietly. 'And all of them still dance and wobble like a spun coin. Dust blown on the wind, a day of rain, a tide that is lower than expected—any and all of those things can change everything. You must know that is true! All I can do is peer into a mist and say, "it looks most clear in that direction". I tell you that our best chance of finding Bee alive is to remain on Paragon until he arrives in Clerres.'

My pride wanted me to be defiant, but my fatherhood was stronger than my pride. What would I not have done to increase the chance that I might rescue Bee, might hold her and protect her and tell her how devastated I was to have failed her? To promise her that never again would she leave my protection?

The others had waited for us. Amber's hand squeezed my arm and I led the way to the bow with them trooping behind me. My guard. My guard that I must protect as I led them into I knew not what.

Amber queried softly, 'Is there a bright light off to our left?'

'There's a lantern on the Vivacia. It's burning very brightly.' Some sort of argument was going on over on her deck, though I could not hear the details. I heard 'anchor' and then a barking of orders to roust someone out of his bed.

Amber had turned her face toward the lantern light and opened her light-gold eyes wide. A slight smile bowed her mouth. Her pale face reminded me of the moon as she said, 'I can perceive it. My vision is improving slowly, Fitz. So slowly. But I believe it is coming back.'

'That would be good,' I said but privately I wondered if she deceived herself.

At the bow of the ship, voices had been rising and falling. I recognized Althea's voice raised in a query but did not catch the words. We were on the outer edges of those who had gathered there, for many of the crew stood between us and the figurehead. It was Paragon who responded. 'No, you of all people should know that I am not Kennit and that Kennit does not petition you for this. Is Vivacia your father or grandmother? Of course not! It is not Kennit that demands this. It is I, Paragon. A ship made from massacred dragons, both embraced and enslaved by a Bingtown Trader family. I, we, had no say in that! No choice but to care, no choice in who we loved as Ludlucks poured out their blood and souls and memories onto the bones of our deck! I do not ask: I demand! Do I not have the right to him, as much right as his ancestors had to me? Is it not fair?'

'It is fair!' A female voice, clear and carrying. Vivacia. And suddenly my mind put together the bits of what I had heard. The liveship had dragged her anchor to come closer to Paragon, not just to hear his words but to add her voice to his. 'Althea, you know it is! Were I setting out on my final voyage would you deny me Boy-O? Listen to them! They have the right to demand Kennitsson, after all they have been through as the Ludluck family ship.'

'What's happening over there?' Wintrow demanded in the moment of silence that followed Vivacia's words.

'What must happen!' Vivacia spoke before any of her crewmen could respond to their captain. 'Did you think I would not hear the truth of what Paragon has spoken? Liveship I am, and a wondrous vessel I have been for your family for generations. But Paragon is right, and deep within we all knew that we had other natures, even before the truth of the so-called "wizardwood" was revealed. I will be a dragon again, Wintrow. I know of no liveship who will not wish to rise up and fly again. So, in this I will follow Paragon. Not just to Clerres but up the Rain Wild River afterward, to demand the Silver that is the right of every dragon!'

'You will follow Paragon to Clerres?'

'You wish to be a dragon?' Althea and Wintrow spoke simultaneously.

'I am considering it,' the ship replied judiciously.

'Why Clerres?' Brashen's voice was raised in complete confusion. 'Why not go directly to Kelsingra?'

'Because a memory stirs in me. A dragon memory, a memory eclipsed by human thoughts and emotions, a memory so over-scarred by human experiences that I cannot be certain of anything except a feeling of anger and betrayal that rises in me at the name Clerres. Dragons recall few memories of their serpent years but . . . there is something that I recall. Something intolerable.'

'YES!' Paragon flung back his head and shouted the word to the night skies.

The exultation that rushed through the ship infected me. I fought against the smile that bloomed on my face. His Skill was so strong, I thought to myself, and then with a shock recognized the implications of that and felt cold and shaky. I lifted Amber's hand from my forearm and said to Spark, 'Please take over guiding Lady Amber. I need a time alone to think.'

Amber clutched my shirtfront. 'You are leaving? You don't want to stay here and hear what is said?'

I took her wrist and tugged her hand free, more roughly than I intended. I could not keep from my voice the unease and the irritation I felt with myself for not recognizing the obvious. 'Listening will change nothing. They will decide what becomes of us, when we travel and who goes with us. I have something else I have to ponder. Spark will be with you, and Lant and Per. But for now, I need to think.'

'I understand,' she said, in a voice that said she did not.

But my insight into the ship's ability to manipulate human emotion was too large to share with her. I strode away to the crew quarters. Empty hammocks. Only a few sailor's trunks and ditty bags remained. I sat down on someone's sea-chest there in the dark and muggy hold and pondered. I felt as if I were assembling the pieces of a broken teacup. The Silver the liveships craved and the dragons so jealously guarded was the same Skill I had seen on Verity's hands when he had carved his dragon. It was the raw stuff of magic, the very essence of it. I'd seen it as a thick slurry on my king's hands, watched him shape stone into a dragon with the power it gave him. In a Skill-sharing dream of Verity I'd seen a river with a wide band of Silver in it, running with the water. I'd seen Silver tendrilling through a vial of dragon's blood, and witnessed how it had rushed the Fool's healing, just as the Skill had healed and changed the children of Kelsingra.

So the Silver was the Skill, and the Skill was the magic I used with my mind, to reach out to touch thoughts with Chade. The Fool had once insinuated that I had dragon's blood in my veins. Tarman had said I had been claimed by a dragon. Was it the stone dragon I had touched, or an echo of Verity as I had known him. I re-ordered that thought now. Had I inherited something in my blood, some trace of actual Silver, that gave me the power to push my thoughts toward others? Silver traces in the portal-stones, in the

Skill-pillars that I could use to travel. Lines of silver in the stones from which Verity had carved his dragon, and in the stone dragons that had slept until, with blood and the touch of my Skill, I had wakened them. Silver traces in the memory-stones that held the records the Elderlings had left for us.

What, then, was the Skill-current I used to reach out for Nettle or Dutiful? It was a force outside me, of that I was sure. And there were others in it, powerful awarenesses that attracted and might absorb me. Who were they? Had I truly felt Verity there? King Shrewd? How did that fit with the Silver?

I had too many thoughts. My mind leapt from wondering about the Skill-current to considering what magic I might be able to wield if I were to drink the vials of Silver that Rapskal had given me. Temptation vied with fear. Would it grant me great power, or a painful death? How much Silver was too much for a man's body to absorb? Paragon had grown much more powerful with the Silver that Amber had given him. The vials in my pack each held more than twice what he'd taken. Now his emotions exploded from him with a force that I could barely resist. Did he know what he did to humans? Did it affect me more because I'd been trained in the Skill? If he understood his power and directed it, would I be able to resist it?

Would anyone?

When the stone dragons had risen in flight and Verity had led them to battle against the Red Ship raiders, they had affected the minds of the warriors below them. With acid breath and the powerful winds of their wings and the blows of their lashing tails, they had destroyed our enemies. But worse had been what they did to their minds. To be overflown by the stone dragons was to lose memories. It was not that different to how the OutIslanders had Forged their captives. Even our own men on the ground had felt the effect; even Verity's presence as a stone dragon had worked it on the guardians of Buckkeep. The recollection of how the queen and Starling had returned to Buckkeep Castle was a hazy one for those who had witnessed it. The most common telling was that Verity had been astride a dragon when he delivered them to safety. Not that the king had become a dragon.

Such was the power of the Skill, of Silver, to confuse and confound. To steal memory and perhaps one's humanity.

As my serving folk had been confounded on the night that Bee was taken. Had they used Silver or dragon's blood to work that magic, to make all my people forget how they had come and stolen my child, to forget that she had even existed?

Could that same magic be used against them?

I dared myself to imagine drinking the Silver. Not all of it, not at first. Just a little, to see what I could do. Just sufficient to make me strong enough to resist the ship's emotions. Enough to heal the Fool without losing my vision to him. Was that possible? Enough to reach out to ask Chade's advice, perhaps to heal his body of the ravages of age and restore his mind. Could I do that? Would Nettle know more of what it could or could not do?

If I drank it all, could I walk into Clerres and demand that all there kill themselves?

Could it be that easy to destroy them and win back my daughter?

'What are you doing down here?' Lant asked me. I turned to see him coming toward me, Per and Spark trailing behind him.

'Where is Amber?'

'She is with the figurehead. She dismissed us. What are you doing?'

'Thinking. Where are the others?'

'Wintrow went back to Vivacia. She needs calming, I think. The queen and Sorcor went back to Divvytown. I think they will try to find Kennitsson and reason with him. Brashen and Althea went to their stateroom and shut the door. And Amber had Spark fetch her pipes; and she is playing for Paragon.' He drew breath and looked around the crew quarters. 'You came here to think?'

'Yes.'

'Can you think while you work?' I turned to Clef's voice. It was humid below deck and his face ran with sweat as he stepped out of the shadowy darkness of the hold. 'I was just coming to look for you. We're short of crew and we need to move freight. Some of the crates have shifted and a few look damp. Captains wanted those ones up on deck. You said you'd pitch in. Now would be a good time.'

'I'm coming,' I said.

'Me, too,' Lant added and Per nodded.

'And me,' Spark asserted. 'I'm part of this crew. Now and to the end.'

To the end, I thought morosely, and rose to follow them. A wave of vertigo swept over me such that I abruptly sat down again on the sea-chest. *There you are!* Satisfaction rang in the voice in my head. *I am coming for you. Prepare for me.*

'Fitz?' Lant asked, concern in his voice.

I stood slowly. My smile held back my fear and confusion. 'Tintaglia is coming for me,' I said.

NINETEEN

Another Ship, Another Journey

Report to the Four

The lurik known as Beloved continues to create restlessness among the other luriks. He was caught attempting to remain in the village when the tide was coming in and the other luriks had already formed up to return to their cottages. He has upset those who have come to have their fortunes foretold by hypothesizing horrible calamities. He told one client that his son would marry a donkey but that the children from that union would bring the family great joy. To another, he said simply, 'How much money do you wish to give me to lie to you? My best lies are very expensive, but this one is free. You are a very wise woman to have come here to give me lots of money to lie to you.'

Twice I have beaten him, once with my hands and once with a strap. He begged me to lash him hard enough to tear the tattoos from his back. I believe he was sincere in desiring that.

As soon as he healed and was to return to his duties in the marketplace, he clambered onto a pile of boxes and proclaimed to all that he was the true White Prophet for this generation and announced that he was being held prisoner in Clerres. He appealed to the crowd that immediately gathered to help him escape. When I seized him and shook him to silence him, I was stoned by some of the onlookers and it was only when two other guards intervened that I was able to drag him back within the walls.

I believe that I have done my duty as well as any might, and I petition to be freed from responsibility for the lurik known as Beloved. With the greatest respect, I say that I consider him both troublesome and dangerous to all.

Lutius

My life had improved, or so I told myself. We were quartered in a nice cabin; the meals were regular and Dwalia had few chances to beat me. Indeed, she seemed almost mellowed by our improved fortunes. Summer had found the seas; the winds were fresh and storms were few. As a result of whatever glamor Vindeliar had cast over me, the crew accepted my presence without comment or interest. If I lived my life from moment to moment, it was not too bad. Very little was expected of me. I fetched Dwalia's meals to the cabin and took away the empty dishes. When she walked on the deck in the afternoons with the captain, I followed at a decorous distance, in a pretence at maintaining the lady's virtue.

But for now, the pretence was small. I sat on the deck outside the door of the captain's stateroom. When he had offered his stateroom to Lady Aubretia, I do not think that Dwalia had realized that he expected to continue occupying it. I heard a rhythmic thudding from inside the cabin and fondly hoped it was the top of her head against the bulkhead. The tempo was increasing, which saddened me. The times when Captain Dorfel was occupying Dwalia were the most peaceful in my constrained existence. She was making little gasping shrieks now, barely audible through the stout plank walls.

I heard shuffling footsteps coming down the companionway. I thought of the sea and the moving waves and how the sunlight glittered on their tops. I thought of the seabirds flying high above us and yet still looking so large. How big would such a bird be if it landed on the deck? As tall as me? What did they eat? Where did they nest or land to rest when we were so many days away from land? I filled my thoughts with those wide-winged, white birds and thought of nothing else. When Vindeliar crouched beside me, I wondered what he would look like if he were a bird. I imagined a beak for him and glossy feathers, and orange-clawed feet with spurs like a rooster.

'Are they still in there?' he asked in a hoarse whisper.

I didn't look at him or reply. Long, shining, grey feathers.

'I won't try to push into your thoughts.'

I don't believe you, I don't trust you, I don't believe you, I don't trust you. I just thought it, but I didn't lower my walls. He was not as powerful as he had been when he first took in the serpent spit, but he was still strong. I was starting to understand that unlike my father's magic that was always with him, Vindeliar's magic depended on the potion. I wondered how long it would take before it dwindled away completely. Before I could trust that my private plans remained private. Don't think of that. *I don't trust you, I don't believe you, I don't trust you.*

'You don't trust me.' He said it with such sadness that I almost felt rebuked. Except that he had taken the words from my thoughts and said them aloud. He wasn't to be trusted. Not at all. I knew that, down to my bones. I desperately needed an ally, but Vindeliar was not one. *I don't believe you, I don't trust you, I don't believe you, I don't trust you.*

'Poor Dwalia.' He was staring at the closed door, a look of dismay on his face. 'He just goes on and on! She must blame me. I made Captain Dorfel see her as the most beautiful woman he could imagine.' He scratched his head. 'It has not been easy, to keep him convinced of his desire for her. At all times, I must be aware of all who see her. It's very taxing.'

'What does he see when he looks at her?' Damn curiosity! The question had been on my lips before I had recalled I must not speak to him. I tried to think only of the birds again.

He smiled, pleased that I'd spoken to him. 'I don't tell them what to see, exactly. I tell them they see something they like. For Dwalia, I told the captain he would see a beautiful woman he wanted to help. I don't know exactly what she looks like to him.'

He looked at me, waiting for my questions. I held them all back and thought of how the tip of every wave sometimes sparkled so brightly that I could not look at them for long.

'For me, I told them all to see "just a serving man". Unthreatening. Nobody to worry about.'

He waited again. I held my silence.

'I told them you were homely and dull and smelled bad.'

'Smelled bad?' Again, I had not meant to speak.

'So they would leave you alone. On the boat before this there were some who looked at you and wanted . . . wanted what he does to poor Dwalia now.' He crossed his stubby arms on his chest. 'I protect you, Bee. Even when you hate and mistrust me, I protect you. I wish you could open your eyes and see that we are taking you to safety, to where you have always belonged. Dwalia has suffered so much for you, and you have rewarded her only with difficulty and physical attacks.'

As if she had heard him and wished more of his sympathy, we heard a series of rising moans from within the cabin. Vindeliar looked from me to the door and then back to me. 'Should we go in? Does she need us?'

'They're nearly done.' I knew that they were mating, but had no clear idea of the mechanics of it. My days as sentry had taught me that it involved a lot of bumping noises and moans and left the cabin smelling sweaty. For a few hours, Dwalia would doze and be uninterested in persecuting me. I did not care what the captain did to her in his afternoon visits.

Vindeliar seemed both foolish and patronizing as he told me, 'She must allow this. If she refused, it would be harder for me to keep him believing that he loves her. She endures this to win us safe passage to Clerres.'

I started to tell him that I doubted it, but bit back my words. The less talk we exchanged, the better for me. Sunlight on the waves. Gray birds flying.

The moaning reached a higher pitch and pace, and then suddenly dwindled away in a descending sigh. A galloping series of thuds and then all sound from the chamber abruptly ceased.

'I will always wonder what it is like. I will never do that.' He spoke as wistfully as a child. Gray birds sliding across the blue sky. Wind in our sails, waves sparkling. 'I barely remember what they did to me. Only the pain. But they had to do it. They saw very soon that I should not make children for Clerres. Girls like me they kill. And most of the boys. But Dwalia spoke for me and my sister, Oddessa. We were twins, born of one of the purest White lineages, but . . . flawed. She kept me alive when all others thought I should die.' He spoke as if I should marvel at Dwalia's goodness.

'You are so blind to her. So stupid!' Anger demolished my self-control. 'She cut you like a bull calf, and you grovel with thankfulness. Who is she to say you should never make a child? She strikes you and calls you names and you sniff along behind her like a dog nosing another dog's piss! She feeds you filth to give you power, a magic she does not understand, and you let her decide how it will be used! She thinks nothing of you, Vindeliar! Nothing at all! But you are too stupid to see how she uses you and how she will discard you the moment you become useless. She hits you and calls you names, but the moment she smiles at you, you forgive it all and forget it! You call me brother but you do not care that she intends to hurt me and then kill me. You know it as well as I do. You could have helped me. If you cared for me, you would have helped me! We should have fled when that last ship made port, and I could have gone home to my family and you could have chosen a life for yourself! Instead you helped her kill a woman who had done nothing bad to you and had been kind to me. And you threw aside the Chalcedean, and left him to die for you after you compelled him to kill for her! You're a coward and a fool!'

But I was the fool. From somewhere in a distant darkness, I heard a wolf's long howl fade. Then Vindeliar was inside my mind. *Be calm, I won't hurt you, just let me see your secrets, what do you fear, be calm, my brother, I won't hurt you, just let me see.* He babbled excitedly as he whirled through my mind, stirring and flinging memories as if they were dead leaves and he an autumn storm. Wall after wall I raised to him, and each he tore and parted as if they were paper. I was dizzy and sickened with the assault of memories, each with an emotion attached to it. My mother fell and died, my mouth was torn when I was slapped, a cat purred still and warm as I stroked him, I smelled bacon and fresh bread in a winter kitchen lit with candlelight and hearth fire, FitzVigilant shamed me, and Perseverance fell as an arrow tore through him. Vindeliar was a greedy child rummaging a platter of sweets, taking a bite of this one and a lick of that one. Dirtying my memories with his eager sampling, as if he could own me by knowing me. *You do dream!* He was exultant.

I felt pushed out of my own mind. I could not find a voice to shriek at him nor fists to batter him. I was writing in my dream journal –NO, he must not see that, he must not read those! And suddenly all I knew were long, sharp tearing teeth and a mouth that breathed hot breath. A father shouted, 'Beware! He is more dangerous than you can know!' and I was suddenly in a cage where I could not retreat and a stinking human hammered my ribs with fierce jabs of a stick I could not avoid. I had never known such pain! It did not stop. Over and over the man shouted curses at me and poked me savagely with the stick, as if he strove to thrust it right through me. I howled and shrieked and snarled, I leapt and fought the bars of the cage, but still the stick struck me, always looking for the softest parts of me, my belly, my throat, my anus and sex. I fell at last, yelping and whining and still the beating went on.

Abruptly, Vindeliar was gone. My mind was my own again. I slammed up wall after wall while my whole body shook with sobs. The remembered pain wracked me and my tears flowed. But through them I could see Vindeliar sprawled on his side, his mouth open, his eyes glassy as if he had lost awareness. Like the wolf in the cage, I suddenly realized. Like Wolf Father.

I give you that pain to use against him. But do not think of me again. He must not find me. He must not know that you can write or anything you have dreamed. And you must stop waiting for someone to save you. You must save yourself. Escape. Get home. But do not think of home right now. Think only of escape.

And Wolf Father was gone as if he had never existed. As if he was something I made up to give me courage. Just as gone as my real father. And I suddenly knew I must not think of him either.

Vindeliar sat up but even sitting he was wobbly. He set his hands flat to the deck to either side of him and looked at me woefully. 'What was that? You are not a wolf. You can't remember that.' His lower lip was trembling, as if I'd cheated him at a game.

I felt a surge of hatred. 'I can remember this!' I told him, and I flung at him every moment of the beating Dwalia had given me on the night when my shoulder had been jerked out of its socket. He recoiled from me, and I added, 'And this!' And I found myself grinding my teeth together as I recalled for him exactly how it had felt to bite Dwalia's cheek, how her blood had tasted and felt as it ran over my chin, and how I had ignored the blows she struck me as she tried to shake me loose.

He put hands up to his cheeks and shook his head. 'No-o-o—' His voice dwindled away. He popped his eyes open wide and stared at me. 'Don't show me that! Don't make me feel chewing her face!'

I met his gaze with a flat stare. 'Then stay out of my thoughts! Or I will show you worse than that.' I had no idea what I could dredge up that would be worse for him, but for now he was out of my mind and I'd make any threats I could to keep him out. I thought about how he had betrayed me, how he'd helped them find and kill Trader Akriel. I thought of how he had pounced on my chain when I'd tried to flee on the docks. I summoned all the hate I could muster and pointed the thought at him in a way I never had before. *I despise you!* His eyes jolted wide and he leaned away from me. I realized that, at this moment, I was stronger than he was. He had barged into my mind when my guard was down, but it had been my strength that forced him out. He had used his full power against me, but I had won.

Just then the stateroom door opened and our handsome captain emerged. His clothing was as immaculate as ever, his cheeks slightly flushed. He glanced down at me, and then at Vindeliar. I saw puzzlement cloud his gaze, as if we were not what he had expected to see. Then I felt the wash of Vindeliar's thoughts against his mind. His brow unfurrowed and the small scowl on his lips became a puckering of distaste. 'Lady Aubretia, this maid of yours . . . well, I vow that when we reach Clerres, we shall replace her with someone clean and pleasant to look upon. Away, wretch!' He nudged me with the side of his foot and I edged away from him and then stood up.

'As you please, sir,' I said courteously. I was half a dozen steps away when I heard Dwalia's voice.

'No, my dear, thank you all the same. Come here, Bee! Tidy this chamber, immediately.'

I halted on the verge of dashing away.

'You heard your mistress! Be prompt.'

'Yes, sir.' I lowered my eyes meekly. Nonetheless, as I walked back past him, he cuffed the back of my head hard, nearly sending me sprawling. I struck the side of the door and then scurried inside, Vindeliar on my heels.

'And that one scarcely looks fit enough to be your bodyguard. He should be replaced with a strong man who knows his business.' The captain shook his head and then, with a sigh, added, 'I will see you again this evening, my dear.'

'Time will move slow as honey until then,' Dwalia said, her voice thick and lazy. Then in an entirely different voice she barked, 'Tidy this room!' as she shut the door.

The captain's chamber was very grand, as wide as the stern of the ship, with windows that looked out on three sides. The walls were panelled with a fine-grained red wood, and the rest of the room was cream or gilt. There was a large bed fat with cream feather pillows, and a table made of wood the colour of rust and moss, big enough for six tall chairs to surround it. There was a deep-cushioned seat by one of the windows, a separate chart-table that folded down from the wall, and a tiny chamber where one's waste went down a chute and out into the sea. Nightly Dwalia locked me in that cramped and noisome space lest I attack her while she slept.

Clothing littered the polished planks of the floor, all of it the excessively flouncy, lacy garments the captain had purchased for Lady Aubretia in the two days before we had left our last port. I gathered the clothing in a slow armful, including a petticoat of stiff lace that crinkled in my arms. It smelled of a lovely perfume, another gift from the captain. I carried the garments to a chest with roses carved into the lid and began to layer them carefully back into it. The chest smelled fragrant, like a forest where spices grew.

'Hurry up!' Dwalia commanded me. To Vindeliar, she said, 'Gather those cups and plates and take them back to the galley. The captain does not like to see his quarters untidy.' She went to the cushioned seat and sat down, staring out over the water. Her long, bony feet and muscular calves were bare beneath her short robe of thin red silk. Her draggled hair was sweaty at the roots, and my bite mark on her cheek was becoming a shiny pink crater. She was scowling to herself. 'We go so slowly! The captain tells me that this is not the right time of year to make the passage to Clerres, that the currents are good for travelling north and west, not south and east. I think he tarries on purpose, to have more time with Lady Aubretia.'

I wondered if she were complaining or bragging, but I said nothing. Lovely clothes, sweet perfumes, carved roses. I kept my thoughts fixed on what I could see and held my walls as tight as I could.

'She has stolen magic from you!' Vindeliar had not even begun to gather the plates and cups from their shared meal. Instead he pointed at me with a shaking hand as he made his accusation.

Dwalia turned away from the window and gave him an angry glare. 'What?'

'She used our magic against me, just now, outside the door. She made me think about biting you and how she hates me!'

Dwalia transferred her angry gaze to me. 'That's not possible.'

'She did it! She stole magic and that's why I can't make her do what you want.' He drew in a deep breath, a tattling child on the verge of tears. I stared hate at him and he recoiled. 'She's doing it now!' he wailed and threw up his hands before his face as if they could stem the flow of what I felt for him.

'No!' Dwalia shouted and fairly leapt from her seat. I both cowered and lifted my fists to defend myself but she ignored me and charged across the room to the carved chest. With a fine disregard for the work I'd just completed, she flung open the lid and began to fling the clothing from the chest onto the floor behind her until she reached her washed but well-worn travelling clothes. She dredged up a leather pouch and peered into it. She drew out the glass tube. The remainder of the serpent spit was clotted in the bottom. 'No. It's here! She hasn't stolen it. Stop making excuses.'

For a long moment, we both stared at her. Vindeliar spoke slowly, his voice full of helpless longing. 'I need the rest of it now. Don't you want me to be able to do everything you ask of me?' A pleading desire was in that last question.

'It's not for you right now. You've had all I can spare.' She looked at him, and then looped the string of the pouch around her neck so that it hung between her breasts. 'There's only a bit left. We must save it for an emergency.'

'She doesn't trust you, Vindeliar. She taught you to want that serpent spit and now she doesn't trust you to not steal it from her.' I flung my foolish words at both of them.

'Serpent . . . who told you that? Vindeliar! Are you telling my secrets to her? Have you betrayed me to her?'

'No! No, I told her nothing! Nothing!'

He hadn't told me. I had found that information in him when his mind was unguarded before me. I wished I had kept that knowledge to myself. Except that it now seemed to be a breach in their alliance.

'Liar!' she barked at him. She advanced on him, her meaty hand held high, and he quailed, crouching down before her, his head ducked and hidden behind his hands. She slapped him, and when her blow fell on his knuckles, she grunted in annoyed pain and seized a handful of hair on top of his head. She shook him savagely by it as Vindeliar shrieked and protested his innocence. I moved closer to the door whilst looking for anything I might use as a weapon. Any moment I feared that both might turn on me and come after me. Instead she flung his head aside with a force that sent him staggering. He fell to the floor and curled there, sobbing. She scowled at him and then looked at me.

'What did he tell you of the serpent potion?'

'Nothing,' I answered truthfully, and then, to deflect her, I shook my head pityingly and lied, 'It's well known, where I come from. But few are stupid enough to use it.'

That made her stare. Then, 'No. No, it is *my* discovery! My new magic, a new ability that some who carry White blood can master. But only some.' She stared at me, hatred burning in her. 'You think you are so clever, don't you? You seek to turn him against me. He told me all, you stupid little chit! How you manipulated him into helping you. How you made him betray me. It won't happen again. I promise you that. And more: I promise you a long and painful life in Clerres. Do you think you have suffered travelling with me? Oh, no. You will know all your father knew, and more.'

I stared back at her. She was edging closer to me. Closer. No weapons. On this ship, everything was firmly fastened down lest wild weather toss things about. She intended to seize me and beat out of me whatever I knew. I wasn't even sure what I knew. Or what I could do with my newfound ability. Was it the Skill, such as my father had? It had to be! Not some filthy magic she'd inflicted on Vindeliar by making him drink serpent spit. My magic, the magic of my family. But I wasn't trained. All I'd read in my father's papers said one needed lots of training to use the magic.

But I'd used it? Hadn't I?

I knew that I'd made Vindeliar feel old pain of mine. And be aware of my hate. Perhaps that had only worked because he was already trying to reach into my thoughts. Or maybe I had stolen magic from him. Was there anything I could do to Dwalia? I stared at her and gathered up my hatred for her at the same time as I pressed down my fear. I looked at her face and gathered up the scar from my bite and how badly she had smelled and how disgusting I found her. They seemed small weapons. What could I do to her, what could I make her feel? Would I be able to make her feel anything or had it only worked with Vindeliar because he had reached into my mind first?

I was panting with fear. Control. My father's scroll said I must have control. I took one long slow breath and then another. She was watching me. How could I focus my thoughts when at any moment she might spring?

Become the hunter, not the prey.

Wolf Father! Faint as a distant bird call.

I found a rolling growl in the back of my throat. Her eyes widened but I marked that Vindeliar had uncoiled and was sitting up. Watch them both. Where was she most vulnerable? She'd grown leaner and harder during our most recent travels. I tried to imagine hitting her. I could, but I couldn't imagine her hurting her enough to make it stop. Once she got hold of me, she would hurt me. Badly. I needed to focus an attack on her, but where?

Her mind.

Be wary. A way out is always a way in.

I had no time to worry about what he meant by that. I pushed at her with all my hatred and disgust for her, hoping she would be hurt by it. Instead, it was like pouring oil on a kitchen fire; I felt her own hatred for me surge and leap like devouring flames. She sprang at me like a cat upon a mouse. And like a mouse, I dodged away, barely avoiding her snatching claws. She could not move as fast as I could, and although she did not crash into the wall, she staggered sideways. When I ducked under the table and emerged at the other end, she pounded on the table so that the dishes jumped and shouted at Vindeliar to 'grab her, hold her!' He got to his feet but he was uncertain and awkward. I shot him a fierce reminder of how I had bitten Dwalia's face and was gratified when he reached with both hands to cover his cheeks.

But Dwalia was still ardent in her pursuit. I kept the table between us but she showed no signs of tiring as she chased me round and round. I slipped under it to catch my breath but she kicked at me and pulled the chairs away from the table and tossed them aside. When I emerged, the tumbled chairs became obstacles for both of us as I strove to keep the cluttered table between us. She was breathing harder than I was but she continued to pant and shout, 'This time I will kill you, you little wretch! I will kill you!'

She halted abruptly, palms braced flat on the table, breathed heavily. In between gasps, she managed, 'Vindeliar, you worthless failure! Catch her, hold her for me!'

'She will bite me in the face! Her magic has promised this! She will bite me!' He stood, rocking back and forth with his hands still clasped over his face.

'You idiot!' she shouted, and with a strength I had scarcely imagined she possessed she lifted one of the heavy wooden chairs and heaved it at him. He shrieked and danced back as it fell short. 'You catch her and hold her for me! Be useful or I'll have the captain throw you over the side!'

I glanced at the door but knew that by the time I reached it and struggled with the heavy latch, she'd be on me. Even if I escaped into the companionway, eventually I'd be found and returned to her. I should not have fed her anger. I should have let her beat me before she became murderous. What to do, what to do? She was breathing more slowly. In a moment, she'd be after me again. She wouldn't stop, not until she'd won.

Give her what she wants.

Let her kill me?

Let her win. Make her think she won.

How?

There was no answer. And a strange trembling went through me as I felt Vindeliar poking at my thoughts, at my being, as if he had just noticed an odd growth on my face. It was tentative, almost fearful, and I slapped it away with another burst of my memory of chewing on Dwalia's cheek. He fell back but it cost me. Heedless of the dishes, Dwalia flung herself flat on the table and reached across to seize the front of my shirt. A vivid memory of the last beating I'd received from her flashed through my mind and crossed to hers. The glittering light of satisfaction in her eyes was almost more than I could bear.

I understood.

I gave her the taste of blood in my mouth, the torn skin inside my cheek, the rocking pain of a loosened tooth. Abruptly, I was seeing myself as she'd seen me, pale, my short hair matted with sweat, a smear of blood down my chin. It took every bit of control I had but I let my weight fall as I went limp in her grip. She did not release her hold on my shirt but as I sank to the floor, she had to slide her body over the table to keep her hold on me. Several dishes struck the floor. I lolled my head as if stunned and let my mouth hang open. She managed an open-handed slap but she was in an awkward position and it had little momentum behind it. I still cried out as if in agony. I gave her, not my hatred, but my fear and pain and despair. And she sucked it in like a thirsty horse at a water trough.

She manoeuvred herself off the table. She kicked me, and again I cried out and let the force of her kick push me under the table. She kicked me again, in the belly, but she was up against the table's edge and it was not as bad as if I'd been in the open. Again I shrieked and offered her an awareness of the pain I felt. Panting, she licked her lips. I lay where I was, moaning. Oh, she had hurt me, she had beaten me to where I was barely conscious, I would hurt for weeks from this beating. I gave it all to her, everything I could imagine she could want.

She turned away from me, breathing harshly through her nose. She had what she'd wanted from me and that anger was satiated. She was done with me, but Vindeliar had foolishly ventured too close to her. She turned on him, and closed her fist before slamming it into his face. He fell away from her, gasping and sobbing, hands clutching his nose. 'You are useless! You couldn't even catch a little girl! I had to do it myself! Look what you made me do! If she dies of that beating, it will be your fault. She is full of lies, and you are too! Stole my magic! What is that tale, something you tell me to explain why you won't control her?'

'She dreams!' Vindeliar had lifted his face from his hands. His wobbling cheeks were scarlet, his little eyes running tears. Blood trickled from his nose. 'She is the liar! She dreams but does not write them down or even tell you!'

'You stupid wretch. Everyone dreams, not just Whites. Her dreams mean nothing.'

'She dreamed the candle dream! She wrote it down, the whole poem! I saw it in her mind! She can read and write, and she dreamed the candle dream.'

I felt a sudden terror. The candle dream! I almost let myself recall it. No! Heedless of any risk, I pushed a desperate thought at her. *He lies. I'm a stupid girl, with no letters. He's just making excuses and trying to avoid punishment. You know he lies, you are correct that he is a liar, you are too clever to be fooled by his lies.*

It was a panicky thrust of thoughts. I think it reached her only because she was already angry at him and was only too happy to have reasons for her anger confirmed.

She beat him. She picked up a heavy metal water pitcher from the washstand and turned it into a weapon. He did not defend himself and I did not intervene. Instead, I huddled under the table. There was blood on my chin from my split lip. I smeared it on my face. I felt the impact of each of her blows on Vindeliar, and I stored those sensations as I winced at each one. I pushed into his mind that she had beaten me more severely, and in his distracted and beleaguered state, I felt him accept that information as truth. He knew the sort of pain she could administer. He knew it better than anyone, and in a gush of information as sudden as a spurt of blood, I did, too. The memory that burst from him sickened me and my walls fell before it.

A way out is a way in.

Then, as the wisdom of Wolf Father's words sank into my mind, I closed my thoughts from him and worked to fortify my walls. Thicker and tighter I built them, until I was aware of the beating he was taking but no longer flinching at each blow. When he had the elixir, he was strong, far stronger than I was in this magic. But I understood now; a way in is also a way out. When I reached out to touch his mind or Dwalia's, it was like opening the gates to them. Did he know that, too? Did he know that when he tried to invade my thoughts, he offered me a highway into him? I doubted it. And after what I'd glimpsed, I never wanted to see inside his mind again.

I lay curled on the floor under the table and tears flowed from my eyes and broken sobs from my lungs. I fought for control. I told myself I must ponder what I'd learned. I had a weapon, but it was not hardened and I did not know how to wield it. He had a vulnerability and did not know it. Information about him and his dismal childhood had poured into me when he'd manifested the power of the serpent potion. I cut away any sympathy I might have felt for him and focused on the edges of those memories.

I'd seen a fortified citadel standing tall on an island. Towers topped with heads like the skulls of monsters looked out over a harbour and the mainland. I'd glimpsed a lovely garden where pale children played, but never Vindeliar. Those children were tended by patient Servants, and taught to read and write as soon as they could walk. Their dreams were harvested and preserved as carefully as soft fruit.

I saw a market with many booths shaded by bright awnings. The smells of smoked fish and honey-cakes and something spicy mingled in the air. Smiling people moved among the booths, making purchases and putting them into net bags. Tiny dogs with barely any fur scampered and barked shrilly. A girl with flowers woven into her hair sold bright yellow sweets from a tray. All the people I saw seemed clean and well clothed and happy.

That was Clerres. That was where they were taking me. But I doubted that the lovely walled garden and doting Servants awaited me, or the bright market under the warm sunshine.

Instead I recalled with horror the searing glimpse of torch-lit stone walls lined with elevated benches, and a bloody creature chained to a table who screamed piteously as Dwalia offered a delicate knife to an impassive man. Pen, ink and paper waited on a tall stand near her. When the person screamed out a recognizable word, she stepped aside to jot it down, and to add notes, perhaps on what pain had torn words from him. She seemed cheery and efficient, her hair neatly braided in a crown around her head. A canvas smock protected her pastel blue garments.

Vindeliar stood at the edge of the theatre, a despised outcast who averted his eyes and trembled at each screech wrung from the victim. He'd understood little of the reasons for tormenting the writhing creature. Some of the seated onlookers were watching with mouths ajar and eyes wide, and others laughed into their hands, with strange shame blushing their cheeks. Some were pale of skin, hair and eyes, and others were as dark-haired and warm-skinned as my parents. There were old people, and people of working age, and four children who looked younger than me. And they all watched the torture as if it were an entertainment.

And then, to my horror, the poor creature on the table stiffened. His blood-tipped fingers strained wide against his restraints and his head thrashed wildly for a moment. Then he was still. The panting sounds he had made ceased and I thought he had died. Then, in a terrible exhalation of breath, he screamed a name. 'FitzChivalry! Fitz! Help me, oh help me! Fitz! Please, Fitz!'

Dwalia was transfigured. She lifted her head as if she had heard the voice of a god calling her and a terrible smile came over her face! Whatever she wrote in the book, she did with a flourish. And then she paused, pen lifted, and made a request. 'Again,' she said to the tormentor. 'Again, please. I wish to be certain!'

'Certainly,' the man replied. He was pale with colourless hair, but the gaudiness of his fine garments made up for his lack of colour. Even the olive apron he wore to protect his jade robe was a thing of beauty, embroidered with words in a language I did not know. His ears were studded with emeralds. He flourished the nasty little tool he held at the four young Whites. Their eyes were very large as he said, 'You are too young to recall when Beloved was a lurik, just your age. But I do. Even then, he was a defiant and obtuse youngster, breaking all rules, just as you break the rules and think yourselves too clever for us to know about it. Look where it has led him. Know that it can lead you here just as easily if you do not learn to master your own wills for the good of the Servants.'

The lips of the smallest one quivered until she clapped a hand over her mouth. One of the others hugged himself, but the two tallest drew themselves straighter and held their mouths tight.

A beautiful young woman with pale gold hair and a complexion like milk stood up. 'Fellowdy.' Impatience ruled her voice. 'Lecture your little darlings later. Force Beloved to utter the name again.' She turned to the spectators and looked directly at one old woman seated next to a man whose yellow robes contrasted with the pale paste on his face. 'Hear it! The name he has concealed so long, the one that proves what Fellowdy and I have been saying. His Catalyst continues to live and they conspire to work against us still. The Unexpected Son has been concealed from us. Has Beloved not done enough damage to us already? You must allow us to send Dwalia forth, to avenge her mistress and win us possession of the Son who will otherwise be our downfall! Over and over, the dreams have warned us of him!'

In response, the older woman stood and fixed the young woman with a glare. 'Symphe, you speak before all these people of things that concern only the Four. Mind your own tongue.' She stood, lifted her pale-blue skirts to avoid the blood and strode majestically from the slaughter floor.

The yellow-coated man next to her watched her go, stood as if undecided, and then sat down again. He nodded to Symphe and the butcher that they should proceed. And they did.

My father's name. That was what they made the tattered creature scream, not just once, but over and over and over. And when the repeated screaming of my father's name was finished and they had tumbled the unconscious body off the table and the guards had dragged the poor wretch away, Vindeliar recalled dashing buckets of water on the spattered floor and table, and then scrubbing them clean.

He cared little for the tortured man. He focused on his work and his fear. A small chunk of flesh had clung to the floor. He scraped it up with his thumbnail and tossed it into his scrubbing bucket. He knew that if he contravened Dwalia's will he might be the next one shackled for a hard lesson on the table. Even now, he knew it still might await him. She would not hesitate. And still he lacked the will to flee or defy her. And I knew in my deepest core that my 'brother' would not risk himself to save me from such a fate.

That memory made me tremble. The poor creature on the table had screamed for my father and begged him to come and save him. I was missing too many links to make a chain of reasons, but my instincts made a blind leap. That was the day Dwalia had won permission to come to Withywoods. That was the day my fate had been sealed. I watched her now as if from a great distance.

And the wretch on the table? It did not seem possible he could have survived. Surely he could not have become the beggar at Oaksbywater. Could not have been my father's Fool. Jagged bits of information stabbed at my thoughts. Dwalia had spoken of a father I did not know. The pieces could not possibly fit together. But her earlier threat to me insisted that they did. That table was what she had promised me.

Dwalia was still kicking Vindeliar but she was panting with the effort. With each kick she grunted and her buttocks wobbled. When she had reduced Vindeliar to a huddled and sobbing mass in the corner, she came back to me. She aimed a kick at me, but I had chosen my shelter carefully and she could not deliver a forceful blow. She flung the now-bloody pitcher at me. It only grazed me. I yelped convincingly anyway and scuttled away, staring up at her dolefully, blood smeared on my face. I made my chin quiver and blubbered at her, 'Please, Dwalia, no more. No more. I will obey you. See? I will work hard. Please don't hurt me.'

I scooted out from under the table, dragging one leg. Hunched over, I hopped about the room, gathering up the clothing she had scattered. With each lurch, I begged her to forgive me and promised obedience and atonement. She watched me, suspicion and satisfaction warring in her expression. I stood weeping by the clothing chest, seeping pain and fear at her and Vindeliar. Inspired, I added a touch of despair and discouragement. I held up each garment, 'See how nicely I'm folding it?' I gulped back a sob. 'I can be useful. I can be helpful. I've learned my lesson. Please, don't hurt me any more. Please, please.'

It was not easy and I could not be sure how well it was working. But she gave me a satisfied sneer and returned to the tousled bed, plopping down onto it with a satisfied sigh. Then Vindeliar caught her eye. He was curled on the floor like a fat larva under a log, sobbing into his hands. 'Tidy up those dishes, I said!' she barked at him.

He rolled and then sat up, snuffling. When he lifted his battered face from his hands, I winced. His eyes were starting to swell and blood had sheeted over his chin. Blood and saliva dripped from his sagging mouth. He looked at me in misery and I wondered if he had felt my inadvertent sympathy. I thickened my walls. I think he felt that, for he gathered his brows and looked at me darkly. 'She's doing it now,' he said in a low, sullen voice, his words muffled by swollen lips.

Dwalia cocked her head at him. 'Think about this, unman. She has learned her lesson. See how she cowers and obeys me? That is all I require of her, for now. And if she can do the magic, if I can teach her what I require of her, what need have I of you? You had best be at least as useful as she is.' Then she looked at me and chilled my soul with her simpering smile.

I heard Vindeliar take a snotty breath. I glanced at him and saw something more frightening than Dwalia's smile. He glowered at me, his face full of jealousy.

TWENTY

Belief

I truly wish I knew more to tell you. I feel as if I should know more, but he has always been private when speaking of his early days. What I do know with certainty can be quickly written. An accident of birth cheated Lord Chade of the power and respect that went to his elder brother and younger sister. Shrewd became king. His younger sister was, some say, the cause of her mother's death, for the birth was difficult and the queen was never healthy after that. Raised as a princess, she was nevertheless doomed to die in her turn, giving birth to a son, August. His sad end you already know. In an effort to Skill through him to his future queen, Verity unintentionally burned out his cousin's mind. August was never sound after that, physically or mentally, and died at a relatively young age in the merciful obscurity of a 'retirement' to Withywoods. Patience, my father's wife and once a queen-in-waiting, had the care of him until he died in his sleep one winter's day. The death of my father in an 'accident' and then August's sliding away were what led her, I believe, to return to Buckkeep Castle to attempt to take on my upbringing.

But it is Chade you wished to know about. He has never been forthcoming about his early days. His mother was a soldier. How she came to bear the king's bastard, we will never know. And I know little of his mother's passing or how he was sent on to Buckkeep Castle. Once he mentioned to me that his mother had left a letter, and that shortly after she died, her husband gave that scroll and a packet of travel rations to the young Chade, set him on a mule and sent him to Buckkeep. The letter was addressed to the king and by some extraordinary circumstances actually reached him. And so his royal family discovered him, perhaps for the first time, but who can truly know about that? In either case, he was taken in.

For all the years in which he taught me, I know little of how he was educated, save that his instructor was harsh. While he was never acknowledged even as a bastard, I do believe that his elder brother treated him well. From what I personally observed, he and Shrewd were fond of one another, and Shrewd counted on Chade as a counsellor as well as an assassin and spymaster.

I have gathered that Chade had a few lively and enjoyable years as a handsome young man before the accident that scarred him and sent him into hiding in the castle walls. I think it likely there is much more to that tale as to why he made himself vanish but we are unlikely to unearth it.

I do know that he desperately wished to be tested for the Skill and educated in the family magic. That was denied to him. I suspect he had other magical talents, namely scrying in water, for more than once it seemed very unlikely to me that his 'spies' could have possibly informed him in a timely way of events that took place at a distance from Buckkeep. But to be denied the Skill both rankled and grieved him. I think it was perhaps one of the most foolish choices our royal ancestors ever committed.

So it is, my dear, that now that he has proven at least an erratic ability to Skill and has access to what remains of the Skill-library, he recklessly indulges himself in trying to master it. He has always been one to experiment and danger does not dissuade him from risking himself or indeed his apprentices.

I do not know if this information can help you persuade him to be more temperate and accord you the respect you deserve as the Queen's Skillmistress. Please, if you can avoid letting him know that I am the source of this information, I would greatly appreciate it. He may have trained me to be a spy but would be the first to object if his old apprentice spied upon him.

Unsigned missive to Skillmistress Nettle

'What does Tintaglia want with you?' Brashen asked me.

I wiped sweat from my face. 'I had some questions for her when we were in Kelsingra. I was hoping to discover if dragons bore a grudge against the Servants.'

'To recruit them to your cause?'

'Perhaps. Or to gain any bit of knowledge to use against them.'

He wiped his hands down his trousers and took a fresh grip on the barrel. 'It might not be the wisest thing to do, sending a dragon in to rescue a child.'

'I wasn't thinking of that at the time. I just wanted Clerres destroyed.'

'But if your child is there . . .'

There it was. The very thought I most wanted to avoid. Bee in the midst of a dragon-attack? I refused the idea.

Brashen cocked his head at me as he stared at my face. 'You don't think she's alive, do you?' His voice dropped low.

I shrugged. It was the last question I wanted to ponder. 'Let's get this done,' I suggested. He nodded grimly.

We had both stopped to breathe. We were taking on a cask of water. It should have been a simple task, but Paragon was determined to make it almost impossible. He had listed away from the small boat that had come alongside with the cask, and then, amid our hoisting it up to the deck, he had listed in the other direction.

It was our second day of struggling against the ship. Paragon had blocked our efforts to offload his cargo. Today's effort to bring on water and fresh food for the crew was twice the work it should have been. In the midst of those difficulties Althea and Brashen had received my news about Tintaglia with a marked lack of interest. As Brashen had said at the time, 'Could a dragon's arrival make our situation any worse?'

Althea had replied, 'I will pass the news to Wintrow and he will let Etta know. They can prepare for her as best they can.' She had added sourly, 'A dragon visit probably presents all sorts of problems. At this moment, all I can say is, I'm glad they're not mine.'

Brashen had nodded grimly. 'We have enough of our own,' he confirmed. And that had closed that conversation.

Paragon delayed our departure in ways I had never imagined. He rocked, he listed, he jammed his hatches shut. Althea and Brashen gritted their teeth and joined in to work the deck alongside their diminished crew. That first day Clef had mustered Per and Spark and then regarded Lant and me with his hands on his hips. 'It may not be the work you were born to, but I need you. Beginning today, while we're still in port, you will each join a watch.' And we had.

Brashen's and Althea's efforts to hire more crew or persuade former crewmembers to return were dismal failures. I welcomed the heavy physical labour, for it sometimes distracted me from dwelling on the possibility of my daughter held captive by fanatical strangers. The idea roused me to heart-pounding fury; I vented it by defying the ship, dragging crates aboard his slanting deck and wrestling them into his hold. Every moment of delay was another moment of agonizing suspense. I no longer cared for whatever news Tintaglia might bring. I wanted only to be on our way again.

Both Amber and the Fool constantly agonized over what Bee might be enduring. Every word Amber spoke about it was a twisting knife in my gut. My anxiety was more than I could bear; his only made mine more searing. I entered her cabin that day to find the Fool hanging upside-down by his knees from the upper bunk. I halted at the sight.

'I knew it was you,' he observed. 'Everyone else knocks first.'

'What are you doing? Do you need help to get down?'

'Hardly. I'm limbering up. They hammered and burned my mind to a mush; what they did to my body was just as shattering. I seek to regain what they sought to destroy.'

He curled up around his belly, seized the edge of the bunk in both hands and with a grunt unhooked his knees and shot his feet toward the floor. He landed, not lightly or gracefully, but still amazingly well for a man who had been half-crippled just months ago.

'Would not practising your tumbler's skills be better done on the open deck?'

'If Amber were sighted, she'd be delighted to run the rigging and dangle aloft and regain all my lost tricks in the fresh air. But she isn't, and so I can't. In this cramped space, I do what I can.' He bent over, seized his own ankles and let out a long slow breath. 'Any news of when we can depart?'

'None that you haven't heard.' I braced myself against his familiar complaint.

'Every day that passes is another day that Bee is their captive.'

As if that were a new thought for me! 'Paragon isn't the only ship in the harbour. We could get a fine price for our Elderling goods here, and book passage directly to Clerres.'

He was shaking his head before I'd finished speaking. 'In my visions of the future, Paragon is the only vessel that carries us to Clerres.'

'Your visions,' I said and closed my mouth. Through gritted teeth, I said, 'Then we must wait.'

'You doubt me,' he said bitterly. 'You refuse to accept that Bee is alive.'

'Sometimes I believe you.' I looked down at the deck. 'Mostly I don't.' Hope was too painful.

'I see,' he said harshly. 'So you are content to wait. Because if Bee is dead, she can't become any deader by our delay. She can't be enduring torture such as they visited upon me.'

I replied with equally harsh words. 'I do not choose to wait. You choose to wait—for Paragon to decide to sail.'

He gripped two handfuls of his own hair, his face contorted. 'Cannot you understand my torment? We must sail on Paragon. We must! Even though I know she is alive and in their power.'

'How?' I roared at him. 'How would it be possible? When Nettle sent her coterie through the pillar after Bee they found no sign of her. Not a footprint in the snow, nothing! Fool, they never emerged from that pillar. They perished within it.'

His blinded eyes were wide with desperation, his face even paler than it usually was. 'No! That cannot be. Fitz, you have been delayed in a pillar, lost for days, and still you—'

'Yes. Eventually, I emerged dazed and half-dead. If I had not been able to summon help, I could have died there. Fool, if they had emerged from that pillar, there would have been signs of it. The dead embers of a fire, a scatter of their bones, something. There was nothing. She is gone. Even if they were delayed for days, we would have seen some sign of their passage when we arrived there. Did you see any such thing?'

He gave a wild laugh. 'I *saw* nothing!'

I kept my temper. 'Well, there was nothing except for bear-sign. So perhaps they did come through and perished there. They certainly did not journey on to Kelsingra, not by foot or by pillar. Fool, please. Let me accept that Bee is gone.' My words were a plea. I longed to return to the numbness of utter loss and the pursuit of pure vengeance.

'She is not!'

His stubborn denial enraged me, so I attacked. 'It scarcely matters. Be she dead or alive, I shall doubtless be killed before I discover her, given how little you have told me of Clerres and its folk!'

His mouth dropped open in shock. Then guilt and outrage shrilled his voice. 'I've done my best, Fitz! I've never planned an assassination before. My memories shy and leap away from me when you interrogate me. And the stupidity of the questions you ask! What does it matter if Coultrie gambles or if Symphe rises early or late?'

'Without exact knowledge, my ability to kill them is diminished to the point of folly!'

'Folly?' He flung the word at me. 'Well, what did you expect from a fool?' He groped angrily for Amber's costume and his voice dropped to a furious mutter. 'I should never have come to you for help. What must be done, I should do myself!' He pulled on her gown with reckless haste, tying laces and fastening buttons blindly and crookedly.

'And all the difference in the world, if you had not come back to me!' The words were reckless daggers. 'And you needn't disguise yourself as Amber. I'm leaving anyway.' I stood up as he fought with a cuff. 'And like most things done blindly and in haste, you've made a poor job of it. I would not go out on the deck like that, if I were you. But you seem willing to do many things I would not do, such as attempt an assassination with no information.'

I slammed from the room, my heart leaping as anger warred with regret. The things I had said! But were any of them untrue?

I leaned on the railing to stare at Divvytown and simmer my fury. The wind off the water could not cool it.

Brashen found me there. 'Wintrow came by. He asked if you knew when Tintaglia would arrive.'

'I don't. Do you know when we will leave here?'

His terse response echoed mine. 'I don't. Wintrow has prepared for the dragon. If you can, he'd like you to let the dragon know that the pens are by the dock.'

I didn't master my anger but I contained it. I stood up straight and pushed the Fool's words and my angry taunt out of my mind. 'I will try, but I am not able to promise she will hear me.'

'I can't ask more of you than that,' he responded.

I closed my mouth and watched him walk away. I stared out over the water and tried to contact the dragon. *Tintaglia. I am at Divvytown in the Pirate Isles. They wish to welcome you with cattle penned by the docks. They would be honoured for you to devour them.*

I felt no response from her. In my heart, I hoped she would not be able to find me. Whatever she wanted of it, it would not be good.

*　　*　　*

Very early on the third morning, Sorcor and Queen Etta called up from a small dory, asking permission to come aboard Paragon. A bleary-eyed Wintrow was with them. All three had the look of people who had spent a long and sleepless night. They were welcomed aboard with steaming mugs of coffee. Sorcor had had the foresight to bring a basket of fresh pastries. To my surprise, Wintrow requested that Amber and I join them.

Etta looked more tough than queenly that day. Her fine jacket was crumpled from being worn all night. The daylight was not kind to the lines around her mouth, and her hair was wilful in the breeze. Sorcor looked as sorrowful as a chained hound when the other dogs were massing for a chase. We settled at the table, and Althea poured coffee. Silence held while Queen Etta toyed with the charm she wore at her throat. Then she straightened and locked eyes with Althea. When she spoke, she was giving orders. 'Paragon Ludluck, Prince of the Pirate Islands, will be travelling with you to Clerres. I know you do not welcome him. I am not enamoured of him making this journey either. Nonetheless, he must go. I offer coin for his passage, and eight reliable hands, experienced at both sail and sword. Though I pray that you will not have need of the latter skill.'

Words and outrage poured from Althea. 'No! When he attempted to board, I turned him away, as you said you wished us to do! As a result, our ship has gone from recalcitrant to dangerous as Paragon has attempted to thwart every task we must do! And now, after all that, you order us to allow him aboard?'

Brashen put his hand over Althea's as she drew breath. 'Why?' he queried Etta calmly.

The pirate queen glared at him and folded her lips.

Wintrow cleared his throat. 'Because his father would have wished it. Or so we are told.' Etta dropped her hand from her throat to the table and glared at Wintrow as he explained. 'Queen Etta wears a wizardwood charm carved in Kennit's likeness. He wore it on his wrist, next to his skin. It took in enough of his spirit to waken. This is his counsel.'

I stared unashamedly at the carved charm at Etta's throat. I half-expected it to move or speak, but it remained still.

Althea leaned toward the pirate queen as she said, 'Kennit desires it? Another reason for me to forbid it!'

'Yet you will take him,' Queen Etta predicted. 'Your only hope to manage your wayward ship is to give him what he wants. Deny me, and you have a difficult, under-manned vessel. All Divvytown has seen his power and his temper. You need what I offer you. Or remain anchored here, with a ship that daily becomes more dangerous.'

Althea clutched her mug so tightly that I expected it to shatter in her hands. Brashen's voice was level as he said, 'Althea and I need a moment to confer. We will join you on deck shortly.' He gestured to the door and waited for us to rise and troop out. He closed the door behind us.

Sorcor and Etta stood side by side, staring toward Divvytown. Wintrow stood apart from them, arms crossed. No one spoke until Paragon called back to us, 'Is it settled? Will I get Kennit's son?'

None of us replied.

They emerged. 'It's a deal,' Brashen said quietly. 'Money for his passage and eight sailors.' Althea's face was as impassive as stone. Brashen continued, 'But he sails as a common deckhand, and accepts ship's discipline.' Althea remained silent as Brashen offered his hand. Etta made a small sound of exasperation, but Sorcor nodded. It was Wintrow who stepped forward and clasped hands with Brashen in the Trader style. 'I'll write it up,' Wintrow promised, and Brashen nodded.

Amber whispered, 'It's the Trader way; a bargain that benefits all.' Very softly she added, 'Althea is not happy, but she recognizes it's the deal she needs if we are ever to leave Divvytown.'

Wintrow stepped back from the handshake. 'We will immediately begin loading supplies.' He lifted his voice. 'Does that settle well with you, Paragon? You've won. You get your way. Kennitsson sails with you. May we now finish offloading freight and come alongside with provisions?'

'You may!' Paragon's voice boomed over the harbour. Satisfaction welled up from the deck and washed through all of us. Even Althea looked relieved.

Brashen clapped me on the shoulder as he passed by me. 'Get ready to work,' he warned me.

And work we did. Kegs of clean water, beer, salt-fish and a great wheel of cheese were soon brought alongside, along with sacks of root vegetables, dried apples and plums, and box after box of hardtack. Our new crew arrived—seven deckhands and a navigator. Clef dared to put them through their paces, sending them up and down the mast, having them coil lines and demonstrate their knots. Not even the navigator was spared these humble chores, but she performed with a disdainful skill that mocked his testing.

The weather had warmed enough that Lant had slung his shirt onto the railing. I was barely able to catch the sleeve and keep both it and Motley, who had landed on it and tangled her feet, from going into the water. 'Be more careful!' I warned the crow as I clutched the shirt. Wings open, she danced and struggled until her foot came free, then announced, 'Tintaglia! Tintaglia! Look up, look up, look up!'

Topaz and sapphire, glittering bright, she came. She was small in the distance, a crow, and a heartbeat later, the size of an eagle. On she came, swifter than I had known any creature could fly. Soon half the crew was pointing and shouting. On shore, folk halted in the street to stare skywards. 'Does she know of the cattle by the docks? Where is she going to land?' I demanded of the crow.

'Wherever she wants,' Per said quietly.

'Look up, look up, look up!' the crow squawked again. I was focused on Tintaglia, but Spark shouted, 'Look, a red one! It's far away, but I think it's another dragon!'

This dragon flew more slowly and seemed to labour heavily. Would it land safely or perish in the waves?

'Heeby! Sparkling Heeby!' Motley cried and lifted in a flutter of black feathers to fly to meet her. I watched anxiously as Tintaglia circled Queen Etta's mansion. *Cattle for you! In a pen by the docks! Food awaits to welcome you!* I flung my thoughts at Tintaglia, but saw no change in her descending spiral.

Folk on the grand green before the royal manor dashed wildly for shelter. The dragon swooped in a final warning circle and then down she came, clawed legs extended and reaching. For such an immense creature, she landed with grace. The crack of her wings as she shook them out carried across the water to me, the sound like wet canvas struck by a sudden blast of storm.

Tintaglia lashed her tail, carving furrows in the green. Some bystanders surged toward the dragon and others fled. The confused babble of folk sounded like disturbed shore birds. Tintaglia rose on her hind legs, sitting up like a begging dog. Her head turned slowly, seeking. Despite the distance, her gaze settled on me. *'FitzChivalry. Approach. I will speak with you.'*

Her words were both a dragon's roar and a commanding voice inside my head. Ordering me. Almost as compelling as Verity's Skill-command had once been. 'Are you going?' Lant asked me, aghast.

'I don't have a choice,' I told him.

'Going where?' Per demanded.

'The dragon summons him, Per. And I'm going with him.'

'And me!' Per added.

I didn't want either of them. I spoke to Per severely. 'Remember that you're part of a crew now. It's up to the captain—'

'Both captains say go.' Althea charged up to us. She had a smear of tar down her cheek and her hair was matted with sweat. 'Take Amber with you. Brashen has the ship's boats waiting for you. Don't dally. I don't want a dragon displeased with someone on my deck. Particularly that dragon.'

Spark dashed to fetch Amber from the cabin. Loaded hastily into the ship's boat, we were whisked to shore. The docks were deserted, but as we neared the manor we had to push through a thickening crowd of folk gawking at the great blue queen. Queen Etta stood in the portico of her mansion with her son beside her. Armed guards surrounded them. Did the guards know how useless cutlasses and armour would be if the dragon chose to spit acid at them? A troop of city guard arrived, shoving through the mob of spectators to surround the dragon and push the crowd back from the green. I hoped I could reach Tintaglia before they irritated her too greatly.

Tintaglia's gaze found me as we forced a path through the massed crowd. 'Part!' she commanded. 'Let that one through!' As confused people pushed in opposing directions she announced, 'I have flown without stopping a day and a night and a day to reach this place. Farseer! I have words for you. Do not be slow to come to me. My hunger has no patience!'

'Out of the way!' I roared and shoved through the crowd with the others in my wake. 'Stay back,' I warned them, and felt naked as I stepped into that open space before Tintaglia.

'I am here,' I said to the dragon. I forced myself to take another step toward her.

She snaked her head toward me, mouth ajar and nostrils wide. Briefly, I saw the lash of a long scarlet tongue. The heat of her recent exertion rolled off her as if I stood too close to a hearth, bringing me the stink of reptile and the carrion waft of her breath. 'I am not blind, and if I were, I'd still know your scent.'

'Is she talking?' Per asked behind me.

'Shush,' Lant warned him.

'I am hungry and I am weary, with precious little time to spare.' Her tone made that my fault.

I bowed low. 'Cattle await you in a pen by the docks.'

Another lash of her tail. 'I know that. You have told me twice.' She spoke as if that were a mortal offense. Severely, she added, 'The docks offer no landing space for a dragon of my size.'

I thought of and immediately discarded the idea of trying to touch minds with her. I had no desire to let a dragon accidentally burn my Skill out of me. She was still speaking. 'First, know this. IceFyre is a coward. A dragon who chooses to bury himself in ice rather than take vengeance for fear of his own safety is scarcely a dragon at all!'

I did not think it would be wise to say anything to this. I stood silent and waiting.

A long breath was blown out through her nostrils, a deep thrumming in her throat accompanying it. She shuddered her scaled skin, resettled her wings and ordered me, 'Lead me to the docks. I will speak as we go. Then I will feed. It is difficult to speak simply to a human, and almost impossible when I am hungry.'

So reassuring to hear. I pitched my voice to carry. 'I believe it has been long since a dragon of your magnificent size descended here. Queen Etta of the Pirate Isles has provided well for your feeding.'

'And we are honoured, most beauteous queen! Azure and amazing you are!' Wintrow charged past the queen's guard and descended the steps to the furrowed green. He flourished an extravagant bow to Tintaglia. 'Perhaps you remember me, glorious one? My sister is Queen Malta of the Dragon Traders of Kelsingra. My younger brother, Selden, has often sung your praises to me.'

'Selden,' Tintaglia said, and her eyes whirled in sudden pleasure. 'Yes, that is a name I well recall. Such a sweet dragon-singer! Is he here?'

'I am saddened to tell you that he is not. And even more mortified to hear that our landing area was inadequate!'

Queen Etta had caught Wintrow's desperate hints. She stepped forward. 'Guards! Clear a path for our extraordinary guest and offer her an escort of honour to the cattle-pen. See that fresh water fills the troughs for her!' A flick of her fingers, and her personal guard peeled away from her and dashed across the green. With sheathed swords, they began to nudge a wide corridor through the gaping mob.

A shimmering of colours down Tintaglia's neck and a rippling of the frills at her jaw indicated, I hoped, her pleasure. 'A fine welcome,' she decided. 'I am pleased.'

Wintrow once more swept his elegant bow and with a sideways glance at me, walked a backwards retreat.

Tintaglia's attention returned to me, and a sensation like a heavy blanket dropped over me. I kept my walls tight against her glamor as she advanced on the avenue the guard had opened in the crowd.

Walking alongside her was challenging. Her pace was neither a human stroll nor a dash. It had been long since I'd been forced to trot so hastily. I glanced back to see Lant and Per following at a safe distance. Spark was guiding Amber toward the portico.

'You,' Tintaglia rumbled, almost quietly. Her tail lashed the ground as she walked, like a lazy cat's tail. 'Presumptuously, you asked me for information in Kelsingra. However, I have cornered IceFyre, and wrung from him with shame and threats much that he should have shared with us years ago. Even Heeby has more courage than he!'

'Your surmise was correct. Whites and their Servants have done great injury to dragonkind. I burn with fury to think that generations of them believed they could wrong us without consequences! That shame is due entirely to IceFyre's cowardice, but I have no belief that he will act. So I will.'

We had reached the warehouse district, an older quarter of Divvytown where the streets were narrower. I walked uncomfortably close to Tintaglia, and several times heard crashes as her lashing tail encountered the fronts of the buildings. If there had been people here, the scurrying guards had cleared them away.

'Understand, Farseer, this vengeance belongs to me. No mere human can deliver the punishment that Clerres deserves. When we come upon it, we will tumble it stone from stone and devour those who have dared to kill dragons, just as we did at Chalced. The satisfaction of those kills belongs to me!'

'Not if I get there first,' I muttered.

Abruptly Tintaglia halted. For an instant, I regretted my ill-considered words. But then she lifted her head, snuffing the air. I smelled it, too. The cattle-pen, where animals were held during the loading or unloading of a ship. We were close.

Emotions battled in me. I wanted my own vengeance. And if the Fool was correct and my daughter lived, I did not want her caught up in a dragon's furious attacks on Clerres. Could I dissuade Tintaglia? Was there any chance that Paragon would be swifter than a vengeful dragon? My doubts that Bee lived were swept away in fear that I might never know. 'You will take revenge on the Servants?'

'Did not I just tell you that? Humans. Everything must be repeated!' She spoke with total disdain. 'Listen, now, before I go to feed. I tell you this in little pieces for your little mind. Yes. I allow you to go to Clerres. As you rudely asserted, if you arrive before me, you have permission to slaughter as you please. I will not count that as your stealing my kills. Do you understand this favour I grant you?'

'Yes. Yes, I do. But we now think it's possible that my daughter is still alive. That she might be a prisoner there in Clerres.'

I might have been one of the flies buzzing on the manure pile for all the heed she gave me. The cattle-pen was before us. The lowing, milling cows had caught her scent. They crowded hard against the walls of the corral. She trumpeted, a fierce, hungry sound that conveyed no words to my mind, and charged forward. Luck, not dexterity, saved me from a blow from her whipping tail.

Then she was upon the poor trapped beasts, trampling them under her great claws and savaging them with her teeth. She seized one in her jaws and flung the bawling animal aloft. Lant snatched at my sleeve and dragged me back as the cow's broken body landed in the street close to where I had been. Per's face was a mask of horror and fascination. The guards who had run ahead to clear her way jeered and roared in the way that some men do when faced with carnage. They were closer than I would have chosen to be, caught up in the barbarity of the moment.

'We should leave her to feed,' I told Lant and Per.

We turned and started back the way we had come. More than one building had suffered damage from Tintaglia's lashing tail. We walked around a splintered loading dock. I moved more slowly than I had, still trying to catch my breath.

'Sir, will you tell me what the dragon has been saying?' Per demanded.

My throat was parched dry from my hasty jog to the cattle-pen. I kept it short. 'She says we have her permission to go to Clerres and kill people there. She also plans her own vengeance on Clerres, when she gets there.'

Per was nodding in a way that he said he didn't comprehend it at all. 'Vengeance for what? Why?' he asked.

'She didn't share the details. Evidently the Clerres folk once harmed some dragons. She is insulted that IceFyre never punished them for it. She warned me that all of them are her rightful kills, but that she will permit us our own vengeance. If we get there first.'

'Perhaps the black dragon thought that caving in half of Aslevjal was enough vengeance,' Lant suggested.

I shook my head. 'Tintaglia doesn't agree.'

'But sir!' Perseverance caught at my arm. 'What if the dragon arrives before us? Amber says that Bee is there! She could be hurt or killed by them! They do not seem to make much difference between us. Did you warn her that Bee was there, did you tell her she must be careful?'

'I mentioned that to her.'

Lant shied to one side as Motley swooped down to land on Per's shoulder.

'Heeby!' the bird announced. 'Sparkling Heeby! Come, come, come! Hurry!' As quickly as she had perched, she lifted from Per's shoulder and flew back toward the manor house.

'I'd forgotten Heeby was coming,' I admitted.

Per muttered, 'Only you could forget about a dragon.' In a louder voice he added, 'Can we hurry?'

My pride forced me to do just that. A crowd had reformed around the green before the royal mansion. Per pushed through, boldly shouting, 'Make a path for Prince FitzChivalry! Make a path!' I was too breathless to object. The pristine green was now as rumpled as a ploughed field. In the middle of the churned earth, Heeby stood. She wore a glorious harness of gleaming red leather and shining brass, topped with a sort of box: a perch for a rider. Hunger and weariness radiated from her like heat from a stove. She was making a sound in her throat as she breathed, as if an immense kettle were about to come to a boil.

In the portico of the manor, Queen Etta, Kennitsson and Wintrow stood, with Amber and Spark to one side at a respectful distance.

A rank of fresh guards, staves at the ready, stood between the queen and her uninvited guest. On a lower step, but so tall he was not looking up at them, clad all in scarlet leather and armour, was an Elderling. 'Rapskal is here!' Per exclaimed in a mixture of surprise and dread. The Elderling was gesticulating grandly and as we circled well away from Heeby and approached the manor, I caught his words.

'. . . and a night and a day, until we came here. We have travelled far, all the way from Kelsingra in the Rain Wilds. My dragon and I bear important tidings for FitzChivalry Farseer. If live meat could be found for her, I would be grateful. Please.'

I had never heard General Rapskal so courteous, but it seemed that for Heeby he could humble himself and beg. Wintrow leaned closer to Queen Etta and said something softly. She did not look pleased, but issued her command. 'Bring her three goats. Let her have them here; the green is ruined anyway.'

'And you are wise, Queen Etta, to let her feed at a safe distance from Tintaglia. I am grateful.' Rapskal looked over his shoulder at his impatient dragon and his face softened with fondness. 'She is so hungry, and I have asked so much of her, to carry me so far. And we have farther yet to go, all the way to Others' Island. And then Clerres.' He saw me then and turned away from Etta, exclaiming, 'FitzChivalry, there you are! I bring you important tidings!'

I advanced hastily. 'Tintaglia has shared them with me already, General Rapskal. I am surprised to see you here.'

'As are we all,' Queen Etta announced icily. 'Especially since you have not yet shared with me the reason for this . . . visit.' There was no mistaking her displeasure. But just as unnerving to me was how Kennitsson was staring at Heeby. He suddenly stepped down, past the startled guard and even past Rapskal, and walked directly toward her.

My breath caught in my throat. The dragon was hungry and he was a stranger. But she only twisted her head at him and regarded him with gently whirling eyes.

'Bring this wondrous dragon a tub of water!' he commanded suddenly. 'She is parched with thirst! No creature so glorious should suffer such privation! And where are the goats? Should not they be here by now? Bring her one of the brown bullocks as well! She is famished!' And the idiot approached the hungry dragon, his hand outstretched.

A murmur of dismay and consternation rose from the gathered crowd. Etta's mouth hung slightly ajar in breathless fear.

'No!' Wintrow cried, starting forward. I expected Rapskal to leap forward to save the prince. But although the Elderling was in motion, he was coming across the green toward me. I noticed Sorcor moving swiftly and too late to shadow Kennitsson's movement. Heeby would eat the prince.

But Heeby only extended her head until her scaled snout touched Kennitsson's hand. My breath eased out of me. I wondered if Kennitsson's display had been true bravery or if he had fallen prey to the dragon's glamor.

He lifted his other hand and set it to her face. 'Lovely one!' the prince said, and the dragon lowered her head to allow him to scratch her brow.

A sigh, a murmur of approval from the gathered throng, told me what I had not guessed before: the people of the Pirate Isles adored their prince. I might have seen him as spoiled man-boy, but his flair of elegance and this show of bravado dazzled the crowd. As the goats came blatting around the corner of the manor house, Heeby lifted her head and looked over her shoulder at them.

'Go!' the prince bade her. 'Satisfy your hunger, you beauteous thing!' He stood fearlessly as she spun and leapt. For the second time that day, I watched a dragon make a kill and listened to a roar of approval from the crowd.

'Ware!' Lant muttered, stepping up beside me, and Per quickly moved to my other flank as Rapskal approached, his hand extended to clasp wrists with me. A wide smile of white teeth looked peculiar in his scarlet-scaled face. I met his hand, but he did not release it after our clasp. Instead he tugged at me as if I had forgotten my manners. 'Don't stand there, FitzChivalry! I must present myself to their queen.' He lifted his voice to cry, 'Enjoy your meal, Heeby, my glorious one! Prince, thank you for such a kind greeting! Now that my dragon is well tended, I shall convey to FitzChivalry all that he must know.'

He took my arm and I let him. We advanced together across the dragon-torn turf, Lant and Per close behind us. A bullock bellowed in alarm and I turned to see the poor panicked creature being dragged and chivvied toward the dragon.

'Release it!' Kennitsson bellowed, and they did. The cattle-boys barely evaded the dragon's charge as bullock and predator savaged another half-acre of garden. This bullock was a fighter and his horns had not been removed. He made several attempts to gore Heeby. She sprang into the air and came down on him with all four feet, a cat pouncing on a mouse. His bellow ended in a terrible wet crunch. Per made a sound of dismay but the mob shouted with piratical amusement. Rapskal could not have planned a better entertainment for them than bull-baiting in the queen's garden. The prince lifted his arms wide overhead in triumph and shouted, 'Fear her not, my people! This scarlet beauty has come in friendship!'

The crowd's resounding approval was deafening.

Queen Etta and her party had retreated slightly from the steps, but Wintrow had remained on the portico and was gesturing to us to join them. Rapskal and I reached the wide white steps and ascended them to where Queen Etta stood transfixed by her son's spectacle. I heard her whisper softly, 'He has his father's gift for winning hearts. This is good.'

We climbed more steps to where a stiffly smiling Wintrow posed. Amber and Spark awaited us there, faces frozen in uncertainty.

'What is this about?' he demanded in a low voice while greeting me in apparently affable fashion. 'What chaos have you brought to our doorstep, FitzChivalry? A mad ship, stealing our prince for your mission of vengeance and now dragons on our green?'

Etta kept her eyes on her son. 'Stand down, Wintrow. We appear to be establishing diplomatic relations with the Rain Wilds.' She gave Wintrow a sideways glance. 'I think the prince who befriends dragons may deserve a bride that comes with a larger dowry.' She lifted her hand from her sword hilt and turned her smile toward Rapskal. There was a lilt of amusement in her voice. 'Greetings. I am Queen Etta of the Pirate Isles. This is my chief minister and admiral, Wintrow Vestrit.'

'Names well known to me.' Rapskal offered them a bow. 'I am General Rapskal of the Dragon Traders of Kelsingra. No diplomat, I fear, most gracious queen, but a loyal messenger for the dragons.' He still had a firm hold on my arm and he patted it fondly. 'When Prince FitzChivalry visited us, he wished to know if the history of the dragons intersected with that of the Servants of the pale folk. We have obtained that information from IceFyre, and it is of great importance that he know that his vengeance may align with ours, but does not supersede it.' He turned to me and added, 'I assure you that I can convey the information much more concisely than Tintaglia, and without her impatience.'

'How comforting,' I replied, and to my surprise, that won a soft chuckle from Queen Etta.

'Doubtless you can then tell me, swiftly and clearly, what an invasion of dragons has to do with this man's mission to rescue his daughter.'

'A coincidence of fate!' Rapskal assured her. 'But I beg you, may I have food and drink before I begin my telling?'

Wintrow chose a smile. 'Please, enter. I'll be with you shortly. I must issue a few orders to the guards. Few of them are familiar with dragons. But I've had enough interactions with them to know that careless words or deeds can bring death.'

'Ask my son to attend me,' Etta directed him.

'Oh, he will not wish to leave Heeby,' Rapskal informed her familiarly and fondly. 'I saw the look on his face and sensed her approval of him. He will stay by her while she is feeding, and possibly while she sleeps as well.'

Wintrow was nodding. 'Likely it will be as he says. They are enamoured of one another. Tintaglia had much the same effect on my brother Selden. She will be unlikely to harm him. And the citizens are taking great pleasure in watching their prince befriend a dragon.' The queen's expression did not change. 'Nonetheless, I will invite him.' Wintrow assured her and left us. Rapskal hooked his arm firmly through mine, a gesture I thoroughly disliked. We followed Queen Etta. I did not like how her guard closed in around us but I held my tongue. As it was with dragons, so it is with queens. A careless word or deed could have severe consequences.

Inside the royal mansion, it was cooler and dimmer. Everywhere I looked, a history of pirate looting prevailed in tapestries and statuary, exotic draperies and foreign treasures. There was a remarkable lack of formality as the queen herself guided us to a sitting room. 'Find food and drink,' she commanded one of her servants.

'Oh, I would be so grateful for that,' Rapskal responded. He turned his attention back to me. 'Heeby could not keep pace with Tintaglia, try as she might. We knew Tintaglia would not wait for us. Our errand is urgent, with little time to spare, even to give this message.'

The queen had taken her seat at the head of a very long table.

There were more than enough chairs for all of us. I manoeuvred Rapskal so that he sat at Etta's left hand and took a chair next to him, leaving a place for Amber beside me. Lant took the next place and after some uncertainty, Spark and Per took chairs. They exchanged a look; seated at a pirate queen's table!

Queen Etta let her gaze rove over all of us. 'Welcome to my home,' she said.

The sarcasm in her greeting was wasted on the Elderling.

'You are so gracious,' Rapskal replied artlessly. 'And far more beautiful than I expected! Oh, and here is the refreshment you sent for. I am so parched and so hungry.' As soon as the serving woman had filled his glass, he lifted it and drank deeply.

For a moment, she stared at him. I waited for her to rebuke him for his ill manners. Instead she suddenly leaned back on one arm of her chair. I saw the pirate who had become a queen as she said, 'And you are much more forthright and simple than I expected an envoy to be.'

'Yes, I am that,' he agreed happily as he held out his glass to be refilled. 'But scarcely an envoy. General I might be, and master of Kelsingra's forces when I am there, but on this errand I serve my dragon, and indeed all dragonkind! I shall be sure that all dragons of Kelsingra hear of your hospitality!'

'How kind of you! Should I be glad of that? Or terrified?' She sent her gaze around the table, and then laughed aloud, apparently finding Rapskal more amusing than offensive. Wintrow entered and took a place at the queen's right hand. 'And my son?' she asked of him.

'He is passing the time with the red dragon and has sent for three more cows.' Wintrow looked at me and added, 'Your crow has joined them.'

'She enjoys the company of the red dragon,' I offered. Questions and concerns boiled inside me, but this was the queen's table.

'So. My son sails with you, to rescue your daughter. And somehow this exposes him to the company of dragons?' Queen Etta stared at me but it was Rapskal who responded. He had cleared his plate of food and was watching alertly the servant approach with a platter of sliced meat.

'Let me make all clear for everyone. We have come to tell FitzChivalry and Lady Amber that the dragons approve and allow their mission of vengeance. Indeed, once our errand is done, we shall follow them to Clerres to finish whatever destruction they have begun. We intend to level the city and raze the surrounding countryside.' He took a long draught of his wine, apparently unaware of Queen Etta's wide-eyed expression.

He set his glass down with a heavy sigh. 'FitzChivalry is not the only one who has been wronged by these Servants. Far more grievous is our injury from them! In league with the Abominations, they have ransacked the nesting beach, stealing dragon eggs, and killing or imprisoning the hatchling serpents! Tomorrow we fly swiftly on to Others' Island to protect the eggs buried there until the summer hatching season. Tintaglia shall stand guard over the nests and shepherd the hatchling serpents as they make their way to the sea while Heeby and I hunt down and kill the Abominations who infest that place.'

'Abominations?' Amber asked softly. She had kept silent and watchful until that moment.

'So we name them. They occur when a dragon who has been too long among humans lays her eggs, and they do not hatch into serpents, but something neither serpent nor human nor Elderling. Grotesque and evil creatures. We will slaughter them. IceFyre alone knew how they had wronged us! How they dug the eggs from the nest mounds or preyed upon the young serpents as they tried to make their way to the sea! Some they killed, to devour or to sell their bodies to the Servants of the Whites! Or worse, imprisoned them for decades, harvesting the secretions of their bodies for potions and medicines!' His scaled lips curled in disgust. 'The Abominations consume those secretions; they claim it aids them to foretell the future and remember distant pasts!'

Wintrow set down his glass with a sharp sound on the table. 'Etta,' he said in a low voice. 'We've been there. On the Treasure Beach. Those creatures. The serpent I freed . . .'

'I recall that,' she said faintly.

Wintrow spoke to Rapskal. 'Kennit took me there to see what the Others might predict for me. He had been there before, I believe. With Igrot. There was a tradition, that if you found something washed up on the Treasure Beach and surrendered it to the creatures that lived there, they would foretell your future. But I found no treasure. Only an immense serpent, held captive in a caged pool. The higher tides would replenish the water around it, but the creature was stunted and twisted from living in such a small space. It spoke to me . . . I managed to free it. Though its passing touch took the skin from my flesh, and I nearly drowned for my efforts.'

'I recall that,' Etta said. 'Sorcor, too, spoke of a previous visit Kennit made there.' A faint smile touched her lips. 'He destroyed what he found rather than surrender it to the creature there.'

'That was Kennit,' Wintrow agreed, and I could not tell if there was fondness or dismay in his voice.

For a moment, a strange silence held.

'Heroic!' Rapskal exclaimed. His fist thudded the table, making us all jump and his eyes shone with tears. 'I will share this tale with Heeby, and with all dragons!' For a moment, he was silent and staring.

Wintrow and Etta exchanged a look. Was I the only one who sensed a flow of communication between him and his dragon? Then, from the direction of the docks, I heard Tintaglia's trumpeting.

Rapskal stood abruptly and suddenly stripped the rings from his fingers. He clacked the cluster of jewellery on the table and pushed them toward Wintrow. There were tears in his eyes. 'A small gift of Elderling jewellery, insufficient for the man who freed a serpent from the slavery of the Abominations! The gratitude of dragons is a rare commodity! You have the gratitude of all Elderlings as well.' He turned his gaze to Etta. 'And Heeby tells me you send your son to accompany FitzChivalry, to aid in taking this vengeance? Heeby is pleased. She wraps him in her highest regard. She promises that when she reaches Clerres, we shall find him!' He lifted his voice to a shout. 'He will ride upon her back to smite them!'

Silence filled the room.

Amber broke it. 'Then the dragons go to Clerres with us, to take their vengeance?' Was there hope or dread in her voice?

Rapskal set down his glass and shook his head. 'Not immediately. Our mission to protect the hatching eggs is the more pressing one. When the hatching season is complete and we are satisfied that every Abomination has been slain, we will come there.'

'When last we spoke, we believed my daughter was dead. Now we believe she may have survived. That Bee may be a prisoner in Clerres.'

Amber broke in. 'If she is in the city and the dragons attack, she may be injured. Or killed.'

Rapskal nodded to that. 'Killed is likelier,' he conceded. 'The destruction we wrought on Chalced was very thorough. Buildings collapsed. The acid breath of the dragons sprayed over people and beasts.' He nodded his satisfaction. 'I doubt that anyone within the duke's palace survived.' Then, as he looked around at the horror on our faces he said suddenly, 'I see your concern. Indeed.'

'And you can speak to Tintaglia and Heeby? Ask them to aid us? Or at least allow us to make our rescue attempt before they bring the city down?' Amber was breathless with hope.

He steepled his long-fingered hands and looked down at their scarlet nails. We waited in silence. At last he said quietly, 'I will tell them. But.' He lifted his eyes and met my gaze squarely. 'I can promise nothing. I think you already know that. Dragons are not . . . they do not regard humans . . .' His voice trailed away.

'They will not consider it important.' My words fell like dead birds.

'Exactly. I am sorry.' He toyed with his fork and added, 'Your best hope is to be there before they are. To try to rescue her before they lay siege to the city. Truly, I am sorry.'

I wondered if he was. I wondered if he were not very like a dragon himself. Unable to grasp the importance of one child.

Rapskal lifted his head as if he were listening to something. 'Heeby is sated. You have provided well for her. I thank you.' Again, his face took on that pensive look. Then he smiled. 'I believe that Tintaglia is as well. Now they will sleep. Such a flight has wearied both of them, and Heeby is close to exhaustion.' He looked at me and quirked one scaled brow, as if to remind me that we shared a secret. 'Luckily I carry in her saddle a supply of a . . . restorative. Tomorrow, she shall have it. But for the rest of the day and all tonight, she must sleep. And so must I.' He turned his smile on Wintrow and Etta. 'Could you prepare a bedchamber for me, and a bath? I confess I am wearied and aching in every limb. Travelling so high above the earth it is always cold! I could sleep a bit in my saddle, but it was not true rest.'

Queen Etta's eyes narrowed to be addressed as if she were a chamber servant. I anticipated Etta coming to her feet with her hand on a sword's hilt, but instead Wintrow pushed hastily back from the table. He knew when his queen had reached her limit for tolerance. 'If you will follow me, General Rapskal, I will be pleased to surrender my own chamber to your use. I'm sure that is the swiftest way to find you a place to rest. Gentlemen, ladies, if you will excuse us.'

And they went, leaving Queen Etta and my party at the table. Abruptly, the queen stood up. 'You need to leave as soon as possible. To have a chance to reach Clerres before the dragons, to save your child.'

'That is so.' I fought to control my voice. I was still trying to accept the fatalism I had heard in Rapskal's words. The allies I had hoped for had now become a different sort of threat.

'And you take my son into a greater danger than I perceived.'

'I consider that likely.'

She nodded slowly. 'He is his father's son. This business with the dragons and their vengeance . . . it will only fire his determination steel-hard.' She fixed me with a considering stare. 'Well, Prince FitzChivalry, you have brought more excitement, disaster and puzzlement to Divvytown than we have enjoyed in many a year.'

I heard the clack of boots and Kennitsson strode into the room. There was a fire in his eyes I had not seen there before. 'Mother. I have come to tell you that I am determined to sail tomorrow, on the first tide. The sooner we reach Clerres, the sooner we can take a vengeance long delayed.' His gaze swept us, and then he turned and departed.

Etta stared after her son for a long moment. 'So like his father.' She turned to me. 'I had hoped to delay your departure. Now, I will give commands that the ship be well provisioned by nightfall.' As she rose from the table she added in a chilling voice, 'Farseer. You have lost your child. Do not lose mine as well.'

TWENTY-ONE

Under Sail

*The first time the mountain burned was in the summer. Some said the
earth's shaking broke the distant mountain. Others that the mountain
woke and that caused the earth to shake.*

*It was not the first time that the earth had quaked under us. Always
there had been tremors. Hence we had always built with stone rich in the
silver threads that could be magicked to stand firm and remember their
purpose in the world. But in that shaking, although most of our buildings
stood firm, a crack opened in the earth itself from the river to the District
of the Tinkers. Later, it would fill with water from the river and we would
accept it as a part of our city.*

*A rain fell on the city that was not only water but contained black
sand. It dusted the streets, and some of the folk and three of the dragons
took a cough from it. Dark clouds gathered over Kelsingra, and day was
like night for twelve days. Birds fell lifeless to the ground and fish washed
up along the shores of the river.*

*All the while, far in the distance, what had been the snowy peak of
Sisefalk glowed like a cauldron of melted iron.*

Memory-cube 941, found in a corridor in Aslevjal
Transcribed by Chade Fallstar

At dawn the next day, the dragons departed.

Etta had been as good as her word. We had worked through the
night, taking on supplies and making all ready to catch the first tide.
I do not think the dragons gave warning or farewell to anyone. They
rose from the ground and our crow circled below, cawing unhappily

as they rose higher and higher into the sky in slow circles over Divvytown before departing to the south and east. As I dropped my eyes, I saw that Vivacia was in full sail below them. Brashen strode past me on the deck and I pointed her out to him.

'Word came late last night. Vivacia was determined to go to Others' Island with the dragons, to see what has transpired there. And afterward, perhaps she will follow them to Clerres.'

I stared after them, wondering what that meant for my mission until Brashen slapped me on the back. 'The ale-casks will not stow themselves,' he pointed out, and I moved to where Clef was putting hands onto a hoist.

Not long after, the Prince of the Pirate Isles came alongside in a small boat. Sorcor was at the oars, pulling hard and well for a man of his years. Two ornate trunks and a canvas seaman's bag rode in the centre of the boat. Kennitsson perched in the bow, with the plumes of his hat nodding in the wind. A youngster, finely attired, sat on one of the trunks.

Clef spotted them and strode purposefully toward the captains' stateroom. A moment later, both Althea and Brashen appeared. Althea's mouth was taut and her eyes narrowed like an angry cat. Brashen looked relaxed and in command.

Kennitsson ascended the ladder first, followed by the youngster. Sorcor joined us on the deck. Two of Etta's sailors clambered over the side to bring the trunks aboard. As Kennitsson looked around, Sorcor spoke. 'Well,' he said heavily. 'Here we are.'

'Paragon Ludluck! To me, young man, to me!' cried the ship. Without a word or a glance at Althea or Brashen, Kennitsson walked towards the figurehead. Over his shoulder he called to the youngster, 'Barla, see to my things! Arrange my stateroom as I like it. Be lively about it.'

Sorcor watched him go, and a blush reddened the old pirate's cheeks. Without looking at Brashen or Althea, he said quietly, 'I'd like to come with you.'

'We've already enough captains on this vessel,' Brashen replied, trying to soften his decision with humour. 'If you're aboard, not only Kennitsson but every sailor you've offered us will look to you before following an order from me or Althea.'

'That's true,' Sorcor admitted. We watched as the first heavy trunk of Kennitsson's essentials was lifted and swung over Paragon's deck.

Sorcor's eyes tracked the trunk's journey. He gave a small sigh. 'You want a free hand with the lad, don't you? Don't want me stepping in if I think you're too rough on our young prince.'

'I do,' Brashen admitted. 'I can't think of him as a lad, let alone as a prince. The ship wants him aboard. You'd like him to learn something of our trade.' He gave a deprecating laugh. 'And I'd like a bit of peace aboard this vessel. That's only going to happen if I treat him like any other hand.'

'So I told him last night, when his mother was chaining that charm snug to his throat. I don't think he heard a word we said to him. But I give him over to you.' A small silence followed Sorcor's capitulation. The old pirate turned to Barla, who was guiding the heavy trunk down to the deck, and said quietly, 'Lass, tell them to take that one back. The canvas sea-bag is all we need brought aboard.' Then he squared his shoulders. 'Kennitsson and Trellvestrit got along well whenever Vivacia was in port. Wintrow threw them together whenever he could. He wanted your boy to get a feel for our politics and to pick up a bit of polish. Begging your pardon, Wintrow's words, not mine!'

Brashen gave a wry twist of his mouth. 'Polish, eh? I'd have said Boy-O had the Trader's polish already. But no offence taken.'

'I'd appreciate it if your lad stood by him now. He could teach him your ways, the same way Trellvestrit learned our ways from Kennitsson. He'll have to learn this deck, and everything above and below it. I know Kennitsson's in for some rough seas before he fits in here. He's never lived aboard a ship. Never been . . .' He shook his big head. 'My fault,' he said hoarsely.

'I'll teach him,' Brashen said in a low voice. 'He'll have to learn to bend a bit. But I won't deliberately break him. The first thing he'll have to learn is how to take an order.' He cleared his throat and gave Sorcor an apologetic look. 'Grit your teeth and stand back, Sorcor.' Then Brashen drew breath and bellowed, 'Kennitsson! Your gear is aboard. Come and stow it. Boy-O, show him his hammock and help him square himself away.'

Boy-O came at a run, a grin on his face, which faded when he saw the trunk being lowered back over the side. Barla shrugged and went down the ladder after it. A moment later, one of the new hands appeared, the canvas sea-bag slung over her shoulder. She set it down on the deck as Kennitsson strode up. He had not loitered but neither had he hastened. He looked at Brashen with his eyebrows cocked. 'My "hammock"?' he queried, a small smile on his lips as if he were certain the captain had misspoken.

'Right by mine!' Boy-O interjected. 'Grab your sea-bag and let's take it below.' I wondered if Kennitsson heard the note of warning in his friend's voice.

'Below?' Kennitsson asked, his eyebrows venturing toward his hairline. His glance flickered to Sorcor and waited for him to intervene.

Brashen slowly crossed his arms on his chest. There was reluctance on Sorcor's face but no challenge as the old pirate offered, 'Good voyaging, Captain Trell. May you have smooth seas and a steady wind.'

'I doubt I'll get either at this time of year, heading southeast, but I appreciate the wish. Please convey my respects to Queen Etta. I would thank her again for all she has done to equip us for this voyage and to help us make amends with our trading partners.'

'I'll be sure she knows you thank her.' I could see Sorcor's unwillingness to leave. Behind him, incredulous indignation was building on Kennitsson's face. Boy-O had picked up the sea-bag.

'Where are my trunks?' Kennitsson demanded. 'Where is my valet?'

'That's your sea-bag there, in Trellvestrit's hands. I packed it myself. Everything you need is in there.' Sorcor turned slowly and made his way to the side of the ship. Below, the dory that had ferried them out awaited him. Barla popped her head up over the railing. Sorcor shook his head and motioned her to return to the dory. Puzzled, she obeyed. Sorcor straddled the railing beside the rope ladder. 'Honour your father's memory. Become a man.'

Kennitsson stared after him, his cheeks going scarlet. 'I *am* a man!' he bellowed after Sorcor.

Brashen spoke in an even voice. 'Boy-O. Drop it.' As soon as his son obeyed, he turned to the pirate prince. 'Can you manage your own sea-bag, sailor? I can tell Prince FitzChivalry to give you a hand with it, if there's need.' His voice betrayed no emotion. He was a captain finding the limits of a new hire.

I had watched the scene unfold as if I watched a puppet-play, leaning on the ship's railing a short distance away. At Trell's suggestion, I straightened and stepped forward briskly to help with the sea-bag. I was a bit puzzled at his request. The canvas bag was not so large that it presented any sort of a challenge. But I had given my word that I'd help sail the ship and I intended to live up to that at least.

'Out of my way! I can manage it!' Kennitsson declared. Captain Trell gave a small jerk of his head and I moved away. Kennitsson had strength more than equal to moving his sea-bag, but he deployed it in the sullen over-reaction of a spoiled boy. I reminded myself that he was not my problem and took myself to Amber's cabin.

There, I found the Fool, sitting cross-legged on the lower bunk, with one of Bee's books open in his lap.

'I wondered if you had changed your mind and gone to Divvytown with the others.'

'Sightseeing?' he asked and gestured at his ruined eyes.

I sat down beside him, bowing my head to avoid hitting it on the bunk above. 'I hoped you were regaining a bit of your vision. You're looking at a book.'

'I'm touching a book, Fitz.' He sighed and held it out to me. I felt a jolt of dismay. It was her journal, not her book of dreams. Open to a page I hadn't shared with him. Did he know? I closed it gently, found the shirt I always used and re-wrapped it carefully. I slid it back into my worn pack. I feared he might accidentally discover the Silver. But I said only, 'We must be very careful with my pack. The fire-brick from Reyn is in here. It must always be stored upright.'

As I placed it carefully under the bunk, I told him, 'Kennitsson has come aboard. We'll be leaving on the change of the tide.'

'Have Lant, Per and Spark returned yet?'

'They won't be late. Lant had some bird messages to send. Per wanted help to get word to his mother. Spark wished to send a message to Chade.'

'So today we finally resume our journey.' The breath he expelled was uneven. 'Yet there is still so far to go, and every moment that passes is a moment that she is too long in their possession. Any moment may be the moment she dies.'

Panic rose in me. I pushed it down and denied it. Hardened my heart and extinguished hope. I tried to share my defence. 'Fool, despite what you believe, despite what you have dreamed . . . If I imagine this is a rescue, not an assassination, I will lose my focus. And it is all I have left.'

Alarm claimed his face. 'But she is alive, Fitz. My dreams make me certain of it. I wish I could share them with you!'

'So you've had more than one dream of Bee still alive?' I asked reluctantly. Could I bear to hear any more of his wishful proof?

'I have,' he replied and then, tilting his head, 'Though perhaps only I could interpret them that way. It is not so much the images as the feel of the dream that makes me certain they pertain to Bee.' He paused and grew thoughtful. 'Possibly I could share my dreams with you? If you touched me with no thought of healing but only of sharing, perhaps?'

'No.' I tried to soften my refusal. 'When we link, Fool, what happens has nothing to do with my intent. Something that feels inevitable begins to happen. Like the current of a river sweeping us along.'

'Like the Skill-river you speak of, like a current of magic?'

'No. It's different.'

'Then what is it?'

I sighed. 'How can I explain something that I don't understand myself?'

'Hmph. When I say something like that, you get angry at me.'

I brought us back to the subject. 'You said you've had more dreams about Bee.'

'I have.'

A short response and a secret unspoken. I pressed him. 'What sort of dreams, Fool? Where do you dream her, what is she doing?'

'You know my dreams are not like windows into her life. They are hints and portents. Such as the dream about the candles.' He tilted his head. 'You recall how Bee wrote of it. I'll tell you something. That's an old dream, dreamed often and by many. It could mean so many things. Yet I think it is fulfilled in us. Bee dreams it more clearly than I've ever heard it, speaking of us as the Wolf and the Jester.'

'How could many people dream the same dream?' I pushed aside his confusing words. Without intending it, my voice had dropped to the level of a wolf's warning growl. His sightless eyes widened slightly.

'We just do. It's one measure the Servants use to consider the likelihood of something happening. It's a common dream among those who carry White bloodlines. Each one is slightly different, but they are recognizable as the same dream. I dreamed it as a fork in a path. There are four candles spaced along the path in one direction. At the end of it, there is a little stone house with a low door and no windows. The place where the dead are put. The other path is lit by three candles. At the end of it, a fire burns and people are shouting.' He took a small breath. 'I stand staring at it. Then, out of the dark, a bee comes, and buzzes in circles around my head.'

'And that makes you think that the dream is about my Bee?'

He nodded slowly. 'But not just because of a bee in the dream. It was the feeling of the dream. But it wasn't the only dream I had.'

'What do the dreams mean?' I asked the question despite suspecting that his recent dreams meant no more than the dreams I had. When I had brought him back from the dead, he had told me he was blind to the new future we had made. Did his mind now play tricks on him, sending him dreams of what he desperately hoped to be true?

'I could say, "you don't want to know" but I would be lying. The truth is, I don't want to tell you. But I know I must!' he added hastily before I could speak. He cleared his throat and looked down at his hands. He rubbed them together as if remembering pain. He had a few fingernails now on his bared hand and the others seemed to be growing. I looked away from the reminder of what he had endured. The body might heal, but the wounds that dedicated torture leave on the mind always seep toxic pus. I reached across and took his gloved hand in mine.

'Tell me.'

'She isn't treated well.'

I had expected that. If she was still alive, her captors were unlikely to be gentle with her. But to hear that spoken aloud was like the fist to the belly that drives all breath away.

'How?' I managed. Dreams, I reminded myself. Probably not real.

'I don't know.' His voice was a hoarse whisper. 'I dreamed a wolf cub licking her wounds and curling tight against the cold. I dreamed a slender white tree stripped of its blossoms and its tender branches bent awry.'

I could not breathe. He made a small sound of pain and I realized I was crushing his fingers. I loosened my grip and found air.

'But I also dreamed a hand holding a dead torch. It was a confusing dream. The torch fell to the ground and a foot ground it out. I heard a voice. "Better to grope in darkness than to follow false light".' He paused and added, 'The confusing part was that it was already dark. An immense blaze of light came up as the torch was ground out.'

'How do you know that the dream was about Bee?'

He looked abashed. 'I am not certain, but it might be. And it felt . . . uplifting. Like something that might be good. I wanted to share it with you.'

There was a hasty knock and an instant later Spark flung open the door. 'Oh!' she exclaimed upon seeing our clasped hands. I released the Fool. She recovered herself to announce, 'Captain Trell wants every able-bodied person on the deck. Time to weigh anchor and depart. Clef sent me to find you. He nabbed Per and Lant as soon as we came back on board.'

I was relieved to leave off our discussion of dark dreams, but the Fool's words haunted me all that day. I was grateful for the times when the distraction of learning the ropes and how the ship moved blocked my anxiety for my daughter. No matter how I moved my thoughts, I was cut. Bee was dead, tattered away in the Skill-stream. Bee was alive and living in torment.

I worked my body as hard as I could, seeking exhaustion, then took a hammock belowdecks with the crew where their talk and cursing and laughter kept dreams away.

We were a day out from Divvytown when a downcast Per came to me. 'Have you seen Motley?'

I had not noticed the crow's absence until he spoke of it. 'I haven't,' I admitted. Unwillingly I added, 'Crows are shore birds, Per. There was plenty of feed for her in Divvytown. That's not true out on the open water. I know that you shared your rations with her when we were running short. But perhaps she prefers to fend for herself now.'

'I'd just re-blacked her feathers. What will become of her when the black wears off?'

'I don't know,' I admitted reluctantly. She was a wild thing at heart and always would be. She'd made it clear she did not want a Wit-bond. I tried to let go of her.

Nonetheless, relief flooded me on the second day when we heard a distant cawing. Per and I were up the rigging that day, leaning on the spar, our feet braced on the foot-lines. At first she was a tiny silhouette in the distance. But as we watched, her steadily beating wings brought her closer and closer. She cawed a greeting and then landed solidly on Per's arm. 'Tired,' she said. 'So tired.' She walked up his shoulder to nestle under his chin.

'I swear, sometimes I am certain she knows every word we say,' I observed.

'Every word,' she repeated, and regarded me with one bright eye.

I stared at her. The tip of her beak was silver. 'Per,' I warned him, trying to keep my voice calm. 'Keep her away from your face. She has Silver on her beak.'

I saw the boy freeze. Then he said in a shaky voice, 'I can't sense magic at all. Maybe I'm immune to Silver, too.'

'And maybe you're not. Please, move her away from your throat.'

He lifted his wrist and the bird transferred herself to his hand. 'What did you do?' he asked her. 'How did you get Silver on your beak, pretty thing? Are you all right? Do you feel ill?'

In response, she turned and groomed her flight feathers. They did not go silver but they sheened blacker than I'd ever seen them. 'Heeby,' she croaked. 'Heeby share. Heeby teach how.'

Ah. Rapskal's tonic back at Divvytown. I should have guessed. And was her time with the dragons improving her speech? 'Be careful with your beak,' I chided her.

She turned her shining eyes on me. 'I *am* careful, stupid Fitz. But so tired. Take me to Paragon.' She clambered up his sleeve to his shoulder again and gave me a baleful look before closing her eyes.

I heard Trell roaring at us to get a move on and stop perching like seagulls. Per looked to me, ignoring his captain. 'Do I take her to Paragon?'

'I doubt you can keep her away. And no matter how careful she is, I want you to be even more careful. Warn any others that she might fly to.'

Brashen roared again, and Per began his hasty descent, shouting that Motley had returned. As Per spidered and slid with the bird on his shoulder, Spark crossed the deck at a run. I began my more cautious descent.

'Are you truly a prince?' Kennitsson asked as I paused beside him.

I hesitated for a moment. Bastard or prince? Dutiful had made me a prince. 'I am,' I said quietly. 'But due to illegitimacy, not in line for the throne.'

He shrugged that aside. 'That lad, that Per. He was your stableboy?'

'Yes.'

'You work alongside him, and he never defers to you at all.'

'He does, but not in a noticeable way, I suppose. He respects me, even if others don't see it.'

'Huh.'

The sound was thoughtful rather than disdainful. Even a few days on board as a common sailor had changed him. He was clever enough to know that if he were quartered with common deckhands such as Ant and Per, he'd best step down from his elevated ways. He had shed his fine clothes and adopted the same loose canvas trousers and cotton shirts that the rest of us wore. He'd braided his hair and tied it after Ant had warned him about how loose locks of hair could get tangled around a moving line and be ripped right off the scalp. He'd also bound the palms of his hands with leather; I suspected bloody blisters on them. Hemp lines are not gentle to handle.

He said no more to me, so I hastened down to await my next order.

It had been decades since I'd worked the deck of a ship, and never had I toiled on a ship like Paragon. The living nature of the ship meant that he could be an active participant in the journey. He could not set his own canvas nor take it in, but he could cry a better heading to the steersman, sense where currents ran swiftest and warn us of a line that needed tightening. He had a fine sense of depths and channels—something that he had proudly demonstrated as he guided his crew out of the harbour at Divvytown, and that he did again now as we sailed cautiously through the waterways of the Pirate Islands and finally into the open sea. As he sliced through the taller waves our diminished crew strove to keep pace with his needs.

I was not alone in marvelling at the ways of a liveship. The crewmembers we had taken on in Divvytown were openly delighted with how Paragon participated in his sailing. Before long the navigator was humbly asking permission to share her charts with the figurehead, and correcting them according to his knowledge. Given his way, Paragon himself became almost affable, and especially so with Boy-O and Kennitsson.

Even so, my transition from passenger to deckhand was not easy. I had always harboured a secret pride in how able I had remained into my sixth decade. Much of my physical strength I owed to the old Skill-healing that still coursed through my body and made unceasing repairs to it. But healthy is not necessarily hardened. Those first days were long ones for me. The calluses earned by wielding a sword or an axe are different to the rough palms that prickling hemp lines award to a sailor. In the rigorous days that followed, I ached in my legs and my back and my arms. Muscle in my limbs and a flattened belly came back to me slowly. My body healed itself, but healing can be as painful as being injured.

Despite the men we had gained in Divvytown, we still had a smaller crew, and fewer who were used to sailing a liveship. The end of my watch was no guarantee of uninterrupted rest. A cry for 'All hands!' might come at any moment. As Brashen had foretold, there was no friendly current to aid us in our south-western journey. Land became a smear of low cloud on the horizon behind us. When I awoke the next day, it was gone.

Spark and Per both thrived. They scampered happily about in the rigging with Ant. Clef was a good teacher, and now they had Boy-O as well, an experienced hand. Lant laboured alongside me, trying to teach his man's body the skills it would have been happier to acquire as a boy. I pitied him, but he did not complain. All of us ate as heavily as we were allowed, and took sleep whenever we could.

There was a hearty rhythm to the days. If I had been younger and had no other goal in life than to earn my bread it would have been satisfying. The animosity of the liveship's crew over how we would destroy the life they had always known was ground away in the day-by-day necessity of working alongside us. I avoided any topic that might remind them that, at the end of this journey, Paragon intended to become dragons.

I marvelled at Brashen's patience with Kennitsson. More than once, the captain had paired me with him. Prince FitzChivalry, Brashen always called me, and I finally grasped that he was making the boy see that even a royal prince did not hesitate to apply himself to the humblest task. But ultimately I think Kennitsson strove for the skills of a sailor not from Trell's orders but his own desire to be seen as equal or better at his duties than any of the deckhands. It was painful to watch. He would race a more experienced hand to a task and loudly exclaim, 'I can do it!' He sometimes scorned offers of help and corrections to his methods. He was not a stupid man, but he was overly proud and desperate to be right. Even more painful was seeing Boy-O caught between his parents and the man he wished to be friends with. Kennitsson treated Boy-O as if he were an affable puppy, sometimes showing scorn of the younger man's maritime skills. I sometimes saw Boy-O surreptitiously recoil a line in Kennitsson's wake or loose a line and reknot it. I said nothing but I was certain that if I was aware of it, his father certainly was. And if Brashen was letting it go by, it was not up to me to say anything. Still, it was darkly fascinating to watch Kennitsson seesaw between a man eager to learn the skills and a prince who could not admit that he did not know something. I hoped for no disasters.

Clef, the first mate, had seen Boy-O raised from infancy, and it was natural the two would be close so I was surprised when he befriended Kennitsson. Clef had been a youngster on Paragon in the days when Kennit had raped Althea and tried to send Paragon to the bottom, yet he seemed to take Kennitsson on his own merits. And when I observed Clef correct Kennitsson, the prince seemed better able to accept criticism than when Brashen intervened. I also feared that Per might be jealous over losing Clef's attention, but instead he attached himself to the group and soon they began to sit together at meals. When Per joined the three of them at dice one evening, I knew he had been accepted into that circle, and I let go of him. Boys seek out what they need.

Over the course of a few evenings, I saw Kennitsson move from ignoring Per to the mockery and teasing that preludes true friendship. I watched Kennitsson and Per conspire to merrily cheat Boy-O at cards until he had lost every dry bean they were using in lieu of coins. Boy-O's mock outrage when he discovered the ploy completed Per's initiation into that group. Clef began to pair Kennitsson with Per for some of his duties. More than once, I saw Per showing the prince the proper way to perform a task. They became friends, and I judged it good for both of them.

But it was not without missteps. I stood aside when Boy-O and Kennitsson undertook to get Per well and truly drunk. Every young man must pass that trial, and I judged that while he would suffer the next day, he would take no real harm from it. Boy-O especially had a heart for mischief rather than petty cruelty. What I had not counted on was that Per would, in his inebriation, invite them to our cabin to see the wonderful Elderling gifts the Rain Wilders had given us. When I chanced to step in, all three were well soused, and my lad was holding up one of Chade's firepots and trying to explain what he thought it was. The Elderling brick was upside-down on my bunk and the blanket had begun to smoulder. That did not upset me as much as seeing Bee's books in proximity to the scorched blanket.

I drove all three out of the cabin with some colourful curses and a solid kick to the rump for Per. He apologized profusely the next day, between bouts of vomiting over the railing, and Boy-O and Kennitsson both offered their contrition more sedately later. It cemented a bond of friendship between the three, and I felt that Per was now as safe aboard the *Paragon* as anyone could be.

Spark came to wake me from much-needed sleep to summon me to Amber's cabin one evening. I went bleary-eyed. The hard physical labour of being a sailor took a toll on me every day. 'It's important!' she hissed at me before wending her way like a cat between the hammocks of the other sailors.

I arrived at the cabin to find Per already there, looking as befuddled as I felt. I was relieved to see that I was meeting with the Fool and not Amber. 'We need to discuss our plans for rescuing Bee,' he announced.

'You are certain that she's alive?' Per asked. His hunger for confirmation made me cringe.

'I am,' the Fool asserted softly. 'I know it is hard for you to believe, after setting out solely with vengeance in mind. But I am certain she lives. And that changes all our plans.'

Per gave me a sidelong doubtful glance that I was glad the Fool could not see. I kept my features grave and still.

'You have all studied the map the Fitz made? It is essential that you have at least that much knowledge of the layout of Clerres Castle.'

They nodded, and Spark confirmed aloud, 'We have.'

'I've told you that the only way to get into the castle is at low tide, when we will join a crowd of folk who will have paid dearly for the privilege of crossing. I will be well disguised lest any recall me. We will think of roles for you.'

I caught my breath before I sighed. I still felt a solo venture in to set some poison or cut a few throats was my best route.

'Once we are inside, we must break away from the main flow of petitioners and conceal ourselves. We may have to separate to do so. Keep in mind that Bee does not know me or Spark. So, after nightfall, when we convene in the deserted washing courts, we must form two parties. Fitz and Per will be one. Lant, Spark and I are the other. Thus each party has a competent warrior. And someone who can open a locked door.' He smiled in Spark's general direction.

Worse and worse. I said nothing. Lant was looking at his hands. Per was listening intently. Spark seemed to have already been a party to this plan for she looked unsurprised.

'There are at most four places that Bee may be. On the roof of the stronghouse, the old harem quarters have been converted to cells for valuable prisoners who must be punished but not permanently harmed. She may be there, or in the cottages where the Whites are stabled.' I knew what his next words would be and dreaded hearing them. 'But there are also two lower levels below the castle. In the first one there are cells with stone floors and iron bars. Little light, and harsh conditions. I dread she may be there.' He drew a breath. 'On the lowest level are the worst cells and the place where torment is deliberate and prolonged. There the waste of the castle flows into an open basin, and then out to the sea. There is no light and the air stinks of excrement and death. That is the worst possible place she might be. And therefore it is the first place I must search for her. My party will begin at the lowest level. Fitz and Per will go to the rooftop cells. If you find her there, go to the washing courts. If not, check the cottages.'

Per opened his mouth to speak. A motion of my hand silenced him.

'Whether you find her or not in the cottages, go to the washing courts.' He drew a breath. 'After we have searched the cells, we will also search for the entry to the tunnel that my rescuers used to extricate me. If we are successful, and we have found Bee, two of us will immediately take Bee out that way. One of us will meet you in the washing courts to let you know where we have gone, and guide you to the tunnel.'

'What if we don't find the entrance to the tunnel?' Lant asked.

'We will bring extra garments for Bee, or perhaps the butterfly cloak. We will again conceal ourselves, and the next day, we will emerge to mingle with the petitioners, and leave with them as they flow out in a crowd.' His hands, one gloved and one bare, clutched one another. He knew how bad his plan was. I didn't need to tell him. It was the desperate plotting of a man who longed for something to be so.

'What if we don't find her?' Per asked in a faltering voice.

'Again, we hide, and leave with the tide of petitioners the next day. That may happen, for my dreams do not tell me if she has already arrived in Clerres or is simply bound there. We may have to wait.'

'And the dragons?' Lant asked. 'Tintaglia and Heeby both seemed intent on their vengeance. What if they arrive at Clerres before we do?'

The Fool's clutching hands rose to his collar and clung there. He licked his lips. 'I must trust that my dreams would show me such a disastrous event. As of yet, they have not. And so I have hope.' He gave a quick shake of his head as if to dash Lant's question from his mind. 'Does everyone understand the part they are to play? Are we agreed?'

I did not nod, but no one seemed to notice that. Spark spoke for the others. 'We all do. And now, perhaps, you can sleep.'

He rubbed his face with both hands and I saw what had escaped me before. He was boiling with anxiety. It took every bit of Chade's training for me to put warmth and certainty into my voice.

'Go to sleep, old friend. Per and I must return to our hammocks, for our watch begins soon. We should all rest while we can.'

'While we can,' he agreed, and Spark nodded to me as we left the small cabin. Lant walked with us as Per and I headed back toward our hammocks.

When we were well away from the Fool's door, Lant caught at my sleeve to halt me. 'Do you believe Bee is still alive?' he asked in a low voice. Per stepped closer to hear my reply.

I chose my words carefully. 'The Fool does. He makes a plan that puts finding her first. I am happy to follow it.' That was a lie. I added, 'It does not interfere with my own plans to take the lives of those who took her from me.'

And so we parted. I returned to my hammock, but could not find sleep again.

Day after long day, the horizon did not change. Water was all I could see when I went to sleep at the end of my watch, and when I arose to my duties. The weather held fine and grew warmer. We all browned in the sun except for Lady Amber, who remained a very pale gold, darker than the Fool had been but much lighter than Lord Golden. Once, the Fool had told me that it was believed that as White Prophets succeeded in their tasks, they would shed skin and become darker. He had become paler, and I wondered if it meant that the Servants had thwarted him in his goals. Lady Amber did what tasks she could, from scrubbing the turnips and potatoes to splicing lines. She ungloved her silver fingers for that task, and the rope seemed to obey and merge where she directed it. It reminded me uncomfortably of Verity smoothing the stone of his dragon, and I avoided watching her at that task.

Amber spent more time with Paragon than either of our captains would have preferred. Paragon welcomed her, and often Kennitsson and Boy-O joined her when she played music for him. Motley also spent a great deal of time with Paragon. Between my duties and Amber's time with the ship, I saw little of the Fool and I had little opportunity to worry about how aloof she had become.

Our progress was slow. The currents of the ocean did not favour us. The weather was kind but the winds were inconstant. On some days the wind slept and the canvas hung nearly limp. Sometimes, looking at the endless water, I wondered if we moved at all. The farther south we went, the warmer the days grew. Summer was upon us and light lingered long in the evenings.

One such a day I retired early to my bunk and closed my eyes. I was both weary and bored, but sleep eluded me. I tried to do as my wolf had taught me: centre myself in the now and refuse to worry about the future or dwell on the past. It had never been easy for me, and that afternoon was no exception. As I lay still, hoping for sleep to find me, a whisper of Skill came to me. *Da?*

I sat up straight, startled, and lost the contact. No, no, lie down, be very still, breathe slow and deep, and wait. Wait. It was like watching a game trail from up in a tree. Wait.

Da, can you sense me? It's Nettle. I got your bird, and I have news for you. Da?

I took slow deep breaths and tried to stay balanced on the knife's edge between sleep and wakefulness. I ventured into the Skill-current. It seemed weaker, almost elusive. *Nettle, I am here. Is all well with you? And your child?* A shiver went through me. Nettle's child, my grandchild. Banished from my mind for all these weeks.

Not yet. But soon. Her response was a whisper on the wind but with it came a warm thread of her pleasure that my first thought had been for her and the child. Soft as thistledown, her words floated to me. *Your bird message reached us, but I did not fully understand. We have sent Lady Rosemary as an emissary there. Why did you wish Skillhealers to go to Kelsingra?*

I believe it would benefit all. I opened my mind to her and shared my pity for the dragon-touched folk there. I added to it my practicality; an unshakeable alliance could be formed with these peoples, and possibly we would gain a greater understanding of the Skill if we had access to Kelsingra and all that the Skill had wrought there. I tempered it with a warning about dragon-Silver and my conviction that it was the same stuff that Verity had slathered onto his hands so that he could finish his stone dragon. *Incredibly powerful and dangerous stuff. Do not let Chade get wind of it or he will long to experiment with it! How is Chade? I miss him and so does Lant.*

Hush! Think not his name!

Her warning was too late. I felt a ripple of something, like a breeze that stirs the canvas before the wind hits a sail fully. Then Chade swept into my mind, obliterating me. He was mad, triumphantly so, and ecstatic with Skill. *FITZ!* He boomed my identity out into the Skill-current. As if he had violently stirred a pot of water, I felt that the Skill whirled and drenched me. *THERE YOU ARE, MY BOY! I'VE MISSED YOU SO! COME WITH ME, I'VE SO MUCH TO SHOW YOU!*

Dutiful! Coteries all, to me, to me! Contain Lord Chade. Contain him!

I was ripped out of myself. Torn from my body, my mind spread as thin as spilled wine on a table. I was a flurry of snowflakes scattered by the wind, the dispersing fog of breath on an icy night. I heard distant cries and shouts and sensed a struggle somewhere. Then, as clear as a drop of icy water on the back of my neck, I felt the uncertain touch of another mind.

Da? Are you a dream? Da?

I had never touched minds with Bee in the Skill-stream. I did not hear her voice; I did not see her face. But the touch of her thoughts was so uniquely Bee that I could have no doubt it was her.

It was feeble and thin, a child's voice shouting into strong wind over water. I reached for her. *Bee! Is it you, are you alive?*

Da? Where are you? Why didn't you come for me? Da?

Bee, where are you? My first desperate question.

On a ship. Bound for Clerres. Da? They are cruel to me. Please help me. Why don't you come for me?

Then, like a great sweeping wind, Chade blasted through my thoughts, scattering me. *Bee? Does she Skill, then? My daughter Skills, my Shine does. She is strong in the Skill, but they keep her from me!*

Da? DA?

Chade was a tumultuous wind, catching and scattering smaller Skill-entities in his roaring passage. I feared Bee would be tossed and broken, torn to shreds in any encounter. I shoved her away.

Bee, flee! Wake up, turn away, break clear. Get away! Don't touch your mind to mine.

Da? She clung to me, desperate and afraid.

There was no time to reassure her. I pushed her then, hard, as if I pushed her out of the path of a runaway horse. I felt her fear and hurt, but I tore myself clear of her reaching thought and engaged Chade to prevent him from scorching her. *Chade, stop! You are too strong! You will sear all of us to nothing, as Verity burned out poor August! Take control of your Skill, Chade, please!*

You, too, Fitz? Will you suppress me as well? Traitor! You are heartless. This is my magic, my birthright, my glory!

Then pour it down his throat if you must! Quickly! Three of the apprentices are having seizures!

That was Nettle, at a great distance, both shouting and Skilling with all her strength. I sensed Chade's anger and hurt that we were conspiring against him. We had all turned on him, he was certain of it, because we were jealous of his magic and wanted all his secrets. None of us had ever truly loved him, not one of us, except for Shine.

As abruptly as a curtain dropping at the end of the puppet-show, all was gone. There was no roaring Skill from Chade, no whisper from Nettle, and worst of all, when I groped for Bee's uncertain Skilling, I found nothing. Nothing at all.

I found I was on the floor beside my bunk. Tears were streaming unchecked down my cheeks.

She was out there, my Bee, tossed and torn in a storm of Skill, captured and treated badly. The Fool had been right all along. I could not give up. I plunged in again, sieving the Skill-current for her, over and over, until I felt my strength failing. When I came back to my surroundings, I was curled in a ball. My body ached and my head pounded. Old, I felt a hundred years old. I had failed and abandoned not only my child but my old mentor.

I spared a thought for him. Chade, poor old Chade, lost in the magic that he had so longed for. Now it mastered him, and he rode it as one rode a runaway steed. We had hurt him tonight, and I knew it was not the first time he had felt abandoned and persecuted. I wished I could be there to sit by his bed and take his hand and assure him that, yes, he was loved and had always been loved. His hunger for that had burned me almost as much as his wild Skilling.

But fiercely as I longed to be with Chade, my anxiety for Bee consumed me. On a ship, she had said, bound for Clerres. Alive. Absolutely alive! But in a terrible situation. But alive. And wondering why I had not come to save her. Her captors were cruel to her. But she lived! The amazement of that echoed through me like bells ringing. The surging joy of being certain she had survived collided with my terrible fears for her. How had she managed, all those months, alone with her captors? It burned that I had pushed her away when she reached for me.

But alive! Indubitably alive! That knowledge was air in my lungs, water after drought. I pulled myself to my feet. She was alive! I had to share the news with the Fool. Our primary quest was now her rescue!

And then bloody vengeance on those who had kept her from me.

'I already told you she was alive.'

I was still shaking, still breathing hard from my rush through the ship to find the Fool. To have Lady Amber be so dismissive of my news was maddening. 'This is different!' I asserted. 'You had a dream that might or might not have indicated that Bee was alive. I felt her Skill. She spoke to me! I *know* she is alive. On her way to Clerres. And treated poorly by those who hold her captive.'

Amber smoothed her skirts. I had found her standing at the railing, staring blindly out over the side of the ship. Waves slapped against us, but I saw no sign we were moving. My need for the ship to be moving, to be pounding his way through waves toward Clerres was a pain in my chest. Amber glanced at me empty-eyed and then turned her face to the sea. 'As I told you. Weeks ago. Months ago! Before we ever left Buckkeep, I urged you to rush to Clerres! Had you heeded me we would be there now, awaiting her arrival. Everything would have been different. Everything!' There was no ignoring the sharp rebuke in her tone. She spoke as if she were the Fool, but she was not.

I stood for a time, simply looking at her. I was on the point of walking silently away when she spoke again. Very quietly. 'It tires me. And it annoys me. All my life, people have doubted that I was the true White Prophet. But you, you are my Catalyst. You have seen what we have done. You took me to the door of death and drew me back again. I do not deny that my powers are greatly diminished. Even my vision of this world is light and shadow.

'But when I tell you that my dreams have returned, when I say I have dreamed a thing, and it is so or will be so, Fitz, you, of all people, should not doubt me. If I were to say that I doubted the truth of your Skilling, if I claimed you had merely had a dream, would you not be annoyed?'

'I suppose so,' I conceded. It was a sharp slap that she would not share my joy in finally being certain but only rebuked me for my doubts. I wished I had not hurried to her, wished I had kept my news to myself. Could she not understand how dangerous it felt to believe that my child was alive? How I feared the fall from such a high hope? Could she not grasp now how painfully I soared, knowing Bee was alive and fearing for her situation? The Fool would have understood that! I was abruptly taken aback at how odd a thought that seemed. Were the Fool and Amber truly so separate in my thoughts?

Yes. They were.

Amber had never saved Kettricken, or carried me on her back through a snowy night. She'd never known Nighteyes. She'd never been tortured and maimed. Never served King Shrewd through danger and treachery. I clenched my teeth. What, exactly, did I share with this Amber? Very little, I decided.

She was merciless as she continued. 'If you had believed me, we would be there, watching and waiting. We would be in a position to recover her before they could take her into their stronghold. As it is, we must wonder now, are they before us, are they behind us?'

I tried to find an argument to make her wrong, but I could not. Her rebuke was too stabbing an attack. I had not shared with her that Chade had been on a Skill-rampage and that Nettle and her coteries seemed barely able to contain one old man, and I decided I would not. I straightened from leaning on the railing. 'I'm going to get some sleep,' I told her. Later, perhaps, when he was the Fool, I'd share my Skill-fears and my agony of worry for Bee. Later, I might tell him how I had pushed her away, out of Chade's path but also away from me. I had come to Amber full of exhilaration from my contact with Bee and devastation that I could not sustain it or find her, but now I had no one to share that storm of emotions. I could not speak to Lant without tormenting him about the state of his father. I did not wish Spark to worry for Chade. Right now, I did not wish to supply Amber with any new quarrels to shoot at me.

'Walk away,' Amber said in a small, deadly voice. 'Walk away, Fitz. From things you don't want to hear. Things you don't want to feel. Things you don't want to know.'

I had halted at her first words, but as she continued, I did as she suggested. I walked away. She lifted her voice to call after me, her words freighted with anger. 'Would that I could walk away from what I know! Would that I could choose to disbelieve my dreams!'

I kept walking.

A ship never truly sleeps. Always, there are sailors on watch and all must be ready to leap to the deck at a moment's notice. But I was deeply asleep when someone shook my shoulder, and I came up ready to fight. By the hooded light of a dimmed lantern, I saw Spark regarding me with a mixture of alarm and amusement. 'What?' I demanded, but she shook her head and motioned that I should follow her. I rolled quietly from my hammock and threaded my way through sleeping sailors.

We emerged onto the deck. The wind was slight, the waves calm. Overhead, the stars were close and bright, the moon a paring. I hadn't bothered with a shirt or shoes but the air was so balmy I didn't miss them.

'Is something wrong?' I asked Spark.

'Yes.'

I waited.

'I know you thought less of me for bringing the book to Amber. For spying on you to see where you kept it. And you had the right to be distrustful of me. When last I tried to speak of this to you, you made it clear you did not wish to know any secrets. Well, now I come to betray trust to you again, and I expect your opinion of me will be even lower. But I cannot keep this secret any longer.'

My heart sank into the pit of my stomach. My thoughts immediately leapt to her and Lant, and I dreaded what she might tell me.

'It's Amber,' she said in a whisper.

I drew breath to tell her that I did not wish to know any of Amber's secrets. Amber's anger at me was a wall I did not want to breach. I felt both sullen and sulky about it. If Amber had a secret she did not wish to share with me, but told Spark, well, then they were both welcome to keep it to themselves.

But Spark didn't care if I wanted to know or not. She spoke quickly. 'She dreams your death. When we were on the river, it was only once, at most twice. But now it is almost every night. She talks and cries out warnings to you in her sleep, and wakes up shaking and weeping. She does not speak of it to me, but I know, for she talks in her sleep. "The son will die? How can the son die? It must not be, there must be another path, another way." But if there is, I do not think she can find it. It's destroying her. I do not know why she does not tell you of her nightmares.'

'Did you leave her just now? Does she know you've come to me?'

Spark shook her head to both questions. 'Tonight, she seems to sleep well. Even when she awakens weeping, I feign sleep. The one time I tried to help her, she told me not to touch her and to leave her alone.' She looked at the deck. 'I don't want her to know that I told you this.'

'She won't,' I promised. I wondered if or how I would let the Fool know that I knew. He had told me that the more often something was dreamed, the likelier it was. During our years together, he had often helped me dodge deaths. I recalled how he had summoned Burrich to the top of the tower on the evening Galen had beaten me. Together they had drawn me back from the edge where I had crawled, inspired by Galen to hurl myself down. He'd warned me of a poisoning in the Mountain Kingdom. Carried me on his back to safety when I'd been felled by an arrow. He'd often told me that in his dreams my survival was so unlikely as to be nearly impossible, but that he had to keep me alive, at any cost, so that I could help him change the world.

And we'd accomplished that. He'd dreamed his own certain death, and together we had defied that.

I believed his dreams. I had to, except when they were too terrifying to believe. And then I always pretended I could defy them.

And now he dreamed my death. Again. Or did he? Was I still the Unexpected Son in his visions, or was Bee? Did we hurtle toward a rescue that he believed could not succeed? I felt supremely unmoved at the thought of my own death. If my death was the price of rescuing Bee, I'd pay it and gladly. And I was suddenly relieved to think that Lant and the Fool would be there to take her safely back to Buckkeep. I knew that Riddle and Nettle would take her in, and probably do a far better job of raising her than I could.

But if he dreamed we would reach Clerres only to have her snatched away into death— No. I would not, could not believe it. I would not allow that to be.

Was that what had made Amber so callous when I shared my news? Did she now believe that Bee lived, but would not survive to be rescued?

No! It had to be me. I was the Unexpected Son, not Bee. Please, Eda and El, not Bee.

Spark was still staring at me, her face pale in the starlight. 'It's not the first time he has dreamed me dead,' I told her. I managed a crooked smile. 'Remember, when he is the Prophet, I am the Catalyst. The Changer. I have no intention of dying, or letting anyone else die. Go back to sleep, Spark. Get rest while you can. What is to be, may be. Or may not!'

She stood silent and I saw a battle waged inside her. She lifted her eyes to meet mine and added defiantly, 'She sees more than she admits to you.'

I nodded to that. 'He always has,' I told her and turned away from her.

I let my gaze wander back over the water. After a time, I heard her light footsteps bear her away. I let out my pent-up sigh. I wished it were all over. All the doubts and uncertainties finished. They wearied me more than any axe-fight. I wanted to be finished with waiting and preparing. Yet the waters stretched endlessly before me like crumpled paper under the uncertain moonlight.

Somewhere upon those waters, another ship moved, toward Clerres, with my daughter aboard. Before us? Behind us? I had no way of knowing.

TWENTY-TWO

The Butterfly Cloak

Wasps sting when their nest is threatened. I went to fetch a clay flowerpot for my mother. I took one from the top of the stack, not knowing that wasps had built a nest between it and the one below. They rushed out in a horde and chased me as I fled. They stung me over and over and the pain was like fire eating into my flesh. They are not like bees, who must weigh an attack against their own lives. Wasps are more like men, able to kill again and again, and still go on living. My cheek and neck were swollen, and my hand was a shapeless lump with sausage fingers. My mother put the sap of ferns and cool mud on the stings. And then took oil and a flame and killed them all, burning their nest and their unhatched children in vengeance for what they had done to her daughter. This was before I could speak clearly. I was astonished at her hatred of them; truly I had not known my mother capable of such cold anger. When I stared at her, as the nest burned, she nodded to me. 'While I live, no one shall hurt you and go unpunished for it.' I knew then I must be careful of what I told her about the other children. My father may once have been an assassin. My mother remained one.

Bee Farseer's journal

There are so many songs about sailing off the edge of the world. Some say one goes over an immense waterfall and reaches a land of gentle and wise people and strange animals. In other tales, the sailors reach a land of intelligent talking animals who find humans disgusting and rather stupid. The one I liked best was the tale of sailing off all known charts and finding a place where you are still a child, and

424

you can speak with the child and warn him to make better choices. But on this voyage, I had begun to feel that when one sailed off the edge of the world, one entered a realm of endless work and boredom and the same watery horizon every day.

The reality of sailing off the edge of all known charts was that one man's unknown territory was another man's pond. Paragon asserted that he had been to Clerres and the adjacent islands when he was Igrot's ship, and that even Kennit had been there as a boy. Igrot had been obsessed with fortune-tellers and omens, a trait that some stories said had been passed on to Kennit. The crew we had taken on in Divvytown included a competent navigator. She had never sailed to Clerres, but had a chart from her grandfather. She was a seasoned deckhand, and as the trade routes familiar to Althea and Brashen were lost in the distance, she spent most of her time with them. Nightly they consulted the stars and she called a course to Paragon and most nights he confirmed it.

The slow days melted one into another. There were minor diversions. One day when there was no wind to speak of Clef brought out a pipe and whistled us up a wind. If it was magic it was a kind that I could not feel and had never seen before. I pretended it was coincidence. Per got a splinter in his foot and it became infected. Althea helped me draw it out and treated it with two herbs I didn't know. He was given a day to rest. Motley had become an accepted member of the crew. Any moment when she was not with Amber, she spent with Paragon. She rode on the figurehead's shoulder or even on top of his head. When the winds were good and he cut through the waves, she flew before him.

The sad thing about boredom is that one only learns to value it when it is exploded by a disaster, or the threat of one. I witnessed the changing relationships among our crewmembers from a distance, watching the tensions that any long voyage or campaign brings. I hoped to see those interior storms break apart and pass us by, yet one afternoon, as I worked alongside Lant mending a sail, he said to me the words I had dreaded. 'Kennitsson likes Spark. And he likes her too much.'

'I've noticed that he likes her.' In truth, I'd noticed that almost all the crew liked her. Ant had regarded her as a rival at first, and Brashen had shouted at the girl more than once for being reckless in her efforts to show herself the better sailor. But that competition had dissolved into a solid friendship. Spark was lively, friendly, capable and hard-working. She wore her dark curly hair in a thick unruly braid now and her bare feet were callused from racing down the deck and up the rigging. The sun had baked her as dark as polished wood, and the work had muscled her arms. She glowed with health and good fellowship. And Kennitsson's eyes followed her as she worked, and he almost always managed to sit across from her at the galley table.

'Everyone's noticed it,' Lant replied darkly.

'And that's a problem?'

'It isn't. Yet.'

'But you think it will be?'

He gave me an incredulous look. 'Don't you? He's a prince, accustomed to getting anything he wants. And he's the son of a rapist.'

'He isn't his father,' I said quietly, but could not deny the lurch of anxiety his words woke in me. I asked the next question carefully. 'Is Spark worried by it? Did she ask you for protection?'

He paused before he answered. 'No, not yet. I don't think she sees the danger. But I don't want to wait for something bad to happen.'

'So are you asking me to intervene?'

He jabbed his needle through the heavy, folded canvas. 'No. I just want you to know before something happens. So maybe you would back me, if it comes to that.'

'It won't come to that,' I said quietly.

He turned to look at me, wide-eyed.

'If you are wise, you will do nothing until Spark asks for your protection. She isn't the sort of girl who runs and hides behind a man. If there's a difficulty, she should be able to handle it. And I think the quickest way for you to make her angry would be to interfere before she's asked for any help. If you want, I'll speak to the captains about it. This is their ship to keep order on. I know you have feelings for Spark, but—'

'Enough. I'll do as you suggest.' He bit the words off and then began sewing with some ferocity.

For the rest of that day I watched Spark and Kennitsson. There was no denying he was aware of her, and that she possibly enjoyed it. I did not see her flirting with him, but she laughed at his jokes. And I could see how Lant, constrained by both honour and duty, might chafe to see it. It made me both weary and envious of their youth. How many years had it been since I had felt the stabs of jealousy and the painful doubts of loving someone I could not claim? It was both a relief to be free of such turmoil, and a reminder of the years that I carried on my shoulders.

I teetered on the edge of interfering. I tried to decide if I should have a private conversation with Spark, but feared that would seem more like a rebuke to her. And if I spoke to Prince Kennitsson, I wondered how he would react. If his attention was but a friendly flirtation, I'd feel like a meddling fool. And if he had genuine feelings for Spark, I imagined he would react as I had when Lady Patience had tried to warn me away from Molly. The situation was complicated even more by my growing friendship with the young man. His pride still made him prickly, but it was evident that he was doing his best to become a solid sailor. He had become more adept at scrubbing out his own garments and generally tending to the tasks that servants had performed for him since his birth, though he was still uncertain of whether the crew was mocking him or joking with him when someone included him in a jest. His pride was a high wall for him to batter through, but he was trying.

More than once now I had slipped the butterfly cloak from its storage and ghosted the deck beneath it. On a ship where there was precious little privacy, it gave me a tiny hidden space when I could sit where no one would tread on me and be ignored by all. My lengthy time as Chade's spy had eroded forever all guilt I might feel at being a party to other people's conversations, but I did not deliberately seek them out on the ship. Ant's close friendship with our Divvytown navigator was certainly not my business, nor did I attempt to hear the morose conversations between Althea and Brashen on the aft deck.

On the evening when I found my usual quiet place occupied by two of the Divvytown sailors having a smoke, I drifted forward soundlessly toward the foredeck. I halted what I hoped was a safe distance away and felt mild alarm to see Kennitsson stretched full length on the deck. I took two more cautious steps and could see that his eyes were closed, but his chest was rising and falling in the slow and steady rhythm of someone in a deep sleep.

Paragon spoke as softly as a parent by a sleeping child's bed. 'I know you're there.'

'I supposed you might,' I said as softly.

'Come closer. I'd like to talk to you.'

'Thank you, but I think I'd best talk to you from here.'

'As you wish.'

I nodded silently. I hunkered down on the deck, my back to his railing, leaned my head back and looked up at the stars.

'What?' the ship demanded. He had crossed his arms and was looking over his shoulder at me.

His face was so like mine as it had been in those years that I wasn't sure if I were talking to him or myself. 'Once, a long time ago, I tried to walk away from everything. From my family, from my duty. For a time, it seemed to make me happy. But it didn't, really.'

'You are referring to me restoring myself. To becoming the two dragons who have been trapped in this wood for six of your generations.'

'Yes.'

'You think I will be unhappy?'

'I don't know. I just think that you might want to reconsider. You have a family. You are loved. You are—'

'I am trapped.'

'I was, too. But—'

'I do not intend to remain a ship. Save your breath, human.' After a moment, he added, 'You may resemble me, but I am not you. My circumstances are completely different. And I did not ask to awaken to this servitude.'

I thought of saying that I'd never desired the role my family had demanded of me. Then I wondered if I had. I watched Kennitsson's chest rise and fall slowly. Very slowly. I started to go down on one knee beside him but the ship spoke. 'He's fine. Don't wake him.'

The small charm engraved with his father's profile lay in the hollow of his neck, the fine silver chain pressed firmly against his flesh. I thought of how much I'd dislike having anything that snug around my throat.

'It doesn't bother him,' Paragon told me.

'Can it speak to him?'

'Why do you care? It's nothing to do with you.'

'It might be.' *Tread carefully, Fitz.* I tried to wonder if discussing it with the ship were less volatile than bringing it up to Althea. I drew a careful breath. 'There is a young woman on your deck named Spark. She is under my protection.'

The ship gave a snort of disdain. 'I know her. She pleases me. And she scarcely needs your protection.'

'She's very capable, but I don't wish to see her forced into circumstances where she has to defend herself. If it came to that, I don't think it would go well for Kennitsson.'

'What are you implying?' the ship demanded and I felt the sudden press of his mind against my defences. I thickened my walls, too late. The ship's upper lip lifted in what was almost a wolfish snarl. 'You think so little of him?'

'I've never heard anyone deny what his father did to Althea. And the wizardwood charm he wears is filled with his father's thoughts. Why should I not be concerned?'

'Because he is not his father! He does not carry his father's memories.' The ship paused and added ominously, 'I carry them. I took them so that no one else would have to bear them.'

And then I was thrown face down on the rough wood of the deck. The skin was torn from my palms and knees by the impact. I tried to rise but a man's weight was suddenly on my back, his thick forearm like a bar of iron against my throat. I struggled to rise but he was bigger than me, and heavier. His beard rasped against the side of my face and his voice was a growl as he said, 'Such a tender little bit of manflesh you are. Buck as you will; I'll tame you. I relish a lively ride.' A hand gripped the hair on top of my head and pressed my face down against the wood. I tried to seize his arm and take it away from my throat, but the thick embroidered sleeves of his shirt slipped and slid in my grasp.

I tried to scream but I could not get any air. I braced my palms on the deck and tried to throw his body off mine. I heard another man laugh as the man on top of me pressed himself against me. As the forearm across my windpipe cut off all air and sparks floated in darkness before my eyes, I felt with horror what he intended for me.

I snapped back to awareness of myself as Fitz. I dropped my hands from gripping at a forearm that didn't exist. I was panting with a boy's fear and outrage. I staggered to my feet. I was furious and affronted and full of a black fear I could not vanquish. *Never again!* I vowed and then became completely myself. Not my pain. Not my fury and shame.

'Kennitsson knows nothing of that,' the ship went on softly, as if the storm of memories had never been. 'Don't leave, Buckman. Stay where you are, and I'll share a bit more of Kennit's youth with you. I've plenty of that. Plenty of hours of him crawling, torn and bleeding, to where Igrot could not reach him. Nights of fever wracking his body, days when his eyes were swollen to slits from the beatings. Let me share with you some of my wonderful family memories.'

I felt sickened but it only increased my outrage. 'If he . . . if that was done to him, how could he bear to pass it on? How could he stand to become the same sort of monster?'

'Interesting that another human does not understand it any more than I do. Perhaps it was his only way to be rid of it. To not be the victim by becoming the . . . victor? You cannot imagine the ways he fought the monsters that assailed his dreams. How he struggled to become everything that Igrot was not. Igrot pretended the finesse of a gentleman, sometimes. It was a façade and I've no idea where it came from.

'The things he forced that boy to do and be, Kennit never understood. To dress as a fine little man in a lace shirt and serve Igrot at table, just so the pirate could later batter him and rip the garments from his body. Kennit was the one who took a hatchet to my face. Did you know that? I held him in my hands as he did it. Igrot laughed as he chopped my eyes away. It was our bargain. Kennit would blind me and Igrot would not rape him again. But Igrot never kept his word to anyone about anything. But we did. Oh, how we kept the promises we made in the dark and bloody nights!'

I heard the ship grind his teeth together. The wave of emotions that assailed me made my heart thunder and my breath come short. I wondered that Althea and Brashen did not come running. The ship spoke to my thought.

'Oh, they guess and suspect, but they do not know all that happened on my decks. Neither are they privy to our conversation now. All those years, with my body trapped as a ship and my mind trapped as a battered boy! Until the day we killed them. He poisoned them all, with chips of my face ground and mixed into their soup. And when they were all sickened, all grovelling and clasping their bellies and too weak to stand, Kennit finished them. With the same hatchet he'd used to take my eyes, he took their lives, one by one and their blood and memories soaked into my decks. Every man who had watched him shamed and humiliated felt that hatchet. And Igrot, last of all. So lovingly he dismembered him.

'So I have all those memories, too, Buckman.' He stopped speaking for a time. He turned his back to me and stared out over the water. 'Can you imagine, human? To have a young creature you love endure such things as you stand helplessly by? Unable to kill his tormentor without killing him? Over and over, I took his memories. Twice, I took his death, and held him safe until he could bear to return to his body again. I could dim those memories for him but I could not erase them.'

His voice became oddly distant as if he spoke of events that had happened a hundred years ago. 'Kennit could not bear to keep those memories. He would have had to kill himself. So he killed me instead. We agreed to it. I no more wanted to live with those memories than he did. We killed them all, one by one, and Igrot last of all. Then Kennit gathered a fine share of the loot that was then on board, scuttled me and watched from the ship's boat as I listed and took on water and finally capsized and sank.

'I tried to die. I thought I would die. But I do not need air and I do not need food. I hung there, upside-down under the water. The waves pushed me about, and then a current caught me. And when I realized it was bearing me home, back to Bingtown, I let it. And so eventually they found me, hull up, in the mouth of Bingtown Harbour, a hazard to navigation. They dragged me in to a beach and pulled me up out of reach of the tides and chained me there. The mad ship. The pariah. And there Brashen Trell and Amber and Althea found me.'

There were stars in the clear night sky above us, and he cut smoothly through the waves, propelled by a light but constant wind. We could have been the only two living things in the world. The young man stretched on the deck had not moved and I wondered if Paragon held him under, immersed in sleep. I wondered how much of this tale he would share with Kennitsson, and why he had shared it with me.

'I will give him none of it,' the ship told me. 'When I go as dragons, it will all go with me.'

'Do you think the human memories will vanish when you become your dragons?'

'No.' He spoke with certainty. 'The memories of dragons and the recall of the serpents that go between the egg and the dragon are what makes us whole. We forget nothing, not if we are properly cased and hatched. I will shake off this ship's body and the shape of your flesh, but always I will carry with me the horror of what humans can do to one another for amusement.'

I found I had little to say to that. I looked down on the sleeping young man. 'So he will never know what his father went through?'

'He knows enough of it. What little Etta and Wintrow and Sorcor knew, he knows. He need not bear the actual memories. Why should he know more of it than that?'

'To understand what his father did?'

'Oh. Does knowing what the child Kennit endured make you understand what the man Kennit did?'

I listened to my heart beating. 'No.'

'Nor I. Nor would he. So why burden him with it?'

'Perhaps so he would never do likewise?'

'That bit of dragon womb the lad wears strapped to his throat, carved in his father's likeness, was worn by his mother for many more years than Kennit. She spent her childhood as a whore. Can you conceive that she thought of Kennit as the first person to treat her with kindness? That she came to love him for saving her from that life?'

'I did not know,' I said quietly.

'Believe me, Kennitsson knows more of rape than he would care to admit, and I doubt he will perpetuate upon others what his mother regards with abhorrence.' He took in air and sighed it out, a sound like waves on fine sand. 'Perhaps that was why his mother bound it so tightly about his throat before she allowed him to board.'

Kennitsson stirred. He rolled over and opened his eyes and stared wordlessly up at the sky. I held my breath and stood motionless. The cloak was not a perfect protection. It took on the texture and colour and seeming dimension of whatever was behind me, but the wind was ruffling it and I suspected that would look peculiar. Still he did not look toward me. He spoke to the sky, or the ship. 'I should have been born on these decks. I should have grown up here. I've missed so much.'

'We both have,' Paragon replied. His voice was kindly. 'There is no going back, my son. We will take what we have now, and keep it with us forever.'

'When you turn into dragons, you will leave me.'

'Yes.'

Kennitsson sighed. 'You didn't even have to think about it.'

'Any other answer would be impossible.'

'Will you come back to visit? Or will you just be gone forever?'

'That I don't know. How can I possibly know?'

Kennitsson sounded very young as he asked, 'Well, what do you hope you will do?'

'I think I will have to relearn how to be a dragon. And there will be two of us, me and yet not me. I cannot speak for what happens after. I can only say that for the days we have left together, I will be here with you.'

I ghosted away. That conversation was not for me. I had enough pain of my own without hearing another child abandoned by a father. I had stayed too long with the figurehead. It might be that both Amber and Spark would be sleeping. I moved across the deck in a series of pauses, avoiding the crew. In the dark of the companionway, I stood outside the door and silently removed the cloak. I gave it a shake and carefully folded it. I tapped lightly on the door three times. No one spoke so I eased it open.

The Fool was supine on the floor. A faint light came in the porthole, just enough to distinguish him there. 'Fitz,' he greeted me amiably.

I looked down at him and then at the upper bunk. 'No Spark?'

'On duty tonight. So. The butterfly cloak again?'

'How did you know?'

'I heard the snap of fabric outside the door. I guessed it was the cloak and you just confirmed it. Where were you spying?'

'I wasn't. It's one way to be alone. To be invisible even when there are others nearby. But I did spend some time with Paragon.'

'That's a dangerous pastime. Stand clear, please.' I moved until my back touched the door. He brought his knees quickly up to his chest and attempted to vault to his feet. He failed, crashing sideways into the bunk with a force that would leave bruises. He made not a squeak at the pain. Instead, he slowly stood, and then sat down on the bunk. 'Not quite able to do that yet. But I will.'

'I know you will,' I said. If will alone could make a thing be, the Fool could master his old tumbler's tricks.

I pulled my old pack out from under the bed. Reaching inside, I found the Elderling fire-brick and made sure it was upright before I tucked the folded cloak beside it. I reached past my folded clothing and Bee's books. The tubes of Silver I felt through the shirt wrapping them. Chade's exploding pots in the very bottom. As I resettled everything securely, I asked lightly, 'Any more dreams, Fool?'

He made a dismissive sound. A moment later, he said, 'I should have known that Paragon would be aware of my dreams. What did he tell you?'

'Nothing about what you dream. But he did share with me, in an impressively vivid manner, a bit of what shaped Kennit.' I wedged my pack back under the bunk in an upright position and sat down beside the Fool. I had to bow my head to fit. 'What monsters humans are! I'd rather be a wolf.'

He surprised me by suddenly leaning on me. 'Me, too.' After a moment, he added, 'I'm sorry. I've been angry with you. That wasn't fair. But it also wasn't fair for you to doubt my dreams. Have you touched minds with Bee again?'

'No. I've tried several times, but I can't find her. I must be so careful. Chade is out there, raging like a storm. Twice he has come at me, demanding I join him. At first, I sensed Nettle there, too, and the coterie trying to bring him under control. To confine him to his body. The last time, I didn't sense them at all. But if Chade is pursuing me and Bee gets caught up in that, it might very well burn out her abilities. She was very tentative, and I pushed her away. I know I confused her.' I stopped. That was enough for him to know. My pain and shame were my own.

'You didn't tell me any of that.'

'You were angry.' I paused. 'So. Your turn. What did you dream?'

He was quiet.

I tried to keep my voice light. 'I suppose we both die. Again.'

He drew in a deep breath and his gloved hand sought my wrist. 'I don't want to sleep, Fitz. I sit up here in the bunk, in the dark both day and night, and I try not to sleep. Because I don't want to dream. But I do. And the urge to speak the dreams, to write them down, is so strong it makes me ill. But I cannot write them down, for I've not enough sight, even if I had ink. And I don't want to tell them to anyone.'

'Not telling the dreams makes you sick?'

'It's like an obsession. The true dreams must be spoken and shared.

At the very least, written down.' He laughed low. 'The Servants count on that. They harvest the dreams of those poor half-Whites like farmers harvesting grapes. Everything goes into their library of dreams and predictions. All is processed, like blowing the chaff from grain. All is preserved. Referenced and cross-referenced. Ready for them to employ, to see what they can predict and how they can profit from it.' He leaned in hard to me like a child fleeing nightmares and I put my arm around him to brace him. He shook his head. 'Fitz. They will know we are coming. They have Bee and they will know we are coming. This can't end well for any of us.'

'So tell me. Don't let me go into this blind.'

He choked out a laugh. 'Oh, no. I'm the one who goes into it blind, Fitz. You die. You drown. In darkness, in cold seawater and in blood you drown. There. Now you know. I don't know what good it does us, but you know.' I felt his shoulders slump in the dimness. 'And I have the small relief of having told my dreams.'

Cold crept through me. My mouth might claim not to believe him, but my guts did. 'Couldn't I freeze to death?' I asked in a falsely light voice. 'I've heard that you just fall asleep and it's done.'

'Sorry,' he said, and I heard the same effort in his voice. 'I don't get to decide how it happens. I'm simply told it does.'

'And you?'

'That's the worst part. I think I live through it.'

I had a moment of relief. Then it died. He was not certain of his survival. 'And Bee?' My voice shook. 'I know you've dreamed her alive. Do we save her? Does she go home?'

He spoke hesitantly. 'I think she is like you. She is a crossroads of many possible futures. I've seen her wearing a crown with alternating spires of flame and darkness. But she also appears as broken manacles. One who frees things. And as the shattered vessel.'

'What is the shattered vessel?'

'Something broken beyond repair,' he said quietly.

My child. Molly's daughter. Broken beyond repair. Some part of me had known that her experience must do that to her. She would be as broken as the Fool and I were. Something inside my chest hurt at the thought. My voice creaked. 'Well. Who wouldn't break? I broke. You broke.'

'And we both emerged stronger.'

'We both emerged,' I modified his words. 'I was never sure I understood what Regal's torture had done to me. Part of me had died in that cell, both literally and figuratively. I was alive today. I'd never know if I'd lost more than what I had found. Useless to wonder. 'What else?' I demanded.

His head lolled forward slightly and then twitched up. I changed my question. 'How long have you been awake?'

'I don't know. I doze off and then awaken and I don't know how long I've been asleep. Blindness is peculiar, Fitz. No day, no night. And not darkness, if you want to know.'

'Any other dreams or thoughts you want to share with me?'

'I dream of a nut that is dangerous to crack. Sometimes I hear a nonsense ditty: "The trap is the trapper and the trapper is trapped." But it isn't always dreams. Sometimes I see . . . like a crossroads, but one with an infinite number of paths starring away from a centre. When I was a youngster, I saw those often and clearly. After you brought me back to life, I didn't see any for a long time. Not until Bee touched me in the market that day. That was incredible. I touched her and I knew she was the centre of a multitude of paths. She saw them, too. I had to draw her back from making too swift a choice.'

His voice faltered to a stop.

'Then what happened?' I demanded in consternation.

He gave a snort of laughter. 'Then I believe you knifed me in the belly. A number of times, but I lost count after two.'

'Oh.' Cold roiled through me. 'I wasn't sure you recalled any of that.' I felt the weight of his body against my shoulder. 'I'm sorry,' I said.

'It's too late for that.' He patted me with his gloved hand and straightened up with a sigh. 'I've already forgiven you.'

What can one say to that?

He continued, 'Paragon. When I looked up and saw Paragon as we came into dock at Trehaug . . . he was shining with pathways. There were others there, at that junction, leading back to Kelsingra or into Trehaug itself, but most were the ones that led to Clerres, the straightest, shortest ones, began with Paragon.'

'So that was why you insisted we must stay with him?'

'Now you believe in me?'

'I don't want to. But I do.'

'I feel the same.'

Silence claimed us both. I waited. After a time, I realized he was deeply asleep. I moved him gently from my shoulder onto the bunk. I lifted his legs up onto the bed. It reminded me of how I used to put Hap back to bed after his nightmares, all those years ago. The Fool pulled his knees in closer to his chest and slept curled defensively. I sat down again on the edge of the bunk. He would sleep and he would dream, whether he would or no.

And I would Skill.

I exhaled slowly, letting my breath blow away my boundaries and immediately became more aware of the ship. 'Excuse me,' I muttered as if I had bumped against a stranger in a crowd. Then I ignored his presence and reached out, feeling for the Skill-current. It was there, but it was calmer than I'd felt it in months. It was as constant as the wind that gently filled the sails and pushed us through the waves. I moved with the Skill-current, letting it carry my thoughts and will toward Buckkeep and to my daughter Nettle.

She was sleeping. I eased into her dream thoughts, woke her gently. *How are you, and your child?*

Chade's dead.

The news flew from her mind to mine, drenching me with her urgency that I know. Her grief swept in and woke my as-yet-unformed sorrow. For a time, that was all there was. I did not ask her how. He was old, it had been coming for a very long time. Deprived of the herbs and kept from the Skill that he had been using for so long to rejuvenate himself, his years had caught up to him.

I blame myself. We gave him delvenbark to quench his Skill. He had grown so randomly strong with it. He would be calm, and then he was like a cold wind blasting. Two of the new apprentices decided to leave the training because his spells were so frightening. Even Shine had come to dread his moments of strength, for no matter how she deadened herself, he would seize her and tumble her into the Skill with him. She was terrified. As were we all!

So I authorized the delvenbark. I changed all the pages who had been carrying out his errands. I suspect they were fetching more than food and wine for him! After three days of it, it blocked his Skill, and he became . . . an old man. Kindly but fretful, and old. We let him have visits with Shine again; I'd had to keep her away from him. He . . . he didn't seem to understand why we had kept his daughter away. He was so confused. He would talk to Shrewd's portrait . . . Oh, Fitz, I fear he died thinking

I was needlessly cruel, that I had taken his daughter and his magic from him, simply for meanness. Simply to control him.

I felt Riddle. He'd heard her crying, I surmised, and awakened. I felt him as if he were armour closing around her, hammered metal holding her in and upright. Anything that wanted to hurt her would have to go through him first. I thought grief had numbed me, but suddenly relief soared in my heart. *I am glad Riddle is there with you.*

So am I. I'll tell him that.

Did you get our bird messages?

Yes. Chade's message from Lant was clutched in his hand. I don't know how many times Shine read it aloud to him, Fitz. He was smiling when we found him. A calm, sweet smile.

I realized abruptly, *I have to tell Lant.* Then, *I can't.*

Your first thought was correct. You must tell him. As I had to tell you.

I will. I didn't know how or when, but I would tell him. And Spark. I wondered if I now understood the Fool's compulsion to speak of his dreams. I did not want to tell them. Yet I desperately wanted to share the news, as if grief were a heavy burden to be spread out among those who must bear it.

Yes, she agreed with me. *And it's good to know you are alive. I have reached out to you over and over these last few days. When none of us could reach you with the Skill, we feared the worst.*

I'm on a liveship His presence is . . . pervasive. Even as I Skilled to her I could feel the ship sharing what I told her. *I am sorry to have worried you.*

I understand. I will immediately wake Dutiful to tell him.

Then my own news burst from me without warning. *The Fool has dreamed that Bee is alive. And the last time I could reach you with the Skill, when Chade so abruptly parted us? I felt Bee. I knew her touch.*

The winds of all the worlds blew between us and the shushing of waves whispered against every shore. What news was more shocking? That Chade had died or Bee might still live?

I felt her shock pour through me. *Where is she? How is she? Have they mistreated her? Does she think we abandoned her? How did she survive passing through that Skill-stone? How is it possible she lived and we gave up on her, for months!*

I don't know. That was the torment of it, so much I didn't know. I was not going to tell my pregnant daughter that her small sister was miserable and mistreated. That I would lie about, with a clear conscience. I agonized enough for the both of us. I would not put that burden on her. *I had just a brush of her against my senses. I know she is bound for Clerres, as are we. I do not know if she is ahead of us or behind us. Only that she is on a ship bound for Clerres. That was all. And the Fool dreamed of her, alive. It's little to go on, but I will take heart from it.*

Her thoughts suddenly swept over me, a mistress of war awakened. *I will muster an army of warriors and Skill-users. Elliania has brought up this proposal more than once to me. We will come. We will take back what is ours and leave nothing but ruins and bodies.*

No! For now, do not send any vast force in this direction. We think our best chance is to go in quietly.

You will negotiate for her return?

That thought had never even occurred to me. I had set out on a mission of vengeance, planning only to kill. The thought of Bee in their hands had only made me more determined to see their blood.

I am still on a ship, bound for Clerres. I will decide when I arrive there and study the situation. Perhaps I shall negotiate. There were many ways to negotiate. Taking hostages immediately sprang to mind. My thoughts went winging off, and I knew that Nettle sensed that.

How are you? I asked her.

Heavy. Tired. Happy. Sometimes.

Sometimes. When she was thinking of her baby rather than the death of Chade or the torment of her small sister. *I'm sorry I woke you. And sorry that Chade is gone. I will tell Lant. And you should rest now.*

She laughed. *Rest. While thinking of little Bee in the hands of kidnappers. Oh, Da, does life ever become simple?*

Only for a few moments, my dear. Only for a few moments.

I drew myself away from her as if we were unclasping hands. For a time longer, I floated in the Skill. I wondered if some remnant of Chade remained in this flow, some ghost of Verity or perhaps even my father. I had encountered presences in the Skill. I was not sure what they were, only that they were far larger beings than I was. Larger? Richer, deeper, more fully formed. Eda and El? Ancient Elderlings or Skill-users who had acquired more presence in that flow?

I gathered my courage. *Bee. Can you hear me?* I formed an image of my little girl in my mind. Little Bee. I saw her in her old-fashioned clothing, I saw her doubting gaze as she looked up at me. I smelled the fading scent of honeysuckle on a warm summer night. Then I saw all the ways I had failed her. No. This was not helping. I'd never find her that way.

I pushed aside reluctance and tried to reconstruct that moment of contact we'd had. With Chade rushing down on us like a summer squall on a small boat, pushing and scattering and threatening.

Fitz, my boy!

An echo in the vast current of Skill. A brief recollection of Chade, like a perfume on a spring breeze. Dead. Gone.

The flood of loss was too much. I tried again to reach for Bee but I was groping in dark water. My child was as gone as Chade was.

I drew back from the Skill-current, and opened my eyes to the darkness of the Fool's chamber. He was sleeping deeply. There was no one else in the room. Sitting on the floor, I pulled my knees up tight to my chest and bowed my head over them. Chade's boy wept.

TWENTY-THREE

Clerres

The Unexpected Son arrives cloaked in a power that none can see but all can feel. It shimmers and floats and confuses both eye and mind. In my dream, he is one, then two, then three creatures. He opens his cloak and fury burns inside him, flames that make me fall back before their heat. He closes his cloak and he is gone.

An Unexpected Son has appeared in various guises and has been dreamed one hundred and twenty-four times. In the last thirty years, it has been dreamed seventy times. In every case, the dreamer reported a sense of foreboding. One described it as the cringing servant who expects punishment. Another reported a sense of shame before justice.

I have dreamed my own form of the dream of the Unexpected Son. I believe it is a dream of justice and punishment to come, brought to those who least expect it. And I have dreamed it more than a dozen times. I believe this dream is an inevitable future. I have studied other dreams of the Son, attempting to find from whence he comes, and to whom he brings judgment. In none of the dreams can I find this information.

Dream 729, of Della of the Corathin lineage

Clerres was the strangest place I had ever seen. I stood on the deck, forgetful of my errand for Dwalia, and stared. Ahead of me was a kindly harbour with water that was impossibly blue. All around the harbour there were square buildings of pink and white and pale green, with flat roofs and numerous windows. Some of the buildings had small pointed tents pitched on their roofs. Greenery cascaded down the sides of some, framing the windows.

Behind the buildings that fronted the harbour, the gentle rolling hills beckoned in shades of gold and brown. There were random, solitary trees with fat trunks and wide-spread branches, although on one hillside an even rank of trees might have been an orchard. The distant hills were speckled with herds of grazing animals. The white-and-grey ones were probably sheep. The other herd creatures were cattle, of a sort I had never seen, with branching horns and hummocks on their shoulders. The small boats of our ship had been deployed and our sails furled. Bare-chested sailors bent their backs to the oars as they towed us toward the docks. Slowly, so slowly we drew closer to shore.

The terraced city followed a curve of land that embraced the harbour. One arm of the embrace was a long narrow peninsula, but the peninsula was broken. Beyond that gap, as if it had broken off from the land, was a big island with a dazzling ivory fortress upon it. The island itself was also white, almost dazzlingly so. Its lumpy shores of tumbled blocks of stone sparkled. Quartz. I'd once found a rock that sparkled like that, and Revel had told me it had quartz in it. All the land outside the fortress walls was barren. Not a tree, no trace of green. It looked to me as if it were an island that had suddenly popped up out of the sea with a magical castle atop it.

The outer walls of the castle were tall and crenellated. At each corner a staunch guard tower rose, each topped with a structure like the skull of some immense and fearsome creature. Each of the empty eyed skulls stared off in a different direction. Within the stone walls and taller than the walls, a sturdy stronghouse stood. And four slender towers rose from each corner of that, the spires even taller than the castle towers, with bulbous rooms at the top, like the top of an onion left to go to seed. Never had I seen towers so tall and slender, gleaming pale against the blue sky.

I stared at it, my destination. My future.

Despair tried to rise in me. I pushed it down with frozen stones. I didn't care. I was alone. I would be enough for me. I'd had two dreams since my father had cast me aside. Two dreams that I dared not think about for fear that Vindeliar might glimpse them. They had frightened me. Badly. I had awakened in the dark of night and stuffed the front of my shirt into my mouth so no one could hear me sobbing. But when I calmed, I understood. I could not see my path clearly, but I knew I had to walk it alone. To Clerres.

I had been sent out of Dwalia's stateroom to return a tray of dirty dishes to the galley. Usually she did not choose me for such tasks. I think she intended it as yet another demonstration to Vindeliar that I was not only trusted but quickly becoming her favourite. I had perfected my grovelling servitude and taken it to levels he dared not approach. I radiated repentant loyalty at her in a small, steady stream. It was dangerous, for it meant I must constantly be on my guard against Vindeliar lest he gain entry to my mind. He had grown terribly strong since he had drunk the serpent spit. But he was strong as a bullock was strong, good at large motions and breaking walls. But I was not a wall. I was a tiny rolling pebble, hard as a nut, with no edges for him to grasp. I'd felt him try, more than once. I had to keep myself very small and let out only the thoughts that had no real ties to me. Like my slavish admiration of Dwalia.

I'd carried my pretence well, even to standing by her bath and holding a towel for her, and then stooping to dry her callused feet and lumpy toes. I'd rub her feet to hear her groan with pleasure, and I'd set out her clothing as if I were garbing royalty rather than draping a hateful old woman. My ability to deceive her almost frightened me, for it involved thinking the thoughts of a defeated slave. Sometimes I feared that those thoughts were becoming my true thoughts. I did not want to be her slave, but living without the threats and the beatings was such a relief that it was almost an acceptance that this was the best life I could hope for.

I felt a familiar squeezing in what I thought must be my heart. I had heard of being 'heartbroken' or 'heavy-hearted' but I had never known it was an actual sensation one felt when the whole world abandons you. I looked out at what I knew must be Clerres, and tried to believe I could make a life for myself there. For I knew now I would never go home. I had felt my father's touch upon my mind. I had felt him spurn me, cast me aside so violently that I had awakened shaking and sick. I had reached for Wolf Father. He had not understood it any better than I had. So. It was done. I was alone. No one was ever going to come and rescue me. No one cared what had become of me.

I had known that for days now, but even more, I had known it for every long night that came between those days. During the days when both Dwalia and Vindeliar were awake, I had no time to dwell on it. I was too busy defending my thoughts from Vindeliar while grovelling to Dwalia and impressing on her how cowed and subservient I was now. During those hours, my father's abandonment of me was a constant humming pain, as permanent as the restless water that surrounded us. During the days, my survival floated on that sea of hurt.

At night, I sank beneath it and drowned in it. My loneliness had become absolute when I had touched minds with my father and he had pushed me away. I had tried to make it less of a rejection in any way I could, but it was like trying to put the pieces of a cup together so it made a teapot. There had been those other voices. One had been my sister's perhaps, but I was not certain. There had been a chorus of others, including one who shouted and roared. I didn't know how I had reached them, but I knew my father had been aware of me. 'Flee,' he had bidden me, as if there were danger, but he did not flee with me. He had not caught me up and kept me safe. He had stayed in the middle of that storm of voices. He had paid attention to them, pushing me to one side. When I had dared to call out to him again, he had shoved me roughly away. He had pushed me so hard that I had not been able to hold onto him. I'd fallen away from him, away from my hope of rescue and a return to a life that had some kindness in it. I'd tumbled back into myself, into my lonely small self, and found Vindeliar already sniffing around my boundaries. I had not even dared to weep aloud.

I'd slammed my walls tight, tight, tight. Wolf Father had warned me. To hold my walls that tight meant that no one could reach me. At that moment, I hoped no one would ever touch my thoughts again. I never wanted anyone to like me again, let alone love me. And I was never, ever going to like anyone else.

The pain in my heart had suddenly become a pain in my belly. It combined with the hurt of holding the dreams unspoken and unwritten. But the dreams that came to me now, I dared not speak. They were frightening and tantalizing, tempting and terrifying. They called to me to make them real. And with every day of our journey, they became more real to me, as if I came ever closer to an inevitable future I would make.

I closed my eyes for a moment and then opened them to the pastel city before me. I made myself see how pretty it was, and I imagined myself as a happy person there. I would trot along those streets, greeting the people I knew, running some useful errand for Dwalia. And some day I would escape.

No. I could not have that thought, nor that plan. Not yet. It was a lovely place, a wonderful place to call home. How happy I was to be here! I trickled out a bit of that thought. I had discovered that I could feed such things to Dwalia even when I couldn't see her. Her mind was a shape I knew now. As was Vindeliar's. Experimentally, I dribbled a bit of my imaginary happiness onto him. For a moment, I felt him warm, and then he slapped my thought away. He did not know how to make his thoughts reach me clearly. Sometimes they did, but I think that was something that happened rather than something he knew how to do. I did not hear his direct thoughts but I felt his distrust of me. And behind his distrust, his hurt. Somehow, he had truly believed that I would become his brother and love him as no one else ever had. He had seen a path for us that I never had.

For a moment, the stinging thought that perhaps he felt as abandoned as I did shamed me. Then I crushed it down and shut it out of my mind. No. He had helped to kidnap me, had aided in destroying my home, and had tricked and helped kill the only person who had befriended me on my horrible journey. He had no right to think anyone would love him for doing those things.

But that fury was a strong emotion, and I was learning that strong emotions made cracks in my wall. I denied my hatred. It made my stomach hurt worse than ever, but I did it. I turned my eyes to the pretty city, with the little rectangular houses like little cakes displayed on a shelf. I would have a delicious life here. I put a cheery smile on my face and carried my tray to the galley and left it there. As I made my way back to the captain's stateroom, I had to dodge hurrying sailors. As we neared our destination, the number and pace of their tasks were increasing. One of them cursed at me as I skipped out of his way. Small boats were hastening toward us as our sailors secured the gathered sails. Coiled lines awaited. The little boat would tow us in to the docks. Our arrival was imminent.

I tapped on the stateroom door lest the captain was making a last-minute visit, and heard Dwalia's charming request that I should enter. 'Pack it all up!' she commanded me as soon as she saw me. She gestured at the scattered garments that she had tried on and then discarded. Every time we had stopped in a port, the captain had purchased more garments for her. I wondered what she would do with them all once we disembarked and she was no longer Lady

Aubretia. She herself was occupied with carefully setting the jewellery she had acquired onto a finely woven scarf, also gifts from her
captain. Once she had them arranged, she rolled the scarf up, folding
the ends in as she went, and then tying it into a small bundle. By
then I was nearly finished layering her gauzy and lacy finery into a
trunk.

'Will you be sad to leave him?' The question had popped into my
head and out of my mouth. At her sudden scowl, I hastily added,
'He treats you so well. It must be gratifying to have someone recognize your true value.'

She narrowed her eyes at me. It had been a bit too complimentary,
but I made my querying face as bland as possible and then turned
away to finish fastening the buckles of the trunk. I managed a sideways glance at Vindeliar. He was very slowly gathering his meagre
possessions and stuffing them into a worn bag. Since I had become
Dwalia's favourite, she had asked less and less of him. I had imagined
he might be grateful to have fewer tasks, but her ignoring of him
only fuelled his dislike of me. I had the uneasy feeling that he was
planning something, but if he was, he had kept it well concealed.
I, too, had a plan, one that was slowly taking shape in my mind. I
dared not dwell on it, lest he catch some flavour of it in my thoughts.
It was the first plan that I should have made, back in winter when
they had first captured me.

No. Don't think about it in front of them when they are awake.
I reminded myself again of the little pastel houses and what an
agreeable life awaited me in this pretty city.

Dwalia responded at last. 'I shall be sad to leave him.' Then she
took a deep breath and squared her shoulders. 'But this is not my
life. I do not depend on a man's position and affection to claim what
should be mine.' She sounded almost angry that she had been well
treated by him. She turned to Vindeliar. 'You remember what you
are to do, as we disembark?'

'Yes.' His agreement was sullen.

She cocked her head slightly at him. 'And you are certain you
can do it?'

'Yes.' His eyes flickered to me and I knew a moment of unease.

'Fine.' She stood, straightened her fine dress and patted at her
hair. I had braided it for her that morning and coiled it carefully at
the back of her head. Now she smoothed it as if she were the lovely

woman the captain imagined her to be. Sparkling earrings dangled, and a network of silver rings dotted with tiny sparkling jewels caged her throat. But above it was her plain round face, ruined forever by the scar my teeth had left. From what I had read in my father's scrolls, I suspected that Farseer Skill-magic could repair her face, but I did not tell her that. It might be a negotiating chip I would need later, an offer that might keep me alive. Or at least make her curious enough to let me live a bit longer. I tried to recall how kindly she had seemed the first time I met her, how motherly and solicitous. Vindeliar's magic.

Vindeliar dared a question. 'Do they know we are returning? Symphe and Fellowdy?'

She was silent and I thought she would not reply. Then she said, 'Sending short bird messages would just have confused them. I will explain myself when I stand before them.'

He took in a little breath as if that frightened him. 'They will be surprised to see we are alone.'

'Alone?' she snapped. 'We bring with us the prize I said we would gain. The Unexpected Son.'

Vindeliar slid his eyes sideways to look at me. We both knew she no longer believed that of me. I thought he would have the sense to be quiet but instead he said, 'But you know Bee's a girl.'

She balled a fist at him. 'That doesn't matter! Stop talking about things you are too stupid to understand! I will handle this. I will deal with all of it. You will tell no one she is a girl. You will not speak at all. Do you understand me? That should not be too difficult for your feeble mind. Just don't talk.'

He parted his lips, then nodded dumbly and emphatically. Dwalia went to the window and stared out at the endless blue sea. Did she wish she were not going home?

In the few extra minutes in which Dwalia did not busy me, I did my best to smooth my hair. I managed to dabble my hands in her used washwater and use the cloth to wipe my face before I bore it away. Wear had not improved my garments, but they were reasonably clean. I made a sack out of my worst shirt and put my few spare garments inside it. I tied the sleeves together to make a handle and slung it over my shoulder. I had chosen my disguise. I would be an honest child, standing straight before all, harmless and intent on pleasing Dwalia. Let no one fear or suspect what I truly was.

We heard the shouts of the sailors and the noises of the town had grown louder. The little boats would tow us right up to the docks that fingered out from the busy streets. Between us, Vindeliar and I managed to carry the trunk full of Dwalia's fine garments up to the deck. Dwalia tucked the packet of jewellery into a lovely embroidered bag that she carried. And there on the deck we stood, mostly out of the sailors' way, and waited for the ship to reach the dock and be safely moored to it, and then for the gangplank to be put into place.

Only then did the captain come to us. He took both Dwalia's hands in his, kissed her chastely on her cheek and told her that he had already sent a runner ahead to secure lodgings for her in a clean and honest inn. Regretfully, he said he could not accompany us, but he had two strong men who would carry her trunk and escort her to the place. He promised that he would come with her to Clerres Castle to consult on her future, for he hoped he would figure large in such a reading.

Lady Aubretia simpered and thanked him. The elegant arched plumes on her hat bobbed in the sea breeze. She reminded him that she had business of her own to conduct in Clerres, but she would see him that evening. And her two servants could manage to take her trunk to the lodgings, so no escort was needed. For a moment, his brow was wrinkled in concern for his darling. Then the lines smoothed as I felt Vindeliar manipulate his mind. Of course she would be fine. He would not worry for her. She was as competent as she was lovely, and he cherished her independent spirit.

Even so, he accompanied us down the gangplank. He again took Dwalia's hands in his and looked down at her as she tilted her head back to meet his fond gaze. 'Be careful, my lovely,' he cautioned her, and stooped to take a final kiss.

I felt Vindeliar do it. He dropped the illusion as the captain's face neared hers and let him see her as she was. His intended kiss did not reach her mouth as he recoiled from her. In less than a breath, Vindeliar had restored her glamour. But by then the captain had stumbled back a step. He blinked, rubbed his eyes with the palms of both his hands and then smiled at Dwalia sheepishly. 'I've been awake too long. I stand on land and feel giddy from the stillness. Lady Aubretia, I will see you later this evening. We shall dine together.'

'We shall,' she promised him faintly. He turned his head, rubbed his brow and made his way back up to his ship. He looked back at us from the deck, and she lifted a lace-gloved hand to wave at him. He grinned like a boy, waved back and turned to his duties. For a moment longer, she stood staring after him. Hurt made her homely face even plainer. Vindeliar stood innocently by, feigning that he did not know what had just happened but, 'He saw me,' Dwalia said in a low, accusing voice. 'You allowed him to see me.'

Vindeliar looked off into the distance. 'Perhaps, for an instant, my control faltered.' He flickered his gaze back to her and then away. I saw his vicious satisfaction but perhaps it was too fleeting for her to catch. 'It takes a great deal of strength to maintain such an illusion,' he pointed out to her. 'The captain is not a gullible man. To make his crew see you as Lady Aubretia every moment was hard. To make the captain see you in such a different form, in every moment he was with you has near drained all my magic. Perhaps now is the time when you should give me—'

'Not here!' she snapped. She glared at both of us. 'Pick up that trunk and follow me.' Vindeliar took one end and I seized the other handle and we walked behind her. The trunk was not that heavy. Carrying it was only awkward because Vindeliar was such a weakling. He kept shifting his grip from hand to hand, and he walked leaning over as if he could barely lift it. The trunk bumped and skipped on the paving stones and knocked against my hip and calf. Every hundred paces or so, she had to stop and wait for us to catch up with her. Vindeliar strove to maintain her appearance. Men were halting to cast admiring looks at her. Two women exclaimed to one another over her hat and dress. She walked proudly and when she glanced back at us, there was a pleased light in her eyes I had never seen before.

We walked down streets crowded with folk foreign to my eyes. Sailors and merchants and workers, I guessed them to be, but in all manner of garb and of all different colourings. I saw a boy with hair as red as rust, his hands and arms speckled with freckles like a bird's egg. There was a woman taller than any person I'd ever glimpsed, and her bare brown arms were sheathed all over in white tattoos from her fingertips to her wide shoulders. A bald little girl in a pink frock skipped beside her equally bald mother whose lips were framed with tiny jewels. I turned my head, wondering how the jewels stayed on and the trunk hit my calf on top of an earlier bruise.

I felt Vindeliar struggling to carry the trunk and maintain Lady Aubretia's illusion. The third time Dwalia had to stop and wait for us, she said, 'I see you are becoming useless again. Very well. You need not try so hard. For now, I wish folk to not notice us. That is all.'

'I will try.'

Her beauty fell away from her. She became ordinary, and less than ordinary. Not worthy of notice.

Dwalia trudged through the crowds, and people grudgingly gave way to her, and we lurched along after her. I could feel Vindeliar's magic failing. I glanced over at him. He was sweating with the effort to carry his end of the trunk and maintaining his illusion. His power sputtered and danced like a dying flame on a damp log. 'I can't . . .' he gasped, and gave up his efforts.

Dwalia glared at him. I wondered if she knew he no longer cloaked her. But as we tottered along behind her, folk began to notice her. I saw a woman wince at the scar on her cheek. A little boy took his finger from his mouth and pointed it at her. His mother shushed him and hurried him along. Twice, pale folk stopped and turned toward her as if they might greet her but she didn't even pause for them. Folk stared at her and she must have known they saw her as she truly was. One grey-bearded sailor gave a caw of dismay at the sight of her. 'A feather bonnet on a pig,' he said to his swarthy companion as they passed, and both guffawed.

Dwalia halted in the street. She did not look back at us as we caught up with her, but spoke over her shoulder. 'Leave it. There is nothing in that trunk that I'll ever wear again. Just leave it.' She reached up and tore free the pins that had secured her hat, threw it to the ground and strode away.

I was stunned. I'd heard tears in her voice. Vindeliar dropped his end of the trunk with a thud. It took longer for me to realize she was serious. She didn't look back. She stumped away from us, and we were both panting when we finally caught up with her. I was quickly aware that I had not trotted nor even walked much in our days aboard the ship. Her pace meant that I had little time to look around. I had only glimpses of a well-kept city, with wide uncluttered streets. The people we passed were clean and their clothing was simple but whole. The women's skirts were wide-belted at the waist and the loose folds came scarcely to their knees. They wore sandals and their blouses either had no sleeves at all or sleeves like bells that fell past their wrists. They were taller than Buck women, and not even the dark-haired ones had curly hair. Some of the men wore only vests over their bared chests and their trousers were as short as the women's skirts. I supposed it made sense in that warmer climate, but to me they appeared half-naked. They were lighter-skinned than Six Duchies folk and taller, and for once my pale hair drew not a second glance. I saw not a single beggar.

As we left the wharves and warehouses and inns behind, we passed some of the pink-and-pale-yellow buildings I had seen from the ship's deck. There were flowerboxes below the windows and benches by the doors. Shutters were opened wide on this fine day, and I saw rows of spinning wheels in one pink building, with the spinners hard at work and I heard the clack of looms from the shadowed room beyond them. We passed a building that breathed out warmth and the smell of baking bread. Everywhere I looked, I saw cleanliness and order. It was not at all what I had imagined Clerres would be. Given how cruel Dwalia had been, I had imagined a whole city of hateful people, not this pastel prosperity.

There was other foot traffic on the road with us. Like the port part of the city, the folk hurrying along beside us were a mixed lot. Most of them were light-haired and fair-skinned and dressed in the garb of Clerres, but some were plainly foreigners and travellers from afar. Mixed in with them were men and women in guard's garb, wearing a badge with a twining vine on it. Many of them stared openly at Dwalia's ruined face, and some appeared to recognize her, but no one offered her a greeting. Those who seemed to recognize her looked shocked or turned away. For her part, she did not offer 'good day' to anyone and set a pace that meant we passed most of our fellow walkers.

Our path toward the white island led us along the shoreline. Water lapped on the beach. Gray-and-white sand sparkled over bones of granite. We walked on a smooth road past houses with vegetable gardens and arbours between them. I saw children, all dressed in the same sort of smock garments, playing in dooryards or sitting on the steps of the houses. I could not tell if they were boys or girls. Dwalia strode on. As she walked, I watched her tug the final pins from her hair and let her braids hang lank about her face. She took off her necklace and lifted the earrings from her ears. I almost thought she would toss them aside, but she tucked them into her bag. With them gone, all traces of Lady Aubretia vanished. Even her fine gown became an oddity rather than lovely.

To my surprise, I became aware of her feelings. She did not simmer and boil as my father had. My father's thoughts and emotions had always surged against my senses; they were why I had first learned to make walls within my mind. Dwalia's were not nearly so strong. I think I sensed them only because for so long I had pushed tendrils of my thoughts into her mind. It was as Wolf Father had warned me. A way in was also a way out. And now her thoughts seeped through to me. I felt from her a resentful anger that she had never been beautiful and had never felt loved, only tolerated because she was useful. I felt her heart wander back to a time when she had known love, once, and loved in return. I saw a tall woman, smiling down on her. The Pale Woman. Then, as if crushed under a fall of icicles, that feeling stopped. The closer we drew to the island, the more I sensed self-justification that was rooted in anger. She would force them to acknowledge that she had not failed. She would not allow them to mock or rebuke her.

And she would have her vengeance.

As if she felt the brush of my thoughts against hers, she glared back at both of us. 'Hurry up!' she snapped. 'The tide is going out. I want to be there early, not caught in the crowds of petitioners. Vindeliar, walk with your head up. You look like an ox going to slaughter. And you, little bitch? Keep your tongue still while the Four are listening to me. Understand me? Not a sound from you. Or I swear I'll kill you.'

It was her first rebuke to me in several days, and it startled me. Vindeliar did lift his head, but I think he was more encouraged by her spitting venom at me than at her order to him. Clearly I had fallen from her favour, at least back to his level. Vindeliar still waddled when he walked, but he waddled faster. I dreaded the meeting with the Four and longed to ask questions about them but kept my tongue stilled. Several times Vindeliar glanced over at me as if almost hoping I'd ask him. I didn't. A few times, my secret plan tried to seep into my thoughts. I dammed it back. I was going to be happy here in Clerres. I would have a good life. I'd be useful here. When I felt Vindeliar looking at me, I turned a vacuous smile on him. I wanted to laugh aloud at his startled face but I restrained myself.

We left the houses behind and walked past a very large building of white stone. There was nothing of grace about it; it was entirely functional. There was a large stable beside it, with its own smithy, and there were several open areas where sweating guardsmen were performing drills. The shouted commands of their instructor echoed from the building's side, and dust rose around the guards as they lunged, clashed and retreated in turn.

Then we entered a section of the town that reminded me more of the Winterfest booths than a true village. Sturdy stone cottages had shade awnings in front of them, and people stood in queues before them. In the shade under the awnings, people paler than me with fluffy white hair sat in embellished chairs that were almost thrones. Some had tiny scrolls to sell. Others had the same sort of cupboard as the man who had told us to find the *Sea Rose*. Some of the sellers wore exotic scarves and sparkling earrings and vests of lace. Others were clad in plain shifts of pale yellow or rose or azure. One had a large crystal ball on a filigreed stand and she or he was staring into it with eyes the same colour as a trout's. A woman stood silently before her, clasping a young man's hand.

There were other vendors there, selling charms for luck or pregnancy or sheep fertility, charms for good crops or to help the baby sleep at night. These wares were cried loudly by younger versions of the merchants, who moved about the crowd carrying trays, their voices shrill and incessant as the gulls over the harbour.

There were food stalls, too, selling foods both sweet and savoury. Their tempting aromas reminded me that we had eaten at dawn and walked a fair pace since then, but Dwalia did not pause. I could have spent the whole afternoon exploring that market, but she strode through it without a pause or a glance to left or right.

Once I heard a hushed whisper, 'I'm sure it's her. It's Dwalia!'

Someone else said, 'But where are the others, then? All the luriks on those fine white horses?'

But not even that turned her head. We hurried past and through folk standing in a thick line, and some cursed at us and others shouted at us for being rude, but Dwalia threaded through the crowd until we came to the head of the line. A short causeway of stone and sand ended in a tall gate made of iron bars. Just beyond the gate, the causeway ended abruptly in water. Beyond that water, on a stony island, was the white stronghold. Before the gate stood four sturdy guards. Two held pikes and stood staring stonily at the queuing people. The other two wore swords. They were formidable warriors, blue-eyed, dark-haired, and well-muscled, and even the women were taller than my father, but Dwalia did not pause or hesitate.

'I am going to cross.'

'No. You are not.' The man who spoke did not even look at her. 'You are going to go back to the end of the line and wait your turn. When the tide goes out and the water has receded completely, then we will admit pilgrims in an orderly fashion, two abreast. That is how we do this.'

Dwalia stepped closer and spoke through clenched teeth. 'I know how we do it. I am one of the Circle. I am Lingstra Dwalia, and I have returned. The Four will wish to hear my report as soon as they possibly can. You should not dare to detain me.' She gave Vindeliar a sideways glare. I felt him try. His thin magic lapped against the guards.

One cocked his head and looked at her carefully. 'Dwalia.' The guard spoke it as a name he knew. He lifted an elbow and nudged the woman next to him. 'Is that her? Dwalia?'

The other guard grudgingly shifted her gaze from the queue of anxious pilgrims to study Dwalia, the wrinkles in her brow growing deeper as she did so. Then her eyes fell on Vindeliar. 'She left here a long time ago. Rode at the head of a troop of white horses and riders. Could be her, but she looks different in that dress. But that one? Him I recognize. He is Dwalia's creature. Vindeliar. He does her bidding. So, if she has him, then, I guess it's her. We should let her cross.'

'But now? While the water still runs over the causeway?'

'It's not that deep. I can tell. I wish to cross now.' Dwalia's tone brooked no argument. 'Open the gate for me.'

They stepped back from her, conferred briefly. One scowled and seemed to indicate her fine dress, but the other shrugged, and he was the one who unlatched the gate and swung it open. We had to step back to allow its motion and that crowded us into the waiting petitioners. And when the gate was clear, and Dwalia stepped forward with Vindeliar and me following, the crowd moved with us, trying to cross with us. The guards with the pikes moved forward, crossing their weapons and pushing them back. We stepped forward alone.

The causeway was of smooth, cut stone, flat as a table. Dwalia didn't pause when she reached the water's edge. She did not lift her skirts or take off her shoes to carry them. She walked forward as if the sea did not still own that space. We followed. The water was shallow at first, not warm but not numbingly cold. As we went forward, it got quickly deeper, soaking my shoes and moving past my ankles to my shins. I began to feel the tug of the ebbing tide. Beside me, Vindeliar was scowling. 'I don't like this,' he said bitterly. Neither Dwalia nor I paid him any mind but I soon began to share his uneasiness. The water got deeper and the pull of the receding waves became stronger. I had waded in creeks and streams, but this was seawater. It had a smell and a stickiness that surprised me. The opposite gate on the far end of the sunken causeway had not looked very far away when we had begun. Now as the water rose past my knees and up my thighs, the safety of the far shore seemed to retreat. Even Dwalia had slowed as she sloshed forward. I fixed my eyes on her back and fought the weight of the water. The tide might be ebbing as they had said, but waves still came and went, and sometimes they wet me to my waist. Vindeliar had begun to make an anxious noise between a hum and a whine. He was falling behind. When I glanced back and realized that, I tried to move faster. The water was colder now and I panted as I pushed my way through it. Leave him behind, I thought fiercely. I think he felt my wish, for his wail grew louder and I heard a splash as he stumbled, and then his hoarse cry as he surged to his feet again. *Drown!* I arrowed that thought at him, and then shut myself behind my walls.

The sun beat down on my head, scorching my scalp through my short hair, while the water pressed against me and drew warmth out of my feet and legs. I folded my arms high on my chest and hugged my bundled clothing to myself. I pushed my thirst to one side along with my aching muscles. Shipboard life had not prepared me for today's hike. The sunlight bounced off the water and into my eyes. I lifted my head and tried to see Dwalia but glittering light dazzled my eyes. I began to feel shaky and ill.

Was the water shallower? Perhaps. I took heart and surged on, head and shoulders bent as I fought the waves. When next I lifted my head and looked for Dwalia, she stood at the far gate, remonstrating and cursing the guards who would not open it to her. Beyond that gate, a huddle of people awaited its opening to leave the castle. Their weary stances and aprons of leather or fabric proclaimed them to be servants of the Servants, probably on their way to their homes.

I sloshed up behind Dwalia. She astonished me by swivelling about, seizing me by my collar and near lifting me off my feet to shake me at the guards. 'The Unexpected Son!' she snarled at them. 'Do you want to be the ones who delayed his arrival before the Four?'

The guards exchanged glances. The taller man looked back at her. 'That old myth?'

Vindeliar came shuddering up beside us. One guard nudged the other. 'That's Vindeliar. No mistaking that treacherous little gelding. So she *is* Dwalia. Let them in.'

Dwalia did not release her grip on my collar as the gate opened and we passed through. I tried not to resist her pulling but it meant walking on my tiptoes. I could not look back to see Vindeliar following but I heard the thud of the barred gate as it shut behind us.

A road of dun sand stretched before us. The sun woke sparkles in it. It was straight and featureless. To either side of it, a barren and rocky landscape spread. It was so flat and empty that I knew that the hands of men had shaped it. Nothing could cross this expanse of ground and not be seen. Never had I seen an area so devoid of small life. The only relief to the eye were occasional stones, and none of them was larger than a bushel basket. Dwalia suddenly released me. 'Don't dawdle. And don't speak,' she ordered me, and then set off at her distance-eating stride again. Her once-fine skirts were wet and slapped against her legs as she walked. I followed, trying to match her pace. When I lifted my eyes to stare at our destination, it dazzled me more than the sunlight on the water. The white walls of the castle glittered. We walked and walked and seemed to come no closer. Gradually I began to realize that I had greatly underestimated how large a fortress it was. Or castle. Or palace. From the ship, I had seen eight towers. This close to it, when I looked up, I saw only two, and the misshapen heads that topped them looked like skulls. I slogged along, head lowered as the sun pounded down on us and eyes half-closed against the brightness. Every time I lifted my head, the aspect of the immense structure at the end of the long road seemed to have changed.

When we were close enough that I had to crane my neck back to see the tops of the walls, the ornate bas-reliefs on the outside of the walls became evident. They were the only marks I could see on the smooth white walls. From this vantage, I saw no windows, not even arrow slits, and no doors. On this side of the castle, there was no access at all. Yet the road led directly to it. White on white, the etched carvings were many times taller than a man, and glittering even brighter than the walls they graced. I stared for a moment and then had to look away and close my eyes. But when I shut my eyes, there the carvings were again, inside my eyelids, like a climbing white vine.

I recognized it.

Impossibly, I knew what it was. I remembered it, from a life I had never lived or perhaps from a future I had yet to see. That vine had crawled through my dreams. I'd drawn it on the front page of my journal to frame my name. I'd given it leaves and trumpet flowers. I'd been wrong. It was an abstract representation. And there was a thought I'd never had before, that an artist could create a picture of an idea, and I would know what it was. I recognized it as the river of all possible times, cascading down from the present and splitting into a thousand, no a million, no an infinite number of possible futures and every one of those splintered into another infinity of possible futures. And among them all, a single gleaming thread, incredibly narrow, that represented the future as it could, should and ought to be. If events were guided correctly. If the White Prophet dreamed and believed and ventured forth to put that world on the path, time would follow it.

I opened my eyes again, for I had only closed them for a moment. There it was again, before me, and despite all I had come through, all I had endured to come here and how much I hated the people who had brought me here, I suddenly felt a lift of belonging. I was here at last.

A certainty rose in me, clearer than anything I had ever known about myself. I was supposed to be here. In this place and in this time, this was where I was supposed to be. A dozen dreams I had had suddenly spun and then interlocked with more recent dreams inside me. The vague plan was no longer vague. I'd felt a similar surge of certainty on the day I had freed my tongue. I'd seen the paths with such clarity only once before in my life, on that fateful day in winter when the beggar had touched me and I'd seen how all futures began at my feet. Oh, the great good that I could do, now that I was here. My fate was here and only I could shape it. It stole my breath away. And as I gazed, I felt my heart lift, just as the minstrels described it could happen. I was here and the great work of my life was before me.

I realized I had stopped only when Vindeliar trudged past me. He looked at me with a gaze full of venom and I found I could not care. A smile pulled at my mouth. Walls up.

'Bee, hurry up!' Dwalia snapped the command over her shoulder.

'Coming!' I replied and something in my tone made her halt and look back at me. I cast my eyes down and bowed my head. This was not a thing to share with anyone. I needed to hold it close inside me. The knowledge was like a glittering stone scooped from a filthy puddle. I saw the shine of it, but I knew that the more I handled it, the cleaner and clearer it would become.

And like a jewel, if I revealed it, thieves would take it from me, in any way they could.

I heard a sound behind us and looked back. The tide was out, and the causeway stood above the water. A snake of people, six or eight wide, now packed the narrow belt of road that ran between the waters. Some were almost across. But even after they reached the island and the waters of the bay no longer hedged them in, they did not spread out but kept to the narrow causeway.

'Hurry!' Dwalia urged me again. No wonder she kept us to such a rapid pace. If we did not keep up our speed, they would overtake us, maybe even trample us.

Ahead, where there had been only smooth wall, cracks appeared, startling black against the white. The cracks became the edges of the doors and then they opened wide. A phalanx of guards, clad in gleaming silver armour and pale-yellow cloaks marched out and formed up in two rows alongside our path. I thought they would halt us, but Dwalia glared at them and made a sign with her hand and we strode past without a word.

It was not until we had passed under the arch of the entry and emerged into a courtyard that a man stepped in front of us. He was tall and thin and wore a sword, but even in his armour he looked skinny and weak. His face was pasty and blemished with splotches of pink, peeling skin. Tufts of greying hair stuck out the sides of his helmet. He narrowed his eyes. 'Lingstra Dwalia.' He made her name an accusation. 'You left here with a mounted guard of luriks. Where are they and their fine steeds? Why do you return alone?'

'Step aside, Bosphodi. There is no time to waste. I must have audience with Symphe and Fellowdy immediately.'

He held his place a moment longer, his gaze wandering over her damaged face, inspecting Vindeliar's ragged garments and then settling on me. His frown became a grimace of disapproval. Then he stepped aside and made a grand gesture for us to pass him. 'Go as you will, Dwalia. Were I coming back from a doubtful quest, scarred and stripped of all that had been entrusted to me, I doubt I'd be in such a hurry to report my failure to the Four.'

'I didn't fail,' she replied tersely.

As we hurried past him he muttered, 'Of all the ones to come back alive, it had to be Vindeliar.' I heard him spit.

The wide courtyard was paved in patterns of white-and-black stone and was as clean as if it had been recently swept. Lining the inner walls of the outer keep were food-and-drink stalls alongside bright carts with multiple drawers that would, I now knew, hold fortune papers inside nutshells. Pennants and garlands hung nearly motionless in the heat. Open-sided pavilions shaded tables and benches that awaited hungry and thirsty patrons. It looked like a celebration, far larger than Winterfest at Oaksbywater. For one instant, childish curiosity made me forget who I was now, and I longed to wander among the booths and buy sweets and bright gewgaws.

'Hurry up, stupid!' Dwalia barked.

These joys were not for Vindeliar or me. I walked away from the child I had been.

She hurried us toward the finest structure within the fortress walls. It was built, apparently, of white ivory. The doors and windows were a filigree wrought in bone or stone. This stronghouse was the base for the four slender onion-bud towers I had glimpsed from the ship. It looked impossible for such towers to be so tall and support such pinnacles. But there they were.

'Come!' Dwalia snapped at me, and for the first time in some days, she snapped a slap to my face. I felt the old split at the corner of my mouth bleed again. I lifted a hand to press it closed and followed her.

Double doors stood open beyond a columned portico. We ascended wide steps to reach them. The cessation of sunlight beating down on my head and shoulders was a shock. My shoes were still damp. I tracked grit from the wet causeway onto the immaculate floor. As my eyes adjusted to the light I became aware of the magnificence that surrounded me.

Here the doorways were edged with gilt or perhaps real gold. Brilliant paintings in opulent frames, the subjects many times larger than life, graced every wall. Tasselled tapestries hung on the upper walls. I had never seen white wood, but every wall in here was panelled in it. I lifted my eyes to see that even the high ceilings were painted with incomprehensible landscapes. I felt very small and out of place in such grandeur. But Dwalia was uncowed by any of it.

The woman who blocked our way was robed in fabric of rich yellow, yellower than dandelions. Her sleeves hung slightly past her wrists and her full skirts brushed the floor. The collar stood up to her chin, and her flowered headdress left only the circle of her pale face showing. The red of her painted mouth was shocking. 'Dwalia,' she said, and waited, scowling. In the distance, I heard a door open and then shut. Two people walked past us and out of the door. As they exited to the pavilion outside, a roar of voices reached my ears. The crowd had reached the outer courtyard. Then the closing door cut off their sounds.

Dwalia spoke. 'I must have an audience with Symphe. And Fellowdy. Immediately.'

The woman smiled nastily. 'This is not a day for private audiences. The Four are in the Judgment Chamber, prepared to hear grievance and assign blame and penalties. You must know those appointments are made months in advance. But,' and she smiled like a snarling cat, 'perhaps I can manage to get you an appointment there?'

At those words, Vindeliar's hands flew to his cheeks and then covered his mouth.

'No. I wish to see Symphe. Alone or with Fellowdy. Only those two. At once, Deneis.' Dwalia gave Vindeliar a glare. He dropped his hands and then hunched his shoulders as if expecting a blow.

The woman in yellow folded her lips, leaving her face all but featureless for her eyes were grey and as I stared at her I realized that she had no eyebrows.

'It can't be done today. Perhaps the day after tomorrow, I can—'

'If you make my news wait two days, I think the Four will slowly remove your skin. Or perhaps allow me to perform that task myself.'

I had thought Deneis was as pale as she could get, but her face turned as white as my father's good paper. 'I will convey your request to their attendants—'

'See that you do,' Dwalia interrupted her. 'We will await their summons in the Joy Chamber. See that refreshments are brought to us promptly. We have come a long way.'

'You do not command me,' the woman said, but Dwalia only snorted.

'Follow,' she ordered Vindeliar and me and led us from the circular entry hall down one of the corridors branching off it like the spokes of a wheel. We walked on spotless white stone past disapproving portraits. Behind us, I heard the outer doors open and looked back to see Deneis greeting a procession of finely dressed folk.

Dwalia moved down the hall with great familiarity and when we came to a door adorned with brass insets of multiple suns, she pushed it open and we followed her in. I trailed curious fingers on the door as I passed it. It looked as if it had been made of large panels of bone or ivory, but what creature would have bones or tusks that large?

'Shut the door!' Dwalia snapped and I snatched my hand back from the panel. Vindeliar was behind me and he pushed it closed. How long had it been since I'd stood still inside a room that didn't shift with the waves? I took a deep breath and looked around me. It was a room designed for waiting and discomfort. Two milky-white windows admitted filtered light but no view. Chairs of hardwood with straight backs lined the walls. A bare table of white wood sat in the centre of the room. There was no cloth on it, no vessel of flowers such as my mother would have placed. The floor was hard white stone, and the walls were featureless white wood panels. Massive white beams crossed the ceiling overhead. With the door closed, no sound came from outside. Dwalia saw me looking around. 'Go and sit down!' she instructed me.

I was extremely thirsty and I needed to pee but I knew there would be no opportunity to appease either need. I went to one of the chairs and sat. It was too tall and my feet dangled. Uncomfortable. I tucked my small pack of bundled clothes behind me. It didn't help.

Dwalia did not sit. She walked slowly around the room like a rat travelling the walls. Vindeliar shuffled along behind her until she abruptly spun about and slapped him. 'Stop that!' He caught his breath on a sob, glared at me, and then took the chair farthest away.

He sat on the edge of it, his toes on the floor and his heels jiggling soundlessly. She pointed her finger at him. 'Nothing left? You have no power left at all?'

His lower lip trembled. 'You well know it has seldom worked against those with a strong measure of White blood. I could not sway Deneis. Besides, I had used so much for you on the captain and crew. It was a lot of work—'

'Be quiet.' She opened the top buttons of her blouse and fished in her bosom. She pulled out the leather pouch and Vindeliar's eyes lit as she took the glass tube from it. 'It is fortunate I saved some. You must convince the Four to listen to me and believe me.'

His face crumpled. 'All Four? It will be hard. It would be hard even if I had a full dose! Coultrie. I might be able to sway Coultrie, but . . .'

'Be quiet!' She had unstoppered the tube, but when she tipped it, the coagulated mess in the bottom didn't shift. She pushed the stopper back in and shook the tube. The clog in the bottom didn't move. 'We are damned!' she said. She opened the tube and thrust her finger in. It was too short to reach the clot in the bottom. She could not touch the residue. She shoved it at Vindeliar. 'Spit in it! Then mix it and drink it.'

I watched as he drooled saliva down the tube and then tipped the tube to try to mix it. I felt my gorge rise and looked away. 'It's not working!' he wailed.

'Break the tube!' she ordered him.

He tried. He tapped it on the floor. Nothing happened. He tried again, harder and harder until suddenly it shattered. The serpent slime was a dried-up wad. Vindeliar picked it up and heedless of the glass splinters that clung to it, put it in his mouth. Dwalia waited, staring at him.

He breathed out hard through his nose. When he spoke, blood flecked his lips. 'Nothing,' he wailed. 'Nothing at all.'

The blow Dwalia dealt him snapped his head on his neck and he fell to the floor. He sprawled there, his breath faltering in and out. She walked away from him and sat down in one of the chairs. She did not utter a word.

Eventually, Vindeliar got to his knees and crawled to a chair not far from mine. He pulled himself up and sat in it like a pile of soiled laundry. No one spoke.

We waited. No one brought the refreshments Dwalia had demanded.

We waited. And waited.

The late afternoon sun struck our obscured windows, making a rectangle of soupy light on the featureless floor. The door opened. Deneis, the same woman who had admitted us, appeared. 'You will be seen in the Judgment Chamber. Now.'

'The Judgment Chamber? That is not what I told you I wanted!'

Deneis turned and walked away without waiting for us to follow. Dwalia motioned me sharply to her side and seized my shoulder in a hard grip. 'Say nothing,' she reminded me. She pushed me along in front of her. The pace she set did not allow me to glance back. We followed Deneis back to the entry chamber and then down a different corridor. This one was broader and more elegant and we walked a much longer distance, my bladder aching at every step.

At the very end of the corridor stood two doors with four shining symbols embedded in them. Even in the muted light of the hall, the symbols gleamed. Perhaps they meant something, but to me they were just shapes in blue, green, yellow and red. Deneis pushed a brass handle and the doors swung wide.

The room was brightly lit, white sunlight streaming in from four openings in the ceiling, and I blinked at the sudden brilliance. Dwalia pushed me past and through spectators who stood motionless and silent. I stumbled forward over the polished white floor. When she halted me, I lifted my eyes to behold an elevated dais with four thrones of carved ivory upon it. One throne sparkled with rubies, another with emeralds. I did not know what jewels were so yellow and blue on the other two. Could there be that many jewels in the world? For a moment that question distracted me from the occupants of the chairs.

Two men. Two women. One woman was young and beautiful with pale skin and hair of white-gold. Her lips had been painted red and her brows and lashes were lined in black. It was a startling beauty rather than a comfortable one. Her pale arms were bare, and her torso encased in red silk so tautly tailored to her that she might have been naked and merely painted red. Her full skirt was black and reached to her knees. Scarlet sandals framed her feet, the laces crossing and re-crossing her calves. I thought her clothing looked painful to wear.

The woman who sat next to her was very grand. Her cascading hair was white and unbound and straight. Her eyes were a very faded blue and her lips were the pink of an old rose. She was dressed in a pale-blue robe that was as simple as the other woman's scarlet garments were complicated. The pearls that roped her throat and dangled in strings from her ears and wrapped her wrists were all of a size and gleamed warmly.

The men flanked the women, one at each end of the arc. One was painted like a puppet, his skin white and his hair moulded to his scalp with white powder. His eyes were dark; those he could not disguise. His jerkin and leggings were dark green, and the rich cloak he wore was the green of spring ferns. His dark gaze was distant and thoughtful. At the other end of the arc was a portly man. He was pale, his hair more white than yellow, but his clothes were all gloriously yellow. Buttercups and dandelions and daffodils could not rival all the shades of yellow in his garments. His hands rested on the top of his belly and each finger was graced with a ring of gold or silver, even his thumbs. Thick hoops of yellow gold hung from his ears, and a flat golden throat piece began under his chin and spread in plates over his collarbones.

I stared at them in puzzlement. The gaudy thrones and their elaborate separation of colours made them seem almost comical. To either side of the dais, two very large guards held spears. They stared impassively at the gathered people. I realized the green man was glaring at me. At the same instant, the pressure of Dwalia's hand on my shoulder drove me crookedly down. I fell to one knee and then got my other leg under me. I glanced to one side and saw that Vindeliar was already kneeling. Past him, I saw a row of pale folk lining the wall. Their garments were loose tunics and trousers in light hues. Hair that was barely blonde, eyes nearly colourless. Like the butterfly messenger my father and I had burned.

Dwalia remained in a deep bow until one of the women on the dais spoke. I heard her years in her voice. She sounded disgusted. 'Straighten up, Lingstra Dwalia. Your bow is more insult than respect. You have returned, after sending us no word for many months. Fitting that you come to us in the Judgment Chamber! Where are those we sent out with you? Luriks and steeds, gone? Stand straight and explain yourself.'

My hair hung over my brow and down into my eyes. I peered

through it as Dwalia spoke. 'Honoured ones, may I tell you my tale from the beginning? For it is a long and complicated path I have trodden. There have been losses, grievous losses, but those lives were not wasted but surrendered to buy us exactly what you sent me to find. I bring to you the Unexpected Son.'

She seized the back of my collar and I was jerked upright, as when someone lifts a pup by the scruff of his neck. I stared at the Four in surprise. Their expressions were startling. The red woman looked intrigued, the old woman angry. The white-painted man appeared startled. The man in yellow leaned forward and looked at me, his eyes gleaming as if I were something delicious presented to him. He frightened me.

'Oh . . . must you?' The old woman said the words as if Dwalia had picked at her nose and presented the results to her. Her scepticism and disdain were manifest. She shook her head slowly and, turning her head toward the painted man, said, 'I told you it was dangerous to let her take those luriks out into the world. She has lost them all, and dragged this ragamuffin back to us as if it were some sort of treasure. A sorry excuse for her failure!'

'Let her speak, Capra,' the lovely woman said. Her voice was taut with anger, but I could not tell if it was directed at Dwalia or for the woman seated beside her.

The older woman let her gaze travel over the people who lined the room. Their eyes were avid to witness Dwalia's downfall. Capra lifted her skinny arm. The bracelets of pearls dangled as she swept the room with a pointing finger. 'All of you are dismissed. Begone.'

I continued to strangle in Dwalia's grip as the spectators slowly filed from the room. I heard the doors thud closed. Capra scowled at someone. 'Doorkeeper. Include yourself in my dismissal. We have no need of you here.' There was a second, softer, thud as the door closed again. I twisted my head to look. All gone. We were alone in the room with the Four and their burly guards.

The old woman's gaze came back to Dwalia. 'Continue.'

Dwalia released my collar and I was glad to sink back down. I heard her draw breath. 'Very well, my ladies and lords. Three years ago, you provided me with companions and horses and funds to allow me to set forth to find the Unexpected Son. Some had claimed that the time of that prediction was past, that we had already endured his meddling with the streams of time, and that the best we could do now was to work with the threads we had. But in light of a flurry of dreams about a new White born in the wilds and peculiar dreams that related to the Unexpected Son, some of you believed I might discover him and—'

The powder-faced man interrupted. 'Why do you begin by telling us what we already know? Were not we there? Do you think us simpletons or senile?'

The woman called Capra scowled. 'She must believe us simple if she thinks that I will not recall that I most ardently wished her to find and return to us the traitor Beloved. That was why I agreed to your quest. To bring back to us the prisoner whose escape you aided!'

'No, I do not think you foolish! No. I but wanted . . . Let me tell you then the full tale of my journey, for I think that if you hear of it, you will begin to share my conviction.' I could feel Dwalia struggling to collect her thoughts and speak them well. 'You will recall that my studies had led me to believe that a man who had once served the Duke of Chalced was the necessary tipping point for the events I wished to trigger. Thus, while some of my luriks both delayed and aided Beloved to lead us to our prey, the first task of my quest was to go to Chalced. Having long studied the dream prophecies, I was certain of my interpretation. I needed to enlist the aid of this man, Ellik. Only with his aid and the service of the men loyal to him could I hope to follow Beloved to what we sought. I found Ellik. I showed him the power of my acolyte Vindeliar and—'

'Be done with your time-wasting!' Capra barked the words. 'Tell us what became of the luriks we entrusted to you? The finest of our creation, the ones with the most promise! Where are they? And the fine white steeds from Coultrie's stables that went forth with you?'

Was the silence long or did it just seem so in the dread I felt?

'Dead. All dead.' Dwalia spoke the words flatly. I opened my mouth at her lie. Alaria was sold into slavery, not dead. And how could she be sure the others had all died? What of the one who had been left behind with Shun?

'Dead?' The woman in red was horrified. Her perfectly-painted mouth hung open in horror.

'Are you certain of their deaths?' Yellow leaned forward over his belly, setting his palms on his round pink knees.

'Did you burn their bodies? Tell me you did not leave their bodies to fall into curious hands!' Green was horrified.

Capra clapped her hands together, and the sound was startlingly sharp. 'Account for them. Account for every one of them. How did each fall, and what became of each body? Tell us this now.'

Another pocket of silence. Dwalia spoke more quietly. A strange calm had come into her voice. 'We had penetrated the Six Duchies, completely unremarked. With Vindeliar's aid and prescience, we crossed that land unseen until we found the youngster. I was, as part of my mission, tracking Beloved as well. He it was who led us to him: the Unexpected Son. We were able to take . . . him. We . . . that is, Vindeliar, blinded their minds to us. We left that place, knowing they would not even remember that such a child had ever lived among them. All was going well. We were so close to boarding the ship to return here. But there was . . . an attack upon us. We were scattered. Some I saw fall. Others fled. Some few I gathered to me. I dared a magic that I did not trust nor understand. We—'

'They fell? They fled? How can you be sure that they died? How can you be sure that our secrets were not betrayed when they were captured? This is unconscionable!' Capra turned her wrath on her fellows. 'Do you see what you have done? Do you understand now? You sent the pick of our luriks, those with the best White blood, the best potential for breeding and for dreaming! Ordinary soldiers were not good enough, no, you had to send our finest. And now they are gone. Dead, scattered, who knows where? Taken as slaves? Living as beggars, selling dreams for food? And who knows who might use them against us?' She turned her fury back on Dwalia. 'You were tracking Beloved? Tracking? Blinded, lamed, and the best you could do was track him? What became of him? Where is he?'

'If you would let me tell my tale,' Dwalia began. Her voice was thickening. Tears? Fear? Fury?

The pasty-faced man in green had been shaking his head slowly through their exchange. Now he spoke. 'Capra asks the most important question last. Where is Beloved? You promised that you would bring him back to us. That was our condition for allowing you to free him and use him. You say it was *part* of your mission! I say it was the heart of it. You promised to bring him back alive to us, or proof that he was dead. Do you have that with you, at least?'

I heard the small sound it made when Dwalia wet her lips. Again, she measured her words carefully. 'No, I do not have proof. But I am certain he is dead by now.' She suddenly stood a little straighter and met his gaze. 'It came about exactly as I had deduced it could, and I made it happen.' Her voice rose and her words made my belly fill with ice. 'You doubted me! You mocked me and said my ambitions were far beyond my means! But I alone studied his dreams and I alone put those pieces together. I knew that I could use Beloved to lead me to the Unexpected Son. And he did! I alone manipulated events to make that happen!'

I felt dizzy as I tried to reconcile her words with all the snatches of information I had gleaned in our travels. The words Dwalia had spoken collided with the words I had read when I had pilfered my father's writings and delved into his secrets. Beloved.

I closed my eyes, for the man in yellow was licking his mouth as if he could barely restrain his enjoyment. The beautiful woman's eyes flamed with a cruel delight. Even the pale painted man's mouth had fallen open in astonishment. I closed my eyes so I would not have to witness their pleasure at my father's pain.

And behind my closed eyes, my own pain ignited.

My marketplace beggar. The man who had touched me and shown me all the futures, the man my father had stabbed, the man he chose to help even though it meant abandoning me, was Beloved. He had been the Fool. The White Prophet. The oldest and truest friend my father had ever had. All my suspicions confirmed. I had so longed to be wrong. I was sick. Sick with knowledge of how I had been part of that betrayal, at how I had prompted my father to stab his oldest friend.

And I was dizzy and weak with the realization that it was all real. They could do it, Dwalia and these Whites. They could sift dreams and make the future become what they wanted it to be. They could lever my father into killing his friend and then leaving me. Because they could give my father what he had wanted so much more than he wanted me. Was his Fool, his Beloved, dead? Or were they together? Was that why he had pushed me away? To make room in his life for his old friend? Bile rose in the back of my throat. If I'd had any food in my belly, I would have vomited it up onto their perfect white floor.

'Proof.' Capra's voice was quiet. Then it rose to a shout. 'PROOF! You promised us proof! You promised you would see him dead or bring him back. I warned you, all of you, how dangerous a creature he was. And is, for all we know!' She had turned to look at her fellows. 'And you conspired against me, all of you, in this foolish experiment.'

'Compose yourself,' the beautiful woman said in a low voice.

'Oh, compose your own self, Symphe!' the old woman snapped. For a moment, they glared at each other like squabbling kitchen maids. 'This disaster is your making! You and Fellowdy cooked it up and served it to Coultrie, and he was gullible enough to believe you and side with you. I'd measured Beloved when first he was brought here. I knew what he was capable of, from the beginning, and I warned you, all of you! I kept him at my side, I watched him, I tried to change him. And when I knew he would not be changed, I warned all of you. We should have done away with him then, when he would not silence his own questions.

'But no, you wanted his bloodlines. And Fellowdy wanted more than that of him, mooning after him like a lovesick ploughboy! So you overruled me! Me, who had actually spent time with him and knew how determined he was to be the White Prophet, to change the world. Was not it bad enough that he escaped our keeping the first time? That he smashed all we had so carefully built and planned for a half a century? Gone. Our Pale Woman, our beautiful Ilistore, and Kebal Rawbread, and the damned dragons set loose again. How could you have forgotten all that? But you did! You ignored all that Beloved had wrought and all he had destroyed the first time he escaped our keeping!'

I turned my head slightly and could see that Vindeliar knelt, his head bowed tight to his chest as if he could make himself smaller and less noticeable. Beside me, Dwalia looked like a cat pelted with rocks. Her eyes were slits and her mouth was dragged down as if she had a fishhook in her lip. On the dais, the three bore the old woman's wrath with varying degrees of displeasure. I could tell they had heard this rant before, but none dared interrupt it.

'We had him here!' Her voice rose to a screech. 'Beloved! Such a name for such a traitor. We could have simply held him here. He'd come back of his own volition. We could have kept him isolated, even kept him comfortable. We could have made Beloved believe we forgave him and that his tasks were accepted by us. Even after you discovered how he was corrupting our luriks and sending them away from Clerres, you still refused to see how dangerous he was. I said kill him. But no. Dwalia, jealous as ever, insisted that he had a secret. And when no pain tore any secret from him, when all you won from him was the name of his lover, you still refused to listen to me! You three thought you were so clever. Allow him to think he's escaped, you said. You said he was too weak to go far, that you could reel him back in at any time. I said no. I forbade it. But you overrode me. You called me foolish and old. You put him back out in the world and concealed that deed from me for months! And when I discovered it? More lies from all of you!'

She seemed drunk on her own fury and righteousness. Instead of calming, she was a storm still building. 'You, Dwalia, you promised you would follow Beloved and he would lead you to his secret. But at the last, he eluded you? Or did you choose to let him escape you?' She pointed a trembling, skinny finger at Dwalia. 'So, set aside, for now, those luriks you led into slaughter. Set aside the priceless white horses, and even the elixirs you squandered on your experiments! Where is Beloved?'

Dwalia lifted her head. She spoke with contained but unconcealed anger. 'Dead. I am certain he is dead. Just as dead as you wished him to be. And he died the way I wished him to die, at his lover's hands! Over and over FitzChivalry Farseer sank his knife into Beloved's belly, for he did not even know him after all I had done to change him! No healthy man could have survived such wounds. And Beloved was poisoned and blinded and broken even before he took them: I had made sure of that.' Dwalia stood taller. 'So I am certain he is dead. And by allowing his Catalyst to take Beloved's dying body, I drew them both away from my prey. From what they both had guarded and thought they had well concealed.' Once again she jerked my collar and hauled me to my feet. 'I tell you, this is the one all those prophecies foretold. And!' she shouted the word as Capra opened her faded lips to speak. 'And I believe this child is not only the Unexpected Son but that she carries Beloved's bloodline! The bloodline that Symphe and Fellowdy and Coultrie so wanted to develop! I bring this to you. I, Dwalia!' Her eyes roved over them and in a low voice she added, 'Do you recall when you would not let me go with Ilistore? When you sent her out without me, with no one to guard her back? Just as I have succeeded with this, I tell you plainly. Had I gone with her, she would never have fallen!'

She held me displayed for them, a rabbit she had snared. The lavishly dressed man in yellow looked at me and said in a low, awed voice, 'She does have the look of Beloved about her chin and the set of her ears. She could be his get.'

'SHE!' Capra bellowed at him. 'Do you know the word, Fellowdy? Do you hear it? Do you understand what it means? Often I have wondered if you know the difference between male and female, or if you care! This is not the Unexpected Son. The best she might be is a bastard daughter of a traitorous wretch. Even if she is Beloved's get, who knows what other blood is mingled in her? She's a mongrel. A mongrel from a tainted bloodline that has brought us nothing but disaster.' She shook her head, and her long silvery hair moved softly. 'Dwalia, you have been gone from us for three years. And in those years, the dreams of the luriks have stacked and multiplied. You speak of how you have shifted events to find this child, yet I know you have shifted them more than you can grasp. We are inundated with nightmares about the wrath of the Unexpected Son. Terrifying visions of the vengeance of the Twice-lived Prophet make the young ones wake crying out in fear. Dreams of a Destroyer! Oh, yes, you have manipulated events, but your petty vengeance has cascaded us into a very dangerous place. "Blind he sees the way, and the wolf comes at his heels!" The prophecy of the Unexpected Son had been fulfilled, to our detriment. It was done, and we looked to the newer dreams to find our way. But you, you have "wakened the sleeping wolf, and stirred the dragons in him to fury." You have set us on a dark path indeed with your vanity and your anger, and your selfish need for vengeance!'

Dwalia was stronger than she looked. I already knew that from the times we had fought. But now she lifted me from my feet and carried me forward, kicking and struggling.

Then she threw me at Capra.

I hit the edge of the dais in front of the blue-clad woman and fell to the hard floor, clutching my bruised ribs. There was no air left in my body. I could not squeak, let alone scream.

'You stupid old woman!' Dwalia did not roar the words but spoke them in a dark, cold voice. Two men with spears seized her by the arms and dragged her away but even as they did so, she spoke on as coolly as if they hadn't touched her. 'You refused to read what my examination of the dreams told me. You wouldn't listen to me the first time that *I* warned *you* about that creature you had taken in. I told you he would free the dragons. You said he could not. I begged you to let me go with Ilistore, that I might protect her. You all refused. You said Kebal Rawbread would be enough. But he wasn't, and so she died. She died horribly, alone and broken and cold, and the dragons you so fear were loosed upon the world.'

Dwalia was not struggling. The guards held her arms but looked as if they felt foolish. Vindeliar was rocking back and forth where he knelt, breathing in noisy nose gasps. I lay where I had fallen, trying for air, watching her.

'Beloved is dead,' she went on. 'I know it, I feel it. I've killed him in the worst way he could possibly imagine, and I've stolen the weapon he and his Catalyst were shaping to use against us. I've brought you the Unexpected Son from the prophecies, and all you can do is sit up there and refuse to let me enlighten you! I expect Capra to ignore my revelations; she has always hated me. And all Fellowdy can think of is his lechery, while Coultrie fears that if he speaks any truth, you will all turn on him and rebuke him for the imposter he has always been. But Symphe? I thought better of you. I thought you were wiser. I always believed that one day you would throw the other three down and rule Clerres as it should be ruled. But no. You hold the threads of all time in your hands and yet you will let them unravel in our lifetime! I've brought you what you need to make up for how stupid you were about Beloved, but you sit there like toads on stones and do nothing.'

'How dare you attack me? How dare you speak to any of us in such a tone? Guardsman! Ten lashes.' Capra ordered one of the guards who held Dwalia, her voice as cold as ice.

The man released Dwalia to his companion's safe-keeping and caught her by both wrists. Still she did not struggle. The first guardsman bowed precisely to the Four and swiftly left the room.

'Twenty,' Coultrie countered. 'Those were exquisite horses. All lost to me now.' There was no regret or sympathy in his voice. He might have been asking for a drink of water.

'Twenty!' Capra was outraged. 'How can you pretend your injury is greater than mine! How dare you!'

'Ten, then. Ten! But those were fine horses.' Coultrie subsided into a sulk, fussing with a green silk handkerchief he pulled from his sleeve. 'Irreplaceable,' he muttered, drawing another glare from Capra.

'So messy. So . . . physical. Ten. Now. Let us be done with this.'

Fellowdy closed his eyes wearily as if it were all too inconvenient for him even to consider.

The beautiful woman, Symphe, spoke last. 'Dwalia, you have gone too far. Too often I have allowed you to speak in blunt terms, but your insults are beyond honesty. I cannot protect you from this. Five lashes,' she suggested. There was regret in her voice, but not a great deal of it.

Capra turned a furious gaze on her. 'Five? FIVE? You insult me, too! You insult Coultrie, who lost a generation of steeds. She does not say she killed Beloved, only that she believes he is dead! She has disobeyed and defied us and—'

'Ten then,' Symphe amended. 'Let it be ten, and let it be over. It has been too long a day already.'

Capra was shaking her head. 'We will have this be over, and leave this chamber. But this evening, I wish to see all of you in my tower chamber.'

I heard the guard's boots, his heels striking the floor very precisely, the jingling of the chain a music to the beat of his footsteps. I sat up slowly, my back to the dais, feeling dizzy and sick. I watched dully as the guard lifted a small panel of the smooth white floor and attached the chains to a ring there.

Dwalia still sounded very calm and rational. 'No. It's not fair. It's not right. No.' The guard who dragged her forward paid no attention to her words or her attempts to sink her nails into his forearm and free herself. She braced her feet on the smooth floor yet he dragged her effortlessly. When he reached his partner, the other man seized her hair and clacked two pieces of metal around her throat. She struggled while he put the clips through the collar. Both guards stepped back abruptly and there she was, Dwalia who had terrorized me for so long, chained like a dog, the heavy loops of metal from the collar around her neck secured to the ring in the floor.

It was a short chain. She could not stand upright. For a moment, she stood bent over, glaring at the Four. Then she hunched down, crossing her arms on her chest and tucking her face in as tightly as she could.

I could hear Vindeliar breathing loudly, a shrill note to each breath he expelled, but he did not move from where he knelt. This was not new to either of them, I realized as the two guards stepped back. One gave the other a stick to match the one he held. No.

Not a stick. Each unfurled short lashes attached to heavy braided leather handles. Whips. They shook them loose in an expert fashion and each took a position to either side of Dwalia.

'You are fools!' she shouted in one last attempt at outrage, but her voice shook with fear as one of the guards made his lash whistle in a practice swipe.

Then it began.

It was not ten lashes. It was forty. Ten decreed by each of the Four. The guards alternated their blows, the lashes rising and falling as rhythmically as a smith's hammer. Dwalia could not escape. Terribly, between blows, she almost had time to decide where the lash would next fall. But the guardsmen were experienced or perhaps just cruel. Always the lash seemed to fall on fresh flesh, or cleverly bisect the welt his partner had just created.

Her garments leapt at each blow. At first, she stayed hunched where she was. The lovely cloth of the back of the dress the captain had bought for his lover frayed and finally fell away. She began to give short shrieks and to scuttle like a beetle all around the ring in the floor. The guards did not care. She could not evade them. Her flesh welted and oozed, and droplets of blood began to speckle the floor and the strong bared arms of the guardsmen. Before they finished, the lashes were slapping raw meat and flinging arcs of blood. Forty had never seemed so large a number before.

I covered my ears. I closed my eyes. Somehow I still heard the sounds that she made. They were not screams nor curses nor even pleas. They were terrible sounds. My eyes kept opening, no matter how tightly I closed them. There she was, the person who had ruined my life, the person I hated most in the whole world, being torn and slashed and ripped and tattered by whips of leather. They did to her what I had so longed to do to her, and it was disgusting and horrifying and unbearable. I was a little trapped animal. I panted and whined and wept but no one took any notice of me. I peed myself, soaking my trousers and making a puddle at my feet. I learned in that afternoon that I would have saved her, if I could. That while I might hate her enough to kill her, I did not think I could ever hate anyone enough to torture them.

Dwalia managed to protect her eyes, but it cost her damage to her hands. The tips of the lashes curled cleverly to slice her shoulder and then lick a scarlet tip across her cheek. She could hide her face in her hands, but then the backs of her hands were vulnerable. She had begun with her arms crossed on her chest and her hands tucked protectively close, but eventually she ended collapsed on her side, her legs drawn up to her belly and her face hidden in the crook of one bloodied arm.

Her punishment was done with swift efficiency but in those long and paralysed moments, I felt the rushing, dragging, shifting currents of time. Every stripe fell in a predetermined place on her body. Every twitch of her shuddering flesh changed that place. But it changed it in a logical and defined way. While my stomach churned at what they did to her, a calm part of my mind made orderly sense of every violent action and her reaction to it. I saw that if she moved this way, the guard would shift his arm, and the lash would strike there, and the blood would fly just so. It was all predetermined. None of it was random.

In that horrifying recognition I suddenly saw how each action we had taken had moved us forward to this place and time and to this event. As late as this morning, there had been a thousand opportunities to choose a different path that would not have led us to this bloody resolution. Dwalia could have chosen to remain Lady Aubretia and gone to the inn to wait for her captain. She could have sent a messenger bird ahead to Symphe and arranged a secret meeting. She could have leapt overboard and drowned herself. Or stayed on the ship. There had been so many ways to divert her path to avoid this disaster. Why had not she seen and known or guessed this would happen?

Why had I not foreseen that she would drag me into this with her?

I did not know enough of these people to predict what would happen to me.

'Thirty-eight.'

'Thirty-nine.'

The guards had been counting, each calling the strike of his own lash. Now they chorused, 'Forty!' and both whips fell. Slowly, slowly they drew the leather straps back and coiled the wet leather thongs around the handle. Their fingers were bloody, their strong arms and stoic faces speckled with blood. Dwalia remained where she was, panting. She had long ceased crying out. What was the sense in crying out when it would avail you nothing? All the nights I had whispered pleas for my father to find me had availed me nothing. The wash of futility I felt left me cold and empty. And free to act.

Capra cleared her throat. If she was moved at all by the horror she had inflicted on Dwalia, it did not show in her voice as she issued her commands. 'Take her to the lowest levels. Confine her there. Vindeliar, go to your chamber and resume your old duties tomorrow.'

Vindeliar was already in motion, scuttling for the door. He looked back once at Dwalia, his mouth turned down in a grimace. Then he was sidling out the door and it closed behind him. It took both guards to get Dwalia to her feet. One unfastened the chain from her neck as the other unhooked it from the floor ring and returned the panel to its place. Then each guard took an arm and stood her up between them. She could not walk but lurched and stumbled and dragged. The sounds of pain she made were pitiful. I stayed where I was. For one awful moment, she lifted her head. Her eyes burned with hatred of me. Her hands had bloody welts on the back where she had sheltered her face from the lashes. She pointed a shaking finger at me and said something.

'What was that she said?' Coultrie demanded.

No one spoke; perhaps no one else had made out her words. I had.

'Your turn now.'

TWENTY-FOUR

Hand and Foot

A rat's head on a stick. No one holds the stick but it is shaken at the dreamer. The rat squeaks. 'The bait is the trap, the trapper the trapped!' The rat's mouth is red, its teeth yellow; its eyes are black and shining. It appears to be the sort of large brown rat often seen near the docks of Clerres town. It has a black-and-white ruff about its neck, and the staff it is fixed to is green and yellow.

Capra's Dream 903872, recorded by Lingstra Okuw

'Well, that was unpleasant,' Symphe muttered.

'Blame yourself,' Capra countered. 'You created that moment. Releasing Beloved, lying to me. Allowing that sour-faced wretch to think she had the perspicacity of a White Prophet. You encouraged her to create this mess. I suppose I must be the one to set events back on their proper course.'

'I will take charge of the child,' Symphe announced.

I heard their voices as one might hear flies buzzing at a window. Dwalia was gone. Only her spattered and smeared blood remained. Vindeliar was gone. I was alone in this place they had brought me to. I stared up at the lovely woman. Pretty did not mean kind. She did not look at me.

'That you shall not,' Capra announced.

'We should all have access to her, to determine her value,' Fellowdy suggested.

Capra laughed low. 'We know what value you would give her, Fellowdy. No.'

Coultrie spoke in a low voice. 'Do away with the creature. Right now. It will only cause division among us, and we've had enough of that. Recall how Beloved's return set us against one another.' He frowned so severely that the cosmetics on his face flaked a sprinkling of powder.

'"Never do that which you can't undo, until you've perceived what you can't do once you've done it." That is among our oldest teachings, you idiot! We need to summon collators and search for any possible references to her.' Symphe spoke smoothly.

'That will take days!' Coultrie objected.

'As you are not the one who will be doing the work, why should you care?' Fellowdy replied. In a quieter voice, he added, 'As if you could understand the dreams, having never had any of your own.'

'Do you think I am deaf?' Coultrie demanded angrily, to which Fellowdy smiled and replied, 'Of course not. You are merely blind to the futures.'

'Enough!' Capra snapped. She glanced at me and I looked away. I feared to have her look into my eyes. Something in her stare seemed to gloat, as if she kept to herself some bit of knowledge. 'Symphe, I propose that we hold her in the upper cells. In safety. In health. Perhaps she is nothing but a blonde child stolen from scutwork in FitzChivalry's home. Dwalia offered us no proof that she is otherwise. If she were truly of Beloved's lineage, she would be dreaming by now, and Dwalia would have offered the records of her dreams to us as proof of her value. I suspect she is nothing but a ruse, an excuse for Dwalia's losses.'

'Then why not leave her with me?' Symphe demanded. 'I could use another maidservant.'

Capra's look was deadly. 'A ruse can be used more than once, dear girl. Dwalia claims Beloved is dead. She said nothing of FitzChivalry, his Catalyst. If this child is his or has value to him we may find that once more we deal with the Unexpected Son. The real one. The one who aided Beloved to thwart us. So, she needs to be confined until we determine if there is any truth at all to Dwalia's tale. Until we have wrung the full truth from both Dwalia and that monster she has cultivated.'

'I do not think that is necessary. What do you—'

Capra spoke over her. 'Or I will have them all killed. As I should have done with Beloved.'

My heart was beating so hard at their words that I thought my whole body shook with it.

A silence fell. Coultrie spoke. 'What right have you to dictate to us? There are four of us.'

'I have the right of my years. My experience. My wisdom. And as you went behind my back with your decision to allow Beloved to "escape", I think it is my turn to make a decision in which none of you have a say!' She paused and satisfaction gleamed in her fish-eyes. 'Oh, look away and pretend you could deceive me! Such a farce. Do you think I do not know how you diverted funds and resources to Dwalia? You think I have no knowledge of the bird messages she used to send back to you?' She shook her head at their naiveté and her smile was a terrible thing to see. 'You have forgotten who dreams better and deeper and more than any of you or your Clerres-bred Whites! You thought you had kept your secrets from me: but I have balanced that scale with the dreams I've withheld from you!

'While you indulged Dwalia's profitless quest for revenge, you ignored our larger problem. Not a child who may or may not be of the White bloodline, but the damnable dragons. All we sought to prevent has happened. Dragons are loose in the world again, and the luriks who remain to us are dreaming dark visions of wolves and sons and dragons. We came within a finger snap of ending them forever! Yet dragons do not forgive. And dragons do not forget. But apparently, you three do forget that, above all, dragons do not forget a wrong done them! It is time you stopped playing at petty politics here and looked to the future. Beloved has cracked the foundation of our knowledge, but we are rebuilding it with new dreams and prophecies. We can take back the rudder and steer the world to our advantage. But all that would end if we were to look up and see wings in the skies over Clerres.'

A silence fell during which I came slowly to my feet. I was ashamed of my wet trousers. They clung to me, cold now. I clutched my little bundle to my chest and allowed the tears to come to my eyes. I'd had time to weave a pitiful shield of lies. I tried to hope they would work. 'I want to go home. Please. I don't understand any of this. I just want to go home.'

Their gazes converged on me, exhibiting various degrees of astonishment and disapproval. I made my lower lip quiver. Symphe, the lovely young woman, spoke sternly. 'You do not speak to any of us unless we tell you to. Is that clear?'

I lowered my gaze. Could I use this? 'Yes, ma'am. Dwalia told me not to talk to any of you. I should have remembered.'

I kept my head bent but tried to watch them through my lashes. Symphe looked uncomfortable. I dared myself and spoke in the most childish voice I could muster. 'Dwalia said we would talk to Symphe alone. Or with Fellowdy. She taught me dreams to say. Do you want to hear them now?'

Symphe must have given a signal, something I didn't see. The swung foot of the guard swept my feet from under me. My elbow struck the floor hard and the pain shot into my hand and my shoulder. I clutched it and curled around it.

'A cell,' Symphe suggested coldly. 'On the lower level. Take her now.'

Again, I was seized by the back of my shirt and handled like a sack. I hugged my little bundle of clothing, hoping it would shield me from the blow I expected. My toes barely touched the floor as the guards dragged me to the tall doors. Behind me, I heard Symphe declare, 'I propose that later tonight we gather. We will talk and then we will go together to see what she has to say. Until then, no one should visit her. No one.'

The old woman laughed. 'Oh, dear little Symphe. Did she start to tell your secrets? Did you really believe that I did not already know—'

The doors closed on her words. My collar was cutting into my throat. I clutched at it with both hands. 'Let her breathe,' said the guard who didn't have hold of me, and I was abruptly dropped to the floor. I sprawled there, gasping. I could smell Dwalia's blood on both of them, and garlic. One of them needed a bath. Badly.

'Get up,' one said, and nudged me with his sandalled foot. I obeyed, but slowly. There were people in the corridor, staring at us. I looked down. Blood smears on the floor. They'd brought Dwalia this way. They were going to put me in a cell near her. With her? Dread froze me.

'Walk or be dragged,' the same guard said.

'Walk,' I said breathlessly. Would there be a chance for me to break free and run? Run where?

Then, from behind us, I heard a call. 'Guards, wait!'

It was Fellowdy who called to us. 'It has been decided we will keep her on the upper level, behind a Lock of Four. Take her there. We will join you shortly.'

'We obey,' one of the guards said. The one that had caught me by the collar gave me a push. I walked past well-dressed folk who turned to gawk after us as they herded me along. A door opened to one side, and I glimpsed a beautiful ballroom. Two girls my age, dressed all in lace and escorted by pages, stared curiously as they passed us and the guards hurried me along to get me out of their sight.

The first flight of stairs lifted in a wide spiral. My guards did not pause on the landing and even though I was panting and half-sick by then, I climbed alongside them up the second flight of stairs and then along a brown-panelled corridor. At intervals, shelves jutted from the walls, each holding a fat lamp shaped rather like a teapot. There were no windows to admit light, but there were doors to either side of the carpeted hall. We moved through a perpetual gloom. The burning oil smelled like a pine forest.

We passed an open door and I had a glimpse of a room that was lined with little boxed shelves with scrolls sticking out of them. From floor to ceiling they went, and it reminded me of a honeycomb, or the chambers in a paper wasps' nest. At long tables, people sat with scrolls unfurled and weighted to lie open beside stacks of paper and inkpots and pen stands. I wanted to stare but when I slowed, one of the guards slapped me on the back of my head. 'Walk!' he reminded me, and I walked.

We passed another chamber full of tables and with the walls lined with books rather than scrolls. Scribes lifted their eyes from the pages and stared as we passed. I saw no windows, but squares of light shone through the stonework. I'd never seen such a thing. Some of the people in there were not much older than me and others were older than my father. Their robes were all a rich green. They were not Whites and I guessed that these were the Servants of the Whites. No one spoke as we passed though I felt their curious glances.

At the end of the corridor was a door and yet another set of steps. These were narrower and steeper, and I struggled to keep moving. At the top, I turned to look back. One of the guardsmen looked away from my gaze. The other never met it. He pounded on a door that had a little barred window in it until a woman with dark hair and brown eyes came and looked through the bars. 'What is it?' she demanded.

'Lock of Four,' one of them said.

She raised her brows. 'For whom?'

He gestured down. She stood on her tiptoes to look down at me. 'Oh,' she said. 'Very well.' I saw her puzzlement, but she unlocked the door and we went into a very small room. She turned away from us and unlocked a second door. Bright sunlight flooded in and she led us out onto a flat, unroofed area. I blinked my eyes and then lifted my hand to shade them. Light bounced back at me from a white floor. I squinted. It was a large area, with tall walls, and I caught a glimpse of a guard walking slowly along on top of the wall. We were on the roof of the stronghold. The tall graceful towers I had glimpsed rose from each corner of the structure.

'This way,' she said. I followed the woman and the guardsmen came behind me. I held one hand over my sun-dazzled eyes, squinting through my spread fingers. It seemed ridiculous: small me in the midst of such vigilance. We crossed an open space and then entered a narrower way, fronted with iron-barred chambers on both sides. Some were occupied but most were empty. I halted when the woman halted.

She looked down at me. 'Now we wait for the Four, for only they have the keys to these last four cells. Give me that sack.'

I surrendered my small carry-pack reluctantly. She opened it and looked inside. 'Just clothes,' I told her. She said nothing as she rummaged through my tattered garments, then handed it back to me.

I heard a door shut and low contentious voices and squinted back the way we had come. The Four. The moment they became aware we were waiting, their conversation ceased. Each had a guard accompanying them. They walked briskly to where we stood. Symphe took an elaborate key on a jewelled fob from a pocket concealed in her skirts. She handed it to her guard, who inserted it into a long bar and turned it with a sharp 'snap'. Then she stepped back as Coultrie handed a key with a white bone handle to his guard. Another snap. When all four keys had been inserted and turned, the woman who had guided us slid the long metal bar to one side and opened the door. She motioned me inside.

As I stepped through the door, I heard a deep soft voice from the next cell. 'What, Symphe? Not even a hello? Coultrie, you should wash your face. You look ridiculous. Fellowdy, have you no youngster to bugger today? Ah, and here is Capra. I see you have washed the blood off your hands for this visit. How formal of you.'

Not a one of them flinched or responded. I was within my cage and couldn't peer into the next one but I wondered who it was who so boldly challenged the Four. Then the first guardswoman shut the barred door with a clang. Each guard stepped forward to turn a key and remove it, and then present it to their master or mistress.

'Child,' Capra said abruptly. 'Tell me your name and your father's name.'

I had rehearsed it. 'I am Bee Badgerlock, of Withywoods. My father is Holder Tom Badgerlock. He manages the sheep and the orchards and the grounds for Lord FitzChivalry. Please, just let me go home!'

Her eyes were flat. I hadn't lied, not at all. I looked at her earnestly.

Without a farewell or words of any sort, they all walked away. From the next cell, I heard that soft voice again. 'Eleven adults to lock up one little child. Are they right to fear you?'

I dared no response. They might ignore him, but I thought they might come back to beat me. Clutching my bundle, I surveyed my cell. There was a pot for waste in the corner, and a low bedstead with a straw-stuffed mattress with a single blanket of undyed wool at the foot of it. The back wall of my cell was of lacy white stone; the openings that let in air and light were shaped like leaves and flowers and seashells. I tried my hand in one. It could fit and I could reach all the way through to the outer wall. The wall was as thick as my hand and forearm. These cells would be unpleasant in winter, I thought to myself. Then I wondered if winter even came to this region, and whether I would live long enough to see it.

The cell was not much wider than the bed, with just room for me to walk past it. The door and the wall that faced the walkway were of bars. I had an unimpeded view of the empty cell across from mine. I would have no privacy here, not for using the waste pot or for changing out of my urine-soaked trousers.

I could not quite poke my head out between the bars. I looked as far as I could up and down the walkway, but saw no one. I had a small amount of private time. I pulled out the blue trousers that Trader Akriel had given me. I'd been wearing them the night they killed her. Her favourite shade of blue. And some brown spots of her blood. There were gaping holes in the knees now and the cuffs were frayed to fringe. But they were dry. I hastily changed and then spread out my wet trousers on the floor of my cell to dry.

I sat down on the edge of the bed. The straw mattress was thin. It crushed flat beneath me and I felt the ropes of the bedstead. It would, I decided, be more comfortable to pull the mattress off the bedstead and sleep on the floor. I went again to the door and peered out. The walkway was still empty. Only then did I allow myself to open the collar of my shirt. I tucked my chin and nose inside it and smelled the elusive, fading scent of honeysuckle from my battered, flaking candle.

'Mama,' I said aloud, as I had not said since I was very small. Tears stung my eyes as if my spoken word had summoned grief from the grave rather than any remembrance of her.

'You are very, very young to be in such a large amount of trouble,' the soft voice said. I froze and made no sound, my heart hammering. The voice was deep and though the words were in Common they were flavoured with a foreign accent. 'Tell me, little thing. What wrong have you done? Or what wrong do the Four imagine you have done, to merit being locked away like this?'

I said nothing. I sat as small as I could, unmoving lest the crackling of straw betray that I was there.

He did not speak for a long time. Then he said, 'When I was a boy this was a beautiful place. There were no cells here then. It had been quarters for an emperor's wives, but by the time I knew this place, it was a lovely roof garden. Latticework pergolas gentled the sun. All manner of flowers and healing herbs grew here in pots. I used to come here in the evenings, when the night-blooming jasmine flavoured the air. And on the hottest nights, when the wind off the sea cooled these chambers, I'd sleep up here.'

He spoke on, not asking any questions, and I listened silently as the light slowly, slowly faded from the long summer afternoon. I heard the woman who had opened the door speaking to someone. No one answered. I sat still. I heard her steps and her voice came again, closer. 'Here you are.'

This time I heard some muttered thanks. I dared to slip silently from my bed and venture to the door. I heard footsteps and the soft clatter of dishes on a tray. The footsteps paused, and a woman said something and received muttered thanks. I listened intently and heard her stop twice more before she reached the cell next to mine. It was the guard who had unlocked the door to admit me. She set a dish on the floor and slid it wordlessly under the barred door of my neighbour's cell. When she came to mine, she frowned and shook her head. 'So small you are. Here's your food. I'll return with water for you.' She took a breath as if to speak more, but then folded her lips and moved on. Only two bowls remained on her tray. I heard her pause twice more toward the end of the corridor. So, seven of us held in what had looked like twenty or more cells.

I drew my bowl closer to me and considered it. The stringy vegetable lumps were a peculiar orange colour. There were six of them, on a bed of a grain I did not recognize. Shreds of cabbage added their strong odour, and some other green herb had been chopped and sprinkled over it. A little paddle was thrust into the pottage. I ate it all, though the herb stung my tongue. And when she came back to take my dish and leave me a little pot of water with a fat base and a narrow neck, I drank almost all of it. A little I set aside, thinking that if she brought me more water tomorrow, this much I would use to wash my face.

A long evening deepened into a darker night. The guard came to light the lamp – a fat pot with a little wick sticking out of its spout. The flame burned very white and gave off a smell like pine trees. The night wind whispered through the walls, bringing with it the smell of the sea. As the sun went down, I heard the gulls crying. I sat on the edge of my bed and thought of the Four discussing what I might be and wondered what I could make them believe. They knew too much. Capra knew my father was the Unexpected Son. So I could not claim that. I told them I was only the child of a servant, stolen from my ravaged home, just a simple little girl. If they believed that, would they release me? Sell me? Or kill me as worthless?

If they knew what my dreams had told me I was, they would certainly kill me.

I wanted Wolf Father, but dared not lower my walls. What if there were others in Clerres who had the same sort of powers as Vindeliar?

Night darkened. I heard whispering from the other cells but I could not make out the words. I wondered who else was held here and what they had done. I stood and shook out the blanket that I scarcely needed in so warm a place. I took off my shoes and put them neatly side by side. I dragged the sad floppy mattress off the bedframe, spread it on the floor in the open space near the door and folded it in half to give it some thickness. I put the blanket on top of it, curled up on it and closed my eyes.

I woke up with tears on my cheeks and my throat tight. I felt my father's hand on my head and I reached up to seize it. 'Da! Why did it take so long for you to find me? I want to go home!'

He didn't answer but gently pulled his fingers through my tangled curls. Then the deep, rich voice spoke again. 'So. Little one. What did you do?'

I caught my breath and sat up. The light from the kettle-lamp barely reached me. I scrabbled back from what the feeble light showed me. A hand had reached around the corner from the next cell and into mine. The skin was the blackest I had ever seen on any living creature. That hand had been touching my head. I tried to quiet my breathing but I was panting with fear.

The voice came again. 'How can you be afraid of me? There is a wall between us. I can do you no harm. Talk to me, little one. For I have been here so very long, and no one else speaks to me. I would like to know what goes on in the great outside world. What brought you here?' The hand turned over, showing me a paler palm. I imagined that the owner of the hand must be lying on the floor of the next cell, shoulder pressed tight against the barred wall to reach through to my cell. He said nothing more and the hand just lay there, open and imploring.

'Who are you?' I asked. And then, 'What did *you* do?' Was I next door to a murderer? I reminded myself of how kind Dwalia had been in the first moments I met her. I would not be tricked so easily again.

'My name is Prilkop. I was the White Prophet of my time, but that was many, many years ago. I've been through many, many skin changes in my life.'

A dim memory stirred. Had Dwalia said that name? Had I read it in my father's papers?

'And why am I here?' he continued. He spoke very softly. I edged closer to the bars to hear his answer. 'For speaking the truth. For doing my duty to the world. Come, child, I'm nothing to fear, and I think you need a friend. What's your name, little one?'

I didn't want to tell him. Instead I asked, 'Why does no one speak to you?'

'They're afraid of me. Or, more exactly, they're afraid of what they might hear. Afraid they might learn something that will trouble them.'

'I can't be in any more trouble.'

I meant my words one way. He took them another. 'I think that is quite possibly true. Nor can I have any more trouble than I already do. So. Tell me your story, little one.'

I was quiet, thinking. I could not trust anyone. Anything I told him, he might tell others. Might that be useful?

'They came to my house in the middle of a bright, snowy day. Right before Winterfest. To steal me. Because they thought I was the Unexpected Son. But I'm not.'

I tried to be so careful of what I told him but once I began to talk to him, words dropped from my mouth, often out of order or choked to a squeak by the tightness of my throat. I never put my hand in his but somehow he ended up holding both my dirty bare feet in his one big black hand.

I talked in circles, telling him part of the tale and then going back to explain Vindeliar and telling him of hiding Perseverance under my cloak, but he was probably dead anyway, and how they had stolen Shun with me, but she had escaped. I started shaking as I told him, and he gently pressed my feet and said nothing. Over and over, I insisted their taking me was a terrible mistake. And when my confused telling was all spilled in splattered tears and words, he said, 'Poor little thing. You are not the Unexpected Son. I know, for I have met him—and his prophet.'

I grew very still. Was it a trick? But what he said next was even more frightening.

'I dreamed you. You become possible the day the Beloved was pulled back from death, undoing so many, many dream prophecies. On that day, I knew something had torn through all the futures and replaced them with new possibilities. It terrified me. I had believed my days as a dream-prophet were well and truly spent. That my time was over, and I could return home. Then the dream of you came. Oh, I did not know it would be you, then. But I was shocked. And afraid of your coming.

'I tried to make it less likely. As soon as Beloved and his Catalyst returned to me, as soon as I could, I persuaded them to part. I thought I had done enough to shift the world into a better path.' The big hand closed briefly around my foot. 'But when I began dreaming about you again, I knew it was too late. You existed. And by your existence, you created many possible divergences from the true Path.'

'You dreamed of me?' I wiped my wet face with my shirtfront.

'I did.'

'What did you dream?'

His hand went lax under my feet. I didn't move them. His words came as slow as dripping honey. 'I dreamed many dreams. Not always about you but futures that became possible when you existed. I dreamed of a wolf that unmasked a puppeteer. I dreamed of a scroll that unwrote itself. I dreamed of a man who shook planks off himself and became two dragons. I dreamed—'

'I dreamed that one, too!' I spoke before I considered if I should.

Silence, save for two other prisoners whispering down the corridor. 'I'm not surprised. Though I am frightened.'

'But why are those dreams me?'

He laughed softly. 'I dreamed a whirlwind of fire, come to change everything. I reached out to take its hand. Do you know what happened?'

'It burned you?'

'No. It offered me its foot, instead. Its little bare foot.'

I snatched my feet back as if I were the one who had been burned. He laughed softly, very quietly. 'Done is done, little one. I know you, now. I knew you would come. I did not expect you to be a child. So. Now will you tell me your name?'

I thought carefully. 'My name is Bee.'

He said nothing. His hand was still there, open on the cell floor. I thought it must be very uncomfortable for him to lie on his floor and reach around to my cell like that.

'If you dreamed about me, can you tell me what is going to happen to me?'

His stillness was like a curtain. The lamp in the corridor outside my cell was running out of oil. I did not have to see it to know how the flame danced on the end of the wick, sucking up the last of it. Finally, the dark rich voice spoke again. 'Bee. Nothing happens to you. You happen to everything.'

Slowly he drew his hand back. He did not speak again that night.

TWENTY-FIVE

Bribes

Our informants have indicated that a large shipment of excellent quality jade and turquoise, both raw and worked, is being amassed at Kerl Bay on the Reden Peninsula. Another ship there is loading excellent hardwood timbers.

In the past six months, three luriks have dreamed about a great storm. Two dreamed of ships broken and wrecked on the rock as clouds parted to reveal a quarter moon.

While we remain uncertain of the exact month of the storm, three luriks felt this event to be close in the future paths.

It is the opinion of this collator that if a ship were stationed in Skalen Cove near the Harke Rocks, following the storm there might be excellent scavenging. It might be a good idea to have on such a vessel the sort of sailors who could deal with those who might dispute ownership of such a valuable cargo as well. Even if our vessel must remain at the ready for six months, the profit would still be substantial.

Report to the Four from Collator Jens of the Seventh Rank

How could I have slept so heavily? I awoke to a woman nudging me. She had pushed the toe of her sandalled foot under the barred door and was poking me with it. 'Move away, please. I will slide your porridge in.' Her voice was low and neutral. Sunlight washed lace patterns on the floor. Shells. Flowers.

I sat up and for a time nothing made sense. Then I remembered. Dwalia beaten bloody, and me in a cell. And in the night, a friend? I stood up and pressed my face against the bars, trying to see into the next cell. All I could see was slightly more of the corridor.

489

The woman who had wakened me had brown hair and eyes. She wore a simple garment of pale blue, sleeveless and sashed at the waist. It stopped at her knees, and on her feet she had simple leather sandals. She stooped and set her tray on the floor, took a bowl of porridge from it and slid the bowl under the barred door. Plain beige porridge in a white bowl. No cream, no honey, no berries. No Withywoods, no clatter of cooking and waiting for my father to come. Just plain porridge with a wooden spoon stuck in it. I tried to be grateful as I ate it. It tasted of nothing. When the woman came back to take the bowl, I asked her, 'May I have water to wash myself?'

She looked puzzled at my request. 'I wasn't told to give you any.'

'Can you ask permission to give me some?'

Her eyebrows rose almost to her hairline. 'Of course not!'

The dark rich voice from the night before spoke. 'She cannot do anything except what she is told to do.'

'That isn't true!' the woman exclaimed, and then clapped both hands over her mouth. She stooped and hastily piled my bowl onto the waiting tray and hurried off so quickly that the dishes jounced noisily on the tray.

'You scared her,' I said.

'She scares herself. They all do.'

I was distracted by the sound of the door opening at the end of the walkway. I pressed my cheek hard to the bars and saw the Four enter one at a time. They were not dressed as grandly today, but still they wore their colours. Four soldiers followed them. Symphe was in a loose red gown. It had no sleeves and fell from her shoulders to her feet in folds, interrupted only by a scarlet belt that cinched it at her waist. Fellowdy was in a long yellow tunic and trousers that barely reached his knees. Some of Coultrie's cosmetics had flaked onto his green vest as if he had just come in from a snowfall. Capra's attire surprised me. She wore what looked to me like a blue shirt with loose flowing sleeves. If she had trousers on at all, they were shorter than the shirt was long. Her bared legs were sturdy but as pale as a fish's belly. She wore sandals of brown leather that slapped against her feet as she walked. I had never seen anyone so attired, and I stared at her when she stood outside my cage.

'Unlock,' Symphe announced, and offered an elaborate fob to the guard. The man took it, then stepped forward and inserted an oddly shaped key into the bar that closed my door and turned it. One after another, each of the other three guards received a key and turned it in the lock. When all four keys had been turned and were standing in the bar, Capra stepped forward and slid the bar aside. 'You will come with me,' she told me as I stepped out of the cell. She spoke to the other three as the guards retrieved the keys and restored them to each owner. 'I will return her here at the beginning of the third watch. You will meet me here then with your key-guards.' She looked down at me. 'Will you obey me and stay by my side, or must I leash you?'

The key-guard who attended her held up for my inspection a chain and collar. I looked from it to Capra. 'I will obey you,' I lied.

'Good. Come along, then.' The others stepped out of our way and I followed on Capra's heels, her guard behind me. I longed to peer into the cell next to mine but her guard herded me quickly past. I had only the briefest glimpse of a black man sitting on a bunk, his head bowed.

Behind us, I heard Symphe say to Coultrie and Fellowdy, 'I do not approve of this. It is true, the girl may be nothing at all. She may not even have White bloodlines. I have heard that folk from the mountains in the far north are sometimes as pale as true Whites. But what if Dwalia spoke true and somehow she is the Unexpected Son from the dreams? Why should Capra have the first opportunity to speak with her?'

'Because you all agreed to it!' Capra called sharply over her shoulder. To me, she said, 'Don't dawdle.' I did not feel that we fled, but we certainly left their company as swiftly as we could. Few of the cells we passed were occupied. The prisoners sat sedately on their beds, doing nothing. As if she heard my unvoiced question, Capra said, 'They are not evil. Simply wilful. We put them here to correct them. They will become useful, and then they will be allowed to rejoin their fellows. Or . . . they won't.' She did not say what else would befall them if they did not become useful.

For a white-haired old woman she moved very quickly as we descended the same steps I had climbed the day before. Down we went, until we reached the ground floor. When we emerged in the main corridor, she swiftly led me off in a different direction. We passed chambers with their doors open, and I glimpsed windows that looked out onto a lovely garden. Soon enough, we entered a room with statuary and cushioned benches. Beyond it was a garden with a large pool in the middle. We crossed swiftly through it, and I felt almost dizzied by the heady fragrance of the trees in bloom. There was a shady portico along the front of a long wall with a series of doors in it. She opened one. I smelled a sharp scent on the cloud of steam that rolled out.

'Go wash yourself. Your hair, your feet, all of you. You will find garments on a bench there. After you have dried yourself, put them on and come out. Do not be slow, but be thorough. You stink.'

She delivered her command and her judgment in an impersonal tone. The prospect of warm water made me swift to obey her. I entered and was glad to close the door behind me. Light came into the room from high windows. My hope that there might be another exit was quickly dashed. In the room was a bench with the promised clean garments and some sandals beneath it, and a drying cloth. There was a pot of something soft like pudding. I dipped my fingers into it and rubbed them together. Soap, I surmised, scented with some sharp herb. A low tub of smoothed and polished stone held steaming water. There was nothing else in the room.

I stripped hastily with many a backward glance at the door. I rolled my dirty garments around my precious candle and set it carefully on the bench before I stepped down into the tub. It was far deeper than I had expected. The water was almost too hot and came up to my chin when I sat down. For a moment, it was all I could do just to sit there. I leaned back and let myself sink completely under the water. When I came up, I saw that pale brown rivulets of dirty water were coming from my hair. I was not surprised but I was still embarrassed. I helped myself to a handful of the soap and stood up to scrub myself with it. After a bit of hesitation, I rubbed it through my hair as well, and then rinsed myself in the now greyish water.

I had not been naked since my time with Trader Akriel, and the fading browns and greens of various bruises still showed on my hips and shins. My toenails were cracked and rub as I might some dirt remained caught in them. The skin of my hands had been roughened by the various tasks I'd done for Dwalia, the hands of a servant, not a high-born Buck girl. I knew a moment of shame that I had not known before that the kitchen girls' chapped hands were evidence of the sort of work that had never been expected of me. So often I had cursed the events that had taken me away from my comfortable life, and now I had a little jolt of realization. How would it have been to be born a slave or a servant, to know that the abuse I'd suffered was to be my daily life?

I put on the garments and felt oddly naked in them. They were loose and the trousers came barely to my knees, but the sleeves of the blouse fell past my wrists. The fabric of both garments was light and a pale rose in colour. There was no way to carry the candle inside my new shirt. The sandals were a mystery but I finally strapped them to my feet. Beneath the clothing, I found a comb. The water had put my hair into tight curls, but I did my best to make it tidy. I folded the drying cloths and looked for a way to drain the grey bathwater but didn't find one. It shamed me that someone would see how dirty I'd been. I steeled myself, tucked my worn garments, with the candle inside them, under my arm and left the bath.

Daylight had grown stronger and the morning was warmer than many a noon in Buck. Capra looked me up and down, with her gaze lingering on my bruised legs. 'Leave those rags. Just drop them. A servant will dispose of them.'

I froze. Then, without a word, I reached into the bundle, and drew out the halves of my broken candle. I let my clothing fall. Capra scowled at me. 'What's that you're carrying?'

'A candle that my mother made.' I didn't show it to her.

'Leave it.'

'No.' I lifted my eyes and met her gaze. Her eyes were peculiar. Today they seemed not pale-blue or grey, but a sort of dirtied white. They were hard to look at, but I didn't break my stare.

She tilted her head to look at me. 'How many candles do you have?'

I didn't want to tell her, yet I could not say why. 'It was one. It broke into two.'

'One candle,' she said quietly. 'That's interesting. But only one. Not like the candles in the dream.' She said this as if hoping to provoke a reaction.

I did not let my face change. But abruptly, the day shimmered around me. I looked up at Capra and it seemed as if light spiked out from her in myriad directions. So many paths leading from her. From this moment, yes, but more than that. She was like the beggar, who was also the Fool. My father's Beloved. I had no words for what I

493

sensed about her. Like a crossroads, I thought, where one could go off in a different direction. I looked away from her, wondering how much time had passed while I had been caught in that moment. None, it seemed, when she spoke.

'Very well,' she said. 'Carry them with you. It's your nuisance to deal with.' Yet from her voice, I did not feel she conceded to me so much as added the candle to my list of wrong-doing. Her guard's expression suggested that I had been foolishly wilful. He was one of the men who had wielded the whips that ate Dwalia's flesh. I set my teeth to keep my jaw from quivering at that memory.

'Follow,' Capra said. 'You will be staying here with us, so I will show you the grounds. Later we will decide what you are to be here. Perhaps a student? Perhaps a scholar? Maybe just a servant.' She smiled at me, a thin stretching of her lips. 'Maybe a breeder. Or a slave to be sold. There are so many ways you might like to be useful.'

I did not think I would like any of them but I said nothing. I walked behind her, her guard next to me. The sandal straps bit into my feet but I gritted my teeth and walked on. She took me back inside, and I was grateful that the sun no longer beat down on my head. I did not realize how I had squinted against the glare of white light on white stone until we were indoors again.

She did not hurry but she did not pause. On the main floor, I was shown a room where five pale children were learning to write and being assisted by scribes in green robes. Each child had a scribe sitting by him, assisting him to guide his pen. The pale children looked very young, no older than three years. But if they were like me, I judged they were older than they looked.

We traversed a long, gently curving corridor and went up grand marble stairs to the second floor. 'Here we welcome those who come to share our wisdom.' She told me this as she opened the door to a room panelled all in rich wood and deeply carpeted. There was a grand table surrounded by carved chairs in the centre, and on it a decanter of some liquor and some tiny glasses.

In the next room six young Whites were at a table. Servants waited behind them. 'Last night, they dreamed,' Capra said quietly. 'They will write down what they dreamed. Then the scribing servants will make copies, and each copy will be sorted into a category and placed with others similar to it. Perhaps they dreamed of candles. Or an acorn bobbing in a stream. Or the dream where one seizes a bee, and is surrounded by a hundred stinging bees.' Her voice dropped. 'Or of the Unexpected Son.' She turned and looked down at me. Her smile stretched her lips flat. 'Or a Destroyer. Over the last year, the occurrence of dreams about the Destroyer have greatly increased. That tells us that something happened, something we did not expect. Some event has made it more likely that a Destroyer exists and will come to us.' She stretched her lips again. 'Have you ever dreamed of the Destroyer?'

I dared not hold a complete silence. 'I often have nightmares of how my home was destroyed by Dwalia and her luriks. Is that what you mean?'

'No.' That word was another mark against me. She led me out of the room. We paced that long hallway and ascended a stair to the next level. Here, the wood that panelled the halls was of a deeper colour. Massive wooden beams supported a ceiling painted with extravagant flowers. 'This is our heart,' Capra told me formally as she escorted me to a door and opened it.

This huge chamber was full of old scrolls and books. Racks lined every wall and reached all the way to the ceiling. I could not see across the room, for orderly ranks of tall shelves, all full of scrolls and large books formed a perimeter around the open centre of the room. In that open space, there were at least a dozen long tables. Scribes who seemed to have little or no characteristics of White heritage sat with pens and inkpots, comparing scrolls and papers and writing busily.

'Here the dreams are studied. We know how many dreams mention candles. We know how long there have been dreams of serpents wielding swords. Dreams of Unexpected Sons, Destroyers and white horses, seashells and teacups, puppets and wolves and blue bucks.' She smiled widely at me. 'Some of these scrolls were written long ago. There is a tremendous amount of information here, and scrolls that go back scores of years, for a truly cataclysmic event might generate dreams dozens of years before it happens. We knew of the Blood Plague before it took its first victim. And before that? The mountain that burst into fire and flame, the earthquakes that levelled the Elderling cities and the great waves that destroyed their stranglehold on the world. Oh, yes, we knew those were coming. If they'd been a bit more useful to us, perhaps the Elderlings would have known them as well. But they preferred dragons to humanity. Their loss.' So much vindictive satisfaction in her voice and words. She told me those things as if I should find them personally hurtful. Then she leaned down and said softly by my ear, 'But not all dreams are here. Mine are in my tower. Known only to me. Last night, I dreamed I pulled up a little white flower by its roots. But the roots were flames and blades.' She smiled. 'I would have been wiser to cut that little flower off at the stem.' She tilted her head. 'Don't you agree?'

She straightened abruptly. 'Come,' she said, and walked briskly out of the room. I hobbled after her, hating the sandals and the straps that bound them to my feet. The next room was identical to the one we had left. The scrolls, the scholars at work, lesser servants coming and going with arms full of paper or large ledgers. And a third room. I could stand it no more. I dropped down and untied the straps from my feet. I stood up, now carrying the sandals and my broken candle.

'As you wish,' Capra said disdainfully. 'Perhaps in time you will become accustomed to wearing shoes and other civilized ways.' She shrugged. 'Or be sold to a household where shoes are not wasted on slaves.'

I could feel myself sinking in her estimation. I battled with myself. Did I admit to her I dreamed and claim a place among her students? Pretend I was stupid and only marginally civilized and hope to be a servant with a chance of escape? Escape to where and to what? I was an ocean away from my home. Wouldn't I be wiser to make a place for myself here?

A different plan bubbled into my mind, the one I had kept hidden while we were on the ship coming here. I pushed it down, out of sight. I might not see Vindeliar, but I had no idea where he might be or if there were others like him. Think about being useful. Think of making a place for myself here. Smile. Pretend to want to be here forever, a part of the web they wove.

As if she could feel my resolve weakening, she led me down a long corridor and down an endless flight of wide, spiralling stairs. Then we turned and went out of a door into an enclosed courtyard. It was immense, and unlike the barren island outside the wall here big trees provided shade, fountains splashed and a little stream wandered through stone-lined channels. Along the walls of this lovely garden were little cottages. Flowers bloomed beside each door, and one tree bore little orange fruits among the shiny leaves on its neatly-pruned branches. Espaliered grapevines bearing purple fruit grew in the loamy soil along the wall, but the twining branches stopped well short of the wall's top. Even if Riddle had stood on my father's shoulders he could not have seen over it. As I watched, a guard walked slowly along the top of the wall. His skin was tanned brown and his long hair was gold. He carried a small bow at the ready. He looked down on the garden but never smiled.

Birds sang—tiny pink birds in cages hung from decorative poles and others perching in the branches of the trees. I followed Capra off the pebbled walkway and onto cool green grass where there were tables and benches under a shady arch festooned with vines. Two women in smocks of bright white arrived from a different door carrying trays of sliced fruit and fresh breads. I could smell the warm bread and my stomach squirmed with desire. They set out the plates on the table and then rang a little silver bell suspended from a branch. The doors of the cottages opened and Whites emerged. 'Oh, I am so hungry!' one exclaimed, and her friend laughed and took her arm. As they came to join their friends at the table, my gaze roved over the smooth faces and white or pale gold hair. They were all dressed in a similar fashion, in short loose robes or garb like mine. And suddenly I could not tell boys from girls at all.

'If you were to prove valuable to us, if you began to dream and could be taught to write them down, this is where you would stay. You'd have your own little cottage, and a servant to keep it tidy for you. You'd share meals here, or on rainy days, in the Hall of Crystals. It's lovely. They dangle from the ceiling and sparkle and shine and make rainbows on the floor. Your tasks would be to think and to dream. Perhaps, some day, to have a child if you desired to, and find a mate among your fellows. See how happy they are?'

They were eating and talking and laughing. No one was frowning or pensive or sitting apart from the others. There were fifteen of them, and I could not tell their ages any more than I could guess their sexes. I tried not to look at the food. The women in the serv-ant-smocks came back with glass pitchers of something pale-brown. They poured it into waiting glasses while those they served exclaimed in anticipation. I stared in raw envy.

'You could be there. Oh, not tomorrow. But as soon as you learned how to write. If you were a dreamer, I mean. But, as you have said, you are not. Still, I imagine you are hungry. Come.'

She led me away from the grassy sward and soon I was forced to limp and hop along on the pebbled walkway. She led me through a gate in a wall, through a washing court with pastel garments hanging on lines under the bright, hot sun. And then another wall and another gate. A lovely herb garden with benches and bowers. The sun beat down on my head as we followed a winding course back to the main structure. We passed under a portico and through yet another door. I forced myself to pay attention, to memorize every turn and door. The corridor seemed dark and the air stagnant after the open garden. Capra walked briskly now, the heels of her shoes tapping on the smooth stone floor. I followed. My head had begun to pound. The long days on the ship, the small meals I'd had and the upheavals of the past few days were suddenly almost more than I could bear. I wanted to simply sit down and weep. If I did, the guard escorting me would probably whip me to death.

Capra turned and opened a door. She stood beside it and beckoned me to enter.

I went cautiously. Three steps in, I stopped and stared all around. The walls were a jungle. Birds called and sang and winged through the thick foliage. I saw a golden-hided predator as a shape slinking through the trees. I looked up, and branches intertwined overhead. A long heavy snake moved along one, the boughs bending under his weight. Underfoot, the floor was a carpet of lush grasses and brilliant flowers and low-growing vines. A butterfly was sitting on a flower. He lifted from it, and I tracked his progress as he flew to another.

None of it was real. I heard and saw, but I smelled nothing, and when I walked, I felt smooth stone underfoot, not verdant turf. 'Is it magic?' I whispered.

'Of a sort,' Capra said dismissively. 'Once, we were trading partners with the Elderlings. One of their greatest artists came here, to line the walls, the floors, even the ceiling with this special stone. Day by day he created this room. It took him almost a year.'

I gazed around, unable to suppress my amazement. 'So this is Elderling magic.'

'You've never seen anything like this before?'

The butterfly cloak! 'No. Never. It takes my breath away.' She watched me closely as I stared about wide-eyed. I stooped and tried to touch a flower. Cold stone and a tingle of magic up my finger. I drew back from it.

'Ah, well.' Her tone was dismissive. 'It's impressive the first time one sees it, I suppose. They were an interesting people. But pretty trickery of this sort was not worth dealing with their self-importance, or their dragons. They exhausted our tolerance. Come. We will eat now.'

There was a table with a white cloth on it and two chairs. There were two plates on the table, and cutlery and glasses. Against the wall, two men stood, holding trays. They were dark-haired and dark-eyed, and for one moment it felt as if I had come home. 'Please, be seated at the table,' Capra said. 'You are my guest today. Let us share a meal.'

I moved cautiously toward the table. My guard closed the door and took a place beside it. Capra gracefully took her seat. I set my sandals below my chair, and then carefully sat with my candle beside me. I folded my hands at the table's edge and waited.

'Well. Not entirely unmannered, I see.' She gave a casual flip of her hand toward the waiting servants and they advanced to the table. Food was set before me and my glass was filled. I waited, watching Capra. I suddenly felt that I represented not only Withywoods but all the Six Duchies. I would not behave like an unmannered dolt.

She took a damp cloth from a covered dish on her right and carefully wiped her hands, paying special attention to her fingers. I imitated her and returned the cloth to the dish as she did. She picked up a utensil that baffled me, and speared a chunk of pale flesh on her plate. I copied her, chewing the bite I took as slowly as she did although it was cold and tasted strongly of fish. 'Tell me about yourself,' she invited me after the third bite. 'You are no servant's child. Who are you?'

I had just swallowed a square of something yellow and sticky. It had been sweet and only sweet, with no other flavour to it. I sipped water to clear my mouth and let my eyes wander the extraordinary room. I decided on the truth. Or some of it. 'I am Bee Badgerlock, of Withywoods. My mother was Lady Molly Chandler, wed to Tom Badgerlock. We are landed gentry. My mother died recently. I lived with my father and our servants. I led a pleasant, peaceful life.'

She was listening. She took a small bite of something and nodded to me to go on.

'On a day when my father was away, as we prepared for a holiday, Dwalia came with her luriks and a troop of Chalcedean mercenaries. She slaughtered my servants and set fire to my stables and kidnapped me. She brought me here.' I took another bite of the unpleasant fish, chewed it slowly and swallowed it before I added, 'If you will send word to my father, it is likely he will ransom me.'

She set down her utensil and looked at me carefully. 'Would he?' She tilted her head. 'Your father would come himself to get you, do you think?'

It was no time to share my doubt. 'He is my father. He would.'

'Then your father is not FitzChivalry?'

I replied truthfully, 'I have always heard him called Tom Badgerlock.'

'And Beloved is not your father either?'

I gave her a puzzled look. 'I love my father.'

'And his name was Beloved.'

I shook my head. 'I have known no one that answers to such a name. Beloved? In my country, sometimes the princes and princesses are given such names. Loyalty or Benevolent. But not such as I.' Nor my sister, it suddenly occurred to me. Nettle and Bee. Never to be princesses. That bothered me for an instant but, *Do not be distracted by self-pity. You are in danger, in the very jaws of a trap. Watch your enemy!*

To hear Wolf Father so plainly made me braver. I sat up straighter.

She nodded to herself. 'Unfortunately, we are unlikely to ask a ransom of your father. To send a messenger so far on such an uncertain errand would be more expensive than any ransom we could wring from him. Late last night, after some earnest counselling, Dwalia admitted that she knew you were female for months. But instead of admitting her mistake then she chose to bring you here, regardless of the loss of luriks and horses! She also conceded that while she once believed she would find the Unexpected Son at Withywoods, she now believes you are no such thing. She concedes to an opinion I have long held, that the Unexpected Son was Beloved's Catalyst. A man named FitzChivalry.

'From Vindeliar, however, we have wrung a different tale. He still believes you are the Unexpected Son. And he claims that you are capable of magic and full of sly trickery.'

On the wall, I had another glimpse of the predator. It was a cat. It sprang, missed and a large bird flew up. I spoke carefully. 'Vindeliar is full of peculiar ideas. When he helped capture me, he called me his "brother". And even after they knew I was a girl, he called me "brother" still.' I gave her my best perplexed expression. 'He is a very strange man.'

'So. He is mistaken about your magic?'

I looked down at my plate and then back up at her. I was still hungry but the food was so foreign to me that it was hard to eat it.

Wolf Father whispered to me. *Eat it. Fill your belly with anything. In this place, you can't depend on anyone to feed you. Stuff yourself while you can.*

I ate two more bites, trying not to make a disgusted face as I got it down. I hoped I looked thoughtful. Then I replied, 'If I had any magical power, would I be here? A prisoner, far from my home?'

'Perhaps you would. If you were a true White Prophet, and you felt you had a task to fulfil here, perhaps you would allow fate to sweep you toward us. If you had dreams that said you must come here . . .'

I shook my head. 'I want to be at home. If I have a home left. I am no Unexpected Son. I'm not even a boy!' Tears suddenly flooded my eyes and choked my throat. 'We were preparing for a wonderful festival. Our Winterfest, when we celebrate the longest night and then the returning light. There was to be feasting and music and dancing. Dwalia came and turned it all to blood and screaming. They killed Revel. I loved Revel. I didn't even know how much I loved him until he came with a blade stuck in him to warn us. His last thought was to warn me to flee! And they killed Perseverance's father and grandfather. And they burned our beautiful horses and our old stable! They killed FitzVigilant, my new tutor, who came to teach me to read. I didn't like him but I didn't wish him dead! If I were a prophet, if I dreamed dreams of the future, wouldn't I have known? Wouldn't I have run away or warned everyone? I'm just my father's daughter, and Dwalia wrecked our lives and killed people for no reason! You had her beaten with whips, but it wasn't for all the terrible things she did! Those things you four sent her to do! She made Vindeliar trick that horrid Duke Ellik into killing all my people. And she didn't even care for her own! She gave him Oddessa for him and his men to rape! Then Dwalia abandoned Reppin in the stone, and she sold Alaria into slavery and she left the Chalcedean to be charged with murder. Did she tell you what she did? Do you even know how horrible she is?' I dragged in a shaking breath. Oh, I'd said too much. I'd vomited out the truth to her, without a thought or plan.

She stared at me, and her pale White's face went even more bloodless. 'Winterfest. The longest night.' Then, as if my words had finally reached her ears, 'Alaria went into slavery?' she said faintly. 'She was sold alive?' As if that were the most dreadful of all Dwalia's misdeeds.

Could a slave be sold dead?

Eat the food! Before she changes her mind and takes it away.

I tried. I stabbed the skewer into a lump of something purple and put it into my mouth. It was so sour my eyes watered. I choked it down and drank. Another unfamiliar taste. I stabbed something else on my plate. It fell off the skewer thing.

When I looked up Capra was gesturing to her guard. 'A scribe, paper, ink, and set up a table here. Make this happen now.' Her guard ran from the room. She turned back to me and her voice was intense. 'Where did this happen? In what city was Alaria sold? What do you mean, Reppin was left in a stone?'

I suddenly knew I had given away things that could have been bartered. I had a piece of food in my mouth. I chewed it for a very long time. When finally I cleared my mouth, I said softly, 'I don't remember the name of the city. I don't think I ever knew it. Dwalia would know, or Vindeliar.' I quickly put more food in my mouth. It was the fishy stuff again and I wanted to gag but chewing was my only way to gain time to think.

She spoke gently. 'A scribe is coming. You will sit with her, and tell her everything you can remember, from the very first time you saw Dwalia's company to the day you arrived here.'

I washed the mush in my mouth down with water then asked innocently, 'And then you will send me home?'

She stiffened. 'Perhaps. Much will depend on your story. Perhaps you are very important to us and even you do not know it.'

'I really want to go home.'

'I know you do. Look. This little cake is my favourite kind. Do try it. It's sweet and spicy.' It had been on a dish in the centre of the table. She did not cut a piece but pushed the whole cake toward me. It was as big as my head and was surely intended to serve several people. 'Try a bite,' she urged me.

I chose a utensil at random, gouged a piece from the cake and took it into my mouth. It was delicious, but I was starting to realize everything on the table had a price. Even so, I took another bite and watched her suppress her questions. What did I have left to bargain with? She probably didn't know that others of Dwalia's luriks were unaccounted for, captured or fleeing in Buck. Did she know of the serpent-spit potion? What would she think of Dwalia's romps with her captain? I wondered if she knew anything of Vindeliar's magic or if that was a secret, too? If I bargained with her, would she keep her word?

'Do you promise to send me home if I tell the scribe everything?' I tried to sound childish and not as wary as I felt.

'You will tell the scribe everything, and then we will decide. I expect it may take more than a day, for after you are done we will have more questions for you. Now, while you chat with the scribe I will find a nice little cottage for you, and a Servant to tend you. What is your favourite colour? I want to be sure you will like your new little home.'

I let my discouragement show. 'I don't think it matters. I just want to go home.'

'Well. Blue, then. I'm glad you enjoyed your meal.'

I had not, and I hadn't finished eating. I made myself set down my utensil instead of trying for a big mouthful of the cake. Servants had entered and were speedily setting up a table, two chairs, inkpot, pen-stand and paper. Just as swiftly, they snatched the plates and dishes from the table in front of me. Capra stood, and so did I. In seconds, that table and the chairs were whisked away.

'And here is our scribe. Pelia, I believe?'

The scribe all but dropped to his knees. Her knees? 'Nopet, if it please you, Highest One.' His voice croaked as wetly as a frog's.

'Nopet, of course. This child has a long tale to tell you. Take care that you take it down exactly as she speaks it. Ask no questions now and dismiss not a word of what she tells you. This is of the utmost importance. Repeat my orders back to me.'

This the scribe did, with his eyes bulging. Was he terrified? No.

The more I looked at him, the more he reminded me of Oddessa. She'd had the same unfinished look, as if someone had begun to make a human and then got bits of it wrong. Nopet's eyes bulged and I wondered if his eyelids could even close all the way. His teeth were like a baby's teeth in an adult mouth. He was setting up his desk and gesturing for me to be seated. When he took up his pen, I tried not to stare at his short, skinny fingers. He drew a page of good paper from the stack at his elbow, centred it in front of him, studied his pen, trimmed it a bit, dipped it and hovered it over the page. 'Please begin,' he said to me in his froggy voice.

It was the last thing I wanted to do. Capra was watching me. I walked across the room and sat down in the chair opposite the scribe. 'What do I do?' I asked him.

He lifted his bulgy eyes to meet mine. 'You talk. I write. Please begin.'

I would not tell him of the day before in the town, where I had first glimpsed Vindeliar. I would say nothing of the dead dog and the beggar and my father going into the stone. Nothing of how my father had abandoned me to tend a stranger.

But Beloved had not been a stranger to him. I pulled my thoughts away.

'I was at my lessons in the schoolroom at Withywoods.'

The scribe looked up at me with a frown. He glanced over at Capra, then the pen in his hand flowed ink effortlessly over the page, his tiny fingers manoeuvring it swiftly. But Capra had seen the pause. She came to stand over us.

'Bee, you must begin with detail. Where is Withywoods? And tell of the lesson and the teacher. Who was with you? What was the day like? Every detail. Every moment.'

I nodded slowly. 'I will try.'

'Try very hard,' Capra warned me. Then she added, 'I will be leaving you for a time. I wish to speak with Dwalia and Vindeliar. Be sure that if I find you are lying to me, there will be serious consequences. Work with the scribe until I return.'

And so I talked. Carefully. Sometimes truthfully. The things I thought should shame them, I told in detail. How Revel had clutched his wound so carefully and how the blood had leaked between his fingers. I told of the women's torn dresses. I knew now what that meant. I lied about some things. I said Perseverance had died. Even as I said it, I wanted to bite my tongue to keep it from being true. The scribe asked me no questions, so I meandered through my story, sometimes going back to an earlier event. Sometimes I wept, recalling how Per stepped over the bodies in the stable. I said that I'd hidden the children in a storeroom rather than telling of the secret passages. I so drew out my tale that the sunlight from the high windows had gone from white to yellow and still I was telling of how they had come to raid my home. My story, I knew, was the only thing I had that they wanted. I had to find a way to use it to my advantage.

At one point, I was hoarse from both weeping and talking. The scribe motioned to the guard who had remained with us and asked that water be brought for me. And a damp cloth for my face and nose. I thought this kind of him.

But if you get the chance to kill him and escape, you must not hesitate.

I caught my breath a little. Shouldn't I try to make them send me home before I began killing people and trying to escape?

You can wait a very long time for them to give you your freedom. Taking it might be faster.

The water and the damp cloth arrived. I took advantage of both. And then I talked on. I had to talk about Vindeliar's magic. If I didn't, none of my story made sense. At Vindeliar's name, Nopet's upper lip curled briefly to show his tiny teeth. Then he wrote, and kept on recording every word I spoke. The sunlight still came in, but it felt to me as if it was weaker and I wondered how many hours had passed.

When Capra came back Symphe was with her. And a moment later, Fellowdy and Coultrie came into the room. Coultrie's white cosmetics looked almost real, as if he had freshened them recently. Symphe scowled and said, 'You put a scribe to taking down her tale without asking us. Surely we should have been informed and allowed to listen in.'

Capra turned to her slowly. She smiled. 'As you informed me before you allowed Dwalia to arrange Beloved's escape? As I recall, you did not include me in the planning of that.'

'And I have apologized for that lapse. Repeatedly.' Symphe bit each word off as if she wished to spit them at Capra.

'Ah, yes. A nicety I should emulate. Dear Symphe, I apologize that I did not tell you that this girl is a veritable font of information about Dwalia's misdeeds. Let me choose one, at random. Let me see

. . . Ah. Do you recall Alaria? Alaria, trained by me in the inter-
pretation of dreams? Alaria, as I recall, was a favourite of yours,
Fellowdy. Did you know that Lingstra Dwalia sold her into slavery?
In the city of Chalced, the capital of the country also named Chalced.
She was sold to buy passage on a ship. For so little Bee told me.
And I went straight away and I wrung confirmation of that from
Vindeliar today. And I look forward to confirming more of her story
with each passing session.'

She gestured the scribe away, turned to the first page in his tidy
stack and ran her eyes over it swiftly. She glanced at me. 'And where
was your father, Bee, on the day Dwalia came to your home?'

No time to think, no time to weigh what Dwalia would have
known and might have told her. 'He went to the big city,' I said.

'Was that after he killed the man with the dog? And stabbed
Beloved in the belly?'

The fog-man had been in Oaksbywater that day. Standing between
the shops, in an alley no one wanted to enter. The fog-man I came
to know as Vindeliar. I could not speak.

I watched them. They all looked at me. Then their eyes went to
the scribe and his tidy stack of pages on the table between us. Then
the men looked back at Capra, but Symphe stared at me. Her lips
looked redder or perhaps the rest of her was paler. After a time, she
realized I was staring back at her. She smiled at me in a nasty way
and I dropped my eyes, wishing I hadn't stared. She spoke. 'And
what else have you told our scribe, little Bee?'

I glanced a Capra, wondering if I should answer.

'I spoke to you!' Symphe said sharply.

I looked from one to another but found no help anywhere. Capra's
face was icy triumph. I gathered breath. 'I told of the night Dwalia
and Duke Ellik came to my home and ruined my life. I told how
they killed people and burned the stable and kidnapped me.'

'Indeed,' Fellowdy said, as if he doubted every word I'd said.

Symphe's voice was sour as she said, 'I shall want those pages
tonight, scribe.'

'No.' Capra's denial was flat. 'I will read them first. I brought her
here and organized the scribe. It is my right to read them first.'

Symphe turned to the scribe. 'Then make a copy for me. No,
scribe, produce three copies, so that each of us may have one to
read tonight.'

Now it was the scribe's turn to look from face to face, his jutting eyes bulging even more. His wavering hand indicated the stack of pages. 'But . . .' he began faintly.

'Do not be ridiculous. You know very well he could not produce copies so swiftly. You shall have them tomorrow. I claim the pages for tonight.' Capra spoke decisively. She smiled around at them. 'And I shall be taking care of this dear child for the night, too.'

'No.' They spoke as one. Fellowdy was shaking his head. Coultrie looked vaguely alarmed and Symphe said, 'She goes back into the cell, under the Lock of Four. We agreed. No one is to have access to her without the consent of all. This interrogation of her already violates the agreement.'

'Child, did the scribe ask any questions of you?'

Yes. Don't say that. 'You told him not to.'

'There. You heard it from her. There was no interrogation. I simply gave her the opportunity to tell her tale.' She turned to me, her mouth kind and her eyes cold. 'Little child, I fear I must walk you back to a cell tonight, instead of to the lovely little cottage I promised you. I am so sorry. But as you see, these three have outvoted me, and we must give way to them.' She turned the smile back on them and I saw Symphe's upper lip lift in a cat's snarl. Did she think I had just been won over to Capra's side? Perhaps if I had not endured those months with Dwalia and been taught so thoroughly to distrust, I might have been.

I stood up, taking my broken candle and then stooped to get the hated sandals as well

'What do you have there?' Coultrie demanded sharply.

Capra said nothing.

'Sandals,' I said quietly. 'They hurt my feet so I took them off.'

'No. The other.'

'A candle that my mother made.' Without intending to, I lifted the two broken halves to my breast and held them protectively.

'A candle,' Capra added smugly. 'The child arrives with a candle.'

A silence fell. I wondered what that pause signified, for it was fraught with something. Respect? Dread?

Fellowdy spoke. 'One candle in two pieces. Not three, nor four?'

'You are thinking of the Destroyer dreams?' Coultrie was shocked.

'Be silent!' Symphe snapped at him.

'It's a bit too late for silence,' Capra said. 'It was probably too late by spring, when the dreams of the Destroyer began falling like late snowflakes. Right after Lingstra Dwalia disturbed a hornets' nest by provoking a finished Catalyst. When she shifted the futures by putting his prophet into conjunction with him again. And stealing his child.' Her eyes swept over them. 'Why did he have the power to make such changes? Because you gave Beloved back to him. You drove him to FitzChivalry's door. You reunited the Prophet with a powerful Catalyst. You restored the power of the Unexpected Son. Perhaps creating the Destroyer he will undoubtedly send to us.'

'What are you talking about?' Fellowdy demanded, his voice going high.

'Why are you speaking of these things in front of this child?' Symphe exploded.

'Do you think I am saying things she doesn't already know?'

I did and I didn't know what she was talking about. I kept my eyes low. Let them read nothing there.

'You three triggered this.' Capra spoke each separate word of her accusation coldly. 'With your stupidity and greed and a thirst for vengeance! As if vengeance ever bore anything but bitter fruit. And now I think we had best put her back in her cell, as that is what you think will keep us safe. As for me, I think I shall be up all night with an army of scribes, reading what she has written and studying the dreams and trying to find a path that does not end in destruction for all of us!' She smiled like a smug cat. 'And reviewing my own dreams. In my personal records.'

'This is highly inappropriate!' Symphe insisted.

'No. What you did was extremely dangerous, and as usual, I am the one who must spring to our defence.' Capra reached into the bosom of her shirt and drew out a key. She pulled it free, snapping the fine silver chain that had held it, and almost threw it at her guard. 'Confine the child and then return the key to me. I do not have time to waste on locking up the harbinger of the storm. I must prepare for the storm itself. One that *I* have long seen coming!'

The guard looked stunned. He caught the key and stared at it as if she had thrown him a scorpion. 'This breaks all traditions!' Symphe shrieked. 'None of the Four can surrender a key to another's use!'

'It broke tradition when you lied to me and aided Dwalia in releasing Beloved. I warned all of you, for so many years, about how dangerous he was. Well, dead or alive, he threatens us again!'

She turned, snatched up the scribe's pages and raged away as if she were the storm she had warned them about. I kept my eyes lowered, watching them only through my eyelashes. Coultrie reached down. He had a pocket somewhere in those loose trousers for he drew out a key on a thick brass chain and unclipped it. He handed it to the twice-stunned guard. 'I go to help Capra, for I fear she is right. I never should have listened to you two. This may be the end of us.'

He did not storm off but went like a shamed dog, head down and shoulders hunched. Fellowdy and Symphe looked at one another. And then Symphe snapped at the guard, 'Well, take charge of her! Do you imagine I will entrust you with my key? Let us lock her up and then I suppose I must go join Capra and Coultrie, to be sure I get the whole truth. Girl! Move.'

And move I did, with the guard's big hand on my shoulder, pushing me along. He was tall and long-legged, and more than once I stumbled as we left that room and went through yet more corridors and up a different flight of stairs. This time, we entered the hall of cells from the opposite end. I could get a glimpse of the man who owned the black hands and rich voice. He was sitting on his bed, his hands folded loosely between his knees. His cell was kinder than mine. It had a little table, a small rug, and a real bed, with blankets. As I passed, he lifted his head and smiled. His eyes were black, as gleaming a black as the rest of him. He caught my gaze as if he had been waiting for me to pass, but said not a word.

They locked me in, the guard fumbling a bit with the two keys, and then they left me. I sat down on my bed and wondered what would next befall me.

TWENTY-SIX

Silver Secrets

I miss the wolf as a drowning man misses air in his lungs. For years after his death, I would have sworn I still felt him within me. Nighteyes. His wry way of telling me I was an idiot, his endless appetite for the immediate pleasures of the world, his solid sense that if only we fully lived in the present, all the tomorrows would take care of themselves.

With this enlarged household at Withywoods, I feel I cannot relax for a moment. Everything is a plan that has gone amiss and must be corrected.

Torn page from journal of Tom Badgerlock, Holder of Withywoods

Spark stepped to the railing. She opened her hand, and Lant's curling locks were blown away in the ever-present ocean breeze. He stood up from the barrel, and rubbed both his hands over his shorn head. His eyes were red-rimmed. He stepped away from the barrel and I sat down on it.

'How short?' she asked me.

'To the scalp,' I replied hoarsely.

Lant twitched and turned back to me. 'He wasn't your father!' he objected.

I could have argued that with him. But it seemed pointless and I was tired of pain. If my shearing my hair for mourning as if Chade were my father was painful to Lant, I need not do it. Chade would never know and it would not change the depth of my loss. 'The flat of your hand,' I said.

I felt her set her hand on top of my head. Her fingers closed to hold my hair upright and she began snipping. My hair was not nearly as long as Lant's had been. Spark piled the clippings into Per's hands. There was a lot more grey in it than I'd realized there would be.

Not my father. I'd never met my father, but Burrich had near-shaved my head for mourning when Chivalry had died. Yet when Burrich had died, I'd not cut my hair at all. I listened to her scissors snipping and thought about that. I'd been on Aslevjal Island, and the news of his death had come to me in a Skill-message, just as tidings of Chade's death had. Why hadn't I cut my hair? No scissors. No time. The gesture had seemed too small. I'd still been a bit angry with him for wedding Molly. So many reasons and no reason at all. Perhaps it was not wanting it to be real. I didn't know any more. Who had that young man been who had thought himself so old and worldly-wise? He was a stranger to me now.

'It's done,' Spark said in a husky voice and I realized it had been some time since I'd heard the snick of the blades.

'That it is,' I said and stood up slowly. Both Spark and Per had taken a hand's breadth off, instead of the traditional lock. The Fool had given me a lock of his pale hair. I think he knew that I wouldn't wish Lady Amber to be the one to hand it to me. I'd released it to the wind and now Per delivered mine to the same breeze. I stood at the railing and watched the steady wind carry my hair away. Scattered into the open air as Chade's memories would disperse. I'd known him longer than anyone at Buckkeep. When I died, a part of Chade's heritage would die with me.

I heard a step on the deck and turned to find Althea regarding me with a mystified look. I'd tried to explain how I could know of the death of someone in Buckkeep, but I think she privately believed I'd had a very vivid dream. I was grateful that she'd allowed us privacy for this small ceremony. And now that time was over and perhaps she had orders for a deckhand.

Her glance flickered over my shorn head and then she pointed out over the water. 'There, on the horizon. Beneath the overcast. Do you see that? We think those are the outer islands, with Clerres on the largest one, and beyond the islands, a mainland. So, Paragon tells us.'

I followed her pointing finger, and saw only clouds. I accepted what she told me. 'How long until we reach there?'

'It depends on the wind and currents. Paragon says less than two days. From what he recalls, there is a good deep-water harbour at one end of the island but he wishes to take us directly to the Clerres harbour. He says he has been there before; that Igrot had dealings with the Servants. Of what sort, he cannot say, but shortly after they visited Clerres, he took Igrot to Others' Island, to have his fortune told.' She fell silent. Perhaps we both wondered what those creatures had foretold for him. 'The wind is up and building; we're making excellent time. If it continues, we could be there late this evening, or early tomorrow.'

'This evening.' I echoed her words. I teetered on the edge of a void. I thought of all I didn't know and could not anticipate. I had studied the crude maps the Fool had helped me make. But knowing the general layout of the Servants' stronghold did not tell me if Bee had already arrived or if she was still on a ship. If she were there, was she held as a prisoner, or housed in the cottages with the other young Whites?

Neither did I know how soon Tintaglia might arrive to take her vengeance. I looked at the distant shadow on the horizon and wondered if she had already finished with them. Would we sail into the harbour of a dragon-destroyed city? And what if Bee had already arrived in Clerres? No. I refused to consider that possibility. I had to believe I still had a chance of saving her.

Knowing Bee was alive had thrown all my plans into disarray. I could poison neither well nor food, lest it make its way to Bee. I could not go in swinging an axe or spreading toxic potions on doorknobs and tabletops. Until I had safely regained my daughter, I could attempt no violence against the Servants. Entering and searching a well-guarded castle to rescue a small girl was a very different task from gaining access and killing as many people as I could before I died. In all my long career, this would be the first time that my primary goal was to save a life rather than take one.

'Paragon wants to anchor well out in the harbour, where the water is deepest. Even so, we must be watchful lest an ebbing tide leaves him aground.'

Brashen drifted up to join her. He leaned back on the railing and said nothing as she spoke. 'We will behave as we always have in a new port. We will go ashore, and visit merchants to see what trade items we might purchase. We've not a lot of coin but it's adequate for a short ruse. We may even buy some goods, on this, our last trading run with Paragon.' Her gaze went distant. 'Perhaps our last time ever to visit a new port.'

I caught yet another glimpse of all we had taken from them and felt shame again. My fate was a runaway horse, dragging destruction like a broken cart through so many lives. I tried to think of something to say. Lant and the others had drawn closer and were listening.

Althea remained silent, staring at the clouds on the horizon. Brashen cleared his throat. 'Before sunset, we'll return to Paragon. We will keep our crew at the ready, for it may be that you will stir great trouble and we will have to depart swiftly.'

I spoke what we all knew to be true. 'You owe us nothing. This was a bargain struck between your ship and Amber. I do not expect you to risk your lives or crew for us.' Dread filled my heart as I offered what was right. 'We will all disembark when we reach Clerres. Whatever trouble we bring down, we will bring down only upon ourselves. Should anyone ask, we will say that we paid for our passage here, and that we hardly know you.' I steeled myself. 'If you judge you must flee before we return, well, then you must.' And I would be in my worst possible situation. Saddled with all of my companions, and I hoped, Bee. With no swift means of escape.

Brashen scowled. 'We do not intend to maroon you. One of the ship's boats will remain at the dock, crewed by Queen Etta's bravos. Should you have to flee for your lives, they will be there, waiting for you. We hope they can swiftly convey you to Paragon and we can flee together.'

A twisted smile crawled across Althea's face. 'Plan for the worst and hope for the best. Given that we know so little of what you intend, it is difficult for us to make specific plans.'

'It's more than what I expected,' I said quietly. 'Thank you.'

She looked me up and down. 'You do what I think any parent would do for a child. I wish that rescuing her had not meant the end of Paragon as ship. Even so, I wish you luck. We will all need a sizeable measure of it to survive this.'

Brashen spoke. 'Per and Spark are young for what you say you will do. Must you take them?'

'I would leave them behind if I could.' Per took a step forward and Spark made a strangled sound. I lifted a hand and my voice. 'But we may need them.'

'Then you have a plan?' Althea pressed.

'Of sorts.' It was pathetic and I knew it. 'We will disguise ourselves as folk seeking a fortune-telling from the Servants. Once we have crossed the causeway and entered the castle, we will attempt to search for Bee. Amber believes she knows where they will be holding her. If necessary, we will conceal ourselves within the stronghold and emerge by night to search for her.'

'And if you find her?' Brashen asked.

'Somehow, we will rescue her. And bring her back to this ship.'

'And then?'

'Bee's safety is my first concern. I would hope that we would immediately leave Clerres.' That part of the plan belonged solely to me. Vengeance could wait until Bee was far beyond the reach of her captors. I had dwelt long on that decision, and had not told Amber of it. I suspected she would agree, but I refused to take the chance that she would not. I glanced at her. Her lips were folded tight and her arms crossed. I reminded them all, 'Tintaglia intends to destroy Clerres. Perhaps we will be content with letting the dragons take our vengeance for us.'

If they had not already.

'How will you get Bee away from them?' Brashen asked.

I had to shrug. 'I hope I will know that when the time comes.'

Althea's face betrayed her shock. 'You've come all this way and that is your strategy? It seems very . . . vague.'

'It is.'

Her smile was strained. 'It's not really a plan at all.'

Brashen put his hand over hers where it rested on Paragon's railing. 'This we can offer you,' he said. 'And it's as thin a plan as your own. The Divvytown sailors know how to fight.' Althea started to object, but he held up a finger. 'As Althea has said, we'll have them wait for you at the dock, and they'll be well armed. If your luck goes sour, get to them, and have them bring you back to the ship. Even if Althea and I are not aboard, Clef will order the ship to pull anchor and set sail.'

Lant's mouth was hanging ajar. I shook my head, 'And leave you in the hornets' nest? I can't ask that!'

'Of course you can't. And that's why we're offering it.' A strange glint, almost merry, had come into his eyes. 'It wouldn't be the first time we have had to hide, or fight our way out of something. If it comes to that, save your little girl, and we'll look after ourselves.'

He put his arm around her and said with a touch of pride, 'We're rather good at that.'

'I don't like that plan,' Althea announced. 'But I admit that I dislike it less than the idea that you might be fleeing with a child and have nowhere to go.' She lifted her hand to cover Brashen's. 'If my ship and my crew can get clear, I'll go along with it. Don't worry about us.'

Those inadequate words. 'Thank you.'

Amber spoke. 'So. Our day is upon us. Time to rehearse. The sea is calm, the wind favourable. Can you spare all of us from deck duties for a time? I think we need to retire to my cabin, assess our supplies and wardrobe and practise our roles.'

Brashen glanced around the deck and gave a curt nod. 'You're free to go.' He tucked Althea's hand into his arm and led her away from us. Her gait matched the motion of her ship perfectly. I tried to imagine her living on land, walking through a market with a basket on her arm. I could not.

'Roles?' Per asked.

A gleam had come into Spark's eyes. 'Yes!'

'I'm not sure that I need to rehearse,' I said to Amber.

'Rehearse?' Per asked again.

'Come with me,' Amber insisted. 'All will be made clear.'

When we had crowded into the cabin, the Fool shed his role as Amber as easily as he dropped the skirts that covered his trousered legs. He kicked them aside. 'I will not be Amber when we disembark.' He looked almost merry as he stooped to drag garments from under the lower bunk. His fingers danced over fabrics and lace, sorting them as he went. I clenched my teeth for a moment. I knew I would not win but I made a final effort.

'I do not think you should disembark at all!' I objected. 'You are known in Clerres. And if they capture you or even if someone sees you and you stir their guard to wariness, you have only complicated my task. No.'

He simpered in my direction. 'As if it were your decision. Be quiet for a time and hear my plan, for I have refined it!' He was fairly quivering with excitement. 'You, Tom Badgerlock, are come to Clerres to find out if your lovely daughter Sparkle should wed Holder Cavala. That's you, Lant. Your serving lad Per has accompanied you. I will be the ageing granny of Holder Cavala, along to be sure that my grandson is not bilked of his promised bride.'

He waited. Per's eyes were as big as plates. Spark was nodding and smiling. Lant was incredulous. We had discussed that the Fool must be heavily disguised if he went ashore, but this was a whole new level of theatre. A simple plan to present ourselves and pay to cross to the castle was suddenly a grand play. I shook my head in slow denial of the inevitable. 'Are you sure this is necessary? That we all have roles and names and an errand?'

He smiled as if he had not heard me. 'No objections? Excellent. I will be doddering along with you, well veiled against the sun. I will carry the butterfly cloak and a few other well-concealed items. We will follow the stream of pilgrims to the merchant square at the end of the gated crossing. There Fitz will pay to have his fortune told. No matter how you are advised, you will express displeasure at how general it is, and offer a substantial amount of coin to have a lingstra determine if the match is well made. I promise you that they will take your coin and give us crossing tokens. We will cross to the stronghold and go in with the tide of fortune-seekers.' He took a breath. 'This will be the difficult part. We must insist that we are taken to one of the libraries of scrolls for the reading. That is a rare and expensive privilege. I doubt we have the coin for it, but we can barter this for that privilege.' He held up the bracelet. The flame-jewels woke in the dim cabin; they truly looked as if they burned. 'We will take the fire-brick as well, but reserve it in case we need a large bribe. It's a practical item. Almost anyone would covet it.'

'But we promised . . .' Per began.

'In dire need, we could part with them. Saving Bee is a dire need,' the Fool said.

I nodded. Not that I liked his plan. I simply had no other.

'In the library, we must find ways to disperse. Perhaps I can insist I must relieve myself, and Lant and Spark will accompany me as I dodder along. When we don't return, you and Per will go to seek us. Instead, you will find hiding-places. You may have to separate . . .'

'I won't send the boy off alone,' I objected.

'I can do it,' Per insisted, but I saw secret relief in his eyes.

'As you will,' the Fool said with a sigh. 'So much will depend on opportunity. But by the time the second low tide of the day comes, and the first wave of visitors is required to depart so that the second wave may come, all of us must be hidden or we will be forced to depart. And go you must, without objection, leaving behind any who manage to remain hidden.'

It had been a terrible plan the first time he proposed it. Details had not improved it.

'How will we find one another after dark when the castle is abed. And how do we know the castle will be abed?'

'Do you not recall what we planned before? We meet at the washing courts: it is deserted at night. That is our rendezvous point. I trust you have all studied our map?'

'We have,' Spark agreed. No one reminded the Fool that he had told us this before.

'And then?' Per asked.

'As we agreed. I will search the lower cells first. If she is there, we must free her as swiftly as possible.'

Per looked as if he might be sick. He sat with shoulders bowed as if expecting a blow. The Fool gave him a sad smile. I pushed aside images of Bee tortured in the dark. I had to think only of the rescue.

'Once we have regained her, we must escape with her. That may be our biggest challenge. When I search the lower cells, we will look for some evidence of how my rescuers took me out. The entry to the tunnel under the causeway must be there. If we find it, and we have Bee, two of us will take her that way immediately, leaving one of us to meet you in the washing courts and guide you out as well.'

He sat back and folded his long-fingered hands in his lap. 'And there it is. My plan, refined.'

He took a breath. 'And we must take with us Chade's firepots and some of Fitz's poisons. Once we have Bee and are certain of our escape, Fitz can place them as he thinks best.'

'I can help with that,' Per said quietly and added softly, 'I have my own vengeance to claim. My father. My grandfather. I recall too well how their emissaries served the men who stood before the doors of Withywoods. I recall how Revel fell.'

A small silence followed his words. Pride and shame warred in me. What had I done to my good-hearted, honest young stableboy?

The Fool spoke. 'Once we have Bee outside of Castle Clerres, that party will not wait for anyone else. She will immediately be taken to the docks and the ship's boat. There we will wait for the others to join us. Unless . . .' He paused and then spoke reluctantly, 'Unless Bee is badly hurt. Then we must get her quickly to the ship and tend to her injuries.' He drew a breath and spoke quickly. 'The rest of us will have to fare as well as we can. But today we prepare. We dress the part; we conceal our weapons.'

'I agree,' I said quietly.

'So let us begin,' Spark announced. She was obviously more informed than the rest of us, for she began to pull out sets of garments from under the bunk.

She set a stack beside the Fool. 'Here is your granny's bonnet on top. I've finished putting on the lace to shield your old face from the sun. Try it on!' Next to the Fool's disguise she placed the butterfly cloak, folded and rolled into a tight packet. Wordlessly, she put out a maidservant's shift and a headscarf. For Bee, I knew. I twitched when she spoke to me. 'Fitz, please set out whatever has survived of your good clothing. Per, here are trousers and a loose vest and your old boots. You've scarcely worn them since we came aboard! Amber says that will pass as a serving boy's garb. Lant, as you are courting me, I've devised some garments for you. And myself. It has been a challenge to remake Lady Thyme's old things into presentable wear!'

She spoke with pardonable pride. She held up for Lant a garment that had been a fussy old woman's blouse. It was now a passable gentleman's shirt with a great deal of lace at the throat and cuff. 'Luckily your father was of a size with you, so Thyme's garments were generously cut.' Her words suddenly choked to a halt. She held the shirt out to him blindly. 'Try it on,' she managed.

The Fool had donned the bonnet and was tying it under his chin. Granny suddenly spoke in a querulous old woman's voice. 'Fitz, we must play the game as the pieces move.' She stopped and looked about. 'What is that smell?'

I knew immediately. Spark's digging for clothing had overset my pack and the Elderling fire-brick was smouldering. Next to Bee's books. Next to Chade's exploding pots!

I fell to the floor and dug like a dog, employing Burrich's finest stable-curses as I did so. I dragged out my pack from beneath a tangle of petticoats. The scorched canvas parted under my frantic fingers. I tumbled the contents onto the deck. The fire-brick was glowing. Lant upended the water ewer over a lavishly embroidered skirt and I flipped the hot brick onto it so that the plain side was up. It hissed as it landed and I stuffed my burnt fingers into my mouth. Not enough to blister, but my fingertips stung. Spark had already stooped and pulled Bee's books from the jumbled pile of my possessions. The books had shielded the firepots from the heat, but my heart hurt that the back cover of Bee's journal showed a scorch-mark. Spark set the books into the Fool's hands and he lifted them against his breast as if they were children in need of comfort.

'Why did you store Chade's pots near the fire-brick?' Per asked incredulously and I had no good answer. Except that if I had been alone, my pack would never have been overset.

Spark had stooped down and was matter-of-factly sorting through my clothes. 'Have you any good trousers left?' she asked me as she pulled a shirt free.

'Let me sort that!' I said. Too late.

'Are those tubes of Silver?' Lant asked in an awestruck voice, for the heat of the bricks had weakened the frayed fabric of my old shirt and the tubes were exposed. I plucked one from the scorched fabric and examined the container. It seemed unharmed. The Silver inside shifted and twirled.

'Silver?' the Fool exclaimed in his own voice. 'Fitz, you have Silver?' He leaned over the tumbled items on the floor, as if peering hard enough would let him see them.

There was no lie large enough to cover what the others had seen. The truth fell out of my mouth. 'Rapskal gave it to me.'

The silence that fell was like a fall of cold snow from steep eaves.

I felt obliged to add more. 'I didn't ask him for it. Heeby convinced him that it was acceptable to the dragons that I have it. He had heard Amber ask for it, and he gave it to me. That day that he helped me home.'

'So it was for me,' Amber said softly. So quickly my Fool had vanished.

'No. He gave it to me,' I replied firmly. 'To use however I thought best.'

'And you kept it secret from me. From all of us, I presume?' Slow nods replied to her accusation. She seemed to feel their assent in the silence. 'Why?'

'I thought I might need it.'

'And you feared I might use it.'

Was there a reason to lie? Not really. 'Yes. I did. And with good reason, I might add,' I spoke more loudly, over her attempt to interrupt me. 'You silvered the fingers of one hand. How was I to know that you wouldn't do more to yourself? Or give it to the ship and let him become more dragon than ship before we were ready to release him?'

'And you thought you might need it,' Amber's voice broke into the Fool's. 'To do far more to yourself than just silver your fingertips. Your hands, I suppose? Like Verity did?'

'Perhaps. How would that be different to what you did? The Silver was a resource, like Chade's exploding pots and the Elderling fire-brick. I don't know how I might use those things. Yet. But I reserve them so I have them.'

'You don't trust me.'

'I trust the Fool. I don't trust Amber.'

'What?' This from Per. The other three were uncomfortable witnesses to this quarrel, and his outburst reminded me of their presence. I glared at him, and he quailed. I was more annoyed with myself, for I could not explain my comment, even to myself. The Fool gave me a hurt look before Amber's mask settled over his features again. There. That was it. He used her to hide from me, and I didn't like it. Whoever the Fool might be elsewhere, when he wore Amber before me, it was a lie and a disguise. I made no answer to Per. He cleared his throat and nervously filled in, 'Motley can do things with her silver beak. She showed me.'

Everyone's attention snapped to Per. 'Such as?' I demanded.

'I've been keeping her feathers black for her. It was time to do them again. The ink wears off. But when I asked her to open her wings, I could see no white. Not even a hint of grey, except on one small feather. And when Motley saw it, she groomed it with her beak. And she made it black.'

'It's a powerful magic,' I said softly. 'Be wary of letting her beak touch you.'

'She is very careful with it.' He made a small sound of regret. 'With me, she is careful. But not with the ship. She likes Paragon, very much, I think. I have seen her grooming the ship's hair as if he were a dragon.'

'He *is* a dragon,' Spark said quietly.

I knelt and put the Silver and my scorched shirt back into the rag of my old pack and bundled them safely. I set the fire-brick to one side. What remained of my clothing was a pathetic heap. I pulled the trousers out of it. 'These will have to do. My Buck cloak is going to be far too warm, but I can wear it thrown back. It may cover that I'm going to be carrying an axe.'

Amber had discarded her grievance with me. Her voice was flat as she said, 'Take something smaller. We can't chance that you'll be stopped.'

I didn't argue. 'I'll borrow a ship's hatchet from Trell.' I found my other shirt and set it on the pile. I began to set out Chade's explosive pots in a tidy roll.

Spark picked up the shirt and held it up. She regarded it critically. 'This won't do. Not for a nobleman showing his wealth and demanding an audience. I'll have to refurbish another of Lady Thyme's blouses.'

'Please,' I managed to say. I reached under the bunk and drew out a separate package I'd brought aboard back in Trehaug and handled little since then. I'd lost some of my poisons and assassin's tools in the bear attack. It held the remains of my supplies. I began to choose. Lock-picks. A garrotte. A little pot of a poison in grease that could go on doorknobs and latches or silverware. Once I'd used it on the back of a book. The owner had died two days later. Here were tasteless powders of death, some fast, some slow. One cluster of packets I set aside.

'You won't need those?' Spark asked. She was watching intently what I was choosing, perhaps thinking of adding concealed pockets. But then, perhaps Lady Thyme's old garments already had plenty of those.

'Soporifics. Sleeping draughts. I doubt I'll need any of them, but I'll take two.' I shifted the packets in question. I added two little knives, sharp, short and narrow as my little finger. 'In-and-outs' Chade had called them. Chade. I took a steadying breath. And here, wrapped in a scrap of paper, was the poisonous pellet I'd made for the Fool. I didn't want to give it to him. I'd said I would.

'Amber, I'm handing you something,' I warned her and reached for her gloved hand. She didn't flinch. I turned her hand palm up and put the packet in it. 'It's something the Fool asked me for. In the event he was captured.'

Amber gave a slow nod as she closed her fingers around it.

'What is it?' Per asked in a voice full of dread.

'A quick exit,' I said. I sorted a few more items into the pile I would take. Abruptly, I could stand it no longer. Everything felt wrong about this. Everything. We were approaching it in the worst possible way, the one I felt was most doomed to failure. I looked at the array of firepots, the tumble of poisons and sly weapons. Spark had already begun ripping a seam out of a green blouse. They were all so intent and united. Like idealistic rabbits plotting to take down a lion. I stood up. 'I need some air,' I said, and left them all staring after me.

Out on the deck I stared over the bow-rail. Paragon was alone save for Motley on his shoulder. I'd greeted him perfunctorily and then subsided into my own silent pain. None of the others had followed me and I was grateful for that. Doubtless they would remain in the cabin and make further plans that I would disagree with. I leaned on the railing and looked toward a now visible landmass. Clerres. My destination. My daughter. I'd abandoned her and then lost her. More than anything, I wanted to be the one to find her and restore her to safety. I wanted her to see my face, be lifted in my arms. Me. I wanted it to be me.

You completely ignore that Amber feels the same way. Paragon's thought thrummed through me. I lifted my forearms from his railing. *As if that would make a difference. I've told you, little man, any time I wish, I can share your thoughts. As I feel her dreams. She blames herself that you saved her and left the child behind. She spends her strength trying to think of what she must do lest others divine it. But this I will share with you. She dreams you dying and does not wish you to die in vain. You should know, if she must choose a death, she chooses yours. Because she believes it is what you would wish.*

I knew a time of stillness. As if all my guts had frozen. Choose a death. Then I knew and I knew the Fool was right. If I must die so that he could live and take care of Bee. That was the better outcome. I framed a thought for the ship. *How do I die?*

In water and fire, in wind and darkness. Not swiftly.

Well. That's nice to know.

Is it? I will never understand humans. Like someone tearing a bandage from a wound, he peeled his mind from mine and left me alone in the wind.

All that day we drew closer to land. It did not seem so, for whenever I looked over the bow-rail, Clerres seemed as distant as ever. The winds were kind to us and the ship sailed with a will, requiring little from his crew. There was too little work and too much time to stew in worry.

I was not the only one pacing and staring. I saw Althea and Brashen, side by side on the roof of the afthouse, staring together toward Clerres. His arm was around her, and as I watched, their son climbed up to join them there. They looked like a family on the brink of a perilous journey. Perhaps they were.

Those of the crew who did not have tasks joined Paragon on the foredeck. Amber was there with them. Paragon was telling tales of what he recalled from Igrot's earliest visit to Clerres. That had been before the ship had been blinded. He recalled a lively town that offered entertainment to seafarers. His merry description bothered me, given that I'd had a glimpse of Kennit's life on the Paragon when Igrot captained him. The Divvytown sailors had a hundred questions about bawdy-houses and gambling dens and what sorts of Smoke would be for sale, and if there was any trade in cindin. Amber sat among them, joining in their questions and jests, telling shore-time adventure tales that prompted the others to recount the disasters and delights of such days. Motley sat on Amber's shoulder and cawed her approval when the others laughed.

I drifted away but found nowhere to go. Per was hovering at the edge of the crowd beside Clef, who listened with his arms crossed and a slight smile on his face. When I grudgingly returned to the cabin to see if the shirt was ready for me to try on, I found Lant there with Spark. She flushed a very pretty pink when I entered, and I made my fitting as brief as possible. 'It looks well enough. Do you wish me to load it, or will you do that yourself?' she asked me.

Had I ever imagined that anyone would so bluntly discuss how I prepared for murder? They both watched me silently as I filled the concealed pockets in the shirt, and then slipped it on again. Spark frowned and said, 'It isn't my best work, but it's the best I can do with what I have. You must wear your cloak and walk a bit hunched, as if feeling your years.' And with that she presented me with a sort of belt with pouches for Chade's firepots to ride in. They would sit at the small of my back, and when I donned my cloak and slouched as she commanded they were well enough concealed.

With that preparation done, I left them to themselves. They were not wise in who they had chosen to love. But I had known that burning passion, and suspected that my father had felt that way about Patience, and that old King Shrewd had not been especially thoughtful about the consequences of taking Duchess Desire as his bride. I withdrew and let them have whatever moments they could.

The day dripped by as slowly as sap dripping from a cut branch. The shoreline grew closer, and as early evening fell, we could make out lanterns being lit in the distant city. Brashen came to find me. 'It will be full dark when we arrive, and from what Paragon recalls of the harbour, it's not one we want to enter at night. We'll anchor outside where the water is deeper, and go in by daylight. The moon is waxing and this time of year we can expect some very low tides. Not a time to take chances in a strange harbour with a ship the size of Paragon.'

I nodded reluctantly. 'We should do the wise thing,' I agreed, even though I longed to set foot on land as soon as it was remotely possible. Just as foolish as my companions, I chided myself, and thanked Brashen for the news.

He nodded gravely. 'Tell your friends that none of them need stand watch tonight. I suggest you get what sleep you can. We have not met under the best circumstances, Prince FitzChivalry, but I wish you luck all the same.' And with that, he left me. And I knew I should accept his counsel, find my friends and advise them to make their final preparations and then sleep. I returned to Amber's cabin to find that Per and Amber had already joined them there.

'Did you see the city lights? It looks so beautiful!' Per asked me.

'It does,' I agreed. 'And another time I would be glad to explore a new city. Brashen says he will anchor just outside the harbour, very late tonight. I'm going to ask if the crew can take me ashore right away to reconnoitre. I'd like to go to the taverns and listen to the gossip there.'

Amber shook her head. 'I share your impatience,' she said, as she unfastened her skirts and let them fall. To my surprise, she picked them up and used the hem to wipe the cosmetics from her face. 'Likely you would be turned back at the docks. Clerres patrols its streets and harbour vigorously. It is a lovely city, clean and orderly and very well controlled. It would be a great inconvenience if you were detained.' She wiped the last of the rouge from her mouth and the Fool added, 'We should sleep tonight and go together, very early. I judge it crucial that we keep our pretence of being eager pilgrims.' He ran his fingers through his hair, standing it up on end. 'Besides, I doubt that Brashen and Althea would allow it. Let a boatload of crew go to town in the middle of the night? Before the ship is anchored in the harbour? Not a good plan.'

Reluctantly, I accepted that advice. We said nothing of how I had stalked out earlier. It was our way of making peace with one another. The others exchanged glances, and I was surprised to see how relieved they were that the Fool and I were not quarrelling any more.

I think he finally realized that my dislike for Amber was real. Within the small room, he reverted to being the Fool, discarding Amber's shawl and slippers on the floor. Once more we spread out our maps and studied them. One was the city and the concourse to Clerres Castle with its towers and courtyards. The other four each represented a level of the interior stronghold. On every map, there were blank stretches where the Fool either did not know or could not recall the exact layout. We discussed routes and possible places of concealment. He recalled, as best he could, how many guards there would be and where they could be stationed. I pretended that our plans had some small chance of success. When I was utterly weary of hearing the repetition of all we had said earlier, I suggested that all of us should get as much sleep as possible. I sent Lant and Per off to their hammocks. The Fool asked Spark to go to the galley and beg a pot of hot water and some cups, 'for a cup of tea to clear my mind before I sleep.' I smiled as she hurried from the room, for I suspected she and Lant would share another goodnight embrace in a more private place.

A strange silence fell when we were alone. There was a distance between us that Amber had created. Before we went into danger tomorrow, I wanted to close it. 'We have small chance of success. I only hope that the others do not fall with us.'

He nodded. His gloved fingers groped along the bunk and found Bee's books. He drew one onto his lap and opened it at random. A woman with golden hair rode a horse through the forest. 'Three hunt as one at the trail's edge. The queen, the foreteller and the stableboy smile to see it so.'

'I think it recalls our time in the Mountains. You, me and Kettricken. Hunting together.'

He smiled sadly. 'How can it be that I recall such a harsh and dangerous journey so fondly?'

'I as well,' I admitted, and the gap between us closed.

We paged through Bee's books, I read to him and we spoke of those times. We were as comfortable with one another now as we were going to be. And in those quiet hours, I had finally realized what Amber had been concealing. My friend was terrified of returning to Clerres, as reluctant to set foot on shore as I would be to return to Regal's dungeons. His torment in Clerres had been as he had described the city. Orderly and well controlled. Carefully and precisely planned in a way that my torture had not been.

'I was too gullible,' he said woefully. 'When first I began to suspect that they were deceiving us, I should have fled. Instead, Prilkop and I talked. And debated. I insisted I must warn you, lest they find you. And I convinced Prilkop that we must leave and seek ourselves for this "wild-born" new prophet and protect him as I was not protected. Was he the Unexpected Son? Of that, neither of us could be sure. But we both knew that a young White would no longer be allowed to pursue his own goals. If the Servants brought him to Clerres, they would use him for their own purposes.'

Bee's book was forgotten in his lap. His splayed hands covered the pages as he spoke.

'The next day, we began to plan our departure. We quietly sold off some of the gifts that we had been showered with and sought to buy passage on a ship, but it had no room for us. Nor did any other vessel in the harbour that day. We tried to bribe a fisherman to take us to the next island. He told us he did not dare. And when we persisted in our efforts, we were ambushed, beaten and robbed of our coin.

'Then the Four abandoned all subtlety. The guards at the gate told us bluntly we were not allowed to leave the island fortress. We were summoned by them and asked if we were unhappy. They told us we were honoured to be kept there in such rich circumstances and that we had a duty to remain. That we should share our dreams and impart wisdom to the younger Whites. And so, began the first phase in our captivity.

'That was when Prilkop agreed we must send someone else to warn you. I had my doubts but we agreed that this new prophet, Unexpected Son or not, must be found and protected. And who else did we have out in the wide world who could undertake such a thing? Only you.' He swallowed but his guilt stuck in his throat. 'And so we sent out our messengers, two by two. I dared not give them clear directions, but sent them off with riddles to solve and obscure references to you. They were as naïve as children, and as eager to be the heroes of the tale. Oh, Fitz, I am so ashamed now. Prilkop and I, we prepared them as best we could, and they were as determined to go as we were to send them. But they knew nothing of the outside world. They were fired with the desire to help us. To save the world. And they went. And they never returned or sent word back. I believe they all met horrible ends.'

There is nothing one can say to such words. One can only listen. After a time, he spoke again. 'One night, after the evening meal, I felt unwell. I took to my bed. And the next time I awoke, I was in a cell. Prilkop sprawled on the floor nearby. Coultrie came to the door of our cell and told us that we were charged with corrupting the young Whites and urging them to run away. And that we could no longer be allowed to move freely about Clerres, but that we might regain our standing if we would help them find the Unexpected Son, the new White born in the wild. Truthfully, we told them we knew nothing of such a child.' His smile was a grimace. 'They held us in cells on the highest level of the stronghouse. The back walls were like filigree or lace, and white as bone, but as thick as my forearm is long. We were allowed comfortable beds and good meals, and given pen and parchment to record our dreams. I knew that we still had value to them. We were locked up securely, with four locks, but we were not mistreated at all. At first.

'Despite our fall from grace, there were a few manipulors and collators who remained loyal to us. We found a message baked into one of the little loaves of bread we were given. It was a valiant promise that they would continue to send messengers until they were sure one got through. I hated to think of the risks they would take, but had no way to beg them to stop. So, I dared to hope.'

He dragged in a breath and closed the book on his lap. His groping hand found my shoulder and clutched it tightly. 'Fitz. One day they moved us. From the pleasant, airy cells down to ones in the bowels of the stronghold. They were dark and damp, and looked out onto a sort of . . . stage, with seating around it. There was a table in the centre of the stage, and tools for torture. It smelled of old blood. Each day, I feared we would face irons and pincers and pokers. But we didn't. Still, that sort of waiting and wondering . . . I cannot say how many days passed like that.

'Each day they gave us each just a small loaf of bread and a pitcher of water. But one evening when they brought our food—' He was gasping now. 'The water pitcher . . . was full of blood. And when we broke open the bread, it was baked full of tiny bones. Finger bones . . .' His voice was rising higher and higher. I put my hand on his gloved hand on my shoulder. It was all I could do.

'Day after day . . . bloody water and bone-bread. We could not guess how many they killed. The second day they separated Prilkop from me. But the pitcher of blood and the bone-bread continued. They gave me nothing else to eat or drink, but I did not give in. I did not give in, Fitz.'

He stopped to breathe, and for a time, that was all he could do. As if he had run a terrible race to escape these memories. But they had caught up with him at last.

'Then, it stopped. They gave me a small loaf of coarse bread, but when I broke it, there were no bones in it. The next day, instead of bread, there were vegetables in a dark broth. I ate it. Bone-flour and blood-soup. For three days. Then, in the bread, a single tooth. And bobbing in the soup, a single pale eye. Oh, Fitz.'

'You could not have known.' My stomach turned.

'I should have known. I should have guessed. I was so hungry. So thirsty. Did I know, did I guess and refuse to acknowledge it? I should have guessed, Fitz.'

'You have not the darkness of heart to imagine such a thing, Fool.' I could not stand to torment him any longer that night. 'Go to sleep. You have told me enough. Tomorrow we take back Bee. And before we leave this city, I will kill as many of them as I can.'

'If I sleep, I shall dream of it,' he replied, his voice shaking. 'They were brave, Fitz. Brave beyond any courage I have ever had. My allies, they did not stop. They helped me when they could. It was not often and it was not much. A kind word whispered as someone passed my cell. Once, some warm water on a cloth.' He shook his head. 'I fear they were harshly punished for those small mercies.'

'Tomorrow, once we have Bee, I intend a different sort of "mercy" for the Four,' I promised him.

He could not smile at my extravagant promise. 'I fear we cannot surprise them. The sheer number of dreams and dreamers they have to consult will betray us to them. And I fear they will be very ready to take me back and resume what they began.' He put his face into his hands. His voice was muffled by his gloved fingers. 'They consider me a traitor,' he confided to me. 'And for that reason, they hate me more vividly than for any other thing I have done. I do not fear that they will capture and kill me, Fitz. I fear they will capture me and never kill me.'

I saw, not his fear, but his courage. He was terrified, but for Bee he would dare to tempt once more the powers of Clerres. I reached over, caught his cuffs and pulled his hands away from his face. Time to be honest. 'Fool. I know what you dreamed. Not just what you told me, but all of it. And I understand your choice.' He gave me a woeful look. 'Paragon told me.'

He gently pulled his hands free. 'I should have known he'd be aware of what I dreamed. I'm still surprised he told you.'

'I think he was concerned for you. As he demonstrated the first day I met him, he is very fond of you.'

'Did he tell you all of it?'

'He told me enough, Fool. You are correct. If there is a choice to be made, and one of us must die, then I would rather that you went on. I have not been a good parent to Bee. I think you might do better. And you will have Riddle and Nettle to aid you in that. And Dutiful will see that you have an allowance to maintain Withy—'

He laughed harshly. 'Oh, Fitz. That is not the choice! I do not choose between you and me living.' A pause. He asked in a choked voice, 'Did you truly think I would choose myself over you?'

'It would be the sensible choice. For Bee's sake.'

'Oh, Fitz. No. The dreams do not even make it my choice. It is simply a divide in the possible ways the future may go.' His voice grew tight. 'On one, the Destroyer dies and the Unexpected Son lives. On the other, the Unexpected Son perishes. So, if it comes down to some act of mine, an act I cannot foresee, but desperately hope it will not, I will do what I must to see that Bee lives. Bee is who I will preserve, at all costs.' His voice squeaked to a halt. Tears glinted in his sightless eyes.

'Of course. Yes. That would be my choice as well.'

'Knowing that still does not make me eager to confront such a decision.'

A tap at the door stopped his words and he hastily wiped his tears on his sleeve. I opened the door. 'I'm sorry it took so long. I had to wait for the water to boil,' Spark said. She angled sideways to carry the tray into the room, pushed aside garments and set the tray on the bunk. 'We've not much left of the Kelsingra teas. What would you like?'

The Fool smiled. Spark looked at me accusingly. She knew he'd been weeping. The Fool spoke. 'Actually, I've a tea I brought from Buckkeep. I've been saving it, but tonight I think I shall indulge myself. It has peppermint and spearmint from the Women's Garden, and fine grated gingerroot dried to a powder. A bit of elderberry as well.'

'Patience used to brew that for me,' I recalled, and he smiled as he groped among his possessions and brought out a little leather pouch.

'I got the recipe from Burrich,' he admitted. 'There is just enough for a pot. Dump it in.' He handed the pouch to Spark, and she upended it into the waiting teapot. As it brewed, the fragrance of a homely time, of simple teas and simple pleasures, filled the small room. Spark poured for us and we drank tea together as if we were not going to face death the next day. The fragrance stirred old memories, and the Fool told her a tale or two of how Buckkeep Castle had been, once upon a time. He spoke of his fondness for King Shrewd and the pranks Hands and I had played in the stables. Of Garetha the garden girl who had loved him from afar, and Cook Nutmeg's wonderful bread. Of Smithy and ginger-cakes and how the Women's Garden smelled when the summer sun struck the lavender.

Spark was reclining on her bunk and the Fool's eyes were closed. When his voice faded to a murmur, I slipped away, closing the door softly behind me. I went to my hammock between Lant's and Per's. I climbed in and to my astonishment sleep came to find me.

TWENTY-SEVEN

Feather to Blade

To Merchants Clifton, Anrosen and Bellidy,

With our greatest apologies, we are unable to fulfil the terms of our contract with you. Our liveship, Kendry, has become unmanageable, and a threat to not only his own captain and crew but to other vessels we encounter. He has twice deliberately taken on water to spoil cargo. He fights the rudder and lists at will.

For the safety and security of our crew, and of your cargoes, we therefore must terminate our agreement. You have the right to bring suit against us for this breach. However, if you are willing, we have made arrangements with the liveship Ophelia, owned and managed by the Tenira family, a fine Bingtown Trader family with a long history of reliable dealings. At no additional cost to you, they will take over our contracts and fulfil them.

We hope you will agree that this is the most equitable arrangement for all of us.

With the utmost respect,
Captain Osfor of the liveship Kendry

The sun had travelled across the sky. Now it entered my cell through the bars and made stripes on the floor. I was hungry, but had probably missed the food for the evening. I tried to put together what had happened to me today. Perhaps tomorrow Capra would come, and would want to know more. If I spoke freely, would she give me the little cottage and clean clothes and good food to eat? And if she did, what then? I could not imagine spending the rest of my life here. I also couldn't imagine ever going home. The only possibility that seemed real to me was that one or more of the Four would be displeased with me, and I'd be beaten. Or killed. Perhaps both.

Or the dreams of what I might do would come true. I felt cold as I thought of them, even though the darkening evening was still warm.

The woman came to light the lamps. They smelled of pine, of a forest. I longed for the forest. I longed to be anywhere that people were not. I put my mattress on the floor but I did not sleep. The lamplight made different shadows from the bars. Their shadows became fainter. I lifted my head to look at the lamp. The flame was barely dancing on the wick. Then it winked out. Only the light from the lamp down the walkway lit my cell now. The world became shades of black and grey.

I heard the black man in the next cell shift on his bed. 'Is it tonight, then? So soon.'

I wasn't sure if he spoke to himself or to me. I waited.

'Little one. Bee. Do you have dreams?'

Who did I trust? No one. Who deserved the truth from me? No. It was too dangerous to be truthful with anyone. 'Of course I do. Everyone dreams.'

'True. But not everyone dreams as we do.'

'How do you dream?'

'In pictures. In symbols. In hints and clues, in rhymes and riddles. Here's one:

'*A piebald bird, a silver ship, oh what are you awaking?*
'*One shall be two and two be one before the future's breaking.*'

A shiver went down my back. That was a poem I'd heard in a dream when I was sick, not long after Dwalia kidnapped me. I'd not spoken of it to anyone. I waited until I could keep my voice level. 'What does it mean?'

'I thought you might know.'

'I know nothing of silver ships or piebald birds.'

'Not yet. Sometimes we don't know what a dream means until after it has become real. And some never become real. Usually when I dream, I can feel how likely it is that a dream will become a future. And if I dream something repeatedly, then I know it's almost inevitable. I dreamed a white wolf, once. With silver teeth. I only dreamed it once, though.'

'Did you dream about the bird over and over?'

'Often enough to know it was going to happen. That it will happen.'

'But you don't know what will happen.'

'No. That is our curse. To know that something will happen, and only after it is over, to look back and say, "oh, that is what that meant. If only I'd known". It can break your heart.' He was quiet for a time. Another lantern flickered and the corridor became dimmer. He whispered, 'Oh, little one. Two flames die. It's time. I'm so sorry.' Almost to himself, he said, 'But you are so young. So small. Can this truly be for you? Are you the one?'

I choked on my question. Quiet footsteps were approaching. I had not even heard the door open and shut. 'Will I die?'

'You will change, I think. Not all change is bad. Change is seldom good or bad; it's only change. A tadpole becomes a frog. A poker is beaten into a blade. A chicken becomes meat. In a dream, I saw a feather slowly hammered into a blade. I saw the hard nut crack and become a mighty tree. I saw the young doe slain and cut into meat. You will become something different, tonight.'

The voice was as slow as falling snow. The silence that followed seemed empty and cold.

Night deepened. The faint light from the sentry towers made soft shapes in the perforated walls. *Da. Why did you push me away? Do you know how much I need you now?* I sent my thoughts out in a careful thread.

Stop that. Wolf Father's warning was severe. *You do not know how to prevent Vindeliar from hearing you. The rabbit that screams in the trap is found by the wolf, and dies more quickly. Be quiet and small until you can free yourself.*

Symphe stood outside my cell door. Her fair hair was braided back and pinned to her head. She wore a simple shirt of white cotton, belted at her waist. Her trousers looked like soft linen, and she wore short brown boots. The cuffs of the white shirt were folded back almost to her elbows, as if she had dressed to scrub a floor. She lifted a finger to her lips, then produced a set of keys from a pouch at her belt. Four keys, spaced out on leashes of silver chains. She selected one and turned it in the lock. And another key, and another clicking turn. A third key.

'How do you come to have all the keys?' I asked her.

'Ssshh.' The lock clicked. The final key.

533

I stood and backed into the corner of my cell. 'I won't go with you.'

You should. She is alone and she thinks you are just a little girl. This may be your best chance for freedom.

The final click of the key. She swung the barred door open. She smiled at me. 'You don't have to be afraid. Look what I have.' She opened a little pouch and shook something out into her hand. 'Look,' she whispered. 'Candy.' The pieces looked like gleaming buttons of red and pink and yellow. She took one and put it in her mouth. 'Mmm. Delicious. Like a cherry but sweet as honey.' She took a pink one between her thumb and forefinger. 'Try it.' She advanced on me, holding it out.

I stepped sideways to avoid being cornered.

'Take it,' she said in a breathy voice. I held out my hand and she set the candy into it. 'Eat it,' she whispered. 'You'll like it.'

'Is it poisoned? Or drugged?'

Her eyes widened. 'Didn't you just see me eat one?'

Pretend to be stupid, stupid!

I nearly laughed out loud. Instead, I pretended to put the candy into my mouth.

'Well?' she demanded. Her whisper was not as soft. She was exasperated.

I nodded, pouching one cheek out. 'Good,' I said around my tongue.

Her smile was relieved. 'See. I am nothing to be afraid of. If you come with me, very quietly, I will give you more candy.' She crooked her finger at me, beckoning.

I assumed my most puzzled expression. 'Where are we going?'

She barely hesitated. 'To make things right. Poor little child. I've come to tell you it was all a mistake. No one meant to hurt you. It was all a misunderstanding. You should not have been taken from your home. So now we must make it right. Come with me.'

'But where?'

She backed toward the open door and I followed her. In the corridor, she closed the door to my cell softly. 'It's a surprise,' she added.

'Surprise,' said the black man and laughed quietly.

She turned toward his cell, her face contorted with hate. 'Why aren't you dead yet?'

'Because I'm alive!' he announced with no effort to lower his voice. He laughed aloud like rolling thunder. 'Why aren't *you* dead yet?'

'Because I'm smarter than you. I know when to stop. I know when to cease being a problem.' She steered me away, her hand heavy on my shoulder.

At that, his laughter boomed. 'You think you know so much. You've seen so many possible futures and you think you can pick and choose. And you have, for so long. For so many generations, you've chosen what you thought was best. Not best for the world, not best for people. Best for you and those who serve you. You chose what would give you the greatest wealth, the most comfort, the most power!'

His words followed us. Other prisoners were waking staring through the bars of their cells as we passed. 'It's nothing, he's mad, go back to sleep!' Symphe spoke the words through gritted teeth, keeping her voice low.

'But the world spins on and there is a destined path. You can tip it only so far before it rights itself! It's all inevitable now. I see, but you refuse to look.' He sounded mad to me. Perhaps he was. How long could you keep a man caged before he went insane?

We reached the door at the end of the corridor. 'Open it!' she snapped at me and I did. We passed into the dimness of the little room. Descending the stairs meant that she loosened her grip on my shoulder. I thought of darting away. Not yet. I'd wait until there was a choice of direction to flee in. But I took the steps faster and the only grip she could keep was on the loose fabric of my shirt. If I needed to, I could tear free of her.

Not yet.

We went down, and down and then down again. 'Where are we going?' I asked her.

'To see some friends,' she replied. 'They have the candy.'

The first two landings we passed were open to corridors I recognized. They led to the rooms full of scrolls and books. When we reached the ground floor, she led me down a wide hall. Door after door we passed, but at last she paused before one. She took out a ring of brass keys, selected one and opened a tall door. 'Hush,' she warned me. More steps, another locked door, and down again. She unlocked a final door and motioned that I should enter.

I stood still. The room beyond the locked door smelled bad, a cross between the low tide in Chalced and a dirty butcher's stall. I didn't want to enter. I should have run from her when I had the chance. *It's a trap!*

'In we go,' she said brightly, putting a hand in middle of my back and shoving me into the room. She pulled the door shut behind us.

I moved quickly away from her into a room with walls and floor of stone. The carrion smell and the stink of faeces grew stronger. I wrapped my arms around myself, for the room was chill and dank. There were fat oil-lamps on shelves at intervals on the walls, but their wicks were low and the light illuminated little more than the lamps themselves. I heard something move and the soft clinking of chain. I squinted and saw a barred door and beyond it, a huddled shape. Did she intend to confine me in a cell down here? She'd have to catch me first! I put more distance between us.

'Come back, Bee! Remember? Candy?'

Yes, she truly thought me that stupid.

Good. Wolf Father's response was terse. *Find a weapon. Kill her. Escape.*

Kill her? I could barely frame the thought. *I can't.*

You must. That smell is old blood. Lots of it. She brought you to a place of bloodshed. Of killing.

I glanced over my shoulder, gave Symphe a vacuous smile and said, 'I want to find the people with the candy!'

She was faster than I had expected. In the second I glanced away from her, she crossed the distance between us and seized my upper arm in a tight grip.

Don't fight her. Not yet. Wait until you know you can kill.

My eyes were adjusting to the dimness. There were other cells. In one, there was someone on the floor, sprawled and still. She walked me past a stone table with metal rings set into the sides and edges. It smelled of blood and old piss. There was a bank of layered benches. Oh. I had seen this place, in Vindeliar's mind. Here they had tormented Beloved. The dim light hinted at ugly stains on the table and on the floor around it. I felt ill. I feigned a stumble and her hand clenched tighter. I dropped to my knees, testing her strength. She kept hold of me but now I knew. She was fast but not as strong as Dwalia. If I had to, I could break her grip.

Not yet.

'Bee! Don't pull away. Soon we will have the candy. It's so delicious.'

She had moved into the dim pool of light of one of the lamps. It was like a big teapot, with the wick poking out of its spout and two handles like ears to pick it up. She reached up to lift it from its shelf. She did not want to let go of me, so she had to lift it by one handle. It was so heavy that her hand shook and the flame on the wick flared up as the oil slopped toward it. She set it on the floor with the scrape of heavy pottery on stone. She poked at the wick. The flame grew taller and it lit a wider circle around us.

'Did you bring her?' Vindeliar's voice.

'Did you get the keys?' That was Dwalia. I shrank back into the darkness.

'Hush. Yes to both.' Symphe laughed softly. 'The keys I've had for years!'

My heart thundered in my chest. Had I missed my chance? What hope did I have against three of them? The brighter light reached into the cell and I feared to look. But Dwalia huddled on a bunk, her hands trapped between her knees. I saw her fever-bright eyes and chapped mouth. Infection had set into her lacerated flesh. Vindeliar was in the same cage, hunkered on the floor. He'd taken a beating; his eyes were blackened, his lower lip split. I could see the chain that bound him tightly to a ring set in the cold stone, barely two links between his neck and the floor ring. How his body must ache from that forced crouch. His only alternative would be to lie on the cold, filthy floor.

Symphe's slender fingers bit deep into my arm. 'Pick up the lamp,' she ordered me.

I stooped to obey her but she did not let go of my arm. The lamp was as big around as a milk bucket and heavy. I wrapped my arms around it with the flame away from me and lifted. I did not like how the flame leapt and stuttered. 'This way,' she said and pulled me toward the cell. I concentrated on breathing calmly and keeping the lamp steady. It was designed to be left on a shelf, not carried. I wondered how long I could hold it.

Weapon, weapon, there was no weapon. I could break free of her and run, but she had locked the door. Was there another way out? Likely it was locked as well. I needed a plan, but I had no plan. I wanted my father desperately. He would know what to do. The night we had burned the messenger's body, he had thought it all through, in just a few minutes. What would he do now?

Stop thinking about doing. Just be ready to do.

I could not imagine more useless advice. Symphe had chosen a key on the brass ring and was turning it in the lock. Break away now? No. She would unlock the others and they would pursue me throughout this chamber. I did not even know how big the room was but they probably knew every nook and cranny. Symphe pushed the door open, tucked the ring of keys into her belt and then reached into her shirt and took something out. It was a dark cylinder, a container of some sort. She held it up. 'And I was able to obtain this as well, at great risk to myself! Not to mention my loss of dignity, in seducing a foreign sentry. You know how closely Capra guards her quarters. When he wakes tomorrow from his long hours of sleep, I imagine he will face the headsman. But it was worth it. Do you know what is in here?' She dangled it before them as she smiled her red-lipped smile. 'It's serpent essence.'

Vindeliar's head lifted and twisted grotesquely. It was both pathetic and terrifying to see him become such a vessel of need. Dwalia looked outraged. 'You said you'd given us the last of it. That there was no more. If I had had that before . . .'

'I had no more,' Symphe snapped. 'No one knows all that Capra has hoarded of treasures and magic, greedy old hog that she is. And she tried to keep this girl to herself.' Her hand became a clamp on my arm as she tugged me into the cell. She kicked the cell door closed behind us. She glared at Vindeliar. 'She had better be what you say she is! You need to prove it. Prove that the risks I've taken were worth it. If you can't, I leave you chained here and let Capra do as she will with both of you.' She spoke as if I were a dog on a leash, too stupid to understand what she said. As if Vindeliar were a block of wood. 'Stand there. Hold the lamp.'

She turned her back on me and spoke to Dwalia. 'I shall let Vindeliar have it all. Then we shall see if he speaks truth, see whether she is or is not the Unexpected Son from the dreams!' She gave a dismissive laugh and stared down at the chained man. Vindeliar's mouth was ajar, his lower lip trembling and wet with saliva. She regarded him as if he were an ugly dog and did not address him as she said, 'Time to use him, Dwalia. Time to take the reins, or give them up. I gave you my promise: help me rise and you rise with me.

That was a promise your Pale Woman never kept to you. But I will, if Vindeliar is truly as useful as you say he is, and if this girl is the prize you said you could win for me.'

She had let go of my shoulder. Now she turned to the door to lock it. As she took the ring of keys from her belt, I tipped the lamp, splashing her back with the hot oil. I did it with no forethought. Doing, not thinking. The smell of a pinewood forest warmed the room. The fire on the wick burned taller and some of the spilled oil on the outside of the lamp flared into flame. I thrust the lamp at her, wick first, as she exclaimed in anger and began to turn to face me.

The lamp was a terrible weapon, one that might work or might not do anything. Flames licked up the fat side of the pot. I pushed it against Symphe, against the fabric wet with oil. The fire made a sound like someone blowing out a candle and the loose cloth of her shirt back flared into flames. The fire leapt up, scorching her hair. It writhed and curled with a terrible stink. Screaming, she aimed a wild slap at me. Instead it knocked the lamp from my hands and it shattered into shards on the floor, spilling the rest of the oil. The wick fell and suddenly the puddle of oil became a flaming wall. I leapt back from it, but Symphe stepped in it as she twisted, vainly slapping at the back of her clothes and hair. Vindeliar was wailing and Dwalia cursing me. But they were chained and Symphe was not. I would deal with her first.

Stooping, I seized the biggest shard of lantern and slashed at her. It cut her arm, a long shallow gash. She grabbed at it, and it cut her hand, but her clothing was well ablaze now, fiery fragments of it spinning off into the air, and she suddenly had no thought for me. She stepped back from the flaming oil on the floor, but the falling bits of burning cloth ignited her wet footprints. She shrieked and began slapping at her clothes with both hands. The brass ring of keys and the long tube of serpent spit went flying. The keys jangled as they struck the floor, but the tube of spit shattered. Vindeliar gave a howl of despair and lunged at it like a dog after a flung bone. The chain around his neck would not let him go far, but he crabbed in a circle around his tether, reaching for the puddle of slime with his hands.

He could barely reach it with one hand. Vindeliar threw himself against his restraints, lunging to reach the spilled potion, ignoring the flailing, flaming woman and Dwalia's angry cries. I'd failed. My shard of lamp was too small to do any serious damage. Symphe would be burned but alive. And angry.

Then I saw the long splinter from the spit cylinder. It glittered, black and gleaming silver, longer than my hand. Long enough to stab deep. I dropped my shard, leapt toward it and snatched it up.

It was sharp. As were the broken bits in the puddle of serpent spit. I cut my bare feet, I cut my hand. It didn't hurt. I looked at the blood welling on my hand. I felt queasy, dizzy and yet full of stillness. Blood seeped from the gash on my palm. It dripped, but the drops fell very slowly to the floor. I saw exactly where each drop would fall. Something was happening; I wasn't sure what it was. A deafening quiet welled up in me and all sound was far away. The moment filled me. I was completely aware of everything that was happening around me.

Symphe danced her fire-dance. I saw the moving tip of every flame and knew where it would lick her. Vindeliar strained toward the slowly spreading puddle of spit, patting his hand in the fluid, not caring that he mixed it with filth from the stone floor. He drew his hand back to his face and licked his palm and fingers. White showed all around his eyes. Dwalia was shouting commands at him. 'Try to reach the keys! Forget the serpent potion! Get the keys! Kill that bitch! Symphe, tear off your clothes! Come to where I can reach you!' Those and a dozen other requests she cried. No one listened to her. I had the splinter in my hand still, its sharp edge in my cut. Abruptly, it hurt. It burned. I had wanted to do something with this. Kill. I was going to kill Symphe and then Vindeliar and then Dwalia. How?

Then the magic surged into me. I felt it race into my body from the cuts on my feet and from the cut on my hand. It burned me with ecstasy. I quivered with pleasure, shivers running up my spine, gooseflesh pimpling on my arms and legs. I laughed out loud. I loved the sound of my laughter. I roared with laughter and focused myself on Symphe. I could see her so clearly, and see, too, all the things that might happen to her. She might collapse to the ground and her clothes continue to burn. She might flee and crash into the bars or carry her flaming body to Dwalia's bunk. But most likely of all was what happened next, for I willed it so. I timed my motion to the movement I knew she would make. At the instant she threw back her head to scream, I stepped in with my shard and cut her throat. I stepped back before the flames could catch me. It was so easy. I knew exactly how the flames would move and precisely where it was safe to step. I knew how firmly to press and how quickly to draw the shard across her throat. Vindeliar had been right! Once I was on the true Path, all became easy and so clear.

I no longer needed the shard. I knew that Symphe would die of burns and blood loss. I saw some futures where I held onto the shard and it cut my hand badly. There were far fewer futures where I needed it to defend my life. In only a few did Dwalia possess it. A few were too many. I tossed it into the far corner of the cell as Symphe fell, her screams now choked with blood. She sprawled and clutched uselessly at her leaking neck. Her feet were in the burning puddle. She kicked them. I turned from watching her. I already knew what happened next. She was finished.

I knew, too, what I should do next. With every action I took, the best Path grew broader and clearer. This was *my* true Path. It was nothing like the one the Servants had envisioned.

I stooped to set my cut hand on the surface of the puddle. I drew breath and felt the magic roar into my blood. I felt it join my other magic, the rightful magic of my Farseer blood. The magics twined and danced in me, red and black and silver. I knew the futures and I knew the past.

And I knew I could command people to create the future I desired.

I felt Vindeliar's power wash over me like a cold wave. A shallow wave. 'Unchain us,' he suggested.

I saw his eyes widen as I slowly shook my head. 'That does not happen,' I told him gently.

'Force her!' Dwalia barked at him, and this time his suggestion was not a wave but a solid slap against all my awareness. It stung, but did not stun. I thought of a little joke. I stooped slowly and picked up the ring of keys. I looked at them. Slack-faced, I held them out toward Dwalia. She lunged. I dropped them, just out of reach. She struggled to get to them, strangling herself against her iron collar.

'Unlock our chains,' Vindeliar repeated the words as a command. But I had found my shields and I cut through his feeble suggestion as a ship cuts through water. I smiled at him and sidled closer to Symphe's unmoving body. I found the dagger at her belt. Its decorated sheath was scorched. I pulled the dagger free of it and put it through my sash. A real weapon. One my father had taught me to use. It felt good. In her pocket I found the other keys on their silver leashes. Those were mine, too.

'Vindeliar!' Dwalia rasped at him, her voice hoarse from her bruised throat.

He tried. I felt him shape his power and thrust it at me. It was like a buffet of wind. I smiled at him. I recalled how my father had pushed me away when I had felt the touch of his magic. I imitated that as I looked at Vindeliar and said, 'Stop that.'

He dropped limply to the floor. Only whites showed in his slitted eyes and his body trembled twice before it was still.

'Is he dead?' I heard myself ask aloud.

'Guards! Guards! Help! Help!'

I had heard Dwalia roar with fury and shout with anger. This was the first time I'd heard her voice ascend to a crescendo of terror.

It took a moment for me to realize that I was what she feared. I stood outside the reach of her chains and knew a moment of panic. Guards would come and I'd be captured. Beaten or killed. No. 'Stop shouting,' I said to her. 'Be quiet.'

And she was, her mouth hanging open. I listened. The dying flames on the oil puddle and on Symphe's body whispered softly. I heard no guards running, no doors unlocking, nothing. Oh. Of course Symphe would have arranged for them to be away from their posts. I smiled at the work she had done for me.

In that moment of silence, my body shouted at me. I had cuts on the soles of both feet. The cut on my hand stung. I looked at it. It was like a smiling mouth carved across my palm and it was sending a smooth sheet of blood sliding from my hand. With my other hand, I pushed it closed and held it.

Oh. I could do better than that. I felt the severed edges of flesh touch and recall each other. They belonged together. 'Be together,' I suggested to them and my body listened. I could almost see the fine net my body wove, like a spider's web to knit my flesh back together. I limped away from the puddle of serpent spit and the dying flames on the oily pool. I sat down on the floor and regarded my bloody feet. I plucked a shard of glass from my heel. Blood followed it. One by one, I closed each cut. When I stood, I could feel that my feet were newly healed. They hurt, but the sharp jab of pain was gone.

There is no time for this now. Kill her. Flee.

Sssh.

I hushed Wolf Father. This was no forest, but a dungeon in a stronghold. Would I need Dwalia to escape? I considered her.

'You were never the Unexpected Son!' she whispered.

'So I told you, over and over. And still you ruined my life. Took me from my home, killed my friends.'

'You are the Destroyer. And we brought you here.'

I was surprised. Her words seemed to shimmer with light and truth. I was the Destroyer? My mind leapt back to the forest and to overheard whispers from Reppin and Alaria. I was that?

'I am,' I said. As soon as I acknowledged it, that Path unrolled before me. I knew what I would do. It did not feel like a choice as I took the knife from my sash. It was a thing I did in so many possible futures that not doing it did not seem possible. I took a slow step toward her. 'I am the Destroyer. You not only brought me here, you created me. I was unlikely, almost impossible. Then you came to my home . . . oh. No.' I stared at her and saw the path she had left behind her. It was like a snail's track on a clean swept floor. 'No. It began years before then. You began to make me when you tormented Beloved.'

She stared at me, her eyes wide. I stepped forward, my knife ready. She slapped my hand, hard, and the knife fell. It clattered on the floor, exactly as I had known it must, making precisely the sound I had expected. I didn't need a knife. I smiled at her. I pushed into her mind as if it were soft butter and I a hot blade. I spoke my word softly. 'Die.'

And she did.

She occupied a space in the world. Then she didn't. I felt the world close up around where she had been. The part of her that had been a living thing became a prelude to earth. Every future that might have sprung from Dwalia living suddenly shrivelled and vanished from the great tapestry of the future. Other gleaming threads writhed in to take their places. They were the futures made possible by her death at this moment. The moment she stopped living, her body began to collapse into something else. I stared at that sack of flesh, wondering how it had held her, and what exactly Dwalia had been. Not the thing that was left behind.

So. That was death. I considered that as I gathered up the brass ring of keys and then Symphe's knife.

I looked at Vindeliar. Tremors were now running over him, jiggling his cheeks and making his eyeballs twitch. I thought of ending him quickly and decided I wouldn't. I was still coming to an awareness of what I had done to Dwalia. And to Symphe? I had not felt her death that way. Was it because I'd had a small tie to Dwalia from attempting to manipulate her? Or was it the taint of serpent spit in my flesh? I feared what I might feel if I killed Vindeliar, for we had had a bond of sorts. I left him to die by himself.

Symphe had never locked the cell door. I walked out of it, thought for a moment, and then tossed the brass ring of keys to the floor. I left that door closed but unlocked. Let them puzzle about that.

My mind moved faster than the wind before a squall. I could flee. They would hunt me through the halls and rooms. And they would find me, for I did not know any way to escape from it. They would find me with Symphe's knife and her keys, they would see the stains of oil and serpent slime on my clothes. They would know me for what I was. An assassin, like my father before me. The Destroyer from their dreams. They would find me and they would kill me.

I didn't want to die.

Wolf Father spoke. *For now, hide your true self. Be what they think you are.*

My true self? I handled that thought reluctantly.

What they have made you. He sounded both sad and proud. *The feather hammered into a blade.*

I hurried now for I could not tell how much time had passed. I left the cell and the ugly table and foul smell behind me. I closed the door. I went back the way we had come. When I reached the main floor I recalled carefully how Capra had led me through the stronghold. I returned to the washing courts and was pleased to find clean garments identical to the ones that I had soiled still hanging on the drying lines. I took what I needed and respaced the hanging garments on the laundry lines to cover up my theft. I splashed my hands and feet clean and dried them on my dirty clothes. I rolled my soiled garments up into as small a bundle as I could manage and buried them in one of the flowerbeds. Then I climbed the stairs to the cells where they had held me. I moved as softly as a ghost as I opened the door and entered the hall. The lamps were out and only the stars and moon looked down on me. The guard was nowhere in sight. Doubtless that was Symphe's arrangement but now it worked to my advantage. I filled my thoughts with sleepiness and slipped past the few occupied cells. No one stirred. Fitting and turning each leashed key was more difficult than I had expected. I had not realized there would be a set order to them. Luck aided me on my third try. I entered and closed the door as quietly as I could manage. It was harder to lock it from inside and I was sweating before I discovered that the order of the keys to lock was the opposite of unlocking them.

I had both a set of keys and a dagger to hide in my sparsely furnished cell. Inside the thin mattress was my only option. I cut the seam just enough to allow me to insert both. I lay down on the mattress and closed my eyes. I could not find the way to sleep. The serpent spit magic coiled strangely through my body and my mind. I could not calm myself.

'So. No Symphe.'

The black voice reached me quietly from the next cell. I held my breath. He would think I was asleep.

'You killed then. I am so sorry.'

I closed my eyes and was very still. The serpent magic twisted through me like a parasite in my belly. I felt it mingling with my Farseer magic. For a terrifying instant, I could feel Prilkop in the cell next to me. I knew there were six other prisoners on this level, and that one of them was pregnant. I felt my magic go reaching, reaching, reaching . . . I slammed my mind shut. If I reached out, who might reach in? I doubted Vindeliar would be the only one they had dosed with serpent spit. I would be small and hard as a nut. I would be still as a stone. I made all things still within me. To my surprise, tears still leaked through my lashes and trickled down the side of my face. I did not weep for Symphe or Dwalia.

I wept for fear of what I had become.

TWENTY-EIGHT

Unsafe Harbour

*This dream does not belong here. It isn't an important dream, except to
me. I only write it down here because I want to keep it forever, for myself.*

*In the dream, I am working in the herb garden with my mother. The
sky is blue and the sun is out, but it is early in the day, so it is pleasantly
warm, not hot. We crawl along the rows on each side of her lavender
beds. She has strong hands. When she grips a weed and pulls, it comes
up with a long white root. I am trying to help her weed, but I am just
pulling off the top leaves. She stops me and gives me a little trowel. 'It is
worse than useless to do things halfway, Bee. For then you think the work
is done, but someone must come behind you later to do it all over again.
Even if you must work much harder and get less done, it is better to do
the whole task the first time.' Then she showed me how to push the trowel
into the earth and pop up the weed I was not strong enough to pull.*

*I woke up with the sound of her voice in my ears. It was so real, but
the peculiar part is that even though it was exactly something my mother
would say to me, I have no memory of such a day. I have drawn here
my mother's hands, strong and brown, as she draws the weed from the
earth, root and all.*

Bee Farseer's dream journal

My foolish choice, often made, is that I do not sleep well and long
on the night before a momentous task. A harsh dream of a rabbit
screaming in a trap stirred me to groggy awareness. The feel of the
ship had changed. Sometime in the night we had anchored. I'd slept
through that?

I'd finally mastered the art of getting out of a hammock, and even in the dark I managed it well enough. I could hear Lant's snoring and Per's childish breathing. My head still felt heavy with sleep and I had no idea of how much time had passed. The belowdecks lantern did not cast light so much as destroy the total darkness. I groped for my boots, pulled them on, and found the ladder to the deck by touch. I yawned, trying to waken myself more fully. I felt dulled and deadened.

On the horizon, there was a promise of light to come. I rubbed my eyes, my body still protesting at being awake. I drifted aft and avoided Althea and Brashen standing close together, looking out not at the city but at the sea outside the harbour. I found my own quiet place on the railing and stared at Clerres as light grew in the sky. The city was even prettier by dawn, a place of manicured greenery and tidy dwellings of pink and pale green and sky blue. I watched the city begin to awaken. I smelled the elusive fragrance of fresh baked bread, and watched several small fishing vessels leave the harbour. I saw the tiny figures of a man and donkey cart descend from the gentle hills to the awakening city. There was only one large ship in the harbour, her figurehead a carved bouquet. So peaceful. My body longed for more sleep. I blinked my eyes, feeling as if I had dozed off standing there.

Our figurehead was as still as if he were truly made of wood. My youthful face stared toward the harbour city and the surrounding low hills. All so peaceful. But likely today I would bloody my hands. If I had my will, people would die. I would do whatever I must to regain my child. I ventured a tendril of Skill. *Bee? Da's here. I'm coming to find you and take you home.*

I felt no response from her, but I remained as I was, my mind open and waiting for her. But it was not Bee who reached me. Thin as a thread, I felt Dutiful's touch. Even more faintly, Nettle's. And then, like a hawser following a messenger line, Thick steadied them. He still had the power. Old and achy and grumpy at being awakened so early, he still reached across the distance and clasped minds with me.

Hello Grandfather!

For a moment, Dutiful's greeting made no sense. Then it did. *The child is born?*

Nettle's Skilling was steady but her exhaustion leaked through.

A girl. Queen Elliania is delighted. She has asked for the privilege of naming her. Riddle and I agreed. Hope. Her name is Hope.

Hope. I said the name and felt its virtue rise within me. I did not need to Skill words to my daughter. All I felt for her and my new granddaughter flooded through our connection. I felt a rush of goose-flesh over my body. *Hope,* I said again, and felt it.

And there is more news! This was Dutiful, as impatient as a child to share something. *My queen has been keeping a secret until she felt it was safe to say it. She goes with child, Fitz. Against all odds, I will be a father again. And she has already chosen a name. Boy or girl, our child will be Promise.*

Tears stung my eyes and every hair on my body stood up. His joy surged through all the distance to lift my heart even higher.

Yes. Babies. Babies everywhere. And we all must wake up so, so early to talk about them. There was no mistaking Thick's opinion that all of this could have waited for later in the day. I pitied the little man for his aching bones.

Waken the cooks! Command a joyful feast! Pink sugar-cakes, ginger-bread, and those little spiced meat pies to celebrate! I suggested.

Yes! I felt Thick's spirits lift at the prospect. *And the little balls of dough cooked in fat, with cherries inside! And brown ale!*

I cannot be there, Thick, old friend, so perhaps you will set the menu to celebrate my grandchild! And eat my share of it for me?

I can do that. More cautiously, *Can I try holding her?*

I held my breath. With Nettle's ears, I heard Riddle's reply. 'Of course you can! Two hands, Thick, just like for a puppy. No, hold her close to your body. So she feels safe in your strong arms.'

She is warm, like a puppy! And she smells like a new puppy! You are safe with me, baby. She's looking at me. Look at her looking at me!

Elliania's voice, fainter to my senses. 'She will grow up trusting you.'

I wish I could be there. My heart rode with the thought.

Do not worry, Fitz. I will be her grandfather until you get home.

Thick's offer was so sincere that all I could do was let him feel my gratitude. It came to me that perhaps my odd old friend would be a better grandfather than I could be.

Where are you now? Dutiful asked.

Anchored just outside the harbour of Clerres. Today I go after Bee.

Emotions, too many to name, simmered in a stew of dread and hope. *Be careful,* Nettle breathed from far, far away.

Be ruthless. Kill them all and bring their city down around their ears. Bring our Bee home to us! This from Dutiful. He looked down at Nettle's little daughter, then over at the slight swell of Elliania's belly. His father's fury awoke. *Destroy the Servants. Make them wish they had never heard the word Farseer!*

At his naming of me, something huge stirred and rose from the depths of the Skill-current. It felt like nothing I had ever experienced before. Nettle, Dutiful and Thick all recoiled. *WALLS!* I cautioned them all, but they were already gone. As Thick lost his focus, they had vanished like mist in the morning, leaving me alone in a rising mire of foreign magic—a magic that felt repugnant and wrong, tarnished and foul, as if a child hissed like a snake. Thick and slimy, it rose around me. But my careless moment of reaching out had opened a door into me. And that awareness flowed in and touched me.

It was a sloppy outpouring of thoughts. I held myself still and small, tight and hard as a nut. I had been taught to use the Skill with purpose and discipline, targeting my thoughts as one might lunge with a sword to skewer an opponent. This was a formless push. There was great strength behind it but no intent. Like having a plough horse lean against you inside a stall. I held still and did not push back.

Farseer. That name. He groped after me. I was breathlessly still. *I feel you. You are close, aren't you? And something is with you. What is that? Not a man.* The flow of thick magic touched Paragon. The ship jolted to awareness and a shudder ran through the deck.

Touch me not! The ship ordered it, and I felt the ship's unease before Paragon put up a wall of his own, the same defence he used to keep his thoughts private from me.

The awareness fumbled at him fruitlessly, then came back to me. His power wrapped me and I was tumbled and shaken as if by a random wave. I could raise no wall against him, for he was already within my mind. His power terrified me, but he seemed to have no idea how to use it. He bumbled blindly in darkness, unable to seize me. I held my stillness and was brusquely dropped as something else caught his attention. I heard the voice that distracted him.

'Vindeliar, awake. I have questions for you.' Then a horrified whisper. *'What have you done? Symphe! Symphe, oh, no, she's dead! What have you done, you wretch? Dwalia, too? Killed your mistress too?'*

Nothing! I did not kill them! No one listens to me. You come here,
over and over, to hurt me, to make me say things that you won't believe!
You are here to hurt me again, aren't you, Coultrie? You like to hurt me!'
Fear hit me a hammer blow that paralysed me. But it was followed
by a surging fury, an outraged hatred, and underlying it in a sick
wave a youngster's hurt at being abandoned. He blasted it out. *Dwalia
is dead! Symphe is dead! You hurt me and hurt me, and I told you Bee
was bad and had magic and would do terrible things, but you only said
I was lying and hurt me more! Now they are dead, and you come to hurt
me again! Well, I will hurt you now!*

He did not aim it at me. If he had, I would have screamed as
loud as Coultrie. I still fell helplessly to Paragon's deck as a sidewash
of agony hit me. I knew them for what they were. Hot pincers,
chains that held me off my feet, tiny blades that wandered over my
flesh. I felt him realize his power.

No screaming! He silenced his target. He was not a swift thinker,
but with strength such as he had, it might not matter. He pondered
as slowly as an ox-cart going up a steep hill. I felt his childish glee
as he realized his power. *Coultrie. Now you love me. You love me more
than anything. You are so sad I was hurt. Unchain me! You will get me
a healer and bring me food. Good food, like the little Whites in the cottages
get! You will take me out of here, to a nice place with a soft bed. And
you will tell Capra and Fellowdy that all I told them is true. Bee has
magic and Bee did this. Bee killed Symphe and Dwalia.*

I felt a Skill-like surge of utter belief that he forced onto someone
else. I had no doubt of the truth he told. He drenched me with
certainty until I feared that it would be Skill-seared into me. For
one terrible instant, I knew that Bee was dangerous, shared his total
conviction that she must die.

*Make them believe me! I tried to warn you before but no one listened
to me. Tell them a Farseer is near! He talks of killing all of us, of destroying
all Clerres. And there are dragons in the harbour. I felt them! I almost
saw them. Tell them that! But get me food first.*

Pulling free of that entity was like trying to wallow out of a bog.
His awareness sucked at me the way mud drags off a man's boots
and holds him fast. I struggled against a strength that was easily the
equal of Thick's at his finest. His mind gripped mine in a disgusting
embrace, and suddenly he was peering out of my eyes, smelling and
touching and tasting all that I did. I could not raise my walls, and

the more I retreated into myself, the more of my senses he claimed as territory. He was on the verge of seizing control of my body and will.

I flung myself at him. He had not expected an attack. Had he no walls? He did not. He had widened the bridge between us; I charged over it. I claimed his vision and his other senses. I stared up at a fellow with his face disguised in white paint and powder, clad all in green the colour of swamp slime. I was lying on a cold stone floor, with the chill bite of a metal collar around my neck. My hands were bloody with fresh small cuts. I was chilled through and aching, with swollen eyes and bruises all over my body. Trivial injuries but I cherished each one as a wrong done to me by my brother. All of this was my brother's fault and now I hated my brother.

In disdain, I peeled my awareness from his. He clutched at me, refusing to let me escape. I let him enjoy how I despised his weakness. None of his injuries would have disabled a warrior. The Fool had endured far worse. His sense of injured self-righteousness weakened him. He was soft and as full of self-pity as a boil is full of pus.

'*I have suffered!*' Somewhere he spoke the words aloud. He found my dismissal of his injuries insulting. So easy to distract him.

'Vindeliar?' I heard someone plead, 'Speak to me. What happened here?'

His wrists were raw from shackles. I chose that pain and focused on it. His hands had little cuts all over them. I brought their stinging to his consciousness. I found an aching, loosened tooth and drove that pain to the front of his mind. He began to make helpless noises. I felt him flapping his hands, and as he paid more attention to his little pains, he built them up for himself. I suddenly snapped his jaws shut on his tongue, hard enough to bloody it. He gave a shriek, as much at my power over him as at the pain. I wanted to do more. I wanted to kill him. I let him know that, and in his instant of panic, he pushed me away from him. I surged back into my own body and flung up my walls. Walls tight, body curled into a tight defensive ball. I was panting as if I'd done an axe bout with Burrich.

'Prince FitzChivalry? Fitz? Fitz!'

I opened my eyes to Brashen crouched over me. Fear and relief warred on his face. 'Are you all right?' In a lower voice, 'What did Paragon do to you?'

I was coiled in a ball on the deck. The strengthening day around us was warm but my clothes were clammy and clung to me with cold sweat. Brashen held his hand out to me and I clutched his forearm and pulled myself upright. 'Not the ship,' I gasped. 'Something much darker. And stronger.'

'Come to my stateroom. You look as if you could use a drink and I've news.'

I shook my head. 'I need to gather my friends. We must go ashore, as soon as possible. Today I must find my child. They are going to kill her!'

He clapped a steadying hand to my shoulder. 'Get control. You've had a terrible dream. You need to let go of it and face the day.'

I started to shake free of his misplaced sympathy but his next words froze me.

'I've bad news for you and it's all real. Amber is missing.'

'What? Overboard?'

He scowled. 'Not in the way you think. We anchored late last night. Both Althea and I went to get some sleep. In the night, some of the crew took a ship's boat and went ashore, eager to see the town they'd heard tales about. Kennitsson among them, and Boy-O, too.' He strangled and then swallowed his anger. 'Did you know of that plan?' It was almost an accusation.

'No! And you think Amber went with them?'

'Yes! She who should have known better as much as Boy-O. I am . . . baffled, FitzChivalry. They talk as if she instigated it. She went garbed as a common sailor, promising to show them the rowdiest tavern they could imagine, food beyond compare, and with men and women trained to satisfy every appetite.' He shook his head. 'Does that seem like her to you? To incite a mutiny on the eve of this rescue she claims is so important?'

I heard Althea shouting orders, and Ant dashed past me with Per not far behind. I stepped out of the way and cut past Trell's confusion. 'How did she go missing?'

'The crew had agreed to return before dawn. When they gathered to leave, she could not be found. They searched. They returned a short time ago, without her. I came to tell you and found you here.'

I realized the ship was in motion. Again. How dazed had I been as I sprawled on the deck? How long unaware? I rubbed my eyes roughly, scratched my face and then gave my head a shake. None of it helped dispel the fog, and I suddenly recognized what I was feeling. 'The tea. He put it in the tea last night,' I said.

'What?'

'It doesn't matter. How quickly can I go ashore?'

'As soon as we anchor, we'll put a boat over the side for you.' He shook his head. 'I'm angrier at my son than I've ever been. He claims his intention was to be sure they all returned. But he should have come to me! And Amber? I feel betrayed and yet full of fear for her. Blind and alone. Why would she have wandered off?'

I had a darker fear, that she had been recognized and taken. 'I don't know. I must get ashore as soon as possible.'

'I'll be glad to help you do that,' he said, and in his voice I heard his ardent wish to be done with me and all the trouble I'd brought aboard his vessel. I could not blame him. He strode away and I was left trying to find my wits. I leaned on the railing and took deep breaths. It was all too much. The Fool had drugged me last night. My fountaining joy at Nettle's news, and my fear of the terrifying presence I had felt, dimmed.

She planned this. She made it happen.

Paragon did not speak aloud. His message was a whisper in my mind.

Why?

I do not know. But now I understand her tales from last night. Be careful! he charged me and suddenly faded from my mind. I felt nothing from the entity that had touched both of us but tightened my walls anyway. Vindeliar. I knew his name now, and his touch. And he would die.

I had seen Per. I discovered that Lant was part of the crew manoeuvring the ship into the harbour. When I knocked loudly on the door of Amber's room, there was no response. I opened it to stillness. Spark was sprawled in her bunk. I shook her and she lifted her head. 'I feel terrible,' she slurred.

'We were drugged. By Amber. Probably with a powder from my own kit.' I talked as I dressed in the prepared clothes.

She swung her feet over the edge of the bunk and sat with her face buried in her hands. 'Why?'

'Because she thinks she has a better chance to rescue Bee than I do. What did she take?'

Spark peered around groggily. 'Not her granny disguise. The trousers

I'd made for Per. They'll be short on her. A hat.' She gestured at pots of cosmetics. 'She disguised how pale she is.' She took a deeper breath and sat up straighter. 'It's hard to tell. Some of your poisons, I think. One of mine. Is the butterfly cloak gone?'

It was.

Spark began going through an assortment of small packets next to her 'fair maiden about to be wed' disguise.

'Did she take any of that?'

'Not that I can see.' She held out a hand to me. There was a pouch and a small paper. 'Cindin or carris seed. You get first choice.'

I took the carris seed. I well knew how that affected me. 'Where did you get this?'

'Carris seed from Chade. Cindin from Prince Kennitsson.'

I ransacked my memory. 'It gives stamina. May cause arousal in some. And may abort a baby.'

She gave me a look. 'He wanted to share it with me. I palmed it.'

'Nice fellow,' I said, feeling strangely disappointed in him.

'He is. He told me what it would do. We were both tired on the dog-watch. It wasn't for romance, only for stamina.'

'Mm.' I opened the pouch of carris seed, gauged how much I needed, poured it into my hand and tossed it into my mouth. I ground the small seeds between my teeth, and the spicy flavour flooded out. Almost immediately my head felt clearer. I watched Spark put the stick of cindin in her cheek against her gum. 'Dangerous habit,' I warned her.

'If it becomes a habit. It won't.' She gave me a sour smile. 'Likely we'll both be dead before that can happen. Are you keeping that carris seed?'

'If I may.'

She nodded and resumed her survey of what remained in the room. I began setting the firepots into the belt she had made. She watched me with an eagle's gaze. 'Remember which fuse is which. Blue is slow. Chade has greatly refined those since you last used one. They are much more reliable and powerful. He is . . .' She lifted a hand suddenly to her lips. 'He was so proud of them,' she corrected herself and I saw her eyes flood.

'I'll use them well,' I promised her.

A moment later she announced, 'The flame-jewel bracelet is gone!'

'I'm not surprised. The fire-brick?'

'It's here. And here's a gentlemanly little shoulder bag I sewed for you yesterday. The brick will fit nicely in the bottom.'

'Thank you.' It suddenly felt companionable and right to be assembling my assassin's gear with a fellow killer. I tucked the fire-brick in the bag. It held it nicely upright. I removed one of the exploding pots from the harness and used a scarf to settle it on the fire-brick. A grease poison, and an extra knife. She watched me.

'Never carry all your supplies in one place,' she guessed, and I nodded at Chade's old wisdom. I watched her putting her picks into a cuff seam and said, 'I'm a grandfather. Nettle Skilled to me this morning.'

'Girl or boy?' she asked without looking up.

'A girl.'

'Chade would have been a great-uncle? No, a great-great uncle.'

'Something like that.' The carris seed was bringing the morning into sharper focus. I would have blurted all my news out to the Fool. I weighed and measured what I knew before I spoke to Spark. How much would she understand? How much would she believe? 'Nettle Skilled the news to me. And then, I sensed something else. Someone else. Vindeliar.'

She was horrified. 'The man who made everyone forget at Withywoods. He Skilled to you?'

'No. Yes. It was like Skill but . . . clumsier. And very powerful. As an ox is to a horse.' Her eyes were getting wider. I told her the worst thing of all as it finally settled into my brain. 'I think he felt me. And Paragon. I think he knows we are coming.'

Her expression looked as sick as I felt at that thought. I spoke quietly. 'Pass me the tubes of Silver.' It was unlikely I would do something so drastic. Very unlikely I would use them.

She moved tossed clothing, looking for them. 'All our plans that we made . . . that was all a ruse? All the work I did?'

'I consider it likely.'

I heard her catch her breath. 'Fitz. There's only one here. She's taken a tube of Silver with her.'

TWENTY-NINE

Accusations

I was troubled beyond telling when I discovered Beloved had been taken from the cell beside mine. Had he died or been murdered, had he escaped or been freed? No one would allow me to ask those questions, let alone give me answers to them. To my cell came luriks trained as healers, and they treated the injuries the torturers had given me, but told me nothing of Beloved. They fed me nutritious food, and when I was healed they cautioned me to silence and released me to live among the luriks at Clerres. No one spoke of Beloved and I dared not ask anything. He faded like an insignificant dream, like the ripples from a tossed stone that spread, travel and are gone.

For a time, they suffered me to continue to live in one of the cottages, and to have access to the youngest Whites. Some of them were pathetic little things, frail of body and feeble of mind, skin white as snow and full of dreams they could barely enunciate. I did what I could with them. Others were keen enough in their thoughts and well able to grasp what I told them of the outside world.

As season after season passed, they grew to prefer my company, and to listen to what I taught them. It distressed me to see the very young girls going with child. I spoke of this to them, and tried to counsel them that this was not the way for men and women to conduct themselves. I spoke often of our duty to the greater world. The lingstras and collators heard of my counsels. Some came to speak with me.

Then the Four sent their guards. They were not unkind. They were not kind. They confined me as if I were a bullock, of little use now but too valuable to destroy. They took from my cottage the dreams I had recorded. They sought to discuss them with me, to add them to their knowledge. *I refused to share my insights. But they must have seen how often the Destroyer figured in my dreams.*

I was placed in a cell on the rooftop, given a comfortable bed, adequate food, pen and ink and paper for my dreams. I was left alone. Those who tended me were counselled not to speak to me.

The writings of Prilkop the Black

I awoke on the straw mattress in my cell from a foul dream of Vindeliar standing over me, gloating. 'You will die today,' he promised me, and I jerked from sleep to wary wakefulness. My walls were slammed tight before I even opened my eyes. I should have made sure of him last night, I decided. It seemed impossible to me that he could be alive after the blow I had dealt him, but perhaps he was stronger than I thought. Perhaps. My heart leapt as I suddenly worried that there might be others like him. I should have made sure of his death. Next time, I promised myself grimly. For if he lived, I was certain that I would encounter him again.

And if he lived, he would tell the others who had killed Symphe and Dwalia. That made my heart beat faster. Had I left any proof of my guilt behind? The loose cuffs of my blouse covered my hands. I pushed them back and examined my palm. The cut was now a fine white seam. It did not look as if it had happened last night. I poked at the marks on my tough soles. A twinge of pain. I sent more healing to them and they eased. I donned the sandals, experimenting with the straps until they didn't strangle my feet. I paced around my cell, practising walking without limping or wincing. It was not easy. Feet remember pain. I thought of the filth and serpent spit I had trodden in. Would the closed cuts become infected? I had no way of knowing. I sat down on the edge of my bunk and waited.

The keeper of the cells came carrying her tray of food-bowls and then returned with jugs of water. The food was neither good nor bad. The vegetables were cooked and the fish was smoked. It was adequate in both type and amount. She moved as calmly as she always did, spoke as little, and the occupants of the other cells were as subdued as ever. Except for my cuts, the faint smell of the oil on my hands and smoke in my hair, the previous night might have been a dream. I said nothing but tension built inside me. How long before someone noticed that Symphe was missing? How long before someone took food and water to Dwalia's cell and discovered the bodies?

The keys and the knife were two lumps in my thin mattress. I avoided sitting on them and tried to imagine how I would behave today if last night had never happened. What if I had slept the night through and awakened to another long day in my cell? What would I feel, how would I think? I must be that girl today. I hoped Prilkop would not betray me. I did not think he would, but scarcely knew why I had that trust in him. He had seemed so sad for me.

I'd killed last night.

I felt every muscle in my body tighten and then go loose. I thought I might faint. No. I could not and must not think of that. I'd done what I had to do. Now as I waited for the murder to be discovered, I had to wait as if I were a girl expecting to spend the day talking to a scribe. I had to be the girl who hoped for her own little cottage and nice things to eat. I practised hopeful smiles. They felt like grimaces.

I did not wait long. I heard the doors open and lay down on my mattress, feigning sleep. I heard footsteps. More than two people were coming. But I did not move nor open my eyes until Capra said, 'Bee. Get up.'

I moved slowly, rubbing my eyes, looking at them through my fingers. Capra was standing at the cell door, looking regal in her long gown of deep blue. She was breathing through her nose, as if some strong emotion raged in her. There were four guards with her, and Fellowdy and Coultrie stood behind them. I did not recognize Coultrie at first for his white cosmetics were ruined. Little remained of them except at his hairline and in the lines of his face. He was weeping and his extravagant green sleeves were smeared with white paint and tears.

I looked from one to another in confusion. Then I smiled at Capra hopefully. 'Are we going out again today? Am I going to tell you more of my story so it can be written down?' I stood, my smile covering how I gritted my teeth against the pain of my sore feet, and came to the barred door.

A fake smile bent Capra's mouth. 'You are coming with us. But not to talk to a scribe today.' She put her hand on the barred door and tried it against the locks. It did not move. She half-turned to Fellowdy and Coultrie. 'Can you see how ridiculous this is? Look at her. Scrawny. Uneducated. Childish. And behind a Lock of Four.' She handed a guard a key. 'Here is mine.' She presented another key to him. 'And here is Symphe's. It was in her pocket.' It dangled on its elaborate fob.

The guard inserted and turned them. Coultrie shouldered past Capra to seize the bars of my door. He shook it and I was glad it was still half locked. His face was livid with rage. 'She is wicked! Vindeliar told me all she has done to him. She killed Symphe and then she killed Dwalia! She stunned Vindeliar with her magic!' He pointed a shaking finger at me. 'You cannot deceive me. I have spoken with Vindeliar myself! I know he speaks truth. When Capra and Fellowdy speak to him, they will know, too! They will give you the slow death you deserve!'

'Be silent, you moron!' Capra snapped at him. 'Your keys, both of you! Present them. And then we take her to a place where this can be done more privately.'

Coultrie pulled a chain and then a key from around his neck. He stared at me with complete hatred as he stuffed it into the lock and turned it. His conviction rattled me, and then I knew. The serpent spit. It had made Vindeliar stronger than I had supposed. He had patted his hands in it, licked what he could reach. And if I had only stunned him, when he woke he would have consumed as much as he could get, regardless of the filth. How much had he taken? How strong was he? Strong enough to touch Coultrie's mind and instil fanatic loyalty in him. And Capra and Fellowdy? My mind raced. Were their thoughts still their own? Whites, Vindeliar had said, were not as vulnerable to his magic. So Dwalia had spoken true when she said Coultrie was no White.

Spittle flew from his mouth as Coultrie shrieked, 'Look at her! She is guilty! She did it, she did it all! She deserves to die! She deserves to die the traitor's death! She betrays every drop of White in her! She killed poor, dear Symphe.'

'Poor, dear Symphe?' Fellowdy asked quietly.

'Step back, and be silent! The knowledge you spew did not need to be shared here!' Capra made a small, furious gesture toward Prilkop's cell. Coultrie clapped his mouth shut.

Fellowdy offered his key. Once it was inserted and turned, the door was opened. Fear held me still. 'Oh, lady, please!' I begged Capra. 'You cannot believe such a wild tale!'

'If you wish to keep your tongue, not another word.' She turned her wrath on her guards as she leaned forward and snatched her key and then Symphe's from the lock. 'Bring her.' And to Fellowdy and Coultrie, 'Come. This is a waste of my time.'

I stepped toward the guards before they could seize me and held out my arms. 'Just move along,' one told me. As we passed Prilkop's cell, I looked in. He sat cross-legged on the floor, at a low table. He wrote on paper. He did not look at me as we passed.

I followed Capra and the others down the corridor, out the door. Down a set of steps, through another door, and then into a small chamber. The guards stayed with us. The moment the door shut behind us Coultrie sprang at me. I shrieked and leapt behind a guard.

'Stop him!' Capra barked. Each seized one of his arms and bore him back, kicking and wailing like a furious child. 'Oh, have done!' she shouted at him. 'You are ridiculous. If I tell you that Vindeliar is controlling your thoughts, can that break through to you? No? Then hold him over there.' As the guards dragged Coultrie back from me, she dropped into a comfortable chair and pointed at the floor. 'Bee, sit.'

I sat down on deep carpet and looked hastily around. Framed paintings of flowers on the walls, a table of dark wood, chairs, a decanter of golden liquid and glasses. Fellowdy took a chair with a martyred sigh.

Capra pointed a finger at Coultrie. 'Coultrie, we have done as you begged. You saw that she was locked in her cell. You saw that we each still had our keys. There is no blood on her, no stink of spilled oil. This scrap of a child could kill no one.'

'Then it must have been Vindeliar,' Fellowdy opined thoughtfully. 'Given plenty of the serpent potion, perhaps he could control Dwalia enough to force her to kill herself.'

'Would he have had Symphe smash the potion on the floor, out of his reach? And I doubt she would fall to Vindeliar's influence and set fire to herself. No. This was not the child and this was not Vindeliar.'

'Listen to me!' Coultrie shrieked. They turned to him, disdain on Capra's face, distress on Fellowdy's. He looked from one to another and panted out his words as he hung between the two guards. 'I tell you what is true. Symphe brought her to Vindeliar's cell.' He twisted one arm free and pointed a shaking finger at me. 'Vindeliar told me all! She threw a lamp at Symphe to set fire to her and broke the serpent-potion bottle on the floor! She told Dwalia to die and she did. She did! Dwalia is dead! My dearest friend is dead!' He roared the words at me and then broke into shaking sobs.

'His dearest friend?' Fellowdy said doubtfully.

'He despised her.' Capra threw herself back in her chair. 'We will get no sense out of him. It is the serpent potion. Vindeliar is stronger with it than I've ever seen. Something good comes of this wreckage: Dwalia leaves us a valuable tool. One we must learn to control. But now is not the time to think of that.' Did she regret uttering that thought in front of them?

Her eyes had narrowed to slits. She considered Coultrie for a moment. In a gentler voice she said, 'Coultrie is not well. His emotions have overcome him. Guards, escort him to his tower room. Fetch for him the Collothian Smoke that was delivered for me yesterday. Poor fellow. He has lost his dearest friends. Keep watch outside his door so he remains there. I would not wish him to harm himself.' Coultrie's eyes had widened at her mention of Smoke and I sensed she conferred some immense favour upon him. She smiled at him, falsely kind, but he seemed eager to believe as she said, 'We will talk to Vindeliar ourselves, just as you have advised us. Put your mind at ease about that. There now. Go take some rest. I can tell that your heart is broken.'

Fresh tears sprang from Coultrie's eyes and trickled down his face at her sympathy. He offered no resistance as the guards moved him toward the door. I heard his sobbing until the door closed behind him. I remained where I was and kept silent. Capra leaned forward and poured some of the drink into a glass. She sipped from it.

'So you think Vindeliar lies?' Fellowdy asked her.

'He told us there were two dragons in the harbour, and that a Destroyer spoke in his mind, threatening to reduce all Clerres to ruins. Have you seen any dragons today? Any signs of an attacking army?' She sipped from her glass again. 'He tells us that Bee did all this. Did you see any sign that she had been out of her cell and in that dungeon?'

'Why would he lie? What would he gain?'

'Finally, you are asking the correct questions. Here are some others for you to ponder. Why was Symphe in that dungeon, with serpent potion, when our supply of it is sadly depleted? Where did she obtain it? What treachery did she plan? And who put an end to it? Vindeliar is not the most intelligent fellow. Did he manage to get enough potion to take control of Symphe? Did she kill Dwalia and then accidentally or purposely take her own life? Coultrie has fallen to Vindeliar's influence. He is useless. But Vindeliar knows exactly what happened. I consider him our most likely killer, and I will have the truth from him.'

'I wish to be there.'

'Of course you do. Because you have no thought for all else that must be managed.'

Fellowdy worked his mouth and then said, 'We all know that you have a supply of the serpent potion you have kept to yourself. Is that where Symphe got it? Stolen from you? Or given by you? How closely must I watch my own back?' She stared at him, her mouth flat, until he dropped his eyes. 'Do we go to Vindeliar now?' Fellowdy asked in a subdued voice.

She rounded on him. 'Do as you wish, I am sure! Go grovel before Coultrie's new friend. That disgusting creature should never have been allowed to survive. I suppose I shall have to deal with all that needs to be done alone. Symphe is *dead*. Have you no thought for that? For what it will mean to the people of Clerres? The first tide has passed. The halls below are full of fortune-seekers, some waiting to see Symphe. And across the water, the crowds for the afternoon crossing are waiting. When the second tide goes out today, we must refuse them. Those who entered this morning must leave. None can enter until we have resolved this. How well do you think that will be received? I need to send birds, to have guards readied to control a mob. And I must consider how we will deal with the loss of several days' income from the fortune-mongers. Details, to you, I know, but these details are what keep our walls standing and our beds comfortable at night.' She gave a great sigh. 'Symphe's death must be announced with the proper pomp and ceremony. The folk of Clerres must see her honoured. Her body must be made to look . . . presentable. They cannot be told she has been murdered. It is unfortunate indeed that so many have seen her body. The guard who shrieked and ran tattling to Coultrie must be . . . dealt with. And Coultrie's babbling before the prisoners means that they must be dealt with, too. Symphe's death must be framed as an accident. A terrible accident.'

'And Dwalia?' Fellowdy asked heavily.

She gave him a disdainful look. 'Forty lashes? Who do you know who has survived forty lashes? Did you expect her to live? I did not. She died of her lawful punishment. And good riddance.'

'What will we say of Vindeliar?'

'Why say anything at all? Few would care if he died, too.' The last she said with measured consideration.

'And who will replace Symphe?' he asked in a low voice.

She gave a snort of disdain. 'Replace her? Why? What did she ever do that was so essential, that I cannot do better myself?' She was silent for a time, pondering something. Then she looked at Fellowdy. 'We should share these tasks. I know you wish to speak to Vindeliar. If you take that task, I shall see to sending the bird-messages and giving the orders for the closing of the gates.'

He mastered his surprise quickly. 'If you wish, I will take on that task.'

'I do. If you would be so kind.'

Fellowdy rose, nodded at her several times, and then almost ran from the room. Even I could tell that she had given him the errand he most desired to be rid of him.

As soon as the door closed behind him, she stood. 'Guards. Let us return her to her cell. There is work to do.'

One guard hoarsely asked, 'Shall I fetch Coultrie and bring back Fellowdy for his key?'

She lifted a shoulder, dismissing it. She almost smiled. 'From now on, a lock of two will suffice, I am sure.'

THIRTY

Barriers and a Black Banner

A big set of scales, like the money-changer at Oaksbywater has. On one pan a bee alights, and the pan is suddenly weighed all the way down. A very old woman, her face impassive, asks, 'What is the value of this life? What is a fair measure to buy it?'

A blue buck comes charging across the market. It leaps and lands in the empty pan. The bee's pan rises and they balance exactly.

The very old woman nods and smiles. Her teeth are red and pointed.

From Bee Farseer's dream journal

I have never liked climbing down a ladder into a ship's boat. I always imagine I will step wrong at that crucial moment. Climbing up the worn wooden ladder onto the docks was almost as bad. The firepots bounced against my back as I climbed. The beautiful Buck cloak was already too warm. And the exposed barnacles on the dock's legs told me that the tide was already starting to go out. Anchoring the ship in the deepest section of the harbour had taken a maddeningly long time. 'Hurry,' I said needlessly to my companions. 'The causeway to the castle is open at the lowest tide. We need to get there, trade the fire-brick for coin and buy our passage tickets.'

One after another, they followed me up on to the dock. Spark was now Sparkle, a very well-turned-out young lady of substance who cursed colourfully when her lace petticoat snagged on some barnacles. Lant looked rather a dandy in his elegant vest, lacy shirt and plumed hat. I did not like my green shirt with the blue cloak, but hoped the contrast would simply mark me as a foreigner and an

564

acceptably wealthy merchant. Per was the only one who looked comfortable in his well-worn clothes. The knife at his hip was long, but not so long as to attract comment.

Brashen and Althea had ridden in with us. There had been little conversation. Now Althea said only, 'Good luck.'

'Thank you,' I replied.

Brashen nodded slowly and they walked away from us. I watched as they turned and strolled toward the warehouses that fronted onto the docks, doubtless to see what sort of merchandise was being loaded out of them. They paced side by side, together and yet apart. Matching stride like two horses long in harness together. I would have had Molly's hand on my arm, and she would have looked up at me and talked and laughed as we walked. They turned a corner and were gone. I blew out a breath and hoped I would not be bringing disaster down on them and their ship.

I turned to my small party. 'Are you ready?' Nods. I looked down at the men who had rowed us to the docks. They looked as merry as sailors who had drunk all night, returned to the ship for a fiery dressing down, and then had to row from the harbour to the docks. 'You'll be here?' I asked them. 'When we come back?' Reluctantly I added, 'It may be quite a wait.'

One of Etta's sailor soldiers had ascended with us and was checking my knots. She straightened, shrugged, and said, 'Every sailor knows how to wait. We'll be here.' She offered me a grin. 'Nice togs, Prince FitzChivalry. Luck to yer. I'd hate to see them clothes get bloody.'

'Me, too,' I said quietly.

Her grin widened. 'Do 'em rough, cap. Getcher little girl back.'

This wish, from a relative stranger, inexplicably cheered me. I nodded and my small party followed me as we moved down the docks. 'Are we going to look for Amber first?' Lant asked me.

I shook my head. 'That would be a useless waste of time. She has the butterfly cloak. If she has decided to hide, we will not see her. And she certainly won't see us.'

Spark frowned as she took my arm, a very proper daughter. 'Why wouldn't she?'

'Because she's blind.'

'No, she's not. Short-sighted, yes, but no longer blind. I told you that.'

'What? When?'

'Her vision has come back to her. Very slowly, and still imperfect. But when you share a room with someone, such a thing is hard to conceal.'

I controlled my breathing, and smiled as if we discussed the weather. 'Why didn't she tell me that? Why didn't *you* tell me that?'

'I did,' she smiled and spoke through her clenched teeth. 'I told you that she saw more than you knew, and you said she always had! I thought you knew, too. As for why she didn't tell you, well, I think that's obvious now. So she could do this. Elude all of us and try to rescue Bee alone.'

Bits of conversations fell into a pattern. Yes. The Fool had considered himself the best choice to enter Clerres alone and find Bee. So he had done it. Just as I had told him I would do if the opportunity presented itself. I fell silent as I considered that.

The day was already warm but a gentle breeze carried the resinous scent of the brushy trees on the hillsides behind the city. The smells of smoked fish, ripe fruit and the fragrance of the tiny white flowers with yellow hearts that seemed to drape every doorway drifted through the air mingling with the expected smells of a seaside town. The streets were extraordinarily clean and well maintained. I saw no beggars and there was a general air of prosperity. The city guards were very much in evidence, stern-faced and well-armed. The Fool had not exaggerated their presence. Many of the buildings were shops, with homes above them. A woman stepped out of a door to shake a small rug as we passed. Two boys in loose cotton shirts and short trousers raced past us. It seemed a quiet day in a prosperous city.

Spark startled when I uttered a short, foul word. Only yesterday, the Fool had read aloud from Bee's book to me. A slip on his part, or had he hoped I would notice? Had he found it humorous? I ground my teeth.

With a whoosh of air and slash of feather against my cheek, Motley landed on my shoulder. I flinched and then told her, 'Go back to the ship. We can't attract attention.'

She pecked my cheek, a sharp jab. 'No. No, no, no!'

People were turning to see the talking bird. I tried to pretend that it was nothing out of the ordinary. I flapped a hand at her and she hopped to Per's shoulder.

'Don't talk to her,' I suggested in a low voice. A crow riding on a boy's shoulder was noteworthy enough. We did not need to be having an argument with her as we strolled along.

Motley chuckled and settled herself for her ride.

We followed a well-travelled road that fronted the harbour, past tidy houses and small shops. The road wound along the built-out docks of the harbour and then the rocky shores of the bay. I saw little fishing boats pulled up on the shore, and healthy children sorting fish they pulled from their parents' nets. The fortune-seekers who walked alongside me were plentiful, and by their garb they had come from many and varied places. Some seemed cheerful, almost merry, as they strolled along. Young couples hoping for augers of good fortune, perhaps. Others were sombre or full of anxiety, snapping and scolding their companions as they hurried past us to try to be the first to the crossing. All of us made a procession of hopes and fears as we promenaded down the well-kept boulevard toward the prediction of our futures.

'Where do you think she is?' Spark asked me.

'There was a low tide early this morning. I suspect that's why she came ashore late last night. She would have had time to sell the bracelet and pay for a pass to cross. She may already be inside the castle.'

'Where should we look for her?' Lant asked quietly. 'After we cross.'

'We don't look for Amber,' I told him. 'We stay to her plan as she proposed it, for that is what she will expect us to do. So we will enter Clerres, find a way to conceal ourselves, and then search the rooftop cells. If we don't find Bee there, we will gather in the washing courts, hoping that Amber will meet us there and Bee will be with her.'

The silence that followed my words was ample evidence of how little any of us liked that plan.

'I don't understand why Amber went without us,' Per said.

'She believes she has the best chance of finding Bee.'

'No.' Spark's hand on my arm tightened. 'I think I know why. I think it's because it is the most unlikely thing. The least practical plan.'

I knew we needed to hurry but her words slowed my steps. 'And?' I prompted her.

'It's the most foolish. You said they knew we were here. Amber has spoken of how they can steer the world's course because they know the likely futures. So she has chosen to pursue the most unlikely one in the hope that they won't have seen it.'

I stopped. 'But all the plans. All our talking, your sewing . . .'

'All to make it more likely we would do it?' She shook her head and smiled up at me, a fond daughter to her father. 'I don't know. I only guess at these things, from all she has told us about the Servants and her dreams.'

'If you are correct,' I said as I resumed walking, 'then they will be watching for us. Our purpose may be to distract them.' To be captured? Held, possibly tortured? Would the Fool have sent all of us into such danger? No.

Perhaps.

How often had he plunged me into mortally dangerous situations for the sake of shifting the fates? He might do it again. To me. But surely not to Spark and Lant and Per. 'You should all go back to the ship,' I said.

'Unlikely to happen,' Lant said quietly.

'Unlikely!' Motley confirmed.

'We can't,' Per reasoned slowly. 'We have to try this. To make it the most likely thing we would do. To keep them watching for us.'

We had followed the half-moon curve of the shore along the harbour. Now the road widened out into a cobble-stoned circle of merchant stalls and shops. The stall fronts were decked with drapery in bright colours and I suspected that, on most days, it was a bustling centre of commerce. But some of the stalls were shuttered today and this seemed to both puzzle and vex the local folk. Some buyers were patiently waiting at a closed booth. The restive crowd milled in the market, asking one another questions. We waded through the maelstrom of people. The shops that were open were offering food or drink or trinkets, broad-brimmed hats and perfumes and tiny dolls of Whites. I saw two money-changers where I hoped to sell our firebrick. A woman had a wheeled cart that held a cabinet with many drawers. She was hawking tiny fortune-scrolls from it. Some of the folk working in the stalls were pale-skinned and blonde, but nowhere did I see any sign of a real White.

'They just closed the stall. A guard came and told them to stop selling passes.'

'They had better let me cross today! I can't stay more than a day here!'

'I paid good coin for this pass!'

Across the teeming market circle, two wooden-faced guards stood before a formidable gate across the causeway to the castle. The water was almost at full ebb. Hopeful people had already formed a thick queue and waited in the bright afternoon sun. They shifted and muttered, reminding me of cattle herded into a slaughter pen. I pitied most the gate guards in their leather armour and plumed helms. They were well-muscled youngsters, and the jagged scar down the woman's cheek said she had seen fighting. Perspiration made shiny trickles down the sides of their impassive faces. They were not responding to any of the folk pelting them with questions.

A shout of relief went up when a skinny old woman pushed open the shutters of her booth. The queue surged forward but she held up both her hands and shouted over the mob's noise, 'I don't know any more than what I already told you!' Her voice was screechy, between anger and fear. 'They sent me a message bird. Told me to stop selling passes. No more folk allowed in today. Maybe tomorrow, but I don't know! Now you know all I do, and it's not my fault, none of it!'

She started to close her shutter. A man grabbed the edge of it, shouting that he must be allowed to pass. Other people surged forward, some shaking carved wooden passage chits at her. Motley lifted her wings, cawing a warning. I feared a riot, and then I heard the rhythmic tread of soldiers coming at a steady trot. 'Move back to the edge of the crowd,' I urged my charges. Lant spearheaded our exit. We came behind him and shoved our way to the edge of the packed people. We found a small alcove between a booth that sold fruit and beer and one that sold meat on skewers. We crammed into it.

'At least three dozen,' Lant observed as the guards arrived. They carried short staffs and moved with the edgy precision of people trained to be ruthless. They formed into a double row, inserting themselves between the mob and the guards at the gate. Once in position, they lifted their short staffs and began to force people back from the causeway. People gave way, some grudgingly, others turning and trying desperately not to be facing the soldiery. The muttering of complaints and pleas reminded me of a disturbed beehive.

'The gates! The gates are opening!' Someone shouted. Across the causeway, the immense white gates of the castle opened slowly. Even before they had swung fully apart, a mob of folk poured forth from the opening and moved in a thick line across the causeway toward us. They moved like herded cattle, with some running along the edges of the road to pass others. Everyone seemed to be hurrying, and as they approached the gate on our end, the guards swung it open. The soldiers pushed back those who had hoped to enter, crying out that they must make room for those departing from the castle. The two crowds met like clashing waves, and there were angry shouts from both sides.

'What does it all mean?' Spark asked.

'It means the Fool is over there, and has done something,' I suggested. I thought of the missing Silver and felt ill.

As if in response to my words, I heard a chorus of wordless cries from the gathered folk. A forest of pointing hands gestured at one of the tall, slender towers. Long black banners had been unfurled from the tower windows. Weighted, they hung straight and still despite the breeze off the water. 'It's for Symphe!' someone cried out. 'That's her tower of residence. She's dead! Skies above, Symphe is dead! One of the Four has died!'

That one shout freed all the tongues in the crowd, provoking a cacophony of shouting, wails and cries. I strove to pick information from the uproar.

'. . . not since my father was a boy!' one man exclaimed, and a woman cried out, 'It cannot be so! She was so young and beautiful!'

'Beautiful, yes, but not young. She has reigned in the north tower for over eighty years!'

'How did she die?'

'When will we be allowed to cross?'

Some people were weeping. One man declared that he had come yearly to have his fortune foretold, and that three times he had actually spoken with Symphe herself. He described her as being as kind as she was lovely, and I watched him gain that aura of fame that comes to one who has touched greatness. Or claims to have done so.

On the far shore, past the causeway gates, a single figure emerged from the castle gates. He was tall and pale and dressed in a long, loose robe of pale blue. He did not hurry as he crossed the bared causeway that had begun to steam and dry in the summer sun. He walked gracefully, and his bearing reminded me of the Fool as he had been in his days as Lord Golden. The crowd's noisy complaints became a chorus of folk calling attention to him, and then became a murmur. I heard someone say, 'Is that not Lingstra Wemeg, who serves Coultrie of the Four?'

The man reached the far gate and the guards, troops and pikemen stepped aside to give the crowd a clear view of him. He lifted his voice and shouted something that no one could make out. The crowd went silent. He lifted his voice again. 'Disperse now, or face the consequences. No one will be admitted today. We are in mourning. Tomorrow, on the afternoon's low tide, those who hold passes will be admitted.' He turned his back and walked away.

'Is Symphe truly dead? What happened to her?' a woman cried after him. He did not even twitch as he walked on. The troops and pikemen resumed their barricade.

The crowd milled, consulting among itself. We waited where we were, hoping a riot would not break out. But the mood of the crowd became more one of mourning and disappointment than frustration. As chaff is blown away by the breeze, so the people slowly dispersed. The conversations I overheard were disgruntled or sad but none seemed to doubt they would be admitted on the morrow.

I fought down the panic that tried to rise in me. 'Oh, Fool, what have you done?' I muttered to myself as I stared across the empty causeway.

'What will we do now?' Per asked as we slowly fell in with the departing pilgrims.

I said nothing. My thoughts were with the Fool, probably inside the castle. Had he killed Symphe? Did that mean he hadn't found Bee and had taken his revenge? Or that he had been discovered and forced to kill? Was he captured? Hiding?

'We won't be getting into the castle today,' Lant observed. 'Should we return to Paragon and wait there until they allow folk in again?'

'Stop!' Per exclaimed suddenly. 'Here. Come over here.' He led us away from the crowded roadway, onto the verge that overlooked the water. He motioned us to draw close to him and then said in an excited whisper, '*We* can't get in!' Per explained. 'But Motley can!' We looked at him in surprise. The crow was sitting on his shoulder. Per offered Motley his wrist and the bird stepped onto it. Holding her level with his face, he spoke to her earnestly. 'Amber told us that the walls of the cells on the top level have holes in them, shaped like flowers and things. Can you fly up there and look through the holes? Could you see if Bee is up there? Or Amber?' His voice began to shake; he pinched his mouth shut. Motley turned one bright eye to stare at him. Then, without a word, she lifted off his arm and flew away.

'She's going straight there,' Spark exclaimed.

But as we watched, the crow flew past the castle and out of sight behind it.

Per sniffed and said, 'Maybe she wants to fly all around it before she tries to land there.'

'Maybe,' I agreed.

We stood, waiting. I stared out to sea until my eyes watered from the glare.

THIRTY-ONE

The Butterfly Man

Your eagerness to be efficient and thrifty is praiseworthy. You are managing Withywoods well in my father's absence. For it is an absence; I am confident he will return.

But as to the changes you suggest, no. Please do not empty my sister Bee's room. Her possessions are to be tidied, and cleaned if necessary, and then restored to their proper locations. Do not put them into storage. I wish them to be left as they should be. I believe that her tiring maid Caution will know exactly how things were kept. Nothing is to be discarded. Let the doors then be closed and locked. That is my wish.

As for my father's chamber, I desire that it be left exactly as it was when he departed. Likewise, close and lock the door. No one need bother with anything in there until he returns. I am confident that he will not rebuke anyone for leaving his possessions untouched. There is a room in the lower halls that he used for a study sometimes. I do not mean the estate study; I refer to the chamber that looks out over the lilac bushes. That, too, I wish closed and left undisturbed.

I believe we have already discussed the room that was my mother's retreat for sewing and reading. It too should be left as it was. That is where her things belong. I do not wish them tidied away.

Before winter closes in on us, both Lord Riddle and I hope to visit Withywoods, if our schedule permits.

Missive from Princess Nettle to Steward Dixon of Withywoods

They made no ceremony of returning me to my cell. Capra inserted and turned her key and then Symphe's to open the door and repeated the task after the door clashed shut behind me.

'What of me?' I dared to ask.

'What of you?' she laughed. 'I may have a use for you. Later. Or sooner.' She smiled and it frightened me. 'For now, just sit there and wait. Everything happens in its own time.' She smiled as if well satisfied, turned and strode off.

Her words did not calm me. She'd sent Fellowdy to see Vindeliar. Was Vindeliar strong enough now to control a White's mind? If he was, he would want me dead and they would kill me. Little I could do about that. I went back to my bed and sat down. The hilt of the knife poked me. I moved over. I wondered how long it had been since one of the Four had died. What did Symphe's death mean to them, and why were there four? Or would they go on as three, now? I clasped my hands between my knees and rocked, trying to find calm.

'So, Bee. What will you do now?' Prilkop's whisper reached me.

I kept my own voice low. 'Sit here, I suppose. I don't have a lot of other choices.'

'Don't you?'

It didn't feel that way. I felt I was water rushing down a stream bed. Water cannot stop itself nor choose to go uphill. 'Water goes where the channel leads,' I said.

I heard him sigh. 'I remember that dream. It was one of mine. Did someone read it to you?'

'No. It was just a thing I thought of.' I moved to the corner of my cell and tried to peer around the wall to see him. It was hopeless.

'Little Bee. Do you see different futures, different paths?'

'Sometimes,' I admitted slowly.

'You can choose any of them. Pick carefully.'

'They all seem to lead to the same end.'

'Not all,' he disagreed. 'I have seen something of what may come. If you remain in your cell and do nothing, they will kill you.'

I swallowed. I had not seen that. Or had I? The dreams faded so quickly when I could not write them down.

He was silent for a long time. Then he reached his hand out, palm open and up, the back of his hand on the floor. He waited. After a time, I put my hand in his. 'You are untaught,' he said quietly. 'I wish you had been born to folk who recognized what you were. I wonder if it is too late now to teach you anything.'

'I was taught,' I said indignantly. I nearly said that I could read and write. I stopped short. It still did not feel safe to admit that to anyone.

'You were not taught the things you needed to be taught, or you would have understood more, sooner. You are a White, descended from a very old race, one that no longer walks in this world. You may grow slowly and live a very long time. Perhaps as long as I have.'

'Will I turn into a Black like you?'

'If you make the changes that fate calls on you to make. I would guess that you've changed at least a few times by now. It comes with a fever and weakness. Your skin peels away. It's how you know you've made a step on your Path.'

I thought about it. 'Perhaps twice I have.'

He made a noise as if he confirmed something to himself. 'Do you know that every White Prophet has a Catalyst? Do you know what a Catalyst does?'

I knew the word from my father's writings. 'A catalyst changes something.'

'That's right.' He sounded approving. 'And a White's Catalyst helps to make the changes that the White needs to change the world. To put this old world on a new and better path.'

I waited for him to say more, but he was quiet. I finally asked, 'Are you my Catalyst?'

He laughed, but it was a sad sound. 'No. I am sure I am not.' After a long pause, he said, 'Unless I am very mistaken, you killed your Catalyst last night.'

I hated him saying out loud that I had killed someone. It made it too real. I made no reply.

'Think about it,' he said softly. 'Who brought you here? Who hammered and pounded you into what you are now? Who set your feet on this journey to this present that was once your future?'

His words were frightening. I found I was breathing hard. No. I did not want Dwalia to be my Catalyst. A question burned in my gut, forced itself out of my mouth. 'Was I supposed to kill her?'

'I don't know. Only you can know what you are supposed to do.' Then he added, 'What you believe you are supposed to do. The Pale Woman opposed my view of the future. She believed it was her destiny to ensure that dragons never returned to our world. She saw

575

a righteous Path in keeping the OutIslands at war with the Six Duchies. She wished to crack the Six Duchies into squabbling minor states, and ensure that the ancient magic of the Elderlings did not resurface in the Farseer lines.'

'You chose the other path?'

He laughed softly. 'Little one, I am older than old. I accomplished my tasks as a White Prophet long before Ilistore came to Aslevjal. When my Catalyst died, I did not want to leave the place where we had done our work. I stayed on, as the snows grew deeper and ice claimed the ruins. Then, when IceFyre came, I chose to remain and watch over him in his icy sleep. I suppose it was well that I did . . .' His voice trailed off as if he now wondered at his choice.

'When Ilistore came to that place and began to make her choices and changes, they rang against my senses like a cracked bell clanging. I began to oppose her. I thwarted her efforts to kill the trapped dragon.'

I heard the strength of his muffled sigh. I knew he skated past painful memories as he added, 'And many events then happened that were not my direct intent. Things that triggered me into a role I thought long finished. My dreams came back to me. That was her doing. Her fault that I awoke to those tasks.' Again, a short silence. 'That is what I want to tell you now. I have glimpsed in some dreams what you might do, so I caution you. Choose carefully, little Bee. Clerres Castle has stood for time beyond memory. Since the Servants have claimed domain over it, it has become a repository of history. The scrolls stored here track not just what may be, if events tumble a certain way. A great deal of history has been recorded here. Wisdom has been gained and preserved in the scrolls and books. The Servants have documented the changes they engineered, and before that, the works of the original White Prophets.

'And then there are the folk who live here, in the castle, and the city beyond that depend on the trade the castle and the Servants generate. Beyond them, there are the rolling hills where flocks graze and farmers till the fields. The fisherfolk, and beyond the inlets and waters where they work, the islands of the archipelago. It is like a child's tower of blocks. If you pull out the bottom block, all tumbles down. Thousands of lives changed.'

I thought for a long time. 'Always in a bad way?'

He paused before answering. 'No. Some benefit.'

'Did you change thousands of lives? Did you know that dragons now raid the flocks and herds of Chalced and the Six Duchies? Did you know that dragons brought down the cruel Duke of Chalced? And that there is peace now between the Six Duchies and the OutIslands?'

His silence was longer this time. 'Some of that I knew. I knew your prince would wed a narcheska of the OutIslands. The rest . . . they give me no news here. I know little beyond what I dream. Capra says that keeps my dreams pure, uninfluenced by the outside world. And I do dream, and I record those dreams. I am like the bird that sings in its cage, with no knowledge of season or mates or offspring. The dreams I write, they take them from me. For good or evil, I cannot say. To dream and record the dreams is my Path. It is what I must do.'

'And you dreamed about me?' I felt a little shiver of importance.

'For many years. At first, you were unlikely. Then . . . I would guess it was nearly ten years ago. It is hard for me to know. Time passes so differently when one is confined.'

'About the time I was born,' I guessed.

'Truly? You are so young to be working such great changes. So small.'

'I wish I could just have stayed at home. I did not want this.' My throat closed and I felt a stirring of anger. 'You caution me about all the people whose lives I will affect. But Dwalia and the Servants cared nothing for that. They killed so many of my people. So many children will go on alone, so many children will never be born. None of that stayed her hand!'

His strong black fingers closed around my scarred white ones. His grip was warm but I felt how thin and fine the bones in my hands were. He could have crushed my hand. Instead he held it warmly and said, 'But you are not her. You are the true White Prophet for this time. You must look for what leads to the greatest good for all. You cannot be heartless or selfish, as your Catalyst was.'

I did not think of what I would do. I was adept at that now. Vindeliar's magic might be weakened but he still had some. And if the Servants had more serpent spit and gave it to him . . . I felt a sudden surge of urgency. I must not be stopped. I think Prilkop felt my resolve in how I drew my hand away from his clasp.

'When people do not know the past, they make the same mistakes their forebears made,' he warned me.

I drew a great breath and wondered if that were true. Then I lay back on my bed and stared at the stone lacework of the wall. I thought of all he had said. 'If I just stay here in my cell, they will kill me, I think.'

'So I have dreamed. A harsh breath, a candle goes out.'

I let the tiny edge of my plan creep into my mind. How much had his dreams told him of me? Did he know my intentions? 'You think I should stay in my cell?'

He heaved a great sigh. 'I only say to you that it is a possibility you may not have considered. Perhaps you should try to see where that decision might lead.' In a very quiet voice he added, 'For us, it is not always about our own survival. It is about the path we believe is best for the world.'

'Vindeliar told me he could feel when he was on the true Path. Well, I feel mine now. It feels right, Prilkop.'

'So many things do when they are the things we want to do.'

'What did you dream me doing?'

There was a smile in his voice. 'I dreamed many different paths for you. Some more likely than others.' He whispered the words to me again, that peculiarly familiar rhyme:

'*A piebald bird, a silver ship, oh what are you awaking?*

'*One shall be two and two be one before the future's breaking.*'

It still made no sense to me. 'I told you before, I have no piebald bird, nor a ship. Prilkop, just tell me. Do I break the future?'

'Oh, child. We all do. That is both the danger and the hope of life. That each of us changes the world, every day.' His smile was sad. 'Some of us more than others.'

'What's that?' There had been a sound, or rather a flurry of sounds. A thud, a muffled yelp, a louder thud. I held my breath, listening. Prilkop drew back his hand, and I imagined that he fled back to his desk and paper.

Down the corridor, a door opened. I slipped back to sit on the edge of my mattress. The footsteps that came now were soft. I waited. Then, a whisper softer than the wind. 'Prilkop? You live? You live!'

'Who is there?' Prilkop asked, his voice deep with suspicion.

'A friend!' A laugh soft as the first patter of rain. 'One who goes cloaked in a gift from you. I have the guard's keys. I will have you out of there!' A soft scraping of metal on metal.

'Beloved? You are here?' Prilkop's voice lilted with incredulous joy.

'Yes. And finding you fills me with delight, but there is another I seek. A child, a little girl named Bee.'

Beloved? My father's friend, the beggar from the market? The Fool? I darted to the bars of my cell, seized them and looked out. No one was there. I could see nothing, but I heard the soft jingle of keys. Inside me, Wolf Father hackled to alertness. We stared.

Prilkop spoke in a whisper, his voice shaking with excitement. 'Wrong keys, old friend. They'll open the other cells, but not this one, or Bee's. But she is here, and she has—'

Both doors suddenly clashed open at each end of the corridor. I heard Capra's voice raised in a shout. 'Advance shoulder to shoulder! Swing your batons solidly. Go! Do not stop until you stand chest to chest with your fellows. The intruder is here!'

'But—' someone objected, and 'Go!' she shrieked. 'Go now, at a run! Strike high, strike low! I know he is there! Trust your batons, not your eyes. Go!'

Someone I could not see made a sound of panic. I heard a scuff. Then, from nowhere, I saw the flash of a disembodied leg. Someone I could not see clearly strove to climb the smooth bars of the cell opposite Prilkop's. He was a rippling shape of nothing, as when one looks through the rising heat of a fire. He went up swiftly, and I had a glimpse of his bare feet curling as if to grip the bars. An edge of a butterfly cloak flared and rolled for an instant.

'There!' a man's voice shouted harshly, and the guards came at a run down the corridors. I stepped back for I heard the harsh clang of short staffs hitting the bars of the cells as they came. I heard exclamations from the other prisoners and then, as the guards reached my cell, the terrible thud of a stick on flesh and a sharp grunt of pain. Wolf Father snarled frenziedly. My leaping heart felt as if the wolf inside me were trying to batter his way out.

'He's here, he's down!' a guard shouted. For a moment, I saw a man on the floor outside my cell. Then he coiled his body and flipped up onto his feet. With the heel of his hand, he hit one guard on the jaw, clanging the man's head against cell bars. Beloved spun, cloak swirling, and I saw only parts of him. An armless hand seized the other guard's staff, and jammed it sharply up under the man's jaw and he fell back with a gurgling cry.

If he'd had only two opponents, I think he would have escaped.
But the guard behind him swung his short staff savagely. It
connected, and Beloved fell. He rolled to his belly, to his knees,
the cloak camouflaging him again. But they knew where he was.
Swift blows rained down on someone I could not see as Capra
shouted, 'Enough! Enough! Do not kill him. I have questions for
him! Many questions.'

I had retreated to the back wall of my cage. I could not get my
breath. Capra came pushing through the guards who now stood like
confused and excited hounds whipped back from a kill. She looked
at the floor, nudged something with her foot. Then she raised her
gaze to sweep from me to Prilkop's cell. 'Oh,' she exclaimed merrily.
'What is this I see on the floor? A butterfly's wing? There's a dream
I've read and even dreamed myself. Come, Prilkop. See your dreams
fulfilled.'

She called to him but I was the one who flew across my cell to
stare down in horror as she stooped and lifted the edge of what
looked like a butterfly's wing. As she peeled it back, it was *my* dream
fulfilled. A pale man lay there. He was barefoot and dressed all in
black beneath the cloak. A ring of keys had fallen from his hand.
Blood was running from a split on his brow and from his nose. His
eyes were half closed. He was motionless. Prilkop groaned deeply in
despair. I had no breath to make any sound.

She stooped beside him and then looked up toward Prilkop's cell.
Her old woman's voice had a musical lilt as she said, 'I still dream
best and truest of all. Here he is. The butterfly-man, the trapper
trapped! Oh, come, do not hide how impressed you are!' She shook
her head coquettishly and added with false sadness, 'Though I am
grieved that you still have not learned who to be friends with. This
was a bad decision, Prilkop. And I fear you must be taught, yet again,
that it is painful to defy me.'

A man has two hands. One of the butterfly-man's hands was
outflung on the floor, the keys just fallen at his fingertips. It was the
other hand, the one still covered by the cloak that darted into sight.
I thought he had struck her with his clenched fist until he pulled
back the bloodied knife and drove it again into her belly. Capra
didn't scream. She made a short sound of disbelief and then her
guards moved in, kicking and clubbing until Beloved lay still and
bloodied on the floor outside my cage.

I covered my ears, but that did not stop Wolf Father's long howl from deafening me to all else.

The guards had dragged Capra back. She sat on the floor, both hands clutching her belly. Her blue robe was dark with blood, and scarlet trickled out between her fingers. 'Idiots!' She tried to shout but had no breath for it. 'Carry me to the healers! Now! And take Beloved and Prilkop to the lower dungeons and throw them in. Put Beloved in Dwalia's old cell! I will see to him myself! Ah!' The last was a cry of pain as two of her guards attempted to obey her.

'We will need the keys for the Lock of Four,' one of the guards pointed out.

'Use those on the floor.'

One of the guards stooped and picked them up. 'Wrong keys,' he said.

Capra said nothing. I think she had fainted. One of her guards spoke. 'Jessim, go ask Fellowdy what we should do. Worum and I will take Capra to the healer. The rest of you, take the intruder to the lowest level. Toss him in and lock him up well. No more mistakes today.' As they lifted Capra, the man added gloomily, 'We shall all wear stripes for this!'

Neither Prilkop nor I spoke as they moved away. They dragged Beloved with them, his head lolling and bumping on the floor as he went. I heard the door slam and then someone said, 'The gaoler's dead. This fellow must have killed her for the keys. Bring the body.'

For a time longer, the quiet held, and then, like startled birds, the other prisoners began to whisper-shriek to one another, speculating, demanding answers, and weeping aloud.

'Prilkop?' I asked questioningly. 'Do you know what will happen now? Do you have any dreams of this time?'

'I do not.'

In my softest whisper, I said only for him, 'I have keys. We could flee.'

'There is no place to flee to, little one. They will have closed the doors and the gates.' He laughed bitterly. 'If I leave here again, it will be when my body flows out of the waste tank with the waste of the castle. The fishes will eat my flesh and my bones will turn into sand.'

'Did you dream that?' I asked in horror.

'Some knowledge comes not from dreams but from life. There is only one exit from Clerres that is not guarded both day and night, and that is the one the dead take. Dwalia and I will share the same resting place, in an eel's belly.' He gulped. 'I wish my journey there would be a short one, but I know it will not.'

He was doing a terrible kind of weeping. Afraid weeping. It made me cry, too.

'Bee! Bee, bee, bee!'

Someone was shouting my name in a hoarse and scary voice.

'What is that?' Prilkop asked, startled out of his terror.

'I don't know. Ssh!' Whoever it was, I did not want them to find me.

The doors at the end of the corridor slammed open again. The tread of many feet. I was frightened but I had to know. I moved to where I could almost see down the hall. Guards. Fellowdy, with Coultrie staggering along beside him. Coultrie looked terrible, both sick and furious. The keys that Capra had used earlier to lock me in now swung from Fellowdy's fist. They marched to Prilkop's cell. They were too close for me to see them as keys went into the locks and were turned. The door was opened. 'Take him!' Fellowdy ordered, and the soldiers I could see surged forward. They emerged, four men gripping one. In the corridor, another man knelt and let fall an armful of chains. Prilkop stood, an ox awaiting slaughter, as the shackles were fastened to his ankles. He did not resist as the guard stood and chained his wrists as well.

I was a coward. *Not me, oh not me!* I radiated the thought. I desperately hoped the serpent-spit magic had not faded from my system. With what Skill I could muster, I pushed it at them. Either it worked, or they had not been told to take me. Wolf Father distracted me.

Stop that. A way out is a way in!

Wolf Father's growl was intense. I obeyed. Walls up. I moved away from the bars and huddled on my mattress. They would drag Prilkop away, to what end? To pain, Capra had promised him. To death? When I had made my decision last night, had I created this future for him? Was it my fault now?

Terrified and selfish, I covered my eyes and I prayed with no god in mind, *Let them not take me. Let it not be me!*

'Hello, Bee!' Coultrie was outside my cell, leaning on a guard's arm. I gave a short shriek and I hated that it made him smile. He had renewed his white paste, but it was badly done. Stripes of his flesh showed through. He smiled at me, a loose-lipped, trembling smile. 'Don't think I don't know! I do. You killed them and I will see that you pay. I will.'

'Stop it,' Fellowdy told him. 'Vindeliar has magicked you. How often must I tell you that? We've caught the killer. When we take Prilkop down, you can see for yourself. It's Beloved. The fool came back. He'd have good reason to kill Symphe. Dwalia was probably just an afterthought. Come on. We need to see Prilkop secured, and then go to see Capra at the healers' chambers. Jessim said it was a short knife. Let's hope it didn't reach anything vital.'

They left. Prilkop walked among them, taking short steps as his chains clattered on the stone floor. Doors slammed again. I had begun to hate that noise. Quiet flowed back in. A lone voice from one of the other cells called out, 'Guard? Guard?'

No one answered.

I sat shaking and weeping. It was too much. Someone had come to find me, to rescue me. And failed. And now Prilkop was gone. I had not realized what a comfort he was until he was snatched away. I felt so cold. I could not stop shaking.

'Bee? Bee, bee, bee?'

The terrible little voice was back. It sounded the way I imagined a pecksie would sound. Not human.

'Bee? Bee, bee, bee?'

It was coming closer. It made my name a random repetition. I heard a soft noise, like a shaken cloth, and a scratching. 'Bee? Bee, bee, bee?'

I could not stand it. 'Leave me alone!' I shouted.

But instead, the voice came closer. 'Bee? Bee?' Now I could tell where it was coming from. It was right outside the perforated stone wall that threw shadows of seashells and flowers on my cell floor. Something blocked the light from one hole and made a scrabbling sound, like a rat in a wall. I was thankful the holes were small and the wall so thick. I did not think it could get at me. But as I stared at the wall in stricken horror, a sharp silver beak poked partly out from it. It moved, jabbing the air. 'Bee?' it queried. 'Bee, bee, bee?'

I was imagining it. It couldn't be real. I didn't want to see it, but I couldn't look away. The beak nudged and poked at air as if struggling to come through and get me. I forced myself to stand

and then to move to where I had a better angle to see inside the wall-hole.

A bird's head. A bright eye. I crouched down to see it better. 'Bee?'

It changed. This had not happened often, and every time it did, it terrified me. The bird's head radiated a corona of pathways. I found a word for it. A nexus. Like the one I had seen in the market with the blind beggar. This could not be good.

'Go away,' I begged in a shaking voice.

'Per,' it said in a whisper. 'Tell Per. Found Bee.'

'Per?' I asked, hope stabbing me. 'Perseverance?' Hope was a different kind of terror. How could Per be near, so far from Withywoods? Was he truly alive? Had the beggar brought him? The bird shimmered, not before my eyes but in my mind. Closing my eyes didn't help. I still didn't open them. I asked a question knowing that the answer could destroy all my hope. 'Is Per coming to help me? To rescue me?'

'No. No. Shut. Gate shut. Closed. Closed, closed, closed!'

I sat back on my heels. This wasn't real. Birds didn't talk like that. Not in a way that made sense. Was I going mad? The shimmering was making me feel sick. 'Go away,' I begged it.

'Closed, closed. Amber? Find Amber? Spark asks.'

It was saying nonsense phrases now. 'Go away.'

A way out is a way in! Tell him that! A way out is a way in! Tell Per. Wolf Father was leaping in my mind, scrabbling at the walls I held so tight. *Tell the bird that!* He flung himself against walls I dared not lower.

The bird seemed to have wedged itself. It was trying to back out of the hole in the wall without much success. 'A way out is a way in,' I told it, with no sense of why that was important. It stopped struggling. Had it heard me? Was it trying to speak to me? A cat had spoken to me once, back in Withywoods. But that had been mind to mind, and somehow less surprising. This bird spoke human words with a crow's beak. It was uncanny. Frightening. 'Bird? Did you come with Per? Did he come with the beggar? They have taken the beggar to the dungeon. Was he supposed to rescue me? Talk to me, bird!' My questions rattled out of me.

'Way in not easy way out. In was easy. Out is hard,' the crow complained. 'Stuck.'

I drew a deep breath. Mastered my dizziness. 'Is Per nearby?' One question at a time.

'No. Per can't help. Stuck. No Per here. Stuck!'

Solve the bird's problem and perhaps she would answer. 'Do you want me to push you out?'

'No!' I heard more scrabbling sounds. Then, resignedly, 'Yes.'

I reached into the hole. 'Careful, careful!' she warned me.

I touched her beak. She braced it against my hand, a hard peck. A push. It was like a lightning flash. Dragons. A red dragon would come. I jerked my hand back.

A way out is a way in. Where the waste goes out from the castle. Tell her!

She wasn't stuck any more. She was backing away from me, taking the shimmering nexus of possibilities with her. 'A way out is a way in! Where the waste goes out from the castle! Tell Per!'

I heard a wild fluttering of wings. 'I think she's gone,' I said aloud. *Did she hear you?*

'I don't know,' I whispered. The wind blew and a single downy feather flew into my cell. I caught it. It was a gleaming red. 'I don't know.'

THIRTY-TWO

A Way In

*There is a walled garden. The sun shines on it, but it is plain to see a
blight has stricken it. Only a few plants stand straight and tall. The rest
are pale and stunted, straggling across the rich soil. The gardener comes.
The gardener wears a wide-brimmed hat covered in butterflies. I cannot
see his face. He carries a bucket. There are silver shears at his belt, but
he kneels in the garden and begins to rip the diseased plants from the
earth. He stuffs them into the bucket. The plants in the bucket writhe
and moan but the gardener pays no heed. He does not stop until every
sickly plant has been torn up by the roots. He carries the bucket to a
bonfire, and throws in the shrieking plants. 'That's done,' he says. 'The
root of the problem is gone.' He turns to me and smiles. I cannot see his
eyes or nose, but his teeth are pointed like a dog's and they drip flames.*
From Reppin's dream journal, dream 723

We stood and waited in the hot sun. I longed to discard my warm,
woollen cloak. Instead I felt the sweat turn into a tiny itching stream
down my spine. 'She's only a bird,' I warned them all. 'It was a
wonderful idea, Per. But we cannot hope for too much.'

'She's smart!' Per insisted stoutly.

'I'm so thirsty,' Spark said. It was a statement, not a complaint.

'I'm hungry,' Per agreed.

'You're always hungry.'

'I am,' Per agreed again. His gaze never left the sky above the castle.

'We passed an inn.' I conceded to ordinary needs. 'Let's sit down
and think.'

I led them back to the road. Most of the crowd had dispersed. Only a few stragglers still trudged along. The guards had plainly wished to clear the area around the gate to the causeway. It was not in our plans to challenge anyone, and so we followed after the disgruntled folk making their way back to the harbour. I had known a moment of hope when Motley had taken flight. Now my renewed despair and agonizing uncertainty were far heavier than anything else I carried.

We came to an inn. I turned aside to it. As we came toward the inn door, Per asked, 'If we go inside, how will Motley find us?'

Personally, I believed that she had flown back to the ship. 'We'll sit outside.' I gestured at some tables under a shade tree beside the inn.

I sat down at a table with Per while Spark and Lant went inside. Per looked at me. 'I feel sick,' he said. 'Hollow.' He lifted his eyes to stare hopefully at the sky.

'We're doing what we can.' Useless words.

At the other tables, folk were drinking and talking loudly. Lant and Spark came back with mugs of ale and a loaf of dark bread. We ate and drank silently as the gossip from the other tables spilled over and washed against us. We heard rumours with no foundation. Symphe had committed suicide. Fellowdy had killed Symphe. Symphe had fallen down the stairs and broken her neck. Someone had poisoned her. For a woman who was spoken of so well it seemed odd that few thought she might have simply died. I listened carefully, but no one spoke of a little girl held captive.

There was gossip of Dwalia's return, with her repulsive henchman Vindeliar. She was universally disliked, it seemed, and two people spoke with satisfaction of the lashing she had received for returning alone without the luriks or fine horses that had gone with her. Neither one of them had witnessed it; one had heard a servant tell of Dwalia being dragged bloody down the halls and thence to the 'deepest dungeon'. They mentioned no child. I had to wonder silently if Bee had been consigned to that dark place with her. Returning 'alone' seemed the worst words I had ever heard.

'Do we go back to the ship?' Spark asked.

I had no will to answer. I didn't know. I didn't know anything. Grief and uncertainty exhausted me as much as if I'd waged a bloody battle. I'd lost. I'd lost everything. I tried to think where it had all gone so wrong, and the answer was that it had begun with every decision I'd ever made, from the time I first said 'yes' to Chade.

And then Per said, 'Here she comes!'

I stared. A small pair of black wings, opening and closing, opening and closing. It could be any bird, really. It came closer. I drained my mug and set it down. 'Let's go to meet her,' I proposed.

We left the inn and crossed the road. There was a short stretch of steep hill with the sort of grasses and brush that can withstand wind, salt and the occasional high tide or storm dousing. We didn't hesitate, but climbed down it and then found a way down a rocky outcrop and onto a beach that was as much stone as sand. The tide was still coming in, but there was enough beach for us to stand on and wait. Whatever news our bird did or didn't bring to us, I wanted no eavesdroppers.

Per stood perfectly still, holding his arm up as if he awaited a majestic hawk. Motley did not come with the slow majestic beats of a raptor, but rocked back and forth as she landed, catching her balance. Per let her settle before asking, 'Did you find her?'

'Bee. Bee, Bee, Bee!' she announced, bobbing her head up and down.

'Yes, Bee. Did you find her?'

'Through the hole. Stuck! Bee. Bee, Bee, Bee.'

I caught my breath. What to believe? Did I dare hope? Was she only repeating Per's words?

'Is she alive? Is she hurt?'

'Does she know we are here?'

'And Amber?' Spark demanded.

The bird was suddenly still. 'No.'

I sharply motioned everyone to silence.

'No what?' I asked the bird.

'No Amber.'

Silence. 'She took the butterfly cloak,' Spark said, a forlorn hope in her voice.

'Did you see Bee? Is she hurt?' I wanted to ask question after question and forced myself to stop. One at a time.

'She talked.' The bird spoke after a moment's consideration. Then, as if working hard to put words together, 'Hole little. Motley stuck.'

I felt a rush of impotent fury, the desire to seize the messenger and crush her in my hands. I needed to know. Wit and Skill, I reached out to her. *Please!*

'Stupid Fitz!' She spoke the words aloud. Without warning, she leaned away from Per and darted her beak at my face. Lifting my hand defensively was a reflex. She seized my hand in her silver bill and clung to my sleeve in a battering of wings. We did not connect as cleanly as Nighteyes and I had but I spied through a tiny crack in her bird-mind. A glimpse of a little girl's battered face, blue eyes wide, her cheek bruised. I scarcely recognized her. Bee's anxious voice. 'A way out is a way in! Tell Per! Where the waste goes out from the castle!' And then an incomprehensible view of the castle and the waters surrounding it, as if viewed from the tallest tower or the top of a mast. It moved and my stomach lurched as Motley showed me what she had seen when she flew over the castle. The roof, the guards pacing there, the cottages in the walled garden, more guards, and then a swooping view of the waters around the castle. Little fishing boats bobbed and cast nets, avoiding the shallows created by the outgoing tide. A plume of grey-ish-brown water in the sea, as if a rain-swollen river had debouched into it. 'A way out is a way in!' Bee's words echoed again, and then the bird released me, dropping to the sand at our feet.

'Motley!' Per cried and stooped to gather her up.

I looked at their anxious, puzzled faces. I didn't smile. It was too slender a hope to support a smile. I spoke the words in a shaking voice. 'Per. Bee told Motley to tell you, "a way out is a way in."' I gathered air into my lungs. 'We have to get ready.'

We didn't go back to Paragon. I sent Motley back to the ship with a simple message. 'Please wait.' I hoped she would remember to deliver it.

The inn room we rented was cheap and bare, and all the noise came up through the floor. We lay on the floor, our grand clothing serving as our beds, and fruitlessly tried to sleep. The inn was finally silent when we rose. 'Leave anything we won't need,' I told them. Spark folded all the clothing and gave the stack a fond pat as if saying farewell. Spark had adapted the firepot belt to ride high on my back. The pack containing the Silver and fire-brick was secured below the belt. I gave Lant my Buckkeep cloak. 'Bring this.' He nodded. On our way out, I ghosted through the kitchen to steal a pot of grease. I raked ash away from the banked cookfire and mixed it generously. Then I caught up with the others waiting on the shore.

We spoke little as we greased our hands and faces with the ashy blend. I had cautioned them that sound carries clear over water. I checked my hidden pockets. I saw Spark making a similar check, and Lant as well. Overhead, there was a full moon, casting more light than I liked over the water. The tide was ebbing. By early morning it would bare the causeway. But that was not our destination.

The retreating tide had left us pockets of packed wet sand and squidgy strands and bulbs of kelp underfoot over a rocky beach. Per fell once, cutting his palms on barnacles exposed on the wet rocks. He made not a sound, but pressed his bloody palms to his belly and held our hurried pace. I had never done anything to deserve such a lad. I looked out at the sea and thought of El, the harsh god of those waters. I had seldom prayed, but that night I offered El both my prayers that he would spare those who accompanied me, and curses for him if he took them from me.

We followed the water out as it ebbed. The stink of low tide surrounded us. The land shelved out gently and I quickly understood why Brashen had chosen to anchor in the deepest part of the harbour. The retreating waves bared rocks and sand usually immersed in saltwater. Small crabs scuttled among the wet stones. I caught the flash of a fingerling stranded in a tide pool.

We caught up with the ebbing waves. 'Now we get wet,' I warned the others.

'Been wet before,' Per replied gamely.

We waded out, trying not to splash. I heard Lant make a small sound as he took the step that filled his boot with water. And deeper we went, pushing against the water that rose past our knees, our thighs and then our waists. Waves slapped against us, as if to push us away from our goal.

The pristine white island of Clerres Castle had slimy green roots. I halted us when we were still in darkness, a good distance from the towers and their archers. As the Fool had warned, stone basins of oil functioned as lights along the island's shore. We huddled and stared.

'We must move slowly. We cannot splash. Whisper as little as possible.' In the darkness, I could barely see their nods. 'We need to move as close to the edge of the island as we can, below the level of what the guards can see in the shore-lamps. It will be a long slog.

This is a gamble. We may or may not find what we seek. We may fail, but we will try this. If you wish to turn back now, I will not think less of you. I have to go on.'

'Such an encouraging speech,' Lant muttered.

Per snickered and Spark said, 'I'd follow him into battle.'

Per said, 'Let's just go.'

The castle had been built on a peninsula of land, and those who had cut it free to make it an island had not cut so deep that some waves did not break white against the barely exposed rocks of the old land. We draped ourselves in the blue cloak to be an amorphous shape on the water. Lant and I were in the lead, holding the cloak's edge clutched tight so that only our eyes were exposed. Behind us, Spark had her hands on Lant's shoulders and Per held my belt. In step we went, in a bizarre dance, slowly, attempting to make no sound. I doubted that the guards in the towers heard our soft whispers.

'There's a low bit here. Watch your footing.'

'There's something in my boot.'

'Ssh,' Lant hushed them.

Talk ceased. We caterpillared on. The waters continued to recede. Wet white rock peered out beneath wigs of seaweed and barnacle. The water grew shallower as we approached the castle's shoreline. Closer and closer we crept as I navigated by the brief glimpse Motley had given me of the waters around the castle. In thigh-deep water we followed the steep rocky shore of the island. Chiselled cliffs loomed high above us, and above them the watchtowers looked out and over both land and sea. The steep angle of the sheer cliffs hid us from the guards slowly pacing the perimeter wall above us. The tide was still ebbing.

'Now what?' Per breathed.

'Now we follow our noses,' I warned him.

We pushed on. The cloak became a dripping bundle in my arms. Every shifting stone underfoot, every harsh breath sounded loud in my ears. The lights of the shoreside town behind us dimmed as we slowly circled their stronghold.

The smell I followed grew stronger – excrement and decomposing garbage. Per made a small disgusted noise and lifted his hand to cover his nose and mouth. The outflow from the castle flowed in an open trench gouged into the rock. It gaped, foul and slimy, exposed rhythmically by the retreating waves. Standing saltwater sloshed shallowly back and forth in the ditch with every wave.

'How deep is it?' Per whispered in trepidation.

'One way to find out,' I said reluctantly. I sat down on the edge of it, the waves lapping to my waist. My groping feet found no bottom in the thick sludge. 'Give me your hand,' I said to Lant, and he knelt to offer it to me. I took it and eased one foot down into the trough of sloshing filth. I was already soaked to the waist, but that had been clean saltwater. Beneath a layer of seawater, my boot sank into muck. I held tight to Lant's hand, stepped down with the other foot, and gasped as I sank. The filth and seawater came halfway up my chest.

The stink and the pressure of the cold water squeezed my voice to breathless. 'Tide is still going out. I think we can go in this way.' I made a final effort. 'No one has to follow me. This trench will become a tunnel into the side of the island, and slope up to the lowest dungeons. It's going to be a foul walk through total darkness. The tunnel will end in the castle's waste tank. The Fool said it was in the lower dungeon.'

'You warned us back at the inn, before we slept,' Per said sourly. 'We said we still wanted to come.'

'If Amber has been captured, I suspect they'll hold her in the lower dungeon,' Spark added.

'Yes.'

'Then let's go. Dawn is coming,' Lant pointed out.

'Step down,' I invited them, and one after another they did. Per gave a shuddering gasp, for the filthy water came nearly to his neck. In a line, we trudged forward. We left the open sky and the sea wind behind us as the trench became a tunnel into the chiselled side of the island. No light beckoned at the end. I led them into darkness. Slowly the incline became steeper. The sludge was slippery and we fought to keep our footing as it sloped slowly upward.

It was a stinking, hunched walk. I led with Per holding onto my belt, then Spark and finally Lant. I cursed quietly when my groping hand encountered vertical metal bars, but more groping found them badly eaten by the sea. Together Lant and I bent two until they broke. I squeezed past the obstacle, my belt of pots catching briefly, and the others came behind me. We went as silently as we could through the breathless stench and clinging muck. I heard Lant ask, 'Will we be able to come back this way?'

'No. When the tide comes in, this will fill with water.'

He did not ask how we would escape the castle. He knew I didn't know. We walked against a slow shallow flow of filth as the castle's tank emptied past us to join the retreating tide out into the bay. We slipped in filth, we clung to one another, we cursed quietly. And still they followed me. The darkness was absolute. The slimy wall I touched with my right hand was my only guide.

We trudged on. Then, in the distance, a faint half-circle of yellow light appeared. 'We should go faster,' Per suggested breathlessly. I understood his wish. My back was cramping and the stench made me even more breathless.

'We don't know who might be waiting for us,' I reminded him. We kept our steady, quiet pace and the dim light grew. I reached the arched opening into the vat and motioned in the dusky light for the others to stay back. The tank had a sloping floor, with the day's fresh excrement and offal to wade through. I heard Lant gag. The light that reached us was less than dimness. I found a corroded ladder by touch and pitied those who periodically descended to shovel out the tank. I turned back to Lant and motioned him forward while signalling the others to hold where they were. Lant joined me at the base of the ladder. 'I climb. You follow. If there is a guard, the two of us handle him.'

He gave a tight nod I barely saw. When I was six steps up the ladder, I felt him mount it behind me. Rung by slow rung, I climbed, trying not to think of what filth I put my hands on. Up, and up and up. The light became marginally stronger. Finally and slowly, I poked my head up above the side of the vat and looked around. Fat pot-lamps burned on shelves at the far end of the long room. I saw no one.

The thick walls of the vat were of worked stone. I clambered out on top of the wall and discovered steps descending to floor level. Of course. The vat's edges had to be above high tide level. I admired the engineering of it. A high tide would flow in to mingle with the waste in the vat; at the low tide, saltwater and waste flowed out again. Lant joined me, and then remained on the top step as I went down the steps, knife drawn.

I moved swiftly and as silently as I could through the large room. I saw what the Fool had warned me would be there. A table where chains dangled. A large hearth, cold now. The racked tools beside it were not for tending a fire. I hurried past them and heard a rhythmic sound. I halted until I was sure of what it was. Snoring. But was it prisoner or guard? I sought the shadows at the edges of the room and crept forward.

A wooden table and a bench outside the cells. A guard slept, face pillowed on his arms and turned aside from me. Only one guard? So it seemed. Quieter than a cat, I crept forward. With one hand I gripped hair and lifted the head. With the other I cut her throat. I clapped a hand over her mouth as her body jerked and pumped blood onto the table. Done. I turned and went back to Lant. I climbed up the steps to speak by his ear. 'I think there was only one and I've done for her.'

He motioned to the others and they came quietly out of the tunnel and into the tank. Spark climbed up quickly. Behind her, Per gave a muffled huff and pointed to a body lying on its back in the sloppy filth at the far side of the tank. It was not quite floating. I walked the tank's edge and looked down on it. 'It's not the Fool, or Bee,' I assured them. It was coated evenly with filth. The tides had not been strong enough to carry it away. A terrible scar marred one side of the bloated face. 'It's just a body,' I said softly, for the boy's face was lit with horror. 'Much too dead to do us harm. Discarded in the waste pit. Maybe Symphe?' I dismissed the body from my thoughts; it could not harm us. Failing to be aware of our surroundings could.

'Where are we?' Per demanded in awe.

'In the lowest level of the stronghouse. The bottom dungeon. Just above the high tide level outside.'

Even in the dim light, we were a sorry sight, wet with seawater, our legs and boots coated with filth. Spark was pale with disgust and as Lant shook filth from his boots, I saw his shoulders heave as he fought to contain his stomach. Per's boots squelched when he walked. He pulled them off, emptied them and grimaced as he pulled them back on. I paused to empty mine, as did Lant, and shook as much filth from my legs as I could. Spark had only shoes, as befit her maidenly disguise. She kicked them off and shook them clear of filth and discarded them. Together, we ventured on.

I led them past the dripping table and the slumped guard, moving quietly into the dimness. I could make out the bars, and then the cells. I peered into the first, and saw only an overturned pot, and a bare mattress. The second was the same. In the third, a terrible sight dizzied me. I saw my worst fear: the Fool, beaten and bloody, lay face down and motionless on a bare pallet on the floor. One hand reached toward us, palm up and empty. I studied him, waiting for the slight rise of breath in his body.

There was none.

THIRTY-THREE

Candles

Then comes a crowned blue buck. He awakens stone. If he awakens stone, then a wolf emerges. A gold man holds the wolf on a chain that goes to his heart. If the gold man brings the wolf, then the woman who reigns in the ice falls. If she falls, a true prophet dies with her, but a black dragon rises from the ice. This I have dreamed, but only twice.

I have dreamed seven times that a blue buck falls, red blood spouting. No stone awakens and the woman becomes queen of the ice. The true prophet turns into a puppet fallen on dead leaves in a deep forest. Moss covers him over and he is forgotten.

Sycorn, White of the Porgendine line, Record 472

After the bird left, I sat on my mattress feeling dizzy and sick. For a time, I had to lie down. I closed my eyes. I don't think I slept. How could I have slept? But when next I came back to myself, the other prisoners were softly calling questions to one another.

'Was that Beloved? I thought he was dead.'

'How badly was Capra hurt?'

'What did Prilkop do? Will they punish him?'

And later, 'Is no one bringing us food tonight?'

'Will no one come to light the lamp?'

'Guard? Guard? What of our food?'

All their questions went unanswered.

The evening light that came through the blocks at the back of my cell faded and died. I peered out through the holes. Above the castle walls, I could see a small slice of night sky. The cooler air of night flowed in with the darkness. I sat on my mattress and waited. I tried to find the feather I had caught, but it was gone. And crows were black. Why had I dreamed a red feather and a silver beak? And a red dragon. It made no sense.

For a time, I puzzled about the crow. It seemed so random. She came, she spoke of Per, she said he couldn't come. Then she flew away.

A red dragon was coming.

Had I dreamed it?

Wolf Father? Why did you make me say 'a way out is a way in'?

To tell them there is a way to reach us. He seemed smaller in my thoughts.

Tell who? Per?

No. Your father. If the Fool is near, your father cannot be far away. I reach for him, but your walls are strong.

My father? Are you sure? I can lower my walls.

No! Do not!

I had begun to tremble. Was it possible? After all these months, after he had pushed me away? *He has come to find me? Are you certain? Are you sure my father is near?*

His reply was faint. *No.*

His presence faded like my hopes.

I carefully pondered what I knew.

I knew Beloved had come. That had been real. If he had come to rescue me, he'd made a poor task of it. He had only made things worse. They would whip him to death, and Prilkop, too. And we'd had no food because he had killed the guard who tended us, and Fellowdy had not thought to assign a new one. I wondered if Capra had died. I wondered if Coultrie and Vindeliar would convince Fellowdy that I had to be killed. I thought that Capra might have stood against them to keep me alive. But if she was gone, or badly hurt, they might come and get me. And kill me.

Was Prilkop already dead? They would kill him slowly, he'd said. Would they kill me slowly? I considered that very likely and the thought frightened me. I stood up, my heart pounding, my hand clasped over my mouth. Then I forced myself to sit back down. Not yet. It didn't feel right yet.

I tried to put my thoughts in order. The crow had been real, because Wolf Father made me talk to him.

If Wolf Father was real.

I pushed all of that away. What did I know with absolute certainty? Coultrie and Vindeliar wanted to kill me. If they could convince Fellowdy, they'd do it.

That left only my path. The path that Prilkop had told me might not be a good one.

It was the only one I had. My only certainty. I could not depend on a talking crow or the dangled hope that my father might be near by. Me. I was what I could depend on. I was my only resource, and the path I had glimpsed was suddenly my true Path.

I felt regret for how my life had gone. I knew it was all over now. I would never sit at the kitchen table in Withywoods and watch flour and water become bread. Never steal scrolls from my father again, never argue with him. I would never sit in my little hidey-hole with a cat that didn't belong to me. That part of my life had been very short. If I'd known how good it truly was, I would have enjoyed it more. But Prilkop was wrong. There had been no choice for me. Dwalia had taken all choices from me when she stole me and brought me here. There was still no choice.

It was silly, but I longed to tell him why he was wrong. To talk with him again. But I suspected he was already dead. I still whispered the words aloud. 'You were wrong, Prilkop. The problem is not that we forget the past. It is that we recall it too well. Children recall wrongs that enemies did to their grandfathers, and blame the grand-daughters of the old enemies. Children are not born with memories of who insulted their mother or slew their grandfather or stole their land. Those hates are bequeathed to them, taught them, breathed into them. If adults didn't tell children of their hereditary hates, perhaps we would do better. Perhaps the Six Duchies would not hate Chalced. Would the Red Ships have come to the Six Duchies if the OutIslanders did not recall what we had done to their grandparents?'

I listened to the silence that followed my question.

Now it was past the turn of the night and venturing toward morning. Now it was time for my plan to be real. Time for me to set the world on my better Path.

I found the little tear in my mattress seam and winkled out my knife and the tethered four keys. I separated the keys. It was awkward to reach through the bars to insert each one in the proper hole and then turn it in the correct order. I was glad I only had to use two of them. It was still a slow process to find which two. Very carefully and quietly, I worked each key in the lock and then slid the metal latch. I opened the barred door just enough to put out my head. I saw no one in the open corridor.

Carefully, I closed the door behind me. I took the time to lock it with all four keys. Done.

For so long on the ship with Vindeliar, I had practised not thinking. And now as I moved silently down the walkway between the cells, I kept my mind as empty as I possibly could. I looked only at ordinary things. The tiles of the floor. The door. The handle. Not locked. Quietly, quietly. I stepped in something. Oh. The guard's blood. Keep going. The stairs. The future I walked toward loomed ever larger, clearer and brighter. With every step I took, my certainty grew. But I pushed my certainty down, folded my Path small and private. Instead, I recalled the fragrance of my mother's candle. I thought of my father, writing in his study every night, and almost every night burning what he had written.

Softly I paced down the steps. One set of steps, and then onto the wider stairway, down to the level of the scrolls and libraries. I edged my way along the wall and peered around the corner. The wide hallways were lit by fat burning pots of oil. No! Not that memory. I thought instead of the forest fragrance of the oil, how sweetly it smelled as it burned. No one moved in the corridors. I moved softly along the panelled walls. I did not look up at the framed portraits and landscapes. I reached the door of the first scroll-room. I entered cautiously lest any luriks or lingstras or collators still be at work, but all was silent and dark. The lamps in here had been extinguished for the night. I waited for my eyes to adjust. The high windows along the back wall let in starlight and moonlight. It would have to be enough to guide me.

I had a careful sequence of tasks to follow. I walked among the shelves and racks, weaving in and out of them, my arms outstretched. I tumbled scrolls and papers and books to the floor. I carpeted the floor with them, weaving among the garden of stored dreams as if I were a bee moving in a meadow of nectar-laden flowers. Old cracked scrolls and fresh sheets of paper, calfskin vellum and leatherbound books. To the floor with them, until I had created a path of fallen dreams through the maze of racks and shelves.

I had to stand on a chair to reach the fat pot of oil on the shelf.

The lamp was very heavy and I spilled some of it as I got it down. Fragrance of forest. I thought of rich earth and called to mind memories of my mother. 'If you weed, you must do it well. Take it all out, down to the deepest root. Otherwise, it will just come back. It will be stronger than ever, and you will have that work to do over again. Or someone else must take on your unfinished task.'

The pot was heavy. I set it on the floor, tipped it like a teapot, and poured the oil in a long, meandering thread as I dragged it up and down the rows of shelves of books and scrolls and vellums. I watered my trail of fallen dreams. When the oil was gone, I walked it again, pulling more scrolls and papers from the shelves and letting them fall and soak in the oil. I saw another shelf with an oil-lamp. Again, I used a chair and again I poured the oil and then tumbled more predictions into it. The shelves were fine wooden ones and I was pleased to see the oils seep under them. A third pot of oil soaked all these possible futures, and I judged my task in this chamber was done.

I thought of my mother's garden as I half-carried and half-dragged a chair into the main hall. Oh, honeysuckle, how well I recalled your fragrance. I took a battered half of my mother's candle. I remembered it as pristine, the rich, sleek amber of bees' wax. It was chipped and dented now, the wax embedded with dirt and clothing fibres. But it would burn.

The lamp shelves in the hallway were higher. I could barely reach the flame with my candle. I lit it, and cupped my hand to protect the flame as I carried it back to the scroll-room. I felt I said farewell to a friend as I let wax from it drip onto the floor. I secured it so that it would burn as it lay there and not roll away. When a thumb's width of candle had burned, the flame would reach the oil. I would have to hurry.

What are you doing?

Vindeliar was confused. Clumsy to let his wondering brush my thoughts. I reached out to him as if I didn't fear him. I let my thoughts soften at the edges as if I were sleepy. *My mother's garden. Honeysuckle, so fragrant in the hot summer sun. The pine forest nearby, breathing sweetly.* I sighed out a long, slow breath and imagined rolling over on the thin straw mattress in my cell. I let my thoughts over-flow with sleepiness as I slipped my awareness into his senses.

He was no longer in a cell but a comfortable room. Fellowdy's room. His tongue had tasted fine brandy but did not enjoy it. His injuries had been salved and bandaged. His mouth held the remembrance of sweet, rich foods. His belly was tight with them. But there was something more to come. He simmered with anticipation.

Fear seeped into my belly like cold water. I knew that eagerness. I knew what he awaited. But I had believed it was all gone.

I'd been careless.

It isn't! Capra had concealed four vials of it! But she can no longer hold it back from us. And when I have it, I will blast your little mind with my magic. You will do whatever you are told to do! I will be so strong that no one can disobey me! I will tell you to die as you told Dwalia! No, no I won't. I know something better I can do! The traitor's death for you! The worms will eat you until your eyes bleed and you plead with me to kill you!

He trumpeted it out, not caring if he awoke me. I slammed my walls shut and his bragging and threats clawed and racketed against them. Oh, how he hated me now. How he hated everyone! Everyone had hurt him, everyone had betrayed him, but he would have his revenge soon. Soon!

Honeysuckle and bees. Bees humming so loud in the fairy rose bush that I could hear nothing else. Only bees. In a deep corner of myself, I was glad I was no longer locked in that cell. I had made the right choice.

Coultrie! Coultrie, heed me! The little bitch is out of her cell! Search the gardens and cottages for her. She thinks she is clever, but she smells flowers and I know it! Quickly! Prepare the traitor's death for her! Hunt her down and deliver it to her!

Vindeliar, I am with the healer and Capra in her tower. She has given me the serpent's potion. I will bring it to you.

Yes, excellent, good! But send out the guards to search for her. Tell them she has escaped and I know it! Begin with the gardens, but find her, find Bee. She is more dangerous than you can imagine!

I stood still. I built my walls, and made them stouter and stronger. If Vindeliar received the potion, could I withstand him? I did not know.

My time was going swiftly. There was still so much I had to do.

I ran light-footed down the hall to the next door that I knew contained a scroll library. I entered the second chamber as cautiously as the first, but it was also deserted and dark. I repeated my serpentine trail of fallen scrolls. I was better at it this time, not struggling to push heavy books to the floor. Let them burn when the reaching flames climbed to them. I made a heap of scrolls and papers under a heavy wooden table that rested on a thick rug. Again, I moved a chair to reach a slumbering lamp. I let the fragrance of the oil fill my mind as I left a trickling trail, in and out and around each towering shelf of scrolls. This was the larger room. I should have come here first. The second lamp was heavy. I watered the tables and chairs as best I could, trying not to spill oil on my clothing. But the pot was heavy and sometimes oil spattered on my feet.

Vindeliar was aware of me now. I thought of my flat little mattress in my cell. I thought of the straw that filled it, and how it crushed under me. It smelled of straw and dust. I filled my mind with the scent of straw and dust. How the broken straws in the coarse fabric poked me. I leaked a tiny bit of that to him. That thought pleased him and I let him savour it. In a distant shout to Coultrie, he demanded more guards sent to the rooftop cells. I slipped away from his thoughts.

The third heavy pot was hard to manage. I staggered as I took it down, and it leapt in my arms. Oil soaked the front of my clothing and made my hands slippery. It was hard to grip it, and hard to think of honeysuckle or pine logs on a fire as I dragged it through the scroll-room. As before, I retraced my steps, tumbling and jumbling scrolls and books and papers from the shelves. They were eager to soak up the oil. I saw ink darken and then spread as the oil took it.

Vindeliar cackled wildly outside my walls. I did not like the note of triumph in his howling, but I dared not give him a thought. A way out is a way in. I would not let my mind focus on his clamour. I thought only of honeysuckle, and pulling weeds out to the last bit of root. How one had to destroy it all or it would all spring up again. I was weeding in my mother's garden. I gathered the leaves into my hands, pulled slowly and steadily to draw the long yellow root from the ground.

My hands slipped on the door latch, and it was hard to keep a tight grip on the heavy wooden chair I dragged into the hall. The dragging legs made a sound. I could not help that. I clambered up. This half of a candle was shorter. I had to stand on tiptoe for its tattered wick to reach the flame. I stood, my hand stretched high over my head, waiting, waiting, until finally the flame moved from the lamp to my candle.

They will find you. They are coming for you now! You will die the traitor's death! I have burned it into their minds, as I burned Coultrie! They will not stop until they find you!

You are too late.

I should not have let that thought escape me, but oh the sweet satisfaction. I showed him the flame, let him smell the fragrance of honeysuckle that my mother and I had gathered and stored in it. Then I pushed him, as hard as I could, with the terrible smell of Symphe burning.

I slipped as I got off the chair. My candle fell and rolled. I pounced on it, and the flame leapt as it licked my oily hand. It did not quite catch. There was oil on my bare feet, and I struggled to get the purchase to open the door to the second scroll-room. I did not leave my candle this time. I walked deep into the room and crouched to set fire to the mounded paper under the tables. I moved past four tiers of shelves, crouched again, and set a tumble of papers ablaze. I lit a third one and was startled when it caught well and the flames darted away from me, following the trail of tumbled scrolls. I ran back to the door, racing the devouring fire. At the door I turned. 'Goodbye, Mother,' I said softly and set her last candle down on an oily scroll.

The flames leapt high, licking the wooden shelves and racks, racing down the narrow walkways between the shelves. They were high enough and hot enough that scrolls on the second, third, even the fourth shelves began to brown and crisp and then ignite. I looked up to see coiling clouds of smoke crawling along the ceiling, like drowned serpents tugged by a tide.

I stood for a time, my back to the door, watching, smelling the smoke and fumes, feeling the heat waft toward me. Burning bits of paper were carried on the waves of heat from the fires. They lifted high, to settle on the topmost shelves like homing pigeons, bringing glowing embers to the papers stored there.

I had to push hard to get the door open. As it did, the air moved and the flames suddenly roared. I leapt out of the room, fearful that the oil on my hands and clothes might catch. The candle in the first scroll-room had done its task. The doors to that chamber shuddered as if the flames were pounding to get out. Thin tendrils of smoke were wafting out with every thud of the doors against their frames. It reminded me of a dog's breath streaming fog on a cold winter day.

I stood still, feeling as if I balanced in that instant. This was my perfect moment. I was where I was born to be, and the task I had been born to do was now being performed. Once I moved, the futures would again swirl and change. But in this perfect moment, I fulfilled my fate. Perhaps I would live. I wanted to live, but only if that path led toward my escaping the Servants. If living meant I was recaptured, if they gave me the traitor's death, if I lived to see Vindeliar's face . . . no. I knew what they meant by a traitor's death. I had seen the poor messenger, tears of blood flowing from her eyes, eaten from within by parasites. If I had to choose between death and capture, I would choose death. My heart beat faster at that thought, and with every beat, I was aware that I was making a decision. Move, don't move. Run back into the scroll-room, and the flames would seize me. It would still be a faster death than that the Servants would give me. Weep, don't weep. Run left, run right. Flee back to my cell and lock myself in, hide in the gardens. All choices I could make, and from each of those choices, an infinite number of futures sprang.

My fire was hot. I could smell the wooden doors charring, and even see the darkening of the wood. The corridor was warmer than it had been. How much damage could I do?

The chairs I had pushed out into the corridor still waited under the lamp shelves where I had kindled my halfcandles. My two candles that had come so far from my mother's hand to help me pull this evil from the world, right down to its roots, were used now. But I could do more, I thought. No time to pause or to wonder. I climbed up on the nearest chair.

The base of the pot-lamp was fat and heavy. And just slightly warm to the touch. I already had oil on my shirt and trousers. One touch of the flame and I could dance and scream just as Symphe had done. *Do it. But do it carefully. Then flee.* Wolf Father's suggestion was a whisper. It made me realize I'd been careless with my walls. I could taste the foul serpent-potion in Vindeliar's mouth.

Do not think of him. Walls.

I could only reach the pot with one hand, and only if I stood on my toes. I pushed at it. Nothing. *Push again.* I heard the baked clay base of the pot grind against its wooden shelf. I pushed again. It didn't move. I felt a wave of dizziness and lifted my eyes from my task to look down the hall. It was hazy. I more fell than jumped from my chair.

My fires were humming behind the doors now. The doors thudded rhythmically in their frames. The wood was blackening. Soon the flames would break through. I wondered if I could pick up the chair and throw it at the pot, to break it or knock it down. Then a little tongue of flame licked from the top of the first door, making a stripe of brown on the wood panelling above the door.

I moved away from my fires. I came to another door and opened it. I stared in awe and disappointment. More scrolls. More books and papers. More harvested dreams for them to exploit. I would not let it happen.

There is no time!

'This is why I am here. This is the future I was meant to create. This is my time, and all the time I need. The Path I make begins here! I have to do this!' I spoke the words aloud.

I was more careless now. I pushed and pulled books and scrolls. I found a lamp inside the library. Someone had left it on a table. This one was only half full. I dumped it in a trail. I found another lamp on a shelf and pushed it down with a great crash. Oil spattered a tapestry and the side of a tall shelf of papers. Good. All good. Now I just needed a flame. I spindled papers and carried them out into the hall with me.

Smoke and haze. I coughed. I suddenly felt dizzy.

Flee. Now! You must get outside. Wolf Father broke through my walls and his urgency could not be denied. I heard a crash and then the fire roared ever louder. Of course. There were other pot-lamps in the scroll-rooms. They would catch and feed the flames. I dropped my spindled papers. Abruptly, I wanted to live. I wanted one more chance to escape and to be alive. I scuttled down the hallway to the stairs. I looked back. Thick smoke was crawling and boiling along the painted ceiling. The panelling above the first door was on fire now.

Abruptly, the doors of the second chamber popped open. Flames leapt out. The pot-lamp beside the scroll-room door hopped and fell. Oil coursed down the wall and across the floor. Flames licked out of the cracked door, and then danced across the flowing oil. Fire caressed and stroked the panelled walls.

The conflagration gave a mighty cough, then the wall of heat struck me. I flew forward with the impact, landing on the hard floor. Elbows and knees and chin. I bit my tongue. I gasped with the sharp pain, choked, and blinked my watering eyes. I gathered myself and stood up. Almost immediately, I dropped down again. Above me was a hovering blanket of heat and smoke. I lay on the floor, trying to pant.

Crawl. Get to the stairs. You must get outside.

I obeyed him.

THIRTY-FOUR

Smoke

'But you know, Fitz, after my brother died, I was more alone than I had thought I could ever be. Shrewd was my king, yes, and the man who commanded my hand, but in the hours after the castle was asleep, when he and I sat at the hearth in his bedroom and talked, he was also my friend.

I've had few friends in my lifetime. When I lived behind the walls, there were a few key spies I met with, often in one of my guises. Perhaps I came to depend on your companionship too much because of that isolation. Was I jealous of your friendships and romances? No. I think the better word would be envy. Even after I emerged from the walls and could move through Buckkeep as Lord Chade, it was difficult to form deep friendships, for always my history and trade had to remain a secret.

Look at your own friends through those days. How many of them truly knew what you were, what you had done and what you were capable of doing?

Missive from Chade to FitzChivalry Farseer

'Fool,' I said. The word barely reached past my lips as I stared into the darkened cell. I saw his pale face, eyes closed, the whiteness of his out-stretched hand and knew with swift certainty that he had taken my merciful exit. Blackness threatened the edges of my vision. I could neither look away nor speak. I'd given him his death. He'd taken it. We were here: we could have saved him. Why had I done it?

I heard small sounds of metal on metal. 'Bring a light!' Spark muttered. I turned my head. She was beside me, picks already in a very old lock. Then Lant came, carrying a fat lamp in both hands. He thudded it down beside her. It did little to light her task, but she laboured on. I studied the Fool in the flickering light. Blood on his face. He'd died alone in a cell. Better, perhaps, than the sustained torture he had feared, but I could not feel any relief.

'Leave it. It's too late. We need to seek for Bee,' I whispered to Spark. Bee, I told myself. Think only of Bee. But Spark gave a sudden grunt as she moved two picks against each other and the lock gave way to her. And I could not help but push the door open and enter the cell to stand over him. Did I have to leave his body here? Could I do otherwise? The others clustered at the door, watching me as I stooped, reaching to wipe the blood from his face.

The swung chamber pot missed my head, but not by much. I felt the noisome wind of its passage and heard the clatter as it hit the cell wall. I jumped back as the Fool came up at me, clawed hands seeking my eyes. I caught him and hugged him tight to me saying, 'Fool, Fool, it's me, it's Fitz! Stop, it's me!'

An instant longer, his body was tense against mine and then he all but collapsed. 'Capra.' His swollen mouth softened his words. 'I was expecting Coultrie. With the hot tongs. While she watched.'

'No. We're all here, to find you and to find Bee and bring her home. Fool, why did you go off without us?' The question that had been fire in my gut all day.

'Get to Bee. Rooftop cells. She's up there. So is Prilkop.'

'Motley told us. We'll find her.'

He pushed his feet against the floor. I let him take some of his weight but didn't drop him. The phrases came from him in gasps as I walked him to the cell door. 'To save Bee. My fault they took her. I led them to her. And to kill them. To do my own dirty work. To fix the mess I'd made. To be the Catalyst this time. As you said I might.'

'Let me help,' Lant said, taking his arm, and Spark leaned in to look at his face, asking, 'How badly is he hurt?'

'I don't know. Fool, I feared you'd eaten the poison I gave you. You didn't. Did you?' A horrible thing, to wonder if he had swallowed it just before we arrived.

'I couldn't. I wanted to, but I couldn't. Not while they have Bee. I can't die until I've made it right, Fitz.' Fresh blood was flowing from his nose. He snuffled and then said proudly, 'I did for two of them. I think. I got to Coultrie's chambers. I had to hide on his stairs, and thought that I might as well climb the rest of the way, and leave him some small mementos. He wasn't there. I think I did it right. On the lip of his cup. In his wine, to be sure, and a powder rubbed into his pillow and linens. More on the latch of his door.' His voice was uneven as we walked him out of the cell.

'That should do it,' I muttered. It sounded as if he had deposited enough poison to kill a dozen people. 'Thorough,' I added. And then, 'How did you kill Symphe?'

'Not Symphe. Capra. She was groaning when they dragged her back. I think I killed her. I put a knife in her belly twice.' He swayed, leaned on me, then determinedly straightened. 'I lost that knife. And the butterfly cloak.'

'Acceptable cost,' I said.

'I found a hogshead of water. I don't know how clean it is,' Per announced worriedly.

'Water? Clean or dirty, give me some!'

We walked him over to it. There was a dipper hooked on the edge of the barrel. Per filled it for him, and he drank. The next one, he poured over his head and rubbed over his face. With his hair slicked to his skull in the dimness, he looked very old. 'More,' he said, and we waited for him, without speaking. When he paused, Spark asked, 'Besides the bruises we can see and the split brow, are you hurt?'

He grimaced, showing bloody teeth, and then spat. 'They hit me with sticks. A lot. Some kicking, too. Brutal, but not precise. They were reserving that for Capra's pleasure, I think. But I hope she's dead. Fitz, my hurts don't matter. We have to get to Bee. The last time I saw her she was held in the upper cells, on the roof of the stronghouse. And Prilkop is here, somewhere. I thought they would put him here with me, but they didn't.' He stopped to breathe, holding his ribs. He coughed, and I winced with him.

'I told you, Motley found her for us.' I wondered how many blows to the head he had taken.

He was silent, then said, 'Of course. She should have been our first spy.'

'Per thought of it,' I said and the boy grinned briefly when I glanced at him. He had dragged the guard's body away from the table and now set the chair out for the Fool. I nodded at him, acknowledging his work. We seated the Fool and Per went back to the water to wash his hands, and then drink. I set my attention back on the Fool. 'We're going after her now, Fool. We can't smuggle her out over the causeway. With Symphe dead, the Servants have shut it down. We are trapped here, unless you can find the entrance to the tunnel that goes under the causeway.'

He squinted at me, trying to master his thought. 'How did you get here then?'

'We came in through the waste chute that dumps into the bay. But we can't go back that way. The incoming tide will flood it. Unless we can find Bee and conceal ourselves until the next low tide.'

'Half a day from now?' He shook his head. 'They'll come back for me long before that. They'll find us here.'

'What was your escape plan?'

'Butterfly cloak and the causeway.'

'One is gone and the other closed. We are back to trying to find the entrance to the tunnel under the causeway.'

He gasped a laugh. 'I liked mine better. How do you know Symphe is dead?'

'They announced it, and hung a black banner from her tower.'

He shook his head and it turned to a wobble. 'Not my doing.'

Spark broke in. 'Dawn comes. We need to go get Bee. Now. Before the castle awakes.'

'And Prilkop, too. Please.' The Fool tried to sit up straighter, failed.

'If we can.' I would make no promises. Once I had Bee, all my efforts would go toward keeping her safe and getting her out of here. 'Fool. How much can you see?'

'In this light? Not much.'

'I killed the guard here. Do you know if or when others will be sent down?'

'I don't know. She was the only one I saw. Fitz, in hundreds of years no one has moved against the Servants. With Symphe dead, my attack on Capra will have alarmed them. Expect to encounter a lot of guards.'

I nodded. 'I'm going up after Bee.'

'They may have moved her. I know they were going to move Prilkop after they saw me there.'

'Well, that's where I'll start. I want the rest of you to stay here with the Fool. Try to find the entry to the old tunnel, the one they took the Fool out of when he "escaped" the first time. Now I must go.'

'Not alone!' Lant objected. Per said nothing. He simply stood and came to my side.

'Let me think,' the Fool replied breathlessly. 'We should go up one level. There are more cells there. A dozen of them, and some will almost certainly be occupied. It is their . . . their main place for torment and imprisonment. They held Prilkop and me there for a very long time. Perhaps he is there.' Unwillingly he added, 'And perhaps Bee is, too.'

I was not sure if I hoped to find Prilkop or not. If he had been as badly treated as the Fool, would we be able to get him out of Clerres? A useless question. We would be unable to leave him. 'The stairs past the water barrel? Are those the ones we want?'

'Yes. The door will be locked.'

'Not for me,' Spark bragged. Fleet as a rabbit, she sprinted ahead of us and up the steps. I saw her bend to examine the lock, and then she rummaged in her small pack to find her picks. While she worked on the latch, I had a more thorough prowl of that level, and quickly came back to my companions.

'If there is a door that leads to a passage under the causeway, I don't see it.'

'The door to a secret tunnel would be well concealed,' the Fool reminded me. Unwillingly he added, 'And it may not be on this level. I was moving in and out of awareness when they freed me from here. Fitz, I know you think I will slow you. I know you fear for Spark and Per. But behind that door, there will be more guards. Possibly more than you can handle alone.'

'It would be excellent if we could find that tunnel.' I let his other words go by me.

Per looked thoughtful. 'It would most likely be on the wall that faces the causeway.'

'Go look again. I may have missed something.' I went to help Spark with the lock.

But as I stood behind her, she gave me an annoyed glance. 'I can do this,' she breathed, and I let her. I knew a moment of terrible guilt. Lant had followed me up the steps. My eyes met his over the girl's bent head as she worked with her picks. I would not waste words telling him to protect her, to protect them all at any cost. He knew. I could see in his eyes that he was as troubled as I about what we might face. The Fool had stirred the hornets' nest, but Symphe's death was not his doing. Accident, disease or murder?

'I've got it,' she whispered at almost the same moment that Per came up the steps to gesture that his search had been fruitless. The 'snick' of the lock surrendering seemed very loud. I held my breath and listened. Nothing from beyond the door. Time to go.

I glanced at Lant. He shook his head, his lips folded tight. He would not be left behind. Per refused to look at me, but his knife was drawn. I touched Spark's wrist, and wagged a finger toward the Fool. 'Protect him,' I mouthed, and was relieved when she ghosted down the stone steps to stand beside him. He looked up at us, his pale features indistinct in the dimness.

I eased the door open and motioned the others to wait as I ventured out alone. Several pot-lamps burned, giving light to the central area of a chamber much larger than the one below. The Fool's horrific tales were made real. There were the tables with their dangling manacles and blade-scarred surfaces. Elevated benches surrounded them on three sides. Comfortable seating for the voyeurs of the torturers' work. A pit for a fire. Beside it, a meticulously tidy rack. Pokers and pincers, knives and saws and other tools I had no names for. I had never understood the hearts of such people. Who could find amusement and arousal in the pain of another? Evidently here it was popular enough to draw an audience.

It was a large room. Along one wall there were barred cell fronts. Along another more steps ascended. I had a terrifying hope; if Bee was here we could break her free and get her out before the tide's turn filled the waste chute with water. It would be difficult to wade out against the incoming tide, but not impossible.

I moved swiftly and silently. There were no guards and while my Wit warned me of flickering life in the cells I sensed no one else within the chamber. I wished for the wolf's ears and nose. I could not stand the suspense. I moved closer to the unlit cells. The dim light from the central area showed me a total of five prisoners, all adults. They slept or huddled on straw. I ventured closer to a cell and saw Prilkop. Asleep or unconscious?

I went back to the door. The Fool and Spark had come up the

steps; they all huddled on the landing. I breathed my words. 'There's no sign of Bee. Prilkop is in one of the cells. It seems clear, but be quiet. We need to—'

There was the unmistakable sound of a lock turning and a door opening. I pushed back in among my followers and drew the door almost closed behind me. 'What—' the Fool began and I quickly placed two fingers on his lips. We all froze.

I could hear but not see. The scuff of booted feet. More than three people. The muttered complaints and curses of guardsmen roused to unwelcome duty. I heard a clatter, a curse, and 'I hate this place! It stinks. Why would anyone come down here to hide? There's no one here; the door was still locked. I told you no one got past us. Now can we go back to our station? I was eating.'

'No.' The leader's reply was terse. 'You're joining us. We're to search every chamber on this level for the escaped prisoner. Rewtor and his troops are searching the cottages and gardens. Kilp's have taken the grounds between the stronghouse and the castle walls. And Coultrie's rousting out his special lads.'

'Whole damn place is on edge since Symphe was killed. Wish they'd done a better job on Vindeliar.' The guardswoman brayed out a laugh. 'Ferb and I had the honour to toss Dwalia into the cesspit. Ferb took a piss on her. Nasty old bitch looked better dead.'

The leader was not amused. 'Let's go. Every room on this level is to be checked, and every door locked behind us. If no luck, we move up to the next level. No one gets past us.'

'I bet it was one of the Whites did Dwalia. Those little snakes have no reason to like her. And Symphe? I think she was an accident. I heard they did some work on Vindeliar to try to get the truth out of him. He was chained there, he had to have seen what happened. They should just make him talk! I wouldn't mind watching that.'

'Let's go!' Their leader was plainly annoyed with the chatter and dawdling. The footsteps moved off. I waited until I heard a door close.

The Fool spoke three words into the silence. 'Dwalia is dead.' I could not read his sentiment. Was he glad, or less fearful, or regretful that he had not had the chance to be present at her death? Maybe all those things, or none of them.

'Prilkop is in a cell in there. And three others.'

'He may know what they did with Bee. He was caged beside her.'

Those were, perhaps, the only words that could have made me delay for him. 'Lant, take Per. Guard the next door. I know they locked it; it doesn't mean they won't be back. Spark, Fool, with me.' I eased the door open and like shadows we moved to our targets. I gestured to Prilkop's cell and Spark and the Fool hurried to it while I seized one of the pot-lamps and brought it over. I did not want the other prisoners to awake, nor to free them. They were factors beyond my control and I already had too many of those.

As Spark went to work on the lock on his cell, the Fool softly called, 'Prilkop, wake up.'

The big man had been curled in a ball, his arms and hand coiled protectively over his head. At the Fool's second call, he dropped his hands and lifted his head. One eye was swollen shut and his lower lip was as fat as a sausage. He stared. Painfully, he uncurled and set his feet to the cell floor. As he shuffled toward us, I heard chains clank.

'Where is Bee?' I demanded of him.

His good eye found me and wandered over my face. He gave a small nod to himself. 'The Unexpected Son. But I expected you.' He coughed out a small laugh. 'The upper cells were where I saw her last. Is this another rescue?'

'It is.' I turned.

Behind me, I heard him say, 'I hope this one is better than the last one.' As I moved away he called, more loudly than I liked, 'There are others up there in those rooftop cells. Free them.'

'Fitz?' Spark whisper-shouted after me.

'Free him. Then search for the hidden tunnel. I'll be back with Bee.'

I didn't wait for their objections. I crossed the room at a run. 'Give me some space,' I whispered to Lant and Per as I drew out my own lock picks. It was dark, but Chade had made me practise endlessly by touch. I wordlessly thanked the old man as I probed, pushed, and levered until I heard the satisfaction of a latch giving way. 'Stay back,' I warned the others.

Again, I eased a door open and peered out. It was the guards' chamber. A table, four chairs. Dice abandoned beside a half-eaten peach and three cups. I slipped into the room. There was fading warmth on the chair, and the fruit looked freshly bitten. I went back to the others.

'Come, but quietly. The guards from this chamber were called away. I fear the whole castle is alerted. They're searching for an escaped prisoner.'

Another door, another lock, but I picked it quickly. Again, I cautioned them to wait and eased a tall, heavy door open. I peered in both directions down a long curving corridor with many doors. There was no one in sight. On shelves at intervals fat lamps burned some fragrant oil. All was calm.

It was jolting to step from a place of bars and torture and bored guards into a gently-lit corridor, panelled in a white wood I'd never seen before, the floor meticulously clean, with framed portraits on the wall. It was like stepping from a nightmare into a dream.

I weighed my plans. I was not cheered to know that all doors on this level would be locked after the guards had searched each room. If we had to retreat to hiding, there would be nowhere to go. One by one, we slipped out. I led the way. Per was behind me with his short sword out. Lant came last, sword in hand. I carried my knife in my left and the ship's hatchet in my right. My pathetic invasion force, challenging a fortified stronghold. But there was no other choice. The corridor curved gently away from me in both directions. At wide intervals, there were tall double doors covered with decorative carving. All was quiet. I recalled what the Fool had told me as we created our map. This ground floor would be audience chambers and waiting rooms and private greeting rooms for very important guests. There were several stairs to the next level. I chose to go to the right.

I tested the first two doors we passed. Locked. I hoped that meant we were following the patrol. But if they turned back this way, we had nowhere to hide.

'What's that sound?' Per demanded.

'I don't know.' It was a muttering, an uneven roar. Lant was looking up, Per behind us. I had no time to worry about it. 'We have to find Bee.' I led them on.

We were like rats as we ran, hugging the walls.

Rounding the curve in the corridor, I saw the staircase. A pale grey fog was drifting down it. I slowed, stared, and then smelled it clearly. Smoke. Now I understood. Above us was the roaring laughter of the fire on the upper storeys. I heard distant shouts and cries of fear. 'She's up there,' I said, and ran. I took the stairs two at a time.

On the first landing, Per passed me. I lost sight of him in the turning of the stairs. I sheathed my knife, hooked my hatchet in my belt and followed.

I heard the slapping of footsteps, coughing and a woman wailing. Four people fled past me, racing down the stairs. 'Fire!' one shouted at me as he passed. Behind me I heard Lant shout and assumed they'd collided with him.

What had been haze became grey, stinking smoke. A dozen more steps, and the smoke was strangling me. My eyes streamed. I stumbled, went down to my knees on the steps and found slightly cooler and cleaner air. I pressed my sleeve to my nose and mouth and crawled three steps higher. It was only smoke. How could it stop me? I'd reached the top of the stairs. There was a landing. Past it, more steps. I couldn't see Per. Bee had been on the rooftop. I continued my upward crawl. Where was Per?

I halted, chest pressed to the last step before the landing. To my left was a corridor thick with smoke, cloaking the dark orange glow of a fire. I put my arm across my mouth and breathed through my shirt. Squinting, I made out flames licking a panelled wall. I heard a pop followed by the sound of falling crockery. Fire skated toward me, gliding on oil as if it were ice.

I recoiled, and felt a body under my hand. 'Per?' I gasped.

I heard shouts above me, panicked cries for help. Someone trod on me as he staggered down the stairs and two others followed, coughing and blindly stumbling over me. Choking on smoke and desperate to escape, they cared nothing for me or the boy sprawled on the steps.

My eyes streamed so that I could not see and the air was becoming too hot to breathe. I shook Per. 'Help me,' he gasped hoarsely.

'Bee,' I groaned. If she was up above us, she was likely dead. I wanted to surge to my feet and try to run up those stairs to her. Was she trapped in a cell as smoke choked and flames roared? Dead already? I wanted to die trying to reach her.

If I left him, Per would die.

I seized his arm and crawled backwards down the steps, bumping him along behind me. It took more strength than it should have. As the smoke lessened, I saw that Per had a tight grip on someone else. A child, a young White by his garb, that Per dragged with us. I gasped in a breath. The smoke in my lungs choked me and fought to be released. A shape reared up out of the haze and seized Per's other arm. Lant. 'Down!' he gasped.

Together we thudded Per and the unconscious child down the remaining steps. When we reached the ground floor, I tumbled onto the floor beside them, barking out smoke. I rolled over onto my back and wiped my sleeve across my eyes. The smoke was not gone; it crawled along the high ceiling of this corridor as a thin grey mist. Lant knelt beside me. He would wheeze in a breath and then choke it out. Two other people clattered and staggered down the stairs. A woman exclaimed at sight of us. The man leaning on her said, 'We must get out!' They left us, hacking and gasping as they ran.

Per and the child were tangled on the floor between Lant and me. 'You idiot!' I wheezed at Per, and then choked. 'Move! Crawl! We have to get back to the others, and then get out of here.'

Per coughed, opened his eyes, and then closed them again. When he didn't respond, Lant and I staggered to our feet. We dragged them laboriously away from the stairs.

When the sound and stink of the fire on the upper storeys faded behind us, we halted. Lant and I both sat down, panting cleaner air into our lungs. The top floors would all be ablaze now. Would the stronghouse collapse on top of us? 'We have to get back to the others,' I said dully. Our quest to save Bee was over. We had to get out. I staggered upright again and stooped to seize the front of Per's shirt. 'Get up!' I ordered him.

Per coughed and tried to stand up. 'Bee,' he gasped.

'Gone.' I spoke the horrid truth. 'We can't get up there. I doubt she's still alive.' My eyes were already stinging and running from the smoke. True tears mingled. It seemed an impossible cruelty that I'd come so close to her and then failed.

'Bee!' Per cried out and rolled free of my grip. It unbalanced me and I fell. I had never known that smoke could so disable a man. I crouched on my hands and knees, wheezing. Per tugged at the unconscious child he'd dragged down with us. 'Bee, I've come to save you,' he said faintly. Then his words shattered into coughing.

The child's clothes were scorched and smudged with soot and his face disfigured by scars. The flesh around his closed eyes was thickened like that of a veteran brawler. There was a scar on his left brow and a split from a more recent beating at the corner of his mouth. The marks spoke of a short life best left behind.

Then the boy opened his eyes and Bee looked at me. We stared at one another. Her mouth formed a word that her breath could not push. 'Da?'

So small. So scarred. She lifted her hands toward me and life surged through me again. 'Oh, Bee,' I said, and had no more words. I reached for her and pulled her to me. Her arms went tight around my neck and I held her close. 'I will never leave you again!' I promised her, and her grip on me tightened.

I rose onto my knees, Bee still clasped to me. Per staggered upright. He was weeping. 'We found her. We saved her,' he said.

'You did,' I told him. With my free hand, I seized Per's upper arm. 'Lant! Come on!' I stood and made a staggering run, dragging poor stumbling Per and jouncing Bee's face against my collarbone. Lant caught up and took Per's other arm. Joggling along, bumping into one another, we fled the smoke down the long gently curving corridor until suddenly my head spun and I crashed to my knees. I managed not to drop Bee but Per fell beside me and Lant went to one knee.

'Oh, Bee,' I managed to say. I lowered her to the floor. She was gasping spasmodically, as if she had nearly drowned. Her eyes had closed again. But she lived. She lived. I touched her face as Per scrabbled over to us.

'Bee, please,' he said. He looked up at me and as if he were a very young child, he pleaded, 'Make her be alive. Heal her.'

'She's alive,' Lant assured him. He leaned on the wall to stand. Then he stood over us, his sword in his hand again. He'd protect us.

She stared up at me wordlessly. I shook my head, too heart-stricken to find even a word for her. My finger traced the line of Molly's jaw, touched her mother's mouth. She coughed and I drew my hand back. No, this was not the little girl I had come to rescue. This scarred and beaten creature was no longer my Bee. I did not know who she was. Still small for her years, as young as I had been when I had begun to act on all Chade had taught me. Bee Farseer. Who was she now?

She rolled her head to look at Per, her breath wheezing in and out. 'You came. The crow said . . .' Her words trailed away.

'We came to find you,' Per assured her, and went off into another coughing fit. He reached over and took her hand in his. 'Bee. You're safe now. We have you!'

'None of us is safe, Per. We have to get her out of here.' No time for reunions and apologies, no time for tender words. I lifted my eyes. I looked up at the panelled ceiling above us and the massive beams that supported it. Wood would burn, but stone did not. Fires always climbed. We might be safe on this level, at least until the heavy timbers that supported the stone scorched and flamed.

Where were we? Had we passed the door and the stairs to the lower levels? We had to find them. Perhaps they'd found the tunnel. If not, we had to fight our way out before the whole stronghouse came down on us.

I coughed again, and rubbed my cuff over my streaming eyes. Time to move. 'We have to go,' I told Per. 'Can you walk?'

'Of course I can.' He staggered to his feet, then bent over, hands on his knees, to cough for a long time. I watched him and slowly it came to me that I knew where to go. I knew where to get help. I had that moment of utter relief one has when the obvious solution to a problem becomes clear. It seemed ridiculous that I had not thought of it before. I came to one knee and lifted Bee carefully. She did not weigh much. Through the loose garments she wore, I could feel her ribs and the knobs of her spine. I stood. I began to walk and Per straightened and staggered along at my side. Lant sheathed his sword. I glanced at him and saw that he, too, felt the same relief. I smiled to see that Per held his knife out and ready. I knew we would not need it.

My brother. Where are we going?

More welcome than cool air or fresh water was the touch of Nighteyes on my mind. I felt my spirits lift and suddenly I knew now that everything would be fine. *Where have you been?* I cried out to him. *Why did you abandon me?*

I was with the cub. She needed me far more than you did. But once she learned to raise her walls, I could not escape them. My brother, where are we going now? Why are you not running? Where is the Scentless One?

I know a place of safety. I know people who will help us.

I saw them, revealed by the gentle curve of the corridor. A troop of twelve guards, weapons drawn, was coming toward us. Spark and Prilkop were with them, guarded by them on all sides. The Fool hung limp between two guards. Leading the way was a small, stout man with a toadish face and bloodshot eyes. A tall old woman hobbled along behind him, clasping her side and two men, one garbed in green and one in yellow, walked beside her. I smiled to see them, and the small man's face broke into a grin. He motioned the guards to halt and they did. They awaited us.

'Vindeliar, I am astonished,' the old woman said. 'You are truly a wonder.'

'You should never have doubted me,' he replied.

My brother, this is wrong. This joy you feel is false.

'I am so sorry,' the woman apologized to their leader. 'From henceforth, you will be honoured as you deserve.'

The men nodded agreement to that, their faces wreathed in doting smiles.

'Fitz? What are we doing? They will kill us!' Per shouted.

Bee lifted her head from my shoulder. 'Papa!' she cried out in alarm.

'Hush. It's going to be all right,' I told her.

'All fine,' Lant echoed me.

'No!' Per shouted the word. 'No, nothing is all right! What is wrong with you? What is wrong with everyone?'

'Papa, walls up! Walls up!'

My brother, they deceive you!

I laughed. They were being so foolish. 'All is well. We are safe now,' I told them and carried Bee toward the welcoming party.

THIRTY-FIVE

Confrontations

I am Bee and Bee is me. My mother knew this from the beginning. Sometimes, at the beginning of a dream, I see myself. I am a bee, gold and black, shining like sparks and charcoal. As I fly, my colours grow brighter and brighter, as does an ember when one blows on it. I am so bright I illumine places that are dark, and in those places, I see the important dreams.

From the dream journal of Bee Farseer

It felt like a dream, the simple sleeping kind, in which one dreams of what one wants most. First Per and then my father were with me, dragging me away from smoke and flame. Per spoke to me, and I heard the voice of my first and only true friend. 'I've come to save you.' The words I'd been longing to hear someone say ever since that wintry night at Withywoods. I could not breathe for smoke and I could not see him but I knew his voice.

But then, magically, it was my father bending over me. He touched my face so softly. Then he picked me up and he was carrying me. I was safe, safe in his arms. He would protect me. He would take me home. He carried me, and I knew his swinging stride from when he had perched me on his shoulders. I put my face into the angle of his neck and smelled strength and safety. His hair was greyer and the lines in his face deeper, but this was my Da and he *had* come to find me and take me home. I lifted my head to smile down at Perseverance. He was taller than he had been, and he looked stronger. He carried his knife before him, as my father had taught me a knife should be carried.

He turned his head and looked up at my father. 'Fitz? What are we doing? They will kill us!'

Then the dream became nightmare.

My father carried me toward Vindeliar. Not just walking, hurrying, as if he could not wait to get there. Capra, Fellowdy and Coultrie walked with Vindeliar, and all of them were smiling. Capra clutched her belly, and a slow leak of blood showed on her garments, but still she smiled. They were so pleased with Vindeliar, so certain they had won. I stared. Did they know of my fires roaring two floors above us? I suspected not; Vindeliar had gathered them and brought them here. They knew only what his will was, and his will was my death.

'Papa!' I shouted at him.

'Hush.' He patted my back. 'You're safe Bee. I'm right here.'

I had held my walls so tight and so strong for so long that only now did I touch them and feel the force beating against them. I allowed myself to hear Vindeliar's lure. *Come to me, come to us. Everything will be well. We are your friends. We know what is best. We will help you.*

And my father was believing them!

'Papa! Walls up, walls up!' I shouted the words desperately as I wriggled to get out of his arms. He looked down at me and slowly a furrow grew between his brows. I think he was starting to realize what Vindeliar was doing to him, but he was doing it too slowly. I kicked free of him, fell as I hit the floor, stood up and pulled his big knife from its sheath.

'Kill her!' Vindeliar shrieked as he saw me seize the weapon. 'Kill Bee now!' Not only his voice but his magic pushed that thought, and the eyes of every person advancing toward us narrowed with hatred as they looked at me. The guards drew their swords and even Capra drew a little belt-knife. I looked up at my father, fearing to see that he, too, would have been turned against me by Vindeliar's magic, but instead I saw a terrible blankness on his face. I turned to face them, alone.

'No!'

Perseverance pushed me to one side as he charged forward. Not for an instant did he hesitate. The full force of his body was behind his knife as he drove it into Vindeliar. Both went down, and Perseverance planted a knee on Vindeliar's chest. I saw Per's elbow draw back and then punch the knife forward again. Vindeliar's terrible pain burst in my mind, edging my thoughts in red. His desperate magic leapt in a new direction.

No! Stop, drop the knife, no, don't kill me, don't hurt me!

So powerful was that sending that my father's knife fell from my suddenly nerveless hands. I was seized with the necessity of not hurting Vindeliar.

But no such compulsion stilled Perseverance. Vindeliar's magic did not touch him. He stood up, drawing out the bloody knife as he did so, and shouted, 'No one will kill Bee while I live!' He had grown stronger than the boy I had known at Withywoods. The terrific slash of his blade had the force of a swinging axe. The edge crossed Vindeliar's throat, and blood flew out in an arc as it ripped free of his flesh. As Vindeliar's magic failed and stilled, Per sprang back. He spun to stand in front of me, knife lifted in one hand and the other pushing me protectively behind him. 'Behind me, Bee,' he commanded. Chaos broke out in the force facing us.

'Why are we here?' Capra wailed, while Fellowdy danced backward into his own guards in his desire to flee.

''Ware!' my father shouted, and took a great stride past us. He stooped, snatching up the knife I had dropped. He had a hatchet in his other hand. He drove himself into the ranks of befuddled guards. He was suddenly among them, using both knife and small axe against their swords. I saw him hook a man's blade with the hatchet and force it down while he thrust his knife into the man's unguarded throat. His only hope was to be closer to them, inside the thrust or swing of their blades. His face was alight, his teeth bared and his eyes brighter than I had ever seen them.

Per remained between me and the melee. 'Stay back!' he warned me, but I cried, 'They are too many for him! We must help him or we will all die!' They were engulfing him as if he were a boot sinking into mud. In the back of their force, something else was happening. I heard a woman screaming, not in pain but in fury as her filthy curses rang out in the hall. A man's deep shouting cut through her words. 'Drop him! Let him be!'

Symphe's knife! I scrabbled to get it from under my shirt, then ducked under Per's arm and went for Fellowdy with it. The great coward had turned away from the battle and was trying to get past the knot of fighters and flee. Perhaps I was as great a coward, for I tried to drive my knife into his back. The short blade skittered down his ribs as if they were a pole fence, and then found a soft place below his short ribs and above his hip. I sank the blade as far as I could, and then seized the haft with both hands and shook it from side to side. I accidentally pulled it free as he jerked away from me.

I was much better at biting than knifing.

Then Coultrie hit me. His open palm slapped the side of my head with tremendous force and my crumpled ear roared at me. Fellowdy was crawling away from me, making short, sharp shrieks. I turned to face Coultrie. 'You dirty little traitor!' he shouted at me. Madness was in his eyes. 'You killed Symphe and you killed poor, dear Dwalia!'

Vindeliar's body was twitching on the floor behind him. I sprang at Coultrie, leading with my knife. He retreated to avoid me, stumbled on Vindeliar and fell backwards. He kicked at me as I jumped at him, a glancing blow that still pushed me sideways and made me lose some of my breath. But I paid no attention to his flailing, slapping hands I would put my knife into the middle of him, into his belly where coiled the parts he needed to live. Wolves always tore for the belly.

I hit him too high. His breastbone stopped my blade. I pulled back my knife and with both hands on the hilt I drove it down again as he battered me with slaps. He wasn't very good at it. Dwalia had hit me harder than that. My knife punched into him. I leaned on it, trying to push it deeper. Coultrie grabbed my hair with both hands and pushed my head back. My head was not my hands. I dragged the knife as he pushed me away. The cracked paint on his face made him look like a ruined doll.

Then someone else's knife carved across his throat. He didn't know he was dead. His lips writhed away from his bared teeth and I lost some hair as I ripped myself free of him.

I'd almost forgotten the other people fighting all around me. Per had hold of my upper arm and was dragging me back, shouting, 'No, Bee, stay clear! Don't get hurt!' The knife in his free hand dripped red.

My father was still engaged with the three guards that were trying to take him down. He was bleeding. Somehow he had gained a short sword and his snarl was a joyous thing. Fellowdy was still trying to crawl away. The guards had dropped the man they'd been carrying. The black man, Prilkop stood over the fallen man, weaponless. Between those two and the remainder of the patrol, a man and a woman stood back to back, and the man was FitzVigilant. Lant was alive! A strange thrill ran through me. Was it all going to come undone, all my hurt and sorrow? My father had come to rescue me, and Perseverance was alive, and Lant, too? Was it possible to hope for Revel? Did I dare?

Then a sword licked in and sliced into my father's thigh. He roared his fury, and it did not seem he could be hurt, for he swung his own blade so forcefully that it cut into the man's side almost to his spine. He jerked the blade out as another man cut at his head. He ducked that blow. 'Help him!' I screamed, but Perseverance dragged me back.

'He can't fear for you!' he shouted, and for a fleeting instant, my father's glance flowed over me. Then I heard Capra screaming, 'Guard me, guard me! Leave off and guard me!' She had broken free of the melee, to lean against the corridor wall, clutching her reddened belly. The five standing Clerres warriors abruptly sprang back from their engagements and formed up around her. She clutched at one of them and he took her weight, helping her hobble along. The others kept their faces toward us, a bristling wall of blades. Capra stumbled and the warrior picked her up. He carried her like a child as they backed away from us. Fellowdy howled at them to help him, and one of the guards seized him by an arm, pulled him to his feet and dragged him off at a staggering run.

My father stood panting, his bloodied blade slowly drooping toward the floor as they retreated. Lant started to go after them, but the girl cried out, 'No, let them go!' and he listened to her.

Capra's retreat saved us. As the curve of the corridor hid them, my father tottered sideways. Per left me and went to him, easing him down to the floor. My father was cursing furiously, clutching at the blood that welled between his fingers. I ran to him. Per was tearing his shirt off. It was the wrong kind of fabric. I wriggled my arm out of my sleeve, and held it out to him. 'Cut this off to use!' I told him, and after a shocked moment, he did.

'Bee!' Lant exclaimed as he came to my father. He looked down at me and I looked up at him. His face was freckled with blood. I didn't think it was his. He looked as if he felt ill and I thought I knew why.

'You wanted to kill me, didn't you? It was Vindeliar's magic. Not your fault. He could make people believe things. Even me.'

My father spoke in a thick, tired voice. 'It was like the Skill, but not. Magic used in a way I've never experienced.' I heard him swallow. 'How could he be that strong?'

'They gave him a potion made from serpent spit. It made him very strong. I could barely hold my walls against him.'

'I couldn't hold my walls. If it hadn't been for Perseverance . . .'

'I felt nothing,' Per said. 'I thought you had all gone mad,' he muttered, almost sulkily. He knelt by my father. 'We should cut the clothing away from this.'

'No time,' Lant said. 'That fire is spreading.' He knelt and took my sleeve from Per and wrapped it snugly around my father's thigh. He knotted it tight and I heard my father groan. The sleeve went red. Then the girl I didn't know came to us, Beloved limping as he leaned on her shoulder. 'They're gone, they ran away,' she was saying to him. Blood was running from the corner of his mouth and his face was lopsided with bruises, but all he said was 'Bee! You're alive!' He reached for me with claw-like hands, one gloved, and I shrank away.

'Bee, he won't hurt you,' Prilkop said quietly.

I had almost forgotten Prilkop. 'He would never hurt you,' he repeated quietly. 'You are his.'

Beloved turned his gloved hand toward me, palm up. 'Bee.' My name was all he said, in a slurred voice.

I drew back from him. 'I can't. He makes me see things when I touch him. I don't want to see things any more,' and it was true.

'I understand,' Beloved said sorrowfully and dropped his hands.

'Bee. He has a glove on one hand,' Perseverance said very gently. 'He has come a long far way to rescue you.' His voice reminded me of a long-ago day when he had said, 'Shall I ready her for you?' and saddled the horse I was afraid to ride. But I was not that little girl any more. I looked aside. I saw my father's expression.

I was still holding Symphe's knife. I wiped the blood from it and put it back in the waistband of my trousers. Slowly I reached out my hand and set it on the back of Beloved's glove. 'I gave you an apple,' I said quietly. 'Do you remember that?'

His mouth shook. 'I do,' he said, and tears welled and ran down his face.

'Oh, Bee, what have they done to you?' Lant asked me. His eyes were moving over my face. My scars sickened him.

I didn't want them to speak of that. I didn't want them to ask me questions about any of it. I looked at the dead guards scattered in the corridor. Blood was pooling around the bodies. The girl was moving among the bodies, looking for something. I saw her take a sword from a dead man's hand. Coultrie lay on his back, covered in blood and unmoving. I'd helped to kill him, and I didn't care. I hoped Fellowdy would die, too. And in the far parts of the castle, I still heard screams and crashes. Fire stops for nothing. Was I truly the Destroyer? 'We need to get away from here.' I reminded them all. Didn't they understand that we could not stand here? 'I set fire to the libraries. It's spreading.'

'The libraries?' Beloved said faintly. He looked devastated as he stared down at me. 'You burned the libraries of Clerres?'

'They needed burning. Burn the nest to kill the wasps.'

My speaking my old dream made his eyes go wide.

'The Destroyer came,' Prilkop said quietly.

Beloved looked from me to my father, and then back to me. 'No. Not her.'

'Yes.' I pulled my hand back from touching him. He would not want to know me now. 'Bee,' he said, but I went to my father. I put my hand on his sleeve.

'We have to get out of here now. If we can.'

My father was trying to stand up. He gave me a crooked smile. 'I know; we need to be moving. But first, are there any more like Vindeliar?'

'He was the only one. I think. They said they did not have much of the serpent potion left, but I think they lied to one another about that.' Could they make another Vindeliar?

'Serpent potion?' Beloved asked. He had drawn closer to us, and Prilkop stood beside him.

Prilkop spoke in his low, deep voice. 'I have heard rumours of this. Is that what they gave to Vindeliar? It is made from the concentrated secretions of a sea serpent. There is an island where dragons used to lay their eggs. The eggs hatched into serpents that wriggled into the sea. Some very peculiar creatures live on that island. Sometimes they capture a serpent or two, and hold it in captivity.'

I was watching my father. He put a heavy hand on Lant's shoulder. His expelled breath made a horrid sound as he forced himself to rise. At first his foot did not touch the ground. Then he set it deliberately to the floor and tested his weight on it. The red on his bandage darkened. 'We need to get out of here. The fire will consume the upper storeys first, and then it will all fall on us. We need to get outside, and then off the island.'

'It may not fall.' Prilkop suggested. 'The bones of this stronghouse are stone and it has stood through many a calamity. It is not the first time fire has visited here.'

My father did not seem to be listening to Prilkop, so I ignored him as well. We started walking. I stayed close to him. My father expelled a harsh, short breath with each step on his bad leg, but he led us. Slowly. 'You should leave me behind,' he said. 'Take Bee and run for the doors.'

'Run straight into their guards?' Spark asked him.

'We aren't leaving you,' Per said quietly.

'Sir, is there a way out of this castle, one that won't be guarded? Or packed with fleeing people?' Spark asked Prilkop. She glanced down at my father's leg as he limped along and said to me, 'We will need your other sleeve.'

Prilkop shook his head. 'This stronghouse was designed to be easy to defend, not to escape from. There are only three entrances. Those who have escaped the flames will flee down the main stairs and go to them.'

I pulled my arm into my shirt and offered her the limp sleeve. She cut it off as we walked, her knife sliding easily through the fabric. 'Wait a moment,' she told my father, and he halted. She knelt to add another layer to the seeping bandage on his leg and a brief snarl passed over his face.

'Let's go,' he growled, and limped on.

'How did you get into Clerres?' Prilkop asked curiously. He walked beside my father. Beloved walked next to me. I think he wished to hold my hand, but Per was doing that. Then he let go of my hand. 'I'm going ahead,' Per said quietly. 'I don't like that we can't see around the curve here. The Fool will take care of you. And Spark and Lant.' He put my hand in Beloved's gloved one, and I let him. He sprinted ahead of us, staying close to the inner curve of the wall. I looked up at Beloved. He looked down at me and offered a cautious smile. It rippled his bruised face. I could not smile back. I let my eyes follow Per.

'We came in by the waste chute on the low tide. It will be flooded with water now. No use to us until late afternoon. I don't think the fire will give us that long.'

Lant asked Prilkop, 'Do you know of a concealed tunnel under the causeway? The Fool believes he was taken out of Clerres that way.'

We were moving, but not swiftly. The scattered bodies of the fallen guards partially blocked the hall. Our bare feet left bloody footprints on the formerly pristine floor as we left the battle behind us. Per was ranging ahead of us, staying close to the wall and trying to peer around the curve of the corridor. He held a short-sword in one hand and his knife in the other. He reminded me of a small hunting creature. I wondered if I were as changed as he was. When he went out of sight, I caught my breath. I wanted him back, right now.

Beloved was limping, his other hand on the girl's shoulder. She held a looted sword and a knife. 'You're bleeding,' I said to her.

She didn't even look at the slice on her forearm. 'It will stop,' she said quietly. She smiled at me. 'Hello, Bee. I'm Spark. I came a long way to meet you.'

Prilkop was talking. 'The tunnel is old, built when an emperor first constructed Clerres and severed the peninsula to make it an island. When I was a boy here, it was not a secret. In those days, the Servants lived simply and had no thought of needing guards or a secret escape route and it wasn't used. I know that Beloved was taken out through that tunnel, as much to avoid Capra knowing as to maintain the pretence he had escaped.' He looked at Beloved as he added, 'They took great delight in telling me what they had done. How they had crippled and maimed you, to make every step an agony. Even so, they knew you would go to him. They trailed you like slow hounds. Not to help, only to keep you from failing. You know that now, don't you?'

'I guessed it then,' he said in a low voice. 'But I had no other path.'

He was the one who had led them to me. And now he held my hand. I saved that bit of information.

'The tunnel under the causeway?' Spark prompted Prilkop impatiently.

'It's very old. It dates back to the creation of Clerres as an island. The emperor who constructed it wished to have a secret egress in case the castle was besieged and falling. When they cut away the land, and pared down the peninsula to make Clerres an island, they cut a trench in the stony earth and roofed it over, and then built the causeway over it. It was failing when they used it to take Beloved out of the dungeons. When the tide covers the causeway, it may leak. Or fill. I don't know. It's considered a "secret" now and not spoken about.' He smiled grimly.

Spark scowled. 'But is it at a higher level than the waste chute? Or lower?'

'Higher,' Prilkop shook his head. 'It was years ago that they released Beloved. It may be collapsed now. After Beloved's "escape" Capra was so furious that she had it bricked up.'

There was a smile in the girl's voice as she said, 'Bricks will not stop us, if you know where it was.'

We heard a distant crash, behind and above us. We all flinched. My father limped faster.

Beloved's voice was soft and flat with a sort of dread. 'Prilkop, how is it you know so much of what has been going on it Clerres?'

The black man gave a bitter laugh. 'I did not betray you, Beloved. Once you were gone, they believed they had all they needed from me and were finished with me—hence the better lodgings and cessation of torture. They took my dreams as I wrote them down. Several times they tried to induce me to contribute to their breeding programme. My dreams and my seed were all they valued of me. One of the night guards was assigned to seduce me. Instead, we became friends. She gave me news, but only what she knew of Clerres. The Four do not encourage news of the outside world here. For the Whites born here, Clerres is all they know.'

Per came sprinting back to us, panic on his face. 'We cannot escape this way,' he whispered hoarsely. 'Ahead is a grand staircase. People are running down it, and crowding at the bottom and milling like corralled cattle in the room before the outer doors. There is no escaping that way; the main doors are locked! I could not get to the front of the mob, for folk are trampling and pushing and hurling themselves against the doors.' He gasped in a breath. 'I ran past them down the next corridor, but there I saw a troop of guards. They were opening each locked chamber and searching it. I think they are looking for us. They saw me but I raced away from them. They didn't follow. I think they thought me just another slave. But I think they will come this way soon.'

I spoke as he drew breath. 'They are seeking me. Vindeliar said he had burned it into their minds. They will not stop until they find me. And kill me.'

For a long moment, none of them spoke. The sounds of the fleeing people came faintly to us. Per sheathed his knife and took my hand.

My father spoke, but he sounded like a different man. One who thought only of what must happen next, without emotion. 'Fool, lead us back to the dungeons.'

It was Prilkop who spoke. 'It is two doors ahead of us. On the left. And I must go there too. We left the other prisoners still locked in their cells when Vindeliar sent his magic to draw us to him.' His voice dwindled away.

My father sounded impatient. 'And down there is the bricked up entrance to the causeway tunnel?'

'Yes, it is also there. On the lower level.'

'We need to get there and secure the doors before the guards come. Run!' my father ordered. And we did, but only as fast as he could limp.

The moment we reached the second door and Lant opened it, Prilkop darted in and disappeared from sight.

My father seized Lant's shoulder. 'Lant. Secure this door and the one to the lower level. Barricade the steps with whatever you can find. Per and Fool, guard Bee with your lives.' He unslung a harness from across his shoulders. It had pockets with little pots in them. He removed three. 'Spark, take these. Have Prilkop show you the bricked-up entry. If nothing else works, blast it open. Get Bee back to the ship.' He put the little pots into her arms. She cradled them like a baby while looking up at him wide-eyed. 'Bee. Listen to Lant and the Fool. Obey them. They will get you to safety.'

'But Fitz—' Beloved said in a broken voice.

'There's no time to argue. Keep your promise to me!' My father's voice was the harshest I'd ever heard it.

Beloved's gasp sounded like a sob.

'Papa,' I said. I held to the cuff of his sleeve. 'You promised me! You said you'd never leave me again!'

'I'm sorry, Bee.' He looked at all of us. 'I'm sorry. Get inside. Hurry.' But at the last moment, he reached over and set his hand on my head. I do not think he knew what would happen. The touch broke our walls. I felt him. I felt his disappointment in himself. He did not feel he deserved anything from me. Not to touch me or even to say that he loved me, for he had failed so badly at being my father. It stunned me. It was like a second wall beyond his Skill walls, something that prevented him from believing that anyone could love him.

Wolf Father spoke to both of us. *You would not feel so terrible if you had not loved her so recklessly. Without limits. Be proud of our cub. She fought. She killed. She stayed alive.* I felt Wolf Father leap from me to my father. I heard his parting words. *Run, Cub. We stand and fight like cornered wolves. Follow the Scentless One. He is part of us. Protect each other. Kill for him, if need be.*

As the wolf went to him, I felt the surge of joy that linked those two. They would stand and fight, not just for me, but because it was what they loved to do. What they had always loved to do. My father stood a bit straighter. They both looked at me from his eyes. Puzzlement and pride. And love of me. It poured out of my father, as uncontrollable as the blood seeping from his wound. It drenched me and filled me. He lifted his hand from my head. Did he know how he had revealed himself? Did he understand that Wolf Father had been with me, all those days, and now returned to him?

Almost gently, he peeled my grip from his cuff. He spoke. 'Please, Lant. Take Bee. Take the Fool, take all of them. Get them safely home. It's the best thing you can do for me. Hurry!' He gave me the softest of pushes. Away from him. He turned away from us, as if confident that we would obey.

He turned and began to limp away.

'Why?' I shouted at him. I was too angry to cry, I thought, but tears came anyway.

'Bee, I'm leaving a blood trail that a child could follow. Per saw guards coming, searching rooms as they come. I will be sure that they find me before they find you. Now, follow Lant.' He sounded terribly tired and sad.

I looked back the way we had come. His bloody footprints were plain on the once clean floor. He was right and that only made me angrier.

Lant stood by the open door. 'Per, Spark, take them in. I'm staying with Fitz.'

'No, Lant, you won't! I need you with them, to be a sword to protect them and to use your strength to barricade that door.'

Beloved didn't move. 'I can't do this,' he said in a very soft voice.

My father rounded on him. 'You promised!' he roared. He seized the front of Beloved's shirt and pulled him close. 'You promised me. You said you would choose her life over mine.'

'Not like this,' Beloved wailed. 'Not like this!'

Abruptly my father seized him in a hug. He held him tight as he spoke. 'We don't get to choose how it happens. Only that you save her, not me. Now go. Go!' He pushed him away. 'All of you, go!'

He turned and limped away from us. His hand left bloody prints on the wall, and his footprints were red on the white floor. He didn't look back. When he came to a door, he halted. We stood in frozen silence. I saw him take something out of his pocket, watched him fuss with the door handle. After a moment, he opened it. Just before he slipped inside, he glanced back at us. He made an angry motion and mouthed, 'Go!' at us.

Then he was gone. I heard him lock the door behind him. Of course. If we were hiding in that room, it was what we would do. There was blood on the floor outside that door. His bloody handprints on the wall and the door. The guards would think they had us cornered.

'Get in here,' Lant said in a dark and savage voice. He took my shoulder and pushed me toward Beloved. I tottered numbly along with him. Per came beside me. I heard him sob once. I understood. I was crying, too. As the door began to close behind us, Per spoke in a hoarse voice. 'Bee, I am sorry, but I am the only one Lant won't need. Spark must set the firepot. Prilkop knows where the tunnel is. Lant is strong and good with a blade. And the Fool promised. And you . . . Saving you is why we came all this way. But me? I'm just a stableboy with a knife. I can stay with Fitz and help him.' He sniffed. 'Spark, quickly. Come back to that door and unlock it for me.'

'Lant?' she asked uncertainly.

'Do it,' he said harshly. 'After all, he's just a stableboy.' He cleared his throat. 'A stableboy who killed Duke Ellik to save Fitz's life. One who stood beside him when Fitz faced down a queen dragon. Go, Per. Be sure he knows it's you And when you've killed the guards, bring him back to us. Two knocks, then one, and I'll open this door without trying to kill you.'

'Yes, sir,' Per said. He looked at me. 'Goodbye, Bee.'

I hugged Per. It had been a long time since I'd hugged anyone. It was even stranger to have someone hug me back, so gently. 'Thank you for killing Ellik,' I told him. 'He was a terrible man.'

'You're welcome, Lady Bee,' he said, and his voice shook only a little.

Prilkop was waiting for us. 'The lad is terrified,' he objected.

Lant spoke. 'That's because he's as intelligent as he is brave. Go, Per.'

'All this talking,' I heard Spark mutter angrily. 'Per, hurry!' But as she turned, she reached up and touched Lant's cheek. Then they left us.

I stood beside Beloved in the dim room. Overhead, something fell with such a crash that the ceiling shook, and bits of paint flaked down. He looked at me and spoke so softly. 'The Destroyer.'

I could not tell if it was a compliment or a rebuke. 'Go down the steps,' Lant said in a low voice. He closed the door behind us.

THIRTY-SIX

Surprises

No, I cannot agree with you that this work should be left to others. You and I, we are the only two with the necessary depth of knowledge to understand and correctly classify the Skill-cubes. In an excess of caution, Skillmistress Nettle has removed from my safekeeping the sack of memory-cubes I myself brought back from Aslevjal. She has given them over to a young journeyman and a team of apprentices. The task she has assigned is that the apprentices should briefly sample each cube, both to teach them how to use a memory-cube and also to teach them the restraint needed to enter the Skill-flow and then to exit from it after a limited time. Each cube is then to be classified as to what it holds, be it music, history, poetry, geography or other branch of knowledge. Each cube will receive a designation so that they can be kept in order.

I consider a 'brief time' in each cube to be inadequate. You and I both well know that a poem can be a history and a 'history' can be a flattering fabrication to tickle a ruler's vanity. You and I are the ones who should be experiencing the cubes, creating clear pages that summarize what they hold and then storing them in order. This is not a task to be left to inexperienced apprentices, and 'sampling' the cubes before storage and classification is inadequate. I understand that the information they hold is vast. Even more reason that each cube should be explored completely by people with a broad base of knowledge.

Chade Fallstar in a letter to Tom Badgerlock of Withywoods

I latched the door behind me. Then I leaned against it. Why had they made it so hard for me? Did they think I wanted to do this?

To leave Bee yet again? I did not mean to slide down to sit on the floor, but I did. It hurt, but it probably hurt less than falling.

I was lightheaded. My body was demanding that I rest, that I sleep. After so many years, I was familiar with its aggressive healing. All my body's attention and resources were going to the slash on my leg, just when I needed to be alert.

How bad was it?

It's bleeding less. Don't poke it.

'Where have you been?' I heard myself whisper the words.

With the cub, doing my best to help her. Mostly failing.

She is alive. That means you succeeded. She would be safer if you went back to her.

She is safer if we draw off the hunters. And kill as many as we can.

I had held back three of Chade's firepots for myself. I reached over my shoulder and took out the cracked firepot that I'd mended, put it back and chose the other two. One had a blue fuse. Long and slow, Spark had said. I wasn't sure I wanted it to burn slowly. I wasn't clear on what I was going to do with it. How slow was slow?

I knew the guards would come. Make all ready.

I looked around the darkened room. It was small, perhaps for private meetings. There were two small windows set high in the wall and no other door. A watery grey light told me that outside, dawn was breaking. As my eyes adjusted, I saw a table with two comfortable, high-backed chairs around it. In the middle of the table there was a little pot-lamp made of glass and painted with flowers. A lovely, welcoming room. An assassin's dream.

I got to my feet, not quickly and not without curses, but I did it. I set my pack on the table and opened it. The folded paper of carris seed was on top. Very little left. I dumped it in my hand, tossed it into my mouth and ground it between my teeth as I set out the fire-brick. The heady rush of the carris seed flooded me. Good. I drew the wick most of the way out of the lamp and set it on the fire-brick. It warmed immediately and soon the wick began to smoulder.

Someone tried the doorhandle. Out of time. I'd planned to have the lamp lit ready to light the fuse. Instead, I uncoiled the fuse from the firepot and set it on the brick. Almost immediately a tiny spark danced on it. A flame leapt and then died back to a steady red glow. The lock rattled once, then turned. I slid the brick along the fuse and lit it closer to the pot. Then I stood. Almost. I leaned heavily on the table. The sword wasn't long enough to be a walking stick. I put more weight on my bad leg. It folded under me and I caught at the table. One can ignore pain. But when the body invokes weakness, determination is useless. I hopped and lurched toward the door. I wanted to be behind it, out of sight when they entered. They'd come in I'd close the door and keep them there until Chade's little pot gave up its lightning.

I made it to the door just as it opened a crack. I leaned against the wall and held my breath.

'Fitz? It's me, it's Per. Don't kill me!'

He stepped in, with Spark peering over his shoulder. I had no time to curse at them. I lunged for the firepot at the same moment that Spark saw it. As I toppled like a cut tree, she stepped past me, slid the fire-brick from under the fuse and flipped the brick over. She evaluated the fuse on the pot. 'We have enough time,' she said. 'Pick him up, Per. We'll backtrack in his blood and be away from here before it goes off.' She nodded to me. 'It's not a bad plan.' She seized one of the chairs and dragged it so that the back blocked the view of the table from the door. 'Nothing for them to see to warn them. Let's go.'

I tried to think of a reason to argue with her. Per already had my arm across his shoulder. He stood, dragging me up with him. The lad had grown stronger. Spark poked the fire-brick, and then picked it up. 'It's cooling already,' she said. 'Elderling magic. Amazing stuff.' With swift efficiency, she resettled it in the pack. I started to object, but she held up the unlit firepot. 'I'm not stupid,' she said and set it upright on the cooled brick. She slung it over my shoulder. 'Go. Now.'

We went, though not as swiftly as I would have wished. I leaned on Per and hobbled. Spark inserted herself under my sword arm. She was barely tall enough to take the weight off my bad leg. She drew the door closed behind us. 'Wish I had time to lock it,' she muttered. My heart sank as I saw the next door open and Lant put his head out. Spark made an impatient motion of her hand and he closed it softly. I tried to move faster.

The rhythmic slap of running feet.

'Drop me. Run!' I ordered them.

No one listened to me. 'Hurry,' Per suggested.

Spark glanced back. 'No. Stop and face them!'

'No!' Per objected, but she held my arm tight to her shoulder and I found myself pivoting on my good leg as she spun me around.

'What are you doing?' Per cried out.

'Trust me!' A hissed whisper. 'Swords up.'

I lifted mine with an effort. 'Get clear,' I warned Per, and at last he obeyed me. I could not walk but I could balance. Somewhat.

'El's balls.' Per's voice went guttural. 'They have bows.'

'Of course they do,' Spark laughed darkly.

They halted well out of sword range, a dozen of them, tall, well-made warriors. Four with bows, six with swords. Their leader barked, 'Capra wants the man taken alive! Shoot the other two!'

'Run,' I suggested.

'Get behind Fitz,' Spark said, and seized Per to drag him in as she stepped behind me. 'And hold here,' she whispered. 'Not much longer. Hold. Hold. Hold.'

The archers were fanning out and advancing. I would not block their arrows for long. They would kill Spark and Per.

'Hold. Hold,' whispered Spark.

The door and the wall leapt out at them as I flew backwards, landing on my companions. In the next instant, the ceiling came down, scorched wood and some stone. A blast of heat and stinging dust struck me, blinding me as the roar numbed my ears. My face felt burned. I dragged a sleeve across my eyes and blinked, expecting to find enemies charging. I still couldn't see. Tears streamed from my eyes. I sat up slowly as Per and Spark squirmed out from under me. The hazy corridor held only the shattered wall and collapsed ceiling and the smouldering beam that leaned across it. I felt a rain of fine debris.

Spark said something.

'What?'

'That worked well!' she shouted.

I nodded and found a stupid grin spreading across my face. 'It did. Let's go!' Per helped me up. His face was reddened from the blast but he managed a smile. I felt something sting the back of my neck and slapped it. I brushed a dart away, looked at it in surprise but Spark was already screaming, 'Ware! More of those bastards! Swords up!'

Chade's firepot blast had deafened us so we had not heard the patter of running feet. A dozen guards had come up on us from behind, completing the pincer movement I had feared.

Four in the front line raised brass-bound tubes to their lips. A blast of those horns would summon more guards. *Kill them first. Fight like cornered wolves!* I agreed with Nighteyes. I raised my sword and Per and I lurched toward them, roaring as the trumpeters puffed their cheeks. But before they could sound their horns, another fall of burning ceiling drove Per to his knees and sent me hopping sideways. The guards wavered as a rush of heat rolled past us and I heard no blast of horns. Was I that deafened? But I'd felt a tiny impact and I looked down to see a dart dangling from my vest. Spark shook another from her hair. It fell away as I hopped in, sword feebly swinging. My blade bit into one before I staggered sideways and fell. Per leapt to stand over me, thrusting and yelling. Spark charged, shrieking as she attacked.

The door to the dungeons swung open right beside them. I roared my dismay. They'd betray themselves! We'd all die.

But it was not Lant who came out, blade in hand, but Bee.

She pointed her knife at them, but that was not her weapon. She widened her eyes and stared at them. *Go away, go away, go away! Be scared, be scared, run away, run away!*

Verity's strength, without his wisdom or control. I slammed my walls against her wild Skilling. Per stared in astonishment as our enemy threw down weapons and fled. I thrashed myself forward, barely catching one of Spark's ankles. She slammed to the floor hard as I tripped her, but in an instant, she was flailing and trying to crawl away from me. 'Bee, stop! Spark, not you! You don't run away, Spark.'

Spark, I didn't mean you!

Bee did not know how to turn down her power. Spark leapt like a hooked fish, and then was still, eyes wide. Like Verity, Bee could influence those whose Skill-ability was so low they had never even been aware of it. Once my king had used that power to convince captains to turn away from the Six Duchies or to steer their red warships onto rocks. Now my daughter sent warriors fleeing. And stunned her allies!

'Inside,' I told them. 'Per, bring Spark.' I hobble-hopped to the door as he grabbed Spark under the arms and dragged her. 'Get inside, Bee!' My daughter held the door wide as Lant thrust his head out.

'What happened?' His face was white with terror. His voice seemed a whisper.

'A firepot brought the ceiling down. And Bee can Skill. Strongly. That was her you felt! But she doesn't know how to target. She frightened off a patrol. But when they come to their senses, if they do, they'll know where we are.'

'I'm so sorry, Fitz!' Prilkop was showing me the bricked-up entrance. 'I told her to stay close.' He had my arm and dragged me in.

'My father needed me,' Bee explained.

'Bee made them run away?' Per asked. He let Spark slide to the floor as he slammed the door shut behind us. We stood in the still-ness of the guard's chamber. My ears were still ringing.

'Spark?' Lant cried, his heart in his voice as his wits returned to him. He knelt by her, crying, 'Where is she hurt?'

'She is Skill-stunned. I think she'll come around in a few minutes. Bee, no one is angry. You saved our lives. Come here, please, come here!'

Per was ignoring the rest of us as he pushed the guard's table against the door. I dodged the chair he flung at it to hobble toward Bee.

She had retreated to a corner of the room, both her hands lifted to cover her shamed face. 'I didn't mean to hurt her! And now they know where we are hiding!'

'No, you saved us! You saved all of us!'

She darted to me, and for a fleeting instant I held my child in my arms and she clung to me, believing I could protect her. For a breath, I felt like a good father. The Fool came up the steps. 'What happened?' he demanded.

'Down the steps,' Lant commanded. He had dragged a dazed Spark to her feet. Her eyes were open and she looked confused. A good sign, I decided.

Bits of paint were already flaking down as the cracks in the ceiling above us ran and widened. 'If the ceiling comes down, we're trapped down there,' I reminded him.

'Even if the ceiling fall hadn't blocked the corridor out there, we haven't any hope of getting out past the guards and gates. This is our only chance, small as it is. Come on.'

I do not like this.

Nor I.

The Fool came to help me follow them. Lant went through with Spark holding tight to his arm. Per put a last chair in his stack of furniture and came to join us.

'You have magic?' Per asked Bee as she held the door for us.

'And you do not. I am so glad. I would have made you run away from us.' For just an instant, a smile crossed her face. It was Molly's smile in that little scarred face. My heart broke.

'Never,' the boy promised her, and his grin was wide. It was all she saw.

Behind me, a corner of the ceiling came down, smoking and stinking and effectively blocking the outer door. I felt a wash of heat with it, pushing Bee and me toward the steps. Per closed the door behind us. 'Well. I doubt we need to fear any enemies coming at us from that direction.' He sounded almost cheerful. I said nothing to contradict him, but I knew that smouldering wood would catch the walls on fire. We were truly trapped now.

Bee and Per descended before us. I looked down the steps. 'Lean on me,' the Fool bade me. At every step, the gash on my thigh gaped. There was light below, but not much. I caught a whiff of fragrant pine oil before the prison stench drowned it. Then I felt an immense thud, as if a giant horse had kicked the wall, and the door jumped in its frame. I judged that more of the ceiling had come down. That was it. We were trapped and would die here if we did not find another escape route.

'No going back,' the Fool said. I nodded numbly. We reached the bottom and I sat down on the lowest step. The Fool sat down beside me and Bee came to my other side. Here we were. All of us alive. For now.

I put my arm around her and drew her close. For an instant, she stiffened at my touch. Then she leaned into me. For a time, I just sat there. My strength was at a low ebb, but Bee was here. My child was beside me.

Above us, fire and falling walls and a furious enemy. Down here, chill and dank and dimness. We were caged in by stone and sea. Prilkop crouched beside the prisoners he had freed. They sat together in one cell, ragged and round-shouldered, huddled close on a single pallet. I could not hear what he was saying to them. Across the room, a shaky Spark inspected a section of the wall. I watched her and Lant run their hands over the stonework, rub at the scratched mortar and shake their heads. They looked discouraged.

'We may have to use a firepot,' Lant suggested.

Spark rubbed her eyes and gingerly shook her head. 'Last resort,' she said loudly. 'Unless we could put it inside the wall more of the force would come at us than into the stone. Chade and I did many tests. If we buried the pot, it blasted a hole. On top of the ground it made a wide, shallow indentation. It could as easily bring the ceiling down on us.'

'I'm so tired,' Bee said. I could barely hear her.

'So am I.' The carris seed had already faded leaving its darkness and weariness.

'Wolf Father is with you now?'

Yes.

'Yes.' Her name for Nighteyes made me smile at her.

'What is he?'

I didn't know. 'He's good,' I said. I sensed approval from him.

'He is,' she agreed. She waited for me to say more. I shrugged at her, and a smile flickered across her face. Then she asked, 'Are we safe here?'

'Safe enough. For now,' I told her.

I studied her face. Her eyes widened. Almost defiantly, she said, 'I know what I look like. I'm not pretty any more.'

'You never were,' I told her. I shook my head at her.

The Fool gasped at my cruelty and Bee's eyes went wide in shock.

'You were and are beautiful,' I said. I freed a hand to touch her lumpy ear. 'Every scar a victory. I see you had many of them.'

She straightened her back. 'Every time they beat me, I tried to hurt them back. Wolf Father told me that. Make them fear me, he said. So I did. I bit a hole in Dwalia's face.'

That shocked me to silence. But the Fool leaned in and said, 'Oh, well done! Would that I could have done that myself.' He smiled at her. 'Do you like your father's nose?'

She looked up at me and I fingered the break in it. She had never seen it any other way. 'What's wrong with it?' she asked in puzzlement.

'Nothing at all,' the Fool told her merrily. 'I've always told people, "There's nothing wrong with his nose."' He laughed out loud, and both Lant and Spark turned to regard us in surprise. I didn't understand his joke, but their expressions made me laugh and even Bee smiled, in the way one does at a madman.

She leaned closer and closed her eyes. The pain from my leg came in surges with my heartbeat. Rest, rest, rest said the pain. I knew I could not. My body wanted to sleep, to heal, but now was not the time. I needed to get up, to help the others, but Bee was slumped against me and I didn't want to move her. I leaned back and the last firepot in the belt poked me. 'Help me,' I said and the Fool tugged it off me.

Bee didn't stir. I looked down at her little face. Her eyes were closed. Her disfigurement told a dreadful tale. Scars, some months old, some fresh, distorted her face. I wanted to touch the cut at the corner of her mouth and heal it. No. Don't wake her. I realized I was leaning heavily on the Fool. I lifted my head to look at him.

'Did we win?' he asked me. His smile was lopsided in his swollen face.

'The fight isn't over until you win,' I said. Burrich's words. Spoken to me so long ago. I touched my leg. Warm and wet. I was hungry and thirsty and so tired. But I had them both beside me. Alive. Still bleeding, and my ears ringing. But alive.

Across the room, Lant was grinding at mortar with his knife. Per knelt on the floor beside him, likewise digging at a seam. Spark had crossed to a rack of tools meant for tearing flesh, not stone. Her upper lip curled back as she selected one of the black iron implements. I turned my gaze away from that and met the Fool's eyes.

'I should go help them,' he said.

'Not yet.'

He gave me a questioning look.

'Let me have this moment. All of you here with me. Just for a short time.' A smile suddenly came to me. 'I have news for you,' I told him. I found I still could grin. 'Fool, I'm a grandfather! Nettle has a baby girl now. Hope! Isn't that a wonderful name?'

'You. A grandfather.' He smiled with me. 'Hope. A perfect name.'

For a time we sat together in silence. I was so weary, and danger still threatened, but that did not steal the sweetness of being here, alive, with them. I was so tired. And my leg hurt. Nonetheless, I had this moment. I slipped into the wolf's enjoyment of the immediate.

Rest a moment. I will keep watch.

I didn't realize I had dozed until I twitched awake. I was thirsty and ravenously hungry. Bee was holding my hand and was asleep against me. Skin to skin, I felt my daughter as a part of me. I smiled slowly as I became aware of her Skill-wall. Self-taught. She would be strong with it. I lifted my eyes to the Fool. He was haggard but smiling. 'Still here,' he said softly.

Through the dimness, I saw that Lant had taken off his shirt and was sweating in the chill. He, Per and Spark were employing our looted swords to dig out the mortar in a section of wall. They had made an opening big enough to admit a man's arm. The stone they had pulled out was as long and wide as a man's forearm but only a hand tall. The blocks in the wall were staggered. They'd have to remove three above to take out the two below. At least six to move before Per could squeeze through. I should go and help. I knew that. But my body had cheerily burned my reserves to try to heal my leg. I cautiously felt the bandaging. Sticky and crusty. No new blood. Still likely to split open again when next I stood.

Lant stood up. 'Stand back,' he said and when Per and Spark did he kicked at the block they'd been working on. 'Not yet,' Spark said wearily. Per went back to his scraping.

'Can't we put one of your firepots in there now?'

Spark gave him a look. 'If you want to chance caving in the tunnel beyond, I suppose we could.'

Per made a small sound of amusement and went on scraping at mortar.

The Fool and I were silent. One of the prisoners came out of the cell. He stumbled slowly toward where Per, Spark and Lant scraped at the mortar. He spoke hoarsely, in a boy's voice. 'I will help, if you have a tool for me.' Spark measured him with her eyes, then she gave him her belt-knife, and he began to dig feebly at a line of mortar.

'I truly feared I had to choose between you,' the Fool said quietly. When I said nothing, he added, 'Her dream of the buck, the bee, and the scale.'

'And yet I am here, and alive, and our enemies are walled away from us by smouldering rubble. Perhaps I am still the Catalyst, and can change even her predictions of what must be. I am not dead yet and I don't intend to die. I am taking Bee home, to Buckkeep. She will be raised as a princess, and you will be at her side to teach and advise her. Her sister will adore her and she will have a little niece to play with.'

Two of the freed Whites rose and went to the rack of torture tools. They made choices and then joined Lant, Spark and Per, chipping away at the mortar. The irony twisted my gut.

'And we will live happily ever after?' the Fool asked.

I watched the bits of mortar fall. 'That is my intention.'

'And mine. My hope. But a thin one.'

'Don't doubt us, or we are lost.'

'Fitz, my love, that is the problem. I do not doubt Bee's dreams at all.'

I opened my mouth and then found wisdom. I closed it. But as a dreadful thought came to me, I asked him, 'The container of Silver you took from the stateroom. Did the Servants get it?'

'I stole it to keep a promise,' he admitted. 'What did you think? That I'd taken it to use on myself?'

'I feared that.'

'No. I didn't even bring it with me. I told Boy-O—'

Beside me, Bee stirred. She lifted her head and took her hand out of mine. The Skill-link held, stretched thin as a thread but still there. I wondered if she felt it. She drew in a deep breath and sighed it out. She looked from me to the Fool. He smiled at her as I'd never seen him smile at anyone. His scars stretched with it, but his half-blind eyes shone with tenderness. She stared back at him and leaned tighter into me. As she looked at him, she whispered, 'I had a dream.'

He lifted a gloved hand and stroked her hair. 'Would you like to tell it to me?' he offered.

She looked at me. I nodded. 'I sit near a fire beside Da and a wolf. He is very old. He tells me stories and I write them down. But I am very sad as I do this. Everyone is mourning.' She finished with, 'I believe this dream is very likely.' She turned worried eyes to me.

I smiled at her. 'That dream sounds lovely to me. I would change only your sadness.'

She frowned at how little I understood. 'Da. I don't make the dreams. I can't change them. They just come to me.'

I laughed. 'I know. The same thing happens to the Fool. Sometimes he is very sure a dream will come true.' I shrugged one shoulder and grinned at her. 'And then I make it not true.'

'You can do that?' She was astonished.

'He is my Catalyst. He changes things. Sometimes in ways I never imagined,' the Fool admitted ruefully. 'And often enough I have been grateful for him to do that. Bee, there is so much I must teach you. About Catalysts and dreams and—'

'Prilkop told me that Dwalia was my Catalyst. She came and made changes in my life. She changed me. Thus she enabled the changes I made. And I killed her. I killed my Catalyst.' She looked up at me. Her eyes were as blue as forget-me-nots, her pale curls matted to her head. 'Did you know that I killed people? And I burned all the dreams so the Servants cannot use them for evil any more. Papa, I am the Destroyer.' Her words left me speechless. In a very small voice, she asked, 'Can you change that for me?'

'You are Bee and you are my little girl,' I told her fiercely. 'That doesn't change. Not ever.'

Bee turned her head sharply to something and I followed her gaze. Another prisoner was making her slow way toward us, her pale face pinched with pain as she limped on a welted foot. 'In my dream, I saw you, little girl,' she said. She smiled at us with chapped lips. 'You were made of flame. You danced in the flames and brought war to where war had never been. With a sword of flame, you sliced the past from the present, and the present from the future.'

Prilkop started toward us, his face full of worry.

The White shuffled closer. 'I am Cora, a collator. I studied in the scroll-library. I had a lovely little cottage. But I spilled ink on an old text. I knew I must be punished. But I also knew that one day I would go back to my ink and pens and fine vellum. To evenings of rest and wine and songs by moonlight.

'But you came. And you destroyed it all. ' She shrieked the last words and flung herself at Bee. Bee screamed in fury and fear, and stood to meet her. My knife clashed against Bee's as they drove into the woman's body at the same moment. She went down under our combined weight as I fell onto her. The Fool gave an incoherent cry over Per's roar of rage. The killing wrath that rose in me obscured all else. Bee was fast. She withdrew her knife and sank it again before I could finish the woman. Cora bubbled a whine that became silence. We sprawled on the filthy floor, my hands slick with blood and my leg searing with pain. Bee rolled off the woman and struggled to rise. The blood on her clothes terrified me. She was not hurt, our Skill-thread assured me. She retrieved her knife and wiped it on Cora's dirty trousers.

Prilkop reached us, crying, 'Cora! Cora, what have you done?' He tried to pull me off the White's body, but I snarled at him and he drew back. Per darted in and pulled Bee to his side as Prilkop demanded, 'Did you have to kill her? Did you really have to kill her?'

'I did,' Bee confirmed. Her eyes blazed at him . 'Because I am going to live.'

Per had hold of her upper arm and was staring at her with a mixture of awe and horror. I rolled off Cora's body and tried to rise but could not. The wounded leg would not bend and my other leg was shaky. Lant came to us. 'Step back,' he warned Prilkop in a deadly voice and hauled me to my feet. I was grateful for his roughness. I wanted no gentleness now.

The Fool's cry cut through the simmering tension. 'Why?'

Prilkop spoke before I could open my mouth. 'Why, indeed, did your Catalyst and his daughter murder Cora? You recall Cora, do you not? She smuggled messages for us.'

'Cora,' the Fool said quietly, and his face sagged and aged in that moment. 'Yes,' he said in a shaky voice. 'I recall her.'

'She attacked Bee!' I reminded all.

'She had no weapon!' Prilkop objected.

'We have no time!' Lant shouted the words. 'She is dead, as are many others. As we will all be dead, unless these stones come out. Prilkop! Come and work. Fool, you also. No time for recriminations or fond reunions. All of you come to the wall. Now!'

I looked down at Cora's body and felt no regret. She had tried to kill my child. I tilted my head toward the nasty black knife that lay by her body. One of their torture tools. 'There are tools for slicing human flesh on that rack near the table. Take what will work best on mortar.' I nudged Cora's knife feebly with my foot. 'Here's one for you, Prilkop.'

He gave me a stricken look and I almost regretted my words. But Bee stooped and took up Cora's black knife. She carried it to the wall and began scraping the mortar around the lowest block. The Fool made to follow.

'Fool. Will you help me?'

'How bad is your leg?'

'Not terrible. It's worse that my body is sapping my energy to heal it.'

'So the half-blind will lead the mostly lame?'

'It's supposed to be the other way round.' I set my arm across his shoulders. 'Watch your step,' I warned him and steered him around Cora's outflung arm.

'She was not a bad person,' the Fool observed softly. 'Bee destroyed her life. Everything she had ever known, the only task she knew how to do, all gone.'

'I don't regret it. Bee sprang like a hunting cat.'

Like a wolf.

'More like a wolf, I am sure,' the Fool said, and his echoing of Nighteyes put a shiver up my back. It was a shiver that made me smile.

Lant looked up and motioned us away from the work area. 'I didn't mean you. No room,' he said. As he spoke, Per and Spark rotated a heavy block of stone. It moved but did not come free. They went back to scraping. Working tools into the crevices to cut the mortar was slow work, as was dragging the freed block out. Above us, we heard something fall. I looked up at the ceiling.

'Do you think they're dead?' the Fool asked.

I didn't need to ask who. 'Dwalia and Vindeliar, yes. Bee killed Symphe. Fellowdy is a dead man, sooner or later, if he touched anything in Couttrie's chambers. And I think Bee stabbed him, at least once, in the corridor. Per cut Coultrie's throat. And Capra was still bleeding from your knife when last we saw her.' I said nothing of all the nameless people who would be dead in the fire.

He was silent for a moment. 'Two for Per: Vindeliar and Coultrie. Two for Bee: Symphe and Dwalia. Perhaps three, unless I claim Fellowdy. She only knifed him, but if they take him back to his chambers, he's sure to die.' His laugh was shaky. 'None for you, Fitz. My fine assassin.'

'And Spark set off the firepot that killed the guard troop. And Bee scared off the others.' I didn't mention the guardsmen I'd taken down in the melee. 'I've lost my edge, Fool. As I feared I had. Perhaps it's time to admit that. I should find a different line of work.'

'Nothing to be ashamed of in that,' he said, but it did not make me feel better. 'Later,' he added.

'Later, what?'

'Later, perhaps, when Bee is somewhere safe, we shall come back and be sure of all of them.'

'If a dragon does not do them first.'

A smile of pure pleasure broke over his face. 'The dragons may have them, if we have Bee.'

I nodded to that. I was so tired, and I had feared that his hunger for vengeance would still be unsated. But as he watched Bee scraping at mortar he seemed only pleased. As if having her with us had driven all other ambitions away from him.

I had seldom felt so useless as I did then. My hunger grew, and my thirst, but I tried to leave our scanty supply of water for those who laboured. When Lant dragged another stone out, I called to him, 'Can you see anything beyond the opening?'

'Lots of darkness,' he replied and went back to work.

At one point, the Fool helped me hobble over to the seats near the torture table. From there, I could better watch the work.

As soon as we moved, the three remaining Whites came to claim Cora's body. They carried her back to her cell and composed her on the straw mattress. Prilkop joined them and they spent a few silent moments standing by her body.

When I quietly commented on it to the Fool, he sighed. 'Our Bee is the Destroyer to them. They mourn the dead, here and above in the fire. Even more, they mourn the loss of generations of knowledge. So much destroyed. So much history gone.'

I looked over at him and thought him blind in so many ways. 'So many weapons destroyed,' I said quietly.

He did not reply to that. We listened to the others scraping mortar and muttering to one another. Lant pushed a poker under one end of a stone and put his weight on it. It did not move. 'Not yet,' he sighed and they went on with their scraping. But the next time he leaned on the lever, a stone broke free. The Fool helped me hobble closer to the work.

Lant reached into the opening, and the muscles stood out in his arms and chest as he gripped the block and pulled it toward him. It scraped, sawed and got stuck, then grated out toward us. It reached the tipping point and he jumped back as it slid out of the opening. With the Fool's help, I hop-limped over to join them.

'One more, and Per can slip through with a torch.'

Per nodded eagerly. He darted away and a short time later returned.

He'd wrapped rags from one of the cell mattresses around a torture poker and drenched them with oil from a lamp. Lant stepped back from the opening as Per kindled it and poked it through the hole. 'Not much to see. Ow!' he cried as the flames licked up toward his hand, and he dropped the torch.

Bee leaned in to peer into the darkness. She dragged her small body up and half into the hole. 'What do you see?' I asked her.

'Steps going down. Not much else.' She wriggled deeper into the hole and then abruptly dropped down on the other side.

'Bee!' I cried in alarm.

She stood up, torch in hand, and peered back at us. 'I'm fine.' She lifted the torch higher and I leaned into the opening. Broad steps led down into darkness. I smelled the sea, and soaked stone. I suspected standing water at the bottom of the steps. I had a glimpse of cut-stone walls and ceiling. The lower parts of the walls were speckled. 'I'm going down the steps, to see what I can see,' Bee announced.

'No,' I forbade her. I tried to seize her but could not reach her.

'Da,' she said, and the hollow beyond echoed her laughter strangely. Her voice was merry as she said, 'No one can tell me "no" any more. Not even you.' She started down the steps. 'I'll be back,' she promised.

My eyes met Lant's. He looked as stricken as I felt.

'I can fit through that hole. I'm sure of it,' Per declared, and pushed past Lant and me to thrust his head and shoulders into the gap. He withdrew, then tried again, leading with his clasped hands this time. 'Lift me and push!' he commanded in a muffled voice, and Lant obeyed. I heard Per's grunts and the scraping of fabric on stone. I dreaded that he would wedge, but after some struggle, Lant seized his kicking feet and pushed him through. I heard him tumble down a step or two. He stood and cried breathlessly, 'Bee, Bee, wait for me!'

'Take a sword!' Lant commanded him, and thrust one through the gap. Per took it and hastened away from us, his body blocking most of the dancing light that was Bee and her torch. 'Don't go far!'

He called something back to us, and was gone.

'They're brave,' Spark said, and I saw her measuring her body against the opening.

Lant caught her by the shoulder. 'Help us free one more stone. At most two. Then I think all of us can escape, if indeed it leads to freedom.'

'I wouldn't go without you,' she promised him and immediately began to dig at the next seam of mortar. After a moment, Lant knelt to pursue the seam adjacent to hers. I stood and stared into blackness. Shadows that were Per and Bee moved with the descending light. It grew smaller and then vanished. I waited, eyes straining, to see it again, but saw only darkness.

'Their torch has failed. We have to send Spark after them.' I hoped my voice did not shake too badly. I imagined a hundred evil things awaiting Bee.

'One more stone, and we can,' Lant promised me.

Time dragged and no one spoke. There was only the endless scraping of tools on mortar to mark the passing moments. Only darkness inside the hole. I wanted to pace. I could not. They worked in shifts, Lant and Spark, then two of the prisoners, then back to Lant and Spark. The ground away mortar sifted down the wall. Behind and above us, the fire muttered to itself.

'Stop!' Lant said suddenly. He leaned past the Whites who had been scraping away to peer into the opening. 'I see light! They're coming back.'

I pushed up beside him. The light danced toward us slowly, barely an ember in the darkness. Lant fashioned another torch and thrust it toward the hole. Now we could see more, but it was still some time before we saw Bee coming up the steps. 'Where's Per?' I called, dreading some disaster.

'He's trying to break an old wooden door,' she called, breathless as she climbed the steps. 'It's partly rotten, but we couldn't get past it. He poked the sword through between the planks and a tiny bit of light came in. So we think it's the way out! The tunnel steps go down, and then the floor slopes down. We had to wade through water for a long way. I cut my feet on some barnacles, but then Per cut one of his sleeves away so I could bind my feet. Then we came to steps going up. A lot of them, going up and up and finally the door. Per said it might have been a guard post once. He said he didn't mind the dark, but I'll want light for going back. We need pokers for levers. Or an axe. We will work on the door while you work on the bricks here.'

It was a sensible plan. I hated it.

We passed the smallest pot-lamp through to her and I surrendered the ship's hatchet. Bee hugged the lamp to her chest, the hatchet and a poker tucked awkwardly under her arm. I watched her carry it away as if I were watching her leave the world.

'The ceiling is burning through,' the Fool said quietly. 'I smell it. And it's getting warmer in here.'

'Work faster,' Lant suggested, and they all did. When Lant judged there was enough purchase for the poker, he pushed it under the stone. 'A moment,' Prilkop suggested, and inserted a bar of his own. 'Now,' he said, and both men leaned on their levers. The stone was adamant.

Behind me, a small piece of the ceiling fell, landing on the torture table and the steps where I had rested. Flames were dancing on it as it came down. The floors here were of stone, as were the walls, but that would be small comfort to us if burning rubble fell on us. I had gained a fearful respect for smoke and heat. We stared wide-eyed at one another.

'Let me help!' Spark cried. She stepped up and balanced on one of the pokers like a bird perching on a twig. 'Now push down,' she told Lant. He and Prilkop leaned on their bars. With a slow crackling sound, the stone moved upward slightly. Prilkop shoved his bar deeper and leaned on it, groaning. The stone grated as it rose out of its bed. It tipped then lodged, making the opening even smaller than it had been. The prisoner who had first come to help pushed the stone deeper into the opening with all his skeletal weight. The stone slid into the maw of the tunnel. It almost but not completely cleared the opening.

Lant threw down his bar and eeled into the darkness. One of the prisoners squirmed in beside him, contributing his feeble strength to move the stone. 'Help me,' the skinny White gasped, and a second crawled through to join him. I heard Lant grunt, then groan and the grinding noise as the stone grudgingly moved. Slowly an escape opened before us. The two prisoners quickly wriggled through and out of the way. Lant joined them on the other side and then turned around.

Lant's face appeared in the opening. 'Quick. Come through,' he commanded Spark, and stepped back to make room for her. But as she stepped forward, the last prisoner suddenly threw herself at the opening. Fast as a startled rat, she was through. I heard Lant's exclamation of surprise and then he cursed. 'They've run ahead,' he complained. That alarmed me; I did not trust any of them.

'Lant. Go after them!' I begged him.

'Sword,' he demanded, and Spark stooped, seized one, and passed it to him.

'I'm going, too,' she declared, and slid into the gap, her sword leading the way.

'Bring my pack!' she called over her shoulder and then raced down the steps and into darkness. Lant was already out of sight. I had to go after her.

I tried to stand and my leg folded under me. The Fool caught my arm and pulled me upright. It simply would not take my weight. Fury welled in me and for a moment I could not even speak. When I had control of myself, I lifted my eyes to Prilkop. 'Will they hurt Bee? Do they mean her harm?' I demanded of him.

Prilkop had picked up the last pot-lamp in his arms. He looked from me to the Fool and chewed his lip. 'I hope not,' he offered me. 'But they are very frightened. And angry. It's hard to say what people will do when they are scared.'

'Can you go after them and stop them?' the Fool asked.

'I don't know if they'll listen to . . .' he began.

'Try!' the Fool cried, and Prilkop nodded brusquely. He pushed the lamp to one side and squeezed stiffly through the opening. On the other side, he laboriously took up the lamp and went down the steps, far more slowly than I wished him to.

'Go,' I told the Fool.

'I can see nothing in there except the flame of the lamp,' he complained. He groped to find the tunnel's mouth and then clambered spryly over the wall. 'I'm handing you a sword,' I told him. I did a slow bend to pick it up and passed it through to him. The blade had not been improved by the use we'd made of it. The ceiling groaned behind me. I spared a backwards glance. A large section of it was sagging.

'Don't wait for me. Touch the wall and go down the steps to the bottom. I'll be right behind you.' The Fool nodded grimly and turned away from me to venture off into a darkness he could not see.

We'd need a torch. I began my limping circuit of the wall, passing

Spark's pack, next to my firepot harness on the steps. I'd get them on my way back. I edged on, gimping from wall to table. At last, I seized a chair and used it as a bulky cane. The deeper I went into the room, the more my eyes stung. By the time I reached the cells and the crude mattress there I knew I'd made a bad decision. Bits of ceiling were flaking and floating in the air.

I dragged the thin mattress onto the chair. Scraping the chair over the floor, I began my journey back. My eyes were closed to slits, and to take a deep breath invited a coughing fit. A piece of ceiling the size of a pony collapsed onto the upper stairs. I looked up at it in time to see another section giving way. As it came down, I threw up my arm to shield my face from the wash of heat. The smoke in the room billowed toward me. I pushed the chair frantically toward the opening in the wall, all thoughts of a torch abandoned. With a groan, a beam fell almost beside me, charred and glowing along its length. A flame leapt up as if rejoicing in its freedom and ran along the fallen timber. Another followed. Paragon's words came back to me. *In water and fire, in wind and darkness. Not swiftly.* Was this my time to die? As if to confirm that thought, a big piece of ceiling fell. The gust of hot wind knocked me over, chair and all. I sprawled on the floor, temporarily blinded and disoriented. I rubbed my sleeve over my eyes. Which way was the opening to the tunnel?

'Fitz? Where are you? Fitz?'

The Fool? I closed my stinging eyes and dragged myself over the cinder-littered floor toward his voice. I bumped into the table, and called, 'Fool?'

'Here! This way!'

I reached the wall. I felt his hands plucking at the back of my shirt and hauled myself up and into the opening. With him pulling and me clawing, I tumbled through into cooler air. He followed me more gracefully. 'What were you doing?' he demanded.

'I wanted a torch.'

'You nearly became one.'

I opened my eyes, wiped them on my sleeve, rubbed them, and opened them again. The scarlet light from the fire in the dungeons behind us gave an unearthly illumination to the worked stone walls and the arched ceiling above us.

'Up you go,' the Fool said. He dragged my arm across his shoulder and stood up. Together we stumbled to where I could put one hand on the wall. I lurched down a step, then two.

'Your legs are wet.'

'There's water at the bottom of the steps. And barnacles on the walls, too. And the tide's coming in, Fitz.'

We both knew what that meant. I let the cold dread creep into me and then asked him, 'Do you think they'll hurt Bee? The Whites who ran ahead.'

He was panting with the effort of helping me descend another step. 'I don't think they can. They're no match for Spark or Lant. For that matter, I don't think Per would let any harm befall her.'

'A moment,' I said, and leaned on the wall to cough smoke from my lungs. When I could draw a full breath, I straightened up. 'Let's go,' I told him. With every step we lurched down, the red light from the burning dungeon room offered less illumination.

'Da?' Bee's small voice floated up to me from the darkness. Both the Fool and I startled. I peered down the steps into a well of increasing darkness. A feeble light glimmered down there.

'Bee? I'm here, with the Fool.' To him, I said, 'Leave me. Go to her,' and he started down the steps.

The light became a dying torch. It bobbed as she reached the bottom of the steps. The light was reflected in standing water around her ankles. She raised her voice in an anxious shout. 'Da, Per broke through the door! Per said we would wait for everyone else. But the prisoners ran up to us, all wet from the tunnel. They were angry. If Per had not been there with his sword— I tried to turn their minds, but I could not.' She paused for breath.

'Per threatened them with the sword, and they ran away. Then Spark came, and Lant. Per told them what happened, and Spark ran after them to kill them. Lant told us to stay where we were and went after Spark. Da, those Whites will run right back to Clerres and tell where we are. I came to warn you: they will come in force and kill us all! Per stayed to guard the door. He'll stop them there if he can.'

Her voice did not shake until the end of her report. As she started up the steps I saw she was wet to her hips. She had come to us through deeper water? How high would it reach? Did we dare attempt to escape that way? As she climbed the steps toward us, her torch revealed old watermarks and barnacles on the wall.

How high could it reach? I didn't like my conclusion. A high tide could come halfway up the steps, completely filling the tunnel below.

Behind us, fire. Below us, rising water. No good choices.

Then the chamber behind me exploded and I flew through darkness.

THIRTY-SEVEN

Touch

The appearance of the Pocked Man is always a harbinger of disaster to come. He was seen not only in Buckkeep Town, but in Grimsbyford and Sandsedge in the weeks before the Blood Plague reached the Six Duchies and devastated our folk. He was seen standing on the balcony of the doomed Fins Tower two days before the earthquake that brought it down on the town. Some have claimed to have seen him immediately before the first Forging at Forge. On the night that King Shrewd was assassinated, the Pocked Man was seen in the washing court and by the castle well in Buckkeep Castle. He always appears as a cadaverous man, pale of countenance, his face marked with red pox.

Six Duchies lore

'Fitz? Fitz? Bee? BEE!' A pause. 'FITZ! She's hurt! Fitz! Damn you, where are you?'

I didn't recall lying down. Had he been calling my name, over and over? I was woozy and tired. The Fool's voice came from far away. 'I'm here,' I replied slowly. Ringing silence answered me. Absolute darkness all around me. 'Fool? Is that you?'

'Yes. Don't move. I'm coming to you. Keep talking.'

'I'm here. I'm . . . I can't get up. There's something on top of me.' I reached for my last memory. Clerres. A tunnel. Bee! 'What happened? Where are Bee and the others?'

'I have Bee!' The Fool's voice was a drawn-out wail. 'She's alive but not aware!'

'Be careful! Don't move—'

657

Too late. I heard him scrabble over loose rubble and then felt his groping touch. Wheezing with pain, he sat down heavily near me. I reached for him and found Bee's small, slack body in his arms. 'Eda and El, no! Not this way, not when we are so close! Fool. Is she breathing?'

'I think so. I can feel fresh blood but I'm not sure where it comes from. Fitz, Fitz, what are we to do?'

'First, be calm.' I tried to move closer to him. I could not. My legs were pinned to the earth. I was on my back. Slowly awareness crept back to me through my panic. My head was lower than my feet. The steps. I had fallen on the steps. And something was on top of my legs just above my knees. I groped toward it but could barely reach it with my fingertips. I tightened my belly muscles and tried to sit up toward it. My back screamed and I gave it up. 'Fool, there's something on top of my legs. I can't get up. Set Bee down carefully. Let me touch her.'

I could hear his uneven breathing as he lowered my child to a rubble-strewn step beside me. 'Are you hurt?' I thought to ask him.

'Far less than I deserve to be. It's my foot, the one they smashed. It's dragging. Oh, Fitz, she is still so small! After all she has been through, must we lose her now?'

'Be steady, Fool.' I had not heard him so emotional since Shrewd died. I forced a calm I didn't feel into my own voice. I could not allow him to panic. 'You must be her strength now. Here is my hand. Set it on her head.'

The darkness was complete. I touched her hair, her ears, nose and mouth. Scars, yes, but no fresh blood from her ears and nose. I next checked her chest and belly. Then I cautiously patted each of her limbs. I ventured along the Skill-thread we shared. I found her awareness, curled small but whole. 'Fool, she is just stunned. Her shoulder is damp, but it's not very warm. It may be only water. Unless . . . is it your blood?'

'Oh. Perhaps. My scalp is bleeding. And I think my shoulder.'

Worse and worse. I had to focus. Order my thoughts. 'Fool, I know what happened. Spark's pack was left behind in the dungeon. She had some of Chade's firepots in it. At least one exploded when the ceiling fell on them. There may be more back there. We must get Bee out of here. Immediately. Help me get free.'

'What of Bee? Can you wake her?'

'Why? So she can be frightened with us? Fool, she will wake on her own soon enough. Let us be ready before she does. Help me get free.'

His hands moved down my belly and then over my thighs. 'A beam came down,' he said quietly. 'It's across your legs. With rubble on top of it.' His hands touched my leg and tried to push under it. I clenched my teeth against the pain that woke. He moved his hand under my leg and tried to force it between my flesh and the edge of the stair. 'You are pinned against the stone steps. I can't dig anything away from underneath you.'

Our mutual silence was a second darkness. I had my hand on Bee's chest. I could feel it rise and fall. She lived. I heard the Fool swallow. I spoke past the ringing in my ears.

'Bee is what matters now, Fool. Remember? We agreed on this. If it came to a choice and you had to make it? The dividing place is now, and there is no choice. You cannot save me. Pick her up and carry her out of here, while you still can. Because if the fire reaches another firepot the rest of the ceiling may come down. And we know the water is rising in the tunnel. No time to wait. Go now.'

I heard him trying to catch his breath in the silence. 'Fitz, I can't.'

'You must. There's no time to argue. I'll say it for you. You don't want to leave me here to die. *I* don't want you to leave me here to die. But you must and you will. I'm done for. Save my child. Save our child.'

'But . . . I can't . . .' He sobbed in a breath. 'My foot is broken again. And my shoulder is bleeding a lot, Fitz. A lot.'

'Come here. Let me feel it.' I tried to speak calmly. I did not feel calm at all.

'I'm right here,' he said.

I had a moment of absolute clarity and inspiration. I felt his hands touch my face, one gloved, one with bare fingertips. Perfect. I reached up and caught his gloved wrist and held it tight. 'You can,' I said, as I peeled the glove from his hand. 'And you will. Take what's left of me, Fool, and save Bee.'

'What?' he demanded. And then, as he realized my intent, he struggled, but with his shoulder torn he had no real strength. I pressed his silvered fingers to the side of my throat. I felt it then, an ecstasy that burned but filled me with joy. Then the connection came, just as it had that time in Verity's tower room. 'Too much', I had said then, and fled from it. Now I wrapped it with my awareness. I felt the Fool and saw his sparkling tumble of life and secrets like the stars in a night sky. No, not taking from him. His secrets were always his to keep. How to do this? He was trying to pull his hand clear of my grip, but I was doing the last thing I expected to do with my life, so I had to do it thoroughly. There could be no mercy for either of us. I threw my other arm around him, pulled him into a hard embrace and held him tight despite his struggles. The boundaries between us gave way. We were merging in a way that felt like a healing. I sensed the torn meat of his shoulder, knew a striating crack in the bone there and the stabbing pain of the little broken bones in his foot. I spoke into his panting mouth. 'Be still. Don't fight me. This must happen.'

I drew a breath and held it. Gripping his wrist hard, I embraced him with more than my arms. As I breathed out hard, I pushed my strength, my healing, my all through the connection I had forced. I recalled how I had taken strength from Riddle. *Let it flow the other way*, I thought, and poured it into him. I needed nothing of what was left. I touched the damage inside him. He shuddered at the pain, and went still.

You leave little for us, my brother.

All the more to save Bee.

The Fool lay stunned in my arms, sprawled on my chest. His resistance was gone. I let my fingers walk over his shoulder. Shirt and skin were torn. The hanging flap of flesh dizzied me. I lifted it into place, held it firmly there, sealed it. Bone be whole and flesh be knit. I healed him fiercely, as swiftly as I could force it, sparing neither of us.

You should go with him, Nighteyes. You should go with Bee.

If we end here, then I meet the end with you. As you ended with me.

How is the hunting where you are?

It will be better with you.

I'm coming to you, my brother.

I willed my Skill into the Fool's body. All of it. I forced his ankle to straighten, pushed the tendon to where Chade's old books had showed me it was supposed to be. *Be made right*, I commanded it, and with my Skill went my strength. I felt myself dwindle. The Fool stirred, then shuddered at the pain; he fainted again. Good. He could not fight me.

But I had a last struggle—with myself. I felt myself soaking into him. If I let go, we would be what I had glimpsed when I had called him back from death. I'd be home, with him. A whole thing. But no.

That was not a decision for you to make. I would not go with you.

I know. I know.

The Fool had to live on as himself. He had to save Bee, not me. We had promised one another.

My arm fell away from him. I peeled my awareness away from him. With the last of my strength, I found Bee's curly little head and set my hand on it. *Eda protect you,* I prayed to a god I'd never known. I found the Skill-thread to her, snapped it. Then, with certainty, I whispered, 'The Fool will save you.'

He was already stirring. Time to leave. Time to make this choice mine, not his. I sighed out a final breath and found Nighteyes waiting for me.

Are you ready, my brother?

Yes. I sank into the nothing.

THIRTY-EIGHT

Ship of Dragons

The white prophet Gerda was barely twenty when she set out into the world to find her Catalyst. She had dreamed of her often since she was an infant. She travelled far from the peaceful green lands of her birth, going both by sea and by land, to a village far in the mountains where a peak smoked in the distance and glowed red at night.

She came to Cullena's home. Cullena was a grandmother who lived with her son and his wife. During the day while her children hunted and fished, she had the care of their seven youngsters. This Cullena did without complaint, though her bones ached and her eyes were dimming. Gerda came to her home and sat down on the doorstep and would not go. Cullena did not know why she had come, or why she would not leave. 'Here is food for you, and now you must depart,' she told Gerda.

But at nightfall, the White Prophet was still there.

'You may sleep by the fire, for the nights are cold, but in the morning you must go,' she said to Gerda.

But in the morning, Gerda sat once more on the doorstep.

Finally Cullena said to her, 'If you must be here, be of some use. Sit and churn the milk to make the butter, or rock the cradle for the squalling baby or stitch the furs into winter cloaks, for we are not far from a time of snow.'

And all of these things Gerda did, without complaint or recompense other than food to eat and a place by the fire. She served a folk not her own just as Cullena had. And so Cullena's family came to love her. Gerda taught the children, too, to read and to write and to understand numbers and amounts and distances. She kept Cullena alive for many a year, and in turn Cullena let her stay, and as years passed

Gerda taught the children of the children as well, to the number of forty children.

And then, their children.

Thus did she change the world, for from among those she taught a woman arose who brought her people together, and they raised sturdy homes and clever children. They lived with the forest instead of upon it, caring for their territory and their people. They served one another well. A descendant of that woman became a man who was a servant to all of the folk who lived in those mountains, and in that way he led them.

As did those who came after him, each one taking up the mantle of one who leads by serving.

And thus did the White Prophet Gerda change the world.

Accounts of the Prophets of Old

I remembered when I was cold and Revel was carrying me into the house. We were going down steps. But I was wet-cold, not snow-cold. My feet were dragging in water. Or was it snow? I lifted my head from his shoulder. 'Revel?' I whispered into the scintillating light.

'Bee? You're awake?' The light was talking to me. It was a nexus, shimmering with possible futures. It was not Revel. This light was a jabbing, glittering thing, stabbing and prickling me. I tightened my muscles to fling myself away but it spoke again, 'Don't do that. It's dark here and water is coming into the tunnel. You took a bad fall. You've been unconscious.'

'Put me down! It's too much!'

'Too much?' he whispered. He sounded confused.

I put up my walls but it did not dim. The light did not illuminate, it blinded. So many possibilities striating out from this moment. 'Let me go!' I begged him.

Still he hesitated. 'Are you sure? The water will be deep for you. Perhaps chest-deep. And it's cold.'

'Too many paths!' I shouted at him. 'Let me go, put me down, let me go!'

'Oh, Bee,' he said, and I knew him. The blind beggar from the marketplace. The one my father called Fool. Beloved, come to save me. I did not like how slowly he lowered me into the water, but he was right. It came to the bottom of my ribs and was cold enough to make me catch my breath.

I stepped back from him and nearly fell. He caught at the ragged shoulder of my shirt. I let him hold onto it. Blessed darkness wrapped me. 'Where is Per?' He was the first safe person who came to mind. Then, 'Where is my father?'

'You left Per at the mouth of the tunnel. We will reach there soon. I hope. It's slow going. Wading against the water is work.' Carefully he asked me, 'Do you remember where we are and what happened?'

'Some of it.' I wished he would speak louder. My ears were full of a ringing. My father had probably gone ahead with the others. To catch the fleeing Whites. I wished he had not left me. I took a step, stumbled, splashed and stood upright.

'I can still carry you if you wish.'

'No. I'd rather walk. Don't you understand? When you touch me, you make me see all the paths. All of them, at once!'

He was silent. Or was he? 'Talk louder!' I begged him.

'I saw nothing when I carried you. No paths. Only the dark that we move through, Bee. Take my hand. Let me lead you.' I felt his fingers brush my bare arm. I twitched away from him.

'I can follow your voice.'

'This way, Bee,' he said with a sigh and began to walk away from me. Beneath the cold water the floor was flat but gritty under my feet. I held my arms above the water. It was hard to take a deep breath that way. I followed him for a few steps and then asked again, 'Where is my father?'

'Back there, Bee. You know there was a fire, and you know about the firepots we carried. There was an explosion, and the ceiling collapsed. Your father . . . it came down on him.'

I stopped walking. With chill water to my waist, with dark all round me, a different, colder sort of darkness was rising inside me. I found there was something beyond pain and fear. That something was filling me.

'I know,' he said hoarsely. But I knew he could not possibly know what I was feeling. He spoke on. 'We must hurry. I carried you down a slope and the water got deeper. Now we are on the level, but the water is still rising. It's the tide coming in. This tunnel may fill completely. We cannot tarry.'

'My father is dead? How? How can he be dead and you be alive?'

'Walk,' he commanded me. He began to slosh forward again and

I followed him. I heard him take a breath and then after something that sounded like a sob, he said thickly, 'Fitz is dead.' He tried to continue speaking but could not. Eventually, he said, 'He and I both knew it might come down to a choice. You heard him say as much. I promised that I would choose you. It was his wish.' In a choked voice he asked me, 'Do you recall your dream of the scales?'

'I have to go back to him!'

He was fast. Even in the dark, he caught my wrist and gripped it tight. I staggered from the light, and then he had me by the back of my shirt. 'I can't allow that. There is no time and there is no point. He was dead when we left him, Bee. I heard no breath from him; I felt no beat of his heart. Did you think I would leave him alive and trapped?' His voice had started out tight and level, but it ended wild. His breathing was hoarse and echoed. 'The last thing I can do for him is take you out of here. Now we go.' He walked on, half-dragging me through the water. I kicked but could not fight him. I tried to twist out of his grip. 'Don't,' he said, and it was a plea. 'Bee, don't make me force you. I don't want to.' His voice broke on the words. 'It is as much as I can do to force myself to go on. I wish I could go back and be dead beside him. But I have to take you out of here! Why did Lant let you come back alone?' He sounded grieved about that. As if I were a helpless little girl. Or it could be someone else's fault.

'He didn't,' I pointed out. 'I told Per to stay and guard the door while I came back to warn you.'

'What of Prilkop?' he demanded suddenly.

'I passed him on my way to warn you.'

'How much farther to the door?'

'We're on the flat part. Then we come to a place where the floor slopes up. Then the long stairs. Then a small flat place and more stairs to the door. Did it . . . crush him?'

'Bee,' he said very softly.

'He said he wouldn't leave me again!'

He said nothing.

'He can't be dead!' I wailed.

'Bee. You know that he is.'

Did I? I felt for him, inside my mind. I lowered my walls and groped to where he had been. No Wolf Father. And the connection he had shared with me since he had touched my head . . . gone. 'He's dead.'

'Yes.'

That was the most terrible word I had ever heard. I reached out and caught the sleeve of his shirt. I held to it and together we walked faster, as if we could run away from his death.

The floor had remained level but the water was getting deeper. We walked on through the blackness. Water sloshed around my chest. The floor began to slant upwards, but the water still became deeper.

'Faster,' he said, and I tried.

'What's going to become of me?' I asked suddenly. It was a terrible, selfish question. My father was dead and I wanted to know what would happen to me?

'I'll take care of you. And the first thing I will do is get you out of here to the ship that will take us somewhere safe. And then I'll get you home.'

'Home,' I said, but the word was hollow. What was home? 'I want Per!'

'We're going to Per. Hurry.' He halted, pulled his sleeve down over his hand, and then seized mine. He dragged me through the rising water, moving so quickly that my feet barely touched the floor. He stumbled when we came to the first shallow step, and we both fell in the water. But in a moment he was on his feet and we were climbing the steps, fleeing the water that seemed to be chasing us. The steps were unevenly spaced. I banged my ankles and tripped and hit my shins. He didn't let go of my hand but dragged me relentlessly on. For a long time, we climbed steps, but the water got shallower very slowly.

'Is that light?' he asked suddenly.

I squinted. 'Not daylight. It's a lamp.'

'I can see it.' His voice trembled as if someone were shaking him. 'Per? Lant?'

It was Lant. He came down the steps to us, holding the small lamp in one hand and his sword in the other. His face was a mask of light and shadow above it. 'Bee? Fitz? Fool? Why were you so slow to follow? We feared the worst!' He came sloshing toward us, talking as he came. 'I feared you were trapped in the tunnel. Only a few more steps and you'll be out of the water. Spark has not come back. She outran me. I came back in time to see Prilkop running away. I would have had to kill him to stop him. Per remains on guard at the door.' His explanation rattled from his lips. Then, as his light reached us, 'Where is Fitz?'

Fool took a breath. 'Not with us,' he said.

'But . . .' Lant stared at him and then looked down at me. I could not bear his expression. I hid my face in Beloved's shirt. 'No,' Lant said on a hoarse exhalation Then, 'How?'

'There was an explosion. The beams of the tunnel came down. Fitz is gone, Lant.'

They were moving as they spoke climbing the steps slowly as if they carried something heavy between them. Lant stopped suddenly. The light wavered as his shoulder's shook. He made a choking sound.

'NO!' Beloved said savagely. He grabbed his shoulder and shook him so that the lamp's light danced. 'No. Not here. Not now. Neither of us can feel that. When she is safe, we can grieve. For now, we plan and we survive. Swallow it, put your head up and walk on!'

Lant did. He took a noisy breath and then strode on. I walked between them and then behind them, trying to comprehend that my father was gone. Again. But he would not return this time. I recalled the dream of the scales. I had known, in some part of myself, that he might buy my life with his. But with every breath I exhaled, something inside me grew heavier. Guilt, fault, grief, or a terrible mixture of those things. I did not weep. Tears would have been too small, an insult to the size of loss I'd taken. I wanted to bleed my sorrow, to let the pain of it drain out with my life.

Lant suddenly glanced back at me. 'Bee, I am so sorry.'

'You didn't kill him. He traded his life for mine.'

He stumbled slightly. Then he said, 'Get up on my back, Bee. We will go faster.'

I thought of refusing, but I was so tired. He stooped and I climbed up. I put my arms around Lant's neck, trying not to choke him. I wondered if the rising tide had filled the tunnel behind us. Would it slosh around my father's body? Would little blind fishes come to eat him?

With me riding on Lant's back, we went more quickly. The steps grew steeper and the water receded. Then, in the distance, I saw a very small light. It was bobbing as it came toward us. 'Get down, Bee,' Lant said in a low voice. I slid from his back and he stepped in front of Beloved and I, his sword ready.

But it was Spark with a brushwood torch. 'I chased them through the bushes and down the hill, to the edge of the town. I couldn't chase them through the streets with a sword. They got away. Where's Prilkop?'

'Per said he arrived after me, and then ran off toward the town. Per stayed to guard the tunnel mouth.'

'I never saw Prilkop! Where is Fitz?' She was close enough now to see that no one followed us.

'Dead.' Lant delivered the news bluntly.

I admitted my guilt. 'He traded his life for mine.'

Spark made a choking sound. Lant put his arm around her. It was as much comfort as anyone could give her. We hurried on.

When the flame on the brushwood torch burned out, Spark flung it against the side of the tunnel. I understood that gesture. 'Where are we going?' I asked in a whisper.

Beloved answered me. 'Out of this tunnel onto a low hillside behind the town, then through the town to the docks. A boat should be waiting for us there. I hope. From there, we go to a ship named Paragon. And then across a lot of water. And home.' He sounded utterly discouraged. He drew a breath. 'Home. We're going home, Bee.'

'Withywoods?' I asked him softly.

He hesitated. 'If that is what you wish.'

'Where else could I go?'

'Buckkeep Castle.'

'Maybe,' I said. 'But not Withywoods. I know too many dead people there.'

He nodded. 'I understand that.'

The adults were walking fast. I caught at his cuff to help me keep pace with them. 'My sister is at Buckkeep Castle,' I told him. 'Nettle. And Riddle.'

'Yes. And they have a new baby! Your father told me. He said, "I'm a grandfather now" . . .' His words faltered to a halt.

'A new baby?' I exclaimed in dismay. It suddenly hurt my feelings. I tried to understand why. There would be no room for me in her life now. Nettle had been my sister, mine, a few moments ago. Now she was somebody's mother. And Riddle would have his own little girl.

'Her name is Hope.'

'What?'

'Your niece. Hope is her name.'

I could think of nothing to say. He said wistfully, 'It will be nice for you to have people to go home to. Your sister. And Riddle. I really like Riddle.'

'So do I,' I agreed.

Spark spoke over her shoulder. 'We're nearly at the door,' she said. 'We need to go quietly now. Lant and I will go first, to see what might be waiting. Fool will guard you, Bee. Stay here.'

I nodded but all the same I took out Symphe's knife and held it, as my father had taught me. A smile twisted her mouth to see me do that. 'Good,' she whispered. Beloved set down the lamp. Spark and Lant ghosted toward a pale-grey light interrupted by bushy shadows.

But no one was waiting in ambush for us. Only Per, hatchet in hand, standing just inside the chopped door. 'Bee!' he exclaimed as soon as he saw me. He rushed to me and hugged me hard, weapons still in his hands. I hugged him back and then held tight to him. I spoke next to his ear. 'Per. My da is dead. The ceiling fell on him. We had to leave him back there.'

'No!' he cried out low, holding me tighter. He breathed harsh, his chest heaving within my embrace. When he spoke again, his voice was angry and fierce. 'Don't be afraid, Bee. I'm still here. I'll protect you.'

'To the ship,' Lant said. 'No tarrying. Not for anything.'

The doors had pushed earth and leaves and the cloaking vegetation aside. No one had guarded this way, or even tended this door, in a very long time. 'So arrogant,' Lant whispered as he worked his way gingerly through the tangle of thistles and climbing vine. 'I doubt they've ever been attacked before.'

'They always believed they could see disaster coming and avoid it,' Beloved said. 'Change the future to save themselves. They knew something of the Destroyer, but I doubt they expected a small girl; I doubt they understood they would bring it all on themselves.' He added, 'And the actions of the Unexpected Son were, as always, unexpected. Fitz had a way of tumbling all their pieces from the gameboard. For a time longer, we may be in their blind spot. Fitz bought this time for us. We must not waste it.'

`Fitz had, I thought to myself. Not Fitz has. Never again. I felt Per's grip on my hand tighten and knew that we shared that thought. We followed them out into a sunny day. I blinked incredulously. I

Robin Hobb

felt it had been a year since I left my cell. Deep grass surrounded the neglected entry to the tunnel and no clear trail led away from it. The tasselled heads of the tall grasses glistened with dew. We could clearly see the trampled grass where the Whites and then Prilkop had gone down toward the town.

'Let me take your arm,' Spark said to Beloved. 'We need to move quickly.'

'I can see. As I once did. Perfectly.'

'How?' Lant demanded.

'Fitz,' he said quietly. He stepped clear of the brambles and looked around him as if the world were a wonder. 'As he was dying. He did a last healing. On me. I suspect it took every last bit of strength he had.' He looked down at me and added, 'I did not ask him for that. I did not want it. But he knew he was trapped. He chose to spend what life he had left on me.'

I looked up at him. He was changed from the first time I had seen him. He was thinner, almost gaunt. The battering his face had taken was almost gone. And he stood differently. It came to me slowly. Nothing hurt inside him any more.

I looked away from him. I was still trying to understand what I felt when Lant spoke, his voice emptied of emotion. 'We need to get to the ship as quickly as possible. We must try to be seen as little as possible. We don't know if the White prisoners or Prilkop have rallied folk against us. So we will assume they have. Per, if we are attacked take Bee and run. Don't stay to fight. Take her, hide with her, and stay there until you can get to the boat and the ship.'

'I don't like that,' I said bluntly. 'Do you think I can't fight? Do you think I didn't fight?'

Per's angry face mirrored mine.

Lant looked down on me. 'It doesn't matter if you like it. My father charged me to protect Fitz. I didn't. I won't lose you, too, Bee. Not unless I go down in my own blood. So, to make that less likely, obey me. Please.' He added the last word as a courtesy, with no plea in it. Per gave a tight nod and I knew I'd have no choice. Months of being on my own. It wasn't even noon and I was relegated to being a child again.

'I will choose our path,' Beloved said. Lant started to object, but he added, 'I once knew every alley in this town well. I can get you to the harbour, and few will mark our passage.'

670

Lant nodded curtly and we fell in behind him. We pushed our way clear of the brambles into a sheep pasture on a hill above the town. From our vantage I looked down at a town that seemed unaware of any disaster. Wagons creaked through the streets. I saw a ship coming into port. The wind off the water brought me the smell of roasting meat from someone's kitchen. The wet grasses slapped against me, soaking me and slicing my bare legs as we strode on. Were the fishermen setting out for the day's work? Did they not know what I had done in the night? How could their lives be so ordinary when my father was dead? How could the whole world not be as broken as I was? I lifted my eyes to Clerres Castle. And there saw thin tendrils of smoke still rising from my handiwork. I smiled. They, at least, would share some of my pain.

Lant spoke. 'This is odd. Don't they see that smoke and wonder what happened there?' He was silent, brows gathered in thought.

I moved closer to Beloved and asked him, 'Where do you think Prilkop went?'

'I truly don't know,' he said, and I heard sadness and a fear of betrayal. 'And we don't have time to worry about him.'

I defended him. 'He's a good man. He was kind to me. I want to believe he was really my friend.'

'I know that. So do I. But good men can disagree. Severely. Now don't talk. We need to move quickly and quietly.'

He led us by a roundabout path, past empty sheep-pens and through a part of the town where vine-covered walls hid gardens and fancy houses. We entered a narrow lane, and trotted past smaller houses and humble cottages. We came to a muddy, rutted road that snaked down to the warehouses. The streets were bereft of people. 'They'll be at the entry to the causeway, asking one another what is happening,' Beloved predicted softly.

I trotted at Per's side as the adults stretched their strides. I was barefoot and my wet trousers slapped against my legs. A man pushing a barrow stopped and scowled to watch us pass. But he did not cry out, or point at us or chase us. 'Run now,' Beloved commanded us quietly, and we did. We dashed past two old women carrying baskets of vegetables and exclaiming loudly about the rising smoke. An apprentice in a leather apron ran across our path, in too much of a hurry to notice us. We came to the harbour road. I had a terrible stitch in my side, but still we ran. We passed other people, but they were all going in the opposite direction. All bound for the end of the road and the causeway to Clerres Castle as Beloved had predicted.

Smoke was rising from behind the castle walls, dark against a blue sky. A fleet of small fishing vessels, some with sails and some oared, were visible on the water. They came around the curve of the castle's promontory, sailing into view as calmly as seabirds.

The docks rang hollow under our pounding steps. We reached the end. I bent over, gasping, my hands on my knees. 'Thank Eda and El,' Lant said in a shaky voice. I took two steps and looked down. Four sailors in a boat, three drowsing in cramped curls in the bottom. But as we clambered down, they woke rapidly and moved to take their places at the oars.

'Where's Fitz?' one asked.

'Not coming,' Lant said tersely.

The tattooed warrior who had asked nodded sagely and tossed her head in the direction of the island. 'I figured that for his handiwork when I first saw the flames last night.' She stared at Beloved's face then shook her head wordlessly. Her eyes came to rest on me. 'So you're the little baggage all this is about?'

'She is,' Lant said, saving me the trouble of replying. He sounded almost proud of me as he added, 'And she's the one who set the fires!'

The sailor woman tossed me a damp woollen blanket, 'Well done, sprite! Well done.' To the other sailors, she said, 'Pull. I think we want to be well away from here as fast as we can.'

The increasing light showed two thin trickles of smoke and one fat black one still rising. The outer walls of the keep prevented us from seeing how much damage I'd done. But I smiled to myself, trusting it was enough. There was little for them to rescue. I was certain of that.

I took a seat next to Per. Spark crouched in the bottom of the boat next to Lant. The warriors bent to their oars. The woman spoke as she pulled. 'Very late last night, I saw flames. Only for a short time. Some of the folk in town came out of their houses and shouted a bit, but then the city guard turned out and chased them all back in. They shut down the taverns, too. We heard all the shouting. "Go home and stay there." And like sheep, they all went! We pushed in under the docks and stayed quiet. We thought you'd all come running then, but no. Before dawn, I saw the lights of three boats come around the far side of the island and go to the shore. I thought they would sound an alarm, turn out the guard. But, nothing.' She shrugged.

Beloved sat up. 'Nothing they'd let you see. But there will be something, I fear.' His face was grim.

The woman nodded. 'Lean into it,' she told her sailors and they rowed faster.

All four were powerful rowers. They bent to their oars and their muscles bunched and slacked in unison as if they were the muscles of a single powerful creature rather than four separate warriors. There were several large vessels anchored in the harbour. We passed one, and then two, and finally I could see the ship we were bound for. The sails were furled and all seemed quiet aboard it. But I saw a small figure in the crow's nest stand up, and then silently scamper down the mast. The lookout raised no cry and I suspected that was intentional. As we approached I saw several sailors looking over the railing.

We came around the side and I saw the figurehead. I could not help it. My father looked down on us, a very slight smile on his face. I burst into tears.

Per grabbed me and held me tight. His chest rose and fell against my back but he made not a sound. No one spoke to us. I lifted my head to see Spark curled as small as a child. Lant held her, his head bent over her as tears dripped from his chin. The rowers said nothing. Their faces were stern. I looked at Beloved. His face was carved of ice. His scars were gone, but he looked older. Tired beyond tired. Too sad to weep.

Our crew brought us alongside and caught hold of an unfurling rope ladder. 'Get aboard now!' a sailor directed us quietly and then left us to our own devices. Spark clambered up the ladder and then stood at the side, offering a hand to Per and then me. Beloved came behind me, as if to guard me from falling. Lant came last of us, and before he was all the way over the railing, two of our oarsmen were clinging to the ladder. A davit swung over the side and lines were lowered to bring up the boat.

A sailor glanced over the side and called out softly to someone else, 'We have them! They're all aboard!'

A woman with her hair tied back in a tail hastened up to Lant. 'All went well then?' she asked him. Then she scowled. 'Wait! Fitz isn't here yet.'

Lant slowly shook his head and her face grew grave. I couldn't bear to listen to his telling that my father was dead. And I had another concern.

I had touched the railing climbing aboard the ship and had felt a deep thrumming of anxiety and awareness. I turned to Per. 'This ship is not made of wood,' I told him, unable to explain what I'd felt.

'It's a liveship,' he told me hoarsely. 'Made of a dragon's cocoon, with the spirit of a dragon trapped in it. The Fool carved his face, a long time ago, to look just like your father.' He looked around. The Fool was in grave conversation with the woman who had greeted us. Lant and Spark stood by them. It felt as if they had forgotten me.

'Come on,' Per said quietly, and took my hand.

'He can't talk to you right now,' he explained as we threaded our way past and through sailors working a suddenly lively deck. 'He has to pretend he's only wood. But you should see him.'

A woman passed us, talking to a man beside her. 'We'll swing him on the anchor and go quietly from the harbour. Not much wind, but enough to get us clear.'

The closer we drew to the figurehead, the more uneasy I felt. My awareness of the ship was intense. I raised my walls, and then set them again, and yet again. Per seemed unaware of the ship's roiling emotions. I tugged him to a stop. 'This ship is angry,' I said.

He regarded me with worry. 'How do you know?'

'I feel it. Per, he scares me.'

My anger is not for you. I felt as if my body vibrated to that immense thought. I gripped Per's hand so tightly he exclaimed in surprise. *I heard what they said. They enslaved a serpent and kept it in misery to make a foul potion.*

They did. Vindeliar drank it. Then he could make people do as he said. I was shaking all over. I wanted not to feel his immense anger. My sadness already filled me. There was no room for his fury. I tried to placate him. *Per killed him. Per killed Vindeliar, and I killed the woman who gave it to him.*

But my thoughts didn't quench his anger. Like oil on flames, I'd fed his fury. *Death is not enough punishment! He took it, but others made it. Yet avengers come. I do not wish to leave until I see Clerres toppled to rubble. I will not flee like a coward!*

I heard Per gasp. I heard shouts from crewmen but what I felt drove all other sensations away. I fell to the deck as a great emotion rippled through the ship. The deck did not rock and heave; still I clung to the planks fearing that what I felt would be enough to throw me into the sky.

'He's changing!' someone shouted, and Per gave a wild, wordless cry. Under my hands, the planks of the deck lost their grain and became scaly. A terrible dizziness whirled through me and heaved my empty stomach. I lifted my head, sick with terror. Where my father's form had been, two dragon's heads now wove on long, sinuous necks. The larger one was blue, a smaller one green. The blue one swivelled to look back toward us. His eyes spun, orange and golds and yellows mingling in pools like molten metal. He spoke, his reptilian lips writhing back from white pointed teeth. 'Per! Avenger of serpents and dragons!'

I was still on my hands and knees. Per was looking up at the figurehead, his teeth bared in a smile, or a grimace of terror. I heard running footsteps on the deck behind me and Lant abruptly pulled me to my feet.

'There you are! I was so . . . Bee, come with me. We need to get you out of the way!'

I bristled, but Per said, 'I'll take her to the cabin.' He pulled me away from Lant, who was gaping at the figureheads, and led me across the deck, dodging running sailors. I let him lead, paying no attention to where we went or how. Disaster was in the air. I wondered if I would ever be safe again. If I would live through the day.

Per tried to deny it as he opened the door to a small, tidy chamber. 'We're going to get away, Bee. Once we are out of the harbour and the sails fill, we'll be clear. Paragon flies through the waves. No one will be able to catch us.'

I nodded, but did not feel any relief. The ship's passions sliced through me like broken pieces of bone in my flesh.

'Just sit here. I wish I could stay, but I have to go help,' he told me. He backed toward the door, patting the air with both hands as if that would calm me. 'Just stay here,' he begged me, and shut the door as he left me there. Alone. I swayed where I sat. I could feel the ship resisting his crew. They wished to flee; he did not.

It was a small cabin. Untidy, but not dirty. A small window. Two stacked bunks and a single bunk. A woman's clothing scattered on the floor. An array of items set out on both lower bunks.

I sat down on the bed, pushing aside a shirt to make room. Buck-blue, my father called this colour. When I moved it, a faint fragrance awoke as three candles tumbled from inside it. Battered candles, impregnated with lint and dust, and cracked. But I knew my mother's work. Honeysuckle. Lilac. The little violets from our stream that fed the Withy River. I gathered them into my father's shirt as if I bundled a baby. I held them and rocked. Were they all I had left of my parents? A strange piece of knowledge grew in me. I was an orphan now. They were both gone. Gone forever.

I had not seen him dead, but I felt him dead in a way I could not define. 'Wolf Father?' I said aloud. Nothing. The loss struck me with numbing force. My father was dead. He had journeyed for months to find me, and we'd had less than half a day together. All that was left to me were the things he had carried so far with him, things he had judged necessary. Such as my mother's candles.

I looked at what he had brought. I wiped my face on his shirt. He would not have minded that. I moved a pair of weather-stained trousers and saw a familiar belt beneath it. And beside it, my books.

My books?

That startled me. My journal of my days and the dream journal of my nights. He'd found them, in my hiding-place behind his study wall, and he'd carried them all those days. Had he read them? The dream journal fell open to the dream of the candles. I looked at the picture I'd painted so long ago, then let my eyes wander to the candles beside me. I understood. I closed that book and picked up my journal. I read a page, then two, and closed it. It wasn't mine any more. It had been written by someone I had once been, but would never be again. I suddenly understood my father's compulsion to burn his work. Those daily musings belonged to someone else, someone who was just as gone as my mother and now my father were. I wanted to burn both books, give them the funeral pyre I'd never given my parents. I would cut a lock or two of my hair for that vanished child and the man who had tried to be a good father to her.

I looked at the other items scattered on the bed beside me. These were his things, I suddenly knew. Little knives and vials; his killing things. Several small pouches. I smiled. I'd killed with less. And he had been proud of me.

I was terribly tired but the feelings of the ship kept washing against me in unpredictable waves. I knew I needed to sleep, and knew also that I could not. Wolf Father would have told me to rest as best I could.

I took the bundled candles and clambered onto the upper bunk. I lay down but my head hit the pillow with a thud. I sat up and pushed it aside. Under a nightshirt was a glass container of something. I picked that up; it took both my hands to do so. It was heavy and when I tipped the container the contents shifted, moving lazily, swirling shades of grey and silver, twisting and twining. My heart sped up. I couldn't look away from it. Something in me knew this stuff, and something in it knew me. Even through the walls of the container, it reached for me and I could not help but reach back.

As I unwillingly clutched the heavy glass tube, I felt flashes of the same hot madness as when I'd cut my feet in the serpent spit. That power lurked and called, just beyond the glass in my hand. I could seize this power. Open the glass, and drown myself in it, and I could be and do anything. I could be like Vindeliar and force people to believe whatever I wished. With a convulsive shudder, I dropped it back onto the bed. I stared at it, tears forgotten. My father had carried that, had possessed that horrific thing. Why? Had he used it? Had he wanted that sort of power? I wiped my wet face on my father's shirt. He was gone and I'd never know the answer to that question. I took the candles and threw his shirt over the glass container so I wouldn't have to look at it.

I climbed down and sat on the lower bunk. I looked at my dirty feet and legs. I considered my hands, rough with work and dirty with soot. Buckkeep Castle. Would I have a place there? I could hear people running and shouting out on the deck. The motion of the ship had changed. Perhaps our time for stealth was over.

Then the ship roared—a wordless cry, of fear and outrage.

'FIRE!' That was a human cry and I sat up, my heart leaping into my throat. I peered out of the little window. Fishing boats surrounded us, but they were not fishing. They were lobbing things at our ship. I heard something break right below the window, the missile shattering as it hit. I peered out, trying to comprehend, and then I saw an archer stand up in one of the other boats. He drew back his bowstring, and another man lifted a flame to his arrow. In a heartbeat, it flew toward us. I could not tell if it struck our ship or not. Then flames leapt up across the little window, obscuring my view. I caromed across the room and flung open the door to the dim corridor. I heard the crew shouting.

'They've chopped our anchor line!'

'Fire destroys liveships! Put it out!'

'Where is Bee?' Beloved's voice. No one responded.

'Here!' I cried out.

'Bee! Bee!' That was Per and he came thundering down the companionway toward me. 'Ship's on fire! We need to get you into a boat!'

'And go where?' I shouted back at him. 'To shore? Those people will catch me and kill me!' My premonition had been right. There was no safety on this ship. We had nowhere to flee. Per and I stared at one another. My heart was thundering in my ears.

A terrible scream, hoarse and deep, rang through the ship. Within the ship. Every plank in the ship screamed and it vibrated up through my bones. Worse was the surge of pain that the ship transmitted to me. Paragon was being burned alive. The pain was not a physical one, but the anguish of a lost chance. An end to his being a ship before he ever had a chance to be a dragon.

Per reached me, seized my wrist. 'We'll decide where to go after you don't burn to death!'

I tugged free and turned back toward the cabin. 'I'm not running. I have a different idea!'

I clambered onto the top bunk and took up the heavy container. Per stared at me. 'I know how to use this,' I told him as it began to whisper its promises to me. I wouldn't let the Servants take me. I could command them to leap from their boats and drown, and they would do it.

'What are you going to do?' Per whispered in horror, then barked, 'Don't do it! Don't do anything with that stuff. It will kill you! The Fool put some on his fingers and the Rain Wild folk said it would kill him . . .'

I pushed past him, the heavy glass cradled in my arms, and hurried toward the deck. His warnings didn't apply to me, I was sure. I'd seen what Vindeliar did with the serpent spit. This was different. Stronger and purer. I wasn't sure how to use it. Did I have to drink it? The Fool had put some on his fingers, Per had said. Did that mean I should put my hands into it? Dump it over my head?

I reached the short ladder that led to the deck. Before I could go up it, a man dropped from the deck, bending his knees deep to catch himself. He straightened and looked at me, pale-blue eyes in a soot-blackened and flame-seared face. He was a nightmare come to life, with the hair scorched back from his brow. He looked wide-eyed at what I carried and shouted up the hatch, 'It's here! She has it!'

Another man dropped down to crouch beside him. The side of his face was blistered and he carried one arm close to his chest. The flesh of that arm was a ruin of fat blisters and burned shirtsleeve. 'Girl, I need that. Amber told me about it the night I rowed her into Clerres. It's for the ship. He needs the Silver.'

'Boy-O!' Per exclaimed in horror as he dashed up beside me. I clutched the container close to my chest. It was singing to me. Power and strength. It was mine.

The ship roared again. It cascaded through the vessel and echoed in me. I could not find myself for his despair. I saw it mirrored on the faces of the men who had cornered me.

The man with the burned face spoke quickly in a shaking voice. 'Fire's spreading, Per. We can't stop it. Whatever they're using, water won't quench it. You need to get the girl off the ship now. But that Silver stuff . . . I need it. For Paragon. He'll sink here and be gone forever unless he can turn into dragons now. Amber told me where to find it. It's the Silver Paragon was promised if he helped you.'

The other man held out his hands to me. 'Please, girl. You can't use the Silver; it's poison to you. But it might be enough to let the dragons break free!'

If I kept it, I could make them obey me. All of them. I'd be like Vindeliar, but much stronger.

I'd be like Vindeliar . . .

'Take it.' I thrust the silvery tube at them. The burned man reached for it.

'No,' the other man said. 'You get them off the ship. I'll get this to Paragon.'

'The flames,' the burned man cautioned him. 'Kennitsson, you'll never get through.'

'It's Paragon. This is my family ship. Blood of my blood. I must.' The man called Kennitsson grabbed the container, cradled it, and scampered up the ladder one-handed.

Another agonizing shriek split the air and raced through the bones of the ship. 'Get up the ladder,' Per ordered me, and I obeyed him as quickly as I could. I gained the deck and stood up into blowing smoke and falling ash. I looked up. Our furled sails were slowly burning, shedding fragments of ash and flaming canvas as they did. On one side of the ship, flame licked up in a wall. We would not escape that way. Smoke rose on every other side, and I had learned how quickly rising smoke could become a sheet of flame. My eyes streamed so that I could barely see.

A gloved hand seized my shoulder from behind. 'Get to the boats!' Beloved shouted in a gasping voice. 'There's no saving him. Oh, Paragon, my old friend.'

'Amber! Where are my parents?' the man with the injured arm shouted, and Beloved shook his head.

'They ran toward the bow. Our attackers have been concentrating the fire there. Boy-O, you won't get through the flames. They're lost!'

But the man chased after his friend with the Silver. They ran forward. I saw them run, I saw them leap, and hoped it was a thin curtain of flames they penetrated and not an inferno. The keening of the ship filled my ears and my whole body. I shook with his fear and anger. This was how we would all end. I knew that as clearly as he did. All this I saw as I was dragged away by Beloved. He was stronger than he looked and, in a corner of my mind, I wondered if it was my dead father's strength that he used.

We reached the other side of the vessel. He looked over the side through the rising smoke and swore. 'They left us!' Per exclaimed and coughed.

Beloved kept a grip on my shoulder. He wrapped his arm over his face and spoke through the fabric of his sleeve. 'They had to, or the boat would have caught fire, too. They're there, trying to wait for us, but we'll have to jump and then swim. And the Servants' boats are closing in on them.'

'Lant?' Per coughed. 'Spark?'

'I don't know.'

'I can't swim,' I said. Not that it mattered. I wondered if drowning hurt less than burning. Probably. But the fishing boats were still shooting arrows at our ships. Two of our sailors dashed up to join us, brandishing their swords futilely.

'Do we jump?' Per coughed. His eyes were streaming. The smoke had a terrible smell and flavour, like burning flesh. Like the body of the messenger my father and I had burned, so long ago.

Then something changed. The whole ship shuddered, like a horse shaking off flies. The deck began to buckle under our feet.

'Jump!' Per shouted, but gave me no time to obey. He seized me by the upper arm and dragged me away from Beloved. He did not give me time to clamber over the railing but pulled me over it, knocking my shins hard against the wood. Strange, how sharp that pain still was in the midst of everything else.

Beloved leapt with us, kicking and flailing as he fell. I saw his flying body for only an instant before the cold water closed over me. I hadn't taken a breath and Per had lost his grip on me. I went down, into cold and sudden dark. The force of my plummet pushed water up my nose. It hurt. I gasped, took in water, and then closed my mouth tight. I hung in cold darkness. Kick, kick, I told myself. Paddle hands, do something. Fight to live. *Wolf Father!*

No. He was gone, with my other father, and I was alone. I had to fight. As a cornered wolf fights. As he had promised my father would fight. I kicked and slapped wildly at the water that held me. I hated it as much as I hated Dwalia and Vindeliar. And then, for an instant, my head bobbed above the water. There was no time to gasp before I sank again. Kick harder, slap harder. Again, I found light and the touch of air on my face. I spat and snorted water, battering my hands on the surface of the water viciously as I tried to stay above it. I gasped in air before a wave slapped me in the face.

Someone caught hold of my arm. I climbed up him like a frantic cat climbs a tree, with no thought that I was pushing him under as I thrust my head into the air. I took a deep breath, and someone else caught hold of me and dragged me backwards. 'Relax. On your back!' a voice commanded me. The world around me was blurry. I could not relax but she held me on my back and the head that bobbed up beside me was Per. He spat, snorted, and caught hold of my arm. He drew himself closer to me. 'Ant. Thank you.'

'Kick!' the girl said suddenly. 'Kick hard!'

I blinked saltwater from my eyes. I was looking up. The ship seemed much larger from this perspective. Fire licked up his sides and the scorched rags of burning canvas drifted up into the morning on the hot air that rose from him. I heard the dismayed and angry shouts of sailors on the other anchored ships and twisted, fearing the flotilla of little boats that had attacked us but they seemed to be drawing back now, satisfied with their handiwork.

I was kicking my feet in imitation of Per and Ant and we were moving away from Paragon, but slowly. The ship towered over us, slowly turning in his own inferno. I saw two more people leap through flames to seek the dubious safety of the water. His slow wallow brought the twin dragon figureheads into view. They had been blue and green, but now both were scorched and burning. The wood seemed to fight the flames. Scorched black, the scales would suddenly reappear, blue or green, but the unquenched oil would ignite again and the flames would flare. Fire licked up the long necks: both heads were thrashing wildly. The foredeck was engulfed in flames. Even at this distance, I could feel the waves of distress from the liveship, and his trumpets of fury and despair echoed over the bay from the rounded hills behind the town.

A taller wave slapped over my face. I came up snorting and blinking water. As my vision cleared, I saw a flaming man leap onto the blue dragon. He clasped it around the neck and shouted something. He held aloft my father's glass container. The dragon opened its jaws to accept it from the man. As he did so, the man fell from his perch into the sea. The blue dragon tipped its head back and closed its jaws. I saw a single silver shard fall from the dragon's mouth.

'Did it work?' Per gasped.

'Did what work?' Ant demanded.

'Catch a line,' someone shouted, and a rope slapped across my chest. Per caught hold of it and so did I. It had been thrown from one of our ship's boats. I recognized the tattooed woman who held the other end of the rope.

'There wasn't enough,' Per said sadly.

The woman began to take in line, dragging us toward the boat. The motion made the waves lap over us more strongly. Another slapped my face and when I blinked the water away it seemed that Paragon was falling to pieces. The masts were tilting and falling, the grand house aft was tipping into the bay. The railings were sagging and the planks loosening and drooping like snow on branches at the end of winter. Per spat out water. Only the hull was holding intact and some of the deck and railings.

'Where's Amber?' Per called to our rescuers.

'Not here,' the woman said.

I watched a ripple of colour run along a plank section as I clung to a line dragging me through the water. Then hands were seizing me and I was hauled over the side and dropped into a few inches of standing water in the bottom of a crowded boat. The ribs of the boat bit mine as I thudded against them. But no one was paying attention to me. Ant and Per were clambering aboard, legs hooked over the sides. I pulled up Per and then Ant.

'Paragon,' Per gasped.

The wreckage of the *Paragon* was settling into the water. I saw someone clinging to a board and hoped it was Lant. My companions were not looking for survivors. Instead they were transfixed by the sight of a great struggle in the water. A green head broke the surface and then its flailing front legs caught at the wreckage. A green dragon dragged itself up onto the slowly sinking house of the ship. It spread its wings and shook water from them. Its wings were patterned with black and grey, the colours of scorched wood and dirty smoke. Abruptly, it threw its head high and gave a whistling cry. Words were mixed with her scream, for as her thoughts slapped my mind, I knew her for a queen.

'VENGEANCE! VENGEANCE FOR ME AND MINE!'

Some of my companions covered their ears against that shrill cry but others raised a cheer. She beat her wings more strongly, stirring the water and wreckage around her. She was not a large dragon, not much longer than a horse and team, but when she roared again I saw her gleaming white teeth and the scarlet-and-yellow lining of her throat. She rose from her perch on the wreckage, fighting her way into the air until she was a green shape against a pale blue sky. She circled twice over us, and her wings seemed to grow stronger with every stroke.

Then she dived onto one of the fleeing boats. I saw her snatch one of the rowers. Three loosed arrows missed her and one bounced from her scales. She lifted the hapless man higher and as her jaws closed, his legs fell to one side and his head and shoulders to the other. We heard our enemies' cries of horror, but no one in our boat cheered. It was too horrific, too great a reminder of what a dragon could do to any human. Even a small dragon.

'A blue one!' someone shouted. I had been so intent on watching the green one that I had missed the blue's emergence from the wreckage. He stood spread-legged upon the wallowing pile of timbers, wings of smoke veined with red lifted wide. He was larger than the green, and the roar he gave was deep and full-throated. He tucked his head and lowered it. I did not realize the body of a man was beside him until he nosed it.

'Oh, sweet Eda! That's Boy-O. He's going to eat Boy-O!'

As if in response to that thought, the blue dragon lifted his head again. His thoughts rode his roar and I began to understand that I 'heard' his speech in my mind while my ears heard his trumpet.

'He lives. My friend is not my meat. I will feast on my enemies!'

His wings beat more powerfully and more slowly than the green's had. He lifted deliberately into the air. Screams from across the water told me that the green was still feeding. We watched the larger blue rise. Our oarsmen were not rowing; we floated in a spreading raft of debris. Higher and higher the blue climbed and then he dived on his prey. He swamped the boat in passing but carried off a stout oarsman in his jaws. He carried the man up until we could barely hear his screams. Like the green had, he sheared off the dangling parts of the man. But then, in a spectacular display of agility, he swallowed and then dived again to catch the man's falling legs and gulp them in passing.

The oarsmen in our boat suddenly seized their oars. I saw why. Another survivor had hauled himself up onto the wreckage. He was crawling toward Boy-O's body across the bobbing planks and debris. 'That's Clef!' Per shouted.

A sailor knelt in the bow of our boat, pushing debris from our path as we made our way toward the most densely packed raft of floating wreckage. Another of Paragon's boats was swifter than we were. I saw Spark climb out, to dance and balance on the floating, tipping pieces until she knelt by the man's body. 'Alive!' she cried and a cheer rose from our company. They rejoiced in the survival of their friends. In life.

I was not such a good person. I turned my eyes from the survivors and watched the two dragons harrying and chasing, feeding and soaring to let bloody bits rain down on the servants of the Servants.

I took my bitter satisfaction from their deaths.

THIRTY-NINE

The Vengeance

Of the Treasure Beach, this is known.

You must anchor in the small bay on the south shore. Watch the tides! A low tide will strand you. A high tide coming in may well drive you into the shore.

Walk the path through the forest with caution. Disaster befalls those who wander from the path.

When you reach the far shore, walk along the tideline in the bay. Do not leave the beach. All areas on Others' Island are forbidden to humanity except the beach and the path.

You may find treasures washed up by the waves. The currents and wind seem to gather them from afar and deposit them there. Collect as many as you wish. None may you carry away.

At the correct time, a being will come to you. Treat the being with great respect. Present the treasures you have gathered. In his wisdom, the being will tell you of your future and suggest the best paths for you to follow. When the telling is done, you may leave each treasure in an alcove in the cliff.

You must not take with you anything you find on the Treasure Beach, no matter how tiny. To do so is to invite calamity upon yourself and all your descendants.

Aljeni's List of Magical Places, translated by FitzChivalry Farseer

I was amazed at the destruction two dragons could wreak, but I was certain that the remainder of the Servants were even more astonished. The blue and the green drove away the small boats that had visited such disaster upon us. The other ships that had been in port raised their anchors and unfurled their sails and fled the incomprehensible destruction. They must have believed that the folk of Clerres had gone mad to visit flames upon a peacefully anchored ship. To have the ship suddenly birth two savage dragons was surely beyond their comprehension.

What shall I say of that chaotic afternoon? All my memories of it are sick and sodden with saltwater and grief and intense weariness. With our enemies fled, we gathered up our friends—living, dead and those in between. Our overladen boat made it to the end of a dock and we claimed that space. Three of our party including the tattooed woman seemed very familiar with battle. Deprived of weaponry, they still organized us in a defensible way and stood ready with knives drawn. Others set out with the boat again, to find our other ship's boats and comrades clinging to the wreckage.

'Will you feel safe if I leave you here and go look for the others?' Per asked me, very seriously.

I shrugged. 'None of us is safe, Per. This entire city hates us, and soon will find a way to show us.' I gestured wide. 'We have no means of escape. The ship became dragons; the other ships have fled or are destroyed by the dragons. We have few weapons and nothing to buy our lives with.' It was all so clear to me. He gave me a stricken stare. I pitied him. Didn't he know we were all going to die here? 'Go,' I told him. 'See who you can find.'

Before he returned, another of our ship's boats found us. Weary survivors straggled up onto the dock to join us. Spark was among them. Lant was not. Boy-O was the man with the burned face and ruined arm. Clef helped him up the ladder to the dock. I was surprised he could still speak, let alone stand. 'Has anyone seen my parents?' he asked. No one replied. His face went slack and he sat down where he was on the dock. Slowly he fell over. The sailor called Ant went to sit beside him. 'Have we any water?' she asked.

We didn't.

Spark came to sit beside me. She was drenched and shaking, and we huddled together for warmth. 'Amber?' she asked me. 'Per?'

'Per is helping find the others. I don't know Amber.'

Spark stared blankly at me. 'Amber is the Fool. But only your father called him that. Or Beloved.'

'Beloved,' I said quietly. I added, 'I have not seen him since we jumped from the ship.'

There seemed nothing else to say. We sat there. No one came to attack us. The Servants' boats had scattered. Some few had fled to the castle, harried all the way by the blue and the green dragons. The dragons were circling the stronghold now, screeching their anger. The archers on the walls were wasting all their arrows with shots that fell short or bounced off the scaly hide. In the town, people watched from their rooftops and the windows of the upper storeys of their homes. We saw no one moving in the streets, and no one seemed to want to attack us. Perhaps the townsfolk did not even know if or why we were the enemy. The sun grew stronger in a bright blue sky, warming us and drying our clothing. I sat on the edge of the dock, swinging my bare feet over the water below, waiting. Waiting to find out who was still alive. Waiting for the townsfolk to attack us. Waiting for anything to happen at all.

'I'm hungry and thirsty,' I said to Spark. 'And I wish I had shoes. That seems so wrong to me. So heartless that I can think of these things.' I shook my head. 'My father is dead, and I am wishing I had shoes.'

She put an arm around me. I found I didn't mind that. 'I wish I could brush my hair and tie it back from my face,' Spark admitted. 'I wish that even as I wonder if Lant is dead, and strange to say, I feel angry with him.'

'That's because if you felt sad and wept, you would be making him dead in your mind.'

She gave me a strange look. 'Yes. But how do you know these things?'

I shrugged and said, 'I'm very angry at my father. I don't want to weep for him any more. I know I will, but I don't want to.' I rolled one shoulder. 'And I am very angry at Beloved. Amber.' I spoke the name with disdain.

'Why?' Spark was aghast.

'I simply am.' I didn't want to explain. He was alive while my father was dead. He was the one who had brought it all down on us. Beloved. The one who led the Servants to the doors of Withywoods. The one who started it by making my father his Catalyst.

I looked at her. I asked a terrible question. 'Do you know about Shun?'

'Lant's sister? Shine? She escaped. Your father found her. That's how he knew you'd gone through the stone.'

'His sister?' I asked in confusion.

Her smile wavered. 'He was as surprised as you are now.' She hugged me closer. 'And he told me that at first, you two did not get along at all. He told me a lot about you.' Her voice trailed away. She shook her head suddenly. 'I'm hungry. Thirsty. And angry at Lant. And ashamed of feeling those things at all.' She gave me a sad smile. 'When things are so immensely wrong, it seems cruel that I long for a cup of tea. And some bread.'

'Ginger-cakes. My mother used to make them for my father.' I covered my mouth. 'My mother would be so furious with him right now.' And the hated tears welled again.

A short time later I saw one of our boats coming back to the docks. Per was pulling one of the oars. We both stood up. There was a body in the bottom of the boat, wrapped in a piece of sail. 'Oh, no,' Spark moaned. Beloved was sitting beside the wrapped corpse.

They came alongside the dock and Spark's first cry was, 'Is it Lant? Is Lant dead?'

'It's Kennitsson,' Per said in a dead voice as he looked up at us. 'The flames took him.'

'Oh!' Spark covered her mouth. I wondered if she hid her face, so no one would know how relieved she was that Kennitsson was dead instead of Lant.

Per climbed up onto the dock. He came to me and opened his arms. We hugged one another tightly. He looked over my head and cried out, 'Not Boy-O, too!'

'He's alive,' Ant said from where she sat beside him. 'But not doing well.' Boy-O lifted his head and then let it drop again. 'Kennitsson,' he said dully. 'He saved the ship.'

It was hard work to get the wrapped corpse up the ladder and onto the dock, taking the efforts of three of them. Beloved did his share, but it seemed to me that several of his crewmates regarded him oddly. He opened the canvas and stooped over the shrouded body to compose it.

Beloved shook his head wearily and looked over at me. A smile slowly curved his mouth, but his eyes were sad. 'There you are. Once I saw Per, I knew you were safe.' He took two steps toward me and opened his arms. I stood still. He let his arms fall to his sides, his embrace unclaimed. He stood looking down at me. 'Oh, Bee. I will wait. I am a stranger to you. But I feel I know you very well.' I do not think he could have said a more irritating thing. My thoughts flickered to my journal and book of dreams, now at the bottom of the harbour. No. No one could be so low as to read another's journal . . . though of course, I had read my father's papers. I looked past him and said nothing.

I was aware of Spark looking at me and then regarding him with sympathy. 'How are you?' she said, and it was a sincere question.

'I am hollow inside,' he said gravely. 'So many masks I have worn, and now they are all empty. I cannot summon even anger to sustain me. The loss is so . . . I want to go back there, I want to look at his body, to make it real to myself . . .' His words ran down.

'You can't.' Spark spoke the words sharply. 'We are too few to divide ourselves. Too poorly armed. And it serves no purpose other than to prolong your pain.' She looked away from him.

'He's dead,' I said softly. I looked up at both of them. 'For a short time, I could feel him. Connected to me. I felt him and I felt Wolf Father. They are gone now.'

He glanced at his gloved fingers, and then cradled that hand to his chest. 'I know,' he admitted. 'But it was a terrible place to leave him. Alone, with the water rising—'

'Do we have a plan?' Spark cut in sharply. 'Or do we just sit on this dock until they come to kill us all?' Her voice was hoarse but level. Her throat was probably as dry as mine, and her stomach as empty. I was coming to like her. She had the same steadiness that Per did. That same in-this-moment practicality. Her words snapped Beloved into a straighter posture. He looked over the huddled survivors and our thin line of protectors.

'Yes. One that is subject to much change, I fear.' He pushed his damp hair back from his face. 'For now, yes, we remain on this dock. We are not a large enough force to protect ourselves if we venture into the town. Here and now, we have a somewhat defensible position.'

And no food. No water. No shelter from the sun. Injured folk. I did not think much of the plan of the man who had replaced my father.

He folded his legs and sat down beside me. Spark copied him

and Per came to join us. Boy-O remained by the body. A muscled, scarred man was looking at Boy-O's arm and the blistered burns on his face and elsewhere. Suddenly Boy-O sagged to one side; the man caught him and eased him down; he had fainted. Ant had a knife and was staring off toward the town. I did not know the names of the others. There were eleven of them. One kept watch out over the harbour. The afternoon sun beat down on all of us. The tide had turned and the waves were retreating, carrying the debris of our ship with them. The other large vessels that had been in the harbour were gone, save for one that was aground and listing.

Per spoke. 'If they come with archers as they did before, we have no cover. If they muster their courage and come by boat as well as on the shore, we will be quickly surrounded. If all they do is keep us here, we have no food and no water. No shelter from the sun. We will end here, I fear.'

'Those things are true. But for now, they are far too busy dealing with dragons to bother with us. And it's only to get worse for the castle. And then the town.' Beloved turned his oddly pale eyes toward Clerres Castle. The blue and the green dragon had finished with the small boats, leaving only floating wreckage on the water. The green one was now high above Clerres Castle, wings spread, rocking in the air as an eagle does when it catches the wind and effortlessly rides it. The blue was actively harrying the castle, swooping and darting in a display of flight that mocked the archers' efforts to hurt him. Arrows still flew but there were fewer in each volley.

As I watched, the blue suddenly changed tactics. Graceful as an alighting swallow, the dragon swept in and up, to perch atop one of the Four's towers. It was not one of the outer watchtowers that he chose, but one of the taller structures within the stronghold. The blue trumpeted loudly as if calling to someone. Then he flung his head back and snapped it forward on his sinuous neck, mouth wide. Something sparkling flew from his open mouth. I heard distant cries.

'He spits acid, in a fine spray. Nothing stands before it. Not flesh nor armour nor bone nor stone,' Beloved told me.

I looked over at him. 'Hap sang to me of dragons. I know what they do.'

I thought of the placid, cheerful Whites in their little cottages. Their spotless flowing garments and picnic meals under the blossoming trees. They would be punished alongside Capra and the Servants and their warrior guards. Did they deserve it? Did they know the harm their cached dreams had done to the rest of the world? I felt a twinge of pity for them, but no guilt. What was happening to them was as far beyond my control as a thunderstorm or an earthquake. Or my own kidnapping and the sacking of Withywoods.

The high-flying green gave a long shrill cry. 'Vengeance!' That was the word that rode on that sound. It echoed, 'Vengeance, vengeance, vengeance!'

Not an echo.

'Oh, my,' Beloved said softly.

The vision my father had given him was becoming keener. He had seen them before anyone else. Two little jewels, sparkling and twinkling in the distance. One glinted scarlet and the other flashed bluer than the sky.

Beloved lifted an arm and pointed. 'Dragons!' he called to our companions. 'Heeby and Tintaglia, unless I am mistaken. Rapskal said they would come!

With a rattle of plumes, a crow suddenly settled on Per's shoulder. I jumped back in alarm but he laughed joyously. She was a strange crow, with a silver beak, and instead of being black she had a glittering blue to her feathers, and several scarlet plumes in each wing. And not the red of a rooster's feathers but shining, as if polished metal could be red. Per cried out, 'Motley! I feared you drowned or arrow-shot! I am so glad you're alive! Where were you?'

The bird bobbed her head as if in agreement. Then she spoke, her voice and inflection oddly human. She opened her wings. 'I fly with the dragons!' Full of satisfaction. Then she turned her bright eyes on me. 'A way out is a way in!'

A shiver went up my back. 'You came to my cell!' I exclaimed. But she paid me no mind. She had turned her head to stare up at the sky.

'IceFyre. IceFyre!'

I saw confusion cloud Per's face but before I could wonder what the word meant I heard him. The black dragon came—not over the sea as the others did, but from inland. He announced himself with one roar. 'IceFyre! I return, and I bring your death!' Every driving beat of his powerful wings brought him closer; he grew ever larger until he seemed impossibly big. How could such a creature exist, let alone fly? But fly he did. And as he approached the castle, we heard only his wings. Then a cry burst from him, a sound so powerful that all of us covered our ears. But while we might hold out the sound of his roar, the sense of it imprinted itself in our minds.

'*Remember me, Clerres? Recall how you poisoned us with a feast of toxic cattle? Recall how you gathered to dance and sing, to welcome us to your treachery? Recall how you butchered my fellows as they lay dying? How when I fought you, you filled my mind with a curse? "Bury yourself in the ice!" Back then, I fled. You shamed me! You made me the last dragon in the world! But I shall not leave even one of you to recall how you all died this day!*'

The blue took panicked flight from the tower, a jay rousted by a raven. The black dragon did not perch. He dived on the turret of one inner tower, hitting it with his talons and the full force of his weight and impetus. It fell, tumbling like a child's blocks. I thought he would ride it down, but his great wings beat and he lifted again. High he rose and higher. The blue and the green dragons circled wide around him, no longer actively harrying the castle. They kept their distance, and I wondered if they feared they might become his meal.

Then he fell like a stone, straight down, and only in the final moment did he change his course with a shifting of his wings, driving himself against one of the skull towers. It was a sturdier thing than the graceful inner towers. Even so, it could not withstand the blow. The fearsome head tipped as if it had taken a monstrous slap. A shocking crack ran down the structure, and as the dragon clung to the skull, pushing and flapping, the crack opened wider. The skull overbalanced and IceFyre lifted away from it as it leaned ever so slowly and then fell. Even at our distance, the sound it made as it struck the earth was impressive.

From her perch on Per's shoulder, the crow opened wide her wings. A string of enthusiastic caws burst from her throat. She bobbed her head and declared, 'Dragons! My dragons!'

Per put his hands on her to prevent her from taking flight. 'It's too dangerous,' he warned her.

'My dragons!' she insisted.

'She has finally found a flock to join,' he observed to me. 'Her own kind always pecked her. But the dragons have taken her in.'

His eyes on the dragons and their destruction, Beloved asked, 'If a flock of crows is a murder, what should we call a group of dragons?'

'A catastrophe of dragons,' someone said, with no humour in his deep voice.

'Stay where you are!' The outcry from one of our guardians jerked my attention back to the land end of the dock. A familiar figure stood there. My heart lifted for a moment and then I wondered. Friend or foe?

'I have no weapon,' Prilkop pointed out. I wasn't sure of that. Two of the Whites we had freed from their cells stood behind him. They had recovered enough to be carrying a large bucket between them.

'I've brought you water. And I offer you shelter in a friend's home.' He turned and gestured at the two Whites to bring the bucket forward. They exchanged a look and one shook his head vigorously. They set the bucket down and retreated farther down the dock. Prilkop stared after them. Then he walked ponderously back to the bucket, took it up and walked slowly toward us, the water sloshing over the brim at each step. We watched him come and all I could think of was the water. He clutched the bail of the bucket in both hands and it was splashing on his legs and feet. I suddenly saw that he was an old man, and not very strong any more.

Behind him in the town, people were leaving their homes, some scampering like frightened squirrels and others moving purposefully, pushing barrows and carrying large packs as they fled. Some of them had clearly understood what IceFyre was saying. I wondered if those who lived here knew tales of how the Servants had killed and driven off the dragons. Had they ever imagined such a vengeance?

Beloved walked past our glowering guardians, went over to Prilkop and took the pail. 'Thank you, old friend,' he said, and left Prilkop standing there as he brought the water back to us.

'Are you sure it's clean? Not poisoned? I heard that dragon say they were poisoners.' This from the tattooed woman.

'It's not poisoned,' Beloved assured them. He stooped and found a ladle in the bucket. He dippered up water and drank it. 'It tastes fine. It's even cool. Come and drink. Water for Boy-O first.'

We gave Boy-O three dippers of water and no one objected. I took one, even though they said I could have more. The guards had not given up their vigilance. I slipped closer to stand near them and hear what Prilkop was saying to Beloved.

'They're destroying it all,' Prilkop called to Beloved. 'What Bee began with her fire, they are finishing with acid and blows of their wings and tails. If they do not stop, Clerres Castle will be nothing but rubble. I come to beg you to call them back. Let us change this path, Beloved. Negotiate a peace for us. Help me return Clerres to what it should have been, what it once was.'

Beloved shook his head, and I do not think he was sad to refuse. 'Easy enough to negotiate a peace with us. Allow us to leave on the first ship that will take us. That is all we ask. We have what we came for.'

Prilkop nodded. 'The Stolen Child.'

In a flat voice, Beloved added, 'We can do nothing about the dragons. Their vengeance is even older than mine. They will be thorough. And nothing will stop them.'

Prilkop said nothing, but his mouth sagged and his face grew older.

The blue dragon had claimed the walkway on top of the west wall. He paraded up and down it. His lashing tail razed blocks of stone, destroying the crenellation. From time to time he threw back his head and then snapped it forward, showering the interior of the fortress with acid. I could not see the green, and then, with a wild roar, a much larger blue dragon flashed past the two remaining skull-topped towers. A smaller red one flew low over the town and then landed at the town end of the causeway. On that dragon's back was something I could not make out at that distance. A rider?

'Heeby! Beautiful Heeby!' the crow cried. She tried to lift from Per's shoulder, but he caught her, his hands moving so fast I barely saw them.

'Motley, she goes to battle. It is no place for you. Stay here with me, where you're safe.'

'Safe? Safe?' And the crow laughed, a terrible cackle. Per had pinned her wings to her side and she did not struggle, but the moment he set her back on his shoulder, she leapt from him. With two flaps of her wings, she was up and then arrowing toward the red dragon. 'I come, I come, I come!'

'As you will,' Per said sadly. 'Likely she is right. There is no safety here for her. Or us.'

The great blue dragon circled back. As IceFyre had, she announced her name with a roar. '*Tintaglia!*' she trumpeted. '*Vengeance! For my eggs stolen and destroyed, for our serpents imprisoned and abused!*' She struck the tower a lashing blow with her tail as she passed. We stared. Nothing happened. And then slowly, slowly the skull tipped back, beheaded from its stone support. It fell, dragging half the damaged tower with it. We heard the distant crash of cascading stones.

'You spent so many years at Clerres. As a child, you laboured long in the scroll-rooms. Your own dreams were stored there. You feel nothing?' Prilkop asked quietly.

'I feel many things right now. Relief is one of them.' Beloved stared coldly at the falling walls of Clerres Castle. 'Satisfaction that what was done to me will never happen to another child.'

'And the children that were in there?' Prilkop was outraged.

Beloved shook his head. 'This is the vengeance of dragons. No one can stop it.' He turned to look at his friend and his voice was terrible. The voice of a prophet. 'I spent him, Prilkop! I plunged FitzChivalry into death, a dozen times! No one can know what that cost me. No one! This is my future, my path, chosen by me, as the White Prophet of this time! Are you so blind? He and I, we did it all! We brought the dragons back into the world.' He turned away from all of us. Arms crossed on his chest he shouted, 'SERVANTS! You made this path! Long before I came into the world, you set us on this rutted route to this future. When you killed and destroyed for your own comfort, when your own wealth and power were all you cared for, this is the path you created! You delayed this reckoning.' His voice dropped lower and suddenly he was coldly calm. 'But my Catalyst and I have won. The future is here, and the vengeance is greater than even a prophet could predict.' His voice, so grand a moment before, cracked and broke as he said, 'Bought with his death.'

The sea wind blew past him and his pale hair stirred slightly in its passage. I did not have to touch him to see that he had been a nexus. For one instant, all the possible paths that had been shone around him. Then they moved, converging into one bright way before it, too, exploded into a thousand, thousand paths. They dazzled my eyes and I could not look away. But abruptly, he dropped his hands and he was just a slender pale man as he asked on a sob, 'Do you think I would undo one moment of my Catalyst's work?'

He knew, as I did, that it all had to end. Beloved was as much the Destroyer as I had ever been. Pull out the deepest root of the weeds. I did not know I was going to do it, but I stepped forward. I took his gloved hand in mine and we stood, staring at Prilkop.

'Will they destroy the town as well?' Prilkop whispered in horror.

'They will,' Beloved affirmed. Our small party had gathered around and behind him. 'Prilkop, I see one narrow path for you. Take those you have and flee to the hills. It is all you can do and all I can give you. This is a balancing of the scales that was long in coming.' He shook his head. 'It did not begin with me but with the dragons. And the dragons have come to finish it.'

Prilkop looked toward the castle, his hands trembling. With no fear, Beloved went to him and embraced him. He spoke quietly. 'Only for what you must feel, old friend, I am sorry. Take those you can. Guide them toward a better path.'

'There were children there,' Prilkop said brokenly.

'There were children at Withywoods,' I reminded him. I did not say I had been one of them.

'They have done nothing to deserve such punishment!'

'And my folk were just as innocent!' Could he not hear what I was telling him?

Per was suddenly beside me, his round face contorted by an anger I'd never seen before. 'Did my father and grandfather deserve to die so that you could kidnap a girl? Your people erased my mother's memories of me, so that she denied me and sent me away. Neither of us will ever get past that! Do you understand that when the Servants came to Withywoods, they destroyed my life as well as Bee's? And now her father is dead, because of what they did!'

I suddenly understood something from a long-ago dream. 'Did you know that they arranged for nets to be set off Others' Island, to capture and kill the serpents so that they would die and never become dragons?'

'But . . .' Prilkop began.

Beloved stepped back from him. His voice was harsh. 'No one deserves to die like that. But very little of what happens to us in life is what we deserve.'

Still the old man stood staring at us pleadingly.

'Prilkop. Time does not pause. Go.'

Prilkop stared at him as if shocked beyond words. Then he turned, and stumbled away. In a few steps he recovered himself and began a dogged trot. I watched him go. Our companions looked at us questioningly but there was nothing more to add. 'Boy-O is awake,' I said quietly. Ant turned and hastened to his side. He was sitting up, but looked worse than he had. Beyond him, out in the water, something moved.

'What's that?' someone demanded, drawing our attention to the other end of the dock.

'There's someone in the water!' Spark cried. All her heart was in her shout, and with no hesitation, she leapt from the dock to swim to the man who clung to a bit of plank and doggedly kicked. We watched her go, some shouting encouragement. She reached him and we saw her take her place beside him on the broken board. They both kicked then, and slowly, slowly they reached a point where Boy-O suddenly cried out, 'It's my Da! He's alive! But where is my mother?' He staggered to his feet, swayed and then Ant seized his good arm to support him.

'Brashen Trell,' Per said. 'Paragon's captain.' His face shone with hope.

Agonizing moments crawled by as they slowly drew closer. The waves pushed them toward us. Boy-O stood, his burned arm held close to his chest, his scorched face full of hope and misery. When they were close enough, Per climbed down to help first Brashen and then Spark to climb out of the water. The moment the man was on the dock, he sank down and Ant lowered Boy-O beside him. The father reached for his son, then drew back, not daring to touch his burned flesh. They both wept as the captain brokenly explained that he had seen Althea briefly when the ship fell apart, but not since. He had been swimming from raft to raft of wreckage, looking for some sign of her, but found nothing. When the wreckage began to drift out of the harbour, he knew he had to try to return to shore before he was carried out with it. Too weary to swim any longer, he had clung to a plank and stubbornly worked his way back to us.

Those who clustered around father and son smiled and wept. Spark, I noticed, isolated herself to sit and weep noisily yet privately.

Lant was gone, as gone as Althea and probably others of the crew I had never met and knew nothing about.

When the captain saw the carefully composed body on the dock, he gave an exclamation of both pity and despair, and Boy-O began to weep afresh. 'I failed, Da. Twice I tried to get through the flames to the figurehead, but the pain drove me back. In the end, it was Kennitsson who saved Paragon from dying. He claimed the Silver from me and ran right into the flames. I heard him screaming but he didn't stop. He saved our ship.'

The man said nothing to try to comfort Boy-O but just let him weep. The two small dragons that had been his ship were like fluttering ribbons in the sky. Though so much smaller than the other dragons, they were just as intent on the destruction of the castle. He watched them. 'So many losses,' he said.

The red dragon rampaged on the ground. The ship's dragons soon joined her. They were thorough in their destruction, moving methodically from structure to structure. They started at the houses and businesses closest to the causeway. There were no flames. The red dragon spat acid and then, when the structures weakened, turned them to rubble with a blast of her wings or a sweep of her tail. We heard the crashes and the shouts, and the stream of fleeing folk became thicker. Some fled up into the pastures and farmland behind the town; others pushed carts and followed the road that wound up into the hills. I sat on the dock and looked up, past the roofs of the warehouse and fine homes, to the hills beyond. People joined the sheep there and then pushed on, to vanish over the ridgeline.

Slowly, slowly the summer evening waned away. There were no flames to light the night. When IceFyre and Tintaglia had finished with the castle, they joined the smaller ones in a very organized destruction of the city. There was nothing random in what they did. The ruination was as coldly calculated as anything Dwalia or Capra had visited upon me. Mothers fled with their babes in their arms, fathers with small children in barrows or on their shoulders ran past. I watched. This was not justice at work, but vengeance.

Vengeance took no account of innocence or right. It was the chain that bound horrific events together, that decreed that one awful act must beget another worse one that would lead to yet a third. It came to me, slowly, that this chain would never end. Those who survived here would hate dragons and the folk of the Six Duchies and perhaps the Pirate Isles. They would tell tales of this day to their descendants and it would not be understood or forgiven. It would, some day, beget more vengeance. I wondered if that was a thread that was wrapped around every path. I wondered if ever a White Prophet would come who could snap it.

Boy-O suffered from his burns and many of the others from their lesser injuries, but we dared not leave our little spot of safety while dragons walked the streets and flew over the houses. I dozed in the night, when sleep eventually triumphed over fear and discomfort.

In the dawn, I wakened to a place I had never been. Every structure in the town was roofless, with walls cracked and crumbled. The harbour was studded with the masts of sunken wrecks. Of the piers and docks, only ours was left intact. The scene was eerie, lifeless: the streets were empty of people. I wakened because Spark shook my shoulder. I sat up to see the smaller blue and green dragons advancing down the dock. 'What do they want?' one of the guards demanded in a shaking voice. Beloved went to him and pushed aside his blade.

'They come for their own. For one they claimed as kin. Step back. For they will pass whether you clear a way or not.'

Brashen stood over his huddled son, for Boy-O could no longer stand for the pain of his burns. Some of the other sailors retreated to the end of the dock, but Spark, Per and I remained where we were.

The planks of the dock complained under their weight as the dragons came toward us, turning their gleaming heads on their serpentine necks and snuffing the air near Beloved. Their eyes spun like twirling silver buttons. The blue opened his mouth, the better to test the air near him.

'Tell me what they say,' Per breathed beside me.

'They have said nothing yet,' I replied. He took my hand in his, and I wondered if he sought to give me courage or borrow mine. It did not matter: I welcomed it. Small dragons were still very large creatures, and they were very close to us but even in my fear and sorrow, their beauty made me smile.

'We have come for him,' the blue one said, and I repeated that softly to Per.

Beloved turned back toward us. 'The dragons that were once Paragon the ship have come to claim the body of Kennitsson.'

I saw the uneasiness that went through all the others. The tattooed woman who had rowed the boat for us asked, 'To do what?'

Beloved looked down at the body and then around at the gathered crew. 'They will eat his body. To keep his memories among their own.' At the looks of horror that his words awoke, he said, 'The dragons consider doing that an honour.'

'Is this a fitting end for the Prince of the Pirate Isles?' Two men stepped forward to stand beside her. Tears tracked wet on one man's face but he held a knife in his hand and faced a dragon.

There would be trouble.

Beloved spoke. 'Is it so different to how Paragon took Kennit's memories, when he died on the ship's deck? Kennitsson goes where his father's and great-grandfather's ship has gone. And that is a fitting end for any pirate.'

Only Beloved seemed resigned that these dragons would eat the body of one who had been a companion to so many of them. But when he motioned to all of us to step back, everyone moved aside to let the dragons pass. The dock creaked and swayed on its pilings as the dragons halted by the body and looked down at it. I had thought there would be some ceremony, some decorous sharing, but no.

Eager to be first, both green and blue dragon darted their heads down to the corpse. We'd had only a piece of scorched sail canvas to cover him with, so nothing shielded us from the sight of the blue dragon seizing Kennitsson by the head and tugging the corpse upright as the green's head snaked in to shear off the bottom half of his body. Before anyone could gasp, the blue had lifted the head half with its now unravelling entrails and gulped it in.

Bits of Kennitsson's guts littered the dock. One of his sailors turned and harshly vomited into the harbour. Ant had lifted her hands to cover her eyes. Boy-O clung to his father like a child and Brashen's face was white. Spark gripped my other hand and swayed slightly.

'It is done,' Beloved said, as if that somehow made what we had seen better. As if the gory bits littering the planks would disappear.

'His memories will be within me,' the blue dragon announced.

'And in me,' the green said, almost argumentatively.

'I will sleep now,' the blue announced. He turned carefully but his tail still swept dangerously close. A step he took, and then he halted. He lowered his head and his eyes whirled as he snuffed Brashen's chest. He turned his head sideways, and regarded Boy-O. 'They burned us,' he thrummed, as if he recalled something from long ago. He made a low sound, like an immense cauldron coming to a boil. 'They have paid,' he said. A longer time he stared. 'Boy-O. I give you the honour of my name. Karrig.' He lifted his head. 'And I take part of yours. Karrigvestrit I shall be. I will remember you.'

Head up, the small dragon moved ponderously down the dock and toward the shore.

The green surveyed us silently. She drew breath and then reared up on her hind legs. She opened her mouth wide, and in the scarlet-and-orange striped maw she displayed, I saw death. Everyone crowded back and one man fell from the dock to the water as she hissed without venom. She closed her jaws and looked down on us. 'I was ever a dragon,' she said disdainfully. The dock swayed from her impetus and I feared it would collapse and spill all of us into the water as she sprang into the air. We cowered like rabbits as the wind of her wings swept us. A few moments later, the blue took flight and we were left as we had been. Ant was weeping with terror. She shot to Brashen's side and he put a sheltering arm around the young deckhand.

Per scanned the skies. 'I don't see or hear any of the other dragons.'

'They are likely gone to sleep off their . . . gorging,' Beloved spoke reluctantly as if he did not wish to remind us of what they had gorged on. But no one was deceived, and an uneasy silence followed his words.

Beloved stood watching them fly against the darkening sky and I could not read his expression. His shoulders rose and then fell. 'I am so tired,' he said, and I felt he spoke the words to someone who wasn't there. When he turned back to us, he spoke briskly. 'The streets are quiet and the dragons gone. Now we must go to salvage food and find a better place to shelter tonight.'

Brashen and Ant and a sailor named Twan stayed with Boy-O while the rest of us ventured out as a tight party, for the tattooed woman insisted we be defended. Clef went with us, carrying a knife and looking as if he wished to be attacked. We soon saw that not every inhabitant had fled. Some peered at us from the doubtful shelter of half-tumbled walls. Others were out salvaging or looting. They were poorly armed and most fled as soon as they saw us. Once, a flung brick struck Spark a glancing blow on the shoulder, but there was no sign of the assailant. Nonetheless, we took that warning to heart.

We salvaged canvas from the tumble of a sailmaker's sheds. Beloved sent sailors back with enough for a sling to carry Boy-O. We made a camp against the standing wall of the sailmaker's house. The night was mild. Per cut a square of canvas for me to sit on. One of the men fetched water in Prilkop's bucket.

Beloved did not wish to let me go with those who went to search for food, but I was too hungry to obey him. It was not a difficult search. This town had lived in plenty, and had not taken much of it when they fled. Some of the gardens had fruit trees. After days of being at sea, we little cared if it was ripe or not. We filled our shirt-fronts. Per found loaves and buns and even little cakes scattered among the wreckage of a bakery, and I found a tub of butter. 'I have heard that grease is good for a burn,' I mentioned to Per.

He looked doubtful but we took it along with our other looted food. 'Boy-O was very good to me, as was Brashen. And Kennitsson,' he added in a tighter voice. 'Althea. Cord.' I had not stopped to think that he might have made fast friends among the crew. I thought of that as we walked, eating as we went. I had Per, but if he had friends here, did I have less of him? Who cared for me in this world? Nettle and Riddle seemed very far away, and now they had a baby to share. Even Wolf Father was gone from me now. As I followed Per and the others through the deepening dark, the world seemed to stretch wider and emptier around me.

When we returned we found Brashen setting cool wet rags on Boy-O's burns. The younger man lay very still. His father had cut away much of his clothing and his burns were more extensive than I had thought. There were places where the fabric of his shirt had adhered to the burned flesh, and there it stayed, colourful flags on scorched territory.

Per knelt on one side of him. 'Do you think we can wake him enough to eat some bread?' he asked Brashen, who shook his head. His face was lined and there was some grey in his dark curly hair.

He looked at me and said, 'So this is the child we came to rescue. All of this death and destruction, to bring her home,' he said bitterly, and I suspected he thought me a bad bargain. Could I fault him for that? I had cost him a ship and his wife. Perhaps his son.

I knelt on the other side of his son with the butter tub. Clef had followed us and stood wordlessly behind me along with the tattooed woman that everyone called Navigator. 'I brought this to dress his wounds,' I told him. His dark eyes were empty of hope and he did not object. I dug my fingers into the soft yellow butter and very gently began to smooth it onto Boy-O's face. The bubbled flesh felt terribly wrong under my fingertips. One of the big blisters broke and oozed fluid that mixed with the butter. Wrong, it was all wrong. What was right? I touched the flesh next to the burn. That was right. That was what his skin should be like. My fingertips dragged on the unburned skin. I wished I could pull it over the scorched flesh like a cool coverlet.

His father abruptly leaned closer. 'Butter does that?' he demanded in a stunned voice.

'No. Farseers do that,' Per choked, and then he lifted his voice to shout, 'Amber! Come here!'

I could not be bothered with any of them. This was fascinating. It was like using a small brush or cut plume to put the colour exactly where I wanted it on a painting. With inks, I could make the bee or the flower precisely as it was supposed to be. With my fingers, I could draw the healthy flesh back over the burned parts. No. That wasn't exactly it. Starting at the healthy flesh was a good idea, but the clean skin was a spreading thing, like green plants growing over scorched earth. I pushed the debris of dead skin out of the way.

'Bee, stop that! Boy-O needs to rest and to eat. Later, perhaps, you can do more. Bee, can you hear me? Per, I dare not touch her! You must do it. Lift her under her arms and draw her away from Boy-O.'

The next thing I knew I sat by the fire, blinking. Per was standing over me, a peculiar look on his face. 'I'm so hungry and tired,' I told him.

A smile quirked one corner of his mouth. 'I imagine you are. Well, we have bread, and butter. And some fish.' My nose told me of chicken spitted over our fire. The others had been as successful in their scavenging. They had a cask of something and were breaking a hole in the top of it. I suddenly smelled beer.

I stood up unsteadily and looked over toward Boy-O. His father was smiling at me, but his cheeks were wet with tears. All doubt of me was cleared from his face. Beloved knelt by the lad. I had not healed his entire face, but he could close both his eyes now and his mouth was intact.

'He's wakeful enough that you should get him to eat. It draws strength from the injured person when a Farseer heals someone.' Beloved gave me a worried look. 'It wearies the Farseer as well.'

A louder voice cut through his words. 'Ah, I see that you have recovered the lost child! And if my ears do not deceive me, she is indeed her father's daughter.'

I startled, for the stranger had come up on us quietly. He was like no one I had ever seen, like a creature from a tale. He was tall and thin, gleaming scarlet, and dressed in bright garb. I stared at him. 'Rapskal,' Beloved said under his breath.

Then Per had handed me a torn slab of bread, the cut end of it dabbled in the butter. I bit off such a large bite that I got butter on both my cheeks. I didn't care. I chewed as I stared at the red lizard-man. His clothing had lots of leather straps and buckles. Things were clipped to him, a water-skin and other gear I didn't recognize. He reminded me of a festival puppeteer, but Beloved and Per seemed daunted by him. He looked around at us, and then asked, 'And where is FitzChivalry? And Kennitsson. I promised he would fly with us, to take our vengeance. Tomorrow, we scour the hills for any who escaped us! He will enjoy that hunt.'

'Neither survived,' Beloved said in a tight voice.

'Oh, dear, I do hope it was not the dragons! My apologies if it was. They are very focused when angered.'

Beloved looked stunned at the man's casual apology. 'No, both died before the dragons came,' he said in a subdued voice.

'Oh, well, that's good then. I would have hated it to have been the dragons. Very sorry to hear it, of course, and that the prince of the Pirate Isles is dead. He seemed quite taken with Heeby and she enjoyed his compliments. I ran into some of your fellows a short time ago. They told me of your other losses, including young Lant. A shame. He seemed such an engaging fellow.'

'He was,' Per said quietly, and suddenly the red man seemed to realize that perhaps his words had been thoughtless.

'Well, I should find some sustenance for myself. Heeby is sleeping and I have some time to myself. Vivacia will soon be arriving. We overflew her on our way here. Doubtless she and her crew will be disappointed to discover they have missed the battle.' He turned and began to walk away, leaving as abruptly as he had arrived.

'Red man!' Navigator called after him. 'Stay and eat with us. And drink to Kennitsson, Prince of the Pirate Isles.'

He turned back, his gleaming eyes very wide. 'I would be welcome here? And my dragon?' He seemed surprised.

'We will remember our dead tonight,' Clef told him.

Rapskal nodded slowly and then suddenly grinned wide. 'We would be honoured to join you. She is sleeping, her belly full of meat. When she wakes, I will bring her here.' He turned and hurried off.

The rest gaped after him, but I filled my mouth again. Spark came to find us, carrying a basket full of onions and carrots. 'I harvested one of the gardens,' she said quietly, as if a bit ashamed. 'There was little left of the house. I do not think the owners will be returning. How is Boy-O?'

'Much better. Bee can heal, like her father. And Vivacia is on her way here. Perhaps we have a way home,' Per told her.

She smiled. 'Good news all round, then,' she said, but her voice held the note of sorrow suppressed. 'I shall be glad to leave this place,' she added.

'As shall we all,' Beloved affirmed.

It was a peculiar night. Someone brought Brashen beer in a bowl. He drank it slowly but did not leave Boy-O's side. Rapskal did come back, and with him a scarlet dragon named Heeby. I was surprised to find that Heeby was shy and held herself apart and did not speak at all. Some of the crew got very drunk and sang songs about loot and sailing. Navigator was as drunk as any, and showing all that her tattoos were actually charts of harbours and waterways. After a time, she and Rapskal went apart from us, for she wished to show him a large tattoo on her belly. Per put my piece of canvas down on the far side of the fire from the singing and laughing crew. When he came to sit beside me, he smelled of beer. Later, Spark came to lie down beside me. She wept quietly in the dark.

Beloved sat apart from us. I watched him until I fell asleep. My last thought that night was that he was as alone as I was.

I awoke to birds calling. I looked up at tree branches with bits of blue sky beyond them. Dwalia! My entire body jerked with fear.

Then Per said, 'Bee? You've slept a long time. Are you waking up now?'

I sat up slowly. Per was bare-chested. Oh. His shirt had been my blanket. I offered it to him wordlessly and he spoke as he put it back on. 'Vivacia came into the harbour early this morning. Well, to the harbour. Too shallow for her to come closer. Their boat came ashore looking for us. That red fellow, Rapskal, he'd overflown them and shouted we were here. They've already taken Boy-O. We'll go next.'

I looked around me, blinking. 'Is there food?' I asked stupidly.

'There is.'

The bread was stale, but he had saved me a peach. He warmed the bread on a stick over the embers and dunked it in the butter. It was good. I washed my hands and face and said, 'The birds woke me. Did you have a blue crow? With some red feathers?' It seemed a dream.

'She went with the dragons, I think. They gave her such colours! She loves them.' He seemed sad.

I changed the subject. 'Who is Vivacia and why has she come?'

'She's a liveship, like Paragon was. She came following the dragons and Rapskal. She'd gone to Others' Island. There was a battle there, too, to kill all the Others who had been taking the dragon eggs or capturing the little serpents as they hatched. Then Vivacia said they must now come here to help Tintaglia take revenge . . .'

'I see,' I said, but only to stop his flow of words. My head felt too foggy to take on so much information. I stood up slowly and looked around. Spark was drifting listlessly about our camp, as if looking for anything that needed to be done. Her eyes were red, her mouth drooping. The others were gone. 'Did Beloved go to the ship with the others?'

'No. He went up into the hills, to try to find his way back to the tunnel. He went before, in the night, but could not find it. So he got up very early, as soon as it was light, to try again.'

'And he didn't wake me to go with him?' Anger coursed through me.

'Nor me, nor Spark. He told Ant to tell us where he'd gone.' He put more bread on the toasting stick. 'I think he needed to go alone, Bee.'

'And what about what I might need?' I raged. The anger that

shot through me was as heady as when the Skill rushed from me. Like the night the serpent spit had got in my cuts.

'Bee?' Per said and stepped a little back from me.

I saw Beloved at the edge of the camp. He walked slowly, looking at the ground. I did not run to him. I shouted, 'Did you see him? You went without me.' I could not keep the anger from my voice.

'No.' His voice was a hoarse admission of defeat. 'I found the tunnel mouth again. But it was as I feared. At a high tide, it floods full.'

I winced. I did not want to think of my father's body floating in cold seawater while fish nibbled at him. 'He's dead. I told you that. I felt it.'

He didn't look at me. With an effort, he said, 'Spark, Per, if there's anything you want to take, gather it. I promised Wintrow I would not delay the sailing. There's probably a boat waiting for us now.'

Per had piled fruit onto a square of canvas. He bagged it up and said, 'That's it. Ready to go.'

'I'm taking nothing from here,' Spark said.

Beloved looked at me. I shrugged. 'Nothing. Taking nothing. Leaving everything.'

'I know he's dead,' he admitted brokenly. He finally turned toward me. The rims all around his pale eyes were red. There were deep lines around his mouth. He looked at me. 'You are all I have left of him now.'

I spoke very quietly. 'Then you have nothing at all.'

FORTY

Warm Water

Battle death to your last breath and even unknown, you are a hero.

Whimper your way into darkness and your name will become a taunt of cowardice.

Chalcedean saying

Dying is boring, Nighteyes observed.

I drew a deeper breath. 'Perhaps you are not taking it as personally as I am.' My voice sounded strange to me. Water had risen in the chamber and I had wondered if I would drown, trapped on my back with my head lower than my hips and my legs pinned between stone and stone. It was among the worst deaths I could have imagined for myself, but it had not even wet my hair. If it had come that high, I probably would have drunk some of it. Saltwater or not, I was so thirsty.

The water was retreating now. The high tide had not reached me. This time. Perhaps the next tide would reach higher. I would almost welcome it, I decided. I had never expected to awaken in my body again, never expected to endure physical discomfort again. Now it seemed unfair that the pain from my trapped legs was not enough to drive hunger and thirst from my thoughts. I wrapped my arms around my body. I was cold. Not the cold that kills, but the cold that makes one stiff and miserable.

Your death is personal, Little Brother. When you go, so do I.

You should have stayed with Bee.

All the same. When you perish, I go, too.

The blackness was absolute. Either I was blind or no light reached this chamber. Likely both were true, but I didn't regret giving the Fool my strength and my eyes. I hoped it had been enough to get them out of this tunnel and back to Paragon. I hoped they had boarded the ship, hoisted anchor and dropped sail and fled without another thought for me.

I tried again to move. The edges of the stone steps dug into my hips, the middle of my back and my shoulders. Cold and hard. The sword slash still hurt, and the back of my neck itched maddeningly. I scratched it again. It was the only discomfort I could do anything about.

So the plan is to lie here until we die?

It's not a plan, Nighteyes. It's inevitable.

I thought you were more of a wolf than that.

That stung. I scowled and spoke aloud into the darkness. 'Give me a better plan, then.'

Make up your mind. Is Death a friend? Then go joyfully to hunt with it, as I did. If it's an enemy, then fight it. But don't sag here like a wounded cow waiting for predators to finish it off. You are not prey, nor I! If we must die, let us die as wolves!

What would you have me do? Chew off my legs?

A brief silence. Then, *Could you do that?*

I don't bend that way, my teeth are wrong, and I'd likely bleed to death before I escaped.

Then why did you suggest it?

I was being sarcastic.

Oh. Bee was not sarcastic. I enjoyed that about her.

Tell me of your time with her.

A longer pause in his thoughts. Then, *No. Fight your way out of this and live, and perhaps she will tell you herself. I am not going to share tales of her hardship while you lie here and moan like a wounded sow.*

Her hardship. *How bad was it?*

Bad enough.

His rebuke stung in a way that only his disdain of me had ever achieved. I tried again to shift my legs. Useless. The fallen beam pinned me just above the knees. I could not get any leverage. I tried to remember if I'd had a long knife in my pack. The wolf was right about that aspect of my predicament. I did not want to linger like this. Would I go so far as to sever my legs to escape? A ridiculous idea. My knife would never go through leg bones. Was the ship's hatchet in my bag?

I groped for my pack. I'd had it slung over my shoulder before the blast flung me down the steps. It was gone. My groping fingers found only loose gravel and rubble. And standing water if I stretched my arms as far as I could past my head. I paddled my fingers in the water and then wiped grit and dust from my face with my wet hand. The warm water felt good. I reached my hand into it again and trailed my chilled fingers in it.

Warm water. Warm water?

I froze.

In my experience, two things gave off warmth: living creatures and fire. My Wit told me there were no other living creatures in my vicinity. A fire in water was not possible. For a single, chilling moment, I recalled that Forged people were invisible to my Wit, yet alive and giving off warmth. But I had not encountered a Forged one in decades, not since the Red-Ship Raiders had created them during our war with the OutIslanders.

We found that hot spring, once.

It stank. I smell nothing.

Nor I.

I opened my eyes wide and strained to see something, anything. But still there was nothing. I firmed my will to iron and reached out again, groping. The water was definitely warmer. I strained my arms in that direction as far as I could. I felt the slash in my leg straining with my reaching. Warmer yet. My fingertips brushed something I recognized at once. The side of my pack. Just a little more. I strained, dragged my fingertips down the sturdy fabric, seeking something to grip. Instead, I felt it overbalance and slip away from me. With a muffled 'tunk' it fell down one step. Hopelessly out of my reach now.

And that sound, the noise of something solid and dense made me recall what had weighted my pack. One of Chade's firepots was in there. With the heavy tube of dragon-Silver.

And the Elderling fire-brick.

I wondered which side of the brick was now up. I wondered if Chade's firepot could explode under water. The brick could not set fire to it. Was mere heat enough to set it off?

What happened to dragon-Silver when it was heated?

Probably nothing.

Some time passed. A lot of time, or a little time. In the dark, degrees of pain, hunger and thirst were more potent measures than time. Occasionally I shifted, to put the pressure of the edges of the steps in different uncomfortable parts of my body. I scratched my neck where it itched. I crossed my arms on my chest; I uncrossed my arms. I thought of Bee, of the Fool. Had they escaped? Had they reached the ship safely? Perhaps they were even now on their way home. I yearned after them, and then rebuked myself. I did not want them here in the dark with me. Much as I might claim to disbelieve the Fool's dream, his prediction had been too powerful. I thought of Bee's illustration in her book. The blue buck stood on one pan of the scale, the tiny bee on the other. And below it, in her careful script, the words of the red-toothed woman were written. 'A worthy exchange.'

It was.

My thoughts wandered. I hoped Nettle's child was growing well. Riddle would be a good father. I hoped Lant and Spark and Per would understand my decision. I thought of Molly and wished I could have died in bed with her beside me.

The Skill was stealing my body's paltry reserves, trying to heal the broken parts while rebuilding the strength I had pushed into the Fool. But my body had nothing left to fuel a renewal. I felt like a lamp flame dancing on the last of a wick. I wanted to sleep but was too uncomfortable. Eventually, I knew sleep would take me whether I willed it or not. Possibly I was already asleep in this total darkness. Maybe I was already dead.

I preferred the boredom to this self-pity. And the water to the left of you is warmer now. Don't you smell it, even with your pitiful nose?

I reached over my head and as far to the left as I could in the darkness. My hand touched water. And it was much warmer than standing water inside a dank tunnel should have been. I strained again, reaching, and the water grew surprisingly hot. The fire-brick was a powerful magic.

As I drew my hand back, my pack exploded.

I was not completely blind, for I knew an instant of gleaming silver light. Water splashed over me, hot enough to scald. I tried to wipe it from my face but it clung, searing and burning, to both my hands and to my face; it was not water. It sank into me like liquid poured into dry sand, permeating me. And my body sucked it in as if it had always craved this magical stuff. One side of my face, my chest and left arm and both hands it coated, and then it spread as if it were something alive, seeking to envelop me. I screamed, but not in pain. It was an ecstasy too large for my body to contain. Four times I gave voice to an experience no human was ever meant to have. Then I lay back, panting and weeping. I could feel it soaking and changing me. Claiming and trapping me.

I tried again to wipe it from my eyes. It had gone into my mouth when I screamed and up my nose. The burning pleasure of it was so excruciating that it was a new kind of pain. I rubbed my eyes and tried to blink it away and saw instead a new world in the dark cavern. The gleaming splashes of Silver that had erupted had spattered the fallen stonework that pinned me. I also understood what the Fool had tried to explain to me back in Buckkeep Castle when he spoke of seeing as a dragon might. I saw warmth, on the spattered silver and splashed water. I watched it fade as the water cooled.

Darkness flowed back in around me. The Silver continued to explore me. I lay still, beyond pleasure, beyond pain. Beyond time. I closed my eyes. I let go.

Fitz. Do something.

I realized I was still breathing. And with that thought, awareness of my body triggered a rush of all the pains. 'Do what?' I spoke the words in a dry whisper.

Verity shaped stone with his silvered hands. The Scentless One shaped wood with his silvered fingertips.

Oh.

With the tips of my fingers, I explored the fallen beam that trapped my legs. I stroked it. No change that I could feel. I scratched at it with my nails. Splinters under my nails. Not pleasant. I smoothed it with my fingertips.

I do not know how long it took me to master the process. It was not a physical digging away that was needed, but a persuasion of the wood. I did not compress it with the strength of my hands, nor shear it away, but I came to know the fallen beam very well indeed.

It was a physical feat to tighten my belly muscles and curl up enough to reach under the pinning wood. Too often I had to lie back and gather myself again. Silver was not food and water. It gave me strength, but still my body was hungry and thirsty. And so very tired.

When my second leg was finally freed, the incredible pain of its reawakening left me weeping and shouting. I slid my body down the stone steps and into shallow water and wallowed about until my head was finally higher than my torso. I crawled up onto fallen debris. I think I fell unconscious for a time. When I awoke, the water had receded slightly. I could not stand, and even sitting was a weariness. I decided I would sleep for a time longer.

No. You can sleep after you have seen the sky again. Up, Fitz. Up and walk. You cannot rest yet.

It was not my human will but the wolf in me that made me struggle to rise. My feet were distant and painful things. There were deep bruises across my legs. The flesh had been compacted and crushed. I could feel that with my fingers, as well as the ragged edge of the sword slash. I was glad I could not see my legs save as warm shapes. My initial progress was a series of stagger, fall, crawl, rest, stand, stagger, fall. The steps went down forever, and every lurch down was a torment. The fall took me into shallow, briny water. I moved through utter darkness. When my groping hands found a section of wall that seemed less damaged by Spark's blast, I followed along it. Barnacles on the wall and floor cut my flesh. I stupidly realized I was barefoot. When had I lost my boots? The blast had torn my clothes, but my boots? I pushed that aside. It was only pain and it did not last long. The steps down seemed endless. I was grateful that the water was gradually receding. I do not think I could have forced my way past its resistance. When the steps finally ended and I sloshed through standing water to my knees, I became aware of a different sort of pain.

It was not just the Skill forcing the healing of my legs. When I touched the sword slash, silver fingers to Silver-splashed wound, I felt as if I had been patched, like a leather jerkin mended with canvas. It did not feel like my own flesh, but there was no stopping it. I might be able to persuade stone to move and free me, but my own body had a peculiar will of its own.

Onward. I had to catch up with the others. The Fool would believe I was dead. That was what he would tell them! My poor little girl! I could not blame him. I had thought myself dead.

You would have been, if I had not held back some life for us. For me. For you. Mostly for the cub. You must stop taking foolish risks. We need to survive.

How long had I been trapped underground? A tide had been rising when the others fled. It had fallen, risen again, and now was ebbing I judged. A day gone, at least. Possibly two. I wondered where Bee and the others might be right now. Had they escaped? Were they even now at sea on Paragon, sailing away from this horrid place, toward home and family?

I tried to Skill to Bee. I had as little success as I always did when I reached for her. Trying to Skill through the pain and the peculiar Silver sensations was like trying to shout when one is breathless and running. I gave it up and trudged on. Catch up with them.

Had they encountered the Servants' guardsmen? Had the fleeing Whites we freed betrayed them? Had they fought and won, or fallen? Had they been taken prisoner? Whenever I wanted to stop and rest I flogged myself with those thoughts and pushed on. I came to steps. I climbed them.

Blackness became dark grey and then a paler grey. I pushed on toward a paler shape of light interrupted by lines and . . . It was a partly open door, overgrown by vegetation. I could barely push past the tangled greenery. Brambles tore at my frayed clothing and skin as I thrust thorny vines aside until I emerged from the hillside thicket and stood under a clear blue sky. The grass was taller than my knees and mixed with twiggy brush.

I collapsed and sat where I was, heedless of the protest of the sword-slash across my thigh. I dared myself to look at it. It was sealed with Silver as if I'd patched myself with tar. I prodded it and winced. Under the patch, my body toiled on with its repairs. My vision was marginally clearer. My palms were silver. I stared at them. My hands were skeletal, bones and bulging veins and tendons. All gleaming as if cast in Silver. I'd eaten myself to make repairs. My clothing hung on me.

I rose and tried to walk on. The ground was uneven and tufts of grass caught at my dragging feet. I stepped on a flattened thistle and fell over. It was hard to see the tiny pale thorns I picked out of the sole of my bony foot with my silver fingers. I could feel what I could not see, the Silver giving me a sensitivity that my hands had never possessed. I looked at my hands in the sunlight. They glittered, gleaming and bright. It was either more Silver than Verity had ever possessed or a much finer quality than he had used. The coating on Verity's hands had reminded me of thick mud; mine looked as if I wore elegant silver gloves that clung to every line and fold of my hands. I reinspected the places where the Silver had struck. Had the blast so shredded my clothing or had the Silver splashed and eaten it? Silver gleamed on part of my chest, in splotches on my legs. I knew it coated more than half my face. I wondered what it looked like. My eyes? I pushed the thought away.

Straggling among the grass were long, crawling threads of clover, both leaves and purple blossoms. Molly had used the flowers to flavour warmed honey and teas. I gathered a handful and put them in my mouth. A faint trace of sweetness and moisture. They helped but not enough.

I managed to stagger upright and stood unsteady on my feet, trying to decide where I was. I was on one of the rolling hills behind the town, I thought. Below me were the ruins of Clerres Castle. I stared. It was castle no longer, but only mounded rubble scattered across the end of the peninsula. Bee's fire had not done that. A slow recognition worked into me. The dragons had come. Heeby and Tintaglia. This was the vengeance they had said they would take. Men would have needed months to topple this stronghold so thoroughly, and men tended to keep and exploit what they conquered. Dragon-acid had eaten the walls, melting stone and dissolving wood. It looked like a dropped cake. I saw two figures moving over the rubble and spotted another man along the shore, pushing a barrow down what had been the road. It was littered with the wreckage of the buildings that had lined it. So few people. I wondered how many were buried under the falling rubble. Were my people among them? Where was Paragon?

Not in the harbour, nor anchored outside it. Paragon was gone. There were no large ships there. Not one. No barrows full of goods moved on the docks, no one strolled the streets of the markets and warehouse areas. All the structures lacked roofs and the walls leaned drunkenly against each other. There was, however, plenty of wreckage sloshing around the pilings of the docks, and many masts of smaller vessels sticking up above the retreating waves.

In the distant sky, something sparkled. Wings of red and blue. Tintaglia and Heeby, finished with their destruction and winging home. And beneath them, a sailing ship. Paragon? I dared to hope. But it was leaving. Leaving me here.

At the edge of the harbour below, a ship was putting on sail. I stared at her. No mistaking that stern and house. It was the liveship *Vivacia*. Departing. Without me.

'Bee!' I shouted her name, and then, 'Fool! Don't go! Wait!' Stupid.

Stupid, stupid. I drew a deep breath, gathered my strength and reached out with the Skill. *Bee! Bee, tell them you hear me, tell them to turn back. I'm here, come back!* I felt no sense of her, not even the rush and rip of the Skill-current. Was my magic as damaged as the rest of me? I tried again, pushing hard, wordlessly trying for a touch.

A wave of vertigo sat me down on the grassy turf. Had she heard me? Were her walls up? I watched the ship, hoping to see the sails change, to see it tack and turn. Was she even on the ship?

Did she still exist for me to Skill to?

If she lived, she had not heard me. The ship moved slowly and gracefully away. Leaving me. I stood, shaking with hunger and tormented by thirst, and watched the ship grow smaller. What did I do now? A rising tide of despair threatened to engulf me. I needed to know what had happened and there was no one to tell me. What should I do?

First you live, stupid. Eat something besides clover. And drink. Find water.

The wolf in me lived ever in the now.

I looked for tell-tale signs of a stream or spring, taller greener grass or bog-grass. I saw an area down the hillside that showed much trampling by hooves. Of the flocks I had seen, only three sheep remained, cropping the grass near the spring. I went toward it. The area around the welling water was bare of grass and carpeted with sheep dung. I was past caring. The mud rose between my toes as I waded out into a shallow pool and found the coolness where the water had welled from the earth. I scooped up water in my silvered hands. I looked at it, my caution warring with my thirst, and then I drank, not caring if it silvered my innards. I was still scooping water and drinking when I heard a caw.

I looked up. A flock of ravens are almost always crows, and a single crow is usually a raven. But there was no mistaking Motley with her silver beak. And scarlet plumes? She circled high above me. 'Motley!' I cried to her. She cawed back and then slid away from me on the wind, down to the town.

'Stupid bird,' I said aloud.

She saw us. Wait. Such counsel was very unlike Nighteyes. I went back to drinking water. When my belly would take no more, I waded to the edge of the muddy watering hole, and then out onto cleaner grass. 'Can I sleep now?'

If you can't eat, sleep. But not out in the open. When did you become so foolish?

When I stopped caring. I did not share that thought with him. It would almost have been a relief to have someone attack me, someone I could throttle and bite and kick. My worry had become anger at everything I didn't know and couldn't control.

I sensed her with my Wit and turned my head before she landed onto the sheep-cropped sward at my feet. Motley dropped a large piece of something and then did a bobbing crow greeting. 'Eat, eat, silver man,' she urged me. She paused to groom her feathers. They had become even more resplendent, with a few scarlet flight feathers in each wing, and a steel-blue sheen to the black ones.

'Silver beak,' I responded to her, and she tilted her head and gave me a knowing look.

'Consorting with dragons again,' I hazarded, and her caw was like a pleased chuckle. 'What is this?' I asked as I stooped to look at a moist brown cube. I didn't want to touch it.

'Food,' she told me, and lifted into the air again.

'Wait!' I cried after her. 'Where are the others? What happened?'

She did a circle around me. 'Dragons! Lovely, lovely dragons! Paragon is dragons now.'

'Motley, please! Where are my friends?'

'Some died, some left.' She called the words down. 'One comes.'

'Which some? Left for where? Who comes? Crow! Motley! Come back!'

But the crow did not heed my cries. She flew away in a straight line, back to the fallen city, probably back to where she had pilfered the food. If food it was. I picked up the sticky cube and smelled it. A rich brown meat smell came from it.

Eat it!

Nighteyes' assurance was all I needed. Without hesitation, I took a bite. It was delicious, salt and beef, a chunk of food almost as big as my fist and doubtless as much as she could carry. I surrendered my annoyance with her. I still needed to know, but my body said that food was more important than information at the moment. And more water. I went back to the spring.

I drank, splashed my face and neck, and then scrubbed at the remaining crust of filth that clung to my trouser legs. Washing my hands had no effect on the Silver that coated them.

The sheep lifted their heads and I looked up with them. Prilkop was slowly climbing the hill toward me. A White followed him at a discreet distance. I stood and watched them come. Prilkop regarded me with dismay and perhaps horror. Did I look so terrible? Of course, I must. When he was close enough that I did not have to shout, I asked, 'Who lived?'

He stopped. 'Of yours or mine?' he asked gravely.

'Mine!' His question angered me with its subtle accusation.

'Bee. And Beloved. The boy you had with you, and the young woman.'

I tamped down my joy with my next question. 'And Lant?'

'The warrior you brought with you? When last I saw your folk, he was not among them. Probably lost in the water when the ship changed into dragons.'

Another jolt to my tottering mind. I waded out of the now muddied water and away from the dung-strewn area surrounding it. Prilkop came and walked beside me but did not offer his arm. I didn't blame him. 'Where did my people go?'

'Another ship came to the harbour and carried them away. They are gone.'

I met his gaze. His dark eyes were full of anguish. 'Why did you come to me?'

'I saw a crow with a few scarlet feathers. I dreamed of that crow, once. When I called to it, it came to me and spoke your name, and said I would find you with the sheep.' He looked around. 'The few that remain,' he added, and again I heard that accusing note in his voice. 'I saw him with your friends, when last I spoke to Beloved.'

'Her,' I corrected. 'You spoke to Beloved?' The grass under my bare feet was relatively free of sheep dung. I sat down like an old tapestry falling from its hooks. Prilkop was more graceful, but not much. I wondered how old he was. The White he had brought with him didn't sit but stood at a distance as if he would flee at any moment.

'Leave the food and wine, and you can go,' Prilkop told him. The White unslung a canvas bag from one shoulder, dropped it, then turned and ran. Prilkop made a sound between a sigh and a moan. He worked his way to his feet, retrieved the bag and seated himself beside me again. As he opened it between us, I asked him, 'Am I that frightening?'

'You look more statue than man, something wrought of silver

attached to a skeleton coated with flesh. Did Capra do this to you? Or a dragon?'

'My own doing and no one else's. A magic gone wrong,' I told him, for I was too weary to bother with more words than that. 'What happened? To Bee and to Beloved? To everyone else?'

'They believe you dead. All of them. They mourn you savagely.'

Vanity is such a strange thing. They mourned me, and I was warmed that they loved me.

He spoke words carefully as he dug a cork out of a web-coated bottle of wine. He set it down between us and began to arrange a strange picnic. 'It's good wine, from the best tavern in town. I had to choose from what folk had left behind. The eggs are raw, from a half-fallen chicken house. The apricots are not quite ripe but the tree was down, so I picked them. The same for the fish; I took it from a fallen smoking rack, and it's still wet inside.'

'And you brought it for me?'

'I was gathering food when I saw the crow. I think you are hungrier than I am.'

'Thank you.' I cared nothing for the condition of the food or its source. I was barely able to restrain myself until he had set out the food on the coarse sack it had been carried in. 'Eat while I talk,' he suggested, and I was happy to comply. The food was as flawed as he said it would be and I devoured it. Raw eggs are fine as long as the belly expects them.

There were gaps in the tale he told me, but I learned much that calmed my heart. He had seen Bee with the Fool and Spark and Per. Lant was possibly lost. Someone had been badly burned. Harder to grasp was that when the ship Paragon had sunk, two dragons had emerged from the waters of the harbour. I had my own thoughts on how that had happened. And other dragons and a scarlet man had come to destroy all of Clerres. I was astounded when he spoke of a black dragon. It had to be IceFyre. The scarlet man that Prilkop had glimpsed was probably Rapskal.

There were things he did not know and could not explain. I could not imagine how Paragon had found the strength to become dragons. Then I recalled the Fool's words about my missing tube of Silver. Tintaglia and Heeby had said they would come as soon as they could, but I was surprised that IceFyre had made the journey. Prilkop knew little of the *Vivacia* other than that a ship with a living figurehead had come into the bay, the dragons had flown in circles above, shouting down to it, and then all the folk that remained from those who had arrived on the Paragon had departed on board.

Logic told me that I should be glad they were safely on their way. But being left for dead, even when one has insisted on it, creates a gulch of hurt in the heart. No matter how foolish, it stung that they had gone without me. It echoed painfully how Molly and Burrich had continued their lives when they believed me dead. Stupid, stupid emotion. Would not I have done exactly the same? I pushed my thoughts into a new channel, forced myself to confront the tragedy in Prilkop's eyes.

'They have treated you badly ever since you returned to Clerres but I know this is not what you would have wished on them. How have the folk of Clerres fared? What of your Whites?'

He made a small sound. 'I have lived a long life, FitzChivalry Farseer. I've seen the fall of the Pale Woman's holdings on Aslevjal, and rejoiced in it. Remember, I had my part in preserving IceFyre's life while he was encased in the ice. But Clerres, here . . . yes, they treated me badly.' He looked down at the white tracery of scars on his black hands and arms. 'Worse than badly,' he admitted. He lifted his eyes. 'As your own family treated you, as I recall from Beloved's telling. But never did you confuse one of your uncles with the others, did you? When I was a child at Clerres, so long ago, it was a place of learning. I loved the libraries! They told me who I was! There were all the deeds of the White Prophets who had gone before me. There were the adventures of them finding their Catalysts, but also there were collections of lore, and accounts of ancient queens, as well as maps and histories of far away places . . . you cannot imagine what Bee destroyed with her fire. I do not blame her; she could not argue with the forces that shaped her and set her on that path. But I mourn what was lost.

'I mourn, too, the Whites in their pretty little cottages, now buried under the fallen stone of Clerres Castle. Some were only children! Their dreams may have been used for selfish purposes, but you cannot blame them for that any more than I can blame Bee for what she became. So many of them are dead. So many.'

He fell silent, strangled by his emotions. I had no reply. Innocents had died. But those who had tormented and tortured the Fool, those who had stolen and abused my Bee, they were dead, too, and I could not regret that. 'So. The Four are dead. What will become of you now?'

He lifted his eyes. The look he gave me was guarded. 'Three are dead. Capra survived.' He studied my impassive face. Could he read my thoughts? 'You and your dragons killed almost all of us. I have gathered seventeen of the Whites. Once there were over two hundred Whites and part-Whites. Those who survived take comfort in Capra's leadership. For generations, she has guided them. Already she tells us that the weakness was that there were Four. She will be the One, now, and will keep our purpose clear. I have spoken with her and she has promised that we will go back to our old ways. I set out to gather food for those who remain. But when I saw the piebald crow and called to her and when she came to me, I knew my best course was to seek you out. To ask for mercy for those who remain. To diverge from your path, just a little. For the sake of those under my protection.'

Was that why he had come? Or only now did he read my intent?

I looked down at the emptied eggshells. Had he thought to buy me?

'I could have poisoned you,' he said, a slight edge to his voice in response to my silence.

'No. You couldn't have. All those years, when you raided the Pale Woman's food supplies, you never poisoned her. I know there is no killer in you, Prilkop. You should be glad of that.'

'And it is a part of you that you can never tear from your soul.'

'That is likely.'

'I brought you food. Can we not trade that for the lives of my Whites?'

I was silent, weighing that. He took my silence as a rejection of his offer. He stood abruptly. 'I do not think we have ever truly been friends, FitzChivalry Farseer.'

I came slowly to my feet. 'I am sad to agree with you, Prilkop, but I give you my greatest respect.'

'And I cede the same to you.' He offered me a peculiar bow, one that involved stretching out one leg behind him. It was more stiff than graceful, and I suspect it cost the old man an effort. I returned a very formal Buckkeep bow to him.

And so we parted. I never saw Prilkop again.

* * *

As the sun grew stronger, I took shelter in a thorn thicket. The bottle of wine was my companion. After I'd consumed it, I slept the rest of the day away. I awoke hungry again, but in much better condition. Even my eyesight had improved, and Nighteyes remarked, *You see in the dark much as I once did.*

And as we once did, we hunt together.

If Prilkop had warned Capra of danger, she had not heeded him. Perhaps he had judged me too feeble to pursue my prey immediately. Perhaps he had thought her well-guarded. It was easy to find her. I ghosted through Clerres until I found a large stone building where the debris had been cleared from the street and a new roof begun. She had a few guards, but I did not have to kill any of them. The guarded doors and windows faced the street front, but I went to the back of the building. Silently, my silver hand slowly eased away old stone and mortar. I made my own entrance.

Somehow, they had found a fine bed for her. The tall wooden bedposts upheld lacy curtains. I woke her before I killed her. My grip silenced her and I whispered to her startled eyes, 'For my Beloved and for my Bee, you die.' It was my only indulgence. With silvered hands I strangled her. My Wit told me of her panic and pain and terror. But I killed her as if she were a rabbit. I did not delay her death, but I did look into her eyes until she was no longer behind them. I hearkened back to Chade's earliest training. I went in, I killed, and I departed. And I took her half-eaten chicken with me.

It was delicious.

As the sun rose, I was moving parallel to the road that led away from Clerres.

FORTY-ONE

Vivacia's Voyage

I mourn the good paper and lovely leather covers of the books my father gave to me. They are gone, sent to the bottom with all the goods and possessions of those who captained and crewed Paragon. I do not miss the writing on those pages. The journal was written by a child whom I barely recall. The dreams she wrote are irrelevant, markers on paths that no longer exist. The few that yet may be will come to pass with or without ink on a page.

New dreams now come to me, and Beloved urges me to write them down. I do not like to call him Beloved. And when I called him Fool once he flinched and the captain of this ship looked at me as if I were rude. Before others, I call him Teacher. He does not seem to mind. I will not name him Amber.

I no longer have a book, but Beloved has given me sheets of paper and a simple pen and black ink. I think he has begged these things from Captain Wintrow.

This is my first dream to record. An old tree blossoms and bears a single beautiful fruit. It falls to the ground and rolls away. It cracks open and a woman wearing a silver crown steps out of it.

I am sad that I must draw this only in black on white paper.

He has told me that he will read the dreams I write. That he must so that he can guide me. I write here what I have already told him, that he may read it again. I will not let my dreams be used to shape the world. And regardless of what he promised my father, I find it intrusive and rude that he reads my words here.

Bee Farseer's journal

We put Clerres behind us, and I was not sorry to do so. The only tear I felt was that my father was left behind, dead and unburned, in such a horrid place.

The ship spoke in my mind the instant I set foot on the deck. *Who are you? And why do you ring so strangely on my senses?*

I walled my mind as well as I could, but that only spiced her interest in me. She pushed at me, and it was like being prodded in the chest with a forefinger. *I don't know why you sense me. I am Bee Farseer. I was a prisoner of the Servants in Clerres. I only want to go home.*

A very strange thing happened then: I felt the ship wall me out. But it was more relief than insult.

We were a rag-tag group that boarded Vivacia. The adults had already spoken to one another while I slept. It little mattered what they had agreed upon. I was like the nut carried in the stream. I was swept along by my fate.

On board the ship, hammocks were hung for us, but there were no walls to divide us from the regular crew. I did not care. The moment my hammock was hung, I clambered into it and fell asleep. I awakened shortly after to incredulous shouts from the deck. I forced myself to roll until I fell out of the hammock. I hurried from the crew's quarters up onto the deck, fearing the ship was being attacked.

The tide had carried some of the wreckage from old Paragon out to sea. And clinging to it was a survivor. Spark's hopes were dashed when they hauled aboard a dazed and sunburned woman. This was Boy-O's mother and Brashen's wife, and she was somehow related to Captain Wintrow. The liveship thrummed with joy, the timbers vibrating. I stayed to see her brought aboard and given water, and then returned to my hammock. I cried—not with joy but jealousy—and slept again.

On this ship, Beloved became a person named Amber. I had no idea why he had so many names, or why he was now a woman. Everyone else seemed to accept it. I thought of how my father had been Tom Badgerlock as well as FitzChivalry Farseer, and perhaps I was the same. Bee Badgerlock, Bee Farseer. The Destroyer.

Bee the orphan.

Two days into our voyage, I woke to Per standing beside my hammock looking at me. 'Is there danger?' I asked, sitting up, and he caught me before I pitched to the deck again. It was not just the hammock. The ship was rolling.

'No, but you have been sleeping a lot. You should get up and eat some food and move about.'

When he mentioned food, my body asserted that it was hungry, and very thirsty. He led me through the jungle of hammocks to a long table with benches alongside it. There were a few people sitting at it, finishing food. And a plate with a bowl covering it. 'To keep it warm,' Per told me.

It was a thick stew that smelled strange, yet was also good. Cinnamon and a creamy but sour smell. Onions and potato pieces. The meat was mutton, Per claimed, but it was not tough and stringy. Per pushed a large bowl of boiled brown seeds toward me. 'It's rice. They tell me it grows in a swamp and they harvest it in boats. Try it with the stew. It's good.'

I ate until my belly felt tight and Per had scraped the bottom of the big black kettle clean. 'Want to come out on the deck now?' he invited, but I shook my head.

'I want to sleep,' I told him.

He frowned at that, but walked back to the hammock with me and helped me into it. 'Are you sick, to sleep this much?' he asked me.

I shook my head. 'It's easier than being awake,' I told him, and closed my eyes.

I awoke again but didn't open my eyes to hear them whispering about me. 'But she sleeps so much. It's all she does!' Per, worried.

'Let her sleep. It means she feels safe. She's getting the rest she didn't get the whole time they had her. And sorting things out. When I came back . . . when Fitz took me back to Buckkeep Castle, for many days after I spent most of my time in sleep. It's the great healer.'

Nonetheless, a few hours later when I opened my eyes, Per was beside my hammock. 'Are you awake enough to talk now? I want to know everything that has happened to you since last we were together. And I have much to tell you.'

'I have not so much to tell you. They stole me, and they dragged me to Clerres. They treated me badly.' I stopped speaking. I didn't want to recount it for Perseverance or anyone else.

He nodded. 'Not yet, then. But I shall tell you of all I have done and seen since you covered me with the butterfly cloak and left me in the snow.'

I climbed out of the hammock and we went out on the deck. It was a fine blue day. He took me to a place near the figurehead, but not in anyone's way. He told me his story, and it sounded to me like a tale of heroes on a quest. I wondered if Hap would ever make a song of it. I cried several times, to hear of all my father and Per had done to seek me. But they were good tears as well as sad ones. In all the days when I had wondered why my father had not come to save me, I had wondered if he had ever loved me at all. I went back to my hammock and my sleep knowing that he had.

It was the ship that woke me the next time. She drilled through my walls. *Please help us. Come to me, at the foredeck. You are needed.*

I thought I would wake the others when I dropped and fell from the hammock to the deck. It was always dark belowdecks, but from the number of occupied hammocks around me, I guessed it was night. There was a single dim lantern, swinging with the motion of the ship. I didn't like to look at it. I made my way through hammocks full of sleeping sailors like ripe fruit hanging on a tree, through shifting shadows to a ladder. I went up onto Vivacia's deck.

The wind was blowing fresh and I was suddenly glad to be awake. I looked up. The canvas was belled out like a rich merchant's belly, and beyond it were realms of stars in a clear sky. The deck of a sailing ship is never deserted when underway, but tonight's wind was steady and kind, so not many sailors were scurrying about. No one noticed me as I moved forward. There was a short set of steps and then I was on the crowded foredeck. All sorts of lines terminated there; they were taut and humming a wind song. Past them was a smaller deck, a feature I'd never seen, that poked out toward the figurehead. On that deck, a man was stretched out. As I stepped toward him cautiously, two other people stirred. I recognized one of them. Boy-O's father, Captain Brashen Trell. Captain of nothing now, I guessed, and his son burned and still. I'd almost forgotten that we'd regained Boy-O's mother. Her face and arms were pebbled; I stared and then recognized that they were the healing blisters from where the sun had burned her. She looked at my scarred face and her brows drew together in pity. I looked away.

Her name is Althea Vestrit. If the past had been a bit different she would be my captain now. Regardless of that, she is still of my liveship family. As is her son. And Trell served on my decks for many years, and I value him as well.

'What do you want of me?' I spoke the words aloud and in my mind.

The ship didn't answer. 'She's here!' Brashen Trell was wearily surprised. 'Althea, this is the child I told you about. The one they came to rescue. She touched Boy-O in Clerres, and where she touched him, his burns healed.'

'Hello Bee,' she said. Softly and sadly she added, 'I am sorry that you lost your father.'

'Thank you,' I replied. Was it correct to thank someone for feeling bad about a death? I knew why the ship had summoned me now. Boy-O smelled bad. When I knelt beside him, I felt how the ship cradled him. It was not that there was a hollow in her deck where she held him. But where he touched her wizardwood, she reminded him how to be alive, and gave him gentle memories of his time on her deck. Memories that were not just his, but his mother's and his grandfather's and his great-grandmother's. All had sailed on this ship. Vivacia held all the memories of those who had died on her deck.

'That's why the dragons ate Kennitsson,' I said to myself.

Yes.

'Paragon's dragons ate Kennitsson?' Althea asked in disbelief.

'They meant well by it. They wanted to keep him with them. They shared the body.'

'Oh.' She touched Boy-O. 'Did you need something?' She wanted me to leave.

'The ship asked me to come here. She wants me to help.'

'What can—' Althea began.

'Ssh,' Brashen warned her, for I had already put my hands on Boy-O's good arm. I wanted to fix him. He was a wrong place on this perfect ship. I should make him right. 'He's thirsty,' I told his parents.

'He hasn't moved or spoken today.'

'He's thirsty,' I insisted. He needed water if I was going to make anything happen.

His mother seemed afraid to touch him as she lifted his head. She trickled water into his dry mouth. He choked a little, swallowed. That was my first way to help him. 'More water,' I told her. She held the cup to his lips while I reminded him how to drink. He drank that cup, and three more. Now I could move within him more easily. 'That salty soup that you make sometimes. It's yellow. That would be good.'

Even without opening my eyes, I knew they stared at me. The woman got up and hurried away. She was frightened and she was eager to do anything that might help her son. She would make the soup.

I rocked gently as my hands talked to his body. I found a little tune, one I'd never known before, and began to hum it as I worked. Two voices began to sing words to the song. The ship and the father sang softly together, and it was a little song about knots and sails, a teaching song like my father's rhyme about the points one looked for in a good horse. I wondered, as I pushed dead skin and flesh away and fastened good skin, if every family and every trade had those little songs. I found a place where something that didn't belong in his body was trying to grow. I killed it and pushed it away. It slid away like slime, stinky and nasty.

His body was working on itself in so many places. I knew them all. He had breathed in hot smoke, and it had hurt his throat and the breathing parts inside him. His arm was burned, and his chest and the side of his face. What was the worst hurt? I asked his body, and it was his arm. I went to work there.

His mother came back with the soup in a pot. 'Oh, sweet Sa!' she exclaimed. She was less fearful as she cradled his head and held the cup to his lips. It smelled wonderful and I remembered how good it would taste, salty and a bit sour. He drank it down, and where I had worked on his throat, he could swallow now.

'What goes on here?'

'Amber! She's helping Boy-O.'

'She has to stop! She's only a child. How can you ask this of her?'

'We didn't ask her! We were keeping a death-watch with him. Then she came and put her hands on him. He's going to live. Boy-O is going to live!'

'But will she?' He was angry. Beloved was angry—no, frightened. He spoke to me now. 'Bee. Stop. You can't do this.'

I drew a deep breath. 'Yes I can,' I told him as I breathed out.

'No. You are giving him too much of your own strength. Lift your hands from him.'

I smiled as I remembered words I had given my father. 'No one can say no to me now. Not even you.'

'Bee. Now!'

I smiled. 'No.'

'Lift your hands, Bee, or I will pull you back from him!'

Did he know that that would hurt both of us? 'A moment more,' I told him, and heard the frustrated noise he made. I told Boy-O's body to fare well, told it to keep working, gently, gently, gently, I had to go now, but it should keep working, yes, we would give it more soup. It was like calming an animal, and I suddenly knew that Boy-O's mind lived inside his animal body, and that was who I spoke to.

I opened my eyes. Beloved reached toward me. I lifted my hands before he could touch me. I folded my arms on my chest and sat back. I hadn't realized how long I'd been crouching over Boy-O. My back complained when I moved. I wiped my hands down my shirt. They were wet and sticky.

And then I knew something. 'Ship, you tricked me! You made me want to do this.'

The carved woman turned slightly toward me. 'It was necessary.'

'She's a child!' Beloved objected. 'You used her ruthlessly.'

'I didn't realize,' Brashen said, and he sounded both guilty and unrepentant.

'It didn't hurt me,' I objected, but when I tried to stand up, I could not.

The mother offered me a cup of the soup from the pot and I drank it in long sips. There were warm spices in it and some of them stung my tongue. Beloved watched me drink. Boy-O was breathing, and it was a good sound. I set the cup down on the deck and said, 'The ship made me love her. I think it was like that thing dragons can do . . .' I was suddenly very tired again. 'When they make themselves so important to someone. I read about that. Somewhere.'

'Humans call it a glamour,' the ship said quietly. 'Your name is Bee? I give you thanks. At the end of this voyage, we will all go our separate ways. It grieved me that Althea and Brashen might have to go without their son. But he will live, and go with them, and be a comfort to them. And knowing that will be a comfort to me, I think. Even as a dragon.'

'As Bee should be a comfort to me. And Per. And her sister Nettle! Ship, interfere with this child again and I shall . . .'

'You have no threat to offer, Amber. Be still. She has done enough for Boy-O. What would I ask again of her?'

He had fallen silent but I could see words piling up in him like unrecorded dreams.

'I will be fine,' I assured them as I stood. I had to smile. 'Vivacia, you are as beautiful and perfect as you told me. I could love you.' I was only a little tottery. And very tired. Don't tell that. 'I am going to go sleep. Good night to all of you.'

Behind me, the adults spoke softly. My hearing has always been keen. Brashen spoke with regret. 'She must have been a very pretty child, once.'

'Such scars! But thank Sa she is here with us now. She has great heart.'

'I beg you to be more careful of her. She is not strong. Not yet.' That was Beloved. He was wrong. I could be as strong as I needed to be. It bothered me that he tried to protect me. That he thought I was weak and tried to make others believe it as well. It made a hot little fire of anger in me.

My legs trembled slightly as I made my way back to my hammock. I couldn't get into it. I thought of the first time I'd had to climb onto Pris's back. My horse. Per was right. I'd be glad to see my horse again.

When Beloved spoke, I startled. 'Bee. That healing was a kind thing. But you must think first of your own health. You are not well yet. I won't ask you to promise me, but I will ask that you let me know if you are going to do something like that. Someone must be with you who has your best interests at heart.'

'I do not think the ship would have let me go too far,' I said. I smiled inside as I felt a warm, wordless reassurance that she would have stopped me. To him, I showed an expressionless face.

'You are like your father. That isn't really an answer to my request.' He smiled, sad but serious.

I sighed. I wanted to sleep, not talk. Even more, I didn't want his concern for me. It wasn't his task. I found a lie. 'You needn't worry. My ability to do this is almost gone.'

The smile changed to a worried scowl. 'What do you mean?'

'The night I fought Symphe and Dwalia and Vindeliar, Symphe had a vial of serpent spit. What Dwalia called serpent potion. I think it had traces of Silver in it, like the Silver Paragon used to turn into dragons.' I yawned wide. Suddenly I wanted to explain. 'In a dream I had, they got it from keeping a sea serpent in a very tiny pool of salt water. Symphe was going to have Vindeliar drink it. He had used it before, and it gave him great power. But when I set fire to Symphe, she dropped the vial and it broke. When I was stabbing her, I cut my feet on the glass and some got into my blood. It made me stronger than Vindeliar. I was so strong I could just tell Dwalia to be dead, and she was.'

He went still. I watched him. Would he fear me now? Hate me?

No. When he came back to himself, his eyes were sorrowful. 'You set fire to Symphe. And stabbed her.'

How could he think it sad that I had done that? I put it clearly. 'I told you when I told my father. I killed them. It wasn't evil, and I have no regret. It needed to be done, I was the one who was in the place and time to do it, and it was my task. So, I did it. I should have killed Vindeliar that night, too. It would have saved us all a great deal of trouble.'

'Did you dream it?' he asked hesitantly. When I stared at him, he said, 'Did you have a dream that killing them was something you were supposed to do?'

I shrugged one shoulder. I seized the edge of the hammock and this time I got into it. I pulled up my blanket. It was summer above, but belowdecks, it was chill at night. I closed my eyes. 'I don't know. I have dreams. I know they mean something, but they are so strange I can't connect them to what I will do. I dreamed a silver man carving his heart. The serpent spit was silver. Was that a dream of me carving Dwalia's heart into death?'

'I don't think so,' he said quietly.

That had been a recent dream. I felt better for having told someone. 'I'm going to sleep now,' I told him. I closed my eyes and ignored him. He did not move. It was very annoying. I'd hoped he would leave. I waited a long time and then looked through my lashes. I was going to tell him to go away. Instead I asked, 'Did you love my father?'

He went as still as a cat. When he spoke it was with reservation.

'I had a deep bond with your father. A connection I had with no one else.'

'Why won't you say you loved him?' I opened my eyes to see his face. My father had given him all his strength, and this man would not even say he had loved him?

His smile was too tight, as if he were forcing a different expression to be a smile. 'It always made him uncomfortable if I used that word.'

'He did not use that word very much. His love was things he did.'

'He never counted up the things he did for me, but he always remembered the things I did for him.'

'So he loved you.' Loved you so much he left me to take you to Buckkeep.

All expression fell away from his face. His peculiar eyes were empty.

'He wrote long letters to you, but he had nowhere to send them. He missed you desperately. He loved my mother, but he always had to be strong for her. He had Riddle, too, and my brother Hap. But the things he wrote about in those letters were things he could not say to my mother, nor Riddle nor Hap. You left him, and all he could do was write them down.'

I watched him carefully and saw my barbed words hit and hold. I wanted to drive him away. I did not care that I hurt him. He was alive and my father was dead. I added, 'You never should have left him.'

His voice and face were expressionless as he asked, 'How do you know what he wrote?'

'Because he did not always burn them every night. Sometimes he waited until the morning.'

'So you read his private papers.'

'I believe you read my journals?'

He looked startled. 'I did,' he admitted.

'You still do. When you think I am deeply asleep, you have looked at my writing.'

He did not flinch. 'You know that I do. Bee, you have endured much, but you are still a child. Your father gave you into my care. I promised to watch over you. Understand me, adults do what is best for a child. Parents especially have that obligation. It comes far before doing what you wish or what you might think is best. You have a White heritage; your dreams are both important and dangerous. You need to be guided. Yes, I read your journal, to know you better. I will read the dreams you write.'

My mind had snagged on his earlier words. 'Do I get my White heritage from my mother?' For I knew my father was Mountain and Buck, and nothing else.

'You get it from me.'

I stared at him. 'How?'

'You are young to understand this.'

'No, I am not. I knew my father and I knew my mother.' I held my breath, waiting for him to tell a terrible lie about my mother.

'Do you know how the dragons change the Elderlings? How they give them scales and colours? How their children are born sometimes with scales?'

'No. I did not know they did that.'

'You saw Rapskal, the scarlet man?'

'Yes.'

'A dragon changed him. A dragon loves him very much. So Heeby, the red dragon, added something of herself to Rapskal, and he changed. And Rapskal's dragon, Heeby, has taken on much of his thoughts and ways.'

I was listening intently.

'For many years, I lived alongside your father. I think we both . . . changed each other.' I saw his thoughts wander into a different trail. 'He said once that he had become the Prophet and I the Catalyst. I thought long about his words. I decided that I wanted it to be so. For once, I wanted to make the change. So I came to Clerres Castle and tried to be the Changer.'

'You were not very good at it.'

'No. But when I first met your father, I would never even have thought of trying.' He gave a great sigh. 'I expect you to be angry at me, Bee. I will tell you this. I did what your father wanted me to do. I got you out safely. When I intrude on your life and privacy, it is because he charged me with taking care of you. My word to him comes first. I had hoped to win your respect, if not forge a closer bond. I understand that you resent that I am alive and Fitz is not. But why unleash this tonight?'

I steeled myself and looked into his pale eyes. 'Tonight, you tried to act like my father. You said things he might have said. But you are not my father. I don't want you to behave as if you are. You can teach me, yes; there are things I need to learn. But you are not my father. Don't pretend you are.'

'Actually,' he began. Then he stopped.

He concealed something. He'd read my dreams and my journal, my most private thoughts, and still try to keep secrets from me? Insult most deep. I struck back. An omission was as good as a lie. 'He wrote you a last letter. One he did not burn, for I think he wrote it mostly for himself. He told you that he understood why you had left. That your "friendship" had never been anything but how you could use him. He wrote that he was better off without you, for my mother loved him for who he was rather than how he could be used. In that letter, he said he hoped never to see you again, for you had twisted his life and robbed him of joy. That he was pleased to take control of his life and determine his own direction now.

'But he saw you again and it happened again. You only came back to him to use him again. You destroyed our home, and he lies dead because of you. All you.'

I rolled away from him, not an easy task in a hammock. I stared up at the timbers and the shifting lantern shadows. My father would not have been pleased with me. I knew I should apologize and admit my falsehood. Even if I didn't mean it? Perhaps.

I looked back at him, but he had fled.

FORTY-TWO

Furnich

And among the remnants of what was burned (And there was not much; your protégé was very thorough!) I found a scorched scrap. I have transcribed it here.

'As soon as they are unable to fight, go forward boldly and bleed them. It is essential to do this swiftly, while most of the poison is in their bellies and has not tainted meat, bone, brain or tongue. Harvest the blood, then the organs and last the meat. Label each tub, for each must be tested separately to see if the poison has been too strong and rendered it lethal. Administer some to at least two slaves. If even one dies, dispose of it. Unfortunately, we cannot control how much each dragon will eat of the bait, and therefore we cannot control how much poison each beast will consume.

The eyes must be preserved in vinegar; they are the most perishable. Slice the meat thinly, salt it and dry it.

Of the entire creature, only the stomach may be summarily discarded. Every other bit must be harvested and preserved, for once we have eliminated dragons, these are the last that we . . .'

And here it ends in scorching. Old friend, you were right. Our Servants deliberately slaughtered what remained of the dragons and serpents following the disaster to the north. Other bits of documents with only dates and the number of casks and barrels would hint to me that the slaughter was carried out in various locations.

Hence the dragons' vengeance. Hence also the longevity of the Four.

Following the murder of Capra, I assumed the care of the few remaining Whites. We have left Clerres for a small farm inland. I am trying to teach the youngsters to grow and harvest food. Many have ceased dreaming.

I fear this letter will take many months to reach you. When last I parted with FitzChivalry Farseer, we exchanged some hard words. Please extend my respect to him. I do not doubt that he will return to you, just as you made your way back to him.

Letter from Prilkop to Beloved

The Fool had told me of how he had returned to Clerres the first time. All I had to do was to make that same journey, in reverse. I had to get to the other side of the island of Clerres, to one of the deep-water ports, Sisal or Crupton. From there, I would find a boat to give me passage to Furnich. There, on the hills around the port of Furnich, I would find the Elderling ruins and a heavily-canted Skill-pillar.

It seems so simple, if one says it quickly. Most things do.

I took shelter in the mouth of the tunnel for the night. It was, as Lant had told Bee, a defensible point. At dawn, I climbed to what seemed the highest hill and looked for a road. I cut across a pasture where two cows regarded me with suspicion, down the hill, past the recent ruins of a farmhouse, and struck the road. There was little traffic but I knew that would change as the news of the fall of Clerres spread. This way would come the plunderers and salvagers and the sort of folk who would be quick to take advantage of the battered population. Rumours of dragons would not deter them for long. I hoped that Prilkop would swiftly seize the leadership position I had left vacant for him. The surviving Whites and whatever Servants followed them might, under his tutelage, go back to the old ways. In any case, I was done with them.

My leg was still healing and ached. I was constantly hungry. Mosquitoes feasted on me and something like a tick had bitten the back of my neck. I could find no little body, but it itched abominably. I missed my shoes badly. That afternoon, a small shadow overflew me. On the next pass, Motley dropped onto my shoulder. 'Take me home,' she directed me.

'Did you miss the boat?' I asked. I wouldn't admit that I welcomed her companionship.

'Yes,' she conceded after a time.

'Crow. Motley. How did you know I was alive? How did you know where to find me?'

'Silver man, but still stupid,' the crow observed. She lifted from my shoulder but called back to me, 'Fruit tree! Fruit tree!'

She flew ahead of me down the road. Within me, the wolf was both amused and annoyed. *In my absence, you bond with a crow? Well, at least she is not prey. And she is clever.*

We are not bonded!

No? Well, you are not bonded as you and I were, that is true. But there are many levels of Wit-bond. She senses you, even if she does not care to let you borrow her senses.

Suddenly, many things became clear to me. I felt offended. *Why does she keep me at a distance?* I wondered.

She knows you will never cede to her the sort of bond we shared. And so she protects herself.

When I made no reply, he added, *I like her. Were I still trotting at your side, I might welcome her.*

I smelled the ripe fruit before I saw the tree. A small orchard. A narrow road led to another collapsed dwelling. The dragons had been thorough. Unharvested apricots had fallen and were fermenting on the ant-covered ground. The heady smell and the buzzing of bees and wasps filled the air. Ample fruit still hung on the tree, and I was not slow to fill my hands and then my belly. The juice inside them eased my thirst as well as my hunger.

When I could eat no more, I picked a generous amount and fashioned what remained of my shirt into a sack. I returned to the road and hiked on, hoping that I would hear a wagon's creaking or a horse's hoofbeats in time to conceal myself. My stomach was cramping from all the fresh fruit, but it was less painful than hunger. From time to time Motley flew a lazy circle over my head. Very cautiously, I extended my Wit toward her. Yes. If I focused, I could sense her. But I also felt a small, indignant push of *repel*. I let her be.

The Fool had never told me how many days the journey had taken. I did recall that he had spoken of travelling at least part of the way in a cart. I had only my feet. I slept in the open each night and hiked on each day. Food was what I could find, and many of the plants here were foreign to me. The few greens I recognized as edible were not filling. The days were too hot, and the nights full of stinging insects.

That evening I tried to find a comfortable spot to sleep where the gnats would not devour me. That wasn't possible. I sat with my back against a tree, slapping mosquitoes, and reached out to Dutiful. I could let him know I was alive and making my way home. I wanted Bee and the Fool to know that as soon as was possible. Perhaps Dutiful could arrange funds for me. The Skill-pillar could take me as far as Kelsingra, and I hoped I'd be welcomed there. But coin in pocket is always useful. Disaster had stripped me down to the Silver-holed clothes on my back, the knife in my belt, and the few small assassin's tools left in my little pockets. I centred myself and pushed away my awareness of gnats and a rock poking me and reached for Dutiful. Only to fail as I had not failed with the Skill in many a year.

I swatted the little bloodsuckers from the back of my neck, pulled my shirt up over my head and tried to think. I tried again. And again. It was like trying to scoop a tiny fly from bubbling soup, always to miss. I stopped and pushed my frustration aside. Calm. What was wrong with me? I hadn't had so much difficulty in years . . . not since I'd been trying to Skill to Verity. Trying to reach him when he was in the Mountains. Verity, who had also soaked his hands in Silver.

Perhaps the difficulty had not been entirely mine? Perhaps there had been more at work than my elfbark habit.

I touched my silvered fingers to my thumb and focused on the peculiar power coursing through me. Pain. No, pleasure. No, it was too intense to classify. I focused on Buckkeep, on Dutiful, and for a moment I was in the Skill-current.

I plunged into a depth that I'd never known existed. I was buffeted and shoved by the mobbed and streaming awarenesses. 'Forgot to feed . . .' 'He's so lovely . . .' 'My boy…!' 'Not enough coin . . .' It was like being in the Great Hall at Buckkeep if all the musicians were playing and all the people were talking at once in equally loud voices. I could not sort one from another. Then, an immense presence, powerful and disciplined, would cut through the prattle like a commander's order being barked above the discord of a battle, or a great fish swimming through a dense school of minnows. All would part and then close up behind it.

Once, long ago, I'd encountered one of those great beings in the Skill-current. I'd nearly lost myself in her. In this strata there were many of them, and as they passed I felt other entities attach to them, combining to grow that awareness. I wanted . . . I wanted to . . . I dragged myself clear of it and came to biting my lower lip so hard I tasted blood.

I tried to puzzle out what might be happening to me. The Silver had increased the power of my Skill, taking me to a level that I could not master. I put up my walls and pondered that. Caution, I decided. If need be I could wait until I reached Kelsingra and then contact Dutiful by messenger bird. There was no sense in taking risks.

As I came to each crossroads or by-way, I chose the more-travelled path. I had to veer widely to avoid villages. I found I was glad that the dragons had not completely slaughtered the inhabitants of the island. Nonetheless, I had no desire to encounter anyone in my silvered condition. Sometimes the crow helped me find a way and other times she was absent and I had to blunder through woods and down trails and hope for the best. I stole shamelessly from outlying farms, raiding vegetable gardens and hen-coops and smokehouses. I took a sheet from a laundry line. There were a few coins left in the corner of my pocket, and I tied them in a shirtsleeve on the line. Even assassins have a bit of honour. Hens would lay more eggs and vegetables replenish, but taking a sheet was a true theft. I knotted the sheet into a makeshift cloak and gained some shelter from both the baking sun and the biting insects. And I walked on.

The weather continued fine and the journey was miserable. I wondered and worried about Bee and the Fool and my other companions. I mourned Lant. I wished vainly that I had seen Paragon transform into dragons. I wondered how long it would take them to get home. I worried what would happen when they delivered the news of the prince's demise to Queen Etta. She had charged us to keep the lad safe and we hadn't done so. Would there be grief, or would there be anger, or both?

Hunger was a given. Thirst came and went depending on streams. And I ached. My weariness was constant.

My body continued to heal and stole my strength to do so. My diet was uneven. I had no shoes. I was hiking and sleeping outdoors as I had not done in years. But even so, my level of lethargy was extreme. I awoke one morning with no ambition to move. I wanted to go home, but more I wanted to be still. I lay on the bare earth in the shade of a tree with drooping leaves. Ants began crawling over my hand. I sat up, slapping them away, and then scratched the back of my neck. The tick bite was slow to heal. I picked the scab away from it and felt some relief. 'Home!' Motley squawked at me from a branch overhead. 'Home, home, HOME!'

'Yes,' I conceded and gathered my legs under me. They ached and my belly hurt.

My brother, you have worms.

I considered that thought. I'd had worms before. What man who has lived by his wits has not? I knew several cures, none of which were available to me right now.

You made me swallow a copper coin when I was a cub.

A copper bit kills the worms but not the pup. I learned it from Burrich.

Heart of the Pack knew many things.

I haven't a copper left to my name. It must wait until we are home. To where I have access to herbs I know.

Then you'd best get up and get moving toward home.

Nighteyes was right. I needed to get home. I imagined embracing Bee. With my silver hands and gleaming face . . . Ah, no.

I pushed that last thought aside. I was becoming adept at doing so. When I was home, it would all come right. I'd see Nettle and my new grandchild. There would be a way to deal with the Silver. Chade would know something, some way . . . No, Chade was dead and so was his son. What sort of a welcome would Shun give me for that news? Had the Elderling woman been right? Was the Silver killing me? It would sink down to my bones, she had said.

Get up. You are lying there while the sun moves. Unless you have decided to sleep through the day and travel by night?

The moon would be full tonight. I'd be able to see. *Yes. I will travel tonight.* I was lying to myself.

At nightfall, I forced myself to rise. The crow had perched above me. I looked up into the darkened branches and to my surprise I could see her. I saw the shape of her body by its warmth. The Fool had spoken of this, when he drank the dragon's blood.

'I am going to travel. Do you wish me to carry you?' Crows did not fly in the dark.

She gave a dismissive caw. She could find me when it suited her. She had shown me that.

The road had become well travelled over the last few days, but there were fewer carts and horses on it by night, and my sheet cloaked most of me. I made good time. Stones heated all day by the sun's warmth gave off a different sort of light than the small mammals that foraged along the edge of the road. Another climb up another hill. The road cut through tilled lands and pastures. Where would I hide this day? Worry about it when dawn came.

I topped the hill and looked down onto a bustling seaport. Lanterns burned bright on the ships anchored in the harbour; lamps gleamed randomly throughout the sprawling town. It was as least as big as Buckkeep Town, but spread out as flat as batter in a pan. How was I to make my way through that, get to the docks, and persuade a boat to take me to Furnich? And all without a copper to my name? Steal a small boat. And go where? I had no charts. I needed a boat and a crew that would obey my will.

Why was nothing ever simple? Why was I so weary?

That night, I raided a chicken-coop and took a hen as well as three eggs. I helped myself to grain from the cattle's shelter, and stared down a watchdog who came to snarl at me. I told him he faced a wolf, and felt the Silver stitch together with my Wit to send him yelping back to his doorstep. It felt peculiar.

I fled with my loot. Man's teeth do not do well on raw meat, but I persevered and stripped the hen down to her bones. I followed with raw eggs gulped down and grain ground between my cow's teeth, and all washed down with stream water. On a rocky berm between two grainfields, I settled for the day.

I waited for night. Before the moon rose full and white, I skulked toward the busy port. Thick had used the Skill to hide himself, but he had always been far stronger in it than I was. I arranged my sheet to cover most of my face and I kept to the shadows even as I sent out 'Don't see me, don't see me' to any I passed in the quiet streets. There were few folk on the street at night. Only two gave me even a glance. The strength of influence I was now able to exert with my mingled magics was unsettling and reassuring. How much dared I trust it? Could I walk the busy streets in daylight and be unnoticed? To test that and fail might be deadly.

I knew my destination and I did not pause. I headed down to the docks.

A harbour never sleeps. Ships unload or take on cargo by night to catch the morning's tide. I chose a dock where an ant-stream of longshoremen pushed carts and barrows to docked ships. I stayed to the shadowed areas as I studied the moving cargo. I was hungry again, aching and weary. I could not allow that to deter me.

I found a ship offloading hides. The Fool had spoken of Furnich being a tannery town. I stepped in front of one of the sailors. 'I need passage to Furnich.' I enveloped him in my friendliness. 'You really want to please me,' I whispered. He halted, glaring at me as I peered from under my sheet. His face went slack. Then he suddenly smiled as if I were an old friend.

'We have just come from there,' he told me. He shook his head. 'It is not a pleasant place. If you must go there, I pity you.'

'And yet I must go there. Of the ships in port, are any bound there?'

'The *Dancer*. The second one, there. Her captain is Rasri, good for most things but a terrible cheat at games of chance.'

'I will keep that in mind. Good evening to you.'

As we parted, he gave me a loose-lipped smile as if I were his lover.

I felt queasy for what I had done to him as I hastened down the dock to the *Dancer*. She was a tidy little vessel with a deep hull and small house, one that could be sailed with a very small crew. A young woman was standing on the deck. I sharpened my will then reached toward her with a wave of good fellowship and trustworthiness as I asked for Captain Rasri. Her eyes widened and she smiled at me despite my drapery. 'I'm Captain Rasri. What business have you with me?' She saw my silvered face and took a step back.

I smiled at her and offered that it was a peculiar scar, no more than that. She politely looked away from it. 'I need passage to Furnich.'

'We take no passengers, good man.'

'But for me, you could make an exception.'

She stared at me and I felt her struggle. I pressed harder on her boundaries. 'I could,' she admitted, even as she shook her head 'no'.

'I can be a handy person to have aboard. I know my way around a deck.'

'You could be a help,' she agreed, as her brow furrowed.

'How many days is it to Furnich?'

'No more than a dozen, if the weather holds fine. We've two ports to visit on our way.'

I wanted to tell her that we would go straight to Furnich, but could not bring myself to do so. Already I regretted what I was doing to her. 'When do we leave?'

'On the early tide. Soon.'

I was no sooner on board than Motley swooped down and perched on my shoulder. The puzzlement on the captain's face gave way to delight. 'Thank you, thank you,' Motley told her, and did the same when the crew approached. I introduced myself as Tom Badgerlock while the crew was charmed and distracted by Motley, and I settled acceptance over them like a blanket. By morning I was on my way.

It was the most miserable voyage of my life. The ship was called *Dancer* for a reason. She bowed and bobbed, rocked and wallowed. I was seasick as I had never been before in my life.

Yet despite how wretched I felt, I did my best to be as useful as I had presented myself. I found that I could remove corrosion from brass by smoothing it with my fingers, and made every fitting on *Dancer* gleam. I smoothed fraying lines so that they ran easily through the blocks and tackles. I ran my hands over stretched and weary canvas to tighten it. I ate no more than one man's share at the table, despite my constant hunger.

The journey seemed interminable. Imposing my will on the crew took strength and focus when my supply of both was dwindling. I dreaded each port stop, for it meant days tied up as they took on and offloaded freight. Each time we made port, I would slip away at night to Skill a plentiful meal at an inn. Sated, I would return to *Dancer* and sleep heavily. When I awoke, I would feel stronger for a day. But then the lassitude would return.

In the long, heaving nights, I thought of Verity and how he had used his Skill to defend the Six Duchies. Even at a distance, he had been able to find the OutIslander ships and influence their captains and navigators. How many had he sent into the teeth of a storm, or onto the rocks? How had he felt to use the power of his magic to kill so many? Had it bothered him? Was that why he had seized on the wisp of an old legend and gone off into the Mountains in search of Elderling allies?

The night we reached Furnich, I conveyed to the captain and crew that they had done a great kindness, something to be proud of. I left them looking puzzled but rather pleased with themselves. Motley settled on my shoulder. 'Home,' she reminded me, and I took strength from that word.

Furnich was a dreary town of bad smells and sour folk. Turning cattle into meat and leather is a messy business but it did not need to be as squalid as Furnich made it. The town was dirty and the air tasted of hopelessness. It crouched in low, ill-kept buildings all around the bay. On the hill above it, I could see the tumbled ruins of what had been an Elderling city. It had obviously been deliberately destroyed. I hoped that no more destruction had been done to the Skill-pillar than the last time Prilkop and the Fool had used it. The Fool had described it as nearly toppled. But if there was any room to wriggle under it, I would take my opportunity and hope that it would take me back to Kelsingra.

There is a danger in using the stones.

Wolf, there is a danger in delaying my return, and I fear that is greater.

I felt his doubt and tried not to be prey to it. As I plodded through the town, I was hungry but saw no tavern where I wanted to eat. They seemed deceitful and untrustworthy places. I would go straight to the Elderling city, find the Skill-stone, and leave this disgusting place. The aura of ugliness was like a stench in the air. In Kelsingra, they would know me. There would be food and kindness there. This place had never known kindness.

I stopped to breathe and leaned against the wall of a stable. My feeling of despair was like a wind that swept through me. The intensity of it was oddly familiar, as was the buzzing in my ears.

Here they betrayed us. For years, they deceived us and pretended to be our friends, and then, when need was upon us and we fled here, they slaughtered us. They ended us as they ended the dragons and even the serpents in the sea.

For a moment, I saw them. The Elderlings ran through the streets, seeking a safety that did not exist. They had fled the collapse of their cities and come here, to an outlying settlement where the air was not poisonous and laden with ash. But as they emerged from the portal stones, hired soldiers were waiting to kill them. For the Servants had known that their cities would shake and fall, had known that both dragons and Elderlings would flee here. To end the dragons, they must end the Elderlings as well.

And they had.

The memories of that bloody betrayal had sunk into the memory-stone of their city. When later generations had salvaged the stone of the Elderling city to build Furnich they had salvaged the horror and betrayal as well. Small wonder that the folk of Furnich regarded the black stone ruins with hatred. The closer I came to the ruined villas on the hillside, the deeper and darker the memories flowed. Skill and Silver writhed in me and I staggered through a flow of ghosts. Men and women shouted and screamed, children lay dead or bleeding in the streets. I threw up my walls to deaden the horror.

Kelsingra was a fountain of Elderling memories of festivals and markets and joyous times. Here the stones had drunk up the blood and the deaths of the Elderlings who had raised them. That terrible legacy of fear and despair had been passed down for generations. Any merry or peaceful memories had been quenched in blood.

I did not know the name of this Elderling town. Grass was trying to grow between the broken paving stones, but too much memory-stone had been used. The streets recalled that they had been streets and did not allow the grass to flourish. Everywhere I saw the signs of hammers and chisels, toppled statues deliberately broken to pieces, fountains destroyed, building walls pulled down.

Where would the standing pillars have been? In the centre of the town, as they were in Kelsingra? Atop a tower? Within a market square?

I wandered the empty streets of the hilly town, wending my way through a tide of screaming ghosts. Motley would lift from my shoulder, circle, and then return to me. Once this had been a beautiful place of opulent manors and walled gardens. Now it was like a fallen buck infested with maggots, all its majesty and graciousness tainted with memories of death and hate and betrayal. Only my Wit assured me that they were not real.

My Wit made me aware that there were real people too, not far from me and following me. In my efforts to keep my walls tight and my mind my own, I had neglected my camouflage of Skill. Perhaps they were just curious adolescents following a peculiar stranger wearing a sheet. Had they seen my Silver-spattered face? Motley cawed overhead. I watched her circle and she suddenly dipped down to light on my shoulder. 'Careful,' she croaked in a hoarse whisper. 'Careful, Fitz.'

They were closing in on me.

I stood still, breathing quietly. I flung my Wit wide, trying to sense how many and where they were. What did they imagine I had that they would want? Were they simply the sort of ruffians that enjoyed giving a stranger a beating? I had no strength left to run, let alone fight. *Leave me alone!* I flung the plea out into the night, but the Skill-infused stones diluted and muted me. I needed to see them, to look into their faces to target their minds. They kept their distance. Doubtless they knew the ruins well. Perhaps they had braved this miasma of fear and hate since they were children. They kept to cover. I would catch a glimpse in the growing dusk of someone flitting from one concealment to another. How many?

Four. No, five. Two were standing close together. I flared my nostrils and took in scent, an almost useless gesture with my feeble human nose.

They are near. Choose your place.

That was my last advantage. I drew my knife as I found a bit of standing wall to put my back against. I discarded my sheet cloak. Perhaps my appearance would give them second thoughts, but in the gathering darkness, would they even see how peculiar I had become? With a sinking heart, I forced myself to question what sort of people would willingly drench themselves in this atmosphere of hatred and blood. It was not a good sort. I heard a low laugh, and someone shushing someone else. It had been a woman's laugh. So. This was sport rather than robbery. I was probably not their first prey.

A rock hit the wall beside me. I flinched and the crow lifted from my shoulder. I didn't blame her. A single strike would kill her. Another rock struck near my head. I stood still, listening. The next rock struck my thigh, and this time their laughter was not hushed. They remained in hiding, unseen. I heard the soft whistle of a sling and that rock struck hard on my chest. I lifted an arm to cover my face but a rock struck me in the mouth with a sharp *crack!* I tasted blood and my ears rang.

Cowards! Nighteyes snarled inside me. *Kill them all!*

When Nighteyes had been alive, our Wit-bond had been so close that I often felt I was as much wolf as human. His body had died but something of him had lived on inside me, all those years. Part of me and not part of me.

And from my earliest time of trying to master the Skill-magic, my beast-magic—my Wit—had been tangled with it. Galen had sought to beat it out of me, and others who had tried to instruct me in the Wit or the Skill had decried that I could not seem to separate the two. When Nighteyes, infuriated by my pain, struck out with the Wit, my Silver Skill rode with it.

I had a glimpse of the woman, moving from a broken wall to a thicket of brambles. I fixed my attention on her. 'Die,' I said quietly, and she was the first to fall. She dropped suddenly and limply as if stunned, but my Wit told me she was gone. Heart stilled, breath stopped.

Foolishly or loyally, perhaps both, two of her male companions ran to her. After all, why not break cover? A cowering, cornered man was no threat. I lifted a shaking Silver hand. I pointed at one. 'Die,' I told him, and as his fellow stood in consternation, 'Die,' I suggested, and he did.

So easy. Too easy.

'He did it!' someone shouted. 'I don't know how, but he's dropping them! Saha, Bar, get up! Are you hurt?' One of them ventured from cover, a scrawny youth with dark, ragged hair. His eyes were on me as he sidled toward the bodies.

'They're dead,' I said.

I hoped he would run. I hoped even more he would fight.

A woman, cautious as a doe, rose and stepped from the tall grass. She was lovely, her loose dark hair curling to her shoulders. 'Saha?' she said, and all laughter had fled from her uncertain voice.

'He killed them!' her companion cried, his voice rising to a shriek. He charged at me, and she screamed as she copied him. I moved my silvered hand across their path.

They dropped just as surely as if my axe had lopped off their heads. They fell, and my Wit immediately told me they were gone. Never had I used my magic in such a way; never had it been strong enough. This was like when I had first tried to learn to Skill and my ability had been wildly erratic. In fear and anger I'd thrown death at people I had not even clearly seen.

I did not know we could do that. Within me, Nighteyes seemed cowed by what had happened.

Nor did I. Had I felt shamed by bending the minds of the *Dancer's* crew? Now I felt numbed with shock—the same calmness I'd seen in a man with a leg lopped off. I spat the blood from my mouth and touched my teeth. Two were loosened. My enemies were dead and I was alive. I pushed remorse away.

I looted the bodies. One of the youths had sandals that would fit me. The pretty woman had a cloak. I took their coins. A wineskin, a knife. One woman had a little paper pouch full of gummy, mint-flavoured sweets. I gobbled those down and followed them with the cheap wine. I looked aside as Motley took bits of flesh from them. How was it different from my looting? They were dead and she took what was useful to her.

Night thickened and the moon rose. The memory of mayhem in the now-ruined streets rose in volume. Motley huddled on my shoulder. Were the folk who had slaughtered the Elderlings the ancestors of those who now lived in the pathetic town below? Was this lingering horror and hatred a terrible unplanned punishment that fell on children who had no knowledge of what their forebears had done? Did the dark humours of this place taint the younger generations of those killers?

I found the Skill-pillars by following the phantom carnage backwards. I waded through ephemeral corpses and shrieking spectres until I came to a place where the ghostly Elderlings milled like sheep surrounded by wolves. They had emerged from the Skill-pillar, seen the slaughter and tried to flee back to dubious safety. At the vortex of that maddened flight, I found the pillar.

It was as the Fool had said. Someone had put a great deal of effort into trying to pull it down. It leaned low, and the full moon above glinted on its scratched upper side. The outer faces of the pillar had been scored with scratches, and there was a strong stench of urine and faeces. After all the years, there was still a hatred so strong that it was expressed in this puerile way?

Humans piss when they are scared.

Tall grass surrounded the fallen monument. Ghostly Elderlings were emerging from it, clutching children or carrying an armful of belongings. I dropped to my knees and pushed my way through coarse grass and tangling bindweed. I wished I'd had the map Chade had given me, of all the known pillars and their destinations. No matter. Gone was gone, and I hope the bear had enjoyed eating it. The Fool had said they had emerged from the downward-facing plane of the Skill-pillar. All I had to do was go back the way he had come. I peered through vegetation into the black space under the leaning stone. Motley clung to my cloak and shirt collar, leaving scratches on my neck.

Are you ready?

I am never ready for this. Just do it.

'Home. Home now.'

Very well. I pushed brambles aside, wincing as the thorns tore my palm. I'd have to crawl to get under the pillar. A moment of the stupidity that weariness brings was all it took. I braced my hand, my Silver hand, on the face of the pillar nearest me, preparatory to crawling under it. It seized me and I had a glimpse of a spoiled rune I did not recognize. Motley gave a terrified caw, and we were pulled into the stone.

FORTY-THREE

Bingtown

To Skillmistress Nettle from Apprentice Carryl:

As you demanded, I confess my fault on this paper, and offer also my explanation. It is not an excuse, but it is a reason why I disobeyed the Journeyman Shers who was supervising me on our visit to Aslevjal. I was aware of our assignment. We were to gather Skill-cubes, note where they had been found, and bring them back to Buckkeep Castle for reading, classification and storage. Shers was most clear in telling me I must stay with the others and touch nothing that did not pertain to our task.

Yet I had heard tales of the map-room of Aslevjal. My desire to see it outweighed my sense of duty to obey. While unobserved, I left my coterie and sought the map-room and discovered it was as wondrous as the accounts had said. I lingered longer than I intended, and instead of returning to where we had been gathering the cubes, I went directly to the pillar that had transported us there.

This is the most important part of my tale, even if it does not excuse my disobedience at all. The others were not yet at the pillar. I was weary, for my bag of gathered cubes was heavy. I sat down with my back to the wall. I do not know if I dozed or was simply taken by the memories in the room. I began to see Elderlings coming and going from the pillar. Some were grandly dressed, and some walked through as simply as if strolling through a garden. But after a time, it struck me that Elderlings either emerged from or entered a facet of the pillar. There was no face where Elderlings both entered and exited.

I believe that we should carefully study the runes on each pillar face, for I believe that some of the issues of time lost or great weakness may be the result of us using the Skill-pillars to travel backwards, counter to

*their intended use. When it came time to return to the Witness Stones,
I felt great trepidation. I attribute our day's delay to entering a facet of
the pillar that I saw Elderling shadows only emerge from.*

*For my behaviour in leaving my coterie, I apologize. It was thoughtless
and reckless. I submit myself for judgment and punishment as you see
fit.*

With great sincerity, Apprentice Carryl

We sailed on. Slowly, I woke to life.

Dwalia had left her mark on me. If the weather was cold and wet,
my left cheekbone ached and sometimes yellow tears ran from my
left eye. My left ear was a shapeless lump; I could not sleep with it
touching the pillow. The bruises and abrasions from the neck shackle
had left sores that were slow to heal.

But that was my body. The rest of me simply didn't want to do
anything. I wanted to stay in my hammock in the dimness. I wanted
Beloved and Amber and the Fool to all stop pestering me. Every
time I wrote in my dream book or journal, I reminded him of that.
Despite the reminders, several times a day he would seek me out. If
I were in my hammock, Amber would sit nearby, and busy herself
with a bit of needlework. Sometimes she left clever little carvings
of animals, and these I guessed were the Fool's work, for my father
had written of such things. I longed to possess them, but I always
left them where Amber had placed them. Mostly I avoided looking
at her, but whenever our eyes met, his peculiar ones were full of
remorse and pleading. He was never less than patient with me.

I had a little fire of dislike for him, and every chance I got, I fed
it. I thought often of how he was here and my father was not. I
imagined what my father and I would have done on this journey
home. We would have talked with the ship, and watched the seabirds.
He would have told me the history and geography of the Six Duchies,
and explained Bingtown and the Rain Wilds to me. My father would
have been steady and fair with me. But he was not here, and every
time I looked at the changeable man who was trying to replace him,
I disliked him more.

Per was more direct with me. He insisted I come to the table for
meals, and while I ate he showed me knots. Boy-O was up and
tottering around. He joined us at table once, and I was so embarrassed

by his gratitude that I could not look at him. His mother always smiled at me. Captain Wintrow gave me a necklace with a gem that glowed in darkness, and a mug that magically warmed whatever was in it.

'You need to know this ship, while you have the chance!' Per rebuked me one afternoon. 'When will you ever sail on a liveship again? Never. They will all turn into dragons. Be here while you can!' I knew he was right, but trying to do anything made me so tired. One day, he insisted on showing me how to climb the rigging. 'Please, Bee. Only five steps up, just so you feel how the ropes are under your feet. All you have to do is follow me. Put your feet where I put my feet and my hands where I put my hands.'

He wouldn't let me refuse. He didn't ask me if I'd be afraid and, just as it had been with Pris, I could not break my pride enough to tell him it terrified me. And so we climbed. And climbed. Many more than five steps. There was a tiny room at the top of the mast, with short walls of webbing. He helped me inside and I was glad to hunker down and feel safer. 'This is the crow's nest,' he told me. His face became sad for a moment. 'Not that I have a crow any more.'

'I know you miss him.'

'Her. Motley. She never came back after she went after the red dragon that day. Maybe she lives with the dragons. She was very taken with Heeby.' He was quiet. 'I hope she is alive. The other crows used to peck her because she had a few white feathers. Would it be worse with shiny red feathers?'

'I'm sorry she's gone. I'd have liked to know a crow.'

He said suddenly, 'Bee, you healed Boy-O's burns. Why don't you fix yourself?'

I turned my face away from him. It stung that it mattered to him, that he noticed the scars on my face and wrists. I knew he had no magic but he still seemed to hear me. 'It's not about how you look, Bee. It's about pain. I see you limp. I see you putting your hand over your cheek when it's hurting you. Why don't you just make them better?'

'It doesn't feel right,' I answered him after a time. I could not say that I didn't want to have to do it myself. My father should have been with me, to smooth my face with his hands, and admit to me how badly I'd been hurt. Why did I have to mend myself? Because

Amber was here instead of my father. But I could not say any of that, so I found other words.

'My father wore his scars. Riddle has scars. My mother wore the marks of all the children she had borne. My father even said they marked my victories. To just make these go away . . .' I touched my crushed cheek. I could feel how the bone was pushed in. 'It wouldn't undo what they did to me, Per.'

He tilted his head at me. Then he opened his shirt. I stared in astonishment as he unfastened the collar laces and laid bare his hairless chest to me. 'See where I took an arrow for you?' he asked me.

I stared. His skin was smooth over his muscles. 'No.'

'That's because your father erased it. He healed me. And Lant, too. And you should have seen what the Fool looked like before your father worked on him! Fitz even took the Fool's wounds and put them on himself so the Fool could heal faster.'

I was silent, wondering how he had done that. It did not increase my respect for the Fool that he had given my father his scars to bear. Per touched my cheek. I realized I had been silent a long time. 'I can see that this hurts you. You should fix it. You can't make it unhappen, but you don't have to carry around what they did to you. Don't give them that power over you.'

'I will think about it,' I told him. 'And now I want to go down. I don't like how we are waving about up here.'

'You would get used to it. And after a time, you might even like coming up here.'

'I will think about it,' I promised him again.

And I did. Two days later, at a time when the winds had died and our sails hung limp, we climbed the rigging again. I wasn't sure that I enjoyed it, but I could convince myself I was not that scared. For several days we were becalmed, and slowly I made the crow's nest a familiar place. Often it was already occupied by a sailor named Ant. She didn't talk much but she loved the rigging. I liked her.

Bit by bit, in the night, in my hammock, I repaired myself. It was not easy. I did it slowly because I didn't want anyone to notice it. I didn't want them to say I looked better, or to praise me for doing it. I could not explain the why of that, not even to myself. But my ear, the crumpled ear my father had touched and called a victory? I left that as it was.

*   *   *

I came to love the ship. I think it was because I could feel how Vivacia felt about me. If I put my hand on the silvery wood of her railings, I could feel her. It was like my mother looking up from her sewing and smiling at me when I came into the room—a small welcome and a good wish for me. I was not bold enough to speak to her very much, but she was full of kindness toward me. That was the only conversation I needed with her.

I heard her have other conversations with her captain. It had taken me some time, but I had sorted out that Captain Wintrow was Althea Vestrit's nephew and that Vivacia was the ship of the Vestrit family, and that Althea had grown up aboard her. Liveships, it seemed, were very important to the families that owned them. That Paragon had turned into two dragons and flown away meant that Althea and Brashen and Boy-O no longer had a ship. And Vivacia wanted to do the same. Then there would be no liveships for any of them. Per was right. Before I was a woman grown, all the liveships would be gone.

That saddened them, but there was a more immediate conflict. I had been sitting in a coil of rope near the foredeck and had dozed off there. I woke to a group of our sailors standing in a respectful row, their hats in hands. I had not heard what they asked of the ship, but her reply made it clear. Vivacia refused to put into the Pirate Isles. Her captain pleaded with her, Boy-O importuned her, but she was adamant. I could see that her black curling hair had the grain of wood, but somehow it still moved when she shook her head.

'Kennitsson will never be less dead, no matter when or how they receive the news. We all know how terrible it will be for Queen Etta and Sorcor and indeed all the Pirate Isles. Do you think I did not care for Kennitsson? He was not blood of my blood, but I cared for him. I knew his father, and perhaps understood him far more than I enjoyed. I respect some of what he did. Nonetheless, I have no wish to be trapped in Divvytown while Etta rages and curses and weeps. And you know she will have a thousand questions followed by a thousand accusations and rebukes. She will delay me for weeks if not months.'

'So what do you intend?' Navigator asked the question.

'I intend to bypass the Pirate Isles. I know you need supplies. I am not the Mad Ship, to care nothing for my crew's lives. I can compromise. We can stop briefly in Bingtown. Then I will go up the Rain Wild River to Trehaug. For Silver. To become the dragon I was always meant to be.'

'What of me?' Captain Wintrow asked discouragedly as he came to join the discussion. 'What will Etta think of me? Do you think I will ever be able to return to Divvytown if I do not bring Queen Etta the news of her son's death?' He shook his head. 'It will be the end of my career there. Perhaps even my life.'

Althea and Brashen and Boy-O were coming to join them. Did they fear a mutiny on the ship?

Vivacia was silent for a time. Then she said, with both firmness and regret, 'I know only that I have been too long a ship. Wintrow, I am trapped. I need to be free. I will free myself. As you should free yourself. It has been years. Etta will never love you as she loved Kennit. She is a woman whose love was won by coldness and neglect. She thought a man who did not beat her loved her. And Kennit? He never admitted to himself that he cared for her as anything more than a convenient whore. He was fonder of you than he ever was of her. Wintrow, go home. Take me home. It is time we both were free.'

So long a silence followed the ship's words that I wondered if they had all left. I opened my eyes to slits and saw Althea set her arm across her nephew's shoulders. The crew stood embarrassed for him, looking aside from his downcast face.

'She's right.' Boy-O whispered the words. 'You know she's right.' But at that confirmation, Wintrow shrugged away from Althea's touch and strode away from both family and figurehead. I judged it better to continue to feign sleep and never speak to anyone of what I had overheard.

Most of Vivacia's crew was from the Pirate Isles. The ship's refusal to put into port there left those sailors bereft and resentful. I felt the tension simmer and was puzzled. The crew knew it was not Wintrow's decision, but the ship's, so what did they expect him to do? But when we were within sight of the Pirate Isles, Captain Wintrow offered his compromise. He gave our ship's boats to those who wished to leave Vivacia's deck and go to Divvytown. Only one boat he would keep back, despite knowing it would not hold us all should some disaster befall Vivacia.

Yet given the opportunity, it was only a dozen or so who chose to depart. Some who had long sailed with Vivacia decided to stay

with her, to see her become the dragon. 'That will be a tale to tell
for years, and a sight I will not miss,' declared one man. And at
that, two who had sought to leave decided to stay. Wintrow bade
farewell to the others and assured them that the ship's accountant
would see them paid. And Boy-O said to the oldest man, 'I trust
this to you, to give to Queen Etta. All of you leaving the ship here,
this must not go astray.' But what he gave them was only a rather
plain necklace with a dull grey charm on it. I did not understand
while the crewmen were so stricken with gravity. They promised
him many times it would go directly to her. The boats were lowered
and we watched them row away across the waves. And we left the
Pirate Isles behind us.

That night Captain Wintrow got very drunk, and Althea and
Brashen with him. Boy-O stood the night watch and commanded
the ship. Clef kept him company, and Per. They sat on the foredeck,
near the figurehead, and sang some rude songs. The next day, they
all went about their work with blotched faces and shaking hands.
Amber and Spark helped to fill the gaps left by the departing sailors,
and the ship seemed almost to sail herself in her drive to reach the
Rain Wild River.

I had another episode of the sickness in which I became weak
and feverish. When Amber sought to reassure me that all would be
well, I said that I'd been through it before and wished to be left
alone. Amber seemed to find that astonishing, but acceded to my
wishes. It was Per who brought me water and soup and when the
fever had passed begged permission of the captain that I be allowed
to take a bath in his quarters. I was given a tub to stand in, a cloth
to use and a bucket of hot water. I had longed for a tub full of
steaming water, but Per explained that given Vivacia's refusal to
stop in the Pirate Isles we had to conserve our fresh water. With
what they gave me, I could rid myself of most of my peeling skin.
I emerged a colour that was a shade closer to Per's skin and feeling
much better.

It was peculiar that the very boredom of our uneventful voyage
became difficult for me. After months of plotting each day how I
would survive, there was suddenly very little for me to do. No one
expected chores of me. Over and over, I was told to rest. In those

idle hours, I was left to recall every detail of what had befallen me. I tried to make sense out of all that had happened. My father was dead. The people who had stolen me were dead, or mostly so. I was going 'home' to Buckkeep Castle, to a sister I did not know well and a niece who was a baby.

I thought of the things that had been done to me, and the things I had done to survive. Some, I could scarcely believe. Biting Dwalia's face. Watching Trader Akriel die. Becoming the Destroyer, and killing Dwalia and setting fire to Symphe and burning all the libraries. Had that truly been me, Bee Farseer?

I had dreams, both those full of portents and the ordinary kind. Sometimes it was hard to tell the difference. I wandered the walls of Withywoods, calling for my father, but only a wolf came to me. Trader Akriel crawled after me, screaming that it was all my fault. I tried to run from her, but my legs were jelly. A blue buck leapt into a silver lake and a black wolf leapt out of it. A dozen dragons rose in glorious flight. Dwalia stood over my bed and laughed to think I had believed I could kill her. I dreamed of a woman who ploughed an immense field, and golden grasses grew up to be harvested into creaking wagons. I dreamed of my mother saying, 'He may not seem to love you, but he does'. I dreamed I watched a grand ball in an immense, festive chamber through a crack in the wall.

Some I wrote down on the paper Beloved had given me, and some I kept to myself. He came to me one evening and said, 'I propose that we sit down together, and you read your dreams to me, and we discuss them.'

I did not want to share them. Writing them down made them important. Reading them aloud would make them even more so. I said nothing.

He sat down beside me on the foredeck. It had become my favourite place to be in the evening. His long hands, one gloved, one bared, were folded loosely in his lap. 'Bee, please let me know you. There is nothing more important to me than that. I want to know you, and to teach you the things you must understand about yourself. Teach you about your dreams and what they might mean and what life may demand of you. Some day you must find a Catalyst, and begin to make the changes . . .'

I noticed that he did not say he wished me to know him.

Amber-Fool-Beloved that he was. I covered my drawing of Trader Akriel. I made a smile for him. 'I found a Catalyst. And I made my changes. I am finished with that.' I thought of what my father would want me to do. I drew a great breath and tried not to hurt his feelings. 'I don't want to be a White Prophet like you were.'

'I could wish that we could change that. But I'm afraid that for you, it's inevitable. Let's set that aside. Would you tell me about your Catalyst?' He tipped his head at me and asked gently, 'Is it Per?'

Per? I tried to hide my dismay for such an idea. Per was my friend! 'I already told you! My catalyst was Dwalia. She enabled me to be who I had to be to become the Destroyer. She changed my life. She took me from Withywoods to Clerres. There I made the changes they all feared I would make. And then I killed her. I am the Destroyer, and I destroyed the Servants.'

He was silent for a time. His fingers, some gloved and some bared, toyed with one another. 'Are you sure that Dwalia was your Catalyst?'

'Prilkop said she was.' I corrected myself. 'Prilkop said he thought she was.'

'Hmm. Prilkop has been known to be wrong.' He sighed suddenly. 'Bee, I thought this was going to be so much easier, for both of us. But then, I had hoped your father might be with us. To help us become friends. To help you trust me.'

'But he's dead.'

'I know.' He suddenly sat up straight. He tilted his head to consider my face. Those eyes. I looked away. He spoke to me anyway. 'Bee. Do you blame me for his death?'

'No. I blame him.' I hadn't known I was going to say that. But now that I had, I felt a surge of righteousness. It had been his own fault that he died, and it was fair that I was so angry with him.

Beloved took my hand in his gloved one. He wasn't looking at me any more. He stared off over the sea. 'I do, too. And I think I am as furious with him as you are.'

I tugged my hand away. As if he were innocent!

We sailed up the shifting coastline they called the Cursed Shores. Day by day we drew closer to Bingtown until the night we could see its lights in the distance. Beloved set out plans for us. We would disembark in Bingtown, send a messenger bird to Buckkeep Castle that we needed funds for passage home, and wait to hear back from them. Althea had invited us stay in her family home until our funds arrived and our passage was arranged, and 'Amber' had gratefully accepted. Until our funds arrived from Buckkeep, we were paupers, dependent on her charity.

The day was sunny as we sailed into Trader Bay and then Bingtown harbour. Vivacia went directly to the docks reserved for the liveships. Our arrival caused a stir and soon the other liveships were calling to her. It was strange to hear ships shouting to one another, demanding news. Apparently the two small dragons that once had been Paragon had stopped in Bingtown to exhort the other ships to follow them to Kelsingra. Now they wanted to know: was it true? Had these dragons once been Paragon the liveship? One liveship named Kendry was the most vocal, roaring that it was past time for ships to be free dragons. His figurehead was a handsome, bare-chested young man. He was tied at a separate dock from the other liveships, and his masts were naked of canvas. Most of the ships were curious, but Kendry's anger was frightening.

It was not only the ships that were in uproar. No sooner were we tied up than a contingent of folk in peculiar robes came down the docks in a gaggle. As I disembarked behind Beloved with Spark and Per they were demanding permission to board.

'Who are they?' I demanded as we passed them by. Men and women alike were garbed in robes of differing colours and wore grim expressions.

'They are members of the Bingtown Traders' Council.' Beloved as Amber spoke quietly beside me. 'Each of the original families who settled here has a vote in the Bingtown Council, to make decisions that bind all. The prospect of the liveships becoming dragons will upset many of them. The liveships and their ability to move up and down the Rain Wild River, as well as their swiftness upon the open seas have long given the Traders a distinct advantage. Their vanishing will affect not only the families fortunate enough to have owned them for generations and to have founded their fortunes upon them, but all who have relied on them to bring first to Bingtown the finest goods from the Rain Wilds.'

'Boy-O told me the council won't be happy about any of it,' Per summed it up. 'They'll likely have a big meeting tonight to decide what's to be done.'

Bingtown was a place of beauty and bustle in equal measure. Folk walked with purpose in their stride. A woman loudly hailed a man, demanding to know where her shipment of fine calf leather was. Two men rose from a table and leaned forward to shake hands over a pot of tea and two cups. A messenger dashed past, her pouch of missives clutched to a bouncing bosom. Clerres had been a town of passive pastels and calm folk. Bingtown roared with colour and commerce. The scents of spices and rich meats floated on the air. Amber grinned as she strode through it, and seemed familiar with the town. She was not certain of every turning, but soon found a place where we could send a messenger bird to Buckkeep Castle. Spark produced a small pouch and counted out careful coins from it to pay.

As we left, Spark hefted the little bag. 'Not much left of our funds, Amber.'

'We are fortunate to have any. Whatever we have, it must suffice,' she said. She was attired somewhere between a man and a woman's garb. We were all in borrowed bits of clothing, for we had come aboard the *Vivacia* with only the clothes in which we had gone overboard. In comparison to the smartly-clothed Traders and the colourfully garbed folk on the streets we looked like beggars.

We were on our way back to the ship when Spark shrieked and bolted away from us. I looked up to see a man charging toward her. He seized Spark around the waist and hugged her tight, then spun her around. I was groping for my belt-knife when Per shouted, 'Lant? How can it be? Lant!'

And it was. He was baked brown from the sun and more ragged than any of us, but it was Lant indeed. His restoration was enough to decree that we would spend what little coin we had to share a small meal. We sat at a table outside a tea-house under a canopy. Lant supplemented our coins with his. 'I was clinging to wreckage when the *Sea Rose* passed me, fleeing the harbour. Her crew threw me a line and I clung to it until they drew me aboard. I begged them to take me back, but neither mate nor crew would hear of that! I'd landed in the middle of a mutiny, for they'd left their insane captain behind them in Clerres.'

It was a fine tale as he told it. He had worked aboard her as a common sailor, and when she put into a port he had left her and taken passage on a vessel bound for the Spice Isles. From there, he had found work on a little boat happily bound for Bingtown. He had arrived within a day of Vivacia and quickly come to find us.

I tried to be glad for Spark and Per, but their joyous reunion made me want to weep. Beloved wore Amber's smile, but in a chance moment I saw melancholy in his eyes. They bought drinks squeezed from fruit and seasoned with a tingling spice. When it came time to pay, the tea-woman refused our money. She touched the wooden earrings she wore and said, 'They've brought me more luck than ever I could have imagined. I am glad to see you back in Bingtown, Amber, and look forward to seeing your shingle once more swinging on Rain Wild Street.'

We were on our way back to the ship only to be met by Althea before we reached the harbour. She grinned to see Lant with us. 'I see you found them! Come. I will take you to my family home.' Her invitation was more of an order than a request. As we fell in with her, she led us up cobbled streets toward a section of the town where gracious homes gazed serenely over garden walls festooned with fragrantly blooming vines. When we had left the crowds of the city behind us, she spoke hastily. 'We go to fetch my mother. The mood of the Traders' Council is a testy one. They assailed us for the Vestrit vote, urging us to forbid other traders from allowing Silver to be given to the liveships. My mother controls that vote. They were very bitter with Brashen and me, accusing us of failing our duties as Traders when we "allowed" Paragon to become dragons.'

'As if you could have stopped him!' Per injected.

'Worse. As if we *should* have stopped him. Paragon was right. Once we knew it was possible, both Brashen and I knew it was the correct choice for him. No matter how hard it was for us.'

'So you will argue that the ships should be allowed to seek the Silver and become dragons?'

'No,' Althea replied grimly. For a short woman, she moved rapidly, her speed making up for the shortness of her stride. 'Brashen and I will not attend the council meeting at all. Nor Wintrow. This way.'

She turned aside from the shady thoroughfare onto a carriageway. A short distance down it we encountered a stout wall of worked stone. But no gate barred our passage and we entered a type of garden I had never seen before. Flat grassy areas spread out to either side, as if sheep had grazed them to an even height, but left no dung.

There were tall trees and beneath them, shady banks of flowers. This vista stretched out beyond us in all directions. To one side, I saw a little building with its walls made of glass. Inside, plants pressed up against the glass like children peering out. We walked and walked, and Althea muttered, 'I should have sent a runner for a carriage. I was too angry to think.'

'The grounds are exceptionally beautiful this year,' Amber observed, winning a wry smile from Althea.

'Money buys good servants. But, yes, they are exceptionally lovely. Nothing like the storm-battered neglect you saw the first time you visited.' She shook her head. 'I wonder if we will be able to keep the grounds like this with Paragon gone? Well.' The last word came out on a harsh exhalation of breath and she bounded up the wide front steps. Without a pause she opened the door and entered, calling out, 'Mother! We're in port! And we've important news!'

Two servants in matching livery were hastening toward us, but Althea waved them off with, 'We're fine, Rennolds, good to see you. Angar, where is my mother?'

We heard a questioning, 'Althea? Is that you?' from down the passage, and then a door opened. Stick in hand, a grey-haired woman emerged. The hand that clutched the stick had knotted knuckles and her face was lined, but the woman stepped briskly as she came toward us with a smile. 'And who have you brought home with you this time? Wait! Amber? Is that you, after all these years?'

'It is,' Amber replied and the woman's eyes and smile widened.

'Come in, come in! I had just requested tea and a bite. Rennolds! Can you please bring enough for a horde? You know how Althea eats when she first gets home!'

Rennolds, who had been hovering, responded with a grin, 'Indeed yes, ma'am. Right away.'

Althea introduced the rest of us. But as she began to explain, her mother said, 'I know more than you think I do, and far less than I should like to. I received your dispatches from Divvytown and was frankly terrified for you and Brashen and Boy-O. But Karrigvestrit assured me that you had survived and that Vivacia would bear you home. How badly injured is Boy-O?'

'Karrigvestrit?' Althea was shocked.

'The blue one. The green dragon was more guarded about her name. She is the decidedly odd one, and I think the one most responsible for Paragon's . . . uneven nature when he was a ship. How is Boy-O?'

'The dragons came here and spoke to you?'

'Would you like to see the mess they made of the iris gardens around the reflecting pool? That is where the two bullocks they requested fled to, and where they feasted. So I knew you were alive and I hoped you were coming directly home, but I know little more than that, and understand still less of it!'

'Well, that saves me some time, but there is much more to tell and an even more immediate worry. A contingent from the Traders' Council met us as soon as we docked. They were very angry that Paragon had become dragons. They all but accused us of treason. And now Vivacia wishes—'

'Trader business is for Traders,' her mother rebuked her firmly. She turned a smile on us. 'Please. I do not even know your names yet, but please, be comfortable here while Althea and I converse privately. In here, if you would.'

'In here' was a spacious room with cushioned chairs near windows that looked over the spoiled iris garden. The room was floored with white tiles, and a table with a white-tiled top was surrounded by six chairs. As Amber ushered us in, I heard the mother say, 'Oh, excellent, Rennolds. In there, and please, a word with you afterwards.'

'Did we offend her?' Lant asked in a quiet voice, but Amber shook her head.

'Not at all. Traders are very private about their business. I am sure she will join us shortly. Oh, my, hot tea! And lemon!'

Rennolds entered with a large silver tray bearing a steaming china pot and cups. As he set it down, I smelled tea and saw a sliced yellow fruit in a little dish on the tray. Two other servants followed, carrying similar trays of little cakes and cold sliced meats and tiny bread rolls.

'Real food,' I said aloud, and Per laughed.

'Like Withywoods food,' he affirmed.

I felt awkward and shy, but Amber was not. She seated herself and dismissed Rennolds with a nod after he had poured cups of tea for each of us. My teacup had a painting of a rose on it and a delicate little handle. The tea was dark and strong. I copied Amber, squeezing juice from the lemon into the tea. Tea had always both calmed me and cleared my mind. Lant put little cakes on a small plate and set them in front of me. I looked at them and my throat went tight as

I recalled a winter feast that had never been. Per bit into one that was dusted with cinnamon. I took one and broke it. It was pink all through. I tasted strawberry. Like my mother had grown. I hid my tears as I ate. The tea smelled like the kitchen at Withywoods in the morning. It was hard to swallow.

Amber was speaking to the others. '. . . funds from Igrot's hoard. I believe Althea put a goodly amount of her share into restoring her childhood home, for it had been neglected due to lack of funds even before the mercenaries invaded and vandalized half the town. I know she fears for their fortune with the liveship gone. But I am sure that Paragon was not Ronica's only business investment. I am confident that Althea and Brashen and Ronica can generate income with any ship, even if it does not speak to them.'

'Would you like more? You've hardly eaten,' Lant asked me quietly. I was surprised at the concern in his eyes. Then I realized that my father's absence would be sharply real to him this day.

'I don't know,' I said, and he nodded gravely. Per was still eating. Amber and Spark had risen from the table and taken their cups to the windows to look out over the destruction. There was a tap at the door and Rennolds entered.

He looked a bit uncomfortable as he said, 'If it please you, Trader Vestrit noticed that the child is shoeless. There are children among the servants who have outgrown shoes and skirts, and she thought I might offer something to you for her.' He spoke to Lant and Amber, as if I were too young to understand him.

I spoke for myself. 'I would be very grateful indeed, for anything that might cover my feet.' I was the most ragged among us, for while the others had been given clothing from Vivacia's crew, nothing they had would fit me. Rennolds had brought several pairs of the soft leather slippers that house servants usually wore, and one set with a harder sole. Fortunately, that was the pair that fitted me the best. I donned the skirt over the ragged cotton trousers that Capra had given me to wear. The skirts tied with a sash, and looked much too tidy to be worn with my stained blouse. It had been so long since I'd worn skirts that it felt strange. I thanked Rennolds for his thoughtfulness, but Per shook his head. As Rennolds was leaving, he marvelled sadly, 'A princess of the Six Duchies, wearing a servant's hand-me-downs.'

'A princess?' Ronica asked as she came in the door. She smiled as she said it, as if it were a fancy of mine.

'That's not quite her correct title,' Amber said. 'But a high-born lady.'

'One who is very glad of shoes,' I put in, lest Althea's mother think me ungrateful. I curtseyed to her in my new skirts and said, 'Thank you so much for your thoughtfulness.'

'She is the daughter of FitzChivalry Farseer. Bee. The girl we went to rescue,' Althea filled in.

Her mother jerked her gaze to her daughter. 'She is the daughter of the Farseer prince who healed Phron?' She looked stricken. 'I did not understand! I grieved when Althea told me that he had died. He was your father? Oh, I am so sorry. Our family owes him a debt we can never repay.'

'And it doubled when she healed Boy-O of his burns from when the Clerres folk set fire to Paragon. Mother, we thought he would lose the use of that arm and be forever scarred. But his new skin is pink and healthy.'

'Boy-O was that badly burned? Obviously, there is a great deal to your tale that you have not told yet!'

'There is, and precious little time to stand here and tell it. Mother, we must get back to the ship. May we use the carriage?'

'Of course. Just let me change my shoes. Rennolds! Rennolds, the carriage, please, as quickly as possible. Althea, come with me while I change. I have many questions for you.'

And they hastened off.

A short time later, a behatted Ronica escorted all of us to the carriage. Per and Lant had left not a crumb or a drop of tea on the table. I'd almost forgotten how to manage skirts, and I stepped on my hem climbing up into the very grand carriage. Per had only a moment to gape at the matched black horses that would take us back to the docks, and then the door was latched behind us and we were on our way.

As we rattled over the cobblestoned streets, Ronica Vestrit leaned across to take my hands in hers. 'Had we time, my dear, there would be a feast in your honour, and I would see you decked out as befits, not your station, but your kindness. Phron and Boy-O are both very dear to me, and your family has saved them both. I regret that our visit will be so short, and I grieve at your loss. I am saddened that you must be on your way again tonight.'

'What is this?' Amber interjected.

Althea spoke tersely. 'I've sent a bird down to the harbour. Wintrow and Brashen will have seen to replenishing our water and bringing on as many supplies as time allows. As soon as the Traders' Council meeting is convened we will be departing Bingtown Harbour and heading for Trehaug. We've sent a bird ahead to Kelsingra, to demand for Vivacia what should be hers by right; enough Silver for her to become a dragon.'

'But . . .' Amber attempted.

'I should have told you first that my mother has received bird-messages from Malta and Reyn. Buckkeep has already sent magic-users to Kelsingra. Some were overcome by the voices of the city, and could not stay long. But others could "keep their walls" as they put it, and they helped many people there. When they went across the river to the Village, they could do even more, away from the stones of the city.'

Ronica Vestrit was smiling as she spoke. 'Including Reyn's sister,' she added. 'And we have sent our bird to let Kelsingra know that we will be bringing you back up the river to them. Your Buck magic-users have some method of travelling between the Six Duchies and Kelsingra using magic statues, as I understand it. And perhaps they will be able to take you home that way.'

'They could,' Amber said quietly. I could tell she was startled by this news. 'And very quickly indeed.' She took my hand. 'It may be a bit frightening, but it would cut many days from our journey home.'

'I've travelled through a stone before,' I reminded her as I disengaged my hand from hers. I fell silent, thinking of being trapped with the others in the ruins of Chalced. Of Reppin falling back into the stone. The coach rattled us along.

FORTY-FOUR

Up the River

A disappointing night. I slipped from my room and went very quietly to my father's study. Last night, I had taken some of his writing from his desk. In them, I read of a day he spent with my mother, when they were very young. He wrote of reading to her something her mother had written for her, a recipe for candles. So strange to read such sentimental words from the pen of one who holds himself on such a tight rein. And he wrote something there that I had never known. On the night she summoned him to tell him that I would be born, when he followed her to the room where I would come out of her body, those were the candles she burned.

How could he not have told me such a thing? Was he saving it until I was older? Does it still exist, that precious writing of my grandmother's? I put his pages back with the edges uneven, exactly as he had left them.

Tonight, when I heard him finally go to his bed, I went again to his study. I wanted to read again how tenderly he thought of her, how astounded he was on the night I was born, and how certain he had been that I would not live.

But the pages were not where he had left them. And when I stirred the dying fire on the study hearth, that I might have a bit more light to look for them, I saw their fate. I saw the words I recalled from the last page 'I will ever regret' curling on the page as the flames ate them. I watched them go, watched them forever lost to me.

Why, I wonder, does he write and then burn? Does he seek to banish his memories? Does he fear that writing it down makes it important? Some day, I hope to sit next to him and demand that he tell to me everything *he can remember of his life. And I will write it down and never let the flames steal it.*

From Bee Farseer's journal

We reboarded Vivacia, but she felt like a different ship. Althea, Brashen and Boy-O were aboard, but Paragon's crewmembers had disembarked. From overheard conversations, I knew that Brashen had seen that they had funds for their immediate needs and promised them that they would be paid their full wages in the next two days, and given recommendations for future work. For some of them, it had been years since they had lived ashore. Paragon had been their home, and most were already pounding the docks looking for a new berth on another ship.

'Why must we leave so soon?' Lant asked Boy-O. We had herded ourselves into the galley to avoid being in the way, and Boy-O had come in to give me a parcel that had been delivered to the ship. It had my name on it. It was wrapped in canvas and tied with string. The knots were complicated but I didn't want to cut the string.

'It's a Trader thing. If we are underway before the council votes that the liveships must not be allowed to turn into dragons, then we don't know they voted that, so we aren't disobeying the Traders' Council. That's something that no Bingtown Trader wants to be accused of, let alone found guilty of and fined. The alliance of Bingtown Traders has become extremely important once the impervious ships started competing for the river trade. If all the liveships go dragon, the Bingtown Traders won't have any way of bringing articles from Trehaug and Kelsingra and the other little Rain Wild towns to Bingtown, unless they hire impervious ships. The Rain Wild Traders will have to start doing business with the impervious boats, and we lose our monopoly on Elderling goods. So we leave tonight and we run hard for Trehaug. And we hope that Malta and Reyn agree with us, and get the Silver shipped down to Trehaug as fast as possible.' He gestured with his pink hand, palm up. 'Once it's on its way, it's a done deal, and to be honourable Traders, we have to accept shipment of it.'

'Can they really stop the liveships from turning into dragons?' asked Per.

'Probably not. But those who don't own liveships, those who think they are just talking boats, believe they can order us to do that. And they could make it difficult for us.'

'Aren't they just talking boats?' asked Per innocently.

'No. They're family,' Boy-O replied seriously and then realized Per was teasing him.

I got the knot undone and pulled the string away. I unfolded canvas to find trousers and a jerkin. The material was like silk, and patterned with golden frogs on a background of green lily pads. They were as colourful as the butterfly cloak had been. I ran the fabric over my hands. It snagged slightly on my broken nails and rough skin. 'They're beautiful. I will set them aside for when I grow into them. Who should I thank?'

Boy-O was staring at the gift open-mouthed. 'My grandmother,' he said breathlessly. 'And you don't have to wait to wear them. They're Elderling made. They'll adjust.'

'Will they make her invisible?' Per asked.

'What?'

'She had a cloak like that with butterflies on it, and it made the wearer invisible.'

Boy-O stared. 'You meant really invisible when you told me that story? You never actually showed us how it worked that night when Fitz chased us out of Amber's cabin! The night Kennitsson and I glimpsed the Silver.' For a moment, he went still, recalling his friend. Then he shook his head. 'I thought you meant she had covered you with the cloak and thrown snow over the cloak to make you invisible.' He sat back. 'Do you still have it? Can I see it?'

As Per shook his head, we heard a shout. 'Boy-O! On deck!' It was his father, and he jumped to his feet. 'And no, they won't make her invisible. But they are worth a small fortune. Try them on!' And he clattered away to his father's command.

That very night we were underway again. Vivacia's mooring lines were slipped and we ignored the shouts of the harbourmaster's underlings. We sailed under a clear sky and when the moon rose and I went out on deck, I saw we were not alone. Kendry trailed us. 'Well. I'm glad his family isn't going to fight him any more,' Brashen said when he came to stand beside me. He looked down at my beautiful clothes, and smiled. 'Aren't you fine?'

But as Boy-O dashed by behind us, he dared to tousle my hair.

'For good luck!' he whispered, and then ran on. More sail blossomed on Vivacia's masts and we easily outpaced Kendry.

Up the coast we fled, with Per and Ant keeping watch in the crow's nest for any pursuit. They saw two ships, but they could catch neither Vivacia nor Kendry. And when we started up the river, Brashen laughed and said the acid would protect us from any pursuit.

We sailed against the current. I watched how it was done and marvelled at it, and marvelled too at a landscape I could never have imagined. In the evenings, our little company gathered at the table. It began with Per telling me of their journey from Kelsingra down the river, and gradually other stories of their travel were shared. Lant spoke of how Per had killed Ellik, a different tale from the one Per had told. Lant's praise made him blush. We recalled those who had died at Withywoods. Spark wept when Per spoke of how his mother had forgotten him. Boy-O remembered Paragon to us, and more than once tears were shed for the ship-turned-dragons. I heard stories of Malta, who I would meet, and her romance with a veiled Rain Wild Trader and how they had wed after many adventures. In my hesitant turn, I began to tell how Shun and I had been taken. Of Ellik. Of Vindeliar's magic. Of the Chalcedean. I even told them of Trader Akriel and her death. But of killing Dwalia and Symphe I said not a word. Silent, too, was Beloved/Amber. I wanted to hear what that person knew of my father, of the years he said they had shared. But he gave me none of that.

Such a strange riverscape! I saw brightly coloured birds, and once, a troop of shrieking monkeys fleeing through the trees. No one asked me to do hard work, no one struck me or threatened me. I had no reason to be afraid. Yet I would wake as often as four times a night, shaking and weeping, or so paralysed by fear that I could not even cry out.

'Come with me,' someone said one night, standing by my hammock in the shifting dark, and I cried out in alarm, for it was Vindeliar commanding me again. But it was Beloved. I followed him up to the foredeck near the figurehead, but not on the special little deck where her family often gathered to speak to her. Vivacia was both anchored and tethered for the night, for the changing currents of the river made night navigation dangerous.

I dreaded long discussion with him. Instead, he took out a little flute. 'A gift from Wintrow,' he said and began to play soft and breathy music on it. When it was over, he handed me his little wooden pipe and said, 'Here are where your fingers go. If it sounds wrong, your fingers aren't blocking the holes completely. Try each note.'

It was both harder and easier than it looked. By the time the sun was threading through the trees, I could sound each note clearly. I ate with everyone, and then found a place on top of the aft-house to curl up out of the way and sleep. I felt like a cat, sleeping in warm sunlight while everyone around me worked. In my sleep, Vivacia spoke to me. *It's like poison working out of a wound. Let the tears fall and let the fear shake you. On my deck or within my hold, you do not have to be strong. Let go of what you had to hide.*

Before we reached Trehaug I could play four simple tunes. And sleep at night in the dark. The ship helped me twice to meet with Boy-O secretly. He did not ask me. Vivacia was the one who told me that something was binding in his elbow and he could not straighten his arm completely. He worked alongside the others and did not complain, but he could not swing through the rigging as he once had. She woke me by night, and I went to him as he stood the anchor watch. I moved very softly and he startled when I reached to take his hand in mine. 'Don't tell,' I whispered, and he stared at me in shock and dismay. He tried to pull his hand away, but I held him fast, and then he felt what I did. 'The ship says it's like loosening a line jammed in a block and tackle,' I told him as I worked.

'How can I thank you?' he asked me as he flexed his arm.

'By not telling anyone,' I said, and slipped away to my hammock.

But the next day, he took me up in the rigging with him, to the very top, and showed me the river and the jungle. And while he named the birds and the trees we could see, I put right a place where the skin on his neck had healed as smooth and shiny as polished wood. 'It pulls sometimes,' was all he needed to say. And then we clambered down, and no one was the wiser save he and me.

I had looked forward to Trehaug after all Per had told me of it. He shouted to me at his first sight of one of the little houses dangling in the trees. He stood beside me and we pointed and exclaimed as we saw little children running along outstretched branches, and a man fishing from a tree branch over the river.

So, I was disappointed when our crew anchored Vivacia out of the channel but in the river, away from the docks. Another liveship, a flat black barge named Tarman, was waiting for us, and we anchored next to him. Lines were exchanged to raft the two ships together. Three little boats from the treehouse town rowed out to us, but Captain Wintrow denied them permission to come aboard or tie to us. 'We are concluding a bargain,' he warned them. Trader custom meant they could not come aboard or speak to us.

I stood at the railing and watched, wishing I were more a part of it, regretting what I had not learned and done. Vivacia reached for me and I lowered my walls. She suffused me with reassurance and a wave of warm gratitude for what had been done for Boy-O and his cousin Phron. *What you have done, no one else could*, she assured me.

The people on Tarman's deck shouted greetings, and Per seized my hand and begged immediately to be allowed to cross to the other ship. Althea said we might, and my heart leapt with a good sort of fear as we crossed over the gap between the two ships and onto Tarman. Had Vivacia spoken to him somehow? He welcomed me, and he felt like a gracious old gentleman as he reassured me that I was safe on his decks. The captain of Tarman saw me touching his railing and as he hurried by me he muttered, 'I should have guessed that would happen!'

On both vessels, the work was swift and frantic. Vivacia's boats were moved and tied off to Tarman. Up from the hold and out of the captain's stateroom came everything of value or sentiment. Charts and chairs, glasses and bedding, all manner of things came across the gap and were stowed in Tarman's hold. At the same time, heavy casks were hauled up from Tarman's hold and arranged in a row on his deck.

Captain Leftrin and his red-haired wife were much too busy to meet anyone new. He told Per to put me up on the flat roof of the deckhouse. He did, and then Per darted away to be helpful. I felt strange to be the only one idle. But from that perch, I could hear snatches of conversations. Several of the crew on Tarman joked with Spark and Per that they had feared the casks would leak. 'We'd be trying to sleep, wondering if we'd wake up in a dragon's belly instead of inside Tarman,' one man called out to Lant. He was greeted with a chorus of shushes. 'Sound carries across the water,' a plump woman warned him, and he grinned and fell silent.

Midway through the day, Kendry anchored alongside us. 'Not sure we have enough,' Brashen called to his captain in a low voice.

'We'll take whatever you can spare,' the captain replied. He shook his head. He was an older man, older than my father had been, and his face was lined. His eyes were the same as Brashen's had been when he knelt by Boy-O and looked at his burns. His voice was thick with sorrow. 'He's been in agony for years now. Time to release him.'

Evidently Kendry had not been sailed for a time, for there was much less to unload from him. As they loaded their few goods onto Tarman, his captain spoke to his sparse crew, thanking them for bringing the difficult ship up the river. He grimly wished them good fortune in finding work again. It was Captain Leftrin who gruffly noted that the Dragon Traders had two impervious ships that could use experienced river crew.

'I'd almost forgotten that Kelsingra had a couple of those,' Kendry's captain replied speculatively.

'They haven't been used much since we captured them. Tarman's better on the river, shallow draught and all. But when his turn comes . . .' They both fell silent.

Kendry's captain nodded grimly, and Captain Leftrin added, 'We'll have a surplus of captains for a time, but experienced crew is always welcome.'

'So. Tarman will change, too?'

'He's not decided yet. At present, he's our lifeline. But if we get the impervious ships crewed, well . . .' Captain Leftrin stroked the railing of his barge as if he were ruffling a boy's hair. 'He is the one who must decide,' he finished.

'Leftrin. We're ready,' Wintrow said.

It still took some time. The day was fine and the wind blew the sweet fragrance of flowers across the water as the crew said their farewells to Vivacia. There were tears. Some of the crew had been aboard her for most of their lives. And then there was a shifting of lines and anchor chains, both to bring the figurehead alongside Tarman's deck and to make it possible to salvage the chain and anchors afterwards. Traders, I saw, wasted very little. If there had been more time I think they would have taken every scrap of canvas and line off her, but there was a limit to what Tarman could hold.

On Kendry's decks, his crew waited uncertainly. The figurehead had his arms crossed over his manly chest, muscles bulging with tension. He was scowling as he looked about. Then his gaze met mine. He hunched his shoulders as if embarrassed and tried for a smile. It was more frightening than his scowl had been.

My friends joined me on top of the deckhouse. Tarman's decks filled with Vivacia's crew. Amber was weeping; I didn't know why. Vivacia's figurehead picked a cask from our deck. In her hands it was like a very large mug. She studied it and then, with an incredible strength, she broke the top with her thumb, raised it and began to drink. Her colours brightened as if she had been freshly painted. Everywhere that she had been built from wizardwood, varnish and paint flaked away. Planks and railings shone with an unusual sheen.

A second keg. A third. 'It did not take that much for Paragon,' Per said.

'He was desperate,' Boy-O said. 'He had to change or die. I think that's why his dragons were so small. He became as much as he could with that small amount of Silver.'

Vivacia was reaching for another cask. She caught my eye and winked at me. I glanced away. That was six casks. I could feel Kendry's tension shimmering across to me. Almost half the casks were gone.

With every cask she drank, she changed slightly. Her face was not so human as it had been. Her wizardwood planks were scaled now. She chose another keg. As she began to drink it, I heard a popping, crackling noise. She dropped the empty cask into the river and gave a shudder, like a horse with a fly on her withers.

'Ware!' shouted Captain Leftrin, but there was nowhere to flee as Vivacia's mast fell like a cut tree. Only good fortune put most of it on the far side of her hull. Spars, lines, rigging came down like a wind-toppled tree. I crouched, my arms over my head, but the bulk of it missed us. The fallen mast and spars dragged the canvas away from us as the river's current tried to carry it off. For a few moments all was frantic activity as sailors cleared fallen lines from Tarman's railing. There was shouting, the thud of hatchets cutting lines, and a lurching as the debris of the ship tugged at Tarman. I looked for Vivacia. I saw only wreckage churning in the river's current.

Then it was floating away down the river, a sloppy raft of wood and canvas. For a moment, Vivacia's aft-house was floating among it, and then it began to slowly sink deeper and deeper. 'Oh, that's going to be a hazard in the channel,' someone said, but I wasn't staring at that. Wallowing among some of the loose wreckage was a large silver dragon. She was twice the size of Paragon's dragons.

'Will she drown?' Althea cried out in a low agonized voice. For the dragon was sinking. Her large head with its glittering blue eyes lingered a moment on the surface and then sank out of sight. Althea screamed, her hands reaching uselessly toward the water.

'Wait!' cried Brashen. I held my breath. I could feel the dragon struggling beneath the water. She fought the current, then let it catch her. It carried her downstream. I turned my head that way and suddenly, in a shallower part of the channel, I saw the water stirring and then there was a wild splashing. 'There!' I shouted, and pointed. A head, a long neck, a spiny back and then, with a tremendous surge of effort, the silver dragon leapt into the air. Her wide wings spread, scattering water not in droplets but as bucketloads. She beat her wings and for a moment I feared she would fall back into the river. But with every heavy stroke, she rose a little higher. A long tail followed her out of the water.

'She's flying!' Althea cried, and her joy and the wave of joy I felt from the rising dragon were one.

'I'm so proud of you!' Boy-O shouted at her. Everyone on the deck laughed and the dragon trumpeted uncertainly.

'I cannot reach it!' Kendry cried out, and his roar of despair was equal to Vivacia's joyful trumpeting. He was listing as his figurehead strained to reach for the remaining kegs on Tarman's decks.

'Move those kegs!' Leftrin ordered and all on deck sprang to his order. 'Quickly!' he added, and I felt Tarman's uneasiness as Kendry leaned on him. It made his deck cant down, and a keg got away from a sailor, rolled across the deck and cracked sharply against the bulwark. Kendry seized it, and it trickled Silver onto Tarman's deck as he raised it to his mouth.

'Oh, sweet Sa!' Captain Leftrin exclaimed, but the Silver soaked into Tarman as if his deck were a sponge, leaving not a trace. I felt a little shiver of pleasure run through him, but no more than that. The other kegs were being transported more carefully and as Kendry came upright, our deck didn't slope. On the shore, people were shouting and pointing at Vivacia's dragon as she tested her wings above the river.

Kendry was on his fourth cask when a small vessel from Trehaug came alongside Tarman. 'Catch a line!' the man in the bow shouted.

No one did.

A small red-faced woman with a thicket of dark curly hair stood up in the middle of the boat. 'Last night, at the agreed-upon hour, a vote was taken. What you are doing is forbidden by a vote of the Bingtown Council. Their prohibition has been affirmed and duplicated by the Rain Wild Traders' Council. You must cease immediately!'

'What's that?' Leftrin shouted back at them. 'Can you say that again?' For as they spoke, a long silver dragon swept over us, trumpeting her joy.

'Stop that immediately!'

'Stop what?'

Her rowers were working hard to stay in place along the Tarman. It seemed as if each time they were almost close enough to catch hold of one of his anchor lines, our ship would sidle slightly away from them. She who had been Vivacia continued to sweep over us in circles that made us all duck from the wind of her wings and pushed the councilwoman's small boat about as if it were a toy. By the time she shouted out at us, that we must not aid any ship in turning into a dragon, Kendry finished the last cask and tossed it casually into the air. Chance made it land with a splash beside the small boat, and the woman shouted in alarm and was barely caught by one of her rowers before she went over.

Captain Leftrin shook his head and made a mocking face. 'Even a child would know better than to stand up in the middle of a rowing boat.'

'You will be condemned for this!' the woman shouted as her rowers pulled their oars and bore her away from us. 'You will be fined for contempt of a lawful council ruling.'

No one was paying attention. Kendry, it turned out, was a very gaudy dragon, with stripes and spots of orange, pink and red on a black hide. His eyes were jade green. He was smaller than Vivacia, and as he rose into the sky he trilled rather than roared. He joined Vivacia over our heads. They sparred twice, there above us, and then both swiftly flew upriver.

Captain Leftrin looked around his deck at his surplus of crew. 'Time to go,' he announced. 'Get those anchors up. Tarman wants to head for home.'

*　　*　　*

'He's done something to himself,' Captain Leftrin muttered to Alise. Alise had been showing me that some sailor knots were the same ones my mother had used to crochet. We were sitting around the galley table when he came in out of the rain. He dripped across to the little galley stove, and made it hiss with rain spatter from his oilskins as he poured himself a mug of coffee.

'Done something?' Alise asked worriedly.

He shook his head. 'We're making good time,' he abruptly announced to all of us. 'Excellent time.' He looked at her and added, 'Better time than we've ever made since I've been captain.' And then he stumped back out onto the rainy deck.

I must have looked worried. 'Oh, don't fret, dear,' Alise assured me. 'The ship is having a bit of a joke. They'll sort it out, I'm sure.'

But Tarman's 'good time' as we went up the river seemed slow indeed to me.

I learned three more tunes on the pipe. Spark and Per insisted I learn more knots. I surprised them with crochet. I could not manage the big lines on the ship; my hands were too small and I lacked the strength. But with very thin cord, Alise and I made tablemats. I spent a great deal of time with her in the galley, helping to make the meals, and in her stateroom listening to her stories of her girlhood in Bingtown. When we walked together on the deck, Captain Leftrin often watched us with a wistful expression.

At night, when the weather was fine, we slept on top of the deckhouse and looked up at the stars in the black sky. One evening when we had tied up to a sandy bank for the night, I went with Amber to find some tall reeds that were like cattails but different. She cut a dozen, and brought them back aboard and made several whistles from them, and Per joined me in learning to play. Their sound was not as fine as her wooden pipe, but we enjoyed them. Often we were banished to the stern of the barge while we practised.

I had other lessons with Beloved, in the small cabin Spark and I shared with him. Beloved spoke of dreams, and changes to my skin, of responsibility to the world, and to my own conscience. He told me tales of other White Prophets and how they had changed the world, sometimes with very small deeds. Despite myself, I enjoyed the stories. It was confusing. I was starting to like him, despite how I nursed my anger for him when I missed my father late at night.

His lessons cautioned me that great events often hinged on small ones. 'Your father was the Unexpected Son. When I was young and dreamed of him, I saw always that the chances of him surviving boyhood were very small, let alone his chance of living through manhood. And so I came, all the way from Clerres, wending my way to Buckkeep Castle, to put myself in service to King Shrewd and wait and hope that I was right. The first time I saw him, he did not see me. He was just a little boy, trudging along behind the stern stablemaster. I looked down on them from my window in a tower and I knew him in that moment. And later that day, when a cart-driver thought to harass him, the boy stood him off without a word.

'Oh, Bee, I put him through so much. It was not a kindness for me to find him and demand that he live through all sorts of beatings and abuse. Time after time I pulled him back from death's door. He endured pain and privation, hardship and heartbreak. Much loneliness. But he changed the world. He made dragons real again.'

That was the day he put his face down in his hands, one gloved and one bared, and wept. After a time, I stood up and left him there. I had no more comfort for him than he did for me.

When we docked in Kelsingra it was so easy that Captain Leftrin was left cursing with amazement. We arrived in the middle of a sunny morning and the sky was full of dragons. Paragon's dragons were there, already larger than when we had last seen them, and Vivacia and Kendry, as well as the red dragon from Clerres and the great blue one called Tintaglia. I saw no sign of the immense black dragon that had helped to flatten the castle.

The city itself had more buildings and larger ones than ever I had seen, even larger than Sewelsby. 'That's because the city was built for the dragons as much as for the Elderlings,' Per told me. 'Look at the steps, how wide they are, and the height of the doors on that building!' He had already recounted so many wonders that I would soon see that I could hardly bear to wait for the time it took to secure Tarman to the dock.

I jumped when Lant suddenly shouted right beside me, 'Hoy, Clansie! By Eda and El! Marden! Nick! Look at them! They're here! They're here, in Kelsingra!' He was literally hopping up and down with excitement, and it was a few moments before I could wring from him that the folk on the dock were from Buckkeep Castle, the Queen's Own

Coterie, my sister Nettle's special Skill-users. Spark had never met them, while Per was as ignorant as I was. There were three of the Buck folk and they looked almost like a different kind of human, with their short stature, dark skin and dark curling hair, beside the tall, slender Elderlings with skin and scales in every imaginable colour and pattern.

'They've come to take us home,' Amber said softly. She put an arm around me and a hand on my shoulder. I tolerated it. I thought of that word as the ropes were tied and a walkway put down for us. Home. It would not be home for me. But I was about to meet the people who served my sister Nettle, those she had chosen and trained. I straightened my shoulders and patted my hair flatter, but felt it pop up again. I did not need to brush my Elderling garb. It hung, sparkling and immaculate, on me. As we drew closer to the dock, I made myself smile. I lifted my hand and waved to them. Per took my other hand. 'He would be proud of you,' he whispered.

Kelsingra was as astonishing as Per said it would be, but it exhausted me. Everything was a whirl and a blur. Elderlings both real and shadowy were celebrating in the streets. We were welcomed as if we were royalty, and it was Per who reminded me that I was. The members of Nettle's special Skill-coterie had their walls up so tight against the city that I could barely sense them. I tried to copy them, but perhaps some residue of serpent spit in my blood made me more vulnerable. All the beauties and wonders of Kelsingra could not charm me enough to make me remain in that cacophony of voices and whirling rainbow of colour and sights. Clansie, the woman who led the coterie, gave me a tea of mint and valerian with a dark, bitter aftertaste. As she had warned me it might, it deadened me to the voices.

But it also freed my sadness from where I had hidden it. Even during the dinners and entertainments, even when the two Paragon dragons demanded to see me, even as I gave my rehearsed speech thanking them for helping to free me, tears would roll. The dragons told me that my father would be remembered as a friend to dragons and a vengeance-taker. As long as dragons flew and serpents swam, he would be remembered. They regretted that they had not been able to eat his body and preserve all his memories. I laughed aloud at this in horror. Fortunately, they took that as my joy at their wish to have made my father their dinner.

Then that was over and I slept. But even sleep was not rest, for the distant voices tugged at me. Even when I rode in a tiny boat on a cable across the river to the Village I heard the voices and knew the story of the shattered bridge in the river below us.

There on the other side the rest of the coterie had been busy with Rain Wilders who were 'Touched'. They had been there for two months, and had done, I was told, miracles for people. Four pregnancies were attributed to their putting their hands on women's bellies and opening something for them. A young man who had been dying from his inability to breathe normally had been revived and healed and celebrated his son's third birthday. All of these joyous things were attributed to my father's wishes to bring them there.

But they could no longer stay, because I had come there. I was resting in a lovely chamber where fish swam in the walls and leapt over my head. They made me ill just watching them. King Reyn and Queen Malta had come to visit me on the day that Clansie told them we all had to leave. 'Only the teas I am giving her are keeping her sane and preventing her from slipping away altogether. You would call it drowning in memories. If we keep her here longer, she will fall into unresponsiveness. We must take her home.'

'Will you travel through the pillars as you did to come here?' Queen Malta asked, and they nodded.

Beloved was still being Amber. She was sitting by my bedside in a chair. She held my hand in her gloved one. The tea and the sadness it gave me had renewed my dislike of her. I didn't like the touch but she helped to anchor me. Per had been best at that. He was so immune to the magic that I could hide inside him. But when I had told Clansie that, she had frowned and said that what I was doing was drawing off his strength, and that doing so put him in danger. So Clansie had separated us.

'It's too dangerous for Bee to travel that way,' Amber objected.

Clansie was very calm as she said, 'The Skillmistress has decided that the whole coterie will travel with you, and take all of you back to Buckkeep at once.'

'I don't agree,' Amber objected in Fool's voice, and Clansie replied, 'It is neither your decision nor mine. Tomorrow we depart.'

I drew a deep breath of relief and sank into sleep. I did not bother to listen to the rest of their long farewells to the king and queen of the Elderlings. I would see my sister soon. And Riddle.

FORTY-FIVE

A Princess of the Farseers

A grey man is singing in the wind. He is as grey as storm clouds, grey as rain on a windowpane. He is smiling as the wind blows past him. His hair and his cloak stream in the wind and tatter away. He tatters with them, until only his song is left.

I awakened from the dream smiling. It is a promise, and a good one. It will happen.

Bee Farseer's dream journal

I was royal now. I did not much like it. I understood why my father had tried to spare me from it.

The journey through the Skill-pillar was uneventful. The horrid procession to it, and the endless farewells and the dragons trumpeting overhead that preceded it, were all extended agony. Oh, how stiffly I smiled, and curtsied and thanked everyone. I had begged for Per and they let me have him. I held tight to his hand on one side and to Clansie on the other, and through we went like a string of beads.

Only to discover that on the other side, there was a welcoming party gathered and there would be another procession, and a feast that night followed by music and dancing. I held tight to Per's hand as they announced it. It was only when he said, 'I feel dizzy,' that I knew what I was doing. I let go of him then. Riddle had been standing beside me on the other side. He suddenly stepped between us and put one hand on my shoulder and one on Per's. We both felt better for that touch.

So many things happened that day. I met my niece, formally, in front of everyone, with a curtsey on a dais. She was draped all in lace with pearls on it and had a tiny red face. Hope screamed through the entire introduction. Nettle looked very tired. Afterwards, we had to have tea and some food in a room full of ladies with extravagant dresses and too many perfumes.

When I said I was rather tired, they showed me a room and said it was mine. The beautiful wardrobe Revel had had made for me was there, with my old things in it. But when Careful came in and curtseyed to me, I shrieked and then cried and could only ask her if she was unhurt, if it was really her, for I had been convinced the raiders could not have left her alive. She began to sob, too, until the woman who had brought me there threatened to call for a healer to drug away our 'hysteria'. I lost my temper and ordered her to go away. Careful latched the door behind her, and we wept alone until we managed to stop.

Careful said she was well recovered, but I knew she wasn't. She had only arrived the day before I did. She was to be my maid here, she told me, as my sister had not wished life in Buckkeep Castle to be too great a change. But then she told me that Buckkeep Castle was immense and full of people and she was almost afraid to leave the rooms at night, and what was she, a simple country girl, doing in such a place?

I said I wondered the same thing for myself. She hugged me so hard I thought my ribs would crack.

She helped me out of my Elderling garb and then we had a tedious time of dressing me in crispy, rustling skirts that she assured me were the latest style from Jamaillia. I did not have lice but she said that was sheer luck for my hair was all tangles and mats despite Spark's best efforts. I left a great deal of it in her comb. There followed a gathering in a room, and walking into a great hall full of people, and trying to eat dinner on a stage. Shun was seated three chairs away from me. She was Lady Shine now, in clothing even more gorgeous than she had worn at Withywoods. I wondered if she still scattered it on the floor of her room when she undressed. We looked at one another once, and then away.

I slept in a big bed in my new room and dreamed that I opened my wardrobe and Revel looked out from the mirror and thanked me for the kerchiefs I'd given him. I woke weeping. Careful came into the room. She slept in the bed beside me. We held hands all night.

Was it the next day we had a ceremony to mourn my father? I burned a lock of my hair, for Nettle said I could not spare more than that. Was it that first day when I was presented to the king and queen? The days were tangled and confused, like a neglected yarn basket. Every day there was someone I must meet, and a meal to share and people telling me formally how sad they were that my father was dead. There was a private meeting with Lady Kettricken, who had taken to her bed as soon as she heard of my father's death and had not emerged from her room since. She was pale and rather old. She gave me a very sad smile and said, 'Look at those golden curls. I wonder if Verity could have given me a little girl like you? If we had had more time.' That seemed very awkward to me.

I was taken to see Lady Shine. 'I am sorry for your loss.' I told her in front of the maids attending her and Lady Simmer, who followed me about. 'And I for yours,' she replied. And what else was there to say? I do not think we even wanted to look at one another. Neither of us wanted to speak of what had happened to us and after a time I excused myself, saying I was still very weary. And that obligation was done. At meals we nodded to one another in passing.

One morning, I asked to see Per and was told I did not have time that day, but was assured that he was being honoured and had been given a matched pair of black horses, from Buckkeep's best stock, and offered a good position in the stables. When I asked if he had the care of Pris, Lady Simmer did not know, but said she would make certain that Pris was given over to his care, if that was important to me. It was.

Nettle and Riddle tried to have a quiet dinner with me but the baby and the baby's nurse and two of Nettle's ladies, and Lady Simmer and one of Riddle's men could not be excluded, and so I sat very straight and we talked of how nice the blackberry tart was. Later, when only the nurse was there, Nettle told me that soon I would become one of the queen's ladies, but I should not fear, for Queen Elliania was actually very kind and Nettle was determined to see that I learned everything that she, unfortunately, had not been taught. To that end there would be a special tutor for me. 'Lant?' I asked, and I did not know if I hoped or dreaded that.

'Lord FitzVigilant has other duties, I am afraid. But Scribe Diligent has taught many a noble child, and will school you in deportment and protocol as well as numbers and letters.'

I nodded to that and glanced at Riddle to see pity and worry in his eyes.

Beginning the next day, there were hours when I must be with my tutor, and more hours when I must attend the queen. I must learn the names of every duke and duchess, and their children, and the colours of their houses, and to know their heraldry. Every evening meal had to be taken downstairs in the dining hall, sitting to the left of Riddle and Nettle.

Daily I spent part of the morning attending the queen. I had been warned to sit very straight, and embroider or knit or weave, as she did, and listen to the chatter of her ladies. They put me in a place next to Lady Shine. We both kept too busy to speak to one another. But on the third day, Queen Elliania bade us continue with our work while she took more rest. The moment the door closed behind her, I felt like a flung bread crust in a flock of chickens.

'Such pretty golden curls, Lady Bee. Will you allow your hair to grow now?'

'Is it true you were kept as a slave in Chalced?' That question came in a scandalized whisper.

'I have not seen before that stitch you used on the pansies. Can you teach it to me?'

'Lord FitzVigilant tells us that you are the bravest little girl he has ever met. Such a charming man! Do you think that you and he would like to join Lady Clement and me for gaming one evening?'

'We have heard so little of your adventures,' Lady Fecund smiled avariciously. 'It makes me shudder to think of a little girl like you and poor dear Lady Shine in the clutches of such monsters!'

Lady Violet, with a sideways glance at Shun, added, 'Lady Shine has told us almost nothing about the day that Withywoods was attacked. You must have been terrified! Chalcedeans, we are told, have no respect for the women when they raid and loot. And they had her for many days. And nights.'

I glanced at Shun. Her chin quivered once and then she clenched her teeth. 'It was a difficult time I do not wish to speak about,' she said stiffly. I knew then that she was not well liked in this room and that Lady Violet would shame her, if she could. Lady Violet was lovely but not as beautiful as Shun with her green eyes and curling hair, nor was her figure as good. I was beginning to learn about such things at court.

Lady Violet pecked at me. 'But surely little Bee could tell us some tales! However did you manage to buy your lives, in the hands of such ruthless men?' She said it as if there were a nasty secret she could wheedle out of me.

I fixed her with a gaze. 'I am *Lady* Bee,' I reminded her, and several of the other women tittered. One gave me a sympathetic look and then put her eyes on her sewing. I tried to find the carrying voice Hap used when I added, 'I lived because Shine protected me. Ill, she nursed me. Cold, she shared her blankets with me. She saw that I had food. At great risk to herself, she helped me try to escape.' My voice had the knack of it. I paused. 'She *killed* for me. And escaped to seek out my father and put him on my trail. She has the heart of a lioness.' I considered her wide green eyes, then turned my smile on Lady Violet. 'If you cut her, I bleed. And if I bleed, Princess Nettle will know of it.'

'Well!' Lady Violet exclaimed haughtily. 'The kitten has claws.'

The tittering laughter was the clucking of hens called to thrown grain.

'The bee has a stinger,' I corrected her. Our eyes met and held. She sneered at me but I smiled. She had no walls at all. 'Rather than my tale, we would all much more enjoy hearing of your tryst last night. With the gentleman who wears a green doublet and far too much oil in his hair.'

Shun's hand flew to her mouth to hold back not a scandalized gasp but a delighted laugh.

'It isn't true!' Lady Violet rose, her skirts rustling like bird's wings, and swept from the room. At the door, she glared at me and said, 'This is what comes of admitting common-borns to a circle of noble ladies!' She scuttled out the door.

I could not allow that to hurt me. Or Shun. I forced a giggle. 'She runs like a startled hen, does she not?' I said to Shine. A ripple of nervous laughter spread out from my flung stone. Lady Violet was popular, but not liked, I saw. I was certain we'd cross swords again.

Shun was sitting taller. She carefully set aside her needlework in a basket at her feet, rose far more gracefully than Lady Violet had, and held out a hand to me. 'Come, little cousin. Shall we walk in the Women's Garden?' she asked me.

I set my own needlework aside. 'I am told that the violets there are actually fragrant.' This time, their laughter was bolder.

We left the room, and none of them followed. Still she glanced back, and 'Hurry,' she said. We went, not to the Women's Garden with its herbs and blossoms, but up to a tower-top garden of potted shrubs and statuary and benches. She used a key to open the door. For an hour, we walked about it, speaking little. When she left, she gave me the key. 'This was my father's key. This is a good place to be alone.'

'What of you?' I asked her, and she smiled at me.

'While my father lived, I had a protector at court. Now I have none.'

'Your brother?'

'He is uncomfortable with me.' She said it stiffly. Sadly she added, 'And I with him.'

'I would rather face men with knives than that circle of bitches with their needles,' I said bluntly.

She laughed aloud, and when she turned back to me the wind had put colour in her cheeks and I saw something of the old Shun in the set of her mouth. 'The "green doublet" is sharper than any knife I've ever held. And I promise you that I will use it well.' She held up her hand, fingers curved, and said, 'Time for the lioness to show her claws.' And she left me there on the rooftop garden, with the wind blowing the scent of jasmine and the clouds running like ships before a wind.

My life began to have a pattern, a hectic one. I saw nothing of Spark or Per. Beloved had donned yet another guise. He was now called Lord Chance. He would call on me once a day, at his appointed time, and we would talk. He always asked if I were well, and I always replied I was. There was a complicated story of who he was now and how he had joined my father and Lant to save me. I couldn't be bothered with it. He brought me little gifts: a carved wooden acorn with a secret compartment under the cap, and a doll dressed all in black and white, and a better pipe than the one we had made on the river. Once he said as he left me, 'It will get better, Bee. Someone else will have a disaster or a triumph, and people will not watch you so closely. Nettle's baby will become less fussy and Nettle will not be so tired. When Queen Elliania's child is born, you can blissfully fade into the background of Buckkeep politics. You will be able to become Bee again.'

It was not an encouraging thing to hear. But every morning another day started, and every night I put another day behind me.

The most serious day was one when Clansie escorted me to Nettle's chamber up in a tower where the Queen's Own Coterie was accustomed to meet. They were one of six coteries that lived in or very near to Buckkeep. One for each prince, one for the King, Nettle's coterie . . . far too many, I thought. I felt a bit offended when Clansie reported to my own sister on my level of Skill-talent and how she had needed to dose me with elfbark in Kelsingra. I learned that some of my dreams, not my White-dreams but my regular ones, had been leaking out of my mind at night and disturbing coterie members. With an apology for being so bold, Clansie suggested that I should be dosed daily with elfbark until I was either able to control my wild Skilling or the Skill was quenched in me. Nettle told her that she would take her thoughts under advisement and consider them.

When I spoke to Nettle as my sister, asking if I did not have some say in this, she replied, 'Sometimes an adult must decide what is best for a youngster, Bee. In this, you will have to trust me.'

But that was hard.

Yet it was not all unfortunate things. Hap Gladheart came to my room very late one night, escorted by Lant and Lord Chance. Careful was scandalized until I reminded her that Hap was my foster-brother. He played some silly songs for me, and soon had even Careful giggling. Then Lord Chance told me that, when I felt able, I should tell Hap every detail of what had befallen me, for it was Buck history and should be preserved. I remembered my sister's words, and told him that I would 'take his thoughts under advisement and consider them'.

Hap grinned and said, 'I thought you might!' and swept into the opening notes of a song.

Days passed, with dinners and introductions and then entertainments with other young nobles of my age that I should cultivate. Lady Simmer organized my social schedule. My brothers came to visit me, some with wives and children, a few at a time. I found that I scarcely knew any of them any more. I loved them, but it was a distant love, the same they accorded to me. I watched them with Nettle and her child, their jests and their advice and their 'do you remembers?', all hearkening back to a family I'd never been a part of. They were kind. They brought me the sort of gifts one would give to a young female relative. Riddle sat beside me for those visits. He spoke to me so that I had someone for a conversation, and taught me how to smile at strangers who loved me and had no idea of my ordeal—especially as I had no desire to share it with them. At such times, I was glad that Per had suggested I erase my scars. When I spoke at all, I told them of seeing ships turn into dragons and moving figureheads and the wonders of Kelsingra. I am sure they discounted half of it as a child's fanciful nonsense, and that was fine with me.

I began to understand why my father wrote at night. And why he burned it afterward.

There came a day when there was an unfilled morning, for the gravid queen had dismissed her ladies. I begged to be allowed to go out riding, and when that was granted, I insisted I would ride only Pris. As I dressed, I was dismayed to be informed that four other nobles, of about my age and two of my sex, would go with me. To my disdain, each would be accompanied by a groom on a mount, and some of their parents would attend us as well. FitzVigilant and Lord Chance would ride alongside me. My heart rose when I saw that Per was there, but he merely held Pris's head while 'my' groom supervised me while I mounted my horse. It was more than I could bear. 'I know how to get on a horse,' I insisted, and even to myself I sounded petulant and spoiled.

I did worse later. We were kept to a sedate pace that allowed the adults to converse and the youngsters to say insipid, dull things to me. Per rode far behind us. I looked back and saw him, and for just an instant our gazes met. I leaned forward and told Pris, 'Run!'

Did I use the Skill on her? I do not think so. But she leapt forth with a will and we burst to the front of the group and I urged her on. She flew. For the first time since I'd been taken, I felt as if I was myself, free and in control, even if I were on the back of a wildly galloping horse. There were shouts behind me, and two shrieks, but I didn't care. We veered from the trail into the trees and up a steep hill. Down a gully she took me, through a muddy stream and up another steep bank. At first I heard hoofbeats behind me and then I didn't. On I went, clinging to Pris like a burr and we were so glad of one another. We emerged from open forest onto a grassy hillside. Below us meadowland unfurled like a green carpet, sheep scattered across it like spilled buttons. Pris halted and together we breathed.

When I heard another horse behind me and glanced back, it was all I had hoped for. Per galloped up on a black mount every bit as fine as they had promised he'd be given. He halted beside me and patted his horse's neck.

'What's her name?' I asked him.

'Maybelle,' he replied. He grinned at me, and then it faded. 'Bee, we should go back. Everyone will be frightened for you.'

'Truly?'

'Truly.'

'A little longer away from them all. They are all so . . .' He waited. There wasn't a word that expressed how they looked at me, and over my head, and that there was always, always someone standing there. 'I never get to be alone.'

He frowned. 'Do you want me to leave you alone?'

'No. I can be alone with you here. You never look at me like I'm something odd in your soup.'

He laughed, and I did, too. 'How is your life? Are you well treated?'

His smile faded. 'I'm a stableboy, one of many. The stablemaster tells me often not to be 'above myself'. Yesterday he chided me and told me I must not have favourites among the horses. I had lingered too long at Pris's stall.' He lifted his hand and rubbed the back of his head. 'He rapped me with the handle of a broom when I said that Lant's mare needed more oats. "Lord FitzVigilant to you, boy! And do not tell me my business!"' He laughed at his own tale. I did not find it funny at all.

'And you?'

I sighed. 'Lessons of all sorts. A great deal of changing my clothes, followed by sitting still and proper in itchy garments. Lady Simmer always trailing after me, correcting me, keeping me "usefully occupied". Always indoors.'

'Do you see much of Spark? Lant and—' he hesitated. 'Lord Chance?'

'Nothing of Spark. Lant and Beloved are almost as good as my father was at leaving me alone.'

Per's eyes widened and I wished I had not said it. But it was true. For all Beloved's nattering, I saw little of him except when he was nosing through my dream book or asking me questions.

'I miss them all,' Per said quietly.

'They do not come to see you?'

'Spark? Not at all. Lord FitzVigilant and Lord Chance? I saddle their horses, and Lant—Lord FitzVigilant always slips me a coin. We look at each other and I know they wish me well. But there are always people watching and appearances to be maintained.' He patted his pocket and it jingled. 'I wonder if I will ever be given time to go and actually spend some of the coins.'

I heard hoofbeats. We both straightened and Per reined his horse a little away from me as first Lant, and then Beloved rode out of the trees. They both looked flustered. Beloved rode close to me and said, very quickly, 'A fly stung your horse and she ran away with you. Per came and caught her headstall. Per, get off your horse and hold her reins. Quickly!' Sternly, he added to me, 'Bee, you must never put Per in such danger of rebuke again. You must look shaken when the others get here.'

Per did as he was told. Perhaps the anger burning inside me could make me look 'shaken'. Every time I began to like Beloved at all, he did something to fan those flames. To hear they neglected Per made me want to spit at him. I drew breath to tell him that.

But here came two grooms and someone's father, all asking if I'd fallen, and the groom sombrely suggesting a more sedate mount 'until the young lady has better riding skills'.

We went by a roundabout way back to the level trail and two of the mothers insisted that we must turn back for they were very unsettled and did not want to witness another incident with 'an unruly horse'. All the youngsters were looking at me with wide eyes. Per dropped back again to the end of our procession.

Later, Nettle called me in for 'a word'. It was more than one word, and her baby cried and she walked up and down gently bouncing her the whole time she was reminding me that I must bear myself with dignity now. I did not ask her if she had decided about my Skill. Now was not a good time to remind her that I was wilful in many ways. Riddle escorted me back to my chambers afterward. As he left me at the door, he said, 'If it is any comfort, your father did not enjoy this aspect of his life either. But he managed it, and so must you.'

I went to bed early that night, thinking that some of Dwalia's beatings had been easier to take then Nettle's lecture and disappointed face. As I did now, I set my walls well before I tried to sleep, to keep my nightmares in as much to keep others out. My window was dark and the castle quiet when I awoke to distant music. For a time, I was still and listened, wondering who would be making music at such an hour and for whom. I could not identify the instrument, but the music suited my mood perfectly. It was lonely and yet not fully sad, as if being alone were not such a bad thing.

I got up out of bed and donned a dressing-gown. The door to Careful's nook was closed: she was a sound sleeper. I stepped into the corridor and hesitated. But no one had ever forbidden me to move alone in Buckkeep at night. I closed the door softly behind me. I listened but could not determine where the music was coming from. I closed my eyes to better focus and walked, away from my chamber and Nettle and Riddle's grand rooms at the end of the hall. Door after door I passed. From time to time, I stopped to listen and get my bearings. Then I would go on.

The music grew stronger. I came to a door and pressed my ear to it. I heard nothing. Yet when I stepped back from it, the music was loud. I argued with myself. My curiosity won. I tapped at the door.

There was no response.

I tapped again, louder, and waited. No response.

I tried the door. It wasn't latched. I pushed it open to reveal a cosy chamber, smaller than mine. There was a low fire burning in the hearth; even in summer, the old stones of Buckkeep seemed chill. In front of the fire, in a cushioned chair with his short legs propped up on a padded stool, a round-faced man was Skilling out the music he dreamed.

I was utterly charmed by this and felt a lift of heart, as if I had stepped into an old tale. A grey cat was asleep on his lap. She lifted her head. *We are comfortable*, she informed me.

'Does he always Skill music when he sleeps?' I spoke softly.

The cat just looked at me. Then the man opened his eyes and looked at me. He showed no surprise or alarm. His eyes were cloudy, like an old dog's. He had odd features, little eyes with fat eyelids and small ears tight to his skull. He licked his lips and left the end of his tongue out. Then he said, 'I was dreaming a song for Fitz's little girl. If I ever got to meet her.'

'That would be me,' I said, and ventured closer.

He pointed to a cushion on the floor near his chair. 'You can sit on that, if you want. It's Smokey's cushion, but he's sitting with me right now. He won't mind.'

Yes, I will.

I sat on the hearth and looked up at him. 'Are you Thick?' I asked him.

'They call me that. Yes.'

'My father wrote about you. In his journals.'

A wide smile opened his face. He was simple, I realized. 'I miss him,' he said. 'He used to bring me candy. And little cakes with pink sugar frosting on them.'

'That sounds lovely.'

'They were delicious. And pretty. I liked to put them in a row and look at them.'

'I liked to put my mother's candles in a row. And smell them. But never burn them.'

'I have four brass buttons. And two wooden ones, and one made from shell. Do you want to see them?'

I did. I wanted simple things, like sharing buttons. The cat made a rumble, jumped off his lap and arranged himself on a cushion. It hurt Thick to get up to open a cupboard and take his box of buttons out, and I knew that he was old. Walking was not easy for him, but his buttons were important. He brought their box back to his chair. His blanket had fallen to the floor. I picked it up and put it over his legs again. As he showed me each button, he told me the story of finding it. Then I asked him, 'Can you teach me to make the Skill-music?'

He grew very still. 'My music?' he said very softly. He was uncertain. Guarded.

I was quiet. Had I spoiled everything by asking for this?

He held out his hand to me. I hesitated, then I set my hand in it and his fingers closed around mine. His touch hummed with power. 'We have to be very quiet,' he told me. 'I'm not supposed to let my music be loud.' He did something to my walls and suddenly we were behind his in a very peculiar way. 'Now,' he said. 'This is how to make the music.' He smiled and said, 'We will start with the cat's purr.'

On that night, I gained a friend and a teacher.

I was back in my bedroom well before dawn. He had taught me a music made of cat purrs, the creak of a rocking chair and the low crackling of a fire. He had cloaked me in 'See her not!' before I crept back to my room. I was sleepy the next day. I didn't care. He

792

was waiting for me when I returned that night. I helped him build the 'tent' as he called it that was stouter than any Skill-wall I'd ever managed. He had saved some gingerbread from earlier in his day, for all his meals were brought to him now. We shared that, and shared our cat-purr music, adding more things to it. I felt honoured when he put in me laughing at the cat as he danced after a dropped spool. It was more fun than I'd ever had with anyone in my whole life.

Even better than the day my father had taken me to the market in Oaksbywater, for there were no slain dogs or stabbed beggars. We just played.

For someone who had never had a playmate, it was astonishing.

FORTY-SIX

The Quarry

The Six Duchies has many folk-tales about people vanishing into Skill-pillars. And many about people suddenly stepping out of one. In many of them, people are fleeing unjust punishment, and the stones give them sanctuary from their attackers. In ones in which foreign or peculiar folk appear, they grant wishes, such as improved health.

All those tales, I believe, are rooted in the inadvertent use of a Skill-pillar by someone who is untrained.

A history of the Skill-pillars in the Six Duchies and beyond,

Chade Fallstar

Something is wrong with the moon.

I blinked my eyes. Yes. There was a moon. A moon in the darkness meant we were not inside the Skill-pillar any more. Nor between Skill-pillars, wherever that 'between' was. We were on the ground somewhere and looking up at the moon. The crow was standing on my chest. As I stirred, she hopped off me and away. For an instant, moonlight ran down her scarlet feathers, then she was gone. Cool night air was soft against my skin. Hard stone was under my back. I lowered my eyes from the moon and saw the Skill-pillar that had dumped me out. Beyond it, forest.

This was not Kelsingra.

The moon, Nighteyes insisted.

I lifted my eyes to it. Oh. It was nearly full. It had been full when we entered the pillar. Either we had come out of the pillar before we had left, or we had been inside it close to a month.

Or longer?

'Where are we?' I asked aloud to avoid thinking about days lost. Or months. Years? There were legends of people vanishing into standing stones and emerging years later, either unchanged or very, very old. I wondered if I had aged. I certainly felt older. Weaker. I imagined Nettle an old woman, Bee a mother. I sat up with a shudder.

Where are we?

Where we need to be. The only place left for us to be.

It took an effort to rise from my sprawl. I rolled onto my hands and knees and stood up. Above me, stars and the almost full moon. I looked up at sheer, rocky walls, and beyond them the dark shapes of evergreen trees. I smelled water. I turned my head and followed the scent. My sandals gritted on sand and small pebbles. The ground sloped down slightly and I came to an immense square pond of standing water. It smelled green. I knelt at the edge, cupped water and drank. And drank some more.

I sat back. I was still hungry but having my thirst quenched also deadened a headache that I had simply been accepting. I looked around in slow recognition. The quarry. The place where the Elderlings had once cut and carved blocks of Skill-stone. I was not far from the place where Verity had ended his days as a man. He had carved his dragon from gleaming black-and-silver stone, and had risen as a dragon to defend the Six Duchies.

Exactly where we need to be.

No! I meant to touch the face of the pillar that would take us to Kelsingra.

I know. But this is where we need to be.

I pushed his words to the back of my mind. I had known this place, once. It had changed greatly, and not at all. I tried to recall where Verity's shabby tent had been, where we had set a fire, where we had camped. The moonlight glinted on the thick silvery veins in the rock. My meandering path took me between and past rejected blocks of memory-stone. Once, Elderling Skill-coteries had come here to select a stone and carve the creature that would become the repository of their memories and bodies. I suspected that it had been an Elderling tradition then was somehow shared with a few Six Duchies coteries. Perhaps somewhere in the walls of Kelsingra or in the memory-blocks of Aslevjal, that tale was stored.

I found Verity's old campsite. Next to nothing was left after all those years. I had hoped to find more, for we had left all behind when we had fled it. What might have been there? The remains of Kettricken's bow, a knife, a blanket? The night was chill and I would have welcomed any additional covering. It was strange to have stepped from summer in a warm land to summer in the Mountains.

Not much left of summer, I fear. Lift your head and sniff, brother. I smell the end of summer, and leaves soon to fall.

Is it possible we were in the stone that long?

Do you remember nothing of our passage? The wolf seemed genuinely surprised.

Nothing at all.

Not Verity? Not Shrewd? Not our passing brush with Chade?

I was shocked. I stood very still, groping back. I remembered the rogues who had attacked us in the old city, and I remembered carelessly putting my hand on the wrong face of the Skill-pillar. I pushed at my memory.

There you are, my boy!

Leave him be. This is not his place, not his time for this. He has a task.

Present that pin and you will ever be welcome into my presence.

I had been lying on my back, looking up at a moon approaching full. Had I imagined those touches of minds against mine? Did I pretend it to myself, now? Weariness swept over me in a wave.

Something is very wrong with us. Something like a sickness, but not.

The pillar journey. I felt this way that time I left Aslevjal and was lost in the stones for a time.

No. This is something else, the wolf insisted.

I ignored that. How long? At least a month we had wandered between the pillars. It was likely that Bee and the others had reached Bingtown now.

It was like the slap of a cold wave. They would all think me dead! I had to let them know I lived. Then I could wait a few days to recover from my pillar journey. Then I would hike the old Skill-road to the abandoned market and its pillar. From there, I could enter that pillar and be back in Buck Duchy. How long before I was home? Before the next full moon! Time to let Dutiful know that I was alive, and as soon as Bee arrived, he would tell her.

I wrapped my arms around myself and stood very still, gathering and centring myself. But I was abruptly aware of how thin I was. I felt my own ribs. And I was chilled to the bone. Make a fire first. With what? The old way. Spinning a stick in a notch if I had to, but I suddenly felt I needed a fire. A light and a warmth to centre myself, and then I would Skill.

Verity suggested you not do that. Remember? Save that strength for your task. You will need it.

No. I remember nothing of our passage. What task? I recall nothing.

You would if you truly wanted to remember.

Such an odd and irksome thing for him to say to me. His sulky words dangled between us as I went looking for wood. The moon gave a ghostly light to the rocky, barren quarry. Rain and wind had deposited branches and dead leaves, but little grew on the stony bone of the earth. My hunger had its claws set in my belly.

Forest rimmed the quarry, and I moved along the edge of it, gathering dry wood. Insects chirred, and overhead bats frolicked in their pursuit of food.

Porcupine!

I sensed it at the same time Nighteyes' excitement burst through to me. I had to smile. Never had he been able to control his fascination with the prickly creatures, and more than once I'd pulled quills from his nose and paws. I dropped my firewood, and then selected one hefty piece from it.

Porcupines rely on their quills for defence. They are slow-moving, one of the few game animals one can kill with a club. He kept his back and tail toward me as I tried to circle around him to where I could bash his head. By the time I killed him I was winded. My dread at the work ahead before I could eat him almost outweighed my hunger. Almost.

I made two trips to get my firewood and my dead porcupine to a place in the quarry near our old campsite. The woods around the quarry were dry as dust. I had no wish to set them alight with a careless spark. But I soon wished for any sort of a spark. My attacker's knife was my only large tool. I sharpened a stick for a fire drill, and bored a hole in the driest piece of firewood. Then I began the endless task of spinning the stick between my palms, trying to build up enough warmth to make the wood smoulder. I kept having to stop and rest. My shoulders and elbows ached abysmally.

Try again! Nighteyes bade me softly and I realized I had dozed off hunched over my fire making. I took up the stick in my silvered hand and began to spin it. It suddenly seemed a hopeless task, and I stabbed the stick savagely into my drill bed, shouting, 'I just want a fire! Is that so much to ask? Fire!'

It burst into flames. Not a spark, not a trickle of smoke. Flames leapt up from both pieces of wood and I scrabbled back and away from them. My heart was hammering in my throat.

I didn't know we could do that!

Neither did I.

Don't let it die!

No danger of that. I piled my wood onto it, and watched it catch. The blaze pushed back the shadows and set the silver in the black stone sparkling. And my silvered hand gleamed in the light as I examined it, caught between wonder and dread. Practicality asserted itself. I plodded back to the forest's edge and came back with as much firewood as I could carry. Twice I did that, and then I turned to my meat.

Skinning a porcupine is as ticklish a job as one might expect. The best way is to hang them spread-eagled and work on them, but I had no string and there were no trees in the quarry. In the end, it was worth the work and nuisance. He was as fat as a fall hog, and as I cooked the meat over the fire, it sizzled and sent up a fine greasy smoke. I ate until I was full, and then slept rolled in a dead woman's cloak. In the dawn's light, I awoke under a wide blue sky. I built up my fire and ate more of my kill. I went back to the water caught in the low end of the quarry, washed my hands and drank deeply. With my belly full I felt as if I could face the day.

I recalled that there had been a stream not far from the quarry. A stream with fish. Starling. On the banks of that stream, I had told her that I did not love her, in an effort to be honest. Then we had joined our bodies in what had been little more than animal comfort, but had begun a strange and difficult relationship that would continue, on and off, for over a dozen years. Starling, in her fine striped stockings with her proud, wealthy husband listening as she sang the tale of our quest. Well, that was a verse she had omitted, I thought, and even smiled.

I returned to our fire. Motley was picking through the porcupine's entrails. She looked up with a bit of gut dangling from her silver beak. 'Home?' she cawed hopefully.

I spoke aloud. 'Today I sleep and catch fish. Some to eat and some to dry. I don't plan to travel hungry again. Three days of resting and eating, and we continue our journey.'

It would be wiser to choose our piece of stone and begin now.

I crouched in stillness by my fire. I knew what the wolf was suggesting. *I'm going home. Not into a stone.*

Fitz. Long have we known it would come to this. How often did we dream of returning here and carving our dragon? Here we are, and it is time, and perhaps we have enough time and strength to do it. I would not wish to remain mired in stone like Girl-on-a-Dragon was.

I framed the thought sternly and spoke it aloud. 'I do not think we have reached that time. I'm not old. Just tired. A bit of rest and—'

'Home?' Motley asked persistently. 'Bee! Bee! Per! Fool! Lant! Spark!'

'Lant is dead,' I told her, more sharply than I meant to.

The wolf spoke more sharply. *Persist in being so stubborn, and you will be dead. And me with you.*

My mind froze.

'Going home!' Motley announced.

'Soon,' I told her.

'Now,' she parried. She ripped a last bit of gut from the porcupine. It wrapped around her silver beak. She deftly pulled it free with one foot, arranged it, and then gulped it down. She preened her feathers, blue-black and scarlet. 'Goodbye!' she added and lifted into the sky. I stared after her.

'It's a long flight!' I shouted. Did she have any idea where we were?

She circled the old quarry, flying low over the blocks of rejected stone, and the piles of rubble from long ago works. At the low end was the rainwater pool. She skimmed it and I spun to follow her flight, she flew straight into the Skill-pillar. I feared I would run to a broken and flopping bird. But she vanished smoothly.

'I didn't know she could do that,' I said. 'I hope she emerges intact.'

Not her first journey through the stones. And she has Skill on her beak.
True.

I could not help her but my heart sank that I might never see her again. I reminded myself I had a plan of my own for my journey. I made several trips for firewood. I roasted the porcupine's bones until they cracked and I could get at the marrow. Then it was time to fish. I had not tickled fish in a long time. I went to the creek and found a spot where I could lay on my belly, where dangling plants overshadowed an undercut bank, where the sun would not cast my shadow on the water. I was pleased that I remembered so well how it was done, and even more pleased with two fine, fat trout. I put a hooked willow wand through their gills and kept them in the water until I was rewarded with two more. Two to eat tonight, and two to smoke or dry for my journey. I felt very satisfied.

Are you sure you 'don't remember' any of what Verity counselled you?

I stumbled into the stone and out of it again. I've no recall of our passage.

You were deep in the Skill. Verity found you. He is a large fish there now, swimming in those deep currents. He told you to carve your dragon and not delay. King Shrewd was there, smaller and thinner. Chade was with him. They wished you well in that effort.

I spoke eventually. 'I don't recall that at all. I truly wish I did.'

I recall it for you. He warned you not to delay it. He nearly failed. Had you not brought Kettle with you, and had she not been who and what she was, there would have been a half-finished dragon and a dead king. And probably the OutIslanders would hold Buckkeep Castle now.

We are not gambling for such high stakes as he was.

Only your life. And mine.

I will think well on it tonight.

Fitz. I do not want to cease being. Make us a dragon. Give me that vestige of life. Let me smell the night air again, let me hunt, let me feel the cold of night and the heat of the sun. There was such hunger in his words. I felt selfish. He experienced the world through me, but my senses were but a shadow of what his had been.

'Nighteyes. What are you?'

He paused. *I am a wolf. You need to be reminded of that?*

'You were a wolf. What are you now? A ghost that lives inside me? A mixture of my memories and me thinking what you might say or do?'

That seems unlikely. For I remember Verity, and you do not. And I sojourned with Bee, apart from you, and she heard me.

I wish I'd had more time to speak of you to her. To tell her the tales I promised she would know.

I was not derelict in that. She knows much of our time together. Much of my life.

I am glad of that.

And I. So, you do not imagine me.

You live in me.

Yes. And if you die, I die with you.

'I want to go home, wolf. I want to see Bee. I need to be with her, and I need to make reparations for the sort of father I was. I need a chance to do better with her.'

That is what you told Verity. I will repeat what he said. Someone else will do that for you. And you must trust that they will do it well. As he did, with his son. The son he never met.

What is this urgency to carve a stone?

My brother, something eats you. From within. I feel it. Stop hiding it from yourself.

I was too long in the stone. That is all. I ran my silvered hands down my ribs. Felt the jut of my hip-bones. *You think I have worms?*

I know you do. They are eating you faster than your body can heal itself.

I thought deeply as I left the stream and made my way back to the quarry. My fire had burned low. I raked coals out and rebuilt the rest of it. I baked two of the fish on the coals and ate them. I looked at the other two. I was still so hungry. I could catch more tomorrow for my journey. I raked out more coals and set the fish on them.

When will you decide?

Soon.

I almost heard his sigh, the same sigh he would give when he wished to go hunting at night and I would stay in, morosely writing on paper that I would burn before morning. I poked at the fish. Almost done. Eating raw fish could give me worms. I smiled bitterly. Would those worms eat the parasites that the wolf insisted I already had? With two sticks, I turned the fish over on the coal bed. Be patient.

It began to rain. I felt two warm drops fall onto my wrist. No. Blood. My nose was bleeding. I reached up and pinched it shut.

What if it doesn't stop?

It always stops.

And your body always heals itself.

After a time, I let go of my nose. No more blood. *See?*

No response.

'Wolf. Are you still with me?'

A sulky acknowledgement.

A thought came to me. 'If you had to. If something happened to me, could you go to Bee? And be with her the rest of her life?'

I would be the shadow of a shadow.

'Could you do it?'

Perhaps. If her walls were down and everything was right. But I would not.

'Why not?'

Fitz. I am not a thing you can give away. We are interwoven.

I poked the fish out of the fire. With a twig, I dusted off the ash. In a less hungry time, I would have peeled back the skin to reveal the flesh and then discarded the skin. Now I scarcely waited for it to cool before I was juggling steaming chunks of fish to cool them before pushing them into my mouth. After the fish was gone, I went back to the water and drank. I felt better.

I looked up at a clear blue sky. Even in summer, nights in the Mountains were chill. I decided I should get firewood. My path out of the quarry took us past abandoned blocks of cut stone. As I headed toward the forest, Nighteyes spoke. *I like that piece.*

It's not very big.

There are only two of us.

To placate him, I walked over to the chunk of rock. I saw why it had been discarded. It had been part of a larger piece that had broken along a thick silver vein. It was gleaming black and richly streaked with threads of Silver. Not near as large as what Verity had used. This stone was about the side of a pony cart. I set my hand on top of it. It was a very strange sensation. Raw Skill-stone was empty, I discovered. Empty and waiting to be filled. It had an indefinable tactile sensation. I wanted to touch it. The sun had warmed it pleasantly. If I'd been a cat, I would have curled up on top of it.

You are so stubborn.

And you are not?

I was as a cub. I wanted to hate you. Do you remember how savage I was when you first saw me in the cage? Even as you were carrying me off, I was trying to bite you through the bars.

You were not much more than a cub. And you'd been treated badly. You had no reason to trust me or listen to what I told you.

True.

He'd been dirty and smelly and bone-thin. Riddled with parasites and full of anger. But that anger was what had drawn us together. Our parallel fury at the paths we were trapped on had linked our minds and for those first few moments, I had not realized our minds were joined. That we had the beginning of a deep Wit-bond, whether we wanted it or not.

'Oh, cub,' I said out loud.

So you called me then.

I realized what we had done. The fused memory had poured from us into the stone. I could feel it under my hand and I knew exactly what I would find when I moved my hand. There was a patch of fur on the back of Nighteyes' neck, where the black guard hairs had a sort of gentle swirl on top of his thick grey-and-black fur. I had a sensory memory of how it had felt to put my hand on him there. Often, I'd put my hand on his back, as we walked side by side, or as we sat on the cliff's edge looking out over the sea. It had been the natural place for my hand to fall. The touch that had renewed our bond like a repeated vow.

It felt good to feel that again.

Lifting my hand was an act of will. And there it was, on the stone. It was not hair and fur and a warm breathing animal beneath it. But it was exactly the size and the shape of my hand, and where my palm had touched, I could see each individual guard hair.

I drew a deep breath. Not yet. No. I walked away.

Nighteyes was silent within me.

I had to pass our old campsite. Kettricken had been so young. The Fool and I of an age and yet not. Old Kettle with her wise old eyes in their nests of wrinkles and her deep-kept secrets. And Starling. Starling, who could annoy me like a humming gnat. I looked around at the view. The trees were taller. Underfoot, on the stone, only sodden and rotted bits of fabric and line. I kicked at it and turned up a layer that had kept its colour. That blue had been Kettricken's cloak. I stooped and touched it. My queen, I thought to myself and smiled. I nudged the rotting cloth. Beneath it, the pitted and corroded head of our old hatchet was scarcely recognizable. I stood and walked on.

Beyond it was the place where Verity had carved his dragon. Chips and shards still littered the empty area where his dragon had crouched. He had used a chisel with a rock for a hammer at first, until he had plunged his hands into raw Skill and carved and shaped with them. My king. Had he truly told me it was time to carve my dragon? Told me it was time to surrender Bee to someone else's care? Time to surrender my man's body for one of stone and Skill?

No. Tomorrow, with the dawn, I would be up and fishing. I would catch a dozen, and eat them all. Then I would catch still more and smoke them and the next morning I would begin my walk to the abandoned market pavilion. I wondered if winter had killed the old bear, or if he would trouble me.

We will die before you get there. Fitz. I know these things. Why won't you listen to me?

I can't.

And that was the truth. I could not let go of the hope that I could go home to Bee. Worms were not so terrible an affliction. Burrich had known half a dozen cures for them. The healers in Buckkeep grew all the herbs in the Women's Garden. Once I reached home, I would rest and grow strong again. Bee and I would be together. We'd leave the court and all its rules. We would travel by horseback. We'd go from keep to keep, as if we were travelling minstrels and she would learn the history and geography of the Six Duchies by seeing them. The Fool would go with us, and Per. We would live simply and move easily and we would be happy.

I won't watch you die.

I don't intend to die.

Does anyone?

I gathered an armload of firewood. There were plenty of fallen branches. I had no way to cut the larger one. I smiled as I recalled how Verity had returned an edge to his sword before giving it to me. I went back for the corroded hatchet head. I handled it, remembering it, and then pushed the rust and corrosion away. I slid the blade between my thumb and forefinger, imagining a fresh edge. Fitting a haft to it took longer. But with it, I chopped a good supply of thicker branches, took an armful and carried it back to my fire. I could smell the fish I had cooked and wished there were more of it. I added a stick or two of wood to my fire and sat down beside it.

I jolted awake in the dead of night. I was lying on cold stone and my fire was nearly dead. I built it up again. I was glad I had enough wood to get through the night, for I had no desire to go blundering through the dark to find the chopped supply I'd left behind. I waited for the wolf to rebuke me for my stupidity and laziness.

He didn't.

It took some time for me to realize he was gone. Just gone.

I was alone.

FORTY-SEVEN

A Wolf's Heart

Revel, if you would, please ride into Oaksbywater today. Marly the leatherworker sent word that my order is ready. I trust you to judge its quality and accept it or ask her to re-do the work. Be sure to see that the pages are well bound to the cover, and that the paper is of a good quality, and that the embossing on the cover is cleanly impressed. Please deliver it only to me, if you find it worth the coin we spent. It is a gift for Mistress Bee and I wish to surprise her with it myself.

Among Revel's papers at Withywoods

I continued to see Thick every night, although it made me very stupid and dull during the days. I did not care that I was chided for not knowing my Chalcedean verbs, and that I had to pick out all my embroidery stitches for making the daisies green. Every night, I went to my bed, and slept a short time before his music would gently wake me. I would hurry down the hall in my night robe for the best hours of my life.

I wanted to give him something. Anything. The bright kerchiefs I had bought for Revel were still in my wardrobe. It took a long time for me to decide that I could give them to Thick. But even those were not enough to express what I felt for the kindly old man. I had ink and brushes for my dream journal. With great care, I sliced a page from it and drew Smokey dancing after the spool. I coloured him, his green eyes and black pupils, his grey fur and tiny white claws.

Thick was delighted with my gifts. He promised he could keep them secret.

I returned to my room and crawled into my bed, tired and happy.

I awoke when Spark sat down on the foot of my bed. 'Bee. Wake up!' she ordered me.

'What? It's you! Where have you been? I've missed you!'

'Shh.' She tilted her head toward the adjoining chamber where Careful snored on. 'I'm here at Buckkeep Castle. I'm busy with many things. When we returned, Lady Nettle took me aside. Lord Riddle had endorsed me. I watch over you. I keep you safe.'

'Because I ran away on Pris that day?' I felt a surge of unhappiness. What a foolish thing I had done. My sister did not trust me now. I didn't deserve her trust.

Spark shook her head. 'From the first day we returned. Years ago, your sister Nettle was a stranger at Buckkeep Castle when she was little more than a girl. She feared that there would be people who would take advantage of you. Riddle agreed. So I watch over you and every few days I report back to them.'

'How is it I don't see you, then? Oh.' My eyes roved the walls of my bedchamber, seeing a spy-hole I was certain would be there.

She smiled. 'I am better able to watch over you if I am not seen. I was taught ways of moving about Buckkeep unseen. Some day, perhaps, I will show you.'

'Why are you here now?'

'To let you know that Thick cannot keep a secret. He will show off his kerchiefs. He wore two of them to bed. And he will, eventually, show Smokey's portrait to someone. He is too pleased with it to keep it to himself. The work is unmistakably yours. No one draws as you do, let alone paints in such detail.'

'Will Nettle say I cannot be friends with Thick any more?'

She shrugged. Her hair, shortened by a mourning cut, had a strand of spiderweb on it. I reached up and took it out for her.

'Nettle will decide. But they will know. Because I must report it back to them tomorrow.'

'Will you tell them you warned me?'

She took a huge breath and let it pour out of her. 'Will you tell them I warned you?'

'No. Absolutely not.'

'I am a terrible spy,' she admitted. I watched her slip out of the door and smiled.

I did not sleep at all. In the morning, I begged Careful to let me breakfast in my room so that I could put off the dreaded business of dressing and hair-fussing. She worried that I was ill, and conceded. I ate, and then submitted to being groomed and decorated with clothing and having my short hair brushed and pinned up as best she could before I went off for my session as a lady to Queen Elliania. Her belly now stuck out like the prow of a ship, and all the talk was of the baby to come, and all our sewing was for the baby. Then I had my lessons, in languages and history.

I went to my midday meal full of dread for what must come. I sat on the dais with the other nobility and ate with them, and at the close of the meal, Riddle invited me to ride out with Nettle and him that afternoon. His eyes were kind, his mouth reserved. I accepted with formal courtesy, and then was trooped back to my room by Lady Simmer. Careful had set out appropriate clothing. My riding garments were green and yellow, Withywood colours. It made me consider how I fitted into the Farseer hierarchy.

I descended, resigned to a gaggle of folk to accompany us. But not even the nurse and the baby were there, and Riddle dismissed all the grooms, even Per who had been loitering hopefully nearby. Riddle tossed me up onto my horse without ceremony, and Nettle mounted hers without anyone so much as touching her elbow. We left at a sedate walk that turned into a canter as soon as we were out of the gates of Buckkeep. We did not speak as we rode, but gave the horses a good gallop on a trail through a forest that led to a secluded glen near a stream. Here we dismounted and let the horses water. And Nettle said, 'I know that you visit Lord Thick every night. You must know it is not appropriate to be running about the keep in your nightgown.'

I bowed my head and tried to look startled.

'Well?' she demanded.

'He is my friend. He is teaching me to make Skill-music. We play with his cat. He has nice things to eat. That is all.'

'And you have learned to erect such Skill-walls that I can barely find you during the day.'

I kept my eyes on the grassy sward. 'It is to keep the music in. He says we must not make the music too loud, for then the apprentices cannot sleep well.'

'Will you lower your walls and let me hear the music you have learned?'

It was a test. Did I trust her enough to lower my walls, so that she might see the truth of what I had told her? If I refused . . . No. There was no refusing this. I dropped my walls. I felt her mind touch mine. I began the purring-cat music.

Wolf Father slammed into my awareness with such force that I sat down flat on the grass. *We must get to the queen!*

Queen Elliania knows of you? I felt dazed, as if the air had been knocked out of me. I could hear Nettle exclaiming and Riddle suddenly knelt beside me, but I knew the wolf was more important. 'How are you here, when my father is dead?' I asked him.

'What did she say?' Nettle asked Riddle in alarm.

He isn't dead. Not yet. And I need to get to the queen, the one who hunted with me. Queen Kettricken. I wish to bid her farewell.

Farewell?

Yes. I felt him hide something from me. Wolf Father was very like my other father.

Very well. I will do my best. I looked up at Riddle and Nettle. There was no simple way to explain it. I would not even try. 'I am not ill. Nighteyes has come to me. I must see Queen Kettricken right away. My father is not dead. Nighteyes wishes to bid her farewell.' The next words came out strangled. 'I think they are dying somewhere.'

Riddle crouched before me. He put his hands on my shoulders. 'Explain more. From the beginning.'

I could feel the wolf's clawing panic. I tried. 'Sometimes, when my father could not be with me, Wolf Father would come. Into my mind. Nighteyes. I know you know who he was! He was Wit-bonded to my father, and after he died, he lived inside my father.'

I looked from one concerned face to the other. Surely they must have known this. They were looking at me as if I were mad.

'When I was taken, Wolf Father went with me. He tried to help me, to warn me or give me ideas of what to do. But sometimes, if my walls were too tight, he could not speak to me. When I saw my father, Nighteyes went back to him. And just now, when I dropped my walls for Nettle, he came to me again. And he says he must see Lady Kettricken. Because my father is dying.' I shook my head and demanded aloud of Nighteyes, 'How can my father be dying when Beloved said he was dead? Why would he lie to me? Why would he leave my father alone and dying?'

He didn't die, Bee. But alone, he will not last much longer. He believes he can rest and be well enough to come home. I know he cannot. He must stay there. It is time for us to carve our dragon.

'Bee!'

What?

'Bee. Answer me. Are you Witted?' Nettle demanded.

'No. I don't think so.' I hesitated. It seemed such a random question as I strove to understand what Nighteyes had told me. 'I don't know. Cats talk to me but they talk to everyone, or anyone who will listen. But this is not the Wit. I don't think it's the Wit. He is my Wolf Father. Please! Let me go to Kettricken. It's important!'

Nettle put her hands on my shoulders. She spoke slowly. 'Bee. Our father is dead. It's hard to accept and even I want to pretend it's not true. But he's dead. The Fool told us all. He was trapped under a fallen timber, and he had bled heavily from a sword slash. He gave to the Fool his last strength. So he could save you. Our father could not have survived, let alone escaped.'

'I wouldn't bet money on that,' Riddle said grimly. 'Not until I see his body. Come. We need to return to Buckkeep.'

'To the healers?' Nettle asked doubtfully.

'To Lady Kettricken,' Riddle asserted. 'Nettle, I know you must doubt this. But we must act as if it were true! We go to Kettricken, to ask what she thinks. And then we will make that other decision.'

'To Kettricken,' she agreed reluctantly.

The old queen had not been well before she received the news of my father's death. On the way to her chambers, Nettle told me that some of the healers felt that news had been the tipping point for her. 'I dread this,' Nettle said to Riddle. 'Might we not be bringing more distress into her life when she is already frail?'

'I do not think "frail" is the best word to apply to her. I think she is resigned, Nettle.'

I had met with Kettricken only that one awkward time since our return. She had been truly ill that day, and full of sadness. Her rooms had been curtained and close. This day, we were admitted to a chamber where the window stood ajar and the sunlight flooded the room. It was a simple room, sparsely furnished. There were chairs to sit on, and a low table, and little else. A vase almost as tall as me held an arrangement of reeds and rushes. That was all. The flagged floor was scrubbed and bare.

Lady Kettricken entered without ceremony shortly after a servant had shown us into the room and announced us. Her grey hair was braided and coiled about her head. She wore a long, straight, pale-blue cotton robe, belted at her waist, and soft slippers. No jewellery did she wear, nor paint on her face. She could have been any old woman at a market. She regarded us with calm blue eyes. The closest she came to a complaint was to say, 'This is a sudden visit.'

I found I was smiling at her, delighted. I almost wriggled. No. Nighteyes within me was delighted. I took a deep breath of the air, seeking her familiar scent. 'You still walk like a forest hunter, light of foot and steady-eyed,' I told her.

'Bee!' Nettle rebuked me.

But Lady Kettricken had only a puzzled smile for me. 'Please, sit,' she bade us, and there was only a slight hitch of stiffness as she lowered herself to a seat. 'I am pleased to see all of you. Should I ring for refreshments for us?'

'Could there be ginger-cakes?' I asked, again without knowing I would speak. Ashamed, I hunched my head down between my shoulders and looked up at her.

She raised her brows at me and with concern asked, 'Is there something going on here that I do not know about?'

Nettle looked hopelessly at Riddle. He kept silent. Nettle tried. 'Bee believes that her father is still alive. She believes that he has sent—'

'No.' I had to interrupt. 'No, he didn't send Nighteyes. He came on his own, to me. And he asked me to come to see Queen Kettricken.'

The former queen was a fair-skinned woman. I did not think she could blanch whiter but she did. 'I am no longer a queen,' she reminded us.

'You are ever a queen to him, but more than that, you are always the hunter with the bow who fed everyone in the dark times. He was glad to be beside you, and glad to run ahead of you and drive game for you, and to offer you what comfort he could when you were sad.'

Her lips trembled slightly. Then she said gently. 'Your father told you tales of our time in the Mountains.'

I folded my arms tightly across my chest and pulled my head up straight. I must not appear mad or hysterical. 'My lady, my father Fitz told me little of those times. Some, I know. But my Wolf Father tells me these things. He has words for you, before he returns to my father. To die, I think.'

'Can this be so? How did the wolf's spirit linger? How can he come to you? And where is Fitz? Still in far-off Clerres, and alive?' Tragedy was in her eyes and drooped her mouth. She became an elderly woman.

I waited for the answer to rise in me. 'No. He is at the quarry, in the Mountains. You know the place well. Where Verity carved his dragon. The Scentless One believed him dead. He was mistaken. Fitz is there, but very weak and riddled with worms. He will die soon, and I will die with him. I wished to see you one last time. To let you know how dear you were to me.' I stopped speaking. I was surprised to find I was standing in front of Kettricken, holding both her hands in mine. The thought he conveyed to me now was only for me. *Your mother was a good mate for Fitz. She gave him what he needed. But this is the woman I would have chosen for us.* A baffling thought and not something to speak aloud. I pushed him back. 'He is very earnest that you believe this.' He offered a memory and I spoke it aloud. 'He remembers this. Sometimes, on the hunt, your hands would get cold and stiff. You would take off your mittens and gloves, and warm your hands in the ruff of fur on his throat.'

Lady Kettricken flowed to her feet as if she were a slow fountain. She looked at Nettle. She was a silver-haired queen again. 'We will need a tent, and warm things, for even in summer the Mountains are chill in the evening. You will take me there. And the Fool. Lord Golden. Whoever he is being today. Summon him as well. Today.'

'Bring food!' I said. Then the wolf told us the last thing I wanted to know. 'He is infected with parasites that are eating him. Day by day he dwindles, and I do not know how long I have been gone from him.' It was strange to hear myself say, 'Ask Bee. She knows of such deaths. She has seen one.'

He faded to the back of my mind as if exhausted. I could understand that. Never had I felt him so intense. But he left me standing in the circle of three adults staring down at me in wary belief.

I doubled over, my hands over my mouth as I suddenly understood. The Traitor's Death. Vindeliar had promised that to me. Had my father taken it for me?

Kettricken's hands on my shoulders were like a raptor's claws. 'Stand up,' she said sternly and forced me upright. 'You will tell me what this means.'

Telling them of the messenger and her death was horrid. I wondered how much Beloved knew of it. The queen rang for refreshments. A servant brought tea and ginger-cakes. I ate a cake with tears fresh on my cheeks, and was astounded at how I savoured the scent and taste of it, while confessing a tale of bloody eyes, a butterfly cloak, and a midnight pyre. I had thought my father might have told Riddle or Nettle. Plainly, he had not. Nettle sank down and covered her face. 'Oh, Da. How could you?'

I swallowed my bite of cake. 'The death is unstoppable. So the messenger said. It is the death they reserved for traitors. Slow, painful and inevitable.' I picked up another ginger-cake. They watched me do it. 'He likes them!' I said through my tears. I looked at the cake in my hands. 'My father is dying horribly. We can't stop that. But ginger still always tastes wonderful.'

'It does,' Kettricken agreed. She put another one into my hands.

I took a large bite of one and for that moment, the ginger and the sweetness was all there was. They were speaking over my head.

'How could he not?' Riddle said, and reminded Nettle of a previous messenger that had vanished, perhaps murdered, during a Winterfest years before the butterfly cloak incident. That made Nettle uncover her face and knit her brows as she connected the two accounts. Kettricken said nothing except, 'It is what he would do. Not what he would choose, but what he felt he must do at the time. Still, Bee, I am sorry that you had to serve him so. But we are wasting time. Riddle. Go request all that we need. We will leave before sunset.'

Nettle held up a hand. 'My lady, I implore prudence.' She took a breath and glanced at me as if reluctant to speak in my hearing. Riddle winced for me as she said, 'I love my sister, but I think we should approach this sensibly. She has suffered a great deal. I was older than she is when Burrich died, and still I had vivid dreams of him coming home to us. I do not think she is lying,' and here she met my eyes, 'but I fear she may be mistaken. Before we mount an expedition, let me send a coterie to see what the situation is. If they find him, they can bring him home! Remember that they will face a journey of days. They must take horses to the same leaning Skill-stone that Lady Shine showed us. I have ordered it righted and cleaned: as it has been used before, we consider it reliable. They will need calm and steady mounts for the passage. Once they have made the journey to the market-circle, I believe there is still a journey to the quarry?'

'There is,' Lady Kettricken admitted slowly. 'At least we still have fine weather for it. It took us days in the winter. We had to hunt for our food, but this time, we will carry provisions. We shall do better without the snow, and I recall the way.'

'My lady. When did you last go out riding?'

Her shoulders rounded and she looked at her curled hands. 'But it is Fitz,' she said softly.

'And a coterie will reach him much faster than a full expedition. I will be sure that they take at least two who are skilled healers. In the event he is actually there, they will bring him home to us.'

Lady Kettricken made a final effort. 'I have a map I have created, of the journey. It will speed us.'

Both Riddle and Nettle kept silent. I stood still, not sure what was expected of me. Then it came to me. They meant to leave me behind. 'I will not be left. I will ride my own horse, and Per will come with me.'

'I will fetch my map,' Lady Kettricken said, as if that were a reply. She stood slowly and the look in her blue eyes was cold and hard. She left the room, walking carefully upright.

'I must gather my things, and find Per,' I said.

But Nettle shook her head slowly. She looked very tired. 'Bee, you need to be sensible. So does Lady Kettricken. And in a few moments, when she is calmer, I will speak to her again. There is no reason to risk her or you on a journey through the Skill-pillars. I will go myself. I will leave Hope with Riddle, and I will take a picked coterie with me. If Father is there, if this is not a terrible illusion you have, then we will bring him back here to Buckkeep Castle where he can be treated and cured. Queen Elliania has brought in two new healers, one from her OutIslands and one who has trained with the priests of Sa in Jamaillia. They both bring new ideas, new herbs and according to our healers, new successes.

'But I will not risk you in the Skill-pillars. You have already been endangered too often in your short life. It's time to be safe and stay here and be a child while you still can. Do you understand clearly what I am telling you? I am not taking you through the Skill-pillars with me.'

I met her gaze. 'I understand,' I said quietly.

'Repeat it.'

I drew a frustrated breath. 'You will not be taking me to Da in the quarry through the Skill-pillars with you. Even though he is probably dying.'

She folded her lips and Riddle rolled his eyes at me. Then, 'Exactly,' she said. She sighed. 'Now off with you. Go about your regular duties and please, speak of this to no one. I myself will inform King Dutiful. Oh, and as to what we were trying to discuss earlier? Of course you may visit Thick, but at a proper time of day and with one of his attendants there, to exercise the restraint that Thick has been lacking. I will arrange that today. You must be careful of him. He is prone to be excitable and sometimes difficult. And the discussion we were to have about your Skill-training must wait until I return. We may need to damp your ability until you are able to exercise more caution with it.'

I had not found him difficult. I did not say that. Instead I curtseyed to my sister. As I turned, she spoke again. 'Bee, I know you think me strict and perhaps cold. But we are sisters, and I so nearly lost you. You cannot imagine how helpless I felt, all through my pregnancy. How I wondered if my baby would ever know you. How Riddle tormented himself that he had not remained there with you. We have you back. We have lost our father. I will not lose you.'

I bobbed a nod to that, turned, and quietly left the chamber. I shut the door behind me. Then I ran as swiftly as I could through the corridors. First, to find Beloved. He could get us through a Skill-pillar. And he owed me some answers. How was it he had told me my father was dead, and now I learned he was not dead, but dying? My anger with him burned hotter, but I knew I would need him. Then I'd find Per. Nettle had not said I could not go, only that she would not take me.

I was thankful I was still dressed for riding. Trousers were much better for hiking than my ridiculous skirts. My mind raced. Could

Beloved pretend that we were going on a picnic and procure food for us? Per could get horses from the stable. We'd need an extra one to bring my father home.

You go to say goodbye, not to bring him home. Food and bedding and something for a shelter are what you should take him. It will help him sustain his life long enough to finish his task.

I am not going to accept his death. Not again.

A page hurried past me, then turned and came back to me. 'Are you well, Lady Bee?'

I realized that tears were running down my face and dripping from my chin. I wiped them hastily. 'Dust in my eyes from my ride. Thank you for your concern. Have you seen Lord Chance this morning?'

'I saw him ascending the stairs to the Queen's Garden, the one on the rooftop of the—'

'Thank you. I know where that is.'

I changed direction and hurried away from him. But in two steps he followed me and seized me by the arm. I spun on him in a fury, shocked to be handled so. But the page suddenly was Spark. 'What is it? What's happened?'

'I must see Lord Chance. Now.'

She folded her lips. 'Change your expression,' she hissed at me. 'Anyone who sees you will know you are defiant. Smile as if we are going on a pleasant errand, and hurry, but do not run. I will be right behind you.'

I recovered from my shock. I wiped my face on my sleeve and stitched a smile onto my mouth. I did as she suggested. The corridors had never seemed so long. I hated the steep climb up the tower steps. Twice I stopped to breathe. I hoped he was still there. The outer door to the tower rooftop was heavy, built to withstand both the winds and the heavy snows of winter. Spark had her picks out. I flashed my key at her, and she exclaimed in surprise. Together we shoved the door open and stepped out into a pleasant day.

High, thin clouds were scraped across a blue sky. Up here, the wind was cooler. I did not immediately see Lord Chance. The large pots full of blooming plants and statues seemed too placid and calm a place for my boiling thoughts. I followed the tiled walkway and at the end saw Beloved standing with his back toward me. He was looking landward.

'Lord Chance!' I hailed him.

He turned to me and a hesitant smile dawned. 'Well. I cannot recall that you have ever sought my company before, Bee. Thrice welcome!' His voice was full of warmth and hope. Then he saw Spark behind me and his expression became one of alarm. 'What has happened?'

I had thought I could be calm. I could not. 'How could you tell me my father was dead, how could you leave him? How could you leave him? How could you not go back for him?'

'Bee!' Spark rebuked me, but I ignored her.

My words tore the smile from Beloved's face. He looked ill and beaten. He tried for a breath, failed, and tried again. 'Bee, Fitz is dead. You yourself said you felt that he was gone.' He clutched his gloved hand in his bared one. 'I felt that link break. He died. I felt it.' His face was full of misery and shock. 'He left me,' he said forlornly, and my fury soared.

'He's not dead!' I bit off every word. 'Nighteyes says he is at the quarry, dying, riddled with parasites, just as the pale messenger died. It's a horrible way to go. You know it. They call it the Traitor's Death. Delivered by a dart. And you left him to it.'

Spark gasped. 'They shot darts at us. Before the explosion. Bee sent them running and he brushed a dart from his jerkin . . .'

Hope and horror vied for possession of Beloved's features. 'He cannot be alive,' he declared. But oh, how he longed to believe my father lived.

'I told Nettle and Riddle. We went to see Lady Kettricken. Nettle is planning to send a coterie through to see if it's real. She says they will bring Fitz back. But Nighteyes says he is dying, even if my father doesn't believe it. The wolf says he should stay at the quarry and carve a dragon. He says they should not bring him back here.'

'Carve a dragon?' Spark looked very confused.

I heard the scuff of steps and turned to see Lant and Per. Per burst out, 'Your father lives!' at the same moment that Lant exclaimed, 'Thank Eda that we found you!' But most shocking of all was when Motley swooped in, to land on Per's shoulder and shout, 'Fitz! Fitz! The quarry. The quarry!'

'We are leaving before nightfall,' Beloved announced. He looked out over the parapet and abruptly announced, 'Kettricken goes with us.'

'And how will we travel?' Spark asked. She sounded sick.

'As you and I did before. From the dungeon-stone to Aslevjal. From Aslevjal to the market-circle. Thence on foot to the Skill-stone quarry. Spark, I recall how it hurt you last time. You need not come.'

'We have no dragon's blood to help you make the journey.'

'I have the Silver on my fingers. I believe I can do it. Any who fear the journey need not come.'

'Of course I will go with you.' She sounded bitterly defeated as she said it.

I spoke up. 'If he can open the stone, I know how to give Skill-strength. And I can draw it from Per, if need be.' Per gave a grim-faced nod. Lant had not spoken, but there was sick determination on his face.

Spark crossed her arms on her chest. 'Kettricken is elderly and her joints give her much pain. She will never be able to keep up.'

'Oh, you do not know her as I do,' Beloved said grimly. 'She will make that journey. I will not leave her behind.'

Spark threw her hands in the air. 'This is mad. And the end of my occupation here at Buckkeep. We are all risking our lives and our sanity.' She sounded angry as she rounded on Per and Lant. 'Why are you still standing here? Fetch all that is needful. Lord Chance, you must be the one to propose this to Kettricken. I will not.' She shifted her attention to me. 'You. Go about your schedule as if nothing is happening. Even to disrobing for bed tonight. Wait until we come to fetch you.'

FORTY-EIGHT

Time

There is a cage made of crawling, squirming things. Inside is something that used to be a man. A black-and-white rat looks at him, and then giggles and turns handsprings as it abandons him.

I make no illustration for this dream. It felt as if it would be true, and I would witness it.

Bee Farseer's dream journal

'Anything a bear can eat, a man can eat, too.' Burrich told me that, long ago, after I died in Regal's dungeon and before I had found myself as a human again. He was looking guardedly at a leaf-buried bear-kill we had stumbled across on one of my supervised walks. He had very hastily cut some chunks from the decomposing fawn and then we had left the bear's cache quickly.

Aged meat is far more tender than a fresh kill. I remembered that meat fondly. But he was correct in all aspects of what he had said. A man can eat grubs from under a rotted log, or a frog. Tender roots and the young shoots of water-grasses. Even pond scum can thicken a soup, if one has something to cook soup in. But pond algae can be eaten by the handful, along with watercress, and the roots of cattails can be roasted in a low fire. Sometimes I wondered if Verity had subsisted in the same way before Kettricken and I had arrived at the quarry to hunt real food for him.

The morning after my wolf left me, I awoke and rubbed my sandy eyes. As I sat up, a terrible coughing spell took me. When I could gasp in a breath, I wiped my mouth on the back of my hand. It left a smear of blood. I looked at it and a sad, sick certainty rose in me. Then, a terrible feeling in my mouth. Not pain. I would have preferred pain. I leaned forward and spat on the ground in front of me. Blood and saliva. And several pale squirming things, no thicker than a bowstring, no longer than a finger joint.

Oh.

I went to the pond, sucked in water, sloshed it through my mouth and spat on the ground. Another one.

Small bits of information tumbled and joined in my mind. An idea threatened me. The pale messenger that Bee and I had burned. I mulled over that memory and then denied it. Nighteyes had insisted that I had worms. I did. That was all. I crouched down to study the creature that had lived inside me. It was a kind I had not seen before, in man or beast. But that was all it was. Just a worm. I wondered if I could be lucky enough to find wild garlic or orangeroot growing nearby. Both were good for clearing parasites from the body. But a more practical plan would be to begin my journey to the ancient market and go from there to Buck. There would be healers there.

I scooped up more water in my hands and rubbed my face. When I dropped my hands, they were tinged pink. I touched my nostrils and looked at my fingers. No.

I touched my fingertips to my eyes. They came away red. And with the blood on my fingertips came a sickening certainty. The messenger had wept blood. She had said the worms the Servants had infected her with were eating her eyes. That she could scarcely see any more. I lifted my eyes and looked about me. I could still see.

But for how long?

I had two tasks every day that I performed faithfully. I gathered more firewood, and I went to the water to drink. I longed to go to the creek to fish, but my strength was failing me. Nosebleeds were a daily occurrence now, and my back and thighs were covered with small, itching sores. The only parts of my legs that were free of the sores were where the Silver had splashed me.

Too late I had come to agree with the wolf. I wished he would return to me so that I could tell him so. By the third day of his absence, the reduction in my stamina was something I could no longer argue with. My wolf was gone, and I knew I was never going home again. I'd made several attempts to Skill and failed at all of them. Perhaps it was the Silver on my body, or my general weakness, or the presence of so much Skill-stone around me. The reason didn't matter. I was alone. And I had one last task to do. I had to prepare a stone for us. And hope that the wolf would return to share it with me.

Once Nighteyes had begun the carving with my handprint it did not occur to me that it would be anything other than a wolf. Daily I toiled on our 'dragon', my silver hand stroking the stone, as I gave it the memories Nighteyes and I shared. I was surprised to see that the wolf emerging from the stone stood with teeth bared and hackles raised. Were the two of us, together, truly so fierce of visage? Yet even as I poured in memories of hunts and shared kills, of wild romps in the snow and mice caught in an old hut, of porcupine quills pulled and his teeth pressing hard against my back as he sheared off an arrow-shaft, I knew that I did not have enough to fill this stone flesh. I knew that when it came time to draw my last breath, I would lean on this cold creature and pass into him. And remain here, mired in stone, just as Girl-on-a-Dragon had stood for so many decades of years.

I should have listened to him. I should have. If Nighteyes had been with me still, there might have been more of us to put into the wolf-dragon.

He had only the colours of the stone, and that bothered me. Before I died, I wanted to once more look into those wise eyes. I wanted, a last time, to see his glance catch the firelight and gleam green and startling. I began to sleep with my back against him, as we used to do. Not that the stone gave me any warmth, but in the hopes that my dreams might permeate it and help the wolf emerge more swiftly.

I woke in the night. There are two kinds of sleep when one is weak and cold. One is the kind where one pretends to sleep as one shivers and shifts and tries to clutch body warmth. I had wrapped my stolen cloak around me, covering my head to keep the gnats from my ears and eyes. Insects do love a dying animal. Then I had fallen into the second kind of sleep, the heavy sleep of exhaustion that cold and pain cannot break. That sleep, I think, is the precursor to death.

Thus I came out of it slowly and reluctantly, unsure of where dream gave way to reality. Voices. Scuffing footsteps. I struggled to untangle my head from its wrapping. I didn't stand up. But I opened my eyes and blinked dully at the startling yellow glare of a swinging lantern coming toward me.

'This way, I think,' someone said.

'We should make a camp and continue in the morning. I can see nothing here.'

'We are close. I know we are so close. Bee, cannot you Skill to him? He said he felt you Skill, once.'

'This stone . . . no. I have no training. You know I have no training!'

The light was so bright I could see nothing else. Then I made out shadows and silhouettes. People. Carrying a lantern. And packs. I feebly pushed my Wit toward them.

'FITZ!' someone shouted, and I realized I'd heard that querying call before, in my sleep, and it had wakened me. And more, that I knew the voice.

'Over here,' I called. But my voice was thin in a dry throat.

The wolf hit me with an almost physical impact. He was a jolt to my dwindling body, almost like an infusion of Skill-strength. *Oh, my brother, I could not find you to return to you. I feared we were too late. I feared you had entered the stone without me.*

I am here.

'Look. Embers of a fire. He's there! Fitz! Fitz!'

'Don't touch me!' I cried out and clutched my Silver hand to my chest. They came to me at a run, shapes emerging out of the twilight. The Fool reached me first, but as the firelight illuminated him, he halted an arm's length away and stared at me, his mouth hanging ajar. I looked back at him and waited.

'Oh, Fitz!' the Fool cried. 'What did you do to yourself?'

'No worse than what you have done, twice,' I managed a twisted smile. 'I did not choose this,' I added feebly.

'Far worse than anything I've ever done!' he declared. His gaze wandered over me, lingering on the silvered side of my face. His expression was more telling than any mirror. 'How could you do this? Why?'

'I didn't. It happened. The container of Silver. The fire-brick in my bag.' I held up a helpless silvered hand. 'Da!' Bee shrieked furiously, and my watering eyes showed me Per with his arms wrapped about my younger daughter, holding her back.

She kicked and struggled, baring her teeth. Abruptly Per said to her, 'Bee, you are not that foolish!' and let her go. She did not rush to me. She came in small steps, studying me carefully. Then she set her small hands onto my arm, touching flesh to flesh with no Silver between us. I could suddenly draw a deeper breath. Hope flowed in me. I could live. I could go home.

Then I realized what she was doing. 'Bee, no!' I rebuked her and pulled my arm free of her grip. 'You do not Skill strength to me.'

But she had. 'I have strength to spare,' she pleaded, but I shook my head. 'Bee. All of you. You cannot touch me now. I am carving my dragon. Our dragon, for Nighteyes and me. Everything I have, I must put into it. And I must not pull you and your strength into it.'

The Fool set his hands, one gloved, on Bee's shoulders. He drew her back gently, but I saw her stiffen with resentment and, for a moment, flash her teeth at his touch. Lant and Per were staring at my silvered face in something between horror and pity.

The Fool spoke. 'Explanations can wait. After we have built up the fire, and made hot tea and soup for Fitz. There are blankets in the big pack.' He lifted his voice to a shout. 'Spark! Over here!' he cried, and I glimpsed another bobbing lantern. Then they were all unshouldering their packs. And he spoke on, of wondrous things, of hot tea with honey and smoked meat and blankets while the wolf capered joyously inside me.

I closed my eyes. When I opened them again, other people had approached and were busying themselves with camp tasks. I sat quietly while Bee told me of their journey home, and described the shape of her life at Buckkeep Castle. The Fool orbited us at a distance, sometimes pausing to listen to some detail of Bee's recitation, but mostly engaged in directing Lant and Per in setting up a shelter and sorting supplies from the packs. I leaned with my back on my partially-carved wolf and tried to take pleasure in what I knew was actually farewell.

But Motley with her silver beak came and perched on my stone wolf. She cocked her head and said nothing but I thought she looked at me sadly. She whetted her silver beak on the stone, once, twice, and I felt something go into the wolf. The memory of a kind shepherd. A man who had taken in a freak nestling. Then she hopped into the air to land on the firewood pile.

I was given a thick wool blanket and Per built up my fire recklessly large, and Lant fetched water for a cooking pot and a kettle. 'Eat this,' Spark said, and set wrapped food before me. I was surprised that she was there, but the smell of the food drove even a greeting out of my thoughts. I opened the sticky cloth. It was cold bacon, thick with grease, wrapped in a thick cut of dark bread. Lant uncorked a bottle of wine and set it within my reach. They moved about me as if I were a rabid dog that might lunge and bite, avoiding my touch as they offered me every physical comfort. I filled my belly with bread and meat, and washed down the immense half-chewed bites I took with the heady red wine.

Spark was brewing tea in a fat kettle. Lant stirred a pot of simmering water enriched with chunks of dried beef, and carrots and potatoes. I could smell it and a deep wave of hunger left me shaking. I hugged myself against it.

'Fitz. Are you in pain?' It was the Fool asking that, in a voice fraught with guilt.

'Of course I am,' I said. 'They are eating me, the little bastards. They eat me, and my body rebuilds itself, and they eat me afresh. I almost think it is worse after I have eaten.'

'I will see to that,' a woman said. 'I have learned a great deal about herbs for pain. And I brought what I thought best would serve.' I looked again, and it was Kettricken. I felt a boyish lurch of joy inside me. My queen. Oh, Nighteyes.

'Kettricken. I did not see you there.'

'You never did,' she said and smiled sadly. Then she called to Spark, asking for a little kettle from her pack and the blue roll of herb-bundles.

'Da, tomorrow, you will feel better,' Bee told me. 'We will begin the journey back to the market-circle, and from there, we can take you home. Nettle says that there are new healers at Buckkeep, from far-off places with new ideas.'

'So Nettle sent you to bring me home?' I suddenly realized how wrong this all was. Was this a dying man's illusion? I looked into the darkness. 'She sent no coterie here?'

An uncomfortable expression passed over Bee's face. 'I left her a note,' she said quietly. Then, at my shock, she added, 'She wasn't going to let me come. She was going to send a coterie after you, to bring you home.'

'Bee, I am not going to go home. I am going to finish here.' She reached out to take my hand and I tucked it under my other arm. 'No, Bee.' She lifted her hands and covered her face. I looked over her head at the Fool hovering at the edge of our circle. I tried to find some comforting words. 'You will have to trust me that this is a better end than I would face if I came home. And this is the ending I choose for myself. My decision, for me.'

The Fool stared at me, and then stepped back out of the firelight. Kettricken came, bearing a small steaming kettle and a thick pottery mug. She offered me the mug and I held it as she poured her brew into it. Her hands shook slightly.

I sipped at the tea and tasted carryme and valerian for pain, and enlivening herbs and ginger all sweetened with honey. It worked swiftly; the pains eased. It was as if I poured life back into my body.

'Tomorrow you will be strong enough, and we will take you back to Buckkeep and the healers there,' Kettricken offered hopefully.

I smiled at her as she sat down beside my fire. Yes. It would be a long farewell. 'Kettricken, you have been here before. We both know how this ends. You see my wolf at my back. I will finish him, and now that Nighteyes is with me again, it will go more swiftly.' I reached behind me to set my hand on his paw. I felt each toe, the space between them, and recalled how his claws had been set. I stroked the polished smoothness of one, and almost expected him to twitch his foot away in annoyance, as he always had.

You always teased me when I was trying to sleep, barely touching the hairs between my toes. It tickled unbearably.

I let that shared memory soak into the stone. For a time, I was alone with him. I heard Kettricken retrieve the mug and her quiet steps as she walked away.

'Fitz, can you leave off that for a time? Stop carving until you have regained some of your strength?' There was a plea in Lant's voice. I opened my eyes. Time had passed. They had rigged a shelter over my wolf and me. The fire was in front of it, and the tent contained the warmth. I was grateful. The Mountain nights were cold. They sat in a semicircle on the other side of the fire. I looked around at them. Little Bee, my stableboy, an apprentice assassin, Chade's bastard, and my queen. And the Fool. He was there, sitting at the very edge of the firelight. Our eyes met and then looked away from me. He had seen this before, as had Kettricken. I tried to help the others understand.

'Once begun, there is no stopping this task. I have already put a great deal of myself into the wolf, and as I add more, I will become vaguer—just as Verity did. This task will consume me, as it consumed him.' I struggled to focus on their anxious faces. 'Bee, know this now, while I can still marshal my thoughts. I will become distant to you. It almost broke Kettricken's heart, how Verity ignored her. But he never stopped loving her. He had put his love for her into his dragon, for he never expected to see her again. It is still there, in the stone. To last forever. And so it will be with my love for you. And the wolf's love for you.' I looked at Lant, at Spark, at Per. 'Everything I feel for each one of you will go into the stone.' My gaze sought out the Fool's, but he was looking past me, into the darkness.

Bee was sitting between Spark and Per. Her hair had grown but it was still short. Golden and curly. I had never seen such hair. My curls and my mother's coloration. My mother. Would I put her into the wolf? Yes. For she had loved me in the time she had me.

'Fitz?'

'Yes?'

'You keep drifting away.' Kettricken looked at me with concern. Bee had wilted over and was asleep by the fire. Someone had put a blanket over her. 'Are you hungry still? Do you want more food?'

I looked down at a bowl with a spoon in it. The taste of beef soup was in my mouth. 'Yes. Yes, please.'

'And then you should sleep. We should all sleep.'

'I'll keep the first watch,' Lant offered.

'I will keep you company,' Spark added.

I finished the soup and someone took the bowl. Soon, I would sleep. But while the taste of the good food was fresh in my mind, I would put it into my wolf.

In the time before dawn, I felt a tug at my sleeve. I'd been putting the roughness on the bottoms of the pads of his feet. Strange to shape something I could neither see nor touch. I looked down at Bee sitting cross-legged beside me. She had an open book before her, and a pot of ink and a brush and a pen, all set out neatly. 'Da, I dreamed of a time when I would sit beside you and you would tell me the tale of your days. I want that now, for I do not think we will have years for you to pass that on to me.'

'I recall that you told me that dream.' I looked around the quarry. 'This is not how I imagined it. I thought I would be an old man, too feeble to write, and that we would sit by a hearth fire in a pleasant chamber, after a long and lovely life together. Is that the book I gave you to write in?'

'No. That one went to the bottom of the bay at Clerres, when Paragon became dragons and we all fell in the water. This is a new one. The one you call Fool gave it to me, along with a book for writing down my dreams. He reads that one, and tries to help me understand them. But this one . . . He has explained how you must put all your memories into your wolf so that he can become a stone wolf, just as Verity is a stone dragon. But as you put them in, if you spoke them aloud, I could write them down. So I would have at least that much of you to keep.'

'What would you have me tell you?' It was hard to stay focused on her. My stone wolf waited for me.

'Everything. Everything you might have told me as I was growing up. What is the first thing you remember?'

Everything I might have told her, had I longer to live. That was a fresh cut of pain. Was it a memory to consider the future we would never have? I considered her question. 'The first thing I remember clearly? I know I have older memories, but I hid them from myself, long ago.' I drew a deep breath. Hiding memories again. Setting the pains and the joys deep into stone. 'The rain had soaked through me. The day was chill and cold. The hand that held mine was hard and callused. His grip was remorseless but not unkind. The cobblestones were icy, and that grip kept me from falling when I slipped. But it also would not let me turn around and run back to my mother.'

She dipped her pen and began to write rapidly. I could not tell if she took down my exact words, and as I began to pour those first memories into the wolf, what she wrote mattered less and less.

Dawn came. Lant and Per followed my directions to the stream and came back with fish. There was bread to go with it, and bacon to cook it in. I felt my strength returning to me as my body finally began to get the sustenance it needed to both rebuild what the parasites were destroying and power me through my carving. They were catching the fish and bringing the firewood. I no longer had to leave my carving at all. It was kind of them and I managed to tell them so, but the more I carved my wolf, the more focus it demanded and the less I cared for any of them.

I knew what was happening to me. It was not the first time that I had poured memories into a stone dragon. Decades ago, I had taken the pain of losing Molly and poured it into Girl-on-a-Dragon. Surrendering that pain to stone had deadened me in a way that was a relief, but there was a darker side to that forgetting. I've seen folk who numbed their pain with strong drink or Smoke or other herbs and always the loss of their pain made them less connected. Less human. And so it was with me.

Every day, I told tales to my little daughter, and every day I gave those same memories to the stone. Sometimes she wept for me as I told her of my days in Regal's dungeons. When I told her that after she was born I was not sure how to love such a peculiar infant, she wept again. Perhaps for her mother, partnered to such a thoughtless man, or perhaps for herself, child to such a man. And the pain that thought gave me, I pushed as well into the stone. It was a relief to have it gone.

Sometimes I laughed as I babbled to her of pranks that Hands and I had played, and sometimes I sang aloud as I told her of learning 'Crossfire's Coterie' from a wandering minstrel. Nighteyes and I had merged more closely than ever into one being, so that it was rare to hear his thoughts as something other than my own. And I told his memories as well, of kills and fights and sleeping by the fire. She asked me when I had first met the Fool, and that tale led to another and another and another, all the stories of how my life had intersected and twined with his. So much of his life was mine and so much of mine was his.

I worked and all about me, the life of the camp went on. Lant and Per hunted and fished, Spark hauled water and prepared the herb teas that kept my pains at bay. Some of the sores on my back opened. It was a distraction when Kettricken insisted on pouring warmed water down my back and using a handful of moss to scrub out the tiny mites that writhed in the sores. When I objected, she asked, 'Would it be better if they ate you alive before your wolf was done?' And then I saw the sense of what she did. She wore gloves and burned them in the fire afterward.

Sometimes, when I had to stop working to eat or to drink, I saw the sadness in their faces. I felt guilt at the pain I gave them. And shame. And those things became emotions that I could put into my wolf.

Several days after the Fool and Bee had arrived, others came. They rode horses into our camp, and brought with them more food. Bread and cheese and wine, once so simple, were now things to be savoured before my memories of them went into the stone. That evening, I became aware of who they were. I looked into Nettle's grieved and shocked eyes. The Skill-coterie who had assisted her in coming set up their own tents at a short distance from ours. They spoke about me and around me and sometimes to me, but it was hard to steal my awareness from my task. Nettle spoke harshly to Bee and Spark and the Fool and Lant. I considered intervening, but I had the wolf to think of. There was no time or emotion to spare for other things.

Nettle brought me food that evening—wonderful camp-bread baked in the fire's embers and sharing its fragrance with the evening sky, sour apples toasted to a soft tang, and a slice from a smoked ham. I ate, savouring every bite twice, for I knew I would put each delightful sensation into my wolf. Nettle kept asking me if I would allow a Skilled healer to touch me.

'It's dangerous,' I warned the waiting man. 'Not only that you may somehow transfer some of the parasites to yourself, but also that I may accidentally take something of yours for my wolf.'

The healer made a very cautious inspection of my infested wounds and attempted to see what might be happening inside me. He was a competent and plainspoken man. 'The damage is extensive. In his weakened state, any herb we give him to try to kill the parasites would also kill him.'

Bee spoke up. 'Cannot the coterie use the Skill to tell the parasites to be dead?'

The healer looked shocked. Then thoughtful. 'If the creatures had minds at all, perhaps a very powerful Skill-user could suggest to them that their hearts stop beating. If they have hearts . . . No. I am sorry, child. There are such multitudes of them infesting your father that, even if we could Skill death to them, by the time we had killed a quarter of them, the rest would have bred enough to replace those we killed. Lord Chance has told us of seeing eggs and maggots in your father's sores. They are living in him like wood ants in a fallen log. I tell you this plainly. Prince FitzChivalry is going to die. In his weakened state, I am not sure we can even take him back to Buckkeep Castle. Our best and kindest course might be to make him as comfortable as we can here. And offer him an end that begins with a deep sleep instead of what I fear is to come.'

Bee lowered her face into her hands. I saw Per put his arm around her, and saw also the unease on Nettle's face.

'I will be going into the stone,' I announced. 'I am not sure that is the same as dying.'

'It's close enough. You'll be gone,' Nettle said bitterly.

'And not for the first time,' I replied.

'Oh, that is so true,' she said, and the impact of her words was like an arrow to my chest.

I tried to clear my throat and realized there were no words that I could speak. Spark poured something into a cup and Lant passed it to me. I drank it. Some kind of spirit and a mixture of herbs. 'What is in this?' I asked when it was gone.

'Carryme. Valerian. Some willowbark. A few other herbs that Nettle's healer brought.'

'As long as they aren't the herbs that will make me sleep my way into death. I do not desire that, at all. I must be awake and aware when I go into the wolf. As Verity was.' I shook my head. 'Let no one seek to drug me insensible to save me pain. Keep me awake.'

I looked over at my younger daughter. Per was standing behind her. He would never be Tallestman, but he would be broad, with the shoulders for an axe. Time to think of these things while I still could. Already the stone was calling to me. It was hard to keep my eyes focused on the people here. I drew a breath and squared my shoulders. Get this task done while I could. I looked at Nettle.

'I have some directives regarding my younger daughter, Bee. I charge you, Nettle, and you, Fool, and you, Lant and you, my lovely queen Kettricken, to be sure that they are carried out.' I had said something wrong. I saw it in Nettle's face. Too late. I had never been good at speeches. And this one had not been planned. 'I would ask my old friend Riddle as well, but he is a wiser man than I, and has remained with his daughter to watch over her.' I forced myself to meet Nettle's eyes. 'Would that I had done so. Not once, but twice over. I felt the decision was not mine, but I now take responsibility for it. My daughters, I am sorry. I should have stayed with both of you.' That pang of guilt was still sharp. No matter how often I put it into the stone wolf, when I thought of my failure, it still cut me. The Fool was staring at me. He shared that guilt. I could not mend what he must feel.

I reined my thoughts back to the task at hand. 'Per. Stand forth.'

The boy came, wide-eyed, to stand before me. No. Not a boy. I'd taken that from him. I'd taken him from a stableboy to a young man who could and had killed—for my sake and Bee's. I could trust him. 'I wish you to remain at Bee's side and serve her until the end of your days, or until one or both of you wish to be freed of this connection. Until then, I desire that no one part the two of you. And I wish you to be educated alongside her. In every discipline. Language. History. And for her to learn the sword and other weapons alongside you. I have nothing of my own to give you in reward for your service. Every valuable thing I ever owned, I've lost along the way. Except . . . wait.' I groped at the ragged collar of my shirt. It was there, as it always was.

It took me a time to unfasten it. I looked at it on my palm. The little fox looked up at me with sparkling eyes. I looked at Kettricken. 'Would you give this to the boy, please? As once you gave it to me?'

'After all these years, you still—' She choked, and held out her hand. I tipped it into her palm. She looked at Per. 'Young man. What is your full name?'

'My lady, I am Perseverance of Withywoods. Son of Tallerman, grandson of Tallman.' Instinct made him kneel. He bent his head, baring the back of his neck to her.

'Come closer,' she bade him, and he rose to do so. I saw now that her fingers were becoming knotted and knuckly. But she made no complaint as she pinned the little silver fox carefully to his Buck-blue jerkin. 'Serve her well and let nothing but death part you from that duty.'

'I shall.'

A moment of stillness. I broke it. 'Nettle, my dear. Please ask Riddle to see to Per's training. He will know exactly what he needs to be taught.'

'I will,' she said quietly.

'I have nothing to give you,' I told her. 'Nothing for you and nothing for Bee. There are a few things of your mother's at Withywoods in the chest at the foot of my bed. You and she must share them out. Oh. And Verity's sword. There is that, but I am sure Dutiful will want it.' Once, we had thought to trade our father's swords, but after a few years, we had traded back. Now he would have both. One for each of his sons.

I looked at Lant and Spark and tried for a smile. 'I suddenly realize that I'm a poor man. Nothing to bequeath to anyone. I dare not even clasp wrists with you a final time.'

'You wrote a letter to my father. It was all I could ever have desired from you,' Lant said quietly.

I looked at Nettle. 'You will provide for Spark?'

She looked directly at the girl. 'She does not excel at following orders,' she said drily. 'I do not know how much I can trust her.'

'Can she do needlework?' Kettricken asked suddenly.

Spark looked dismayed, but quietly replied, 'Embroidery and crochet. Yes, my lady.'

'I recall how well Patience was served by Lacey. Young woman, I am getting older. I could use a youngster in my service. At Buckkeep, and in the Mountains. Would you wish to accompany me to the Mountain Kingdom?'

Spark's eyes flickered a glance at Lant. He lowered his eyes and said nothing. 'I have heard of Lady Patience's Lacey. Yes, my lady. I believe I could serve you in a similar capacity.'

There was a sadness there. I should have remembered something about it. But the itching, burning pains inside me and the unfinished wolf tugged and worried at my thoughts. It was so hard to focus. But there was something important left to do.

I had only one bequest left. 'Bee. In all things, and in a better way than I ever was, the Fool will act as father to you. Is that acceptable?'

'But Riddle—' Nettle began, but Bee interrupted. 'Riddle has a daughter. As do you, my sister. I would that you were my sister and Riddle my elder brother rather than you become my parents.' She smiled and it was almost real. 'And recall that I have my brother Hap Gladheart also to look over me.' She brought her gaze back to me and spoke earnestly. 'And I have had a father. You were my father, and I will go on without one now. You need not worry for me, Da. In your own way, you have well provided for me.'

'In my own way,' I conceded. Pain. Bitter disappointment in myself. Something more to put into the wolf.

Are we finished? I asked the wolf.

I believe so. But they may not be finished with us.

And they were not. I went back to the wolf, muttering my tale while Bee sat near me and noted it all down. Sometimes, I saw, it was not words but a painting or an ink sketch. She did not ask questions but simply accepted the things I told her about myself and my days. I noticed her head drooping lower over her book. The next time I looked at her, she was on her side, curled around her book. Her pen had fallen from her hand and she had not stoppered her ink. But I was putting into the wolf a picnic with Molly and I could not pause.

'Fitz,' said the Fool.

I looked down at him. He had the ink-bottle in his hand and had pushed the stopper in. I had not seen or heard him come near. I saw him set the ink to one side. He drew the book out from under Bee's hand, and settled a blanket over her. He sat down cross-legged, his back straight, and opened the book on his lap. He began to page through it.

'Does she know you do that?' I asked.

'She allows it, but not graciously. It is something I feel I must do, Fitz, for she reveals very little of herself to anyone. She told me earlier today that you had put a great many memories of me into the wolf, and that she was writing them down as well. I found that a bit alarming.'

I took my hands from the wolf and sat down beside him. It was difficult to do. I folded my hands in my lap, Silver over Silver. So bony. Absently I stroked my hand, whetting one against the other, repairing the damage to the flesh and tendons beneath the Silver. I could do that. At a cost. He watched me do it. 'Cannot you do that with your whole body?'

'It costs me to do this. Flesh and strength from elsewhere. And already they attack me again. But I need my hands, and so I do it.'

He turned a page, smiled and looked up at me. 'She has written down the names of the dogs that were under the table with you the first time you saw me. You remembered all their names?'

'They were my friends. Do you recall your friends' names?'

'I do,' he said quietly. He turned a few more pages, reading swiftly, sometimes smiling, sometimes pensive. He scowled at one page, and then closed the book gently. 'Fitz, I do not think I am the best person to be Bee's father.'

'Neither was I. But that is how things turned out.'

He almost smiled. 'True. She is mine. And isn't. For she doesn't want to be. You heard what she said. She would rather go on with no father than have me.'

'She isn't old enough to know what is best for her.'

'Are you sure of that?'

I paused to think. 'No. But who else should I ask?'

It was his turn to pause. 'Perhaps no one. Or Lant?'

'Lant's life is complicated and likely to become more so.'

'Hap?'

'Hap will be there for her, but as her elder brother.'

'Chivalry or one of Molly's other boys?'

'If they were here, I might. But they are not, and they have no concept of what she has gone through. You do. Are you asking me to release you from being her father? Because I cannot, you know. Some duties cannot be shed.'

'I know,' he said quietly.

I felt a vague tug of alarm. 'There is something else you'd rather be doing than staying with Bee? Something you feel called to do?' Would he leave her as he had left me?

'Yes. But in this, I take your wishes more seriously than my own.' He blinked back tears. 'I have made far too many decisions for both of us. Now it is time for me to accept one of yours, no matter how difficult it is for me. As you so often did.' He leaned forward suddenly and put his hand on a paw. 'I give you how startled you looked in the moment that King Shrewd saw you there, eating scraps with the dogs.' After a moment, he drew his hand back from the stone wolf and shook his head as if dashing water away. 'I'd forgotten what it felt like. Giving life to stone.' He clasped his hands on Bee's book and looked down at it as he said, 'There is much more I could give you for your wolf. If you wished me to.'

I recalled something that Nighteyes had once said to me. 'I have no desire to see Bee fathered by a Forged One. That is what you would be if you gave up too much of yourself to this stone. Save your memories and feelings for yourself, Fool. Putting some of yourself in stone is not a good idea.'

'It has been many a day since I had a good idea,' he replied. He slid the book under Bee's hand and quietly left my shelter.

* * *

One night, Kettricken came to me. Despite all my warnings, she set her hand on my shoulder. 'Stop that,' she said. 'You are tearing your back to shreds.'

The itching had become an unbearable distraction, and I had picked up a piece of firewood to scratch my back. She took it from my hand and tossed it into the fire. I realized it was very late and the others were all sleeping in their shelters. 'Who has the watch?' I asked her.

'Spark. And Lant is keeping her company.' She spoke without judgment. I could not see either of them. Bee was curled in her blankets nearby. She had pulled a corner up over her face to keep the gnats at bay, and pulled her book in under the covers with her. I looked up. Kettricken was gone.

Time had become so peculiar. It moved in jerks and slides now. And then Kettricken was back with a pot of something in her hand. She crouched down behind me and I heard her knees crackle. 'In the Mountains, sometimes in winter the children had lice. Grease smothers them. I brought this with me, thinking perhaps you could be saved. Now, it may at least ease the itching.'

'Don't touch them!' I warned her, but she had a small scoop like a little spoon.

There were many pustules on my back, and she had me turn toward the fire and take my shirt off. The shirt surprised me. It was intact, a nice shirt. When had they put that on me?

'Keep still,' she told me, and she dabbed a touch on each sore. It was grease, goose or bear, with some fragrant herbs mixed in. Mint. Mint keeps many pests at bay. With each touch, the itching eased. She spoke in a low voice as she worked. 'I want to go with you. I truly do. But there is Bee to think of. And we have another grandchild on the way. Elliania hopes so for a girl, but I will be content with whatever we get. Think on it, Fitz! If she is a girl, she will be a narcheska, and help secure our continuing peace with the OutIslands. And the Mountain Kingdom will be formally accepting Integrity as their Sacrifice and duke. That is part of why I will be going there. To ease that transition.' She caught her breath and said, 'Do you recall when we first met in the Mountains? How I tried to poison you because I thought you had come to kill my brother?'

'I do.' Something warm fell on my bare shoulder. A tear. 'Do you weep because you wish you had succeeded?' I asked her, and succeeded in wringing a hiccupped laugh from her.

'Oh, Fitz, the changes we wrought in the world. I do wish I were going with you.'

I'd never even considered such an idea. 'On the way here . . . I lingered in the Skill-pillars. I am not sure how long. I do not remember it, but Nighteyes claimed that Verity spoke to me there. He said I would have to bid my child farewell and trust that others would raise her well. Just as he had to do.'

'Oh.' That was all she said at first. Then she added, 'I promise. I will take her as my own. I have always wanted such a child!'

I was startled at her offer. 'But I have already asked the Fool to take her. Though it is hard for me to imagine him as anyone's father.'

She made an amused sound. 'That is true. I expect he will make his own decision in that regard. It surprises me that he has not already.' Then she leaned forward and fearlessly kissed my cheek. 'In case it is my last opportunity,' she explained. 'Tomorrow, I am taking Spark with me to go visit Verity-as-Dragon. Try not to leave before I get back.'

I nodded. She rose with creaking knees. I listened to the swishing of her skirts as she walked away. Then I leaned forward and carefully put the kiss into the wolf. I knew it was actually his.

'I would just like to finish this,' I said to the Fool. I stroked the wolf's rough stone coat. He still had no colour. The fur of his tail looked lumpy to me. His eyes needed work, and his bared teeth. The tendons in his hind legs. I closed my eyes. I needed to stop numbering what was missing.

It was relatively quiet now. Dark had come and the cool of the Mountains night was descending. The shelter helped but the chill still reached in. I was sitting in the open front of it, leaning back on my wolf. I felt as if I must always be touching him now. For safety.

The Fool was sitting on the ground next to me, hugging his knees and drinking a cup of tea. He set it down carefully. 'You did not really think you would be allowed to die privately, did you?' He flapped a long, narrow hand at the encampment that had sprung up in the quarry. There were multiple campfires and tents softly billowing in the night breeze. At the forest's edge, someone kept watch on the picketed horses. How many people? I could not guess. More than thirty. More had arrived today. All come to watch me die.

Dutiful had come with his Skill-coterie. Over their mother's objections, both Integrity and Prosper had come as well. Shun had wanted to come but still had a terrible fear of Skill-pillars. Hap had talked them into bringing him, and was now lying in a tent feeling disoriented and nauseated. He had even suggested he might ride a horse home through the Mountain Kingdom rather than brave a Skill-pillar again. Integrity had liked the idea and proposed to accompany him 'since I am soon bound for the Mountain Kingdom anyway'. Dutiful was uncertain. They were waiting for Kettricken to return from visiting Verity-as-Dragon to discuss it. I could sense Dutiful's impatience. His wife would soon be brought to bed with their child. He should be there, not here to watch me die. Earlier I had promised, 'I will go into the wolf as soon as I can. For now, you should just go home. There is nothing you can do here. Be with the woman you love, while you can.'

He had looked troubled, but had not left yet.

I did not want to ponder any of it. My body was beginning to feel like a rickety shed on a sea cliff's edge. I still ate but there was no pleasure in it. My gums were bleeding and my nose was continually crusted with blood. The world tasted and smelled like blood. And I itched everywhere, inside and out, as new pustules erupted. I had a terrible itch in the back of my throat, and one high inside my nose. They were maddening. I felt regret for the sturdy body I had taken for granted. With my fingers and thumb, I worked a lump from Nighteyes' tail.

'What did Dutiful say to you?' the Fool asked.

'The usual. He promised to care for Nettle and Bee. He said he would miss me. That he wished I could see his third child born. Fool, I know that what he says is so important to him. It should be to me. I know that I loved him and his boys. But . . . there is not enough left of me to feel those things.' I shook my weary head. 'All of the memories that kept those connections, the wolf has taken. I fear I hurt him. I wish he would just go home and take his coterie with him.'

He nodded slowly and took another sip of his tea. 'So it was with Verity at the end of his days. It was hard to reach him. Did that hurt you?'

'Yes. But I understood.'

'And so does Dutiful. And Kettricken.' He looked away from me. 'So do we all.'

He lifted his gloved hand and considered it. The first time he had silvered his fingers, it had been an accident. He had been acting as Verity's manservant and had accidentally touched his silvered hands. 'Fitz,' he said suddenly. 'Is there enough of you to fill this wolf?'

I considered my wolf. It was a small block of memory-stone compared to what Verity had chosen, but much larger than a real wolf. The top of his shoulders was level with my chest. But somehow the size of the stone did not seem related to how much I needed to fill it. 'I think so. I won't know until I go into him.'

'When will that be?'

I scratched the back of my neck. My nails came back bloody. I wiped them on my thigh. 'When I have no more to give him, I suppose. Or when I am so close to dying that I must go.'

'Oh, Fitz,' he said mournfully, as if it were the first time he had considered the idea.

'It will all be for the best,' I told him, and tried to believe it. 'Nighteyes will be a wolf again. As will I. And Bee will have you to watch over her and—'

'She doesn't like me, I fear.'

'There have been many times when Nettle or Hap disliked me, Fool.'

'I might feel better if she disliked me. I don't think she feels much one way or the other.' In a lower voice he added, 'I was so sure that she would love me, as I love her. I thought it would just happen, once we were near each other. It has not.'

'Being loved by your children isn't really what being a parent is about.'

'I loved my parents. I loved them so terribly much.'

'I have no basis of comparison,' I pointed out to him quietly.

'You had Burrich.'

'Oh, yes. I had Burrich.' I laughed grimly. 'And eventually, we realized we loved one another. But it took some years.'

'Years,' he repeated dolefully.

'Be patient,' I counselled him. I touched one of the wolf's toenails. They were smooth. That wasn't right. They should be ridged. I remembered the smell of a buck's blood on a winter dawn, and how it had clotted into tiny pink balls in the ice. I corrected the toenail.

'Fitz?'

'Yes?'

'You were gone again.'

'I was,' I admitted.

'Have you put much of me into him?'

I thought about it. 'I put in your room in the tower at Buckkeep, the time I climbed those broken stairs, and you were not there and I stared around in surprise at what I found. I put in the day we had the water fight in the stream, not so far from here. And that horrid song you sang to me to embarrass me in the halls of Buckkeep. And Ratsy. Ratsy is in there. And I put in treating your wounds the day Regal's thugs put a bag over your head and beat you. And you carrying me on your back through the snow, when you did not know me.' I smiled. 'I know what else. I put in how you looked at me that time King Shrewd gave me his pin. I was under the table and there had been a feast. The keep dogs and I were sharing all the leftovers. And then Shrewd came in, with Regal. And you.'

An uncertain smile had dawned on his face. 'So you will remember me. When you are a stone wolf.'

'We will remember you, Nighteyes and I.'

He sighed. 'Well. There is that.'

I had to cough. I turned my head aside from him and coughed. Blood spattered the wolf, and just for an instant, before it sank in, I saw his colours as they would be. I coughed again, drew breath and coughed some more. I put my arm on the wolf and leaned my forehead on it as I coughed. If I must cough blood, let not a drop be wasted. When I could finally draw a wheezing breath, my nose was bleeding.

Not long now, Nighteyes whispered.

'Not long now,' I agreed.

It had been quiet for a time. Then the Fool spoke beside me. 'Fitz. I've brought you something. It's cold tea. With valerian in it. And carryme.'

I sipped it. 'There's not enough carryme in there to do anything. I need more.'

'I don't dare make it stronger than it is.'

'I don't care what you dare. Add more carryme!'

He looked shocked and for a moment, I jolted back to being Fitz as I once was. 'Fool, I'm so sorry. But they are gnawing on every part of me, inside and out. I itch in places I can never scratch. I feel them rattle in my lungs when I draw breath. The inside of my throat is raw and all I can taste is blood.'

He said nothing but took the cup away. I felt ashamed of myself. I put it into the wolf, enough to define the lift of his lip. I startled when the Fool spoke. 'Careful. It's hot now. I had to use hot water to make the carryme blend.'

'Thank you.' I took it from him and drained it. The hot tea mixed with the blood in my mouth. I swallowed it. He took the cup quickly from my shaky hand.

'Fool. What were we?' It wasn't an idle question. I needed to know it. I needed to finally understand it to put it in the wolf.

'I don't know.' His reply was guarded. 'Friends. But also Prophet and Catalyst. And in that relationship, I did use you, Fitz. You know it and I know it. I've told you how sorry I was to do it. I hope you believe that. And that you can forgive me.'

His words were so intense, but that wasn't what I wanted to talk about. I waved them away. 'Yes, yes. But there was something else there. Always. You were dead, and I called you back. For that moment, when we returned to our proper bodies, as we passed one another, we . . .'

We were one thing. Whole.

He was waiting for me to continue. It seemed ridiculous that he could not hear the wolf. 'We were one thing. A whole thing. You and I and Nighteyes. I felt a strange sort of peace. As if all the parts of me were finally in one place. All the missing bits that would make me a complete . . . thing.' I shook my head. 'Words don't reach that far.'

He set his gloved hand on my sleeved arm. The layers of fabric deadened that touch but it still sang in me. It was not the stunning touch he had shared with me once in Verity's Skill-tower. I recalled that well. I'd been left huddled in a ball, for it had been too much, too overwhelming to know, so completely, another living entity. Nighteyes and I, we were simple creatures and our bonding was a simple thing. The Fool was complex, full of secrets and shadows and convoluted ideas. Even now, insulated from it, I felt that unfurling landscape of his being. It was endless, reaching to a distant horizon. But in some way, I knew it. Owned it. Had created it.

He lifted his hand.

'Did you feel that?' I asked him.

He smiled sadly. 'Fitz, I have never needed to touch you to feel that. It was always there. No limits.'

Some part of me knew that was important. That once it would have mattered terribly to me. I tried to find words. 'I will put that in my wolf,' I said, and he turned sadly away from me.

'Da?'

I tried to lift my head.

'He's still alive,' someone said in a wondering voice and someone else shushed him.

'I brought you tea. There's a strong painkiller in it. Do you want it?'

'Gods, yes!' That was what I meant to say. I had draped myself over my wolf. I had feared I would die in the night and worried that if I were unconscious I could not slip away into him. I opened my eyes and saw the world through a pink sheen. Blood in my eyes. Like the messenger. I blinked and my vision cleared slightly. Nettle was there. Bee was beside her. Nettle held a cup to my lips. She tipped it and liquid lapped against my mouth. I sucked some in and tried to swallow. Some went down. Some ran down my chin.

I looked beyond her. Kettricken, weeping. Dutiful had his arm around her. His sons were with him. The Fool and Lant, Spark and Per. And beyond them the ranks of the curious. The Skill-coteries and those who had come with them. All gathered to watch my final spectacle. I would do at last what the Witted had long been rumoured able to do. I would transform into a wolf.

It reminded me of my final days in Regal's dungeon. They had tormented me there, trying to force me to reveal my Witted nature so they could justify killing me.

Was this so different?

I wished they would all go away.

Except the Fool. I wished he would join me. Somehow, I had always thought he would join me. Now, I could not recall why. Perhaps I had buried that in the stone.

I heard music. It was strange. I cast my eyes to one side and saw Hap with a strange stringed instrument. He played a handful of notes and then began to softly sing 'Crossfire's Coterie'. I had taught him that, years ago. For a time, I was carried away by the music. I recalled teaching him the song, and then how he had sung it with Starling. I recalled the minstrel who had taught it to me. I let the memories seep into the wolf, and I felt them lose their colour and vibrancy within me. Hap's song became only a song. Hap became only a singer.

I was dying. And I had never been enough for anything.

It's time to ask him. Or time to let go.

It's not the sort of thing one asks of a friend. He hasn't offered, and I will not ask it. I will not tear him that way. I am trying to let go. I don't know how.

Do not you recall how you shed your body in Regal's dungeon?

That was long ago. Then, I feared to live and face what they would do to me. Now I fear to die. I fear that we will simply stop, like a bubble popping.

We may. But this is excruciating.

Better than being bored to death.

I do not think so. Why don't you ask him?

Because I already asked him to look after Bee.

That one needs little looking after.

I'm letting go. Right now. I'm letting go.

But I could not.

FORTY-NINE

Lies and Truths

I have endeavoured to record the events of my father's life as he has put them into his wolf-dragon. I can tell that when I am near and writing, he selects what he will share with great caution. I accept that he must have many memories that are too private to share with his daughter.

Today he spoke mostly of his times with the one he calls the Fool. It is a ridiculous name, but perhaps if my name were Beloved, I would consider Fool an improvement. Whatever were his parents thinking? Did they truly imagine everyone he ever encountered would wish to call him Beloved?

I have observed a thing. When my father speaks of my mother, he is absolutely confident that she loved him. I recall my mother well. She could be prickly and exacting, critical and demanding. But she was like that in the confidence that they shared a love that could withstand such things. Even her angers at him were usually founded on her taking offence that he could doubt her at all. That comes through when he speaks of her.

But when he speaks of his long and deep friendship with the Fool, there is always an element of hesitation. Of doubt. A mocking song, a flash of anger, and my father would feel the bewilderment of one who is rebuffed and cannot decide how deep the rebuke goes. I see a Catalyst that was used by his Prophet, and used ruthlessly. Can one do so to one he loves? That, I think, is the question my father ponders now. My father gave, and yet often felt that what he gave was not considered sufficient, that the Fool always desired more of him, and that what he desired was beyond what my father could give. And when the Fool left and seemingly never even glanced back, that was a dagger blow to my father that never fully healed.

It changed what he thought their relationship was. When the Fool returned so abruptly to my father's life, my father never trusted his full weight to that friendship. He always wondered if the Fool might once more use him for what he needed, and then leave him alone again.

And apparently he has.

Bee Farseer's journal

'They should leave,' I whispered to Nettle. 'He's our father. I don't think he'd want even us seeing him like this.' I didn't want to see my father like this, draped on the stone wolf like laundry drying on a fence. He looked terrible, a patchwork man of smooth silver and worm-eaten flesh. He smelled worse than he looked. The clean robe we'd put on him yesterday was now soiled with spilled tea and other waste. Lines of crusted dried blood stretched from his ears down his neck. Bloody saliva collected at one corner of his mouth. Yet the silver half of his face was smooth and sleek, unlined, a reminder of the man he'd been so recently.

Last night I had watched a grim-faced Nettle bathe the parts of his face that were flesh. He had tried to object, but she had insisted and he'd been too weak to fight her off. She'd been careful, dipping the cloth and folding the soiled part away from her, never directly touching his skin. Little writhing creatures had come away from his sores. She had thrown the cloths into the fire.

'They don't care for him. They simply want to be here if the wolf comes to life.'

'I know that. They know that. Da knows that.' She shook her head. 'It doesn't matter.'

'It would matter to me. I would want to die privately. Not like that.'

'He's a Farseer. Royalty. Nothing is private. Learn that now, Bee. Kettricken has it right. Servants to all, and they take from us what they need. Or want.'

'You should go home to your baby.'

'If that decision were solely mine, I would. I miss her and Riddle terribly. But I cannot be seen to leave my father and sister now, in these circumstances. Do you understand?' She looked at me with my mother's eyes. 'I'm not doing this to you, Bee. I will try to protect you from it. But to protect you, I must ask that you be as unremarkable as possible. If you disobey me, if you are defiant or wild, all eyes will be drawn to you. Appear to be mild and uninteresting, and you may have a little bit of a life that is all yours.' She gave me a tired smile. 'Even if your sister will always know you are anything but mild and uninteresting.'

'Oh.' I didn't say that I wished someone had told me all this before I'd made it so difficult for her. I did take her hand.

'Nice walls,' she said. 'Thick taught you well.'

I nodded.

The day grew brighter. The drapery of my father's shelter had been tied open to let in the early warmth of the day, and to let out the smell of death. I sat by his wolf, clutching the book I'd been keeping of his memories. It had been two days since he'd spoken coherently enough for me to understand him. But still I'd stayed beside him, adding illustrations to the memories he had spoken aloud.

Nettle had explained to me what little she knew of the process. Once, it seemed, ageing coteries from the Six Duchies had made their way here, to carve dragons and go into them. They had learned the custom from the Elderlings. It offered one a limited immortality. 'The vitality of the stone does not seem to last long. Verity fought as a dragon until the Red Ships were defeated. Da was able to rouse the sleeping dragons and win them to Verity's cause, but how he did that has never been fully discovered. Some of the coteries I have founded have said that, when they are aged, perhaps they will attempt this feat. Da once told me that the old children's song "Six Wisemen came to Jhaampe-town" is actually about a coterie going up into the Mountains to carve their dragon.'

'Did they all die in such an ugly and painful way?'

'I do not think so. But any records of how it was done were lost when Regal sold off the Skill-scroll library. I hope we may find information in the memory-cubes from Aslevjal. But as yet, we have not.'

I took no comfort from anything she had told me. My father's worm-ridden body was on display like that of a caged criminal in a Chalcedean town. If die he must, I wanted him to do it in a comfortable bed in a well-appointed chamber. Or to be like my mother, and simply fall down in the midst of doing something he loved to do. I wanted to be able to take his hand and offer him comfort. I sighed and shifted my feet.

'You do not have to watch this. I can ask one of my Skill-users to take you back to Buckkeep Castle.'

'You have already explained to me why I cannot.'

'True.'

Night fell and we built up the fire, and he still had not died. I felt I might die of this before he did. There was a terrible tension in the air. We wanted him to die now, and hated that we wanted that.

His real family, as I thought of us, sat in a tight circle by the fire, our backs to the quarry. 'Can we help him?' Per asked suddenly. 'Could each of us put something into his wolf?' He told the first lie I'd ever heard from him. 'I'm not afraid to try it.'

He stood up. 'Per!' Nettle warned him but he slapped his hand onto the wolf. 'I don't know how to do this. But I'll give you my mother forgetting me and turning me from her door. I don't need that memory. I don't need to feel that.'

My father's human hand twitched slightly. Per stood, waiting. Then he lifted his hand. 'I don't think anything happened,' he admitted.

'Don't feel bad,' Nettle told him. 'I think you must have a bit of the Skill to be able to do it. But I think it's a good idea. And he's in no position to prevent us from doing it.' She stood, graceful as she always was. She put her hand on the wolf's muzzle. 'Dream Wolf, take something sweet from my memories of you.' She did not say what it was, but I could tell by how she stood that she gave him something.

When she sat down, Lant stood. 'I want to try,' he said. 'I'd like him to take my first meeting with him. I was terrified.' He set his hand to the wolf's shoulder. He stood for a very long time. Then he put his finger on my father's fleshly hand. 'You take it, Fitz,' he said, and perhaps he did.

Spark tried but failed. Kettricken gave a small smile. 'I already gave him what I wished him to put into our wolf,' she said. She left us all wondering.

'No,' Hap said. 'I'm keeping every memory and emotion I have about him. I need them. How else do you think minstrels make up songs? He knows that. He wouldn't want me to give them up.'

Dutiful stood, and motioned his two sons back. 'Lads, you need to hold tight what little you knew of him. But I have something. There was a night we fought, and I hated him. I've always regretted that. Perhaps it will be useful now.'

When he was finished, he wiped tears from his cheeks and sat down. I glowered at the Fool. For he was the Fool now, all of Lord Chance and Lady Amber and Lord Golden scraped away by sorrow. He was no one's Beloved now. He was a sad little man, a broken jester. But he did not stand and say he would give anything to my father. I was very still. I needed a strategy, for I knew they would drag me away before I could succeed. I hung my head as if I feared to try, and after a moment, people shifted and Spark offered to bring tea for us all.

'And some cool water,' Kettricken requested. 'I'd like to try to at least moisten his mouth. He looks so uncomfortable.'

Not now. I must not do it while there were onlookers. They were accustomed to me sleeping near my father's wolf. Some of them, at least, would fall asleep. Don't die just yet, I thought fiercely at my father. I dared not Skill the thought, and I kept my walls tight lest Nettle hear what I intended.

Night had never deepened so slowly. We shared tea, and Kettricken wiped my father's broken lips with a wet cloth. His eyes were closed and likely to remain so. His bony back rose and fell with his slow breaths. Spark persuaded Kettricken to lie down and sleep. Then she and Lant went to the upper lip of the quarry to keep watch. Dutiful and Nettle had withdrawn a small distance to have an intense conversation. The princes sat back to back, leaning on one another and drowsing. Hap sat at a distance, his fingers wandering on the strings of his instrument. I knew he played his memories and I wondered if the sound could sink into the wolf.

I curled up and pretended to sleep. After a very long time, I opened my eyes. All quiet. I edged closer to the wolf, moving as if I shifted in my sleep. I slid my hand along the gritty stone toward his leg. As I lifted my hand and opened my fingers to clutch the wolf's leg, the Fool spoke. 'Bee, don't do it. You know I can't allow it.'

He did not leap to stop me but leaned forward to put two more pieces of wood on the fire. I drew my hand back a little. 'Someone has to do it,' I told him. 'He's holding on, experiencing the pain so he has something more to put into the stone. Because he doesn't have enough to fill it.'

'He would not want you to pour yourself into his wolf!'

I stared at him, refusing to look away from his eyes. I knew the most terrible truth. My father would not want me to join him in the stone. He would want his Fool. I nearly said the words aloud. Nearly. Instead I asked a question. 'Why don't you go, then?'

I wanted to hear him say that he wanted to live, that he had important things still to do with his life. That he was afraid. Instead he said very calmly, 'We both know why, Bee. You wrote it, and he said as much to me. It's his decision to make, and finally it's his own decision. Your dreams spoke of it. You wrote it all down for me to read. A black-and-white rat that runs away from him. His final letter to me saying that he wished I'd never come back, wished that he could reach his own decisions without me. That he knew how I had used him, so very many times.' He took a sudden gasping breath and covered his face. A terrible sob shook him. 'If he ever wanted vengeance on me for all I did, he has it now. This is the worst thing he could do to me. Now I know how it feels to be left behind. As I left him.'

What had I done?

Old words came into my mind. I'd heard them from my father, read them, heard them from others. 'Never do a thing until you consider what you can't do once you've done it.'

Slowly he lifted his face. 'Not a perfect quote, but close.' He looked ill and dwindled. '"Don't do what you can't undo, until you've considered what you can't do once you've done it." The words I dreamed so long ago. The words I came so far to say to King Shrewd, so that he would not let Prince Regal kill Chivalry's bastard. I knew if I could but say those words to him, I could keep Fitz alive. The first time.' He shook his head. 'The first time of many that I intervened, to push him through a tiny hole in his fate. To keep him alive, to be a lever I could use to alter how the future might unfold.'

And the world re-ordered itself around me. I spoke each word carefully. 'You are so stupid.'

Astonishment broke through his pain.

Could I still undo what I had done? So that he could do what he should? 'I lied!' I spat my whisper at him. 'I knew you read my journal. I knew you read my dreams. I wrote there what I thought would hurt you most! I lied to hurt you. For letting him be dead while you lived. For being loved by him more than he loved me!' I took a breath. 'He loved you more than he ever loved any of the rest of us!'

'What?' His mouth hung open after that word, his eyes wide. He made a stupid face of astonishment.

As if he hadn't always known he was loved the best. That he was the Beloved.

'Stupid again! Asking stupid questions. Go with him. Go now. It's you he wants, not me. Go!'

When had my voice risen to a shout? I did not know, I did not care. Let it be a spectacle, let all the camp be roused and folk stare at me. For that was what was happening. Dutiful had come to his feet, a sword in his hand, looking around for an enemy. They were all half-awake, roused by my shouts. Hap was staring with his mouth hanging open, Nettle's hands clutched her face in horror at the truth I had shouted.

And my father lifted a hand. His face was so ravaged, it was like looking at death itself. Except for the smooth, silvered part of it. By creeping degrees, his human hand lifted. He turned it over, showing a bloody palm. His cracked lips moved.

Beloved.

He could not say the word, but I knew it.

So did his Fool.

He rose, the blanket that had draped his shoulders falling to the earth. He pulled the glove from his hand and let it fall. He walked uncertainly, like a puppet with his strings pulled by an apprentice puppeteer. He reached my father. So tenderly, he set his hand into my father's. Then he leaned down until he lay upon the wolf, his face turned to my father's face. He put his arm across my father's bony back. He drew him close and then set his silver fingers to the wolf.

For a moment, all was still. Then I saw Beloved's fingers stir the soft fur of the wolf's back. The firelit bodies of my father and Beloved softened and merged. I felt something I could not describe. Like the whoosh of air when a door opens, and then closes again, but it was in the Skill-current, and so strong that I saw Nettle flinch at it, too. Briefer than an instant, I saw light striate out from them. A nexus, a node on the path of fate. Then it was finished. Something finally complete, as it should have been.

Their colours dimmed and the wolf's eyes gleamed. It was slow and it was sudden, that they were gone and only the wolf remained. The snarl faded. The wolf's ears pricked and swivelled. His broad head turned slowly. He lifted his muzzle and snuffed the night air. Such eyes he had! They were a darkness full of the brilliance of life. For one brief instant, light caught in them and glowed green. We were all as motionless as if a huge predator faced us. Then, like a wet dog, the wolf shook himself and tiny fragments of stone flew in all directions, as if he had rolled in them.

His slow look roved over us, pausing at each in turn. His gaze lingered on me the last. His eyes were both hard and amused. *Those were astounding lies, cub. And the very last one the most inspired of all. You have your father's talent for it.* He gave a final shake of his coat. *I go to the hunt!*

His claws left deep scratches on the stone as he leapt, not only over the fire but over all of us. For a moment, he was motion in the darkness. Then gone.

'He did it!' Dutiful shouted. 'He did it!' He seized Nettle in his arms and whirled her round.

Hap rose to his feet and in his minstrel's voice, he declaimed to the half-roused camp, 'And so the Wolf of the West rose from the stone! And so he will rise again if ever the folk of the Six Duchies call to him in need.'

'Seven Duchies,' Kettricken corrected him.

FIFTY

The Mountains

I think the Skill-road through the Mountains will remain long after humans, Elderlings and dragons are gone. Stone remembers. That is what the Elderlings learned, so long ago, and the lesson they have left us. Humans die and the memories of who they were and what they did fade. But stone remembers its task.

From the writings of FitzChivalry Farseer

'This is a bad idea,' Nettle said again.

'It is an excellent idea,' Kettricken replied. 'And Fitz gave her to me. Do not fear I will be too indulgent with her. You know I will not.'

Less than a day had passed. All the tents had been struck. Dutiful had already surrendered to his mother's wishes, taking Prosper, Lant and his coterie with him and hastening back to Queen Elliania's side.

Integrity and Hap remained. As did Per, Spark and I. Nettle's coterie stood in a huddle, awaiting her. Everybody was anxious to return to Buckkeep, to share their versions of what they had seen. I had already felt a flurry of Skilling from them to other coteries.

Dutiful had looked from his sons to me, and then at his mother. 'I don't fear you will be too indulgent with either of them. I have known you too many years to fear that. But I will speak plainly. Even with you using our horses, this will not be an easy journey for you.'

Kettricken sat well on a grey mare. 'My dear, the journey home is always easier than any other. For me, at least. Now, you must let us go. We have daylight still, and I would use it well.'

My sister opened her mouth to speak. Kettricken nudged her horse. 'Farewell, Nettle! Give our love to Riddle and Hope.'

Spark, not too comfortable on her bay mount, fell in behind her. Integrity moved his horse up beside her. I heard him say, 'You'll get used to it.'

Hap moved to flank her other side. 'Don't listen to him,' he warned her. 'Likely you will be horribly sore tonight. If we are not eaten by bears before then.'

'Lying minstrel,' Integrity observed, and they all laughed, Spark nervously. Motley had claimed a perch on Hap's shoulder, and she chortled along with the others. The minstrel had been pleased that she had chosen him. I knew she was waiting for a chance to steal one of his gaudy earrings.

Per stood nearby, holding the reins of both our horses.

Nettle hugged me and I allowed it. Then I demanded better of myself and hugged her back. 'I am going to try much harder,' I told her.

'I know you will. Now go, before you are left behind.'

Per stepped forward, but it was my sister who boosted me onto my horse. 'Behave!' she admonished me sternly.

'I will try,' I replied.

'Watch over her,' she told Per and turned away from us. She was not crying. I don't think any of us had any tears left. She walked toward her coterie. 'We're leaving,' she told them.

And so we parted.

I rode side by side with Per. I had the smallest horse. He was brown with a black mane and tail, and a star on his brow. We had already discovered that he liked to bite. Per said he could teach him better. Per rode a gelding the colour of creek mud. The fox pin glittered on his breast.

I was thinking about things like that: biting horses and fox pins. Thieving crows. How soon we could send for our own horses to be brought to the Mountains. What Spark and Lant felt for each other and what they might do about it. Hap was trying out lines and rhymes. 'Nothing rhymes with wolf!' we heard him exclaim in annoyance.

'There must be something,' Integrity insisted, and began to suggest nonsense words.

As we left the quarry behind, I was astonished to find that we were on a smooth road, with little encroachment from the forest. The Skill-road. I lowered my walls slightly and heard whispers of the many travellers who had once come this way. It was annoying. I closed my walls again.

'Did you hear something?' Per asked us suddenly.

That startled me. He had no magic. Of that we were now certain.

'The crow isn't worried,' Hap observed and then 'Ow!' as she made her first try for the earring.

Per was serious. 'Stay close beside me,' he warned me and urged his horse to a faster walk. He looked all about us as we moved through the dappling shade of the forest. When we were closer to Kettricken, he said worriedly, 'There's something stalking us. Off to the side of the road, moving through the forest.'

Kettricken smiled.